NINE THOUSAND FEET UP . . .

and Brady eased the small plane's climb. The sun had sunk below the horizon, and the eastern sky was dark, showing its early stars. Brady looked about him, enjoying the relaxation the flight gave him. He saw a light high above and to his left, descending slowly . . .

He knew it couldn't be a satellite when it continued to expand in brightness and size. At the same moment he knew it was rushing directly toward him.

Brady tensed, his mouth agape. Holding formation off his left wing was a huge disc. It maintained its position, unmistakable, absolutely clear, unbelievably real. He saw the rounded dome above the disc, a wide-bellied protrusion beneath . . .

Brady felt the pounding of his heart, and he took several deep breaths, forcing himself to calm down. But now he knew he was right. *The discs were real!*

ENCOUNTER THREE

MARTIN CAIDIN

PINNACLE BOOKS • LOS ANGELES

ENCOUNTER THREE

Copyright © 1969 by Martin Caidin

A Pinnacle book, originally titled *The Mendelov Conspiracy*, published by special arrangement with Hawthorn Books, Inc., New York.

First printing, September 1974
Second printing, May 1978

ISBN: 0-523-40350-X

Cover illustration by Paul Stinson

Printed in the United States of America

PINNACLE BOOKS, INC.
One Century Plaza
2029 Century Park East
Los Angeles, California 90067

for
LES ROBERSON
just because

Encounter Three

CHAPTER I

"Crap."

The word came out ugly and flat.

Cliff Brady watched for the reaction he knew would come. With a little more experience the man across the desk would have remained poker-faced. But the captain didn't know how to mask his emotions when someone called him a liar. A cheek muscle twitched and he tightened his lips. Brady smiled. The other man was fighting to keep in mind that he was an officer in the United States Air Force. As such—unless you're prepared to have your ass raked over hot coals—you don't get into a fight with a top newsman from World Press. Even when the son of a bitch is doing his best to provoke you.

Captain Walker remembered his orders. He

1

leaned forward and slowly stubbed out his cigarette. "Maybe I don't read you right, Mr. Brady."

Brady snorted. "The hell you don't. I can recognize a snow job, Walker."

"I've told you everything I know," Walker broke in.

"That's a matter of opinion," Brady retorted, "and right now I don't mind telling you that mine isn't very high of you."

The officer shrugged. "That's up to you, Mr. Brady. Congress pays me to do a job. Including," he added sarcastically, "being insulted by influential newsmen."

Brady didn't take the bait. He knew better. He went back to worrying the bone. "What you're saying, in effect," he said smoothly, "is that half the people in Barstow are insane, or subject to hallucinations, or liars. Those people out there"—he stabbed a finger in the direction of the nearby town—"saw something. They saw it, Walker, they heard it. They know what happened. They weren't frightened by any mass hallucination. They—"

Walker threw up his hands. "Hold it right there, Brady," he snapped. "Don't put words in my mouth. I don't *know* what the people in Barstow saw or didn't see. I was sixty feet underground when this whole flap took place and—"

"WHAT flap?" Brady barked.

Walker eased back in his chair. "Nice try," he said. "The flap *you* are telling me about.

2

Like I said, I was sixty feet straight down in a command post."

"Then how come I'm not talking to someone who *did* see what happened?"

"Because, Mr. Brady," Walker said, "we don't have anyone at this base who saw anything. At least not what you're claiming took place."

"I talked with forty people who saw it, Captain. Who saw it and who heard it and observed its effects. There must have been a few thousand more eyewitnesses. Hell, the town's only a dozen miles away—everybody can't be deaf, dumb, and blind. Why the cover-up? What are you people so afraid of?"

A blank look appeared on Walker's face. "Afraid?"

"Yeah, afraid," Brady said dryly. "The symptoms are all over the place. I've never seen so many people so determined to deny that something happened."

"Look, Brady, we're not denying anything," Walker said. "We simply aren't going to confirm what we didn't see—even if you tell me the whole town saw your UFO. I give you my word I didn't see anything at all." Walker sat back and glared at Brady.

"So you've told me a couple of times," Brady replied. "Sure, you're telling the truth. *You* were sixty feet down. *You* didn't see anything." Brady held the eyes of the other man and then dropped his trump card.

"How about my talking to some of the men who made up that combat team?"

3

Walker's eyes were ummoved. "What combat team, Mr. Brady?"

"The team you sent out by helicopter and ground vehicles to find whatever it was that landed about eight miles from here."

The silence held between the two men. Brady realized that Walker's instructions to deny everything didn't cover this sort of thing. Brady knew far more than the captain had realized; he knew far more than he should have known. And the captain didn't know what to do. He was a missile-control officer who spent most of his time riding herd on a group of Minuteman missiles buried in silos that were shotgun-scattered across the Nebraska hills and mountains. Walker didn't like newsmen. He wondered just how much Brady did know.

Brady knew enough to make a good story—but for a wireservice story he wanted hard facts, something definitive. He wanted confirmation from experienced observers. He wanted something official into which he could sink his teeth. He wasn't getting what he wanted. The captain in whose office he sat was making sure of that.

Barstow Auxiliary Air Force Base was essentially a command nerve center for an unspecified number of missile silos spread out in all directions. The town of Barstow, twelve miles distant, had learned to live with the presence of the missile-command sites. The Air Force people mostly kept to themselves, and those who came to town were pleasant, intelligent people. They should have been; they were handpicked for the job.

Nobody rocked the boat. Until a few days ago, when Barstow leaped onto the front pages as the center of a UFO flap. Brady had checked out the initial news reports. When the story failed to die down, World Press had packed him off to Barstow to see if he could make a wire-service feature out of it. Reliable UFO sightings were rare and they made good copy.

Brady expected one or two days of first-person interviews and that would be it. He hadn't figured on a town scared half to death. They weren't just excited. The people in Barstow had been frightened. The missile command post was involved. But Brady couldn't break through.

The first person he interviewed was the chief of police in Barstow. Brady's immediate impression of John Cotron was of a solid, reliable, phlegmatic man who knew his business and who wasn't likely to go off the deep end because of something he might have seen in the sky. Chief Cotron's first words made this clear.

"Maybe you want to call it a UFO," Cotron had said, measuring his words carefully. "I don't. UFO means 'unidentified.' This thing here was a disc. No doubt about it."

"You're certain of that?" Brady prodded.

Cotron nodded. "Yeah, no doubt in *my* mind. Course, it was a long ways off. But I saw it high up, when I could make out the disc shape easy enough. Then I saw it over the hills to the north, where it dropped below sight. The shape changed, but it was a disc, seen from the side."

"Could you make out any details?" Brady prodded.

"Uh-uh. Too far away. But it was a disc, all right."

"Anything in particular?" Brady knew enough to let the man respond to brief questions.

"Silver. It was silver. Metallic, I guess you might call it." Chief Cotron was emphatic. "The way it reflected light. Couldn't have been anything else."

"Could you see any markings, or windows? Perhaps a dome or control cabin?"

Cotron shook head. "Like I say, it was too far away for that. And I know better than to try to guess."

Brady jotted down some notes. "Oh? Are you a pilot, Chief?"

"Was. During World War Two. Flew dive-bombers in the Navy, got a couple thousand hours before I quit. I got plenty of experience looking at things in the sky. It was a disc, all right. Nobody going to make me change my mind about *that*." He finished his final words with a snort of disdain.

"Anybody try changing your mind?" Brady asked.

The chief nodded. "Sure did," he said. "Bunch of professor types. Said they were from the Air Force, came out to investigate the UFO report. Told me I didn't see a disc at all. Said what I saw was probably a swept-wing

6

airplane that reflected light to look like a disc."
His gaze arrowed to Brady's face. "I *know*
what I saw."

Brady thought quickly. Cotron's eyewitness
report was strong enough to be worth something. But there was more. "Chief, what about
those reports that the UFO—the disc, I
mean—interfered with radios and electrical
equipment? Is there anything to that?"

Again Cotron nodded. "Hell, anybody in
town could tell you that. Never saw anything
like it before. Every damned radio for miles
around went crazy. Static. Like to drive us
nuts. TV wouldn't work, radios just buzzing
and sputtering. Half the lights in town were
dimming, you know, like going on low power.
Couple of people out in the hills called in later
complaining that the thing, whatever it was,
had killed their cars. Engines just quit, I mean.
They saw the disc drop down below some hills
to the north. A little while later it showed up
again, this time going like hell. Faster than any
airplane I ever saw. It climbed up real steep.
Just kept on going until it disappeared from
sight. Everything worked fine again."

You said it landed beyond some hills to the
north?" Brady queried.

"I didn't say it *landed*," Cotron said quickly.
"I said it dropped from sight. Long ways from
here. I don't know if it landed or not. Maybe
the Air Force people know."

"Why do you think they might know?"

Chief Cotron dug a black cigar from a shirt
pocket, talking between puffs as he lit up.

7

"They got combat teams—security teams, I guess you'd call them. They go out regularly to check the silos. Sometimes they get a report that someone's fooling around or something, and they get out there fast. Use helicopters. Well, they sent out a chopper from the main base to investigate. I wouldn't have known anything about it except that the chopper's engine quit. Just like that," Cotron snapped his fingers to emphasize his point. "Conked out. One of my men saw it go down and he got there right away. Pilot put it into a field without hurting it none. My man talked to the pilot. Said he couldn't figure out why the engine had quit. But you know something? His radio wasn't working either. Same thing with the radio in the police car. It wouldn't work. Not until"—Cotron spit out a piece of tobacco—"that damned disc left the area."

"What happened then?"

Cotron shrugged. "Pilot started up the chopper and took off. That's all."

Brady didn't learn much more. Hundreds of people had had a long, clear look at the UFO. Chief Cotron, an experienced observer, insisted it was a disc. Other witnesses insisted just as strongly it had a torpedo shape, or was curved in the form of a scythe. It was the same old eyewitness problem. They'd all seen something, but they had a dozen different descriptions.

But everyone agreed about the strange interference with mechanical equipment. That by itself didn't mean much. It had happened before, hundreds of times. Scientists explained it away

8

as electrical discharges in the air, and there wasn't any reason to become hysterical over phenomena that was perfectly natural. Dead end. Except for the disc in the air.

Even *that* could be explained away. Plasmoids were weird things. They were made up of a mass of ionized gas that formed into a visible shape for a few hours, held together by a self-generated magnetic field. While they lasted they shone brightly—and then took on a disc-shaped appearance. They also produced strong magnetic and electrical fields that screwed up radio and television and electrical systems. The plasmoid—the ionized gas— reflected both light and radar. It could move with tremendous speed. It was *real*. It was also perfectly natural.

Brady mentioned this to Chief Cotron. He wouldn't buy it. He'd seen electrical apparitions before; just about every pilot sees them, sooner or later. And this thing, Cotron said flatly, wasn't "no damned bunch of electricity. That was a solid object, and I don't give a damn what else anybody says about it."

The story would have died right there and then. Except for the combat team that had gone out in the helicopter and had lost all power without any known reason except that it was within a few miles of the strange object lost to sight beyond the hills. Even that, Brady admitted, could have been nothing more than coincidence.

But something was wrong. Two things, really. They irritated Brady, who didn't like loose pieces lying around.

First, the eyewitness reports that the UFO had been observed to *ascend* from behind the hills. Did ionized gas drop down from high altitude, wander about out of sight, and then take off again? Some scientists insisted it was perfectly natural. Okay. Brady would have relegated the story to just what it seemed to be— a good UFO feature with eyewitness reports.

But, second, the Air Force gave him the fast shuffle. Or tried to. They should have left Captain Everett Walker sixty feet below ground. He was a dead giveaway.

Brady didn't know *what* had the Air Force in such a snit that they would order an officer to throw up a wall of denials. Why should they be afraid to admit what they had seen? UFO's were common enough—birds, airplanes, planets, balloons, plasmoids, and a hundred other things in the sky had all been identified as strange and frightening objects. So why the sudden blanket refusal to admit *anything*?

Brady's sixth sense, his long experience as a newsman, jarred him.

Captain Everett Walker was, if not frightened, damned well shaken by something. Officers selected for missile-command duty do not rattle easily. Before they ever get near the red buttons with which they can send a dozen nuclear-tipped ICBM's racing toward the Soviet Union they go through intensive psychological screening. They live in a psychological glass cage. It takes a lot to rattle that cage.

Walked was rattled.

Brady wanted to know *why*.

And he couldn't find out.

CHAPTER II

Cliff Brady ripped the paper from his typewriter and crumpled it angrily. A quarter to four in the goddamned morning and he couldn't sleep. Worse, he couldn't write. At least thirty sheets of paper lay scattered about him in the wide first-class seat of the TWA jetliner.

Before he'd left New York to cover the UFO incident he'd virtually written the story in his mind. This wasn't his first UFO flap, and almost all of them turned out the same way in the end. He'd brought to mind the usual cutting phrases about the nuts and the thrill-seekers who kept seeing all sorts of things in the sky. Every so often they wandered into the press room in New York demanding protection from the government. Sometimes they brought photographs of strange lights and shapes in the sky as proof of a monstrous plot to take over the world. They'd been around for years.

There were the serious ones, of course. Experienced pilots who saw strange objects that appeared to defy all explanation. Sober observers in the air and on the ground who couldn't fathom shapes or lights in the sky. But they didn't leap to conclusions. They remembered that anything seen at night or at long range could *seem* to be anything but what it really was. St. Elmo's fire sometimes turned an airplane into a violent, multicolored fantasy of twisting light. Harmless enough when you knew what it was, but it could scare the hell out of you if you didn't know what was happening. And if you were on the ground and looked up to see a plane wreathed in kaleidoscopic electrical violence, well, it was natural for a man to run for the nearest telephone.

But the pattern didn't fit what had happened at Barstow or at the ICBM command post twelve miles away. Before Brady left the area he had checked out a hunch. The military field would have its own source of electrical power for emergencies, the regular cut-in switches that were part of any emergency system. But for normal power, like most fields, they used the same electrical power source that fed the town of Barstow. That was Brady's lead. He visited the central power station. Within ten minutes he knew just how right he was. There had been serious interference with normal power outflow. So serious that the emergency systems at the missile-command center had kicked in and automatically set off the war-alert alarm.

That wasn't all. The communications center of the Minuteman command complex had almost been knocked out of touch with its remote command posts. Radio transmitters and receivers sixty feet below ground had thrown out so much static that for several minutes they were useless. The main power station in Barstow had automatic recorders that told Brady the exact times electrical current interference took place and just when the missile-command center radios started acting up. From that point on, the rest was checking out other figures. The results had Brady convinced he was on the brink of a story all out of proportions to the run-of-the-mill UFO flap.

No wonder that captain had been on edge! He'd been sixty feet down, shielded by steel and concrete, and all his critical communications had gone haywire. Cause? A strange unknown object in the sky, apparently.

Apparently. Bardy warned himself not to jump to hasty conclusions. But why had Captain Walker played the role he'd presented to Brady? And what had happened to the combat team in the helicopter? Had they seen anything? Why should the Air Force be so hot and bothered over a UFO—which they claimed they had never seen in the first place?

The more he thought about it, the angrier he became. At the moment he didn't have his story. Nothing would fall into place so that he could turn in the copy that World Press expected later that day. At six hundred miles an hour, New York was coming up too damn fast.

He glared at the almost empty drink in his hand. It was time to stop chasing the shadows skipping just beyond his reach. He needed perspective. Shit, he needed another drink. He buzzed for the stewardess.

Ann Dallas looked up at the glowing light on the "alert" board and smiled. That would be Brady again, wanting another martini. He'd put away four already, double the quota she was permitted to serve. Even as she thought about not serving another drink, she twisted the cap loose from the small bottle to pour the martini over the ice. She dropped in two olives. With only two others passengers in the forward section, and both of them asleep, it really didn't matter.

She wondered about Brady. She knew of him through his column. Most of the crews did. Brady's byline was one of the few that promised accuracy in writing about the airlines. The pilots couldn't fault Brady when the newsman twisted their noses just a bit—not when Brady himself was a veteran at the controls.

She wondered about the man, and wondered equally at the fascination he held for her. She was twenty-six and knew from reading about Brady that he was about forty or forty-two, enough of a difference for her to dwell briefly on the matter before she dismissed it. He certainly wasn't physically attractive. For one thing he was too short. He made up for his lack of height with a body that might have been assembled from a tree trunk. He had thick sloping shoulders and powerful arms. You watched Brady walk and you expected the man to go charging right through a wall rather than to follow an aisle.

She'd felt an electric shock when he boarded the airplane. No smile. He was very clearly *not* in a smiling mood when he stomped his way up the ramp into the cabin. He stopped in the doorway and she stared into startling, clear black eyes. For a moment he didn't say a word, and in that instant she studied him. Not the casual appraising glance with which she judged boarding passengers. She was studying, evaluating. Not for TWA. For herself. His eyes held her fast. His face was a guide to years of violent battering. Somewhere in his past Mr. Brady had taken a right to the nose that left a thin white scar running from the bridge down across the side of his nose almost to his cheek. His chin and one side of his forehead showed the knotty bumps of scar tissue. She was startled to notice his lips, not quite full, strangely sensuous to her against that battered face.

His voice came straight, deep, and demanding. "Who are you?"

Experience came to her aid. "Miss Dallas, sir. Welcome aboard. May I help you with—"

"No. You can't help me with my things. I'm in first class. I have work to do." No nonsense

17

with him. "Soon as Captain Marvel or whoever it is up front gets this thing in the air, bring me a martini."

He started past her before she could issue another automatic, if not shocked, "Yes, sir." Then he stopped and turned. "Miss Dallas . . . Make that a double." She nodded, afraid to say a word. His face split in a wide grin. "You're a beautiful thing, just in case no one ever told you."

And he was gone to his seat. Before she had collected her thoughts she heard the typewriter clattering.

The fierce intensity Ann Dallas noticed in her first meeting with Cliff Brady was a characteristic that marked him well throughout his profession. To his peers and those who wished to emulate him Brady was intense, confident, knowledgeable and possessed of brawling cynicism. He was also one hell of a good writer. Brady's physical appearance and belligerent demeanor masked an incisive mind. He didn't simply report his subjects, he *knew* whereof he wrote. It gave him a powerful calling card in the industry, and his rapier slashing of individuals and agencies made his column "essential reading" to millions of people daily.

As a war correspondent early in his career, Brady had carved a mild fame for his in-depth reporting from the thick of battle in Indo-China, and had bceome known as the most heavily armed noncombatant in any war. He had sworn never to be taken alive by Communist troops. From the debacle of Indo-China

18

Brady had followed a natural evolution to covering military hot spots as they erupted around the world. He had reported on the testing of atomic and hydrogen bombs, missile and space shots, and become an expert on new developments in science, war, aviation and space.

Brady's marriage never really had a chance. News came first and his wife a poor second. Perhaps if Greta had known the art of "staying loose" rather than fighting for her own conception of wedded bliss, if might have worked. Perhaps not. Too quickly Brady discovered he didn't care. After their divorce something of Greta remained with him, but he knew he never really missed her; in the long run she just wasn't his cup of tea.

As a professional newsman Brady strove for perfection and accepted nothing less than the attempt to reach that state. Thus his growing irritation with the UFO incident at Barstow. He could easily have put together a story wholly acceptable to the wire service. He could make light of the affair and apply the screws to the Air Force for its inexplicable censorship. Safety lay in that direction.

But there was a story, significant and meaningful, behind what had happened at Barstow. The elusive nature of that story rankled every professional fiber in his system. And there was more. Deception, deliberate misinformation, and fear. The wrong people were afraid. Men in charge of nuclear-packed missiles aren't those you expect to . . .

Where the hell was that drink?

He really hadn't looked at her before. Now he stared. She sat on the armrest of the aisle seat, the overhead light a halo glow through the edges of her hair—raven hair . . . And full lips, a delightful, friendly smile . . . Without speaking, he reached out slowly for the drink.

Brady saw that her nose was perfect. Why the hell her nose meant so much eluded him, but it was perfect for her dark eyes and delicate brows. He looked and admired. He had remembered Ann Dallas when he climbed the boarding steps. He judged the legs of stewardesses with epicurean zeal. Hers made him want to snort and paw the ground. She was also as well proportioned as any female he had ever known. The curving lines of her bust, her waist, her hips and legs . . . everything was just right. "Thank God," he murmured to himself, "she isn't too stacked." Proportion was everything in a woman.

The stewardess gestured to the paper strewn about the seat. "You seem to need this." She smiled, looking again at the glass she was offering. "Trouble finding the right words?"

His fingers closed around hers for several seconds before he accepted the drink.

"Uh, huh." He mumbled his acknowledgment with the glass to his lips, drank deeply, and sighed. "Jesus, that's good."

She smiled again. "I've heard my father say the same thing when he was fighting a story."

Brady glanced up.

"Westerns," she anticipated the question. "Brawling, horsey Westerns of the old school.

20

Dad always believed in martinis and type-writers."

Brady raised his glass in a toast. "Smart man." He searched his memory. "Dallas, Dallas. Hmm." He looked up at her. "*Sam* Dallas?"

She was delighted with his recognition. "One and the same," she said.

"Hell, I know him. He's one of the best."

"I always thought so," she said. He liked that. She was proud of her old man and didn't hide it.

"I read him for years," Brady continued. "Sam Dallas . . . sure, he believed that cowboys and horses went together and women in the West should be kept for occasional thumping, cooking, and doing the laundry. Right?"

"You're very good, you know." She shifted the conversation to him without pause.

He raised his brows in surprise. "I didn't know that girls read my column," he said. "No sex, no scandal. Hardly interesting to a beautiful young thing like you."

"You're interesting," she persisted. "That's the second time tonight you've called me a beautiful young thing. Thank you."

"It's true."

She nodded. "I know."

The frankness of her words caught him off balance. She said it with pride in herself, not ego. He couldn't believe it. He didn't think there were such women. His interest in her grew swiftly.

21

She glanced at his typewriter. "Problems?"

He closed the case on the machine and dropped it heavily to the floor by his feet.

"All writers have problems," he snorted. "Ask your old man."

"I don't need to. Remember, I made his martinis." She laughed quietly. "The more problems, the more martinis. What's your problem, Mr. Writer?"

He sighed and mumbled a curse. "It's a will-o'-the-wisp."

"A what?"

He glanced up. "You could also call it a UFO." In the dim light of the cabin he would have missed it. But the reading light was still on. The moment he said UFO she stiffened. He couldn't have been mistaken.

"You act as if I said something dirty."

She moved her hand in a sign of agitation. "UFO," she said. "In this business that's a dirty word."

He waited for her to continue but she kept silent. "Going to tell me why?" he asked finally.

This time the smile was guarded. "You're putting me on," she said softly. "You know what the papers have done to pilots who've reported seeing UFO's."

He nodded.

"Everything but castration," she continued with a flash of temper. "The way those stories are printed, you'd think the people flying airliners were all crazy." She looked about the cabin to confirm the other passengers were still

22

asleep, and asked Brady for a cigarette. He held a match for her and she inhaled deeply. "As far as the crews are concerned, when it comes to talking about UFO's, newsmen are lower than dirt." She held his gaze.

He grinned. "Including me?"

She was still on the defensive.

"That depends, I suppose, on how you treat the report of a competent and serious man. That's for starters."

Brady shrugged. "You read my column. Apologies don't go along with it."

She nodded. *"Touché."*

"Think nothing of it." He grinned again. "Anyway, according to some people, I'm the one who's going off the deep end."

"Did you see—"

"Uh-uh," he said quickly. "Nothing *I* saw. But a few hundred people, including some very solid citizens, saw something. They saw it clearly, they know what they're talking about. Some other people, however . . ." He let his words trail off. "You really interested? Seriously, I mean?"

"I am." She stubbed out her cigarette. "Tell me about it, please."

He told her what had happened. As much as he was enjoying talking with her, being with her, he was also interested in her reaction. By the time he'd related the events of the past few days, the SEAT BELT sign was on.

"We're starting down for JFK," she said.

"Wait a moment." He held her wrist. "I don't want this to just break off and . . ." He

23

finished his meaning without words. She nodded. "I couldn't sleep now," he added quickly. "Not with this"—he tapped the typewriter—"bugging me. Besides, I don't want you to disappear. How about a dinner-breakfast or whatever they call it at this ungodly hour? I know a great all-night restaurant in the city. Chef's a great friend, make you anything you like. Date?"

"Date." She smiled.

"Where do I pick up up?"

"You know the Lexington Hotel?"

"Uh-huh."

"I have work to finish after we land," she explained. "I'll go into town with the rest of the crew. Six o'clock? In the lobby?"

"Great."

"See you there."

He was surprised with himself. He was eager for six o'clock to roll around.

Breakfast was more than he had bargained for. At six o'clock sharp he walked into the hotel lobby, where he found Ann with another stewardess and a man wearing the three stripes of a co-pilot on his sleeve. Ann introduced Keith Johnson, the copilot of the jetliner in which Brady had flown. Brady looked at Johnson carefully.

"Chaperon?"

The others laughed. "No, not really," Ann explained quickly. "Those two are engaged, and you and I are keeping them out of bed." The other girl showed pink on her cheeks and smiled at Brady. He liked these people; they were crisp and clean-cut and honest. "But Keith wanted to meet you," Ann was saying.

"That's right, Mr. Brady. I've been a fan of yours for a long time. I wanted to see if there really could be a newsman who didn't have horns," Johnson said with a smile.

Brady pawed at his forehead. "Not yet, anyway."

Keith then became serious. "Ann mentioned you were on a UFO story."

Brady nodded and waited to see the point of Keith's seriousness.

"It would mean something to a lot of us if a writer . . . I mean, a writer with your background and scientific knowledge—you're an airplane driver, aren't you?—well, someone with *your* qualifications . . . we'd like to see your reactions to what we've got to say. That is, if we can agree ahead of time on . . ."

"Ann's told me about your problem," Brady said. "I don't blame you."

"No names?" Johnson queried.

"No names," he promised as they shook hands.

The copilot took a deep breath. "Okay, Mr. Brady. Let's go to breakfast."

An hour later Brady said good-bye to the others and walked Ann to her hotel room. He hesitated at the door.

"I'm leaving for three or four days, but dinner's open tonight."

"It's a date. I'll call you later and let you know what time."

She kissed him lightly on the cheek.

He hesitated. "Ann, I want to ask you something . . . What Johnson said, during breakfast, I mean. Is all that for real?"

"It's for real, Cliff. He was very serious. So are the others."

He rubbed his chin. "If what they say is true . . ." He realized his words could be taken two ways. "I don't mean their honesty or integrity," he added quickly. "It's a matter of interpretation, I suppose. But if what they've seen is what it seems to be, and there are more cases like Barstow—" Abruptly he cut short his own thoughts, self-conscious for keeping her in the hall. "I'm too tired for all that right now, anyway."

"Do you want them to join us for dinner?" she asked.

"The hell I do," he said with mock anger. "Tonight's for me and thee. Strictly. Music and flowers and all that."

She kissed him again.

Brady went to his apartment to wrestle with his typewriter.

26

CHAPTER III

Milt Parrish sucked noisily at his pipe. He withheld it from his mouth and tapped the stem against the story on his desk.

"You're putting me on, Cliff," he said, glancing at the typewritten pages. "At least—I *hope* you're putting me on."

Brady's response was tense. "That story is straight."

"But everyone knows this UFO stuff is bullshit!" Parrish snorted.

"Who the hell is 'everyone,' goddamn it!" Brady shouted. "You? The guy in the next block? Your sainted aunt? Where are all your experts coming from? What the hell do they know about this stuff?" Brady jammed his cigarette in the ashtray, scattering ashes across the editor's desk. "I don't get you, Milt. You never tried to second-guess me on a story before."

"You never gave me drivel before," Parrish retorted.

Brady came slowly to his feet. His voice dropped to an angry growl. "Drivel? You're sitting here on your fat ass. I was there and suddenly you're an expert—"

"Now hold on!" Parrish cut in. "You know I'm responsible for what passes this desk. It's got to carry my personal okay, and that means I'm supporting what the story says. Not this time, Cliff."

Brady returned to his chair and studied his editor. "You canning the story?" It was a challenge, and Parrish knew it.

"I didn't say that." He frowned, hesitating on Brady's demand for a decision.

Brady rolled his eyes. "Then what's this all about?"

Parrish picked up the story and thumbed through the pages. He was friendly and concerned. "Cliff, according to this, the Air Force people you talked to are liars who are—"

"Goddamn right they are," Brady snapped.

"Who are," Parrish continued, "deliberately concealing information from the public about a UFO, or a disc, or whatever it is—"

"That's what the story says," Brady threw at him.

"Will you shut up and let me finish? You're saying that not only are UFO's real but that they're threatening our missile bases and—"

Brady couldn't remain quiet. "That is *not*

what I said!" he shouted. "I've given you a report on what happened at Barstow. I didn't say UFO's, plural. I said a disc. *One,* singular, disc. Not strange things buzzing around in the air. *A* disc. With eyewitness, with—oh hell, it's all there and you're interpreting it the way you see fit."

Parrish's eyes gleamed. "That's right," he said softly. "That's the way I interpreted it. How do you think everyone else is going to see it? The same way I did."

"Then you've got a streak of stupidity I never saw in you before," Brady retorted, still unmoved.

Parrish dropped the story back on his desk and spent several moments stacking the pages neatly. "All right." He sighed. "Let me ask you some questions."

Brady gave him an unintelligible grumble in reply.

"You quoted the eyewitnesses. Right?"

"You know how to read," Brady said ungraciously.

"Never mind the wisecracks. You quoted eyewitnesses, but the Air Force will not admit to seeing anything. That's true, isn't it?"

"I *told* you what happened with—"

"Stay with me, damn you," Parrish broke in. "Isn't that true? I'm talking about what we're going to put on the wires."

"Yeah."

"Okay. So as far as the Air Force is concerned, the people in Barstow saw what thousands of other people all over the country have

29

seen. Strange lights or shapes in the sky. Right?"

Brady's eyes narrowed. "Go on."

"All right. There isn't any way for you to disprove what the Air Force says. It's your word against theirs."

"What's that got to do with—"

"It's your word against theirs," Parrish hammered at him, "and you weren't there. You got there when it was all over. Anything you've got to go against the Air Force is so much hearsay."

"You're twisting the facts and you know it, Milt."

Parrish slammed his hand against his desk. "You're damned right I am! And so will everyone else who reads this copy." He took a deep breath. "Now let me ask you something else." Brady didn't comment and Parrish went on.

"Were the missile sites damaged in any way?"

"I told you about the readings at the power station. It's right there—"

"Please. Answer the question. Do you know, do you have any *proof*, that the missile sites were damaged? Do you have anything else except some squiggles from a civilian power station?"

"No."

"So. There's no *proof*—nothing to show that the missile sites were damaged. If you can't show that, if all you've got are those squiggles and a power-station engineer with a vivid

30

imagination, *why* should the Air Force lie to you or anyone else?"

"That's what I would damn well like to know."

Parrish sighed with relief. "But you *don't* know, do you?" He held up his hand to forestall a reply. "Hold it, Cliff. That's my whole point. Your story is based on inference. You're drawing conclusions without meat to them." He tapped the story with his fingers. "It won't hold up. More than that, it's not like you to turn in something you can't back up. And you *can't* support what you say in here."

Brady dug in his shirt pocket for his cigarettes. Jesus Christ. What the hell was he supposed to do? Out there at Barstow it was clear as ice. No mistakes. It came up and belted you right in the face. But the way Parrish threw the story back at him . . . Of course he couldn't *prove* . . .

"We're right back where we were before," Brady said. "I'll ask you again. You canning the story?"

Parrish shook his head. "No, I'm not. There's nothing wrong with the story. It's the conclusions that bother me." He looked directly at Brady. "I want you to run this through the typewriter again. You don't need to change much. Write it as it was, as it is. Tell what happened. Let it wind up as a mystery. Just don't end it with a warning that the Martians are invading us."

Brady thought back to his conversation with Keith Johnson. He recalled what the veteran

31

airlines pilot had said about the discs he and his pilot had seen, on at least three occasions. Clear sightings. Unmistakable. Not a doubt in their minds. And when they tried to explain it to someone else, it was all a big joke. Very funny. Now he knew how they felt.

He climbed heavily to his feet and picked up the story. "All right, Milt. I'll do it the way you want. I *know* I'm right, but apparently that's not enough."

"It is for me, but not for the wires." Parrish felt grateful the session was over. A lopsided grin appeared on his face. "You pissed at me?"

"Go screw yourself."

"How about a drink when you're through?"

"You buying?"

"We'll toss for it."

Silence.

Parrish sighed. "Okay. I'm buying."

The cab pulled up before the hotel and Brady saw Ann waiting for him. "Hold it here a moment," he told the driver. He climbed out and helped Ann into the cab and leaned forward. "Make it Sixty-Seventh and Third," he said.

Ann leaned over to kiss Brady lightly on the lips. "Hi, there," she said. It came out light and with a musical sound to her voice and Brady felt better than he had all day. He held her hand tightly and sighed.

"Oh, my. Bad day at the office?"

"Yeah," he grunted. "Did the Barstow piece over again to please an editor who thinks

UFO's show up only on mornings after. And then—oh shit, it's not worth recapping." He waved his hand to dismiss what had happened as unimportant.

Ann laughed. "Welcome to the crowd," she said. "Now you know what it's like. I saw one of your mysterious visitors one night, you know."

"Oh? You didn't tell me."

"Keith told you about it. The time we were flying through high clouds. You know, those cumulus buildups at night. Bright moon and it's all so lovely, like flying in the midst of clouds made of marble." He nodded; he knew the sights and the sensations. "Remember? He told you that something—no lights, just reflecting the moon like polished silver . . . when it came around, *not* through, but around, a cloud?"

"Sure," he said. "Took up formation with you."

"The pilots called us in the back and told us to look. Wanted proof that they weren't drunk or something like that. We had plenty of witnesses. Half the passengers were glued to the windows. 'It' stayed with us for several minutes."

"You see anything the pilots didn't?"

She shook her head. Brady didn't reply and Ann studied the passing crowds. The streets were filled on the warm summer evening.

The cab pulled to the corner of Sixty-Seventh and Third. Ann looked out and exclaimed. "Oh, Oscar's! I've heard about this place—"

"Out, out," he broke in. "Let us rather have at it."

Ann looked up at the sign. "Salt of the Sea," she read aloud. "Is Oscar real, or is it just a name?"

Brady opened the door for her. "It's real—I mean, *he's* real, all right. I used to eat here when this place was only a seafood bar. Now look at the damned thing."

Ann looked with dismay at the people crowding together behind a rope barrier, waiting for tables. "Oh, Cliff, it'll take us hours."

He ignored her, waving vigorously to someone beyond the crowd. A heavy-set man in dark slacks and an open black shirt pushed through to them. Before Ann could collect her senses, Oscar had them seated. He waved off a waitress approaching with menus. Their host cracked Brady smartly on the back and was off again toward the impatient crowd waiting to be seated.

"Is it always crowded like this?" she exclaimed.

"Always."

"The food must be marvelous."

"Better than that," he said. "No one does lobster like you get it here."

"But you didn't ask me if I like lobster."

"You do, don't you?"

"Yes, but—"

"So what's the bitch?"

"Cliff, you're impossible. Aren't you going to ask me if I want a drink?"

"Nope."

34

"Are you always this uncooperative?"

"Sure," he said.

She studied him carefully. She wasn't accustomed to someone like him. It tugged at her vanity, but at the same time Brady was accepting her as a woman who didn't need the standard routine of boy-meet-girl. That pleased her.

Oscar reappeared and vanished as quickly. Brady was pouring wine into a glass that seemed mysteriously to have leaped into existence on the table. She held up the wine and studied the gold liquid in the light.

"What is it, Cliff?"

"Taste. Don't talk." He filled his glass and brought it against hers.

"I've never had anything like it," she marveled. "Going to tell me what—"

He didn't let her finish. "To be honest, I don't know. It's private stock, and Oscar never tells. I don't know a damn thing about wines or vintages or what's a good year or anything else, Ann. All I know is what I like, and Oscar keeps his private stock close to the vest. Except," he said, smiling, "when I show up with a beautiful girl."

She drank to that.

Dinner, he told her while he slowly tore his lobster to small pieces of claw and shell, was celebrating a small victory.

"Did you shoot your editor, Mr. What's-his-name?"

"Parrish."

"Well, did you?"

35

"Milt's all right, and no, I didn't shoot him."

"All right?" She shook her head. "That's not the impression you've given me. A while ago you sounded as if you'd like to boil him in oil. Slowly."

"Not really. Milt backed me against the wall. But he's fair. He put me on the spot and told me to prove what I'd written." Brady shrugged. "The long and short of it is I couldn't prove—and the emphasis is on the word *proof*—anything."

She slammed a lobster claw to her dish. "Cliff, you're the most exasperating man I've ever known. What are we supposed to be celebrating?"

He looked smug. "I did some backing against the wall myself," he replied. "Had a couple of drinks and a long talk with Parrish after I did the rewrite. I got the okay to do an in-depth series on UFO's."

"That's marvelous," she said. "How did you manage it?"

"I told you Parrish was a square shooter. Although," he hastened to add, "he's not exactly doing handsprings about the idea. He thinks this whole thing with UFO's is really way out. Kooksville and all that."

"He hasn't flown in formation with one of them," Ann said grimly.

"Of course not," Brady agreed. "That's the trouble. You go along for years laughing and pointing the finger at the people who insist something screwy's going on in the skies. Then one day a UFO comes along and kicks you in

36

the slats and *whap!* just like that you're a believer."

"And everyone else then thinks *you're* nuts,"
she added.

"Uh-huh. Right now Parrish is, like I said,
against the idea."

"Then how did you—"

"News," he said brusquely. "No matter what
else it is, a good UFO story is news. Get
enough people seeing swamp gas under their
beds or chasing them down country roads, and
you've got news. Parrish is a newsman first
and an editor second. He can smell the stories. I
made a deal with him."

"Go on."

"Well," Brady shrugged. "I backed off today.
I don't do that very often, and Milt appreciates
that fact. I met him halfway. It was up to him
to do the same. He had me down to cover a
meeting of atomic scientists in England, but I
got him to assign someone else to that. He
knows this Barstow thing's got me bugged.
Which it certainly has." He emptied the remains of the wine bottle in his glass and toyed
with the stem.

"I'm in something of a quandary," he said,
suddenly moody. "I know how I feel about the
Barstow story, but I can't pin it down. It's the
sort of thing you know absolutely, but if you
were to tell your case from a witness stand in a
courtroom, you'd sound like an idiot."

"Is that how you feel, Cliff?"

"Yes and no," he said candidly. "Every instinct I have as a newsman is screaming I'm

right. I also know the first rule in this business, Ann, and that's to get your facts straight. *Facts*. Of which I have distressingly little. Sure, I *know*. Maybe, that is. I know what Keith Johnson told me and what he's said about other pilots. But even Keith on a witness stand would have his story torn to shreds."

He drained his glass and placed both hands flat on the table. "That's what's so maddening about all this," he said, his face serious. "You're fighting shadows. Are millions of people off their bird? Because millions of people have seen things. I don't know. I don't believe in mass hallucination, but I've seen what suggestion can do. People will believe anything—and swear on a stack of Bibles they really saw an object when in fact they saw nothing more than a reflection of light or something of that sort. The trouble is these people are telling the truth—as they believe the truth to be. But there's a long way to go between what someone believes and what's really so." He looked at her and grimaced. "It's a can of worms, Ann."

Then a thought hit him. He came upright in his chair. "Ann, you said you'd be gone for a few days, didn't you?"

"Yes."

"All right, I'm starting this series—starting my interviews and research, I mean—tomorrow. I'm taking the company plane out to Ohio to get the ball rolling. Could you do something for me?"

"Of course. If I can," she amended.

38

"Would you start collecting the details of these airline incidents? You can get the stories. You know the stewardesses; I know how you share these things with each other. You can get for me what I as a reporter can't. Dates, names, places, just what happened, the . . ." His voice trailed off as he noticed the hard lines that had suddenly appeared on her face.

"What the hell's the matter?" he said. "Did I say a dirty word or something?"

"Names, Cliff?" She let the sentence hang.

"Of course I want names! I've got to document . . ." His expression showed realization for her sudden withdrawal. "Oh. I get it. *Names.*"

"That's right," she said.

He shook his head and gesticulated with a hand. "No sweat, beautiful. Same conditions I gave your boy Johnson."

"You don't know how these people have been smeared," she said, still protesting.

He didn't answer her right away. The intensity vanished as if he'd pulled a plug within his brain. He looked at her as if she were a stranger, and shrugged. "Forget it," he said slowly. "It didn't occur to me that my word isn't enough."

Her eyes flashed with anger. "You owe me an apology for that, Cliff. Of all the— Aren't you forgetting a few details, like Keith Johnson, and what I've already told you?"

"It's an old cliché," he said with a grin, "but you're even more beautiful when you get mad."

Her eyes stayed level with his. "Go to hell."

39

He stood and bowed slightly, mocking her. "Apologies are in order and are hereby extended to the beautiful young lady who is pissed off at me," he said loudly.

"Cliff! People are looking at us. Please!"

"Why shouldn't they? We're both beautiful. Oscar!" Heads turned.

"Cliff!"

"Apology accepted?"

"My God, yes, *yes!*"

Oscar stood by the table.

"The lady," Brady said with a deep bow, "would like to buy us a drink."

CHAPTER IV

"How do you want it, Mr. Brady? We can run you through this whole thing from any angle you like. We can start off with the reports we've discarded—sun dogs, airplanes, comets, meteors, stars and planets, birds, ice-crystal clouds, balloons, satellites, plasmoids and corona discharges, cloud reflections of search-lights, cloud formations, flares, fireworks, noc-tilucent clouds, contrails, rockets, skydivers: you name it, we've got it." Lt. Col. Jim Trap-nell, USAF, director of Project Blue Book, swung his feet to his desk top and grinned at Cliff Brady.

Brady was at Wright-Patterson Air Force Base near Dayton, Ohio, headquarters for Proj-ect Blue Book, the Air Force investigation of UFO phenomena that extended back to the late summer of 1947. Brady had been assured before his departure from New York, the assurance stemming directly from the highest Pentagon levels, that the staff of Blue Book would open all their files for his perusal, and would, as well, respond to whatever questions he brought to them. But his experience at Barstow made him wary of Air Force brass.

He didn't return Trapnell's grin. "What else?"

"Hallucinations, delusions, illusions, hoaxes, pranks," the colonel rattled out quickly, ticking off each item one by one on his fingers. "Deliberate acts, misconceptions, autosuggestion, hypnotism—the whole ball of wax that has nothing to do with really seeing anything in the air. You can exclude from this the effects of mirages, inversion layers, refraction, reflection, and other similar effects."

Brady whistled. "You sound as if you've lived with this for a long time," he said at last. "Maybe I'd better find out right away if you've got any bona fide sightings."

The colonel waved a hand airily. "Oh, sure," he said easily. "Thousands of 'em." He gestured to an adjacent room filled from one end to the other with filing cabinets. "The master file, in there," he went on. "We break down reports into categories that enable us to dismiss many of them quickly. Saves time, and all that. After you've worked on this sort of thing as long as we have, you can do a run-through faster than you might think. At least ninety percent of everything we receive here gets into the 'immediately identified' files. That's the first group I gave you. Airplanes to balloons, planets to plasmoids. The lot. All quite ordinary, except"—he chuckled—"to the inexperienced onlooker. *He* can see anything."

Brady chewed his lip. He hadn't expected this breezy attitude to UFO investigations by the Air Force. Then he realized he didn't truly know what to expect. He'd heard the Air Force's Project Blue Book was a sinister plot kept under security cloaks so as to carry out a monstrous deception against the public. He'd heard, almost within the same breath, that the whole thing was a front, that the Pentagon assigned harebrained administrative clerks as a sop to public demands for UFO studies, and no one really gave a damn. Neither of the two extremes proved valid. What Brady found had him still off balance.

Lt. Col. James R. Trapnell, for example. A clean-cut, intelligent and alert officer who, by the ribbons on his chest, had managed to get in some violent, and successful, air combat. With his own Korean air-combat experience behind him, Brady could recognize a pro when he ran into one. Trapnell was a pro. He was also, from what Brady had learned of him, a man with several degrees in engineering and science. If anyone were qualified to act as chief honcho for the Air Force's UFO shop, Trapnell was the right man. And that threw Brady. With all those attributes to his credit, Trapnell was unexpectedly open, calm, and quite objective about his job. Not very many people were paid the salary of a lieutenant colonel to look after errant UFO's.

"What about the unidentified files, Colonel?" Brady still didn't know how he was going to hack this thing.

"More than enough of those." Trapnell was all courtesy and cooperation. Brady pushed it.

"Are they . . . will they be open for my inspection?"

"Of course," Trapnell agreed quickly. "I know quite a bit about you, Mr. Brady, and I assure you complete cooperation is the order of the day."

That was overdoing it. "The Pentagon," Brady said, more in statement than in question. "They told me—"

"Forgive me," Trapnell interrupted. "Of course we've got the TWX from the funny farm. I wasn't referring to that."

Brady waited.

"You don't know my voice, Brady," Trapnell said. Brady didn't miss it. The colonel had dropped the "Mr."

"But I know yours," Trapnell went on. "Quite well, in fact." He laughed.

"Have we met?"

"Not face to face," Trapnell said. "I flew support missions in Korea. Thunderthuds." Brady grinned at the pilot slang for the old F-84 fighter-bomber. "And if I remember correctly, your call sign was 'Dingbat Seven-Two' wasn't it?"

Brady stared. "I'll be damned."

"You flew one of those air-control jobbies,"

Trapnell continued. "We used to watch you going in." He shook his head in open admiration. "It was bad enough getting down there in one of the iron birds. But in something with fabric on it; Jesus . . ."

No question about it, Brady knew. He *would* see everything the Air Force had on UFO's.

Project Blue Book occupied office space in the Air Force System Command's Foreign Technology Division. Instead of being shunted to some remote office as a sop to public outcries for official UFO investigations, as part of the Foreign Technology Division Blue Book had available the highest level of engineering and scientific intelligence. Rather than having to forage for themselves, Blue Book investigators could call upon the best scientific and engineering talent in the country. It was a priority effort with quality. Brady hadn't expected that. Trapnell convinced him, through the first minutes of their meeting, that the people assigned to Blue Book were of excellent qualifications. But that the UFO investigating staff had access to so much professional talent was new to him. It also confirmed his decision to utilize the results of more than twenty years of professional investigation. Brady never could have gained access to sightings from around the world, attended with the results of investigations, and specifically how those studies were carried out. Trapnell assured him he would also be given access to whatever the Air Force

45

had available in the way of photographs and films.

Brady received Trapnell's words with growing hope he could dig through the morass of material to produce concrete results. But there was another bridge to cross.

"How much of your material is classified?" he asked Trapnell.

"You mean UFO's? None," the colonel replied. "However, certain files are classified, but that's got nothing to do with UFO reports." Trapnell noted the disbelieving look on Brady's face. "I know," he added quickly, "that sounds like a convenient cover-up. It isn't, believe me. The classification has to do with military equipment or facilities, and—"

"That's going to leave me with a couple of blank spaces," Brady said. He didn't like this part of it. Under the blanket of security you could hide anything, no matter how open he would find everything else.

"We anticipated that," Trapnell said. "Your name, as you know, carries weight in the Pentagon. Your record, plus the fact that you had top-secret clearance when you were in uniform, allowed us to do something that doesn't happen very often. Under the restriction—we'll have you sign some papers for this—under the restriction that you agree not to print material that's obviously classified, we can give you access to everything we've got."

"That can be a two-edged sword," Brady muttered.

Trapnell nodded. "Of course it can. We're not trying to lock you inside any—"

"Look," Brady broke in. "I appreciate the confidence. I mean that. But signing papers is out. I can't do that, Colonel. *You* are cooperative. Maloney in the Pentagon is cooperative. You may not be here next month and Maloney can get hit by a truck. That leaves a piece of paper with my signature on it. If someone then questions what I write, you've got me over a barrel. I don't mean you personally. Hell, man, you know the score. Signing papers on a subject this broad is idiotic. I'm sorry, because you're obviously trying to help. But I won't sign any documents."

Trapnell digested what Brady had said. Abruptly he leaned forward and made some notes on a pad. "All right," he said. "I see your point." He looked up at Brady. "I can't authorize your getting into our classified files on my own. You say you know General Maloney well?"

"Real well. We flew a couple of missions together in Korea."

"I'll put a call in to the general this afternoon and see what we can do. If Maloney's found your word good enough before, I can't see why he'd change now."

Brady nodded. "That's fine." He looked around the office. "How's the coffee supply in this scientific nuthouse of yours?"

"Strong enough to curl your toes."

"I might need it," Brady said.

"You will." Trapnell laughed.

The first order of business, Brady learned, was to separate the wheat from the chaff. With the full-time help of Jim Trapnell, he went through the "obvious" rejections of UFO reports. "Obvious," in this instance, meant actual objects sighted in the sky that *seemed* to be anything but aircraft or balloons, but at the same time definitely were not unexplainable, no matter how bizarre. High-altitude balloons were one of the better examples. Balloons made of highly reflective material were sent to heights of more than 130,000 feet. During certain periods of the day, especially at dusk, when the sun's rays struck the balloon at a low angle, the balloon became a tremendous disc hurtling through the stratosphere. It picked up winds as great as 400 miles an hour. Put a few clouds between the observer and the balloon and the speed relative to the eye became several thousand miles an hour. Sometimes the balloon left in its wake a swirl of ice crystals and dust, and these, also caught by the sun, became the blazing exhaust of a great disc that just *had* to be a huge machine in the upper heavens—when it wasn't anything of the sort. Sometimes research balloons went out in clusters and accounted for reports of discs in formation.

There were other times when the balloons were responsible for reports of great disc craft hurtling with tremendous speed through the upper air and making right-angle turns at thousands of miles an hour. Temperature inversions in the air, Trapnell explained, gave the optical effect. To the naked eye, to a motionpicture camera, the disc *was* moving with tremendous speed and *did* make right-angle turns. Inversions, layers of air of different temperatures, distorted, bent, twisted, and otherwise affected light rays so as to create what could properly be termed a mirage.

The same inversion effects in the air, Trapnell went on, caused thousands of reports on every type of UFO. Venus setting near the horizon could change color rapidly, expand swiftly in size so that it seemed to be hurtling through the air, and became so bright it appeared to the eye as a dazzling searchlight.

"That's something that throws me," Brady said. "I've seen the planets plenty of times from the ground and when I've been flying. I just do *not* understand how you can take a planet for something whizzing through the air."

Trapnell listened with signs of growing amusement. "Brady, I felt the same way before I got in this business," he said. "Now I believe *anything* can happen in terms of what people see. You know that Venus is so bright, sometimes you can see it in broad daylight?"

"I've heard about that, but I've never been able to see it, and I've looked."

"Well, take my word for it. Sometimes Venus even throws a shadow after dark."

"I didn't know *that*."

"It's true. You get a combination of inversion layers, haze and mist, smoke, or whatever, and you've got a bona fide UFO on your hands.

Especially where there's flat country, such as Florida, where Venus has been responsible for God knows how many UFO reports. Something else, too," Trapness said as a thought came to him. "If someone stares for any length of time at Venus, or Jupiter, for that matter, and he doesn't have a balancing point of reference, *then* things get even wilder."

"You mean problems with the eyes?"

"Uh-huh. Most pilots know the dangers of staring without depth-perception reference. Other people don't. But when they don't have a balancing point of reference and they stare, you know what happens?"

Brady did. "Sure," he said. "You've got something wandering all around the sky."

"That's right. And it expands so swiftly because of inversion layers that it seems to be rushing back and forth and doing right-angle turns and all sorts of fancy maneuvers. All the time you're looking at plain old Venus."

Brady made some notes. "You mentioned mirages before. I know something about them, of course. How often do you figure mirages figure in your reports?"

Trapnell clasped his hands behind his head and leaned back in his chair. "More than is indicated in the files," he said finally. "That's because most people don't understand what makes up a mirage. They think it's got to be water in the desert or the effect of water on a straight road during the summer when it's hot. The fact of the matter is a mirage can happen just about anywhere."

50

Brady frowned. "That sort of screws up what you're trying to do, doesn't it?"

"Man, is that ever the truth," Trapnell said with a vigorous nod of his head. "Mirages, inversion layers, refraction, reflection, something we call reflectional dispersion—it's all there in one big grab bag. The problem is, the observer doesn't know what's in the air. Haze, ice crystals, industrial smoke particles, clouds, water droplets, sand, dust, all of them stirred up by the wind, all of them layered in different temperature strata—Jesus, Brady, it's a wonder we don't get more UFO reports from these effects. What you've got to understand is that all these things, the list I just gave you, form atmospheric lenses. *Lenses*," he repeated with emphasis, "just as much as if you've rigged a system of lenses and mirrors in the air." Trapnell leaned forward again. "Look, you've seen the reports of discs in formation? As many as twenty or thirty or more?"

"Right."

"You've seen how they move through the sky at different speeds? Sometimes at a few hundred miles an hour, sometimes at thousands of miles per hour. Okay?"

"Go on," Brady said.

"Do you believe there're discs moving in formation through the air? At thousands of miles an hour?"

Brady smiled. "No."

"Got any ideas as to what they might be?"

"Never mind the guessing games," Brady said, his irritation quick to show.

51

Trapnell laughed. "Forgive me," he said. "I don't often get an intelligent audience for this long, and I can't resist the tweaks every now and then. Okay. Would you believe automobile headlights?"

Brady made a face that spoke his thoughts for him.

Trapnell buzzed his secretary. "Set up the New Mexico films for Mr. Brady, will you? I'll want to see them in about ten or fifteen minutes."

"Right, Colonel."

Trapnell turned back to Brady. "We'll let that one lie for the moment and come back to it when you see the film. You want some more poop on mirages?"

"If it applies."

"It applies, all right. Let's take this one from the beginning. You understand how light rays travel through the air?"

Brady groaned. "Give me a quick run-through."

"It's simple enough. Normally light rays travel in a concave path that intersects with the horizon. 'Normal' means when temperature distribution through the air is normal. Often it's not. We get two conditions that set up a mirage."

Brady took notes steadily.

Trapnell waited for Brady's pen to stop moving. "Sometimes the air just above the ground becomes exceptionally warm," the colonel continued. "The air expands and it becomes less dense. Then, the convex path shortens. If it's

52

really hot, the air itself becomes concave. Whap! Light starts playing tricks because it's everywhere it shouldn't be. And since all the human eye sees is reflected light, things start moving around or ending up where they shouldn't be. Now, you also get the temperature inversion. In this case you get a layer of warm air over another layer of cold air. What happens is that the path of light rays lenghtens. The light rays parallel the earth's surface at greater distance."

"And you get more optical . . . um . . . effects isn't the word I want," Brady mulled aloud.

"Mirage is as good as any," Trapnell offered. "Let me relate it to seeing things from the air. The distortion and the displacement can really be fantastic. Under the conditions I've described, for example, a city that's over the horizon will show up to a pilot as being in view, and sometimes a few hundred feet, or even a few thousand, above the horizon. Castles in the sky and all that. This is why we get reports sometimes of land areas distorted into unusual shapes that seem to float in the air. Now, if it's a lake that's being reflected, and you feed in the factors of the observer, the pilot in this case, also at altitude and moving, what you can end up with is—"

"A huge silvery shape rushing through the air," Brady finished for him.

"Affirmative," Trapnell said. "The next thing is that the speed of your great silvery shape changes rapidly. It can move slowly or with explosive bursts of speed. It can pick up lights from the ground, other aircraft in the sky, just about anything. We had someone report in that he'd seen a huge torpedo shape rushing through the air at night. He said there wasn't any question, that twenty people in the airliner confirmed the sighting. Said the torpedo shape had windows, that it left a wake behind it. The man was telling the truth."

Brady sighed. "I've learned a lesson from you," he said, "and that's not to lead your trick questions. So I won't ask what he saw."

Trapnell grinned at him. "Right. It was a mirage. Fortunately this observer—a pilot, by the way—had an exact recording of time, altitude, position, and course. We were able to backtrack on an occasion when the temperature inversion conditions were right. Know what he saw? A yacht."

"A *yacht?* Jesus, that's hard to believe."

"Sure it is," Trapnell said affably. "Nevertheless it's true. One of our investigators saw the same object a few nights later when he duplicated the flight path of the original observer. It turned out the yacht was thirty or forty miles away in a small harbor. Which, incidentally was very well lit up. The yacht was moving slowly. The temperature inversion picked it up, projected it as an image in the sky. What the pilot, and his passengers, saw was the hull—they didn't see the superstructure or the masts. Just the hull, and the portholes, which were lit up. The wake the pilot saw was just that—the wake of the boat in the harbor.

But when it was picked up by the particular optical conditions and transmitted as a mirage, the torpedo shape—the hull with the ports— seemed to be moving at thousands of miles an hour. Since the pilot was convinced he was seeing something in the air, he *knew*—he was interpreting with his eyes, of course—he *knew* that what was trailing his mystery ship just had to be exhaust of some kind."

Brady stared glumly at his notepad. What the hell did this do to the reports of Keith Johnson and the other pilots? Surely they would be able to distinguish between a mirage and something that really was in the air with them. Brady had flown enough formation so that he had experience with objects close by and at great distance. But according to what Trapnell was telling him, what the observer saw had nothing to do with his eyes playing tricks on him. A delusion was a mental condition. A mirage was something else. Optically the mirage was *real*. A camera's film recorded it. It had nothing to do with delusion.

What about that disc at Barstow Air Force Base? From what Trapnell was saying, it could have been a mirage or a similar optical effect. The eyewitnesses saw something. Their eyes didn't play tricks on them. But it could have been an optical eff——Wait a moment, Brady thought. Mirages don't cut off radios sixty feet beneath the ground and knock out power stations!

"You got something special?"

Brady looked up at Trapnell. "Nothing for

the moment," he said. "I'll come back to it later. That film of yours ready yet?"

The colonel glanced at his watch. "Should be. Let's take a look at it and then break for lunch."

"Good deal."

Brady ordered a double shrimp cocktail, steak rare, and a stiff martini. He went through the drink quickly, to the amusement of Jim Trapnell. "You look as if you needed that," the colonel observed.

"I did," Brady agreed, ordering a second. "That's a hell of a movie show you got there."

"Sure is," Trapnell said. "Straightens out a lot of enthusiasts." He hesitated a moment. "How about yourself?"

"I'm not a believer," Brady said cautiously, "in the sense that I've seen UFO's skittering through the air. But I've talked with . . ." He shook his head. "Never mind," he said. "Not yet, anyway. I want to save my questions for later. That film of yours was enough for lunch."

It had been all that. Perfect formations of discs hurtling through the night air. Sometimes four objects, sometimes as many as fifty or sixty. And every one of them, Trapnell said in a running commentary with the film, was simply a mirage. A reflected light, or lights. Auto headlights thirty miles away, shining into the air as cars drove along an incline. The lights flashed into the night sky, were bent, separated and bounced against another inversion layer many miles distant. The observers looked up and saw discs in formation, ghostly, silent, but terribly real.

Was there proof they were optical effects? Proof enough. The Air Force scientists set up an experiment. When the inversion-layer effects were prominent, they drove cars up the same incline. This time they capped the auto headlights with transparent plastic. Presto: great formations of discs in yellow, red and blue sailing through the sky. End of case.

Trapnell had an even more interesting film to kick off the afternoon session. "We've put together in a sample film a group of sightings," he explained.

"You mean of actual sightings? UFO's?"

Trapnell shook his head. "Uh-uh. IFO's. Identified Flying Objects." He signaled the projectionist to start the picture. "I'll give you a running commentary as we go along."

Brady studied two DC-8 airliners flying through a hazy sky. Ordinarily DC-8's don't fly in formation. And certainly they don't fly in formation with one airplane holding a perfect *inverted* position over the other.

"This effect is common enough," Trapnell said. "Not ordinary, but not rare. There's only one airplane, of course, and it is miles away. You're not seeing the single DC-8, but its mirror image reflected from another part of the sky. Sometimes you get this double effect with the planes flying side by side and sometimes you see it like this—one airplane inverted."

The film clip ended and a new sequence began. Brady started from his chair. In the film, shown near the horizon, was a disc-shaped craft, absolutely clear in its outline, rushing through the air, the speed accented by clouds between the camera and the disc. What startled Brady was its color and the dazzling exhaust trail it left behind. Along the top of the disc the color showed as a bright blue. The bottom was a brilliant red, and a reddish-orange exhaust trailed behind. Suddenly the disc shot upward in a steep climb, hovered for several seconds, and plunged vertically.

"What the hell is *that!*" Brady exclaimed.

Trapnell's chuckle was the answer. "Hang on to your seat," he said. "You're seeing the planet Venus again. That's our old friend under a really wild temperature inversion. To save time, we kept the camera in place. See the clock on the side? Okay, this next scene was taken several minutes later."

The mixture of color was gone. A dazzling light in the sky replaced the multicolored disc. Now its shape was perfectly round.

"Keep watching," Trapnell urged.

Several minutes later Brady watched an ordinary picture of Venus sliding toward the horizon. He shook his head.

"Ready for the next one?" asked the colonel.

"Christ, I think I'm ready for anything," Brady said. "Let's have the works."

Two scenes showed in rapid sequence. The first appeared as a long broken streak in the sky, something glowing, brilliantly, moving with tremendous speed. As it disappeared, it left a phantom glow in the night sky. The second sequence was much like the first, but the original light was more circular. As Brady watched, it broke up into a loose cluster that ripped across the screen.

"I recognize the second one," Brady said. "I've seen that myself. Fireball, wasn't it?"

"Right. Big meteor. When it heats up, it sometimes explodes into several chunks. They come in all colors. The ones that shake people the most are the green and yellow fireballs. People just won't believe they're meteors."

"What about the first scene?"

"Warhead reentry. It was taken from Ascension Island. You saw the entire sequence. Tracking camera stuff." In the gloom Brady saw Trapnell turn to him. "Now comes dessert."

By now Brady was ready to expect anything. He got more than he bargained for.

A huge disc showed on the screen. Sunlight reflected brilliantly from its curving upper dome. Between the top and bottom shell was a row of ports or windows. The disc, slicing at a steep angle toward the ground, rushed in and out of clouds but tracked steadily by the camera. Brady saw the thin exhaust trail behind the disc.

Trapnell stopped the film. He turned again to face Brady. "Give up?"

Brady pointed to the screen. "Unless I've lost all my marbles, I saw a disc. A real, live, bona fide dyed-in-the-wool disc with ports and an exhaust trail and . . ." He glared at the colonel. "Are you going to tell me that god-damned thing is also an illusion?"

"We call this the Congressional Special," Trapnell said by way of reply. "It shakes up everybody."

"You're shaking *me*."

"You ready for the rest?"

"You mean there's more?"

"Sure. Lets you in on the secret."

Brady leaned back in his chair. "Christ, let's not stop now."

The film started again. The disc was still there, still rushing through the sky. Then something strange began to happen. The curving metal shape distorted, shimmering in the bright sunlight. Near the rear of the disc Brady watched a great tail begin to appear. As he studied the screen, his eyes wide, the curvature of the disc evaporated. Brady stared at a Boeing C-135 in a steep descent. The lights went on.

"That little gem," Trapnell said, "teaches us several things. One, cameras can be dangerous things. Two, never interpret with the eye—use the brain. Three, always have all the facts at hand. Four, always ask to see the full run of any film. Five, understand temperature inversions and meteorological phenomena. Six—"

"Hold it right there," Brady said. "Just tell me what was going on, will you?"

"The disc was a reality," Trapnell said, "but only in the optical sense. What you saw was part of a steep and rapid descent test of the Charlie 135. The bird started down from forty-three thousand feet. On that particular day the temperature was minus eighty. That's Fahrenheit. The bird came down quickly and went through an inversion layer. Moist, warm air; that sort of thing. The metal was cold and the ship was near sonic velocity. With all these conditions put together, you can get a condensation shock wave. Which, to the eye, or the camera," he added, "turns an ordinary airplane into a disc going hellbent for leather for the ground. A condensation shock wave also reflects light in the same manner that metal reflects light. When the plane went through the inversion layer . . . well, you saw for yourself."

"Does that sort of thing happen very often?"

Trapnell shrugged. "Hard to say. We've got one hundred and ninety-four intelligence people around the world, assigned to different bases—they pull double duty by investigating reports for us—but this is the only film I've seen that shows so clearly the upper and lower shock wave. Of course the shock wave itself is common enough. You've seen films of the B-70, haven't you?"

Brady nodded.

"Have you seen the shots where it's riding a visible shock wave?"

"No."

"Again it's a matter of understanding meteorological phenomena. You get shock contrails from wingtips, propeller tips, and when you're near Mach one. Not the same as the exhaust trails. It's not rare. But one like you saw on the film appears to be quite uncommon. If it happened more often, we'd be deluged in here with 'positive' sightings of discs."

Brady pondered what he'd heard and seen, and checked off a list on his notepad. "While we're on meteorological," he said, "give me a quick rundown on sun dogs, will you?"

"Make that sun dogs and moon dogs," Trapnell said.

"I didn't know there was a nighttime effect with that stuff," Brady admitted.

"There is. It's a reflection of the sun in a layer of flat ice crystals," Trapnell explained. "Technically, when that happens, you get what the scientists call a sub-sun. We've bastardized it into sun dog. The thing that shakes you when you get a good one is that the sun dog appears at a point adjacent to the real sun. What's important is that the apparition, so to speak, can be just as bright as the actual sun. It doesn't always appear as a single source point of light, either. It develops several sun dogs, so you have a cluster or a formation. The moon dog is the same thing at night. Except people get a lot more shook about something at night than they do during bright daylight."

"What do they look—I mean, how do they appear to a pilot?"

"Depends. Viewing angle, size of ice crystals. That sort of thing. But if conditions are right, it will take up formation with a plane. It may even chase the airplane. Remember, the pilot actually sees a source of light. It's real. Sometimes we get a fighter jock who's irritated and he goes to hot guns and turns toward the thing. He gets confused very quickly. The sun dog, or moon dog, will either speed up, slow down, hold a constant separation, or even seem to attack the airplane."

Brady felt overwhelmed. "How effective—or meaningful—are radar sightings?"

Trapnell shifted in his chair. "For tracking UFO's?"

"Yes."

"Unreliable, to sum it up in a word. Radar picks up ice crystals, birds individually and in formation, balloons, and all sorts of things. If it's near the ground but out of sight of the operator in the radar room, it will even show Ferris wheels as something moving through the sky. Then there's the effect of inversion layers when the radar beam is bent—"

"Wait a moment. I thought radar waves were strictly linear, always straight-line stuff."

"We thought so too for a long time," Trapnell admitted. "Now we know better. An inversion layer will bend a radar beam just as it bends light. We've had UFO flaps where radar picked up things moving at tremendous speeds—and no one could see anything. It turned out the radar waves were bending and reflecting planes a few hundred miles away. In fact, we've even had UFO voices—ghost voices."

"How could that happen?"

"Same effect," Trapnell said. "VHF radio especially. Inversion layer bends the radio signal and we pick it up when nothing's in the air. Shook up a lot of communications people."

Brady shook his head. "I'll bet."

One more thing remained on his checklist. "Anything else that contributes heavily to your identification of UFO's? I mean as a major source of reports?"

"That would be electrical."

"Plasmoids?"

"You know about those?"

"Some," Brady said. "I've seen plenty of St. Elmo's fire and I've done research on plasmoids and corona discharges."

"How about ball lightning?"

"Uh-uh. Fill me in on that."

"Let me give you a quickie course on ball lightning and atmospheric plasma. It won't take long and it might straighten out a few points for you."

"Okay; shoot."

"Well, for starters, a plasma is essentially an electrified gas. Its electrons flow freely. But they do so in the middle of positively charged molecules without becoming attached to the molecules. This makes them electrically neutral. A plasma cloud has its own magnetic field. Still with me?"

"Yeah. I've almost but not quite got a headache. Don't quit now."

"All right. The magnetic field of the plasma, and surrounding magnetic fields that are always in the air, accelerate the electrons. The electrons also collide with neutral molecules, those without electrical charges. The long and short of it is that energy is always being increased or released. And that energy is radiant—"

"Can it be seen?"

"Sure can," Trapnell said. "It oscillates, or vibrates, in the ultraviolet, the visible spectrum, and in the infrared. If it's in the visible blue or visible red part of the spectrum—that's electromagnetic, by the way—the plasma glows in blue or red colors to the human eye. And when people see glowing blue or red clouds, especially when they move erratically or travel in a long straight line, well, they get shook, and we've got a rash of UFO reports on our hands." Trapnell looked at Brady and grinned. "You ready for the ball lightning now?"

"I may not last much longer."

Trapnell guffawed. "I'll get Charlene to rub your fevered brow," he said. "Charlene's attended to more UFO headaches than any other living human. She's my secretary, by the way. I wasn't always this calm about things from somewhere out there. It took me months to quit growing gray hairs." The colonel lit a cigarette. "Okay, to the ball lightning. Short and sweet, it's simply a special kind of plasma. I really can't tell you too much about it—"

"Don't tell me it's classified, for Christ's sake."

"Your headache is showing."

"Sorry about that. Seriously. Go on."

"I can't tell you much about it because no one really knows much about ball lightning. It doesn't show as frequently as other phenomena. But when it does, wow! It comes in about every color, shape, and size you can imagine. Unless you're hep on the scientific end of things, you simply won't believe—"

"Never mind the rah-rah," Brady interjected. "I'm hep enough. And my headache *is* showing. Lemme apologize ahead of time."

Trapnell nodded in acceptance. "Okay. Size first. People have seen ball lightning more than twenty feet in diameter. The most common colors change from orange to red and then they skip back over the spectrum to higher energies. That's the electromagnetic radiation, by the way. They go up into green, blue and violet."

"What about the shape?"

"You name it, we got it. Spherical, discoid, torpedo, wobbly, firm—the works."

"Any pictures?"

"Plenty. I'll show you some stills and movies. Sometimes they have edges that are . . . well . . . fuzzy is a good description. At other times they're sharply defined. And sometimes you see them surrounded by a glowing haze, or a blur. They also rotate when they feel like it. And they're not quiet."

Brady looked up at that last remark.

"Not all the time, I mean. They've been known to hum, whir, and pulsate. The sound sometimes is rasping, sometimes, well, it's a smooth keening cry. Some people have also reported it as sounding like a bass fiddle at its lowest pitch."

"That's great. It does everything but sing opera."

"Just about," Trapnell agreed. "I didn't mention that it hovers, or drifts slowly, or can go scooting across the countryside at hundreds of miles an hour. Maybe thousands, for all we know. It can also make right-angle turns, which upsets people rather easily. What shakes them up even more is when it tears down a road and then reverses direction faster than the eye can follow. *Without* turning, I should add."

". . . when it tears down a road," Brady said. "Could ball lightning be responsible for all those reports of UFO's following cars?"

"Uh-huh. That's our baby, all right. It can also knock out ignition systems or just screw up car radios and lights. It's happened many times."

Brady nodded. "Is that the course? Are you—"

Trapnell held up his hand. "One final item. That is, if you're still able to go on like this. You look like a man who's taking a beating, Cliff. You're getting in a few days what's taken me many months to absorb."

"Hell, the final straw can only break my back. Let's have it."

"In a nutshell, it's auroras. The northern lights. Or, for that matter," Trapnell append- ed, "the southern lights as well. Are you familiar with—"

"I did a couple of stories on the subject," Brady said. "Give me the visual effects."

"Okay. You know, then, that auroras are

67

created by intense electrical activity in the upper atmosphere—sometimes hundreds of miles high. I'll give you one shining example of what auroras can bring on. This incident was seen by thousands of people across almost all of northwest Europe. The reports apparently were all accurate, that is, from different sources. What people saw was a huge and brilliant disc that showed up on the east-northeast horizon and then moved slowly across the sky. During its passage it changed shape from a disc into an elongated ellipse and then *back* to a disc before it went over the horizon. I should mention," Trapnell emphasized, "that many scientists tracked the disc. They were the ones who confirmed the color as white, pearly-white, greenish-white, and yellow-white. You ready for the finale?"

"Don't spare me now."

"It was seventy miles long by ten miles in diameter when it assumed the elongated ellipse shape."

"My God. It must have been seen for hundreds of miles," Brady said.

"It was."

"Any photos?"

"Some. It was seen at night and they weren't too good."

"How about radar?"

Trapnell shook his head. "Nope. No radar tracking."

"But why? How could they miss something that big?"

"Oh, they didn't miss it. It's just that no one had any radar for tracking. You see, this particular disc was seen about eighty-five years ago."

CHAPTER V

Brady saw a large red barn, a silo nearby and, set off to the side amid a stand of high trees, a neat farmhouse. It was a perfectly normal scene of a Midwest farm. "Look at the details," Trapnell advised him through the flickering gloom of the projection room. "Get them fixed in your mind." Brady made out several trucks; a group of horses beyond a whitewashed fence.

"Anything special you want me to pick out?" Brady asked.

"Not yet," came the reply. "The action takes place in a few moments. I want you to get the scene clear in your mind so there won't be any outside interference with what happens."

Brady concentrated on significant details, picked out a power line in the distance, then saw several people and a dog enter the scene from behind the farmhouse. But that was it. Impatient to get with the heart of the matter, he realized he was losing his cool. He was still in a funk about the previous day. Trapnell had overwhelmed him with sheer weight of information on UFO's. Or, to cut it closer, with IFO's—identified phenomena. If the man had tried to conceal information, if he'd once been evasive, Brady might have felt some measure of triumph. Even if it were negative. But nothing of the sort had happened. Trapnell was responsive in every way to Brady's pointed queries. Even General Maloney had come through from the Pentagon with the verbal okay for Brady's access to anything in Blue Book files.

Yet there was still hope. Agreeing to Brady's request, Trapnell concentrated first on the 90-odd percent of UFO reports, photographs, and films that fell into the identified category. Brady wanted as much grounding as possible before he entered the remaining 10 percent loosely regarded as "unknowns." Even there, Trapnell cautioned him, unknown could mean anything. It certainly did not mean, he emphasized, that an unknown could be equated conclusively as a mechanical object. It *might* be. Then again, if might also be certain phenomena wholly beyond comprehension of the scientists who attempted to categorize and identify every reliable UFO sighting report they received. Unknown, Trapnell stressed, was a literal identification. No one knew for certain what the phenomena, or "whatzit," might be.

Trapnell's voice cut into his thoughts. "Okay, here we go. This is going to be a beaut."

It began along the right side of the screen. Three white objects—no, gleaming white, Brady corrected himself—floated through the air. For a moment their movement prevented him from confirming their shape. Then he saw they were spherical. He tried to guess their size but knew it was impossible without depth references. The three gleaming spheres drifted slowly through the air above the farmhouse. Brady saw the people on the screen turn, hands pointing, gawking. Abruptly the spherical objects picked up speed. Brady couldn't tell the acceleration. One moment they moved slowly, almost lazily. In the next instant they streaked over the ground as if propelled from a gun. The photographer almost lost them.

Brady couldn't believe what his eyes saw. The three spheres took up a loose rotating and whirling formation as they raced over the ground. The camera showed them disappearing briefly behind several trees and a billboard along a road. *That's no illusion. Illusions or mirages don't disappear behind something and then show up on the other side!*

As if reading his mind, Trapnell commented on the same point. "We've already run timing tests," the colonel said. "The speed maintained by the objects for a period before they reached the billboard checks out. In other words, there's no change in the speed between the time they go behind the billboard and when they emerge from the other side. Now watch what they do."

The spheres seemed to go crazy. Their motion of whirling one about the other became a frenzied spinning. Then they re-formed as a loose cluster, rotating vertically one about the other, the cluster itself racing low over the ground, dodging trees and other objects. Brady had never seen or even heard of anything resembling what he now saw on the screen.

"All right," Trapnell said. "Do you see the key? Those things are following the power lines."

Brady hadn't noticed that before, but this was his first viewing of the film and Trapnell had seen it many times. The other man confirmed his thoughts. "We weren't certain about the power lines until we sent some of our people to the area. They checked out everything on the ground, flew the route in a helicopter—the works. There's no question of it. The power line has something to do with those objects." By now the spherical shapes were receding in the distance. Brady blinked. They had vanished.

"What happened?" he fired at Trapnell.

"Just as you saw it," the colonel said. "They vanished." He motioned for the overhead lights and turned to Brady. "Want to see it again?" Brady nodded. The second time around he concentrated on the spherical white shapes.

74

When the lights went on, he hadn't the faintest notion of what they might be.

"The science boys have pretty much ruled out a plasmoid or corona-discharge effect," Trapnell commented.

Brady shook his head slowly. "Any ideas?"

"Some. Mostly guesswork, however. One of our eggheads is holding forth a theory that the spheres represent a form of life."

"You're putting me on."

"Nope." Trapnell said it matter-of-factly. "We have other films of these things. High-altitude stuff, playing in and out of thunderstorms with strong electrical activity. That's a definite tie-in. They *always* associate with electrical force of one kind or another."

"But—Christ, you said they might be living creatures!"

"I know it sounds crazy," Trapnell admitted. "But look at it from an objective viewpoint. Have you ever compared a jellyfish like the Portuguese man-of-war with an elephant? What two more dissimilar forms of life could there be? Or take a shrimp or flounder that lives seven miles down at the bottom of the ocean, in the Marianas Deep. The pressure down there would squeeze a man into the shape of a thin wafer—yet sea creatures get along quite nicely, thank you. Or take the things that fly. Did you know the largest flying creature today weighs over a billion—that's *billion*—times more than the smallest? That's the ratio of the smallest gnat to the largest bird, the albatross."

"Man, you are asking a lot," Brady said with open disbelief, when you ask me to accept those things as *alive*."

"Got any better ideas?"

"No, I don't. But that doesn't make me buy *your* answer."

"It's not a matter of buying it," Trapnell countered. "I said it was a theory. Which is growing in acceptance, by the way. That there are electrical life forms—based on electrical phenomena—that exist in the higher atmosphere and sometimes are attracted to lower levels. They're no more preposterous than the jellyfish and the elephant." The colonel smiled. "But like I say, we don't *know*. I just wanted you to be sure we weren't overlooking any possibilities."

Trapnell motioned for the projectionist to set up another film. When he turned back to Brady, the colonel's face was deadpan. "I'm talking off the record now," he said. "Okay?"

"Yes."

"This next reel is classified."

Brady's interest quickened. "I was hoping we'd get around to the hard stuff," he said.

"Sure, sure," Trapnell replied, a slight irritation showing. "I want to caution you again not to leap to any hasty conclusions." A smile flickered and was gone. "Not that you won't, though."

"You seem pretty certain," Brady said.

"I am." Trapnell said it with the finality of long experience. "I've been here before, remember?"

Brady nodded. He'd come to pay close attention even to Trapnell's side remarks. "One other point," the colonel added. "No running commentary during the first run-through."

"Any reason for that?"

Trapnell shrugged. "There's a lot to see. Better for you to take it in without interference. I recommend you save your questions for later."

It was Brady's turn to shrug. "You're the conductor on this ride," he said. "Let's go."

The lights went out.

It took Brady several seconds to recognize the scene. He watched the camera panning across the high, sloping structure of an early-warning radar. No question that this lay somewhere north of the Arctic Circle; huge snowdrifts and ice-sheeted buildings testified to that. Several men crossed before the film, shuffling awkwardly in heavy clothing, bent over to avoid a wind evident by the snow it whipped before its passage. Brady wished the scene had more light. The sun low on the horizon confused him for a moment until he realized he was watching the Arctic sun. They had more than twenty hours of daylight out of every twenty-four. He'd ask Jim Trapnell later about the time the film was shot.

The camera crossed the small confines of the radar station and started panning back in the other direction. Along the left corner of the screen Brady saw a momentary flash. Apparently the cameraman had seen the same flash of light. The camera stopped, blurred in an awkward motion, then swung quickly back to place the light close to the center of the screen. At this point all that could be seen was the white snow foreground, an indistinct horizon, the sun off to the right side of the picture, and the object.

It appeared to move. Without buildings in the foreground and only a single ice-encrusted radio mast in the distance, the motion at first was difficult to detect. Brady watched the slightly changing reflection and expanding size of the object. He looked carefully for, and saw, its position change relative to the top of the radio mast. It was approaching the cameraman.

The motion ended. For several seconds, during which Brady caught himself holding his breath, the object remained still, hovering in one place. He didn't know specifically why, but somehow Brady was convinced the object wasn't an airplane or a balloon carried by the wind. Christ, of course he knew. Trapnell would never have screened a film with *Secret* emblazoned across the opening frames unless
. . .

Suddenly the object began to glow. Brady corrected his first impression. He didn't know if the object glowed or the air around the shape had suddenly begun to glow. He couldn't tell. He saw the effect for only a second or two. Before he could adjust his eyes to the new scene, the object streaked off at a steep angle. The cameraman followed it briefly. In the changing angle Brady swore the shape became defined clearly as a disc. Until a few days ago he would have insisted he'd seen a disc. But after Trapnell's interrogation he knew he couldn't be certain of anything at first glance.

He heard the colonel's voice. "Stay where you are, Cliff. We'll run through it a second time in slow motion."

Brady didn't answer. All his attention riveted to the screen.

This time he *was* certain. Unless he was seeing an optical projection—and under those Arctic conditions he was convinced that wasn't the case—he had just watched a film of a disc in flight.

Brady let out a deep breath. "What the hell *was* that?" It was more demand than query.

The colonel held his gaze. "We don't know. We—"

"What do you mean you don't know!" Brady shouted. "You saw it big as life out there. You saw how it moved. That damned thing accelerated to a few thousand miles per hour before it went out of sight!"

Trapnell's bearing had stiffened. "I said we don't know. That's precisely what I mean. The official listing for the object you saw in this film is a 'good unknown.' " He rose to his feet and motioned for Brady to return to his office. As they walked along the hall, Brady pressed the colonel.

"I don't see how you can call that thing an unknown," he persisted. "It was damned obvious to me it was a machine and—"

"I'll grant it *looked* like a machine," Trapnell said.

"Looked hell. Do you want it to come out of the screen and bite you?"

Trapnell laughed harshly. "Yes." Abruptly he stopped and turned to face Brady. "That is exactly what I would like to have it do. Bite me, or anyone else. Or knock down a building or shoot down an airplane or sink a boat or steal the Taj Mahal, or *something.*"

"I don't get you."

"Jesus, we've got more film like the one you saw. Perhaps not as clear in terms of the UFO, the object," Trapnell corrected, "but we've got film up the ass. We've got movies taken over the Amazon River, over the North Pole, in Antarctica, over cities, and deserts and oceans. But we're not able to make a positive identification of what we see on that film."

"Including that disc you showed me?" Brady was incredulous.

"Including that disc." He started walking again. "Let's get some coffee while we continue this, okay?"

"All right," Brady said with ill-concealed anger. "I'll take it your way. You'll agree it wasn't an airplane, a helicopter, a dirigible, a blimp, a balloon, a—"

"Save your breath, Cliff. I'll tote it up for you. Nothing we discussed fits the bill. Every possible condition of which we know was considered. We don't know what the object was. No," he said with his hand raised to ward off the interruption, "wait a moment and hear me out. I'll tell you what the film *didn't* show us. We've got nothing for size—only crude guesses. It might have been huge and a long ways off or fairly small and close in; you can't tell from the film. No reports of any sound. The men were wearing earmuffs and heavy head covers, and with the strong wind they didn't hear a thing. There wasn't any sign of external control surfaces, of a cabin, of an antenna. Nothing in the way of propulsion was evident. There—"

"Hold it right there. What about that glow I saw?"

"Just before it accelerated?"

"Yep. Right then."

Trapnell shrugged. "We don't know and you don't know," he threw at Brady. "It could be a camera fogging effect ..."

"Bullshit."

". . . or it could have been, and probably was, some form of ionization in the air."

"It sure looked like that."

"As the madam said, 'In this business looks don't count.' " Trapnell grinned.

Brady sat back in his chair. "I don't get it," he said finally. "I don't get you or this outfit or the Air Force. What the hell. You've just given me a clear film of a disc, you have radar tracking, you have visual identification, you have ..." He shook his head again and reached for the coffee. "You've got the whole thing locked up and all you tell me is a good unknown. That damned thing," Brady said angrily, spilling his coffee as he gesticulated, "was a machine just as much as you and I are sitting in this room together."

Trapnell laughed softly.

"What's so goddamned funny?"

"You know the film you saw yesterday? The one on the Charlie 135 in the dive test?"

"So?"

"Run it through your mind again, will you?" Trapnell urged Brady. "But leave out the second part. Where you see the condensation shock wave dissipating. Okay?"

Brady thought it over. Before he could respond, Trapnell went on. "Just remember that film and what you saw. Perfect conditions of visibility. All meteorological, electrical, optical, and other factors well known. Broad daylight. Tracking cameras that are the best in the world. Radar tracking, with transponders in the big metal bird. Everything perfect, even better than the film we just saw at that radar station. So you see this disc coming lickety-split through the air, and you tie in all the other factors, and what have you got?" The colonel grinned hugely at the box into which he shoveled Brady. "We have, on the basis of your logic and common sense, absolute and unquestionable proof of a flying disc. A genuine, bona fide, caught-on-film disc.

"Which," the colonel added with a pointed finger, "was never there in the first place."

"Big deal," Brady sneered. "You don't twist me around that fast. From where I sit, you *refuse* to make a positive identification."

Trapnell studied him carefully. "You don't

mean that," he said after a pause. "We don't refuse anything of the sort. We also don't go off half-cocked."

"That's a matter of opinion," Brady said rudely. "I think it's just as much your responsibility to make a positive finding on something like this as it is to bend over backwards not to, as you said, go off half-cocked."

Trapnell applauded lightly. "Bravo."

"Sorry for the sharp teeth," Brady apologized with an abashed look. "But I meant what I said, Jim."

"I know you did. Maybe you can answer something for me?"

Brady waited.

"We've got that film. We say it's not enough. We need more, much more," Trapnell emphasized. "Could you bring that disc back to us again so we could take more pictures?"

"I don't get you."

"We put cameras in every radar station in that part of the world," Trapnell said, "hoping for a repetition. We got a lot of lights and strange things in the air that glowed, glittered, shone, pulsated, quivered, danced, and did a great many other things, but never sat still long enough to get its picture taken. One sighting isn't enough. *Ergo*—a good unknown is the answer."

"Don't you have other reports," Brady pushed, "from other parts of the world?"

"Sure do. Thousands of them."

"I don't mean the whole barrel of fish," Brady said, again impatient. He felt he was always permitted to get almost within reach of what he sought and then it was snatched away from him. "Hard sightings. Stuff you would call a good unknown?"

"That covers a lot of territory. Do you know what shapes we've seen in our 'good unknown' files?"

Brady shook his head.

"Discs, torpedo or cigar shapes, doughnut rings, spheres, discoids, stars, wheels, glowing lights of every color and size, formless objects pulsating in different colors, diamonds, squares, rectangles, pie-shaped, in the form of kites, like ice-cream cones, like balloons of every shape and size; we've got them in the form of huge ovals with sledlike runners, we've got spinning wheels, we've got central nuclei with blazing lights orbiting the center, we've got them like conventional aircraft but without wings or engines, we've got them in the form of rockets, delta-wing airplanes, submarines, scythes, eggs and ovals and boomerangs and ovoids and teardrops and crescent moons with bubbles in the center and God knows what else. And those are in the reliable and good unknown files. Any comment?"

"Yeah. You're a son of a bitch to deal with," Brady said.

"Thanks. I consider that a compliment in this job."

"I meant it to be," Brady came back. "All right, I'll lean on your experience. Out of all the material you've studied, if you had to pick the most reliable sightings—I mean the kind of shape—which way would you turn?" Brady motioned for Trapnell not to answer yet. "Let me add something to that. You've got things fixed in your mind from your side of the desk," Brady continued. "Try to take it from my side of the fence. Come into this thing cold, then consider everything. Not simply in the shape of the UFO, but the details of the sightings themselves. On that basis, what would you choose?"

Trapnell looked unhappy. "You're asking me to be two people at the same time, aren't you? Maybe I didn't make myself clear before." The colonel shifted in his chair. "I've lived with this thing"—he motioned to the offices about him—"for quite a while. I don't believe UFO's represent anything more than natural phenomena, no matter how weird or mechanical they may sometimes appear to be."

Brady nodded. "Okay, okay," he said, gesturing in impatience. "We'll come back to *that* in a little while. But stay with what I asked, will you? Make it theoretical or whatever else you want to."

Trapnell drummed his fingers on his desk. "You understand this has to be entirely unofficial?"

"Sure."

"Not so fast," the colonel admonished. "I've got to hear this said. No assumption. This conversation is strictly off the record. It's between two people. Officially it never happened."

"Agreed."

"All right, then. If I were to play Alice in

Wonderland, there wouldn't be any question. The discs."

Brady snapped it out. "Why?"

Trapnell shrugged. "I'm playing by your rules. "They fit best of all."

"Break it down for me, will you?"

"Everything else—elongated shapes, spheres, glowing lights, all of it—doesn't fit into a pattern. They've *got* to be some form of natural phenomena. A good many of the discs are the same, but in this business you learn that what someone describes as a disc can be a sphere seen without depth perception. That's just an example. If we go back to the old rule of separating the wheat from the chaff, then the discs emerge as the only likely possibility."

Brady slammed a fist into his palm. "Damn it, I *knew* it!"

"Now just hold on," Trapnell said loudly. "Let's not go off the deep end because of what I just said."

"Deep end?"

"Hell, yes," the colonel said with almost a glare. "I gave you an Alice in Wonderland simile. Don't go pasting 'authentic' labels on the discs so fast."

Brady almost whooped with laughter. "Jim, let me ask you another one from way out in left field. What would it take to convince you one of these things is real?"

"Real, shmeal. You're making the same mistake the nuts and kooks make. You're setting up artificial standards of proof and judging from *your* viewpoint." Trapnell shook his head. "It won't hold water."

"If I see something that looks like a duck, quacks like a duck and waddles like a duck, then I think I'm safe in assuming the goddamned thing is a duck."

"And you could easily be wrong!" Trapnell cracked the palm of his hand against the desk. "That's my whole point, man! If I saw my sainted grandmother go whizzing by in one of those things, I wouldn't believe it."

"I'll ask it again: What would it—"

"I heard you the first time," Trapnell said. "We would want to examine it. Kick the tires, work on it with a wrench and a hacksaw, take pictures, examine its teeth, the whole bit. We'd want to run lab tests, metallurgical samples, X rays, the lot. And *not* until then."

"Jesus," Brady said, "you people are hard to convince. That's my entry for the understatement of the year."

"Oh? Maybe you're missing the point of all this."

"I sure as hell am."

Trapnell nodded, his face serious. He rose from his seat to pace the room. "I think I screwed up," he said at last, and turned to look at Brady. "Do you know why this office is here?"

"Sure, to check out UFO reports and to—"

"Wrong."

"Wrong? Then what the hell is all this"—Brady swept his arm through the air to take in the Blue Book files and offices—"doing here?"

"Not to play nursemaid to UFO reports, as you—and everyone else, apparently—might think."

"I'm all ears."

"The long and short of it is that we're here to study and evaluate reports of UFO's only in the respect that they may constitute or pose a threat to the security of this country." Trapnell took a deep breath. "If that sounds like a speech, it is. But that's also on the level. We judge everything we see on the basis of an alien or a foreign or a whatzit being a danger to the United States. If it doesn't fall into that category, we're satisfied. I hope I've impressed that on you because it's our only justification for being here. Do things—objects, UFO's, whatever you call them—threaten air safety in terms of interfering with military, civil, or general aviation? Do they threaten people's lives, or installations? That sort of thing. If they don't pose a threat, we stick them in the files."

Brady didn't know what to say. Finally he knew what he wanted. "I'd like to lean on you for just a few more hours," he said to Trapnell.

"Sure," the colonel agreed. "I haven't had a good fight like this for a long time. Name your poison."

"Could you pull from the files, oh, say about two or three dozen of what you consider the most reliable sightings of discs?"

"No sweat. What else?"

"I'd like to study those and then ask you some questions."

Trapnell looked carefully at Brady. "You holding back on me?"

"Might be," Brady grinned. "We'll let it lie fallow for just a bit."

"Good enough," the colonel said. He glanced at his watch. "Just about closing time."

The next morning Brady buried himself behind a desk in Trapnell's office. The colonel personally had selected from the vast file of more than twenty thousand sightings two dozen of those he felt were disc observations that defied all possible explanation. Other, of course, than that they were machines and not natural phenomena. But as he cautioned Brady again, any conclusions to be drawn were not and could not be, in the view of the Air Force, any manner of proof that they *were* of an artificial nature. Bradly grumbled at Trapnell to go away and dug into the reports.

Several hours later he planted himself before Trapnell's desk. "You ready?" he growled.

The colonel looked up and grinned. "Don't you ever learn?"

"Nope."

Trapnell sighed. "Okay. Let's have at it."

Brady drew up a chair. He kept firing questions at the colonel, the latter doing his best to answer. Brady smiled grimly. The answers were less certain than they had been before, and there weren't so many ready explanations for certain situations raised in the reports.

"All right, then," Brady said, "what about this sighting? You've got a small passenger ship, I guess you'd call it a coastal steamer, that's been going up and down the African coast for years. British and Dutch crew, all well known, all with experience, all reliable, *and* they're familiar with every inch of the coastline. Are we agreed on that so far?"

"Sure."

"So these people, on a night without clouds, perfect visibility, see something huge moving toward the ship. Something moving through the air and descending. It takes up position between the ship and the shoreline that's less than a mile away. No question; these men— and there are nine of them—have been watching things at sea as far back as they can remember. Then a beam of light, a searchlight or something, comes from the bottom of this thing and plays straight down. Against the water. The light reflects back, it's bright, real bright. And in that light those nine ship's officers see a disc. They see it clear. No question. None," Brady said with emphasis. "It stays with them for several minutes. The light goes out and the thing—the disc they've seen clearly for several minutes under perfect seeing conditions—climbs away and disappears." Brady shoved the report before Trapnell. "How the hell do you explain that incident?"

"We don't," Trapnell said. He remained un-ruffled. "We don't because we don't *know* what

90

that thing was, even assuming every aspect and detail of that sighting report is correct. Even assuming all that we don't know. All we do know is that nothing in that sighting shows any kind of threat to this country. It's not the only one of the sort, you know." Trapnell noticed Brady's surprise. "You can't go through all the reports without spending months here," the colonel explained. "I gave you a cross section. There are quite a few other sightings, some, no, most, less reliable than this one, but all of a disc that turned a searchlight downward." He returned the report to Brady. "Let me turn the tables a moment. Could you tell me what a disc, not of any known manufacture, is doing running around the ocean and playing searchlights on the water? What's the purpose, the reasoning, behind something like that?"

"How the hell would I know?"

"Then why ask me to come up with the answer?" Trapnell threw at him.

Brady didn't have a ready response. As he mulled over Trapnell's blank wall placed before him, the colonel caught him off balance. "Have you ever thought what all this signifies?" Trapnell asked. "If these discs are real, what the devil are they doing wandering around the Arctic and the Antarctic? Why do they show up over the oceans and the deserts and every kind of terrain imaginable? *Why* should there be such a vast expenditure of energy, and whatever it costs to keep such things going, without any rhyme or reason? What's it all about?"

Brady rubbed his chin as he thought. "There's one obvious reply to that," he said finally. "Only some of the disc reports are accurate. The others aren't."

"And there's no way of knowing which is which, is there?" Trapnell said immediately.

"I—Christ, I don't know," Brady admitted. "That's what's so exasperating about all this. *Some* of these things have *got* to be real. I'm absolutely convinced of that. But the authentic sightings are all mixed up in this hodgepodge of reports. What I'd like to do is separate the authentic sightings from this whole mess."

"When you do"—Trapnell laughed—"how about telling us? We could use the help."

It hit Brady suddenly. The notes he'd made a few days before. "Wait a minute," he said slowly, thinking as fast as he could, putting pieces together in his mind. "Wait just one ever-loving minute." He snapped his fingers. "Barstow!" he exclaimed. "There's one that's completely outside even your magic bag of tricky explanations."

Trapnell looked carefully at Brady. "You mean Barstow Air Force Base?"

"You bet your sweet ass I do," Brady said in triumph. "You've got that report, don't you? It's a recent one."

Trapnell showed little enthusiasm for continuing the matter. "Cliff, I don't want to sound evasive but—"

"—Barstow is under full security wraps, right?" Brady finished it for him.

"How did you know?"

"I went there. I talked with one of your missile-control people. Everything he *didn't* say made it obvious something screwy was going on."

"I can't give you any information on the ... on Barstow," Trapnell said. He sounded stiff and formal.

Brady was astounded. "Why the hell not? You've let me crawl through everything else you've got here."

"I know, I know," Trapnell said, "but this one is out of my hands."

Brady sat back in his chair. "Better explain that to me."

"The security classification—and it's way up on top—is from Strategic Air Command," Trapnell explained. "That's out of our jurisdiction."

"That stinks."

"Maybe," Trapnell said, "but it obviously involves SAC weapons in one way or the other."

"It sure as hell does," Brady said grimly. "Like blanking out all communications of a Minuteman complex command post sixty feet beneath the ground."

He saw Trapnell start suddenly. It was the first time Brady had seen the other man caught off guard. "Found a sensitive nerve, didn't I?" Brady chuckled.

"Where did you get that information?" Trapnell said. It was a demand.

"Uh-uh," Brady replied. "Sanctity of sources and all that. It doesn't matter. What—"

"It matters," Trapnell barked.

"I'll take that up with you some other time," Brady quipped. "Let's stay with the subject, huh?"

"I can't discuss it with you."

"Why not?"

"I told you. It's SAC, and it's got top security on it."

"To hell with SAC. I'm not interested in the missiles. I'm interested in something you've been telling me for days isn't real, can't be real, and you don't care about it because it doesn't pose any threat to national security. Them's your words, Jim, not mine. But this thing, this disc, or whatever it was, *did* interfere with the untouchable SAC, didn't it? Don't answer. I *know* it did."

Brady shoved aside the reports he had been studying. "I think I'm getting warm," he said. "The disc, the UFO, fits too many categories, doesn't it?" Trapnell didn't answer, and Brady rushed on. "If it's a plasma, what the hell was it doing at a hundred thousand feet before it came down to ground level and went back up again?" He noticed the frozen face of Trapnell and laughed. "You're trying too hard not to show any reaction," he said. "The eyewitnesses who saw it *all* reported a clearly defined object. Experienced pilots among the eyewitnesses, by the way. So we have something that went from a hundred thousand feet down to the deck and back up. It disappeared from sight for a while. It was seen visually, it was tracked on radar. It generated enough of an electrical field, or electromagnetic, or *something*, to knock out

94

automobile radios and engines, to screw up a five-thousant-watt commercial broadcasting station. It even fouled up a main power station. And it cut off all communications with a superbly shielded, fail-safe command post sixty feet below the ground."

Brady watched Trapnell for several moments. "Any comments?"

"I know this doesn't sound good," Trapnell said, "but you've got to believe me. We can't cut across lines of a security rating by SAC."

"Look," Brady said, doing his best to sound earnest. "You've been great with me, Jim. I mean that. But I've got to be honest with you. What you've just told me stinks to high heaven. It's censorship. You've impressed upon me for several days that censorship is the last thing you people want. Now you build a great big wall of censorship and you hide behind it."

"We've not hiding behind anything," Trapnell glowered.

"No? What would you call it, then?"

"I *told* you! It's out of our hands."

"My, my. How convenient."

Trapnell sat back in his chair. His voice was cold. "Do you think I'm lying to you?"

"Christ, of course not," Brady said. "If I've even given you that inference I apologize. "No, *you* are not lying. But SAC is sure as hell covering up something. By *your* own ground rules, something mucked up an ICBM complex. And *that* constitutes interference with the security of the country, doesn't it?"

"I can't make any comments on the matter."

"Orders?"

Trapness shrugged. "You've been in the business for a long time and you wore the blue suit yourself," he answered.

"So there's an official blanket over the case, huh?"

"I can't even comment on that," Trapnell said, obviously unhappy with his defensive role. "All I can tell you is that like any other case, when we break this one down, it goes into the open files."

"From what I know of this case"—Brady grinned—"we could both have long white hair by that time."

"I told you: no comment."

"I guess we've wrapped it up, then, haven't we?"

"I wish," Trapnell said, "you weren't leaving here with a sour note about all this."

"Sour? By no means," Brady said. He was almost chortling. "You've just proved to me what I've wanted to know. Not in any details, perhaps, but enough."

"Which is?"

"You know the answer to that one. *Something* is out there. You don't know what it is. You can't do anything about it. You—I mean the Air Force, of course—is in a flap about it. Otherwise SAC wouldn't have its heavy hand in the middle of it all."

"Cliff, you can't prove a thing, and you know it."

"Why'd you say that? I didn't say I could *prove* anything."

Trapnell recognized the slip. Brady held up a hand. "No sweat. This conversation never happened."

The colonel nodded. "Thanks."

Brady rose to his feet. "I'll be in touch with you," he said. "If I have any questions about certain sightings, can you give me answers by phone?"

"Sure. Everything—except Barstow—is open to you."

"Thanks. What about those reports? Can you make copies for me?"

"Will do. You want to wait for them, or have me mail them to you?"

"Mail will be fine."

Trapnell drove Brady to the flight line where his Aztec waited. The newsman was jubilant.

He *knew* he had been right all along.

CHAPTER VI

Brady cupped his hand over the phone and shouted to Ann. "Whaddya' want? Corned beef or pastrami?"

"Pastrami."

"Rye or roll?"

She looked at him from across the room and shrugged. "Hell, I'll order for you," he muttered. He spoke again into the phone. "Make that one corned beef and one pastrami. Both on rye. What? Sure, mustard, catsup, relish on the side. So I like relish on my corned beef! Yeah, two orders of French-fried. Hey, wait one. Stick two six-packs of Budweiser in the bag. Got it cold? Great. Uh-huh. Apartment nineteen-B. Right, thanks." He dropped the phone onto the cradle and walked back to Ann. "I'm starved," he complained. "Forgot all about the time. Didn't you have anything to eat?"

Ann sat on a high barstool, her hands clasped about her knees. She'd removed her uniform and slipped on a Japanese lounging robe from Brady's closet. She moved her toes back and forth and sighed.

"Nope," she said. "I wonder sometimes if I'm in an airliner or a restaurant. God, we were full. Not a seat open. By the time we got through serving dinners and cleaning up the mess . . ."

"Bumpy flight?"

"Not too bad. Couple of urpers in the crowd, but it could have been worse. Anyway, we were letting down by the time we got everything ready." She wrinkled her nose and made a face. "After you get through cleaning up somebody's dinner, when they've thrown up all over themselves, it sort of ruins your appetite."

Brady laughed.

"But I'm hungry enough now," Ann added.

"It'll be here in a few minutes." He gestured at the papers strewn across his worktable. "C'mere," he said gruffly. "I want to show you how this is working out."

Ann slipped from the stool to join Brady and kissed him lightly on the cheek. "What's the delivery boy going to say when he sees me lounging around in your bathrobe? I'll ruin your reputation."

Brady smiled. "That's not a bathrobe. It's a happy coat."

"Happy coat?"

"Sure. That's what the Japanese call it. Got lots of happy memories. I wore that at a hotel spa in Japan when I went there on leave for a month."

She ignored the robe. "What happy memories?" she prodded.

"Ummm, you know."

She moved her thigh against his. "Don't know," she murmured. "Tell me."

"You're not old enough."

She giggled. "That's what you think." She leaned forward to tickle his ear with her tongue. "You can tell me," she whispered. "I'll never tell."

"Knock it off," he growled with mock anger. "My former love life isn't for publication."

She blew in his ear. "Get laid much?"

"Enough."

"How much?"

"Enough, goddamn it."

"How many times?"

"Jesus Christ," he exclaimed, "I didn't keep score."

"Was she good?"

"Who?"

"Your Japanese lover."

He couldn't resist the dig. "Which one?"

"Oh, any one of them. All of them. Tell me."

He glared at her.

"Did you make love to one at a time or did you have a gang bang? That's what they call it, isn't it?"

"Will you knock it off?"

"Tell me then."

"That's none of your business."

"Oh." She pouted. "Now you'll ruin my survey."

"*What* survey?"

"A study of your sex life."

"Who's it for?"

She pointed a finger at herself. "Me," she said brightly. "I was wondering when you were going to make a pass."

"I don't make passes," he retorted.

She stuck out her tongue. The doorbell rang as he lunged for her.

"Saved by the bell." She laughed. "Food?"

"Guess so," he said as he crossed the room to the door. He handed Ann the package and paid the delivery boy. They spread out their sandwiches and beer on the bar. Ann bit into her sandwich and nudged Brady with her foot. "You want to be serious for a while?"

"No. You've got me all excited. Let's get laid."

She chewed lustily. "Sorry about that," she murmured through her food. "Out of the mood now. Besides, I'm too hungry."

He grabbed his sandwich, bit in and shouted with pain.

"What happened?"

"Miserable goddamn— I bit my tongue," he rasped. "Son of a bitch, that hurts."

She laughed quietly. "Serves you right," she said. "Here. Soak it in some cold beer."

"Fat help you are."

"So I'm a lousy nurse." She shrugged.

"Shut up and eat," he admonished her. "We got work to do."

He assembled the reports into neat piles and tapped the large chart spread before them. "There it is," he said after a long pause. "The pattern. It's beginning to show."

Ann looked over his shoulder. "Only discs?"

"Uh-huh. Everything else is eliminated." He pointed to the reports. "Not only that, but I'm using only disc sightings I feel are reliable. No lights in the sky or that sort of stuff. Every one of these," he emphasized, "refers to a confirmed disc. If there's any doubt at all, the report gets thrown out."

"How many reports do you have."

"With that you brought back, over three hundred and eighty."

"That should be enough," she said.

"Maybe. I hope so." He turned to her. "You were a big help with these, Ann. More than you know."

She kissed his nose. "Thank you, kind sir."

"No, I mean that. I could never have gotten those people to loosen up for me."

"What's the next step?" she asked.

He climbed from the table. "I'm still trying to pin something down," he complained, starting to pace the floor. "I need more than I've got. Somewhere in all this"—he jabbed his thumb at the papers covering the table—"there's a key. I haven't quite got my finger on it."

"Shall we fight about it?" she asked.

He stopped in mid-stride. "Fight?"

"I mean it," she said, nodding. "Whenever my dad got into a real hassle with a story, when he couldn't get it all together smoothly, we'd have a rip-roaring argument about it." She laughed. "People who heard us thought we were really angry. Dad shouted and cussed and I gave it right back to him. Sometimes he'd cut the fight short in the middle of a sentence and rush off to the typewriter. He'd usually solved the problem."

Brady walked up to her and kissed her on the forehead. "Sweetheart, I'm not writing a story," he said. "I'm trying to find the missing piece, or pieces, to a puzzle."

"Same thing," she insisted.

"I don't feel much like fighting."

"I don't mind," she said. "A good fight always clears the air."

"Sure. And sometimes makes for bloody noses."

"So what makes you so special?" she demanded.

"What?"

"You heard me, Cliff Brady. If it worked for my old man, it'll work for you."

"Oh, Christ." He reached for his cigarettes.

"Do you believe there's a government plot behind UFO's?" She threw the question at him as a challenge.

"A plot? No."

"Why not?"

"Couple of good reasons. That captain at Barstow was frightened. The Air Force doesn't

104

go around scaring its own people. Not when they're in critical positions like playing nursemaid to a brace of citybuster missiles. Besides, SAC takes a dim view of anyone screwing up their ICBM sites." Brady rubbed his chin while he thought. "The open-house attitude of Blue Book *could* be a blind. You know, let the yokels in to gawk at the pretty things and they go away thinking they've seen it all. But Trapnell isn't that good an actor. He leveled with me. The discs have been reported from all over the world. Some of the best reports are from Brazil and Russia. That lets out the discs being something we've put together. If it's that good, we wouldn't dare risk the loss of such a machine by letting it wander all over the planet. So that's out. Besides, it can't be ours."

"Why are you so positive about that?"

"I've already told you. Not only that, but the propulsion system . . ." His voice trailed off. Ann watched, silent, knowing he was buried in thought. Brady could have been her father in that same position and with the same facial expression.

"That could be the lead," he said. She could barely hear him.

"The drive," he mumbled.

"The drive, Cliff?"

"Oh." He emerged from his fog of concentration. "What makes those things go. It sure as hell isn't any kind of push I know about." He returned to the table and the sighting reports. "Ann!" he called over his shoulder.

He pushed a stack of papers to one side of

the table. "Go through these, will you? Look for anything that refers to propulsion. Engines, jets, exhausts, a glow . . ."

"Glow?"

"Uh-huh. Ionization field. It's been reported a few times. A glow or a haze around the disc."

"What's it from?"

"Later, later," he said impatiently. "Just go through these, will you?"

She sighed to herself. Here she was half undressed in the apartment of the man who interested her more than anyone she'd ever known, whose maleness aroused her, and now they were burying themselves in reports of UFO's.

She stood to his side and studied his profile. She wondered if she was falling in love with the big ape.

Relish on corned beef? My God.

"It's *got* to be some form of electrical propulsion!"

Brady slammed a powerful fist into his palm again and again as if to pound reality into his convictions. He spun around and jabbed a finger at Ann. "There's nothing else, *nothing*, that could account for such performance!" The words poured from him with a breathless rush.

She laughed and threw up her arms in mock fright. "I'll agree to anything," she cried. "Just don't beat me any more!"

He grinned self-consciously. "Sorry about that," he mumbled. "I didn't mean to get carried away."

"Think nothing of it," she said with a wave of her hand. "Whatever it is you were shouting about, that is."

"The drive for the discs," he snapped.

"What makes them go," she said.

"What the hell do you think I've been talking about?"

"You're raising your voice again. Do you always get so carried away when you have relish on your corned beef?"

"Will you listen, damn it?"

She threw herself into his arms, forcing him to hold her tightly or they would both have tumbled to the floor. "Ann, for Christ's sake, will you . . . mmmm . . . well . . . I mean . . . mmm."

Brady's head swam as she embraced him. Ann stepped back, her eyes dark and wide. A little more of that and Brady would never be able to control himself. She'd felt that. Good Lord . . .

"I think you'd better tell me about how those things go," she said, still breathing hard.

He didn't move. She knew that kiss had banished everything from his mind except her and the bed in the next room.

Silence. "Cliff, answer me!"

"Oh. What?"

"Tell me about the engines."

"The engines. You want me to tell you about the engines."

"Stop mumbling."

"What engines?"

"The—oh stop it. You know very well."

"I don't want to talk about the goddamned engines." His hands were clenched tightly and he looked as if he were standing on eggshells.

"I told you I don't make passes, Ann. I want very badly to make love with you, but I won't play games."

She looked at his face and thought of the pain that had carved those lines and scars. She wanted nothing more in the world at that moment than to cradle that scarred head and face in her hands. But she didn't move.

"Cliff, will you listen to me?"

He swayed slightly, his hands still balled into fists. "I'm listening."

"I want to tell you something. I know how you feel, that you want me. I hoped that you would." She motioned for him not to interrupt. "Hear me out, please. I want you, Cliff. I want to make love with you." She shook her head and he watched her hair and the light changing across her face, and he knew he was falling in love with her. What the hell was she saying?

"But not now, Cliff. Not yet."

He didn't answer her immediately. "Any good reasons?"

"Not for anyone else but me," she said slowly. "It's just too soon."

He let out a long breath and she saw him start to relax. He shrugged. "I always figure a door works both ways," he said.

Instantly she stiffened. "Are you asking me to leave?"

"No, no," he said, careful to be gentle with her. "You're reading me wrong, baby." He saw her confusion. "You know what I want with you," he went on. "That's only a part of it, but it's an important part." He sighed audibly. "But you're an equal partner and I told you I don't push. I can't figure why you want to wait but that's up to you." He moved closer to her and took her hands.

"It's out in the open and I'm glad of that." She nodded. "You know how I feel," he said. "Now it's up to you to come to me."

"Yes." Her voice was a whisper.

"You're something, Ann," he said gruffly. "You get to me, and you do it good. I don't understand it all and I'm not going to try. I know I want you and I'm mixed up about you. I'll let it ride right there for the moment."

She kissed him lightly. "You're marvelous. Do you know that?"

CHAPTER VII

Strange, he thought, just how the feel of her against me can be so important. Ann slept soundly, her hair silk-soft against his arm, the pressure of her body warm and satisfying. The jetliner rocked gently in turbulence and Ann murmured in her sleep. Brady smiled and turned his head to look through the window. Except for cumulus build-ups over distant mountains, the sky was a clear, deep blue. He glanced at his watch. Another hour and they'd start letting down for Phoenix.

Ann's presence was the result of a last-minute decision to take advantage of Brady's trip to Arizona and Colorado. He told her he'd be spending several days out west.

"Where?" she asked.

"Fly commercial to Phoenix," he said. "I'll

rent a plane there and take it up to Flagstaff.
Be there for one day, I guess. Then I'll go on
up to Denver. I want to spend some time with
Walton."

"And who is Mr. Walton?"

"Not 'Mister.' Professor. He's the mucky-
muck running the UFO investigation for the
University of Colorado. Under contract to the
Air Force."

She looked up at him. "Why Phoenix and
Flagstaff if you're going to Denver?"

"Denver's last in line. I've got a meeting
first in Flagstaff with Dr. Taggert. He's supposed to be pure genius with electrical-propulsion systems."

"Oh."

"Oh, what?"

"Isn't Flagstaff near the Painted Desert?"

"Uh-huh. Why?"

"And Monument Valley?"

"You on a scenic kick?"

She was suddenly excited. "Cliff, I've always
wanted to see those places," she said. "Why
don't I go along with you? Will you have
enough time to . . ."

"Sure," he said in anticipation of her question. "By plane it's only a few hours out of the
way." He looked at her and grinned. "Unless
you're planning to go by horse."

"Silly. Seriously, Cliff, I'd love to go with
you."

He didn't waste any time on the matter.
"Great," he said. "What about your job?"

She waved her hand to dismiss any problems. "I've got plenty of time coming to me, and there are more than enough girls to handle the flights, and besides, I'd love to be with you, and—"

"Hold it, hold it!" He laughed. "I get the message." He smiled warmly. "It would be great to have you."

She kissed him. "What flight are you on?"

Five minutes later she was gone, rushing to her hotel to prepare for the trip. The next morning he picked her up by cab and they drove together to the airport.

He shifted carefully in his seat so as not to disturb her. For the first two hours of their flight she'd prattled gaily, as happy as a young girl starting a summer vacation. Then, tired from the heavy workload she'd had for the previous week, up late the night before, she fell asleep.

It gave him the opportunity to think, to run through his mind what he might accomplish with his appointment in Flagstaff.

Taggert—Dr. Kenneth Taggert—was a long shot. Brady had no way of telling what were the odds, but it was the kind of bet he couldn't pass up. Taggert was supposed to be the kingpin of electrical-propulsion research. If anyone might answer the questions Brady found so frustrating, Taggert was the man. But it would help if he came to the scientist with a solid grounding on the subject.

If the discs were real, then they used a propulsion the likes of which the world had never seen. What made them go?

Everything pointed to electrical propulsion. It was anybody's guess as to what type. It could be electromagnetic, electrogravitic, something to do with static electricity or—Brady shook his head. He was out of his depth. It could be just about anything and probably was a type of which he had no knowledge. Something revolutionary in concept and in practice.

Once again. What could be the propulsion, the drive? He reviewed again in his mind the many reports of the ionization in the air, the dimly glowing corona that confirmed an electrical energy disturbance of some kind. Most sighting reports made it clear the discs could move at thousands of miles per hour, and they moved that fast within the atmosphere.

Brady stiffened as a new thought came to him. They could move at thousands of miles per hour *within* the atmosphere. *But no one had ever reported a sonic boom.* Here was another piece to the puzzle. It tied in with a program underway by the Federal Aviation Administration. The FAA was gung-ho to solve the problem of sonic booms. When the supersonic transports showed up, all hell would be breaking loose on the ground beneath the SST's flight path. The boom would break windows and crack walls and have many thousands of people up in arms. The most promising research into eliminating the boom was electrical. A sonic boom was the result of a pressure wave. The air piled up like the forward wake of a speeding ship. The air moved with the speed of sound, but the SST went faster. It left behind it a continuous shock wave that traveled to the ground and woke up people and disturbed chickens and smashed windows. The trick, the science boys had figures out, was to break up the air so that the shock wave couldn't form. They were testing electrical fields. They were *ionizing the air*. It worked in tests. If if worked for supersonic planes . . . and no one had ever reported a sonic boom for a disc . . . They've *got* to fit, Brady thought grimly. And Taggert would know how.

With minimum movement Brady reached for the briefcase at his feet. He glanced at Ann. The shifting of his body stirred her, but only for a moment. Her eyes opened sleepily, she smiled and was almost immediately fast asleep again. Brady opened the briefcase and withdrew his notes on the scientist.

Dr. Kenneth Taggert was unusually young to have earned the prominence he enjoyed in his research circles. His background and experience belied his thirty-eight years. Taggert had been through Cal Tech and MIT . . . Brady wasn't surprised to see he had performed advanced rocket-engine research in the Santa Susana laboratories—and, yes; there it was. After two years he left Rocketdyne to get into electrical-propulsion systems with Republic Aviation in Farmingdale, New York. The notes triggered Brady's memory. Taggert, he recalled, had worked on a plasma pinch engine, leaving Republic when the National Aeronautics and Space Administration moved the research program into one of NASA's own laboratories. Taggert followed wherever the most advanced research beckoned; he smacked of the scientist who insisted on going his own way. That made him a rarity in today's world of "scientist teams" within which individuality faded and "group genius" was the goal. Group genius, my ass, Brady thought—a bunch of pencil pushers hot after job security.

Taggert lasted only a year with NASA and then answered the call of Lockheed's nuclear-propulsion program for the AEC. Brady saw the word "Nerva" penciled in his notes, and without going further he knew that Taggert had left *that* program as well. Nerva had become a funds-depleted foot-dragger that would make a mind like Taggert's ache for release.

For the last two years Taggert had been the director of research for Blackburn Aero, a division of the huge Blackburn industrial empire. Brady searched his memory. Blackburn Aero had invested heavily in production of huge commercial air freighters, intended primarily for cargo hauling on international routes. Brady recalled they were especially interested in South America where, Frazer W. Blackburn was convinced, the movement of heavy cargo by air had tremendous promise. According to Brady's files, Taggert was directing an engine research program for the great air freighters.

Blackburn constituted one of the true industrial empires, and Blackburn Aero was only one in a family of divisions that ran the gamut from locomotives to huge tankers, from concrete to a massive plastic industry. And power. Everything else old man Blackburn considered transitory. Shipbuilding empires came and went and so did others. Except one. Commercial power, in any form, was Frazer Blackburn's key to industrial might. Steam plants, electric generating plants, and more lately nuclear-power plants. Blackburn investigated everything in the way of power, from tapping volcanic fires to nuclear coil heating of enclosed bodies of water.

Brady couldn't be certain, but he'd give odds that Blackburn had snatched up Taggert with the one offer no scientist of Taggert's ilk could possibly refuse: open-ended research in his chosen field—electrical propulsion. With unlimited funds, facilities, and personnel. If Taggert was really into something that revolutionary in the power field, then whatever Blackburn spent would be a pittance against the potential return.

"My, you're all wrapped up, aren't you." Ann squeezed his arm gently as she smiled at him.

"I thought you were asleep."

She nodded and yawned. "Was." She stretched and snuggled against him. "One thing always wakes me up when I'm flying."

Brady glanced out the window and noticed they were in a steady descent. "Built-in alarm clock, huh?"

"Never fails," Ann said. "Just let an airplane start down and I'm Miss Alert. How much longer?"

Brady studied his watch. "Less than thirty minutes."

She disengaged her arm and sat up, reaching for her purse. "Time to powder my nose."

He studied her walk down the aisle. That girl, he thought fondly, has just got to have the most beautiful ass in the world.

"Cliff. Just *look* at it!" Ann pulled Brady's arm. The horizon swung through a sharp arc as the sudden movement jerked Brady's hand on the control yoke. He righted the Aztec and glared with mock anger at her.

"You wanny fly this thing?" he growled.

She muffled her laughter. "Sorry about that."

"What's got you so fired up?" he asked.

"Over there." She pointed toward the fiery patterns of the Painted Desert. "Aren't we going to fly over it? You said we could..."

"On the way out," Brady replied. "I don't want to be late for Taggert."

"Nuts to Taggert. I thought you were giving me the grand tour." She pressed her face to the window. "I've always wanted to see this from up close. Cliff, isn't that a volcano? It is! Look!"

Brady laughed at her excitement. "The whole country is lousy with volcanoes. You'll see plenty more of them," he promised. "We'll take it all in when we leave here."

Brady swung toward the airport in Flagstaff and the cindered wasteland exploded into lush forest. Brady fought increasing turbulence as he descended through his traffic pattern. The runway was seven thousand feet above sea level. He didn't like the field. He couldn't remember a single time when the air was calm. The Aztec protested the bumpy ride, and Brady surprised himself when the tires squealed satisfactorily in a letter-perfect touchdown.

Twenty minutes later they were in a cab on the way to Taggert's office in Blackburn Aero. It wasn't until then that Ann thought of her presence with Brady.

She linked her arm in his and leaned against him. "Who am I, Cliff?"

"What kind of nutty game are you playing now?"

"The man who thinks of everything," Ann said, shaking her head. "Am I your wife, sister, broad, secretary, friend—"

"Secretary."

Ann looked doubtful. "Are you sure you want me along? I should think I'd only be in the way."

"Anything but," he reassured her. He opened his briefcase and withdrew a small folder. "Pad and pen in there," he said. "I want you to sit and listen. If you hear anything that strikes you as odd, or different, or important, anything at all, jot it down."

"But—"

"I don't know what it'll be or even if there'll be anything," he said quickly. Blackburn Aero appeared at the end of the road. "But you've been around this stuff enough to know it almost as well as I do. Play it by ear, will you?"

She nodded. "You're the boss."

"And don't you forget it," he quipped.

It didn't go well at all.

Dr. Kenneth Taggert was brilliant, cooperative, friendly, and bland. Brady was almost convinced the scientist patronized him, but there remained a shadowy doubt that kept Brady off balance. The newsman had a surgical skill in eliciting information from those he interviewed, but the knife scraped ineffectually against the urbanity of the man who had received them. Taggert was not an imposing man in the sense one expected of a scientist with his reputation. He was meticulous in every aspect of his appearance. Right down to the manicured fingernails which, Brady knew, damned few scientists ever permitted. There wasn't a visible trace of scientist in Taggert who, even after twenty minutes, seemed almost a carefully packaged nonentity. Brady couldn't find a flaw or a major distinction about the man. That he was a loner Brady had already discerned from his research on the man; he confirmed this opinion within the first few minutes of conversation.

Usually Brady could connect with some form of rapport. He couldn't make it with Taggert and from growing signs of impatience Brady knew he'd better cut the mustard and not continue with pleasantries. Brady shrugged to himself and went to the point. He had already told Taggert of the series he was preparing; in that conversation Brady made certain not to include his personal involvement or convictions. He knew how necessary it was for him, Brady, to appear the objective outsider.

"One of the safety directors of the airlines," Brady was explaining, "and his business involves anything to do with passengers and aircraft safety, is concerned about interference with electrical and electronic systems. He doesn't give a fig about UFO's one way or the other. He sees everything in the light of its effect on safety."

Taggert nodded for Brady to continue.

"In certain disc sightings, pilots have reported some manner of interference. Ignition systems, navigation equipment, communications; that sort of thing."

Taggert moved his hand and Brady waited. "Discs?"

"That's right, Dr. Taggert."

"Or disc-shaped plasmoids?" Taggert smiled.

"The pilots were emphatic about the disc shape," Brady said.

"I'm sure they were," Taggert said. And that was all. Brady couldn't figure the question ending right there. He had no choice but to continue.

"I'm familiar with plasmoids, corona discharges, and similar effects," Brady said. "I thought I'd save your time by simply stating that as a fact. My point is that with complete descriptions of such effects, including St.

Elmo's fire, the pilots insist a clearly defined disc has been involved."

"Interesting." Again only the brief murmur from Taggert.

"To review," Brady said, "when holding formation with the aircraft—this includes commercial, military, and private—the discs have shorted out systems, blanked out radios, and made hash of VHF radio navigation equipment. Some radios have even been burned out completely."

"What do you make of all this, Mr. Brady?"

I'll be damned, Brady thought. He's tossed the ball right back to me, and I came to him for help. "From everything I've researched," Brady said with s shrug, determined to remain casual in his approach, "the discs, if they are some sort of machine, utilize a form of propulsion that's electrical in nature. What kind, I have no idea. But whatever it is, it gives off a tremendous electrical field that's picked up by the electrical and electronic systems of the aircraft involved." Brady gestured to indicate he wasn't yet through. "I'm not that well up on electromagnetic systems, *if* that's involved." He forced a grin. "But if anyone is, you're the man. I don't think anyone is more qualified than you are to—"

"Mr. Brady."

The newsman stopped in midsentence. Brady wasn't sure if he'd been rebuked.

"Mr. Brady," Taggert repeated, "I do not wish to appear unkind, but aren't you carrying a process of elimination for rather a long distance?"

"I'm not carrying anything anywhere," Brady said quickly, "except something that's baffling a great many people. If I'm doing any carrying, it's bringing this to you in the hope you can shed some light on the matter. Of course," he added as a thought came to him. "I'm perfectly willing to consider this as wholly conjectural."

Taggert nodded slowly. "I do think that's wisest. You see, you're starting off with a premise that in itself is doubtful. I don't know very much about your UFO's, Mr. Brady, but to have interference with the high-capacity systems of a modern aircraft, from an outside source such as you have described, calls for an intense force field."

Taggert shifted in his seat and smiled at Ann, then turned his gaze back to Brady. "What you're talking about could easily mean an electromagnetic field, although, to be strictly accurate, all force fields, no matter of what appearance, are electromagnetic in nature.

"All?"

"Most certainly," Taggert said. "They must be, of course, since they all function with the same subnuclear energies. What we see as variations in energy dispersion or direction, Mr. Brady, are only the results of our inadequacies in judging correctly the forces that are involved."

Brady glanced at Ann. She was sinking fast.

Who the hell ever expected Taggert to get into elemental basics? Goddamn it, he couldn't pin the man down!

"Well, no matter what the system—I'll buy the electromagnetic force field, of course, since you're the one who knows best—but no matter what the system, could there be some sort of leakage from the propulsion unit? Whatever drives the discs?"

This time Taggert's smile could only be, and was, patronizing. "Once again, Mr. Brady," he said in that soft voice, "you're starting off with a premise, and then asking me to build upon that. I suppose, if you wish to continue this as strictly theoretical, that *if* you did build an electromagnetic drive, and if you did place it within a disc-shaped machine—although for the life of me I don't know why, since aerodynamically you're introducing a host of problems; but, to stay with your premise, if you did all this, in your disc—it is possible there could be some, umm, leakage would be an acceptable term, I would imagine."

Brady felt a headache coming on. "Would that leakage interfer with aircraft systems?" he asked.

"If all your ifs work out," Taggert said, "which is accepting a great deal on faith, why, yes, it's possible."

"Dr. Taggert, do you feel an electromagnetic drive of some sort is feasible?"

"Anything, given proper knowledge, is feasible. There are certain limiting factors, of course, which—"

"Forgive me, but I mean feasible in the contemporary sense."

Taggert, Brady swore, almost laughed aloud. "Mr. Brady, we have electromagnetic drives right now." He did laugh at the expression on Brady's face. "In fact, we've had them for years. So, for that matter, have the Soviets. We have both carried out extensive testing of plasma-pinch, photon, and magnetohydrodynamics-propulsion systems." Without even a pause, he turned again to Ann. "Did you get that all right, my dear?"

Ann looked up with a vacant expression on her face and nodded.

"Not only that," Taggert went on, "but we have flown several of these in different spacecraft. The Russians as well, I repeat."

Suspicion nibbled at the edge of Brady's mind. Taggert's next words brought confirmation. "Of course, the energy distribution of these systems leaves much to be desired," the scientist continued. "The truth of the matter is that the thrust developed by even the most successful drive flown—they have been orbited, you understand, as part of certain satellite experiments—well, the greatest thrust achieved to date has been exactly a tenth of a pound, and the maximum duration is somewhere on the order of eight days."

Shot down in flames, Brady cursed himself. Shit, I knew all that before I got here. Time to change the routine.

"Dr. Taggert, are you involved in any research in this area?"

Taggert was openly condescending. "Company research is hardly a matter of public discussion, Mr. Brady." The scientist held up his hand to forestall Brady's expected apology. "However, I understand the manner of your question and I can answer it for you. It would be, ah, more convenient for me if no direct attribution were made."

"Of course," Brady said.

"Your reputation is sufficient assurance," Taggert said with unexpected praise. "But to the point. Every major firm in the nation is engaged in a maximum effort to produce a new system of power. Mr. Blackburn's emphasis on this matter hardly needs to be examined; it's too well known. As I say, all of us in the field are engaged actively in the search for new power systems, for drives, as you have put it."

"Including yourself?"

"Of course," Taggert said.

"Are you into any antigravity programs, Dr. Taggert?"

"We are *all* interested—intensely—in such a matter. I know of at least twenty corporations in the country, each of which spends a small fortune every year trying to find *that* holy grail. However"—Taggert chuckled—"there is a slight problem. We're all of us no closer to the heart of the problem than we were twenty years ago. We've eliminated some blind alleys and we all feel we're smarter than we were, but really . . ." He shook his head and smiled again.

126

"Could you identify, well, as you might put it, the major problem?"

"Oh, to be sure. We don't even know, you see, what *is* gravity. Really, we have no idea in terms of indisputable fact. We wrestle with Einstein's Special and General Theory of Relativity and we go tramping through the woods of his Unified Field Theory, and we dabble with Lorentz and wonder if quasars will shed some light on the matter; but really, we simply don't know."

Brady noticed that Ann had given up completely.

"I'll sum it up for you, Mr. Brady. If you can bring to me an unquestioned solution as to what constitutes gravity, I can assure you," Taggert said, "you will, overnight, become wealthy beyond your fondest dreams."

Brady made a final stab at it. "What about electromagnetic systems?"

"Mr. Brady, gravitation and electromagnetic forces, or energies, as you will, are separate and distinct. They are also inseparable. We are wrestling with philosophical as well as elemental mysteries. I assure you they are all quite profound."

Before Brady could reply, Taggert rose to his feet. "This is most interesting," the scientist said, "and I would like to continue our discussion. However, time presses." He pushed a desk button and a secretary appeared through a side door.

"Good day, Mr. Brady. It's been a pleasure,
127

Miss Dallas." Taggert was gone before Brady could say another word.

"Well, how did you figure him?" Brady demanded.

Ann slumped in the cab. "My head's splitting," she complained.

"Never mind the skull bumps," Brady snapped. He was irritable and it showed. "Something was goddamned well wrong in there and I still can't figure it."

Ann lifted her hand, then dropped it. "Oh, it was wrong, all right. It has nothing to do with what happened. That old devil, woman's intuition, however."

"Well, go on."

"For a while"—Ann sighed, kneading her forehead with her fingers—"I felt as if your brainboy was patronizing us." Brady nodded. "Then it occurred to me—the intuition bit, I mean—that he wasn't."

"Patronizing us?"

"Uh-huh."

"So?"

She turned to look at Brady. "Cliff, I've never felt smaller in my life." She grasped his hand. "He just didn't *care* whether we were there or not," she went on. "He had to see you because of your reputation, I suppose. Or someone in the front office felt he should see you."

Brady nodded slowly.

"Do you know what he did? Taggert, I mean. The whole interview was like brushing a fly off his sleeve. That's what you and I were.

Two flies. He brushed us and went about his business. That's all we meant to him."

Ann hit it smack on the head. The Blackburn outfit spent millions every year to build their public image. So why would they brush off one of the top reporters from the second-largest wire service in the world? It didn't fit, it didn't add up. It felt *wrong*.

What the hell was Taggert hiding?

Maybe, a small voice said to Brady, he just thinks UFO's are so much crap, and anybody who pushes the subject has got to be a nut. Are you a nut on UFO's, Mr. Brady?

He couldn't turn off the pip-squeak dancing around in the back of his head. The unhappy fact of the matter was that Brady had yet to find a single scientist who believed the UFO's—no, he corrected himself, the discs— were even worth bothering about. And they all smiled politely at those who pursued the matter.

Like Cliff Brady.

CHAPTER VIII

Brady looked at his watch and cursed. Who did this son of a bitch Walton think he was? Despite his scheduled appointment, Brady had been cooling his heels for an hour in Walton's outer office. Brady couldn't figure what would keep a college professor closeted in his office while he had a visitor from two thousand miles away sitting on his hands. I'll give him another twenty minutes, Brady thought. Then he can go fuck himself.

The previous day's events had already soured Brady. First there had been that infuriatingly nonproductive interview with Taggert. Ann did her best to get the supercilious scientist off his mind, but it didn't take. They left Flagstaff in the rented Aztec, and Brady kept his promise to Ann with several hours of daz-

131

zling scenic flight. He circled Meteor Crater, did the Painted Desert from six thousand down to only ten feet above the ground, keeping Ann breathless until he hauled the plane up in a soaring climb. Monument Valley overwhelmed her as Brady approached the vast arena of carved buttresses and sculptured formations from two miles above the ground. Then he took the plane down to a hundred feet, twisting and turning amidst the great stone monuments that gave the valley its name. Finally he eased into a climb and turned for Denver. He'd never felt closer to Ann. He felt as if the final barriers had been dissipated, that this night Ann would give herself completely. They landed in Denver and everything fell apart. Brady cursed Ann's sense of responsibility. If only she hadn't checked with her airlines' operation office. Damn it. But she had, and there was an urgent request for all stewardesses on leave to report in. Something to do with crews on the East Coast being down with food poisoning. Brady didn't know and he didn't care. There'd been an apologetic look in Ann's eyes when she kissed him good-bye. There wasn't time for anything else as she ran for a waiting plane.

Brady cursed and went to bed alone. Early the next morning, still exasperated with Taggert and irritated because of Ann's absence, he showed up at the University of Colorado. His appointment was for nine sharp, and here it was a quarter after ten, and that son of a bitch Walton was playing games. Well, maybe it would be worth it. Brady hoped so, for this trip had so far turned out to be about as useful as teats on a boar.

Five minutes before Brady's imposed limit of telling Walton to go screw, the professor's secretary ushered him into Walton's office. It took Brady no more than sixty seconds to realize he had again come a cropper. The white-haired scientist with whom he sat would have been better off mating rabbits or guinea pigs. Brady fumed as Walton tut-tutted the newsman's sense of urgency in establishing the discs as controlled machines.

"Utter nonsense," Walton said heavily. He made deprecating gestures with his hands and motioned Brady to silence. "The notion that these things, what everyone has popularized as UFO's, might be mechanical contrivances is preposterous. Even the term UFO is ridiculous. It represents an unidentified flying object. The only phrase with any accuracy, young man, is when we say 'unidentified.' "

Brady clamped a tight rein on his temper. The frosty old bastard. He'd rehearsed this goddamned speech of his so many times, it came out of him like water from a tap. Brady pressed his lips together and forced himself to continue writing down notes. Notes, shit, he told himself. I want to quote this mother word for word. I don't want to leave out a thing. The pompous old—

"Are you listening, Mr. Brady? My time, really, is quite valuable."

It should be, Brady thought. The taxpayer is shelling out six hundred grand for your line of

133

crap. "I'm all ears, Professor," Brady said aloud.

"As I said before, the very phrase UFO is responsible for much of the confusion attending this phenomenon. Certainly what people are seeing is unidentified. Much of it exists only above their eyebrows. Hah, hah, it's a cranial sighting, that's what it is. All in the mind. Take the rest of UFO. Flying, eh? Most of these things don't *fly*, Mr. Brady. How can they fly? How can sun dogs fly? Or mirages, or—"

"Colonel Trapnell filled me in pretty thoroughly on the atmospheric effects," Brady broke in.

"Umph. Very good. But to finish, eh? The last word. Objects. Come now, Mr. Brady. If the good colonel provided you with a thorough interrogation, then you of all people should know these are not objects. Not in the sense we regard solid, substantial matter. How could they possibly be objects? We are referring to what I already mentioned briefly. Mirages, reflectional dispersion; that sort of thing. UFO, indeed!" A finger wagged annoyingly at Brady. "I'm afraid it's people like yourself, Mr. Brady, who are responsible for much of the mess in which we now find ourselves. Yes, yes. The newspapers." He says newspapers, Brady grimaced, as if a squirrel had just shit in his mouth. Maybe it did. Brady did his best to ignore Walton's stigma of irresponsibility.

"Professor Walton, I wonder if you would hear me out for a few minutes?"

"Eh? Oh. What on earth about?"

"Discs. Not UFO's. Discs," Brady repeated with emphasis. He didn't wait for Walton's acquiescence but plunged into his research study of UFO sightings. He detailed the extensive pilot reports. He described the film taken at the radar station which even the Air Force could not explain. He went through the discs from beginning to end. He emphasized what had happened at Barstow Air Force Base. He didn't leave out a thing. He hammered home to Walton that he had gone through every possible precaution in retaining only the authenticated, reliable sightings. When he had finished, he sat back in his chair and waited for the reactions of the other man.

He didn't get what he expected. No scientific defense of the Air Force position or even that adopted by the University of Colorado. Walton smiled benignly, as if Brady were a congenital idiot. Brady had expected anything but derision from a man who was this deep into a serious study of reliable sightings of UFO's. No man with an ounce of common sense, Brady knew, could have studied the reports and the photographs and the films, could have judged the radar sightings confirmed by visual observation; no man could have done all these things and emerge from such an effort without acknowledging that, if nothing else, at least the matter demanded impartial evaluation.

Walton acknowledged nothing of the sort, and he took little pains to conceal his reaction to Brady's presentation. The scientist fairly twittered with amusement. He made a steeple of his fingertips and peered owlishly over them at Brady.

"My. Oh, my, but you *do* sound like one of those, hah, hah, one of those enthusiasts we get here so often." Walton snuffled with quiet laughter. "You know what I mean, of course. They frequent those UFO conventions or séances or whatever they call their nonsense, where they have all manner of visitors from Venus and other worlds. Including," Walton said drily, changing his facial expression, "the astral. I'm surprised that someone in your position would—"

"Just hold it right there," Brady said. He knew he was now snarling at the professor, but he no longer cared. "That's enough, Professor. I didn't say a word about visitors from anywhere. I came here hoping to get an objective scientific viewpoint regarding those UFO sightings that appear to have merit to them. I didn't expect a canned speech from you."

"Canned speech?"

"You'll forgive my seeming lack of respect in such august surroundings," Brady said with open sarcasm, "but you've just recited your stock speech number four, or whatever you call your little talk."

Walton was no longer amused. "Your insults are quite unnecessary, Mr. Brady." He spoke in icy tones. "My position toward aerial phenomena is quite scientific and requires no defense from me. I find it quite interesting, however, that your tirade and your lack of good manners is precisely what we encounter with all the other rabid enthusiasts—and I'm being kind—who come flocking to our doors. They *all* have revelations, Mr. Brady. All of them, I repeat. They come in—no, I advise you to listen. Don't interrupt me. You came here for an evaluation, and that is exactly what you are getting. You may quote me if you like—"

"I'll do that, Professor."

"By all means, Mr. Brady, and I would be most interested to read that you are honest enough to include yourself amongst those I am describing to you. To repeat, those like you who come here are always burdened with some deep and dark secret that purports to let us in on solving the mystery of UFO's. There is no end, it would seem, to their ingenuity. If you have indeed spent time with Colonel Trapnell at Blue Book, then you are aware of those poor souls who know, who absolutely *know*, Mr. Brady, that they are in the right, and we deluded folk of science are all obstinate, thickheaded, muddled, and God knows what else because we don't agree with them." Walton leaned forward over his desk. "That description, I am sorry to say, Mr. Brady is one that applies to you."

Brady had regained his composure. He stood up and closed his briefcase. "You remind me of Trapnell," Brady said slowly. "Not that you're in his league, Professor, but you both have the same party line."

"You've lost your amusement value, Mr.

137

Brady," Walton said coldly. "Be good enough to leave."

"Oh, I'm going, all—"

"Professor Walton, Mr. Brady, I'm sorry to disturb you like this. . . ." Brady turned to see Walton's secretary in the doorway.

"Yes, yes, what is it?" Walton wasn't exactly sweetness and light to his own employees, Brady noticed.

"It's Mr. Brady's office," the woman said. "A Mr. Parrish, I believe. They say it's extremely urgent."

Brady looked at the telephone on Walton's desk. "May I?"

Walton frowned, then nodded. "Of course."

Brady picked up the telephone and waited for the operator to connect him with his office in New York. In a moment he heard Parrish's voice. It had been a long time since he'd heard it with such excitement.

"You listening, Cliff?"

"Go ahead, Milt. What is it?"

"Better sit down, boy."

"Get with it, will you?"

He heard Milt Parrish chuckle. "Okay. Hang on to your hat, fella . . ."

Several minutes later Brady replaced the telephone on its cradle. Professor Walton studied his face. "I hope, Mr. Brady, it's not bad news?"

Brady turned to the scientist. "Thanks for your concern, Professor." He said it simply and meant it. At least the old bastard *could* be decent. "No, it's not bad news. Not for me, anyway. I think even you would find it interesting."

"Mr. Brady, I am really very busy, and there are other people waiting to—"

"That was my editor in New York, Professor Walton. He's just had a report from Cape Kennedy." Brady paused deliberately. "It seems that a Minuteman missile was fired a short time ago from the Cape."

"Now, really, Mr. Brady, I don't wish to be unkind, but—"

Brady looked down at him and smiled. "It was a failure, Professor. Not a normal failure. Do you follow me?"

"I do not. I wish you would go."

"In just a moment. I'm almost through. I said it wasn't a normal failure. Parrish said the missile was about three thousand feet up, just beneath a cloud deck, when it exploded." Brady picked up his briefcase and remained silent.

"Missiles have exploded before," Walton said, his exasperation evident.

"They also got some tracking film," Brady said. He smiled again. "But that comes later. Apparently there were a number of newsmen on the press site at the Cape. They were watching the launch. Very carefully, I'm glad to say." He placed the briefcase on the floor and rested both hands on Walton's desk. He looked directly into the eyes of the other man.

"At least a dozen people saw it, Professor Walton."

"Saw what?" Walton shouted. "Will you either get to the point or get out of here?"

Brady relished the moment.

"A disc," he said slowly. "They saw a disc. They saw it emerge briefly from the clouds. The reporters saw it through binoculars. Quite clear, too. They saw some sort of light flash from the disc. At the missile. *At* the missile, Professor. The Minuteman exploded, but you know what? It didn't explode until after that light beam had cut the missile in half."

Brady laughed harshly. "Any comment, Professor Walton? For the record, of course."

The elderly scientist looked back at Brady. A long moment of silence passed. Brady could hardly believe his ears when Walton chuckled and gave Brady a look of pity.

"Do you truly"—Walton sighed—"believe that rubbish?"

"Rubbish, my ass! I told you we had confirmation from—"

"I know. I know." Walton made a lazy gesture with his hand. "Mr. Brady, I *do* wish you would listen. That report you received just now . . ." Walton shook his head and smiled. "If I have heard one such report, I have heard a thousand. You'll see, Mr. Brady. Once the initial excitement dies down, what you heard will most certainly be altered drastically. Discs coming out of the clouds and firing ray beams at missiles. Pah! Rubbish, I say, and rubbish it is!"

Brady grunted to himself. "I should have known," he said. "What if I told you there was

140

film confirmation of what happened? Tracking cameras were—"

"Did your editor in New York see the film, Mr. Brady?"

"No. He—"

"Has *anyone* seen the film?"

"I don't know, of course, but—"

"Yes, yes, I've heard it all before," Walton said in his final dismissal of his visitor. "In due time you'll learn, Mr. Brady. Will you have the courtesy to leave *now*?"

Goddamn all scientists, Brady thought acidly. He left without another word.

CHAPTER IX

"Goddam it, that's *great*."

Brady slammed the newsreel cameraman violently on the back. "Phil, that's tremendous. You don't know what that's going to do for me." Hendricks gasped for breath as Brady poured drinks for himself and the three newsmen crowded into their motel room at Cape Canaveral. Brady waved the bottle at arm's length. "Run that son of a bitch through for me again, will you?"

Hendricks grinned at Brady. "Man, you've already seen it three times."

"And we'll see it three times again, if necessary," Brady cracked. He almost chortled with glee. All the bile he'd accumulated during the past several days had spilled out of him.

Fats McCabe from the *Washington Chroni-*

cle made a rude sound. "Screw him," he said. "I know what I saw. You should have been there. It was clear as a bell. You tell this Professor What's-his-name *I* said he should go play with himself. Maybe"—McCabe smirked—"that's his trouble."

"I'll bet." Someone snickered.

"Phil, how come you got this film, anyway?" Brady asked of Hendricks. "You don't usually cover the Minuteman launches. I didn't think anyone came out for that bird anymore."

Hendricks shrugged. "Usually we don't," he said. "But I had a long lens I wanted to try out for the next Saturn in a couple of weeks. This was the only shot between now and then." Hendricks showed a toothy smile. "Jesus, I never thought it would turn out like *this*."

Brady threw his next question to the group. "Anybody see the tracking film?"

Hendricks, McCabe, and the third man, Ben Rogers, exchanged glances. "What's the mystery?" Brady demanded.

McCabe tapped the projector. "Good thing Phil got this," he said, his demeanor serious. "The Air Force classified their film."

"What?"

"Yeah. Real cute, ain't they?"

"But the Minuteman . . . that goddamned thing's been wide open for years!"

"Sure," Rogers said. "But suddenly it ain't so wide open anymore."

Brady lit a cigarette and dragged deeply. "What's their story?"

144

"What you'd expect," Rogers replied. "Some crap about a new warhead on top of the bird."

"It's all baloney," McCabe assured Brady. "They had that warhead on display for a week before the shot. No one cared enough about it to take a look."

Brady buried himself in thought. He looked up at Hendricks. "Phil, who else knows about this film?"

"Five people," Hendricks said immediately. "The four of us and Parrish. It's World Press film." He nodded at McCabe and Rogers. "What they know is strictly off the record."

Brady glanced at the others. "Keep it that way, will you? At least until we think it's ripe to break this."

"Sure."

"Of course."

"What about copies?" Brady asked the cameraman.

"Haven't had a chance yet," Hendricks replied. "Jay said he'd let me use the NBC lab soon as they clear some rush work out of the way. I don't want to take this to a commercial house," the photographer emphasized. "I want this baby right in my own sweet little hands."

They laughed with him. "Good deal," Brady said. "Can you make up some stills at the same time?"

"No sweat. How many?"

"Um, maybe six of each. Pick out a few of the best shots, okay? Hey, what about copy negs?"

Hendricks nodded. "Same time I print the film."

"Fine."

"You want to see this now?"

"Let's go. Douse the lights, will you, Fats?"

For the fourth time within an hour Brady devoted his full interest to the screen. The film was short. It would be, of course, with a cloud layer only three thousand feet up. The Minuteman came out of its silo so fast, the whole launch sequence would be over in seconds. Brady watched the Minuteman pad expand in size as Hendricks played around with his telephoto lens. The camera zeroed in on the pad and Brady noticed the red flasher lights warning of a hot bird in the silo. Hendricks panned back so he wouldn't lose the missile when it erupted from the ground. The fire came. A searing burst of flame, clouds of boiling smoke and a giant smoke ring leaped upward. Through the flame Brady saw the Minuteman already pitching over in flight. It ripped away from the ground.

"Phil, slow motion."

Hendricks slowed the projector and the screen flickered as events took place at half speed. Brady wished the damn thing were clearer, but with an overcast sky they were fortunate to have even this much. Before the missile started into the clouds, a disc appeared to one side. Brady strained his eyes to catch every detail. There wasn't much, but something suddenly appeared on the film. A glow, not quite a clear beam, flashed between the disc

146

and the missile. Just as the Minuteman was swallowed up by the clouds, it appeared to break in two.

That was all to be seen for the first sequence. The only sound in the room came from the projector and the heavy breathing of the four men. A faint glow appeared in the clouds.

"That's the blast," Rogers said. "We checked the timing. Range safety officer set off the destruct charges just about then."

Moments later blazing chunks fell from the cloud layer. Several huge pieces plowed into the Cape to throw up sandy geysers. The film flickered, then ended. Someone turned on the lights.

Brady grunted as he made a decision. He grabbed for the phone and dialed the motel switchboard. "Operator, this is Mr. Brady in two eighteen. I want to make a person-to-person call to New York. Right, code two one two. I want to speak with Miss Ann Dallas at the Hotel Lexington. No. Call the information operator in New York for me, will you? Thanks. Right, I'll wait here for you to call back." Brady hung up the phone and looked at the others. "There's a certain young lady who'll be very interested in this film. *Very* interested."

He stood up and stretched, grinning hugely. "Who wants a drink?"

Every World Press office had been instructed to teletype to New York all reports of UFO's. No sooner had the story broken that a disc might have been responsible for the loss of a

Minuteman ICBM at Cape Kennedy than the UFO floodgates burst wide open. Overnight Brady came to appreciate, as he hadn't before, the frustrations of someone like Jim Trapnell at Blue Book. The deluge included virtually the complete spectrum of sightings Trapnell had described to Brady. People were seeing UFO's everywhere, and the usual rash of strange visitations plagued the news media. Milt Parrish assigned three secretaries to Brady, who in turn put them to work weeding from the mass of incoming material the reports he wanted. He stuck with his original plan. Disc reports only. Everything else to be discarded. All other shapes, lights, objects, or phenomena were tossed aside. The girls then broke down the disc reports into more detailed categories for Brady to study.

An oddball curve had shown up in the pattern and he couldn't figure it. Reports of discs from South America had increased tenfold. Normally that would have meant little. Brazil gloried in its reports of flying discs and had done so for years. The Brazilians saw discs scooting along harbors, dashing over mountains, landing in the jungle. The Brazilians muttered darkly of secret liaisons with the mysterious occupants of discs that landed in high plateaus. They even had a few juicy murders on their hands that thrilled every lover of suspense in the South American country. Several men with strange radio equipment and crude lead face masks had been found dead nine thousand feet along a plateau. Their

148

grief-stricken families told police of secret meetings at night, of trips to fog-shrouded valleys. The stories assumed the proportions of mass contact between a secret organization and the disc occupants. Brady laughed aloud. When it came to direct contact with disc occupants, he wanted the same terms as Jim Trapnell from Blue Book. He'd want to kick the tires, cut off a piece for lab study, and take a ride in the thing. Until then? Just some more good stories to tell on a dark night.

But the news reports from South America—and Central America as well, he noted—had nothing to do with secret conclaves. These were within the reliable-sighting category, discs reported by airline crews, military pilots of local governments, and even by the crew of American military aircraft in that part of the hemisphere. The discs had all been sighted along the West Coast or over the Pacific. Nothing over the interior or to the east. He shrugged and stacked the reports. He could worry that one for weeks and still come up with a blank.

One report among all the others gnawed at his professional curiosity. He wished he had more information. He withdrew the teletype from the file and read the cryptic sheet again.

INFORMATION ONLY. STORY FOLLOWS. MAC-DILL AIR FORCE BASE NEAR TAMPA, WEST COAST OF FLORIDA, SCENE EARLIER TODAY OF FIRE DISASTER. BASE CLOSED OFF, SECURITY. BEST REPORTS INDICATE SEVERAL BAKER FIVE TWO BOMBERS ON

COMBAT READINESS FLIGHT LINE DESTROYED DURING SEVERE ELECTRICAL STORM. UNABLE CONFIRM BUT APPARENTLY BOMBERS LOADED WITH HYDROGEN BOMBS. VIOLENT SQUALL LINE HIT MACDILL BEFORE DAWN HEAVY RAIN STRONG WINDS. POSSIBLE TORNADO FUNNEL NO CONFIRMATION. CIVILIANS OUTSIDE BASE OPEN VIEW FLIGHT LINE CIRCULAR SHAPE SIGHTED IN GLARE LIGHTNING IMMEDIATELY PRIOR FIRE AND EXPLOSIONS. NO COMMENT RADAR TRACKING. CIVILIANS WHO SAW CIRCULAR SHAPE CLAIM VERY BRIGHT BEAM THEN FIRE AND EXPLOSIONS. FLAMES SET OFF FUEL TANKS. ESTIMATES LOSS EIGHT BAKER FIVE TWO BOMBERS. AIR FORCE STATES NO DANGER NUCLEAR WEAPONS INVOLVED. MORE FOLLOWS.

Within an hour from the World Press initial report, the Air Force issued official statements that a tornado had struck the flight line and destroyed a number of B-52 bombers. Brady didn't believe it. Civilians along the fenced perimeter of MacDill had seen a circular—or disc, Brady thought—shape, and then the same sequence of events that had taken place at Cape Kennedy. The disc appeared briefly beneath the clouds, there was a light or energy beam of some kind, and then all hell broke loose. Everything matched too closely to be sheer coincidence. Brady wondered how the civilians could have seen the disc and the fires along the flight line, but never see the thundering tornado the Air Force claimed was responsible for the loss of the bombers.

There was something else. . . . *If* the MacDill report turned out to be true, then, tied in with what had happened to that Minuteman at Cape Kennedy, the discs *had* to be machines, constructed through techniques far beyond anything with which Brady was familiar. Their propulsion, what appeared to be an energy beam of some form, their performance . . .

But that smacked of something from *beyond* the Earth! Try as he might, Brady couldn't accept this solution. And that left . . . A big nothing squeezed itself between Brady's ears. He was ready to start his series on UFO's and still he couldn't come up with the final answers he needed. Russia, England, France, China, West Germany, Japan . . . every one of them had the means of creating the discs. They were in the same technological league with the United States. Well, cross China off the list. The Red Chinese had produced the hydrogen bomb and they were working on long-range missiles, but everything they did, and Brady judged this without deprecating their accomplishments, rested on the pioneering and established results of others. Originality in concept, design, manufacture, and operations lay, especially at this time, beyond the ken of the Red Chinese.

If the Russians had produced the discs; well, goddamn it, they wouldn't be stupid enough to wander all over the United States, tearing up real estate and weaponry in the bargain. The Russians may have been crazy but they weren't stupid, and the arguments against the Soviet discs were so apparent that Brady wasted no further time on *that* subject. Unfortunately, the same arguments applied to the other countries on his list. Each one had the technological acumen, but nothing else fit. Why would they perform in a manner that would be utterly stupid for the United States or the Soviet Union?

They wouldn't, of course. That knocked them out of the box.

So who had the answers? There wasn't a doubt in Brady's mind the Air Force said as little as possible about the disc sightings that had *them* buffaloed. Oh, sure, Trapnell did a convincing song-and-dance routine. He could afford to because everything he said about the discs, lumping them in with the rest of the UFO's, was true enough. It was what the Air Force *wouldn't* say that fouled things up so badly. Maybe, Brady thought, they're just as messed up over all this as I am, only they won't admit it.

There lay the backbone of his series. The discs were real as far as he was concerned. He couldn't pass the Trapnell Test by dragging one into a laboratory, but he could come pretty damned close. His series would lay it on the line, tell the facts in a logical, sober, and yet dramatic manner. He didn't have to hoke up what had happened. One of the beautiful things about putting together a series like this, Brady knew, was that you didn't need to act like a pitchman selling a cure-all snake oil. He would lay it on the line as he saw it, and—

His office buzzer snapped him out of deep thought. Brady pushed the switch. "Yeah?"

"Milt here. We got troubles."

Brady straightened in his seat. "What's up?"

"Rather tell you face to face."

"Be right there." He cut the switch and started for Parrish's office.

Parrish hit him in the belly with it. Nice and clean.

"Phil Hendricks just called. He lost the film from the Cape."

Brady's face spoke for him. Parrish couldn't remember that last time he'd seen Brady gape.

"Maybe 'lost' is the wrong way to say it. Phil said the film was stolen."

"But . . . Jesus, I mean . . . what about the copies?"

Parrish shrugged. "Gone."

"How? Where? What the hell happened?"

"Don't know. Hendricks is beside himself. They were stolen from his apartment sometime last night." Parrish looked up at Brady. "You ready for the rest?"

"There's more?"

"The Air Force released the tracking film of that Minuteman launch."

"Christ, that's something. At least that'll show—"

"There's no sign of a disc. Randall just called from Washington. He saw the film. The Air Force ran it three times for him. Nothing showed."

"But what about the goddamned missile?" Brady shouted.

"It's there. Also the failure. But no disc. Randall was positive about it."

"Milt, that fucking disc was on that fucking film!"

"So you told me. But it's not on the Air Force film."

"Do you think I'm—"

"Don't bother saying it. I know better. Besides, even if I wanted to question you, there's Hendricks and McCabe. And Rogers. Do you think the Air Force doctored their film?"

"What else?" Brady said through clenched teeth. "The sons of bitches. It wouldn't be hard to—"

A copyboy came into Parrish's office with a Teletype sheet. "Sorry to bust in, Mr. Parrish, but you told me to—"

"Thanks, Jimmy." Parrish scanned the sheet. "Well." He sighed. "Here it is." He looked up at Brady with sympathy on his face. "Read this," he said "You're being shot down in flames."

Brady read quickly. Parrish watched the newsman's face whiten with renewed anger.

LATEST ADD. WP SPECIAL. PENTAGON. THE DE-
PARTMENT OF THE AIR FORCE STATED OFFICIALLY
TODAY THAT AN EXHAUSTIVE EXAMINATION OF
THE TRACKING FILM OF THE MINUTEMAN MIS-
SILE THAT EXPLODED IN A RECENT TEST AT CAPE
KENNEDY SHOWS ABSOLUTELY NO SIGN OF A

UFO AS HAS BEEN CLAIMED BY CERTAIN NEWS
SOURCES. THE FILM WAS EXAMINED BY PROFES-
SOR DAVID A. WALTON OF THE UNIVERSITY OF
COLORADO, BY MISSILE SCIENTISTS FROM THE
EASTERN TEST RANGE, AND BY OTHER SCIENTISTS
WHO SPECIALIZE IN AERIAL PHENOMENA. THE
AIR FORCE ADMITTED THAT THE SEQUENCE OF
EVENTS OF THE MINUTEMAN EXPLOSION COULD
HAVE BEEN MISTAKEN BY INEXPERIENCED OB-
SERVERS AS INDICATING ANOTHER OBJECT IN
THE AIR. IMMEDIATELY BEFORE THE MISSILE EN-
TERED THE CLOUD LAYER ABOVE KENNEDY
THERE WAS A PREMATURE IGNITION OF THE
SECOND-STAGE MOTOR. A JET OF FLAME ISSUED
AT A RIGHT ANGLE TO THE BODY OF THE MIS-
SILE. THIS SUDDEN LIGHT WAS REFLECTED FROM
A NEARBY CLOUD, GIVING THE IMPRESSION OF A
CIRCULAR OR DISC-SHAPED OBJECT NEAR THE
MISSILE. SEVERAL NEWSMEN CLAIMED THIS OB-
JECT, IN REALITY THE CLOUD THAT WAS RE-
FLECTING LIGHT, SENT AN ENERGY BEAM OF
SOME MANNER AT THE MINUTEMAN. THE AIR
FORCE HAS NO KNOWLEDGE OF ENERGY BEAMS.
HOWEVER, A LINE OF LIGHT DOES APPEAR ON
THE FILM. THIS HAS BEEN IDENTIFIED AS THE
FLAME JET THAT ISSUED FROM THE MISSILE
WHEN THE SECOND-STAGE ENGINE IGNITED PRE-
MATURELY. POOR VISIBILITY AND LOW CLOUDS,
STATED THE AIR FORCE, COULD PRESENT TO AN EX-
CITED OBSERVER AT A DISTANCE THE OPTICAL IL-
LUSION OF A PHYSICAL OBJECT AND A LIGHT RAY.
THE AIR FORCE NOTED THAT THE PRESS SITE ON
CAPE KENNEDY USED FOR OBSERVING THE MIN-
UTEMAN LAUNCH IS A MINIMUM TWO THOUSAND

FOUR HUNDRED YARDS, OR APPROXIMATELY ONE
AND A HALF MILES, FROM THE MINUTEMAN PAD.
UNDER CONDITIONS OF POOR VISIBILITY, THE
VIEWING DISTANCE, THE FLAME AND SMOKE
FROM THE MISSILE SILO, AND THE SPEED OF THE
LAUNCH, MISIMPRESSIONS AND OPTICAL ILLU-
SIONS ARE QUITE COMMON. THE REPORT THAT
THE MINUTEMAN WAS CUT IN HALF BY THE
ENERGY BEAM IS OF COURSE ERRONEOUS, STATES
THE AIR FORCE. THE PREMATURE IGNITION OF
THE SECOND-STAGE ENGINE INITIATED THE STAGE
SEPARATION SEQUENCE AT THE SAME TIME,
BRINGING ABOUT A NORMAL BUT PREMATURE
SEPARATION OF THE FIRST AND SECOND STAGES.
THIS EFFECT APPARENTLY WAS ALSO MISINTER-
PRETED BY PRESS MEIDA PRESENT AT THE CAPE.
PROFESSOR DAVID A. WALTON COMMENTED THAT
SUCH MISINTERPRETATIONS ARE COMMON. THE
PROFESSOR. . . .

Brady felt sick. There wasn't any use in
reading further. He could anticipate well
enough what Walton would have said. Brady
tossed the sheet back to the desk.

"What's next, lover boy?" Parrish quipped.

"What the hell are they so scared of they've
got to steal films from—"

"You don't know *they*, and I assume you
mean Air Force," Parrish broke in, "stole the
film."

"Who else could have done it?" Brady
snapped. "Only the Air Force knew about it."

"You're too mad to see straight," Parrish
said, not unkindly. "I believe like you do. The

blue-suiters had something to do with copping the film. But you can't prove it and I can't prove it. However," Parrish said with a tight smile, "it does involve me a bit more than it did before."

"How so?"

"I don't like my film being stolen."

"How do you think Hendricks feels?" Brady asked.

"Lousy. But I wasn't finished. We were scheduling the series to start a week from Monday, right?"

"You changing things around?"

"Sure am. You're going to have a busy weekend. This is Friday. I want to start the series *this* Monday. We're pushing it up a week."

Brady hesitated. "But that means—"

"I know what it means," Parrish said quickly. "It means you don't sleep this weekend and you don't get laid and what you will be doing is to write your fingers to the bone. I want the copy in here no later than ten Sunday night. We start sending at two A.M. Monday to make the morning papers. Anything else?"

Brady shook his head.

"You don't look happy," Parrish observed.

"Like you said, I don't sleep or get laid. I just write. Hell of a weekend."

"Yeah, my heart bleeds. This is your baby and I'm letting you run with the ball. Any complaints?"

Brady grinned at his editor. "None."

"Take off."

Brady held up his middle finger and went back to his office.

Ann Dallas pulled the covers gently over the sleeping form of Cliff Brady. She slipped into the pajamas she'd brought to his apartment and eased into bed next to him. I could blow a bugle, she thought, and it wouldn't bother him. Brady slept with complete exhaustion. He'd worked all Friday night and through into Saturday without rest. Ann found his urgent message waiting at flight operations when she landed from a West Coast trip. She called him to learn of his marathon stint at the typewriter.

"You know how to make coffee?" he barked into the phone.

"Y-yes," she stammered, taken aback with his brusqueness. "Why?"

"Get your beautiful ass over here fast as you can," he said. "I need you, baby, and not for the sack. You can make me coffee and cook for me and keep me awake." He told her he must deliver his first four articles no later than Sunday evening. If he could do it, he added, he wanted to complete the series by then.

"I'll be there," she said, sighing audibly into the telephone. "Although I have had better invitations—"

"I think I love you," he said gruffly. "Hurry up. Bye." The phone went dead.

She made drinks for him, cooked, rubbed his aching shoulder and neck muscles, and was kissed fervently as the result of sudden inspirations on his part. He gulped down Benzedrine capsules to stay awake and attacked the typewriter with almost religious fervor. She studied him with growing admiration. He never slowed his pace except to stretch and groan with complaining muscles, which brought her hurrying to him with soothing fingers.

By four o'clock Sunday morning he couldn't work anymore. The words were there, but he couldn't get them straight. His fingers stumbled on the typewriter keys. He knew it was time to break. He stood up, clothes rumpled, his face bearded. His eyes were hollow. "I need six hours' sleep," he said hoarsely. "Get me up no later than ten. I've got two more articles to do and then I want to edit the stuff." He blinked several times as if to confirm she was really there.

"Did I tell you I love you?" he asked.

She nodded, a smile on her lips.

"Christ, I think I do." He went into the bedroom and collapsed.

She moved closer to snuggle with him. He mumbled in his sleep and turned, his arm resting across her breasts. In the darkness she smiled to herself.

CHAPTER X

"I thought *you* were the fucking editor around here!" Cliff Brady gestured with open contempt. "Ass kisser is more like it."

Despite himself Parrish whitened. His voice came out like a hiss. "If I were you, Cliff, I'd—"

"Thank Christ you're not," Brady snapped. "At least I can look in the mirror without throwing up. The first time, the very first goddamned time you've got to stand up and be counted, you fink out." Brady stabbed a finger at Parrish. "Well, you fooled me. That's a hell of an act you've been putting on all this time. Where's your fucking skirt?" Brady sneered. "Because you sure ain't got any balls to fill those pants."

Parrish eased himself slowly into his chair,

161

never taking his eyes off Brady. My God, he had no idea Brady would flip this way. They'd killed the UFO series after the first three installments, and Brady acted as if it were the end of the world. Parrish forced himself not to lose his temper. One madman in the office was enough.

"Will you let me get in a word?" Parrish said it with a thin smile in an attempt to regain the warmth that usually existed between them. It didn't take. Brady was too far gone to bring this back to a gentleman's level.

"Get in a word? You unholy son of a bitch. Bad enough you killed the series. *You*! Not anyone else!" Brady shouted. "So long as that fucking sign on your desk says 'Managing Editor,' you run the show. At least that's what you've told me all these years." Brady gesticulated wildly. "But the first time they put on the pressure, you crack like an eggshell. Get in a word, huh? Where the hell were your words when you killed the series? The least you could have done was to pick up the goddamned phone and—"

"I tried to reach you!"

"I just bet you did. For ten years you've always been able to get hold of me no matter where the hell I was. Now I'm in the same goddamned city and all of a sudden nothing works." Brady was close to becoming physical. Parrish didn't want that. If Brady blew his cool completely, there's be a breach so wide neither man would ever be able to close it.

Parrish put all the sincerity he could manage

162

into his voice. "Cliff, I told you I did everything possible to get you," the editor said. "There wasn't that much time. I was told to kill the series immediately." He shook his head. "Jesus, I know how you feel. I'm sorry as hell about—"

Abruptly, Brady calmed down. Where before he had exploded with anger he was now cold. "All right," he said with a release of pent-up breath. "We'll hear you out. Who ordered you to kill the series?"

"It came from the top."

"Don't play games with me, Milt. I asked you *who.*"

Parrish shrugged. No use hiding it. "Wilkinson."

The name stopped Brady, as Parrish knew it would. Wilkinson *was* the top, the president of World Press.

"I've been trying to explain," Parrish continued. "It was Wilkinson personally. Himself. No secretaries or flunkies. He called me directly and said he would confirm it in writing." Parrish made a face. "He didn't ask or recommend. He *told* me to kill the series effective immediately."

"And you just took it lying down?" Brady was incredulous. "You're supposed to be the big goddamned lion of Editors' Row, and you get a lousy phone call and just like that"—Brady snapped his fingers—"you blow everything I've done for all these weeks? Either I don't know you very well or you're lying."

163

The words hung ominously between them. Parrish preferred not to hear that Brady had called him a liar.

"No, I didn't just take it lying down."

Brady made an obscene gesture. "It looks like it. You killed the series just like the good little boy you were told to be, and you tell me you didn't take it lying down. What kind of shit is that?"

Parrish flared. "You asked me what happened and I told you!"

"Like hell you did." Brady smiled coldly at the other man. "You told me you got a phone call and you went to see the man. *Now* tell me what happened in your little tête-à-tête."

"Wilkinson said it was a matter of policy," Parrish said. He knew it was lame but it was the truth.

"Policy!"

"That's what the man said."

"Since when have you let someone tell you how to run your shop?"

"It's not the same. This is the first time that—"

"Don't crap me," Brady said. His voice was quiet. "I've known you too long, Milt. Just don't shit me."

"I told you straight."

Brady's disbelief mirrored in his eyes. "Just like that, huh? You didn't say anything. You just took your castor oil and crawled back under your desk. You—"

"I've had it," Parrish burst out, his own anger pouring over his self-control. He came to his feet and shoved a finger against Brady's chest. "Have you stopped to think *why* Wilkinson killed the series?"

Brady knocked aside Parrish's hand with an easy blow that sent pain stabbing up the editor's arm. He tried not to wince. Brady didn't know his own strength and ...

"You're asking *me* why?" Brady asked. "I've been trying to find out from *you*. Quit the games and lay it out, will you?"

"You're way out in left field."

"Did Wilkinson say that?" Brady demanded.

"Not in quotes but in so many words. He——"

"Did he say why I was out in left field?"

"No, but——"

"Did you *ask* him?"

"I talked about it for a while."

Brady's quiet was ominous. "You talked about it for a while," he mimicked Parrish. "Did you tell him *you* were the editor here and that if he didn't like it he knows what he can do?"

"You're awfully free with *my* job, aren't you?"

"Did you tell him even that?" Brady was almost pleading for Parrish to tell him he'd stood up to Wilkinson.

Parrish paled. "No."

"You going to tell me why?"

"I don't have to tell you *anything*," Parrish said coldly. "Not a damn thing."

"No, you don't," Brady agreed. "You haven't got any balls either."

"All right, damn you. As far as Wilkinson is

concerned, you sound like a nut." He saw Brady stiffen but plunged on. "Some of your stuff *is* way out. I've told you a hundred times it's not enough to feel you're right or even be positive about it unless you can *back up* what you're saying. The—"

"And I can't back it up, huh?"

"That's the way it is," Parrish snapped. "You can't back up what—"

"Even with the eyewitnesses to what really happened at Cape Kennedy. Funny," Brady said, "you were awfully willing to accept what I saw in the film because it was supported by Hendricks and McCabe and Rogers. You made me pretty speeches about getting involved because of stolen film. You—"

"You wait right there," Parrish broke in. "I called your eyewitnesses. I spoke with all three of them. They admitted that if it came down to the kind of questions you've got to answer from a witness stand, they couldn't be positive about a disc. They said maybe the Air Force was right. They think they're right, but they couldn't swear to it."

"That's not what they told me."

"It's what they're saying now!"

Brady didn't answer for a while. He took a deep breath. "All right. I won't interrupt. Let's hear the rest of your fairy tale about Wilkinson."

"You just won't believe you might be wrong about this whole scene, will you?" Brady refused to answer. "Okay, okay," Parrish said, "we'll lay it all out nice and neat. The way your copy reads it sounds as if you're accusing someone of carrying out a monstrous scheme against the country. Or the world. It's hard to tell," he said, sticking it in deeper. "But you don't know *what* kind of plot. Or *who's* carrying it out. *If* anyone is carrying it out. Whether it sits well with you or not, you *do* sound like a nut. If you . . ."

Brady lifted his hand and Parrish lapsed into silence. "Maybe," Brady said softly, "I'd better get something clear. Do you think I'm a nut?" He held up his hand again. "No speeches. Just a plain yes or no."

Parrish sighed. "Of course not. No." He emphasized the word.

"Thanks for the towering vote of confidence," Brady said. He was ungracious about it and he didn't care. "If you don't think I'm some kind of nut, then you must have confidence in my work."

"You know I do," Parrish said, hoping the thaw had started. "We've worked together for a long time, haven't we?"

"Yeah, we sure have," Brady agreed. It was the most pleasant tone of voice Parrish had heard from him since the fracas started. "And. you've always backed me up all that time," Brady continued. "We've made a hell of a team."

Christ, Parrish thought with overwhelming relief, the storm's over. "Damn right we have," he said.

"That's why I'm asking you to tell Wilkinson to go shit in his hat."

Parrish stared.

"And run the series."

Parrish didn't believe what he was hearing. "Are you out of your mind?" he shouted. He knew his voice was shrill but he couldn't help himself. Here it seemed everything was back to an even keel and now . . . now *this*! "You know I can't run the series if Wilkinson refuses!"

To his astonishment, Brady remained calm. "You ought to take lessons in lying, Milt." Brady smiled at him. "I could buy your argument about the series, about my being off base," he said, "except for one little mistake you made. Sunday night, just four days ago, you read this series. It didn't bother you then. It bothered you so little, you committed the full nine articles. Now that Wilkinson has made his little speech, suddenly you don't like the series. Not until now. Quite a switch, wouldn't you say?"

Parrish fought for the words.

"You got no balls and you're a liar to boot," Brady said. "Shove your job up your ass."

Ann tried for hours to reach him. The World Press operator said he had left the office and she had no idea when he would be back. Ann's flight left in only two hours. But she *had* to reach Brady. Thirty minutes before flight time, she talked another girl into standing in for her. Every twenty minutes Ann dialed Brady's number. At ten thirty that night he finally answered the phone. Ann could hardly understand him.

"Darling, will you listen? *Please.* I must talk with you."

"Shure. Wanna talk with *you.* Ever tell you I'm in love, in love wish you?"

My God. Of all the times . . . "Cliff, I'm *serious.*"

"So'm I. Where the hell are you?"

"At the field. Will you wait there for me?"

"I'll wait anywhere for you. Till hell freezes over. Even till it melts. Howzat? Pretty good, eh? Till hell melts over. I'll be waiting for youuuuu."

She had never heard a hairy laugh before. She looked at the telephone as if it had turned into a snake. "Cliff. Cliff? *Listen* to me."

"Shure. I'm . . ."

"Never mind," she said firmly. "Take a cold shower. Do you hear me? Take a cold shower. Drink coffee. Lots of hot coffee. All right?"

"Thas' silly. Why should I take a hot shower and drink cold coffee? Never heard' anything so silly in m'life."

Ann groaned. "I'll be right there. Just wait for me." She hung up the telephone and took a deep breath. Well, it didn't matter if he *was* smashed. What she had to say would sober him. And fast. She hurried through the terminal to get a cab.

She pushed open the door to his apartment and heard the shower. Thank God for small favors. She glanced at the table in the living room. She couldn't tell if he had spilled more coffee than he managed to get into him. But at least he'd tried. The bathroom door was open. She stood outside and called him. "Cliff?"

"That you, honey?"

"Are you all right, Cliff?"

A waterlogged head peered around the edge of the shower curtain. At the rim of the bathtub. The head grinned sheepishly at her.

"What on earth are you doing down there?"

"Trying to drown myself. Gimme a kiss."

"You're getting me all wet!" she exclaimed.

"Good for what ails you."

"Me? You're the one who needs—"

He kissed her again.

"Cliff, you idiot. Let go."

He grinned at her. "You're beautiful and I love you and I'm glad you're here and what's so all-fired important?"

"Later," she said. She straightened her skirt.

"What's wrong with now?" he asked.

"Later," she repeated. "Hurry up out of there. I'll put up some fresh coffee. By the way, what were you doing in there before? Drinking coffee or washing the table with it?"

"Can't remember."

"I'm not surprised. Head hurt?"

"Just minor agony."

"Want an Alka-Seltzer?"

"Gaagh. Yes."

"I'll bring it to you."

Fifteen minutes later he came into the living room and grabbed for the coffee. They didn't say a word until he had downed the second cup.

He leaned over and kissed her gently. "All right," he said. "I'll probably last through the next few hours. Where are my cigarettes?" She lit one and placed it between his lips. He dragged deeply and leaned back on the couch.

"Okay. Let's have it," he said.

"I don't know where to begin."

"Punch hard. It's easiest that way."

She placed her hand on his arm. "We received the word just this afternoon."

"Ann, stop playing games." He showed his annoyance. "*What* word?"

"We're forbidden to talk with you."

He stared at her. "You mean the crews?"

"That's right."

"Spell it out, will you, hon?" She tried to read his expression but couldn't get through. She sighed. "It's simple, I suppose. Your articles are having a tremendous impact. Someone found out—you've been seen with me and several of the crews, of course, so it wouldn't be difficult—anyway, the company found out you'd been talking with some of the crews, and"—she shrugged—"everyone has been told not to speak with you. Any inquiries on your part, about anything," she emphasized, "are to be directed to the front office, blah, blah. That's about the size of it, Cliff." She squeezed his arm. "I'm sorry."

"Sorry? What for?"

"Isn't it obvious?" His poker face and the question flustered her. "I mean, here we're all being told to have nothing to do with you, as if, as if"—she groped for words—"you're some-

171

thing terrible who would contaminate us. Cliff, that's a terrible thing to do to someone!"

He smiled at her. "No, it's not." He drew deeply on the cigarette and blew out a long plume of smoke. His face had a lopsided grin. "Besides, you haven't heard *my* news."

She gestured toward the half-empty bottle of Scotch. "Were you celebrating?"

He snorted sarcastically. "I suppose you could say that."

"I must say you don't seem very disturbed over what I told you," she said. She felt exasperated, as if Cliff should have reacted more strongly to the news she had brought him. If something like that had happened to her . . .

"Shit, I'm not disturbed."

She noticed a sudden change, as if a cloud had passed over his face. "What were you going to tell me?" she prompted.

He was buried in thought and she waited for him to respond. "By God, it might just fit." She was annoyed. Cliff was talking to empty air and not to her.

"Will you tell me—"

"Sorry. Didn't mean to be rude," he said. His apology surprised her as much as his fleeting moods and the rapidity with which he changed. "Pour me another coffee? I want to get something straight in my own mind."

The cup was almost empty when he came to a decision. "Ann, I started to tell you before." A rueful grin appeared on his face. "Yeah, I've got some news all right. First, WP cancelled the UFO series."

"Oh, Cliff . . ."

He held up his hand. "That's only for starters."

"But *why*? The series is wonderful! Everyone who's been reading about it is . . . why," she almost spluttered in indignation, "even the passengers are talking to us about—"

"Wait, wait a minute, baby. Hear the rest of it first."

"Well, it can't be any worse."

"Hah. I quit today."

She didn't have any immediate response to his announcement.

He grunted in reflection. "I told Parrish to shove it."

Finally she found her voice. "Was it because . . ."

He patted her hand. "What else? I couldn't do anything else. You've either got balls in this game or you don't. And one of the things you *never* do to a byliner is pull the rug out from under his feet. Especially when you don't notify him first, and, most especially, when you haven't got more than a pisspor excuse about policy for creaming the guy."

"Policy?"

"That's what they told me." He reviewed the episode with Parrish. "It's a blind. It's *got* to be a blind. Policy, my foot. They were putting the screws to me, Ann. Bearing down with the pressure."

He turned and held her eyes. "Someone is trying to shut me up."

"But who, Cliff? And why would they want

to do such a thing?" She tried desperately to stay with his thoughts.

"The only 'who' I know is the bastard who gave the orders. Wilkinson. He's top dog for WP. But what puzzles me is that Wilkinson has never stepped into anything before. Jesus, even when we did that series on trying to look at communism from *their* side of things. We practically had mobs stoning the office. But no one interfered with us. But *now*," he shook his head, "now the roof caves in. And because of what I've been saying about the discs."

He reached for another cigarette. "I didn't have any leads until you showed up here," he said. "I mean, I couldn't figure Wilkinson. And I still can't figure Parrish sucking eggs the way he did. But what you told me begins to put some light on this whole thing. First Wilkinson steps into the picture. That's all wrong. I've never even *seen* the man. Did you know that?" She shook her head. "I don't even know what the mother looks like. Then right out of the blue he sticks his heavy hand into things. Parrish walks the plank and cancels the series."

He turned again, his face grim. "Do you know what they did today? They boxed me in. They *knew* I'd quit because they knew I'd *have* to quit."

He scratched his chin, lost again for the moment in thought. "They're squeezing me. Get rid of the one weapon I've got—my column. If they fire me it's too obvious. So they squeeze me into a corner and they force me to quit.

Neat. Oh, baby, it's neat. I did just what they wanted me to do."

"But—but, who is 'they'?"

"I don't know," he confessed. "Maybe Wilkinson, or maybe someone who got to Wilkinson. I don't know. But they're out to get me, to turn me off. Look, I've talked to pilots and crews only from your airline, right?"

"I—I guess so, Cliff."

"Sorry. You couldn't have known one way or the other. But that's what I did. Most of my airlines sightings have come from your outfit. I never identified the pilots or anyone else. I never identified the airline. I made sure *not* to do that. Yet the very same day the series is killed and I'm boxed into quitting, it's *your* airline that sends out notice I'm poison. That's a damned convenient coincidence. Want to take odds no other airline got the word like yours did?" She started to speak, but he motioned for her to wait. "There's something else I want you to consider. How'd they know I was talking with you and the others? I never told anyone. I never even told Parrish what outfit you worked for."

He stubbed out his cigarette with an angry gesture. "Someone's been watching just about everything I've done. That means organization of some kind."

"Don't you have any idea of who they might be?"

"Uh-uh. Not yet, anyway. Maybe Wilkinson is tied in or maybe he's doing someone a favor.

175

I don't know. From the way it looks, Wilkinson figures to be a part of the picture. Parrish I can't figure. Maybe he's getting old and he's scared that good jobs are hard to get. I wasn't able to latch onto the size of the effort that's going into this. Not until you showed up."

She felt her body relax. At least she knew she'd done right, that what she had to say was important to him.

He brought the telephone to the table. "Ann, call someone you know at one of the other lines, will you? Stewardess, pilot; doesn't matter. Just so long as they're crew. Ask them if they got any word like you people did."

She called stewardesses of three separate airlines. None of them knew anything about company orders not to discuss UFO's. Only one of the girls knew Cliff's name.

"See?" he said when she completed the calls. "There's a direct tie-in all right. I never mentioned your company and yet they're in a sweat about me. They got the word from someone, Ann. Someone who's got a hell of a lot of influence with the line."

She tried to be practical about matters. "What happens next, Cliff? What will you do?"

He dragged the Scotch to the table and poured for both of them. "Do? First things first. Try to figure this out." He took a stiff drink and sighed. He put his feet up on the table and wriggled his toes. She wanted to hold him. The import of what he'd been saying was beginning to sink in. The series canceled, he'd lost his job, he . . .

"So first they label me as a nut," he was saying. "A lunatic who's gone ape over UFO's. No one makes any distinction about the matter. I'm just a nut who's scrambled his marbles. It's easy to do. There are plenty of kooks around who come from Venus or screwed Miss Mars of 1969, or God knows what. I'm lumped with the rest of them. Ready-made character assassination. The more I protest, the worse it gets. Instant shithead, that's me. They don't have to say a word. Anyone with an ounce of common sense," he said sarcastically, "*knows* that UFO's aren't real. They're not even there. If you say publicly they *are* real, then you're one of the lunatics. It's perfect, almost as if the whole thing were set up in . . ." His voice trailed away and he stiffened visibly as a wild thought came to him. He put it aside, not rejecting it, but filing it mentally for attention later.

"Okay," he said, "we'll take this piece by piece. For some reason, someone's decided I've got to be turned off. Nothing drastic like a concrete bath. Just turned off. Made to look like a jerk who's gone off half-cocked about UFO's. Next question," he said, holding up two fingers, "is why."

"That's what I'd like to know," Ann murmured.

"It's obvious. I'm on to something. I've gotten home. Why else would they steal that film from Hendricks, unless I'm under their skin? They're not worried about my saying that UFO's are real. Entire organizations devoted

177

to UFO research, like NICAP, have been saying just that for years. But in my own way I've been sorting out the nonsense from what's real. I'm on to something and I've got—I *had*—a column with millions of readers every day. So the next question is, Whose cage have I been rattling? The whole idea sounds so wild I don't even want to say it out loud." He looked at Ann. "Am I making any sense?"

"I'm not sure," she said.

"I don't blame you," he replied. "Stick with me. Maybe the pieces will start to fall into place. We'll assume I hit the right nerve with someone. I'm agitating them. They're upset. Whoever they are, they've got influence. That much is obvious or I wouldn't be out of a job. But I don't know *who* it is. This thing with Parrish isn't kosher, Ann. Milt wouldn't balk at a story if I told him I turned into a werewolf every time the moon was full. Two guys have worked together as long as we have . . ." He shook his head. "So it can't be Parish. Someone got to him, all right."

"How do you mean that?"

"They played him like a fish on a line. He backed me up, but he never really bought the 'UFO's are real' bit. They didn't ask too much of him. Just get Brady off his kick with UFO's and little green men from Mars. They tell him there's opposition, people are complaining, and they don't ask him to go out and break my back. From his viewpoint he's supporting me as a matter of faith. He'd rather have me doing something else, anyway. So he passes on the word and—I forgot his canceling the series the way he did. I don't know, honey, maybe they told him to do it that way or maybe he felt a nice clean cut was the best answer. It really doesn't matter, I suppose."

He leaned forward to rest his face in his hands. Ann knew he was talking aloud to himself as much as to her. She didn't mind. Cliff would share it with her when he had his mental affairs in order.

" . . . worry about myself except for a couple of other items. First, the film. Unless the film proved something that this . . . this group, whoever or whatever they are, didn't want before the public, why the devil would anyone want the film? But the biggest mystery of all is Wilkinson."

"Maybe," Ann smiled, "he just doesn't like UFO's."

"Christ, that's about as valid as anything I've come up with," Brady muttered. "But seriously, Wilkinson shouldn't give a damn one way or the other—hell, I've already gone through that with you. He's the chairman of the board of World Press, but he's also on the board of a dozen corporations. He's not a newsman, he's a financier. He's a shrewd money handler. Brilliant, for that matter. Wilkinson's not the kind of individual to get involved in policy matters with news. He's—hey, maybe that's it!" Brady's sudden shout made Ann jump.

"W-what's—"

179

"Hold it," he barked at her. "Goddamn it, if I'm right . . ." He dialed his office. "Ralph? Brady here. Yeah, I know. Thanks. Later, will you? I need something. Pull the file on Wilkinson, huh? Right. Wilkinson, Drew David. Sure, I'll hang on."

He cupped his hand over the telephone. "Cross your fingers or pray or something, baby," he told her. He wouldn't say another word but waited with mounting impatience.

"Yeah, I'm here. Got it? Good. Okay. Read me the list of corporations he's involved with." Brady's face was a mask as he listened to the other man. Suddenly he came alive.

"Give me that again," he ordered. "I'll be damned. Are you sure? Jesus. Ralph, thanks. And keep it close to the vest, will you? Sure thing. S'long."

Brady's face showed triumph when he hung up the phone and turned to Ann.

"My hunch was dead on," he said.

"Cliff, I haven't the faintest idea of—"

"I know, I know," he said. He burst into a roar of laughter.

"It turns out that Mr. Mucky-Muck himself—Wilkinson—is a member of the board of directors of Blackburn Aero."

He waited to let it sink in.

"And that ain't all, baby." He grabbed her by the arms and kissed her roughly.

"Umm, I ought to do that more often," he said gleefully.

"Will you tell me what—"

180

"Our friend Wilkinson, it just so happens," Brady said, serious again, "*also* is a member of the board of directors of a certain airline. You should recognize the name. You fly for them."

CHAPTER XI

Brady watched the Salt River sliding through the peaks of the Superstition Mountains. Beyond the upcoming range Phoenix sprawled across its valley. The jet banked steeply as the crew took the airplane down in a heady descent. Brady leaned back in his seat, judging he had time enough for one more cigarette before they'd be on final approach.

His face remained passive, his attention seemingly on the terrain drifting beneath the jet.

Ann . . . She had been with him for hours before he became aware of the change in her. The aftereffects of drinking and his preoccupation with being pushed out of his job crowded almost everything from his mind. Not until midnight did he realize he hadn't eaten and, for all he knew, neither had Ann. He asked if she'd like to go out for a midnight breakfast when, for the first time, he noticed her bags in the foyer.

"Didn't you check into the hotel?"

She shook her head.

"I'd better call for you," he said.

Again she shook her head.

He was struck by the look on her face. It hit him then. Without another word.

Ann started for the kitchen. "We'll eat here," she said. "How's the refrigerator?"

"Huh? Oh. Christ, I don't know. There should be a couple things in there."

He sat on a stool, leaning his elbows on the bar that doubled as a breakfast table. For several minutes they didn't speak. He was content to watch as she explored the kitchen. Finally she stood quietly. "This place is a gastronomical horror."

He shrugged.

"Well." She sighed. "There's enough for a Western omelette. Daddy Dallas style."

"One of your old man's creations?"

She nodded. "Very exclusive."

"What's in it?"

"Tell you later. With what you have here, I'm going to experiment a bit."

"Blargh," he said.

"Even before you taste it?"

It went like that for the next hour. Comfortable small talk. A feeling of being contented.

Brady wondered about it. With his wife it had been a whirlwind. Moonlight and nights out on the town and mixing with friends and being social as hell. The right perfume and the dresses that appealed and tantalized just enough, everything fitting within the accepted boundaries of courtship, modern style. Almost as if the whole damned thing had been ordained.

There'd been none of this with Ann. He didn't poke around in his mind to pluck his emotions like a violin string, hoping for the right chords of understanding to come back to him. He'd been that route and ended up with a marriage that went to hell in a wheelbarrow. He didn't know if he loved Ann, but he didn't care. Not that it wasn't important; he just didn't care if all the factors were right. He followed the way he felt. He wanted her with him, he missed her when she wasn't around.

When they ate they sat around and talked for another hour. It wasn't as if we were hesitating, he thought, as if there were some inner delay in sharing the bed. We were just plain enjoying being with one another.

Finally Ann kissed him. "Go to bed," she said. That was all. He slipped between the sheets and heard her turn on the shower. In the soft darkness of the room he saw the outline of her body. Then she was with him and their lips met.

Afterward, they lay together, warm and close. He felt marvelous, the knot of tension gone completely. He wondered if he loved her, if she, like him, had yet to resolve her emotions.

When you were off to a start like this, things took care of themselves. Just stay loose, he told himself. They slept together like children.

There was still the crying immediacy of the events that had shattered his professional life. Brady intended to patch up the pieces. Fast.

Discovering Wilkinson in a web that included World Press, TWA, and Blackburn Aero was the first solid break in the wall that had so thoroughly baffled him. He didn't know yet what the breach signified. Somehow the discs were involved. They *had* to be . . .

He was making someone damned uncomfortable with the needle he had threaded through the overwhelming mass of UFO material. Now he was getting the backlash of his effective stinging. Someone was out to shut him up.

Brady kept returning to the thought that the discs *were* real and they were connected somehow with the group he had angered with his series. Angered? If they were of Wilkinson's class and they were linked somehow with the discs, "angered" might be self-praise. "Annoyed" might be more realistic, Brady thought wryly.

Whatever the extent of his irritation, it had certainly provoked a reaction. The unknown group was turning him off. Within a few hours of his storming out of Parrish's office the word was being passed among the major news services. And the papers. *Cliff Brady's a leper. Don't touch him.*

Officially he was poison, but he had good

friends in the right places. Even those who couldn't work with him in their professional capacity would do almost anything he asked as a personal favor. Those favors included some immediate research.

If he had suspected before that Dr. Kenneth Taggert's position with Blackburn was a blind, he was almost convinced of it now. Brady had kicked himself for missing what should have been obvious to him. Blackburn Aero was supposed to be developing huge transports to wrap up the entire air-cargo market of Central and South America.

Once he took a deep look into the claims of Blackburn Aero, the pitch of giant new air-cargo transports rang hollow. To develop giant cargo planes involved astronomical costs. Not even Blackburn could easily absorb that staggering dollar drain.

The Blackburn air-cargo program was a sham. Blackburn Aero's research center was in Flagstaff, Arizona. Okay so far. But where was their facility for flight-testing their giant airplanes? Into what manufacturing complex would flow the machinery and matériel, the skilled workers, and all the other demands of a huge industrial effort?

The flight-test center for Blackburn was an isolated area within the Colorado Plateau, east-northeast of Flagstaff and just south of the Arizona Mountains. But that was madness. The country was unspeakably desolate and forbidding. There weren't any major roads leading into the area. No rail lines of any kind.

That part of the United States was as savage as the worst of the Gobi Desert. It was insane to move a vast facility into such a Godforsaken part of the country. None of it added up. Brady had flown through that general area with Ann in the Aztec and there hadn't been the least indication of something big. Of course he could have missed it in so vast and desolate an area. Brady intended to cover it all this trip. He would rent a plane and fly over the Colorado Plateau and look for that damned airstrip himself.

CHAPTER XII

"Good morning, Mr. Brady."

Brady stared at the tall brunette behind the receptionist's desk.

The brunette favored him with a radiant smile. "It's a pleasure to see you again, sir."

"Uh, sure. Good morning."

Brady felt like an idiot. He knew Blackburn Aero, or whoever was involved with Wilkinson, might be keeping tabs on him. Obviously they were, to some extent. But when it worked so well down the line that secretaries recognized him on first sight . . . Christ, what had he gotten into? He knew his whereabouts were simple enough to trace and that a TV monitor could have picked him up as he climbed from the cab in front of the building. Someone else who recognized him on sight could pass the

189

word to the girl behind the desk. That didn't bother him. He could figure out plenty of ways to carry out this routine. Why they'd go to the trouble was something else.

Even as he stood before the reception desk he was contemplating the "why." If nothing else, it confirmed that he'd affected the group involved with Wilkinson to such an extent they would keep tabs on him. It was more than that, he realized. They were *anticipating* his moves. He didn't like that. He liked it less the more he thought of it. It smacked of organization and control well beyond anything an outfit like Blackburn Aero should require.

Brady rallied. "I haven't got an appointment," he said, "but I would like to see Dr. Taggert. He, uh, we've met before, and—"

The girl nodded. "I'm so sorry, Mr. Brady, but Dr. Taggert is unavailable."

Brady thought of the long trip to reach Flagstaff. "I know he's busy," Brady said, "and I'm barging in. I can wait or come back later in the day."

"I'm sorry, sir, but that won't be possible."

"Is Dr. Taggart out of town? Perhaps you could tell me when he'll be back."

The brunette tossed her hair aside. Brady studied her and knew this girl had been selected carefully and trained down to the last detail. She was beautiful, crisp, efficient, poised and . . . he spotted it then. Even her speech. Letter-perfect. Receptionist, hell. Whatever she was, it smacked of a professional handling difficult visitors. For all he knew, they'd yanked the regular girl the moment they had confirmed his arrival at Flagstaff.

"I'm sorry, sir," the girl repeated, again with that dazzling smile.

"Sorry about what?" Brady snapped. "I just asked if he was out of town and when he'd be back."

He didn't ruffle a single hair. "Dr. Taggert is unavailable, Mr. Brady," she said, her tone unchanged. "Is there anything else I can do for you?"

Brady wanted to go right over her desk and through the doors beyond. What that would accomplish he didn't know, but he damned well wasn't going to be stopped here.

What did he do now? The girl led him by the nose. "Is there anyone else who might help you, Mr. Brady?"

He hadn't expected that. Who could there be? Should he try to beard Frazer Blackburn in his den? He didn't believe the industrialist would even be here. Who else that he knew was involved in one way or another with this mess? Drew Wilkinson? What he might be doing in Arizona was something Brady couldn't figure and didn't expect.

"No," he said, trying to keep the anger from his voice. "But I'd like to find out when Taggert will be back so that I—"

"Mr. Brady."

The voice came from behind him. Brady turned. He stared at a woman who was the most physically perfect female he had ever

191

seen in his life. He had never seen her, and yet, again, he was being addressed by his name.

"I'm Dianne Sims. Perhaps I can help you."

"What? I mean . . ."

She bailed him out of his flustered reaction. "Would you come this way, please?" She turned and walked through a doorway Brady hadn't seen before. Then he realized it wasn't a doorway; a wall panel had slid open.

"Dianne?"

The blonde stopped and returned to the desk. "Of course. How careless of me." She picked up a security identification badge extended by the receptionist. "If you would, Mr. Brady?" The newsman took the badge. He blinked as he clipped it to his jacket. *The badge had his name and his photograph sealed in plastic.*

Dianne Sims brushed by him as she returned to the open panel. Brady caught the scent of a fresh breeze. Her physical presence was over-whelming. He shook his head and walked after her. As he stepped through the doorway, the panel closed behind him. He turned and looked at a blank wall. Not a trace of a sliding panel.

"Very neat," he observed.

She nodded and flashed a smile for answer. Brady walked with her along a pale-green cor-ridor, through a structure unlike anything he knew. The floor appeared steel-hard yet ac-cepted his steps with the resiliency of soft car-peting, absorbing the sound of their shoes. It took him several seconds to notice the absence of lights. Yet the walls and ceiling glowed in a softly pervasive illumination. He did find what he expected: the concealed lenses of closed-circuit TV scanners. Had he not sought them out he would have missed them in the pattern of ceiling panels. What was this building that demanded such security?

Dianne Sims stopped before an elevator for which there were no buttons. After a brief interval, a door slid aside noiselessly and she motioned for Brady to precede her within. He couldn't tell whether they rose or descended. They left the elevator and walked another corridor identical to the first. At the far end they stopped before a blank wall. Brady spun around as a soft hiss sounded and steel bars barricaded the way behind him. Before he could question the girl, another panel opened at the corridor end.

"Mr. Brady?" Dianne Sims waited with her arm extended. Brady stepped forward into a large office paneled in dark wood. Soft light glowed from ceiling and walls.

Standing behind a large desk was a giant of a man. Brady recognized him at once.

"Ah, Mr. Brady." The voice was low but filled the room with its power. The giant smiled warmly.

Brady shook the outstretched hand of Vadim Mendelov.

Of all the men who were listed among the great scientists of the world, none looked less the part than Dr. Vadim Mendelov. The sheer physical bulk of the man was overwhelming. He stood six feet four inches tall with a frame

193

of huge girth. Yet this physical mass detracted nothing from the tremendous impact of presence the man radiated. His green eyes were startlingly clear and penetrating. Some big men were cursed with voices disproportionately high or weak. Not Mendelov, who commanded attention with a subdued tone in a closed room. And Brady discerned in the scientist the rare example of a huge man who moves with swift reflexes and unusual agility. If he ever decided to quit the brain business, Brady mused, he'd be a natural in the wrestling ring.

A socioscientist of the first order, Mendelov was equally famed as an anthropologist and a doctor of medicine, and he was an expert in many allied sciences and technologies. One of Mendelov's gifts was photographic memory. Being able to correlate what he imprinted in memory, he had the astounding capacity to cross-reference in his own mind the disciplines of the many sciences in which he delved. At Princeton University, where Mendelov was on the faculty as a professor in the humanities, his colleagues considered him a socioscientist who taught the applied science of constructive planning for the social structure of man.

Within a limited circle of intimates, Mendelov was as famed for his personal life as for his extraordinary mind and his physical bulk. The Russian-born scientist lived with his sister off the Princeton campus. Fortunately for the tastes of the scientist, Rachel, his sister and housekeeper, professed an objective outlook of her brother's equally huge capacities for philosophy, food and wine, and a discreet but unnumbered flow of women tempted by association with the great man. Never married, Mendelov preferred such fleeting relationships, some lasting no more than an evening, others enduring for weeks or even months. Beautiful women moved, bag and baggage, into his capacious home, where they were tagged with the status of "research assistant."

And yet, reviewing in his mind the background of the scientist, Brady wondered if Mendelov ever slept. The scientist was an established writer whose works were brilliant. His textbooks, translated into dozens of languages, brought him a steady and sizable income.

In those few seconds of meeting Mendelov, Brady reviewed in his mind all that he knew of the scientist. He knew instinctively that this strange association of Mendelov, Taggert, Wilkinson, and Blackburn contained the solution to the enigma of recent weeks. But the presence of the scientist who now greeted him with such open warmth raised an obvious question.

What was an evolutionist doing in the midst of a scientific and technological empire?

Brady took the seat before Mendelov's desk, noticing as he did so that Dianne Sims had left the room. He looked directly at Mendelov. "The receptionist made it obvious I was expected," he said carefully.

"Of course. We didn't question your return

here." Mendelov's voice rumbled from his huge chest. He sat behind the desk with the poise of a granite mountain.

Brady reached for a cigarette and lit up slowly. Now that he was here and had more than he'd bargained for, he didn't want to blow the whole thing with stupid questions. Had he encountered Taggert, he would have been crisply efficient from the outset. Mendelov was something else, and the newsman wasn't sure of his ground.

"You were that certain?" Brady said, his words as much a statement as a query.

"We were." Mendelov nodded and clasped his hands across his stomach. By his expressions and movements he made it clear to his visitor that an equal exchange was under way.

"You're aware of my professional, ah, fields?" Mendelov smiled as he saw Brady's nod. "Well, then, you know that among other things I am a psychologist. Let me assure you that your actions have been wholly predictable. Ah, that appears to cause you some distress. It shouldn't," Mendelov said with a slow movement of his head. "You function within a human skin, and it would have been remarkable had you acted other than you did. Any intelligent man would do his best to run down the names of those individuals who have been responsible, or even who appear to be responsible, for the upheaval in his affairs. "So"—the giant shrugged—"there is no magic involved.

196

You had no choice, really, except to seek answers to your questions. You are here."

"You make it sound as if someone is pulling strings and I'm dancing to your tune." Brady didn't disguise the anger in his voice.

"Not at all!" Mendelov boomed, his eyes twinkling. "No one guided your destiny but yourself."

"It doesn't sound like it," Brady grumbled.

Mendelov unfolded his hands and swung the chair around. "Mr. Brady, you are a man of strong will. Your past record makes that evident. No, please, if you will," Mendelov said with a motion to avoid interruption from his visitor. "I am not playing games with you. I have no need to fabricate." The scientist chuckled deep in his throat. "You're also a creature of curiosity," he said with a brief smile. "That established the pattern you'd follow. It's quite simple, Mr. Brady. The only person who pushed you was yourself."

"Okay. I'm curious," said Brady. "Then maybe you can answer the questions I'm here to ask?"

"Perhaps I can," the big man said amiably.

"For starters, I'd like to know how *you're* mixed up in all this," Brady demanded. "What the hell is going on around here?"

"What am I doing here?" Mendelov had the smile of a hungry cat. "If you came here to question Dr. Taggert, then surely I don't interest you. Didn't you wish to question Dr. Taggert about, um, I wish to use the very words you yourself have employed; would flying discs be correct?"

"That's almost right," Brady said coldly. "Almost, but not quite. I came here before to ask Taggert about electrical propulsion systems. He did a fancy song-and-dance routine and the neatest disappearing act I've ever seen. I didn't come this time for a repeat. As far as I'm concerned, Dr. Mendelov, there's a direct tie-in between Taggert and Wilkinson *and* Blackburn and certin disc sightings, and—"

"And yourself, of course," Mendelov interjected.

"And myself," Brady snapped. "I won't pull out the crying towel. But one way or the other, today or tomorrow or the day after that, I'm damned well going to find out *why* someone's put the screws to me."

"And I can help?" Mendelov asked. *Too* innocently, Brady thought angrily.

"Maybe," Brady answered. "Since I don't know how you fit in, you can answer that better than I."

"Ask away, then," Mendelov said with a wave of his hand.

"All right," Brady said, his mood grim. "As far as I'm concerned, the discs—not *all* discs, but those I've been singling out—are real. Somehow there's a link between Wilkinson and this place. Wilkinson made sure I was squeezed out of my job. That's the way it goes, sometimes. But not this time. It's too pat. Wilkinson is tied in with Frazer Blackburn and that's too much coincidence. I don't know how you figure in all this, but—"

Mendelov had motioned to Brady and the newsman interrupted himself. "Please, Mr. Brady. I apologize for breaking in like this. But I have nothing to do with Wilkinson's association with you. That's between the two of you. But this matter of discs—"

Brady broke in. "That's right," he said. "Discs. Discs that fly, discs that—"

"You're referring to mechanical objects?"

"I am."

"Of a disc shape?"

"I made myself clear, Dr. Mendelov."

"So you did, so you did."

An uncomfortable silence rose between them.

Finally Mendelov sighed audibly. "Normally, Mr. Brady, I wouldn't even entertain a conversation that has as its basis a preconclusion that UFO's are mechanical."

"I didn't say UFO's. I said discs."

"Yes. Forgive me. Being specific, then, *I* do not believe discs, or any other object embraced within the broad description of UFO's, represent anything even remotely artificial in nature." Mendelov leaned forward. "I don't wish to have an exchange with you on the subject. I know your attitude toward this, and—"

"Do you really?"

"Yes, I do," Mendelov said, showing the first sign of pique since Brady had met him. "I read your articles. Perhaps"—Mendelov smiled warmly—"I should mention that I have read your work for some years. You're outstanding in the field. Which is why"—the smile vanished as Mendelov went on—"your preoccupation with the subject is somewhat distressing."

Brady studied the other man and waited.

"You didn't come here for an exchange of views on the subject, did you?"

"No," Brady admitted. "But if the damned things aren't real, why's Wilkinson so hot and bothered over it all?"

"I must repeat that's between you and—"

"So hot and bothered he's gone to the trouble of getting me out of my job," Brady said, ignoring Mendelov's interruption. "That's a hell of a lot of *non*concerned action. And now I find *you* tied in with everything else. You'll forgive me, Doctor, but I don't believe you."

"Specifically what don't you believe?"

"I don't believe you know nothing about the discs," Brady shot back. "And I believe even less you're not aware of Wilkinson's involvement. And to top it all off, somehow *this* outfit is involved."

Mendelov drummed his fingers on the desk. "I'm not going to respond to your, um, allegations, Mr. Brady. Not point by point. Discussing UFO's is like arguing the validity of God in a physical sense. It would lead us nowhere. However"—Mendelov leaned back in his chair with a creaking of springs—"I don't wish to be uncooperative. What *can* I tell you that will set your mind at ease?"

"Well," said Brady, "let's begin again.

What's *your* place in all this? You're a psychologist and an anthropologist. I didn't know Blackburn Aero had gone into the head-shrinking business."

"Oh, but they've been in the head-shrinking business, as you put it"—Mendelov laughed—"for many years. The psychological approach to machine design, to controls, to any system where there is a man-machine relationship . . . well, the better the psychological preparation, the more efficient the final product in its use. But to answer your question directly, in reference to my being here with Blackburn . . ."

The scientist appeared to reach a decision. "I'm not at liberty to discuss details of our project here," Mendelov said. "I believe I have the discretion, however, to discuss it briefly under certain conditions."

"Which are?"

"Nothing is for publication, Mr. Brady."

Brady shifted uncomfortably in his seat.

"Your word is necessary," Mendelov pressed.

"All right," Brady said, giving in. He really didn't have much choice. Maybe what Mendelov had to say would fit a few of the pieces together.

"How familiar with nuclear propulsion are you?"

Brady's heart leaped. Finally . . . !

"I'm fairly well up on it." He didn't want to say another word, delay Mendelov even a second.

"Including Nerva?"

Brady knew the nuclear-rocket program well enough; he'd written several articles on the project. He nodded.

"Do you know of Draco?"

Brady's expression answered for him. "No, I don't," he said, confirming the look on his face.

Mendelov nodded. "Of course not. I didn't expect you would. Draco—the dragon—is an unexpected derivative of Nerva. I must repeat your promise of silence is critical. I have, ah, well, let's say I have breached a security code. Draco is a nuclear drive, Mr. Brady, that at present has the highest national priority for its development. You can understand the stress I have given to security when I explain that Draco is not simply an engineering study. Every emphasis is on producing Draco as an operational machine."

Brady felt elation. "Is Draco flying now?"

"It has been for some time," Mendelov said. "The name comes from the distinctive sound of the nuclear-thrust unit. Forty thousand pounds thrust through a nozzle throat of narrow diameter is, ah, rather spectacular. Someone likened it to the cry of a dragon"—Mendelov smiled— "and the name stuck. It's appropriate."

"What kind of ship—I mean, how's Draco being used?"

Mendelov read the double meaning of Brady's question. "Oh. I think I see what you mean. I'm sorry, Mr. Brady, but there is no disc form involved. The test aircraft are of delta planform."

202

Brady didn't reply. Mendelov showed the barest hint of a shrug and went on. "In all fairness to you," he said, "I must say that many UFO—discs, in this instance—reports are attributable to the Draco flight tests. The machines fly at very high altitude and the delta form, seen at a great distance and moving in the supersonic regime . . ."

Mendelov paused. "Well, those are the details. But if you will understand the need for security, you can see how you've been misled. I have taken a risk and I don't mind saying so, in even discussing Draco with you. Obviously, Dr. Taggert could not do so and—"

"Is that his tie-in here?"

"Of course. Taggert spent some time on the Nerva program with Lockheed and the AEC."

Jesus Christ, Brady groaned to himself.

"I believe," Mendelov continued, "this should explain his presence."

Brady nodded. He felt crushed. He'd never thought of any of this. The nuclear-propulsion project of the Air Force had been dropped years ago, after more than a billion dollars had vanished into the maw of inefficiency and corruption. It had been stupid of him to think the Air Force would have left it there. And Blackburn Aero. Sure, the air-cargo story was a farce. It was a cover for the Draco program, and he had turned it into a monstrous scheme. . . . No wonder Taggert had seen him out as quickly as he had. But there was still . . .

"Dr. Mendelov." Brady faltered for a moment. "You're a psychologist. I don't see how you fit into—"

"Of course." Mendelov nodded. "Draco has a flight endurance of twelve days." The scientist smiled in sympathy with Brady's discomfort. "Keeping flight crews efficient for that period of time, even with double crews, when they're working immediately adjacent to a nuclear furnace, well, the problems are obvious. The solutions are more psychological than mechanical."

Brady felt numb. He rose to his feet. All he wanted was to get out of there. He'd made enough of an ass of himself without compounding his stupidity with more questions. "Thank you," he said to Mendelov. "You've been generous with your time. If you'll have someone take me back to . . ." Mendelov nodded and as if by magic Dianne Sims appeared in the room.

"Good-bye, Mr. Brady," Mendelov said, offering his hand. "Perhaps I'll see you sometime at Princeton." He chuckled. "We can discuss anthropology, if you'd like."

"Sure. Thanks again."

Behind him the sliding door opened and Brady turned to leave.

"One more thing, Mr. Brady."

He turned back to the scientist. A strange smile played across Mendelov's face.

"To save you time and disappointment," Mendelov said, "you'll find your tape recorder won't have worked very well. But you'll have an excellent recording of an electronic interference signal. It's been a pleasure, Mr. Brady." Mendelov grinned his hungry-cat grin. "Good luck with your, ah, discs."

CHAPTER XIII

Still smarting from the humiliation of his interview with Vadim Mendelov, Brady took a taxi to the Flagstaff airport. He wanted to get up in a plane again. To clear his mind, if nothing else.

Thirty minutes later he was in the grip of renewed vexation. He couldn't find the Blackburn flight strip on the Arizona charts. He checked the dates and confirmed the charts were the latest issued. Brady cornered the airport operator, asked him if he knew where he could find the strip.

"Nope. Don't know a thing about it," was the reply.

"How can that be?" Brady persisted. "It's supposed to be a ten-thousand-foot strip. It's got to be on a chart somewhere."

The other man studied Brady carefully. "You got business there?"

What the hell was this? Brady thought. "All I'm asking you is: Do you know where the strip is?" Brady said patiently.

The airport operator shook his head slowly. "Don't know a thing about it. Anything else I can do for you?"

Brady took off, pointing the nose of the Debonair away from Flagstaff along a course of seventy degrees. Every time he found something else connected with Blackburn Aero, he was jarred off balance. A strip two miles long and nothing showing on the flight charts? Brady would have given a hundred to one that any flight-testing facility would also have its own VOR homing and communications facility, but he couldn't find out a thing about that, either. Interesting, he mused. Someone's got a finger in with the FAA and the Coast and Geodetic Survey offices. They'd need a strong contact somewhere to keep a strip that big off the charts.

Brady was well aware of the difficulties in locating even a two-mile strip in the vast area of the Colorado Plateau. But he could cut down the area of search. He was almost positive the strip would lie generally east of the Little Colorado River that cut in a diagonal line across the northeastern quarter of the state. There stretched the Colorado Plateau and its deep gorges, washes, canyons, and desolate terrain. To find the airstrip Brady decided *not* to search it out. He wanted no part of looking for the needle in the haystack. If Blackburn Aero had any sizable facility in the remote plateau, it needed power, and power meant long lines marching across the ground. Power lines that stood out far better than did any airstrip. Brady figured, as well, that the power lines would be new and they wouldn't be on the chart. If he was right, it would cut down greatly the search pattern he needed to fly.

It took him just under two hours. He was crossing the Oraibi Wash, six thousand feet above the rock-strewn terrain, when he saw the power lines. He studied the chart. Nothing. *Goddamn!* he exulted. He swung the Debonair around in a steep turn to follow the power lines he knew would take him straight to the field he sought.

Straight as an arrow the lines led him to the Blackburn airstrip. What he saw bothered him. There was enough power feeding through those lines to fill the needs of a small city. Brady circled the strip from six thousand feet, looking for any trace of industrial or research facilities. Nothing. Why all the power then? Nothing he saw gave even a hint for all that inflow of energy. Brady took several pictures of the strip and the surrounding countryside. The sun was low on the horizon and he got some excellent shadow effect. But he wanted more than he could capture on film from this height. He pulled the power and dumped the airplane in a swift, steep spiral.

As details enlarged with his descent, he

made out several four-engined transports and a half dozen small jets and executive planes. Several hangars were aligned neatly near the airstrip, but there wasn't anything even remotely large enough to accept a giant cargo plane the size of the C-5A or the 747. Nothing. Down to five hundred feet he made out the power substation into which the lines flowed, and again he was struck with the enormous energy available to the limited facilities. Something else tugged at him—no roads! Not a single road leading to the strip. A few dirt paths, but that was all. Flight-test facility, my ass! Whatever's going on down there hasn't got a thing to do with any cargo planes, that's for sure!

He readied his camera and took a series of photographs. A group of people by a truck flashed a red blinker light at him to climb away. Brady thumbed his nose and laughed. The laughter died when red flares hissed into the air, several of them streaking close to the plane. Brady lost his temper. Everything that had happened during the day boiled over. He shoved the prop control to flat pitch and pushed the throttle against the panel. When he came around out of his diving turn, he was flat on the deck, the Debonair wide open at nearly 230 miles an hour. He whooped loudly when he saw people diving wildly for the ground as he ripped scant feet overhead, pulling away in a high climbing turn.

He was at nine thousand feet, climbing

slowly as he homed in to Flagstaff. The sun had sunk below the horizon and the eastern sky was dark and showing its early stars. Ahead of Brady showed the faint light lingering after the desert sunset. Brady looked about him, drinking in the scene and enjoying the moment of relaxation the flight gave him. He saw a light high above and to his left, descending slowly. Brady twisted in his seat for a better look, believing he was watching one of the lower and brighter satellites traversing the early night sky.

He knew it couldn't be a satellite when it continued to expand in brightness and size. At the same moment he knew it was rushing directly toward him, he saw the circular shape. Brady tensed on the controls, his limbs reacting automatically in case it was necessary to hurl the plane away from the onrushing shape. At the instant he was about to haul the Debonair into a climb, the disc slowed.

Brady stared with his mouth agape. Holding formation off his left wing was a huge disc. It held position, unmistakable, absolutely clear, unbelievably real. Brady saw the rounded dome above the disc, a wide-bellied protrusion beneath. He judged it at more than a hundred feet in diameter. Instantly he searched for every detail of which he had heard during all these weeks of studying disc reports. The rounded windows, the ionized flow before the disc, a lesser glow behind. He remembered a warning: Never believe what you see through glass. That was stupid; what the hell did pilots

211

do when they took off and landed? Despite the thought he pulled open the narrow vent window to his left. A small explosion of air sounded through the cabin. Brady hunched down in the seat to look through the opening. He sat up straight as the air about the disc glowed suddenly. The disc accelerated with blinding speed. As fast as it moved forward it burst upward, faster than Brady could react. Cursing, he hauled back on the yoke to lift the nose. In those few seconds the disc became a faint light that in the next moment winked out of sight.

Brady felt the pounding of his heart and he took deep breaths, forcing himself to calm down.

The thought rose with absolute clarity in his mind: What the hell do I do *now?* For instantly, completely, he knew that no one would believe what he had seen.

He wasn't sure he believed it himself. He was right. The discs were real. And Vadim Mendelov was a goddamned liar.

CHAPTER XIV

Brady studied his drink. Wunnerful drink. Wunnerful bartender. Made margaritas *exactly* right. Perfect. Thas' what they were. Perfect drinks. Brady wanted heavy on the salt and he got heavy on the salt. Marvelous bartender. Splendid fellow, he. This was the fifth drink and it was perfect. Fifth? Maybe it was the sixth. He couldn't care less.

When Brady had landed at Flagstaff, he felt numb. He rented a car and drove to the hotel downtown. He wanted to run down the middle of the street waving his arms and shouting about the disc. But since he knew he would end up spending the night in jail or in a padded cell or laced tightly into a straitjacket, he kept his mouth shut. He signed in for his room and sent the bellboy hustling for a drink. He had to tell *someone*. But who would believe him? Of course; he had grabbed for the phone and put in a person-to-person call to Ann. No dice. She was on a flight and wouldn't be in for several hours. The operator found out she would be landing in San Francisco. Brady sent a telegram that would be waiting for her on arrival. He asked her to call him. He even used the word "urgent."

But Ann was hours away. Brady took a shower, shaved, and slipped into fresh clothes. He went to the lounge and climbed onto a barstool. It took three drinks to shake the feeling of numbness. He drank another quickly and felt it coming back. Oh, Christ, he thought, I should have remembered. He had spent several hours at high altitude during the day. And Flagstaff was about seven thousand feet above sea level. And alcohol always hit you harder at altitude where there was less oxygen . . . Jesus, but I am getting *stoned*. A sloppy grin appeared on his face because he didn't care. He wanted to get stoned. He was tired of thinking, tired of trying to unravel the spaghetti of contradictory information, all the hints and the shadows, and chasing ghosts, and after what he had seen today, knowing that everything he had done had been right . . . And he couldn't tell a single goddamn human being because Ann was mixing drinks for someone thirty thousand feet up. . . .

Piss on it. He tipped the glass, licking the salt from the rim and draining the drink. He motioned to the bartender for another. Wunnerful. He felt the warm glow spread through his body and he accepted it greedily. "Just right for what ails you," he announced to himself. He lifted the glass again and sipped slowly. His hand froze as he looked into the mirror behind the bar.

Dianne Sims. She stood just within the entrance, looking around, obviously missing someone. Brady slid from the barstool, steadied himself, and made his way toward her. He tried not to sound too much like an idiot and asked her to have dinner with him. No, she didn't have a date. Yes, she'd love to join him for dinner. Right here in the hotel, the finest steaks in Flagstaff. Brady sat across from her at the dinner table and he marveled at her beauty. She was breathtaking and he told her so. She smiled and thanked him, and in the way she responded to his compliments she was more beautiful than ever.

He leaned forward and rested his hand on hers. "Would you believe me if I told you," he said with deliberate slowness, "that today I saw a giant purple elephant flying through the sky and towing a bright-orange barge with sixteen naked broads on it? And they were all throwing flowers at me as he flew alongside each other?"

She laughed. Brady noticed she didn't remove her hand from beneath his. Well, he thought smugly, goddamned evening may not be a complete bust after all.

"Well, d'you believe me?"

"I don't think so." She tasted her drink.

"How about a, um, an ahh, how about a whale in an oxygen mask? At nine thousand feet. Wouldja believe *that?*"

"No, Mr. Brady, I wouldn't." She frowned with mock seriousness.

"No?"

She laughed and said "No," again.

"Well, then, how about a great big flying disc a hunnert' feet across with round windows and a blue glow that goes *Zap!* through the sky? How about that, huh?"

"Purple or orange?" she said lightly.

"Forgot to ask," he mumbled.

"If it was bright orange, I might believe it," she said.

"Oh." He pouted and provoked more laughter from her. "Then you'll never believe me because this disc was white with turquoise stripes."

"Oh, my."

" 'S' fact," he said.

"It must have been very pretty."

"Beautiful, beautiful." He looked at his glass. "Whaddya know. 'S empty. Wanna drink another one, or would you like to eat?"

"I'm starved, Mr.—"

"Cliff."

"Cliff." She smiled, squeezing his hand.

Dinner was a hazy memory. The steak didn't slow down the tequila. Brady tried to remember what Dianne had said about why she was at the hotel, but he couldn't remember—and what the hell, it didn't matter. He ignored it

216

and concentrated on her. God, but she was beautiful. He pictured himself with her on cool sheets and he knew he could make love to her through an entire night. Goddamn, she—he shook his head. The evening blurred and he remembered leaving the restaurant, driving in her car, going to her apartment. She pushed him gently onto a wide couch and removed his shoes. "Make yourself at home," she said, brushing her lips against his. Moments later a drink was in his hand, and she was gone again. He removed his jacket and tie and took her at her word, relaxing completely. He watched her and marveled at her body and felt the heat rising within him. He wondered if he was too drunk to make love. The hell I am. He grinned idiotically. Dianne turned on a gas fireplace, started a tape with soft music, and dimmed the overhead lights. Brady felt as if he were watching a scene from a movie. Things just didn't happen like this. But it was happening, all right. Even to the point where she reappeared in a filmy negligee and sat next to him on the couch. He took a stiff drink from his glass and stared at her. He had never seen a woman so beautiful and . . .

Brady felt a compulsion to talk. He wanted to talk. He wanted to throw away his clothes and strip the negligee from her and bury his face in her breasts and crush her lips and love her and at the same time he wanted to talk, to let the words run free from him. He couldn't understand himself. What the hell was the matter with him? "Make love to her, you fool," he shouted to himself. But he couldn't stop. The compulsion to talk overwhelmed him.

He talked about the discs, about everything that had happened to him, even about Ann, to his astonishment. He told her Mendelov was a liar and he knew it and until a few hours ago he hadn't known why, but *now*, by God, he did. He told her about the disc, he repeated every detail his eye had captured. He told her he had fitted the pieces together, that Taggert was tied in somehow with the propulsion system of the disc. He felt—he didn't know, but somehow he was positive—Vadim Mendelov was the mastermind of whatever was going on. He knew now why Wilkinson had acted as he did, how and why he was involved.

"But how could Dr. Mendelov be involved?" she protested mildly. "You said he was the mastermind, Cliff. About what?"

"I don't know," he said, raising his voice. "But I'm sure ash hell going to find out. You can bet on *that*," he concluded in drunken assurance.

She pressed the point gently. "But what good will it do? You said no one will listen to what you have to say, Cliff. If you do find out what he's doing with the discs, you can't do anything about it."

Brady grinned. "Ho ho ho," he said slowly. "Ho ho."

"You must have someone very special in mind, Cliff."

"Do," Brady said in a conspiratorial whisper. "I sure do."

218

"And he'll really listen to what you have to say?"

"Whaddya' mean, *lissen?* He'sh in a position to do sumpin'."

Dianne waited. Brady couldn't remain silent if he wanted to.

"Know who he ish, I mean, is?"

She shook her head.

"Old Felix, thash who."

"I don't know him, do I?"

"Doubt it."

Again she waited.

"Felix ish m'Russian buddy. He'll listen t'me. Don't you think the Russians wanna know what happened? Don't you think they'd like t'know what wash over Moscow when they fired all their missiles? When they tried to shoot down those pretty lights? When alla time they were discs, huh?" Brady waggled a finger at her. "Oh, they'll lissen, all right. Y'don't know Felix Zigel, do you? Hah, I'll bet y'don't. Old Felix ish Doctor of Science at the Russian Aviation Institute. How y'like them apples? Pretty good, huh? Not only that," Brady ran on, "but he'sh in charge of UFO inveshti . . . invesh . . . UFO studies of th' whole Russian guv'mint." Brady threw his arms open in an expansive gesture. "Whole Russian gov'mint! How 'bout that?"

Brady's eyes narrowed and he leaned closer to the beautiful woman on the couch with him. "Wanna know sumpin' else? Felix, he'sh a believer. That'sh right." Brady's head bobbed up and down vigorously. "Believer, all right. And

219

I know him and he knows me and he trusts me and he'll listen to me and we'll by God do sumpin' about all thish. Howzat, huh?"

He thought Dianne had a strange, sad expression on her face. "I'm sorry to hear that, Cliff," she said, so quietly he could barely hear her words. There was a blur. He would remember her holding a small aerosol can. He thought she turned it to him. He couldn't remember the spray coming at him, but he remembered the can. It didn't matter. The aerosol spray enveloped him and the lights went out with a crash.

CHAPTER XV

Brady awoke with a cottony mouth and a skull fragile as a Ming vase. He made certain not to move. He opened his eyes slowly. He was seated in a wide, comfortable chair, arms relaxed, his body cushioned pleasantly.

Slowly focus returned to him as he stared directly ahead. He blinked several times and blurred images contracted into clear definitions.

The huge form of Dr. Vadim Mendelov took shape. Mendelov was also seated, watching him silently. Brady turned his head slowly, scanning. He was in an enclosure of some kind. The room was small, and was filled with these wide, thick chairs, which were luxuriously upholstered in leather. He pressed down with his feet and felt soft carpeting. He looked higher along the walls and saw steel plates.

"You may remove the seat belt, Mr. Brady."

Brady grunted at the sound of Mendelov's voice. For the first time he noticed that he was fastened in his seat by a shoulder strap. He released the belt catch and stretched slowly. His limbs ached; he judged their soreness from too many hours of inactivity. To his left he saw Dianne Sims, who favored him with a quick—and apologetic?—smile. Brady sighed. He would learn where he was in good time. Mendelov's presence made it all too clear that Brady exercised not a whit of control over his immediate situation.

"Headache?"

"What?" He turned to Dianne.

"How's your head?" she asked, not unkindly.

"It's been better."

She smiled again and rose to her feet. He watched her open a sliding panel behind which there was a bar of some sort. She handed him a glass.

"What is it?"

"It's a head-straightener," she said. "Please drink it, Mr. Brady. It will help, I assure you."

Brady drank quickly. There was a faint lemon taste, almost bitter-sweet. He couldn't recall anything similar to it. He closed his eyes and took a deep breath. She was right; he began to feel better almost immediately. Among other things, he judged, the drink must contain a stimulant. Suddenly he craved a cigarette. He returned the glass to Dianne. "All right if I smoke?"

She nodded and slid back a panel in the chair armrest, revealing an ash tray. Brady lit up and dragged deeply, savoring the taste. He felt almost human again.

He looked at Mendelov. "Okay. I give up. Where am I?"

"That will become clear soon enough," the scientist said curtly. "First, it appears necessary for us to continue our conversation." Mendelov's eyes were steady and piercing.

Brady didn't miss the change in Mendelov's tone, or the difference in mood. The last time they had faced one another Mendelov had been the congenial host. That man had vanished. In his stead was a man accustomed to power and totally in control of the situation.

"I would appreciate your relating—without holding back, please—the entire story of the discs as you understand them," Mendelov said. "This time, however, I want your thoughts to their final conclusions. No matter how unlikely they may seem. Your life may depend upon your answer, Mr. Brady. Especially the sincerity, the honesty of that answer."

Brady licked dry lips. Not for an instant did he doubt what he heard. He took a deep breath and leaned forward. Without hesitation, he began. Added together—Brady ticked off one point after the other—one conclusion only withstood all examination. The discs, Brady said carefully, *had* to be real. Even before the shattering experience of encountering such a

223

vehicle, he had believed this to be so. Now all events led him inevitably to the conclusion that Blackburn Aero and those involved, including Mendelov, *must* be related to the discs. He was through. He leaned back in the chair and gazed steadily at his adversary.

"Remarkable," Mendelov said quietly. "However, we still have need of sharing our thoughts." The smile vanished as if Mendelov had turned some switch within himself. He leaned his great bulk forward, his eyes burning into Brady.

"I wish to ask you something," Mendelov said slowly. "Why are we doing all this?"

"Doing what?" Brady countered.

"Assuming everything you have concluded is true," Mendelov said, unperturbed, "why are we involved in this, ah, effort of ours?" Mendelov leaned back in his chair, his expression unreadable.

Brady wrestled with his thoughts. Several times he started to speak but changed his mind. He realized that he had no clear idea of the purpose behind the vast expenditure of time and money and energy that must have been required to create the disc he had seen. He would have to guess, to probe, and attempt to draw Mendelov out into the open.

"It's a power play," he announced finally. "You people are obviously in a position to pull off some of the wildest capers the world has ever seen. You've got millions; millions, hell, you've got hundreds of millions to back you up. You've got a tremendous organization, you've got power, brains. All that adds up to freedom of action. What you've got going for you makes all those fiction ideas of an international crime group look like a Sunday picnic. . . ."

Mendelov had relaxed his stern visage and Brady caught the expression of disappointment clouding the scientist's features. He may be the world's greatest semanticist, Brady thought, but he's got a few things to learn about playing poker.

Brady leaned back in his seat and stabbed a finger at Mendelov. "Everything fits into what I've said except one thing. *You.*" Brady smiled. "You're the fly in the ointment. Someone like Wilkinson could be in this up to his teeth for power to control things. Groups, people. Taggert's the kind of scientist who'd follow his holy grail anywhere. That makes him easy to understand. But *you're* not," Brady stressed. "You're the antithesis to money, or even power, when it comes to complicated involvement and risks. I just don't think you care one way or the other about it."

"Why is that, Mr. Brady?" The voice rumbled from deep within the chest of the huge man.

Brady didn't answer at once. He reached for a cigarette and glanced at the woman with them. She hadn't made a sound. She sat easily in her chair, completely relaxed, following every word of the two men. Brady made a mental note to find out just where she fitted into the picture. He turned back to Mendelov.

"Because of time, Dr. Mendelov, because of

225

time," Brady said slowly, convinced he had his man pegged. "Time is too precious to you to throw it away." Brady didn't miss the glance that passed between Mendelov and Dianne Sims. Finally she had reacted to something. What could there be in what he had just said that would bring her out of that cool composure? He *had* to be right....

"For there's not enough time. Every week, every day, is fleeting. You don't have enough time. I think you're more the philosopher than the scientist. Maybe they're both the same; I don't know. I've read your works. Pretty thoroughly, too. You're an evolutionist and you're worried the human race is going to cream itself all over the map and you haven't got time to screw around. So there's only one conclusion left."

"Which is, Mr. Brady?"

"You're a zealot. Like other zealots, you've got great dreams." Brady allowed an edge of sarcasm to enter his voice. "You think you've found the miracle cure. Some new way to keep the world from destroying itself.

"It's not hard to figure, I suppose," he said after several moments of silence. "Somehow you people have put together a new drive. From what I've seen, it makes anything else in the air look like a bark canoe. Maybe it's a weapon. If what happened at Kennedy and MacDill is true, then obviously it *is* a weapon." Brady made a weary gesture. "And your little club figures now it's got the upper hand and maybe it's time to step in, right?"

"You have emphasized time, Mr. Brady." Mendelov spoke slowly and carefully. "But I doubt you understand its true meaning as it relates to the present moment. Nature often arrives at critical junctures in the survival pattern of any race. The race of man is right now at such a crossroads.

"What road we take will determine," Mendelov said, "not whether man moves into a future where certain forms of prosperity are guaranteed, but whether or not man survives. Whether or not he selects or avoids the massive devastation he is preparing to wreak upon all peoples."

Mendelov shook his great head in a gesture of sadness. "You think you know the weapons, don't you? No, hear me out. I'm aware of what you know and I say that you know all too little. That's why we have Hoffsommer with us, why we also have in our midst a Soviet air marshal. . . ."

Brady felt a mild shock. Stanley Hoffsommer? He was the number-one man in nuclear-weapons development . . . a brilliant Israeli scientist. And a Soviet air marshal . . . ! Until this moment he had never thought that Mendelov and those about him might include within their group opposite numbers of other countries. Jesus, how big was this thing? He listened with complete attention.

". . . because we *know* what we're facing. You're aware that years ago the Russians tested bombs as powerful as a hundred million tons of high explosives. But the hundred-mega-

227

ton bombs, Mr. Brady, are *toys!*" For the first time Mendelov revealed the intensity of emotion for which Brady had waited. "Toys, I repeat. The weapons now available, that have already been emplaced . . . they are a hundred times more powerful than a hundred megatons. Do you understand what I'm saying, Brady? *Think*, man, *think!*" Mendelov slammed a huge fist against his armrest.

"They are so powerful they cause a gravitational warp where they detonate. Do you realize the enormity of that statement, Brady? They are disturbing the space-time continuum. They are literally shredding the fabric of space itself. I told you these weapons were emplaced, and so they are." Mendelov's powerful voice shook. "More than thirty of these monsters are ready for use. In five years there will be more than a hundred of them ready. Can you possibly comprehend the energy we are preparing to unleash upon ourselves? These are planet-busting forces, man! Planet-busting! And we—the United States and the Soviets—are preparing to use such monstrous devices in the name of self-defense!"

After a long silence, Brady felt compelled to respond in some manner. "From everything you've said"—Brady chose his words with care—"I take it you, and whoever forms your organization, believe there's no alternate solution?"

Mendelov nodded. "Not merely an alternate solution. There's only one course to pursue."

"Sure," Brady said. "Take away everybody's guns. Then no one blows up anyone else."

Mendelov frowned. "You seem flippant about it."

"Who, me?" he asked, his voice mocking the scientist. "That's an old refrain you're playing. Disarming everybody puts all the guns in the hands of one group. That group—I take it this means you—then watches everybody so they can't build any more bombs. The next question is easy. Who watches the watchers? Who decides who's to play God?"

Mendelov grimaced with distaste for Brady's choice of words.

"Of course, of course," the scientist said after a pause. "Whenever any one nation has attempted to practice what you've just preached, it was with the heaviest hand possible. They used the same weapons available to everyone else. The result was inevitable. Wholesale slaughter. In this particular respect history has only repeated itself." Mendelov's voice became grim. "We choose not to build upon a repetition of past tragedies."

"That's got a nice sound to it, I admit, but—"

"Be still for a moment," Mendelov snapped. "Do you understand what is meant by an ultimate weapon, Mr. Brady?"

Brady waved his hand. "I'll defer to your description. I have the feeling anything I said would be wrong."

The scientist ignored the barb and went on. "Simply stated, it's a weapon vastly superior to anything that may be arrayed against it. But its superiority exists only within a limited time. In other words, the weapon must be used when the time is opportune. That weapon, Mr. Brady, includes destructive power as only one—*one*, I repeat—facet of its strength. It is a weapon combining many strengths—easy availability, flexibility, psychological impact to achieve a desired effect, virtual immunity to the user—all of these are important criteria of the ultimate weapon.

"And, Mr. Brady . . ." Mendelov paused. "We possess that ultimate weapon . . . now."

Brady didn't speak, didn't move.

"Do you understand why I've told you all this? Why I have asked you to respond so carefully to the questions I've asked?" Mendelov's face was impossible to read.

"Frankly, no," Brady said.

"Because in our, ah, organization," the scientist said, "I believe there's a vital place for you."

"Me!"

Mendelov nodded, a half-smile appearing. "Yes, you. I confess my colleagues don't share my opinion. However, I think they may be persuaded to—"

"Now you wait just a moment!" Brady shouted, half out of his seat. Brady stuttered in his sudden rush of anger. "If you th-th-think for one moment you can shanghai me into joining your holy-rolling, save-the-world crowd of do-gooders, you're out of your fucking mind!"

Mendelov held up his hand as a light flashed on the wall. "Later, Mr. Brady, later," he soothed. "Perhaps before too long we can bring about a change in heart. In the meantime I have a surprise for you."

"Go to hell!" Brady growled.

"Please sit here next to me," Mendelov said, his voice suddenly warm. He gestured to the seat to his left. Brady shrugged and took the chair. The scientist turned his own chair on a pedestal and motioned Brady to do the same.

"Settle yourself well, Mr. Brady. This often comes as a shock, I daresay, to those exposed for the first time." Laughter boomed from the scientist. "You're a pilot, aren't you, Mr. Brady? Yes, of course. Um, how high have you flown?"

"About seventy thousand feet. Why?"

Without answering, Mendelov depressed a button. In front of them, steel plates began to slide back from wide, clear ports.

Brady gasped, his stomach twisting.

He looked down on the earth.

Sixty miles down.

CHAPTER XVI

Brady stared in wonder at the curving planet three hundred thousand feet beneath him. Questions surged to his mind but what he saw told him more eloquently than could any words the awesome power that surrounded him. Sixty miles high, they rushed through wispy atmosphere without sense of motion. Brady was struck with the clarity of the stars, like those at sea or on the desert at night. The stars did not twinkle but shone with a steady, faultless gleam. Then, in the awesome silence of the void stretching before him, a star moved. He watched it rise from the distant horizon, gaining in brilliance as it drew nearer. A star made by man, a satellite spinning its orbital web as it plunged around the world. Deeply impressed,

Brady watched the gleaming orb moving across the star field.

The faintest orange glow on the horizon brought his attention down once more. Lower than the gently curving rim of the world he saw the scalloped edges of clouds snaring the first light of the coming day. The horizon brightened swiftly, the orange deepening until finally it glowed red with yellow-orange shadings. The clouds reflected pink and then whitened swiftly. Brady saw for the first time the massive skeletal ridge of the South American continent, the thundering march of the Andes, a huge tidal wave of stone absorbing the dawn light.

Still cloaked in silence, Brady looked upon an expanded dimensional map of the upper regions of South America. He needed no questions to supply what his eyes and memory brought to him. In the brightening shades of the early day he watched the reflection of rivers snaking through still darkened jungle and plains. Far to his left he saw the ocean becoming richly visible.

"Careful of your eyes. Watch out for the sun." Mendelov's voice was a thousand miles away. "Here." Brady paid no heed. A hand jostled his shoulder. "Here," Mendelov repeated. "Take these." Brady accepted dark glasses and turned his eyes back to the miracle about him. Barely soon enough, he realized. Savage light flared above the horizon. Above the protecting atmosphere the stellar furnace stabbed wickedly at the unprotected eye.

234

A bell chimed. Mendelov glanced up at the speaker. "Mendelov here."

"Sir, we're starting descent," said the voice from the speaker.

"All right," Mendelov replied, his voice carrying to whatever part of the disc—Brady assumed it was the upper dome—contained the controls and the crew. "Take the course I ordered."

"Yes, sir."

Brady took a deep breath and exhaled slowly. He nodded toward the sight beyond the viewglass. "It's quite something," he said simply.

"It sobers a man," the scientist replied. "It's a shame the sight has been shared by so few. There's something about the perspective from here . . ." Mendelov's voice trailed off in a mental shrug.

"Mr. Brady." He hadn't heard Dianne's voice for some time. "Your belt, please."

Brady joined the others in fastening the belt across his lap. He smiled awkwardly. "According to the science-fiction stories I've read," he said, "people in discs don't need belts. They're surrounded by electrogravitic force fields or something."

"Something is as good a description as any," Mendelov said dryly. "Unfortunately we haven't yet learned how to repeal the laws of motion and inertia." The scientist tapped his own belt. "A good thunderstorm—if we ever blundered into one—could give you a good knocking about."

Brady ran his thoughts backward. "Speaking of force fields," he said, "what makes this thing go?"

"All in due time," Mendelov said. "I'm not being evasive, Mr. Brady," he explained. "Bear with me a while longer, however."

Brady shrugged. "Forget it. Let me try another. I've never been, obviously, anywhere this high. How fast are we moving?"

Mendelov thought over the question. "Much less than optimum," he said finally. "Umm, the Mach numbers don't apply at this altitude. Insufficient density." Brady nodded; he knew that. "In more familiar terms, then . . . oh, I'd say about eighteen hundred miles per hour."

Brady's face remained blank. "And that's much less than optimum?" he asked.

"Yes, yes. We've been holding back. I didn't want to start our descent until dawn." Mendelov pointed. "Ahh, there. We're on our way now. I recommend your undivided attention to this, Mr. Brady."

Brady didn't need further prompting. His eyes were already glued to the view straight ahead. The flanks of the Andes splashed back the sun now well above the horizon, and Brady could discern the different hues of jungle green and the browner stains of the higher plateaus. The horizon lifted in a smooth, flowing motion as the forward rim of the disc lowered to match the path of flight. Brady was astonished with the smooth movement despite their tremendous speed. He dismissed the mechanics and threw his attention into the exhilarating sensation that swept before his eyes.

The mountains expanded swiftly as the disc plunged in a heady swoop toward the earth. The planet closed in from all directions as their height vanished, the western coast of South America sliding beneath the uprising flanks of the now tremendous peaks. Almost as swiftly the disc shredded its way through growing cumulus clouds. For the first time the disc rocked gently from strong vertical air currents.

The peaks appeared now at eye level. The forward motion of the disc increased as the thick jungle carpet expanded into individual details. Then the peaks were well above them and they plunged forward in a dizzying rush low over the thick matting of trees. At two hundred feet they hurtled across miles of raw jungle. The disc eased into a shallow ascent. Brady noticed their height above the ground remained constant. They had swung to the southeast and now, he judged from the shadows, the disc raced along the southwestern heading as it came upon a vast plateau. Clearings in the thick growth appeared more frequently and scattered native villages flashed into sight.

Brady was astonished to see the natives in clearings look up as the disc burst into sight and *waving at the disc*. Not once did he see a single action he might interpret as fear. Few natives, he judged with growing wonder, even seemed surprised at the sight of a great disc tearing along almost directly overhead.

The disc moved deep within a valley, great mountainous walls flanking them on each side and directly ahead of their course. Their speed diminished steadily. Brady judged their forward movement at no more than a hundred miles an hour. Still they slowed, the flanking mountains closing to narrow the valley until, after twisting along a gorge, he knew peaks surrounded them from every side. There was no way for him to know where they might be. Brady saw a huge waterfall. Along the sheer sides of a mountain appeared the power lines and other facilities of a hydroelectric plant. Brady studied the scene carefully, noting the generating plant was set well back from the slope within a cavelike depression. From a distance it would be virtually invisible. More signs of vast work; the depression had been gouged out by some terrific force. Brady looked about the area. No roads led away from the hydroelectric facility. Whatever equipment had been used here had been brought in by air.

Still their speed fell. Directly ahead lay a towering pinnacle of rock. The disc hovered, a startling sensation. Brady leaned forward and saw a faint blue ionization of the air along the rim of the disc.

Obviously the crew was waiting for some signal or—suddenly the massive stone walls directly before them split, the rock outfacing slid aside, and Brady looked into a cavernous opening. The disc eased forward. Brilliant lights stabbed into life within the cavern and Brady saw a landing cradle with flashing approach lights. He felt a slight rocking motion and then nothing. They had landed.

Moments later he felt new movement, a service tractor drawing the landing cradle farther into the cavern. Brady looked ahead and to the sides. Overhead floodlights made the vast interior almost as bright as day.

By now Brady had ceased to be surprised by anything he saw. He counted a flight line of eight discs similar to the craft he had seen over Arizona. Far to one side was a single disc at least twice the size of the others. The forward movement stopped. Brady heard air hissing from valves. His ears popped slightly as pressure equalized and a green light flashed in the cabin.

Part of the curving cabin wall slid away to form a ramp to the cavern floor. Brady unbuckled his seat belt when he saw Mendelov and Dianne release theirs. The girl started along the ramp and Mendelov motioned for Brady to follow. Brady left the disc, his eyes trying to take in everything at once.

Then he heard his name. "Mr. Brady."

He turned. Dr. Kenneth Taggert greeted him with a broad smile.

"Welcome to Condor, Mr. Brady."

CHAPTER XVII

"No guards," Taggert said. "Until you know your way around, you'll need a guide. But no one will be, um, standing watch over you." The scientist smiled. "Really, it makes it much easier on all of us."

Brady shook his head as they walked along a wide corridor. "I don't get it," Brady admitted. "You can't tell what I might do."

"Brady, we don't *need* guards. Do you know where you are?"

"Somewhere in the northern part of South America," Brady said. "From what I saw on the way down, we're east of the Andes. That puts us in the plateau that, well, it could be Brazil or Colombia along this latitude."

"That's good enough," the scientist said. "The point is, you're isolated. By more than

241

simply distance. We don't believe a white man has ever crossed this part of the continent. Not"—Taggert smiled—"that they haven't tried it. You're in the midst of dense jungle," he explained. "You saw the mountains around here, the rivers. The natives for two hundred miles in every direction serve us. Our organization is on excellent terms with them. There are no fences or other barriers. Just impassable jungle, rivers, savage animals, dozens of different types of poisonous insects."

Brady forced a smile of his own. "I'm convinced!"

"I didn't finish," Taggert warned. "The natives will kill anyone who leaves this base on foot. *Anyone*. You, me, Mendelov. It doesn't matter. If anyone attempts to leave here under his own power, he's as good as dead. No exceptions. It's the best security system ever devised."

"Yeah, hurrah for you," Brady said.

A frown crossed Taggert's face. "I'm sorry you had to come here the way you did," he said. "I know it must have come as a shock—"

"Think nothing of it," Brady said airily. "I'm used to being suckered in by beautiful blondes and being knocked out by drugs and kidnapped. Happens all the time."

Taggert hesitated.

"Forget it," Brady said. "It's not your worry. Besides, I have no intention of leaving. I wouldn't miss this for the world."

Taggert nodded. "Thanks. This has bothered me, I admit."

"I said forget it."

Taggert motioned toward the main chamber where Brady had seen the discs. "I'm supposed to give you the grand tour," he said. "Would you like to start now or would you rather clean up? You look tired."

Brady glanced down at his clothes and rubbed his chin. "I do feel sort of gritty," he said. "Cleaning up sounds good. Besides"—he smiled—"I'm not going anywhere. All this can wait."

Taggert slapped him on the shoulder. "Okay, let's go. This way." He turned off along a side corridor. "All apartments down here," he explained. "Number Fourteen is yours."

"Apartments?"

"That's right." Taggert glanced at Brady's stocky frame. "What size flight suit do you wear, by the way?"

"Thirty-eight. Why?"

"We'll get your clothes cleaned for you and you'll need something to wear in the meantime. We use jump suits," Taggert said. "Much more sensible."

The scientist opened a door marked "Number 14" and motioned Brady in. The newsman looked around a comfortably furnished living room, bedroom, and kitchen bathed in a pleasant artificial light. "Neat," he said. "All the comforts of home."

Taggert showed him the bathroom. "Everything you need is here," he explained. He glanced at Brady's shoes. "What size?"

"Nine D," Brady said. "More of your haberdashery service?"

"Sure." Taggert laughed. "Flight boots coming up. You smoke, ah . . ."

"Luckies."

"Anything else?"

Brady shook his head. "Just that shower and a shave."

"Go ahead. I'll phone in for the suit and boots. And the cigarettes," he added. "I could put some coffee on while you're getting squared away, if you'd like."

"Great." Brady looked at Taggert. "You're quite the host."

"Took a Dale Carnegie course," Taggert replied. Brady laughed and turned on the shower.

Well, Brady thought, a couple of wars prepared me for anything. He tried to be objective about his reactions to the events of the past twenty-four hours, events that should have overwhelmed him completely. But after a while the mind refuses to absorb any more and creates a natural defense against the unexpected. Something like this had happened to him during the Korean War when he was a prisoner of the Chinese. After being kicked and punched and tied with barbed wire for hours in excruciating positions, he had reached the point where fear vanished. It wasn't that he had gained courage. He just didn't care anymore. He couldn't do a thing except die. Once he felt that he *would* die, they couldn't reach

244

him anymore. You stop caring about events you know you can't control.

Obviously he hadn't been very much in control of his actions for quite a while now. And what Taggert had told him about the natives enforcing a zone of death for two hundred miles in every direction had sunk home. Brady was a realist. He accepted the fact that someone else was calling the shots.

He turned the shower to hot and felt the steaming needles against his skin. Anyway, he laughed to himself, this was being kidnapped in style. Brady scrubbed his body and rinsed off.

Ten minutes later he was dressed in a flight suit and boots. Taggert had produced new underwear and socks as well. They must have a complete quartermaster and commissary to support the many people working here at—what had Taggert called it?—*Condor*. The name fit, Brady thought.

Taggert waited with a pitcher of steaming coffee. Several packs of cigarettes lay on the table.

"I understand you may be joining us," Taggert said.

Brady looked up slowly. "Who told you that?" His voice came out flat, unfriendly.

"Why, Vadim. He—"

"Next time try asking me, huh?"

Taggert was flustered. "I didn't . . . I mean, Vadim said you and he . . ." Taggert put on the brakes. "From what I understand, you and Vadim discussed this organization."

245

Brady knew how to keep someone off balance. "We discussed it," he interrupted. "That's a long way from signing on the dotted line."

Taggert nodded slowly, confused by Brady's hostility. "Apparently I misunderstood."

Brady fixed his gaze upon the scientist. "Look, Taggert, I'm not holding you responsible for my being here or even the way I got here. I know that's out of your bailiwick. Let's get that straight. But as for joining up with this crowd"—Brady shook his head—"uh-uh. I still don't know what makes all of you tick or what you're really doing with all this talent, but I'll tell you one thing straight out: I'm a long way from agreeing with self-appointed cops."

"Just a moment, Brady," Taggert said. "You've got to understand—"

"I've got to understand nothing," Brady snapped. He rose to his feet. "I don't want any fights with you," he said. "I told you I don't figure you in the fun-and-games department. Let's leave it at that." Brady reached for a fresh cigarette. "Are we ready for your grand tour?"

Taggert came to his feet slowly. He took a long breath before replying to Brady. When he did, it was with a definite coolness. He wasn't out to make anyone happy. Not anymore.

"Yes, I'm ready," Taggert said. "It's rather a long walk, and we can discuss any technical questions you may have."

"Long walk to where?"

"The servicing area for the discs," Taggert replied, opening the door and stepping into the corridor.

Brady followed, walking at Taggert's side down the hallways. "That hydroelectric plant I saw on the way in," he said. "All that for here?"

Taggert, relieved to change the conversation, nodded. "Yes. The hydroelectric facility supplies all our base power. For housekeeping. There's another plant about a mile to the east; you couldn't see it the way you came in. It's an alternate source in the event of failure. We use two nuclear generators to provide the energy feed for the discs. They—"

"Two nuclear generators?"

"Yes."

"I don't understand. What is—how did you put it?—energy feed for the discs?"

"We feed energy to the drive unit in the discs," Taggert said. "Whatever we direct into the energy storage system provides a return outflow directly proportional to the—"

"Whoa there!" Brady halted his stride and held up his hand. "Right then and there you lost me."

Taggert smiled in understanding. "I know it sounds difficult at first," he admitted.

"Look," he said, "I understand propulsion systems pretty well. I can tell you how piston, turbojet, fanjet, solid and liquid rocket engines work. I'm even pretty good on balloons. But maybe you'd better go *all* the way back."

Taggert nodded. "It's a long story."

"I don't want the nuts and bolts and especially I don't want the math," Brady said quickly. "I've already had more than my share of headaches this week."

Taggert laughed. "Yes, I can well believe you." He motioned down the corridor. "Shall we continue?" They started up again.

"You know my background, don't you?"

"Pretty well," Brady said. "I did a biog search on you before I went to Flagstaff. Rocketdyne, Lockheed, AEC. I'm fairly well grounded. Before you joined Blackburn, that is."

"Right. I think it's best to give you my philosophy on power systems first," Taggert said. "Not a long story, though."

"Shoot."

"Well, the long and short of it, Brady, is that for years I was convinced the power systems we employed were hopelessly archaic. Were you aware that the most efficient form of transportation is the steel wheel on the steel rail?"

"The railroad?"

"Strangely enough, yes." Brady noticed the rising enthusiasm of Taggert as he moved into his narrative of power-systems development. Brady had pegged Taggert perfectly in his discussion with Mendelov. Dr. Kenneth Taggert cared little or nothing for politics as he pursued the holy grail of science.

"I knew," Taggert went on, "that sooner or later even the most advanced propulsion we used would become extinct, like the dinosaur.

You're aware I left Nerva after only one year, aren't you?"

"Uh-huh. Any particular reason?"

"Good Lord, yes. It was a dead end from the start," Taggert replied with a grimace. "Nerva was simply a nuclear application of large rocket engines. Trying to squeeze hotter gases through a smaller throat nozzle about summed it up. It was a better rocket. Period. It was still a giant with feet of clay."

"So you quit?"

"Not quite that way," Taggert corrected. "When I saw the dead end, I moved on to what I'd always believed was the key to energy control. I discovered I'd been on the wrong track all the time. It was like trying to make the piston engine more and more powerful when the answer was to get rid of pistons and go to jets. I drew the same conclusion for all propulsion systems. They were hopelessly archaic. Nothing was really new, including the jet. What we needed was a complete breakthrough. So I undertook some studies of force fields, magnetic fields, subnuclear structures, such things as the effect of supermagnetic fields against electron orbits. That was really the key, and I—"

"I hate to bust in on you again," Brady said, "but just as your audience of one, I don't know the first thing about supermagnetic fields against electron orbits. Would you believe I never even heard of it?"

"I'm sorry," Taggert said. "No nuts and bolts, right?"

"Right. And no math."

"Difficult to do without it, but I'll try." Taggert chewed his lip. "I made certain never to lose sight of the first law in this business of power. In any power system the key factor is your efficiency in extracting energy. For example, you can burn a mixture of crude oil and you get heat. Burn high-octane gasoline and you get far more heat. But everything then depends on how well you use that heat. You can burn gasoline to heat water to operate a steam engine. Not terribly efficient. It makes a lot more sense to burn gasoline in a piston or jet engine or use it as fuel for a liquid rocket engine. That will use the gasoline's energy with the greatest efficiency." Taggert glanced at Brady. "All right so far?"

"Fine," Brady said with enthusiasm. "I like to keep things in my own mind in the form of analogies. In my business I fall back on that pretty heavy. You're doing great," he emphasized.

"Well, then. We have the basic law: maximum source, plus maximum efficiency, equals maximum power. When you understand the law as we've simplified it, you know in what direction you must move. Do you realize that power exists all about us in quantities that strain the imagination? But we don't know how to use that power. Again—to use an analogy—you can burn a lump of coal in a stove or, if you know how to go about it, you can split the atoms of that coal. Let's say it's a lump weighing about two pounds. Handled efficiently, as nuclear fuel, that amount of coal would give you a power return of something like twenty-five billion kilowatt hours of energy! That's about equal to all the energy produced by every power plant in the United States running at maximum output, day and night, for six weeks without interruption. So there it is. The problem and the road to its solution, I mean. Find a way to really use all the tremendous energy that's always about us."

"You make it sound simple," Brady commented.

"It *is* simple," Taggert replied. "Everything is simple, once you know how to go about it. Few things were easier for the American Indian than making fire. But put an inexperienced man in a field of flint, stone and dry brush and he wouldn't know where to begin to make his fire. To the Indian it's simple."

"What happened after you found the right road?" Brady asked.

"Force fields started me off," Taggert said. "Energy fields invisible to the eye can contain other forms of energy. Again, going to analogy, you can have a forced draft of air within an enclosed space to keep out air."

"I know what you mean," Brady said. "They call those air doors. High-speed fans blow air downward in a doorway. It keeps out bugs. Air, too, I suppose."

"That's right," Taggert said. "You're using air to contain air. A better analogy would be ice. It's a form of water that's also used to contain water."

"So this set you off?"

Taggert chuckled. " 'Set me off' is an excellent way to put it. I was doing theoretical studies of force fields when I was introduced to some new work involving the collapse of electron fields. In effect, this meant being able to compress or reduce the diameter of electron orbits about an atom. The key was that the atom wasn't broken up."

"Wait a moment," Brady said. "Orbital mechanics—maybe that's the wrong phrase, but it'll do—is the same for electrons or planets. When you tighten up an orbit, you increase its speed, right?"

"Exactly. The moon orbits the earth at just over two thousand miles an hour. A satellite at a few hundred miles above the earth has orbital volocity of about seventeen thousand miles an hour. Let's say this satellite was first put into a very high orbit. If we then bring it closer to the earth we increase its speed—along with its mass, of course—but the nature of the satellite itself doesn't change at all."

"This apply also to electrons?"

"I thought it would," Taggert confirmed, "and as it turned out, it did. That's why I spent so much time working with the bevatron at Cal Tech. The experiments I was able to do there, along with theoretical calculation—I rather hogged a computer for several months—established that I was on the right track. There was a lot of trial and error, of course. But I moved closer and closer to the answer. I discovered I had to use a certainly alloy, a metal of absolute purity that—"

"What kind of metal?"

"Sorry." Taggert smiled quickly. "Very few people know that, and we believe it's wiser to keep it that way."

"I can see that. Forget the question."

"Thanks. Anyway, I found out, in theory, that electron orbits could be reduced in size. Tremendous energy would be needed to create a force field, a super force field—you might call it a field of compression—but finally"— Taggert shrugged—"I put all the right pieces together. It worked."

"What happened next?"

"Oh, I wasn't quite out of the woods yet. It was one thing to arrive at a theory, but something else to prove it in repetitive demonstration. That took some doing, but we managed to get the funds.

"The next breakthrough came when I discovered that if we poured energy into the compression field, and then halted that energy input, what we had poured into the field would be returned in precisely the same quantity."

"Could you break that down?"

"Look at it this way," Taggert said, drawing figures in the air as he spoke. "You put a thousand tons of fuel in a rocket. When you light your fire you burn that fuel within a few minutes. You get heat and thrust for a specific period of time. You're operating with relatively low efficiency, of course, but it works. If you could burn that fuel with three times the efficiency you have, you'd get three times as much energy. In other words, if your big rocket could put thirty tons into orbit, just by burning the fuel with more efficiency you could triple that payload and orbit ninety tons without using an extra drop of fuel."

"No sweat so far," Brady said.

"All right. In essence, we discovered that the compression field was acting as a . . . consider it a storage battery. If we put in x quantity of energy to collapse the electron orbits, we discovered that over a certain period of time we got back that same x quantity in power outflow. It was like putting energy into a bank. The moment we stopped pouring it into the bank, the bank started to return the deposit. We found out that if we primed the force field for a period of thirty-eight days, we would get back thirty-eight days of equal output of energy. The moment we stopped feeding the compression field, the electrons, still within the force field, remember, began to return to their normal paths. That meant they were giving up the energy required to collapse their orbits in the first place."

"I see," Brady said slowly. "And you were there to catch all that outflow in your own bucket."

Taggert chuckled. "Not a bucket, exactly. Let's say a paddle-wheel. As the energy began pouring out from the force field, our drive unit the paddlewheel—was there to be turned."

"You said a period of thirty-eight days. Does that mean you can charge up your system and have power coming back to you for thirty-eight days?"

"Exactly," Taggert said. "The energy outflow is constant. For thirty-eight days we get energy at a maximum rate. Whatever we don't use is lost. Or we can use that energy at maximum rate for the full thirty-eight days."

"And that's where your nuclear reactors come in?" Brady asked.

"Right again. We use the hydroelectric plants for housekeeping, as I said. But we can't take a chance on a power interruption to energize the disc drives, so we decided to ship nuclear reactors here. There are always a few discs in the chamber, being energized."

"Can I see that being done?"

"Certainly. We're on our way there right now."

"Good. Can you translate your energy output—what's coming out of the force field—into normal measurements of power?"

"It wouldn't be completely accurate," Taggert cautioned.

"Use a ball-park figure," Brady urged. "If you had to translate it into pounds thrust or horsepower, how would it add up?"

Taggert thought for a few seconds. "All right. It would work out something on the order of two million horsepower."

"Two mill—"

"Difficult to accept," Taggert said to the astonished Brady. "It's true enough. However, that's an equivalency we're using. Six pounds of oranges don't make six pounds of apples, even though in both cases you're dealing with fruit. In the same way, pounds thrust, or horsepower, can't always be translated accurately."

"I know, I know," Brady said quickly. "But, Jesus Christ, you're talking about—" He shook his head. "I can see now how the discs get such tremendous performance. Can I ask you some other questions?"

"I'm here to serve," Taggert said with a smile. "In your own idiom ... shoot."

"That ionization—the blue glow around the discs, I mean. Is that a result of your energy outflow?"

"Yes. We use—no, let me back up a moment. I consider the disc drive an electrostatic-field drive. Some people here feel the proper term is electrogravitic or perhaps purely electromagnetic. What's important is that the disc operates through resistors incorporated around the entire rim of the disc. We not only control the energy flow at any given level, but also with a positive or a negative field. What we do, in its simplest form, is to have two different electrical fields, each of tremendous disparity, on opposite poles of the disc. It operates as a giant magnet chasing itself. I realize," Taggert explained with an unhappy expression, "that doesn't explain it too well. I can show it to you much more clearly with the formulas that—"

"Perish the thought," Brady said quickly. "What you've said is fine. Would I be correct in saying your energy field pushes against itself?"

"No, you wouldn't," Taggert said. "But the effect seems to be that, just as much as a rocket pushes against itself."

256

"Let me ask you another. Does your drive leak?"

"Leak?"

"Well, there must be some leakage. I mean, your energy output is so great there must be electrical discharge of some kind beyond the disc." Brady sought for another analogy. "What I mean is this. You've driven your car, when your radio was playing, alongside power lines, or past a truck with poor shielding in the engine, haven't you? The result is static in the—"

"I see what you mean," Taggert said, nodding. "Yes, you're right. We can't always contain all the energy outflow perfectly, so leakage is sometimes present."

"Would that account for airplane radios and ignition systems going out of whack?"

"Certainly."

"Could the disc be responsible for car engines conking out? I mean, if it was low enough?"

"Oh, yes. It could blanket out just about any electrical system within its field."

Brandy told Taggert the story of Barstow Air Force Base. Taggert explained the incident. A disc overflying Nebraska at more than a hundred thousand feet had suffered a failure in the drive. The energy pouring from the partially collapsed force field had been enormous. With the collapsed force field, the energy had penetrated hundreds of feet through solid objects. Including radio equip-

257

ment of the underground missile complex and the power station in the town.

"I've got an idea why there haven't been any sonic booms from the discs," Brady ventured. "The ionization effect . . . is that it?"

Taggert confirmed what Brady had deduced. The electrical field broke up the air molecules before the moving disc. The turbulent ionized air was unable to form a clear shock wave. Therefore, no sonic boom reached the ground. One more puzzle solved.

They climbed a metal stairway, passed through doors entering the huge, hangarlike cave, and walked down a catwalk that curved along its upper walls. Brady marveled at the size of the cavern below and the ingenuity with which complex machinery, astonishing in its variety, had been installed and was in use. Taggert led him away from the main hangar through several air-locks, each time opening and closing the doors with ship-type dogging handles. Finally they stood before leaded glass viewports.

Brady leaned close to the glass. Within a giant metal chamber a disc rested on its landing cradle. Access plates had been removed and four cables led into the bowels of the machine.

"This one's been here for just about a month," Taggert said. "Another week and we'll remove it."

"And it's got power for thirty-eight days after that?" Brady asked. Taggert nodded.

"What are all the radiation signs around here for?" the newsman queried.

"We're working with tremendous energies," Taggert explained. "There's some ionizing radiation involved."

For an hour Brady studied the disc carefully and questioned the scientist closly on details of the scene spread out before him. When he had absorbed as much as he could, he turned to Taggert. "Is this a natural cavern?" he asked.

"You mean this chamber?"

"That's right."

"By no means. We did this ourselves."

"Christ, this must have taken a lot of explosives." He couldn't believe they had hollowed out so vast an area without spending years at the job.

"Not dynamite," Taggert said.

"Then how . . . ?"

"Two men were responsible for this," the scientist explained. "Harry Boener and Wayne Priest. You'll have a chance to meet them if you like. They determined how to channel the energy output of the disc drive into a beam—"

"The missile at Cape Kennedy!" Brady exclaimed. "And the bombers at MacDill . . ."

"Yes." Taggert frowned.

"You mean what your two geniuses did was to turn the drive into a weapon, right?"

"I can be either a weapon or a tool," Taggert said, "just like any other device or implement or force. Boener and Priest adapted the drive system to create a beam. It acts something like a laser beam, but its power is increased by a very high multiple. Directed against a solid object, like the rock here"—Taggert swept his hand through the air—"it causes complete molecular disruption. Not destruction, although the physical effect seems to be just that. The energy beam slices through rock as if it were so much fog. We used it to hollow out this cavern. It was really quite simple. We—"

"Simple, my ass. It took more energy than building the Panama Canal."

"Yes, but that's a matter of utilizing the energy that's available," Taggert insisted. "We had high utilization. We used two discs, hovering outside the mountain, to start the job. The entire task was completed in a month."

"What's the range of your little toy?"

"Well, it's affected by inverse law, of course. If—"

"Just the range, Doctor. Please."

Taggert sighed. "Yes, of course. The extreme effective range would be about a thousand yards. Close up, for the job we had here, we could expand the beam to a width of about two feet. It cuts through rock quite nicely."

"It certainly looks like it," Brady observed. "Where to next?"

"My office," said Taggert. "This way."

"Just what are you people trying to do?" Brady resumed, coffee cup in hand. "You've performed a scientific miracle with the discs. You can revolutionize global transportation. *Global.* Christ, you could go to Mars on one of these babies. Half the people in this world are on starvation diets—not because we can't produce enough food, but because we can't get the food to the people who need it. The discs could wipe out the logistics problems or colonize another planet. And instead you're off on this half-baked crusade Mendelov seems to have started. Surely, one of the first tenets of science is that you can't turn your back on a new frontier. Seems to me"—Brady grunted contemptuously—"you're doing just that."

"You through?" Taggert said.

"Yeah I made my little speech for the day."

"Then let me clarify something for you," the scientist said, thoughtfully. "I'd like to go to the moon. Personally, I mean. The idea fascinates me. Good Lord, to walk the surface of the moon . . . and *Mars*. I'd give almost anything to do that."

"Then why—"

"Because, for one thing, Brady, we don't *know* if the discs can operate safely above ninety miles. We don't know what will happen when we're out of the electromagnetic field of the earth. We have to make tests first. Extensive tests to eliminate the margin of error. All that means time. We don't have that time. And as far as using the discs for revolutionizing transportation, for food, as you put it, that's nonsense."

"That's debatable. If—"

Taggert didn't give him the opportunity to reply. "Maybe from your viewpoint it is," he said with a touch of anger, "but not from mine. The people involved with us, Brady, include some of the best minds in the world. Not only in the physical sciences but in sociology, economics, geopolitics; we cover the range pretty well. Do you know Robert Kroot?"

"I've heard of him."

"Kroot is a first-rate politicometrics scientist," Taggert said. "Whatever there is to know about the matter of food and world population, including logistics, Kroot knows it. Don't you think we've thought of, and examined, at great length, every possibility that you brought up? When I first became involved in this with Dr. Mendelov, I sounded a lot like you. That's not an insult, Brady. I believed the drive would provide power anywhere in the world, help lift that part of the world that's still in the dark ages to new levels. I was wrong," Taggert said harshly. "I was wrong because I looked at things from a restrictive viewpoint. The solutions I thought of were the same old solutions. Their effect would be temporary. The point is *survival*. People with full stomachs and television sets in their front rooms die just as easily as people who are hungry and don't even know how to read."

"Sounds like the master planner himself." Brady laughed without humor. "Your Mendelov is brilliant. I'll admit that. He's more than brilliant. He's pure genius. But I'm not sure if he's an evolutionist or a benevolent Genghis Khan."

"He's a long way from that," Taggert said angrily. "But even if he were . . . well, I'll tell you this, Brady: The worst that man could do, and I mean the *worst*, would be a damn sight better than what the world is heading for."

Brady's reaction came instantly. "Who the hell says so, Taggert? You? Him? His entourage? Who appointed him God?"

Taken aback at Brady's response, Taggert didn't answer immediately. When he spoke, his voice was calm. "It's not a case of anyone playing God," he said.

"The hell it isn't!" Brady shouted. "I don't know all the answers yet, but I can sure figure some of them. This drive, the discs, the energy beam—all this gives you and Mendelov and this whole bunch absolute power, doesn't it? Aren't you thinking that way, Taggert? You've got something so powerful no one can touch you. Right?

"Absolute power corrupts absolutely, mister, in case you've never heard that phrase before." Brady slammed his hand on the armrest of his chair. "Do you really think you're original about this business of saving the world from itself? Jesus Christ, man, every tyrant who's ever been in business has used that line!"

Taggert had become ice, "You seem certain of what we're trying to do."

Brady gave the scientist a scathing look. "Don't give me that," he shot back. "Just show me where I'm wrong."

"Don't lecture *me*, Brady!" Taggert shouted suddenly. "You're insulting. It's clear enough that this is quite *different!*"

The newsman laughed harshly. "It's *always* different."

"But it *is* different, damn you!" Taggert cried. "Mendelov's found an answer that's evaded us all." He stopped when he saw the sarcastic smile on Brady's face and struggled visibly to control his temper. "You're hardly the objective type, are you? It must be wonderful to draw such perfect conclusions before you've heard a man fully. Saves time, doesn't it?" Taggert rose to his feet. "Sometimes I wonder what Mendelov sees in you or why you're here," he said. "He must have his reasons. I'm willing to wait and find out. Do you realize you're the first man who's ever come here, knowing what you do, before he's even been accepted as a part of what we're doing?"

Brady smiled bitterly. "I'm touched. I really am. A bunch of megalomaniacs get *me* branded as a lunatic, thrown out of my job, blackballed in my profession; they drug me, drag my ass out of the country, hold me a prisoner, threaten to cash my chips for me, and *you* think I should be grateful! Har-de-har-har!"

"Sometimes, Brady, one man isn't that important in the—"

"Shove it," Brady snarled. "That's the easiest thing in the world to say when that 'one man' isn't you."

CHAPTER XVIII

Brady faced Dr. Mendelov across a low table. They were alone. Mendelov might have been comfortably at home in his Princeton study. The huge scientist wore an open-necked shirt, and his booted feet rested comfortably on a hassock. On the table to his left stood a pitcher with cool wine and glasses. Mendelov smoked a calabash, with obvious relish, Brandy noted sourly. Even the room rubbed Brady the wrong way.

"Damn it, Mendelov," Brady said, "it's time we stopped beating around the bush."

Mendelov blew smoke from his nostrils and gestured with the pipe. "Have we forgotten something?"

"Yes," Brady said angrily. "How long do you intend to keep me here?"

Mendelov swung his feet from the hassock and faced Brady. "That depends."

"Thanks a heap," Brady said caustically. "Upon what?"

"On many things," Mendelov said with open good humor. "I thought I'd made it clear . . . You're being considered for this organization."

Brady waved his hand in a gesture of disdain. "*You've* got big plans for my joining your circus. But not me. Saving the world isn't my cup of tea."

"Isn't it? I should think it would be the avowed interest of any sane being."

"Goddamn it," Brady raged, "it's not a matter of 'could' or 'would'! To hell with you and your games. I just don't for one damned minute believe you could prevent a nuclear war if that's what the major nations of the world decide to get into. Not you or anyone else. This circus of yours is very impressive. But do you really believe you've got the power to affect what countries like the United States or Russia or Red China intend to do?"

The scientist shrugged. "You realize what you're trying to do? You're saying, Brady, that what always has been will—must—always be. That history is repetition without hope for change. Really! It's not so, not so. You've ignored the saturation factor." A sad smile appeared on the scientist's face. "Everyone, it appears, struggles desperately to ignore the saturation factor.

"You won't admit that war has reached its point of saturation. The popular idiom refers

266

to doomsday weapons. Their power is so great that casualties mean nothing anymore, simply because there won't be enough of us left to compile the casualty lists. Sad to say, that possibility is no longer remote."

Brady glared at the other man. "And you've got the answer to all that right here?" he said. "Is this the big speech you've been building me up to? Because if it is, you sure haven't—"

"No, Mr. Brady," Mendelov broke in. "This is not 'the big speech,' as you put it."

"Then what are you waiting for?"

"The right moment, Mr. Brady. You haven't had sufficient conditioning yet. You see I—"

"The Chinese tried that 'conditioning' long before you showed up," Brady snapped.

"Forgive me. I had no intention of compelling a change of heart. My beliefs don't run that way. I don't want to alter your basic convictions. No pressure is being placed on you, Mr. Brady. I have much more confidence in your native intelligence than you think."

Brady waved his hand to cut off Mendelov. "Never mind the bouquets. Taggert tells me you've discovered the flaw in everything the human race has ever done. That's a tall order"—he laughed without humor—"even for you. He claims you've found the key to world peace."

Mendelov was suddenly brusque. "You have never heard anyone here say our interest is in world peace. Bah! Peace as it's commonly defined is literally impossible. Man is incapable of existing without strife."

Brady stared at Mendelov. What he had just heard baffled him. "You're right," he said. "I *don't* understand."

"Obviously," Mendelov retorted. "We're not searching for an emotional nirvana that doesn't exist. You must understand that we're not pursuing unattainable goals. Nor is our interest the imposition of global peace—an impossible task. Our interest, Mr. Brady, lies in preventing the destruction of the world civilization. Do you understand? The two concepts are wholly distinct from one another. You must distinguish between the two, or you'll never understand what our effort represents."

Mendelov laid his pipe on the ash tray. He leaned back in his chair, both hands on the armrests, facing Brady like a judge passing sentence. "Nothing is ever black and white," Mendelov said. "Nothing. Neither in nature nor in the affairs of men. But every sign, every indication, every lesson from the past fairly screams its warning. Man is headed for a final conflict with thermonuclear weapons. We have the chance to avert this mass suicide. The means at our disposal, some of which you've seen, much of which you have *not* seen, give us the hope we pursue so urgently."

A thick finger stabbed in Brady's direction. "That is what we're after. It has nothing to do with peace—as you've been using that most imprecise word."

Brady sighed. "Look, don't get me wrong," he said. "No doubt what you're trying to do is . . . well, I don't want to use the word 'noble' because I don't think it would sit well with you."

"Bloody well right," Mendelov growled.

"All right, so you've got good intentions. But everything you've told me avoids the crux of the matter. You—and this includes everyone with you—believe you've come up with the right answers. You also believe you've got the means to enforce what you feel is the only way for the world to behave. So you're all convinced you can rule better than anyone else. *You* know what's best for—"

Mendelov's roar filled the room. "Rule! Good Lord, man, are you blind?" The giant had come bolt upright in his seat and was staring at Brady. "The *last* thing in the world we want is to *rule* anyone!"

Mendelov cut himself short with a sudden laugh. "Never mind," the scientist said. "I believe we've gone far enough for the moment. Let me change the subject. You'll be told what you need to know in good time. In the interim, Brady, I do wish you would think deeply on what we've discussed. Because we need you— your knowledge of the public mind, the press, the world of the well-informed laymen. We need that knowledge for what we have in mind."

"You need *me?* Very flattering." Brady laughed. "You got off to a hell of a start. Do you go after all your help with knockout drops?"

"Spare me, Brady. Your ego's been damaged. You're supposed to be a realist," Mendelov said with no attempt to conceal his irritation. "What we did was necessary because of your persistence in tracking us down. That interested me, and I can see great value in recruiting a man who managed to do what no one else has accomplished. But we've gone over that ground before. It's done. Don't confuse my interest in you with weakness. That would be stupid." Mendelov's eyes gripped Brady. They were cold and heavy-lidded. "If it becomes necessary . . . You may as well hear this without any room for doubt . . . If it becomes necessary, you will be killed."

CHAPTER XIX

Brady was lucky. He was out of the city when it happened. He drove along a narrow country road edging the Neversink River near Fallsburg, New York, about a hundred miles northwest of New York. It was about three o'clock in the morning and Brady was returning to the city when the night tore apart with a soundless scream of light. One moment the road was clear in his headlights and the next instant everything vanished from sight. Light, all-pervading, intense beyond description, blinding the universe. New York was a hundred miles away, but in that split second Brady knew what was happening even as the savage glare from a hundred miles away clawed at his eyes. With the pain ripping upward through his sockets, everything took on the false tones of a photo negative with the glare behind it.

Instinct brought his foot slamming onto the brake pedal, his hands clutching the wheel. But he was going too fast and the turn rushed at him. The car bounded into the ditch and flipped crazily over and over. When everything came to a stop and the sound of metal tearing ended, the car lay on its side and something wet and sticky ran down his face. He tried to clear his head. He knew he was bleeding, that he had been hurt. He struggled from the wrecked car. Despite the dancing lights in his eyes and the needles of pain, he could see. Ignoring the pain, he turned to the southeast. Toward, he realized with a sickness in his belly, where New York *had been*.

In the sky writhed something monstrous, boiling and writhing within itself, twisting upward. A flowery head disgorged itself from the glowing stalk. Brady remained numb, stangely calm. He realized he was watching the funeral pyre of what had been millions of human beings. He started walking and looked at the spreading sky glow that filtered down through the trees and illuminated the clouds. When he had climbed a small hill and could see for miles there came another terrible glow in the sky from a much greater distance, this one to the northeast. A steel fist grinding into the bowels of a city. Then, dimmed by an ever greater distance, still another. Then the heavens took up a slow, uneven pulsing, a throbbing of nuclear hells that no longer faded completely. Slowly the shock ebbed from his body and the pain, stabbing more deeply, brought the distant nightmare into focus. He heard the sound of a car, the engine racing. Brady turned and signaled with his hands, but the car rushed past, a glimpse of white faces within.

Twenty minutes later he reached a small crossroads village. People milled about the streets, many carrying rifles, all of them grim, listening to a car radio blaring loudly. The man in the car turned up the volume and still the throng pressed closer. Brady joined them. No one seemed to notice the blood caked on his face or his torn clothes. Brady knew the emergency networks had come into action. He heard what he expected to hear. Confused, angry, frightened men behind the microphones, themselves lacking hard information to pass on to their millions of invisible listeners. The voice blaring from the car radio spoke falteringly of mass nuclear attack. There were no reports from the cities that had been attacked. How could there be, Brady queried himself, when there isn't anyone left to report?

Brady listened to the pleas for the public to stay off the roads. The announcers were more hysterical, Brady noticed, than the grimly calm people about him. Those who weren't calm would do what they pleased or felt compelled to do. Those close to the cities who saw the leaping flames and the spreading clouds downwind would run for it. They'd run madly, impelled by years of fright building to this moment. They wouldn't have anywhere to go,

273

but they'd run there in cars and on foot and any way they could move. The highways would swiftly become clogged. The man nearest Brady blurted suddenly. "Thank God we're off the main roads." The others nodded, and Brady noticed a tightening of hands around rifles and guns.

The radio was reporting massive tidal waves along the Pacific Coast. Brady felt it was true enough. One of the recognized dangers for many years had been the threat of the Russians sinking monster hydrogen bombs along the sea bottom from fifty to two hundred miles from the West Coast, and then setting them off by remote control. Brady closed his eyes and shuddered. He thought of tidal waves a thousand feet high, rushing inland from the sea with a roar such as no one had ever heard since man first walked the planet: a wall a thousand feet high and moving at eight hundred miles an hour, boiling with radioactivity. He thought of the massive radioactive clouds and the steam that would cross the high mountains and flow inland, drifting for hundreds and even thousands of miles, a sticky blanket of slow death.

Brady felt a hand on his arm. For the first time since he had arrived, someone took heed of the blood on his face. A man tugged him away from the crowd, led him to a doctor nearby. Brady remained only half conscious as the doctor attended his injuries. Two broken ribs, lacerations, bruises, one deep cut requiring sixteen stitches. Brady remained with the doctor for the better part of an hour. Then the lights went out. The doctor lit two kerosine lamps. The old man lit two cigarettes and passed one to Brady. His hand paused as the deep roar of passing jets bounded from the sky. The hand continued its motion. Brady sucked greedily on the cigarette.

"Well, it's come finally."

Brady didn't have any comments for the end of the world.

"They must be hitting everywhere." The old doctor talked as if his words gave him release. "Everywhere. Whole country is being torn apart. . . ."

The words came from Brady without bidding. "At least the Russians must be getting it three times as bad. There won't be a city standing anywhere in the Soviet—"

In the flickering light of the lamps he saw a strange expression come over the doctor's face. "Does it make you feel better? What's the difference, mister? Does it do them"—he pointed in the direction of New York—"a damn bit of good? Why don't you go down there and tell everybody that we're really giving it to the Russians? Why don't you . . ." The doctor's voice trailed away.

Before dawn the first white ash fell from the sky. A ghastly pallor appeared over the trees and on buildings, on the ground, on cars and animals and people caught outside. A warm snow that wouldn't melt. They all knew what it was. The fallout. The deadly ash from the bomb. It was everywhere, drifting before the wind, swirling along the breeze. It wouldn't be so bad, Brady thought, if it thundered or roared or did something. But it doesn't. It doesn't make a sound.

The invisible death brought with it the signs of fear. Widened eyes, spasmodic movements, high-pitched voices, tight lips. The doctor had returned with Brady to the village center. With many others they collected in a small diner. The owner kept it open "because I wouldn't know what else to do." They were in the diner when the ash came from the sky.

The wind piled it against buildings, on street corners. It lay everywhere, weighing almost nothing but pressing against them all with a terrible finality. Brady sensed the first waves of hysteria. The shrill laughter, sudden cursing. He, they, all of them; they were helpless. You always thought of mass death with violence and horror and the world crashing down all about you. Outside, not a single twig was broken. Not a window shattered. Still the death flowered down from the sky.

It fell for hours. No one remained near the windows any longer. The doctor smiled to himself. He knew the diner was no protection. He didn't say that aloud.

Later, they saw someone walking in the ash, an alien creature in a rubberized suit and hood, wearing a mask and heavy boots, in his hand a shining metal-and-glass instrument. Measuring the radioactive count. They didn't need the man and his goddamned instrument to tell them what the vomiting was telling them better. The weaker among them were feverish,

276

nauseous, wide-eyed with fear. They knew they were all walking dead, everything so quiet and peaceful, the ash raining softly in its death kiss from on high. They saw the hooded, caped, booted, masked figure gesture in anger or disgust, they couldn't be sure, but he flung away his Geiger counter and tore off the hood, threw away the cape, kicked off the boots, and walked toward and into the diner. They shrank away from him because the ash was on him. Brady tried to see his face, but too many people were in the way. He heard the stranger's voice. ". . . goddamned counter's no good anyway. Right off the scale, right—off—the—scale; it's so damned hot out there, that stuff is so hot!" The figure paused, framed in the doorway, and Brady moved to see him. "You're all dead!" the man laughed, the laughter swelling into a cackle. "Dead, dead, dead! In a day or two, you'll all be dead!" He roared with mirth, his arms spread out and his head thrown back, a standing crucifix, then he brushed the ash from his body, swirling it through the room toward them. Abruptly he reached up and with a wet, sucking sound ripped the mask from his face. Brady knew a shock of horror. There was no face: He stared into empty skull sockets, heard the jawbone clattering as the cackling laugh roared at him. Cursing, Brady hurled himself at the skeletal thing in the radiation suit. He heard himself screaming as he clawed at the thing, but he couldn't raise his arms or batter with his fists; he struggled to rip and tear and destroy but he couldn't move and the laughter

277

swelled like a balloon inside his brain, calling *Brady, Brady, BRADY!*

He stared wildly, gasping, trying to focus his eyes, the grinning skull a fleeting retinal shadow mocking him as it faded slowly. Brady jerked himself to an upright position, perspiration matting him everywhere. "Brady! Are you all right?" Mouth open, he looked up. Taggert. Bending down over him, grasping his arm. "Are you all right?" Again the question. Brady nodded slowly. "You've been having a nightmare."

"Uh-huh." Brady's throat hurt, he was hoarse. He swung his feet to the floor, the sweat-salt stinging his eyes. He shuddered. It had been so goddamned real! He looked up at Taggert, saw the concern in the other man's eyes. "I—I'm all right," Brady stammered. "Just let me get, get my wits about me." He couldn't shake the dream. It came back in spasms, breaking waves of horrible memory. Brady stumbled into the shower, jolted himself with a stream of icy water, turning it hot until steam billowed about him. He sagged against the wall as the water washed over him, cleansing him.

Christ, how had it started? He remembered now. He had left Mendelov to visit with several of the top men in Condor—Wilkinson, Kroot, the others. It had all been too much for one day, for the night before. Crammed from beginning to end, thoughts, conflict, anger, all of it churning in his mind.

278

He didn't stay long with Drew Wilkinson. To the financier the situation and events necessary to meet that situation were cut and dried. Within several years there was every chance his entire financial empire would crumble in ruin. "Because," Wilkinson told Brady, "financial structures collapse just as readily as mortar and stone when a nuclear shock wave arrives." Wilkinson gave Brady the impression of being involved with Mendelov strictly for his own purposes. Personal interests spurred on the man, not a sense of avoiding war, as Mendelov judged the matter. Brady spoke his thoughts to Wilkinson. The financier laughed in Brady's face.

"For the life of me I can't understand what Vadim sees in you," Wilkinson lashed out. "You fool! You put *your* values into everything! Isn't that it, Brady? You've bitched and complained about the dangers of do-gooders. Yet I've been flatly honest with you and told you I was committed up to my ears for personally selfish reasons. And what does that call for me to do? To risk everything I have so that we might avoid a total nuclear disaster. Because if the country is destroyed, I go down with it. And because I *am* honest with you, and because I detest dishonesty in these things, because I agree with you that do-gooders are a dangerous breed, you still insist we're misguided zealots wasting our time.

"Let me ask you something, Brady. You're aware that even the most optimistic computer studies give us barely three chances in ten for staying out of a total nuclear war. You agree it appears inevitable. You know it means the destruction of everything in the world that's meaningful to us." Wilkinson slammed his hand against his desk. "Just what the hell have *you* done to prevent its coming? As far as I'm concerned, you're a blind fool with a loud mouth. You can harp and snipe and wallow along with the rest of the world, wailing about the savagery of man, but you're not *doing* a goddamn thing. You make me sick. Get the hell out of my office."

Brady was still brooding over Wilkinson's words when he first met Robert Kroot. The economist was worlds removed from Wilkinson. Retiring almost to the point of physical discomfort, he seemed to fade into his surroundings. Yet the small man looked upon his visitor with eyes that were electric. They moved almost constantly, darting about, reassuring their owner that nothing would escape his notice. Kroot didn't have any speeches for Brady. He responded to Brady with adding-machine efficiency.

From Brady's point of view, Kroot made more sense than everyone else put together. He lacked the high-flown idealism of Taggert, he remained remote from the calculating self-interest of Wilkinson, he had nothing of the philosophical depth of Mendelov. What Kroot did have was a dispassionate and calculating appraisal of the facts of life. He was a scientist of applied economics, and in clipped sentences he stated flatly to Brady that the industrial-economic society of the world had accepted that nuclear war could not be avoided.

"Accepted," Kroot repeated. "The international community has geared itself to a nuclear war economy. Hard business had been currupted with a compelling need to increase the capacity for mass destruction. I use the term 'corrupted' advisedly. Once you achieve an industrial goal, a senseless repetition of that goal, resting on national debts of prohibitive proportion, is a corruption of all logic." Kroot shrugged as if none of it mattered beyond his evaluation. He was totally impersonal. "It's simple enough," he went on. "There exists the capacity to destroy civilization many times over. The hair-trigger balance has lost its stability. With the introduction of nuclear weapons to new countries, beyond France and China —and I know at least eight other nations now developing their nuclear arms—the whole delicate structure is set in quivering motion. It has the substance of jelly. It's impossible by any normal means to stop the vibrations now sweeping the mass. One day"—Kroot shrugged again—"it comes apart at the seams, like a bag of water split down its side. There are many signs attesting to this."

"Are you referring to specific items?" Brady asked.

Kroot looked with disdain at Brady. "I deal only in specifics," he said coldly. "The sum of national knowledge is microfilmed in underground vaults. Redundancy and lead-shielded vaults are the theme. Vast stores of materials, weapons, the like, are cached. There are secret deep underground shelters that can withstand anything save exposure to the nuclear fireball. The select members of our society to occupy these human vaults are aware of their role. They number in the thousands. The public, however, can't be told of the existence of such facilities." Kroot smiled as Brady started to interrupt. "You of all people, Mr. Brady, are aware of the ramifications of such news being made common property.

"Did you know that at least twenty nations have sperm banks in cryogenic storage? Those sperm banks are buried far beneath the sea, in underground caverns, high in mountains. They have only one purpose, Mr. Brady, and it has absolutely nothing to do with economics. They have been prepared for the day when all mature males left alive will have been rendered sterile by radioactivity."

A smile flickered on Kroot's face and fled, the grim humor of a man who sees the future and cannot help smiling at the madness of man.

"Dr. Mendelov and our associates, Mr. Brady, believe the world is rushing into an accidental nuclear war that's inevitable. I don't agree with them."

Kroot's words startled Brady. "No, Mr. Brady," the economist said in that same quiet voice. "There's nothing accidental about it. *The world is perparing deliberately for that war.*"

After his meeting with Kroot, Brady had returned to his apartment and had fallen asleep. And had dreamed. Even now, after running the shower alternately cold and hot to sting him fully awake, the nightmare haunted him. Maybe Mendelov and the others were right, he thought wearily. Maybe anything they did was better than waiting to be trampled under a rain of atomic hell. Every time Brady fought back from whatever rationale he could muster that an all-powerful group meant the greatest of all dangers, he heard Kroot's words that the world was preparing deliberately for its own self-destruction. The dream swirled through his mind. He could ignore the scenes of the terrible light, the towering mushroom stalks that punched their way far into the stratosphere. But he couldn't push from him that silent, terrible rain of lethal ash. The silence of that horror pounded in his ears.

He dried himself quickly and dressed. Taggert studied Brady's face as he came into the living room.

"You all right?"

"I'm fine now," Brady replied, managing a weak smile. "That was like nothing I've—" He cut himself short and dropped gratefully into a chair.

Taggert nodded. "I think you could use something a bit stronger than coffee this time," he said. He reached into a zippered pocket and withdrew a flask. "Scotch?"

"Christ, yes," Brady said with relief.

Taggert unscrewed the cap and handed the

flask to Brady. He drank long and slowly, letting the fire settle in his system. Finally he lowered the flask and took a deep breath. "Thanks. It helps."

Taggert replaced the cap. "I've got some news for you," he offered.

"Oh? What about?"

"Your fiancée."

"Who?"

"Why, Miss Dallas. Ann Dallas. She is your fiancée, isn't—"

Brady's eyes narrowed as he came upright in his chair. "What about her?" he demanded.

Taggert was taken aback by Brady's intensity. "Mendelov told you about her, didn't he?"

"No. What about her?"

"You should be proud of that young woman, Brady. She's a wildcat."

"Goddamn you, get to it, Taggert!"

"Sorry. She showed up at the Blackburn office in Flagstaff."

"Oh, good Christ."

Taggert's smile was friendly. ". . . and when she discovered you'd checked out of your motel, and she couldn't find you, she tore the roof off."

Brady eased carefully back into the chair. "How?"

"She threatened to tell the police that the Blackburn company had kidnapped you."

"She'd be dead right."

"Yes, of course. But Miss Dallas didn't *know* that. Either way it could have been embarrassing to have the local police tramping through the building."

"Never mind. Where is she? What's happened to her?"

Taggert held up his hand. "She's on the way here."

"*Here?*" Brady echoed.

"Yes."

"But why in the name of God did you have to—" Brady came angrily from the chair.

"Please. She's perfectly all right. Will you let me tell you what happened?"

Brady sat down again and waited.

"Miss Dallas threatened to go to her father."

"Her father?" The whole thing was mad.

"Sam Dallas, it turns out," Taggert said with a wan smile, "has some very powerful friends in Washington. In the White House, in fact. We couldn't permit that."

"Don't tell me you—"

"No, no, of course not," Taggert said, anticipating Brady's words. "No abduction this time."

"Then how could you—I mean, how did you get her to agree to come here?"

Taggert couldn't resist the grin. "Love is a powerful force, apparently. We simply told her the truth."

"You mean . . ." Brady stared at Taggert. "And she just went along?"

"That's right."

Brady didn't know what to say.

Taggert glanced at his watch. "It's six now.

Your, ah, fiancée will be here in about six hours or so. About midnight, I should say."

"Hold it, hold it," Brady said as the question occurred to him. "How can you cover up a second disappearance? The airline will be looking for her, and if she's reported as missing, and her old man's got the friends you say he has, you've got a can of worms on your hands, haven't you?"

Taggert laughed and stood up. "Not at all. She's not missing. She called the newspapers and told them you and she had eloped."

CHAPTER XX

Brady walked through the disc servicing area with Dianne Sims and Dr. Kenneth Taggert. Mendelov, called away for the night, would see Brady the next morning. Brady glanced at his watch. The disc would be arriving within minutes, descending almost vertically from high altitude.

"When do I find out just where we are?" He addressed the question to both Taggert and Dianne Sims. They exchanged glances and Taggert picked up the query. "He has a good idea right now," he told the woman. "It's all right. Vadim said to tell him what he wants to know."

Dianne smiled at Brady. "Have you ever heard of Palenque?"

He searched his memory. "No," he admitted.

"Palenque is a form of quasi-statehood," she said. "Not really a country in the legal sense, but a country in pratice. Its existence is neither recognized nor challenged."

"Challenged by whom?"

"Palenque forms part of Venezuela, Colombia, and Brazil. The countries involved look the other way as far as Palenque is concerned," Dianne went on. "We're in the high plateau and rain forests east of the Andes chain. You had a good look at the terrain on the way down. You can see why it's considered the most inaccessible region anywhere in the world. The winds that blow off the mountains make this entire area very difficult for airplanes. Several have been lost, in fact."

"It's what you'd call an atmospheric trap," Taggert broke in. "The currents are strong and no one has any idea of their flow. Most aircraft couldn't stand up under the turbulence."

"There are about a hundred thousand natives in Palenque," Dianne continued. "To outsiders they're the most hostile savages anywhere in the world."

"You seem amused about that," Brady noted.

"I am," she said. "That's why I was so careful to say 'outsiders.' Among themselves they're a peaceful and gentle people."

Brady laughed. "That isn't the story I got."

Dianne smiled gently. "That's because you haven't lived with them, Cliff. Otherwise you'd know better."

Brady stared. "*Lived* with them? I thought

288

no white man had ever gone through this country."

"They haven't," Dianne said. "My mother was part of a missionary group attacked by the natives. She was the only survivor. One of the chief's sons took my mother as his wife."

"So you're, I mean . . ." Brady halted, embarrassed.

"That's right. I'm half-Jicaque."

"That's why we're on such excellent terms with the natives," Taggert said. "As far as the Jicaque are concerned, Dianne's one of them."

"But how did you—I mean, you speak English so perfectly and . . . and . . . just *look* at you," Brady said, still baffled.

"Have you heard of Dr. Francisco Valdivia?" Dianne asked.

Brady shook his head.

"Dr. Valdivia—that's his name in Brazil, not his name among the Jicaque—became a great friend of my mother. She taught him to speak Portuguese, Spanish, and English. He learned so swiftly, she convinced Ah Tutul that Valdivia should be sent to school in Brazil. He saw that the modern world was bound to encroach upon this territory and that the Jicaque would need several of their own people who understood civilization. He—"

"Wait a moment," Brady broke in. "Who's Ah Tutul?"

"Ah Tutul is chief of the Jicaque Indians. He has been as far back as I can remember. His word is law throughout Palenque."

"Right," Brady said, keeping track. "And what happened with Valdivia?"

"Mother was right," Dianne explained. "Francisco fulfilled the promise Mother saw in him. With the languages he commanded, besides Mother's instruction in other subjects, he had no difficulty in school. While he was attending the university, he struck up a close friendship with Carlos de Landa and—"

"General de Landa?" Brady asked.

"Yes. Have you heard of him?"

"Heard of him? I've known him for years," Brady said. "He was a Brazilian Air Force observer with us in Korea. I even flew him on a few missions. Is de Landa tied in with all this?"

"Only indirectly," Dianne answered. "Francisco became close friends with General de Landa. They were pretty much agreed about Palenque. Francisco became the liaison between the outside world and the Jicaque, and General de Landa worked closely with Francisco. There are some things about civilization Francisco felt could benefit our people.

"The Indians were happy to receive medicines," Dianne continued, "and Francisco felt that the outstanding Jicaque should receive an education on the outside."

"Sanitary engineering; that sort of thing," Taggert added. "But Ah Tutul's a wise old bird. He won't permit anything to interfere with the sanctuary of Palenque. The natives will still slaughter anyone who tries to penetrate this area."

"If that's the case," Brady said, "how come this place is here?"

"Francisco Valdivia and Vadim Mendelov are close friends," Taggert replied.

"Dr. Mendelov," Dianne explained, "met Francisco during a study of different tribes in South America. Mendelov had been warned not to travel within Palenque. So, having heard of Francisco, he arranged a meeting. That was many years ago," she explained. "All this, the discs and this base, I mean, came much later. When Dr. Taggert developed the drive for the discs, and the group began to form—"

"Mendelov plans to fill you in on that tomorrow," Taggert interjected. Brady nodded.

"The discs must be pretty impressive to savages—"

"Indians," Dianne corrected gently. "Not savages."

Brady grinned ruefully. "Sorry. But what I meant is that for people who've lived the same way, apparently, for thousands of years, the discs are rather overwhelming, aren't they? I should think the natives—Indians"—he smiled at Dianne—"must look on you as gods."

Dianne shook her head vigorously. "Absolutely not," she said quickly. "You mustn't underestimate the intelligence of these people. Once the Jicaque ruled much of the northern part of this continent A long time ago they accepted the white man. They paid for that trust." She bit her lip. "They won't make the same mistake again. The position the Jicaque take is they must rule within their own territory before mixing. They're quite prepared to die first."

Brady thought over what he heard. "Then what's the position of Ah Tutul with Mendelov and the rest of you?"

"Mendelov persuaded Francisco to set up a meeting with Ah Tutul," Dianne said. "During that meeting—it was after the first discs had flown secretly—Mendelov arranged for this base to be set up here. To protect the sanctuary, they agreed upon the rule that no one ever enters or leaves here by any other means save the discs."

"That's what I meant when I told you no one, including Mendelov, can ever move through this country," Taggert said. "Dianne's case is different. This is her home."

"You said Ah Tutul doesn't regard Mendelov or anyone else as gods," Brady persisted. "What brought him to accept this base right in the middle of his home grounds?"

"Ah Tutul's an Indian," Dianne said quietly, "but he has great wisdom, and he's not unworldly. I've never confused his lack of what we call schooling for ignorance on his part. Francisco acts as his ambassador to the outside world, but Ah Tutul judges for himself. After Dr. Mendelov first met Ah Tutul, Francisco went with Mendelov to Princeton. It was then that Mendelov told Francisco about the discs and his plans. After all," Dianne said with a quick smile, "if the world is covered with radioactivity, Palenque also will be affected."

"I suppose," Taggert said, "Ah Tutul considers what we're trying to do as a holy mission. Not in the theological sense, of course. He—"

Taggert broke off as a warning horn echoed through the great chamber. Red lights flashed over the huge sliding doors.

"They're here," Taggert said briskly, motioning for them to move inside, away from the doors. Moments later the bright floodlights winked out and guide lights for the disc crew came on. The doors rumbled aside to reveal a starry night. Several hundred feet away, motionless, glowing in the night air, the disc waited for the doors to open fully. Brady heard a low hum as the disc pilot increased power and the machine glided forward to settle on its landing cradle.

Moments later Ann was in his arms.

"But what made you go to Blackburn and start screaming I'd been shanghaied? How did you know?"

Ann placed a finger gently against his lips. "Shh. You're not letting me tell you." She kissed him and pressed her body close against his on the couch. She sighed and placed his hand by her cheek "You feel so marvelous. . . ." She let her words trail off and held him tightly for several moments.

"Anyway," she sighed, picking up her story, "when I called and the motel told me you'd checked out, I just *knew* something was wrong."

"Woman's intuition?"

"I just had this awful feeling, Cliff." She shuddered. "I called the airlines in Flagstaff and they didn't have your name on any reservations, and I knew you wouldn't have taken the plane you rented somewhere else—"

"How'd you know that?"

"Silly. I know what they cost to rent. Remember, no more expense account?"

He kissed her on the nose. "Go on."

"I even called all the car-rental agencies in Flagstaff. Nothing," she said sternly "Absolutely nothing. As far as I was concerned, you were either still in Flagstaff, or . . . or, well, or you'd been taken away against your will."

"That sounds pretty grim," he said. "Against my will, huh?"

"Cliff, stop it. I was frantic. I took the first flight to Flagstaff and went straight to the motel.

"I asked the motel desk when you'd checked out. They showed me the time on their ledger and I asked the man what you were wearing."

"What I was *wearing*? Why would you—"

"Cliff, shut up! I knew what I was doing," Ann continued. "The man, the one at the desk, thought about it for a few moments, and *then*," she said with a note of triumph, "he said he didn't know. I asked him if he meant he didn't remember, but he said, no, he couldn't possibly know because you hadn't checked out personally, that another man had checked out for you." She looked at him with her eyes bright.

"So I *knew* you were in trouble," she exclaimed. "You didn't know anyone there, you went to Flagstaff alone, and . . well, that was it. I went straight to Blackburn and demanded to see Dr. Taggert. You know the rest."

Brady exhaled slowly. "What a woman."

"Cliff, when I—I mean—when you were gone . . ." She threw herself into his arms. "I was so afraid. I love you so much. . . ."

"Say that again." His voice was dry and husky

She clung tightly to him. "I love you so much . . . and I was so worried. . . ."

He pressed her close to him. "Yeah. And so you put yourself into hot water right with me."

She sat straight, studying him. "I don't understand."

He told her of his conversations with Mendelov and the others. "And the long and short of it, honey, is that it's a one-way trip down here."

Her eyes widened. "You mean . . ."

"You don't think the friendly giant is going to turn us loose after what we know, do you?"

"Turn us loose?"

"Yeah. Or else . . ." He drew his finger across his throat.

"But why would he want to do that!"

He squeezed her hand. "At the risk of using an old cliché, Ann, we know too much."

"Know too much? But you're part of them now!" She shook her head. "I don't understand."

295

"Hey, hold on," he said harshly, "I never told you I'd signed up for the crusades. Where'd you get that idea?"

Ann was flustered. "Why, after what they told me at Blackburn about your being somewhere, at a secret base, I mean, and the *way* they said it, I assumed . . ."

"I haven't agreed to a thing."

"But Cliff! What they're doing is wonderful. A chance to prevent a nuclear war. How could you *not* want to help?" She stared at him in disbelief.

"Oh Christ," Brady groaned. "Not you, too."

"You mean you won't help?" she blazed.

"Sure, sure I would," he said soothingly. "If I believed in how they were going about it and if they really had a chance of making it stick. Now, hold on," he said quickly as he saw another outburst starting. "All you know is what you've been told so far and that spectacular little ride down here. You don't *know* anything else. Remember that. You don't *know*. So far it's all been their story, and no one else has come up with any arguments. I'd say that was good cause not to take everything they offer at face value."

He rose and stretched, smiling down at her. "But right now, sweetheart, no more. I want you in that bed."

"Oh, no, you don't," Ann said, rising to her feet and placing her hands on her hips. "Not so fast."

"Ann, it'll wait until tomorrow."

"Why can't we talk about it now?" she demanded.

"I *told* you," he said, vexed. "I don't want to talk. I want to make love to you! *Now* will you shut up and come to bed?"

CHAPTER XXI

Mendelov and Ann were still exchanging small talk. Brady chewed his lip, trying to force from his mind another period of subconscious terror. Last night, Ann in his arms, he had dreamed again. The same dream, everything the same. Ann told him he was thrashing wildly and screaming. He snapped out of it again soaked from head to foot in perspiration. He left her in bed, puzzled and alarmed, while he went into the next room to smoke in the dark and wrestle with himself. Later, in bed, he spent most of the night awake, afraid to drop off, afraid he'd return to the terrible white ash drifting silently from the sky.

Today Mendelov would get down to cases. The longer Brady thought about the organization and the people who were involved, the more he realized that both his and Ann's lives *were* at stake. Vadim Mendelov would not give a signal for execution with a wave of his hand, but there were other ways to ensure a person's silence. Drugs or a wire-thin needle in the brain would do it. Hell, they needn't kill anyone.

Ann took to Mendelov. What he and the others were attempting appealed tremendously to her. Brady looked at her with affection and smiled to himself. He wondered if she had ever marched in student demonstrations. The way she had snapped at him last night for not leaping into Mendelov's schemes had surprised him.

Mendelov and Ann finished their pleasantries and the scientist fixed his gaze on Brady. "Mr. Brady, I've told you that our organization neither wants nor feels capable of ruling the affairs of men. What we do want for all men is a guarantee of freedom from nuclear war. Everything we're doing is directed toward this one purpose. The world needs a reprieve from threatened self-destruction. A reprieve; time. Time for the social sense to mature, for mankind to mature, for nations to engage in competition without brandishing nuclear arms. We need—this is empirical, of course—not a single power to control all governments, but an enforced international conscience whose sole responsibility is race survival. *Survival* only. And we need your help to bring this about."

"You have said your outfit," Brady replied,

"doesn't want to rule." The scientist nodded slowly. "You have also said," Brady went on, "that it is impossible to achieve peace because man is determined to fight no matter what."

Ann looked on with astonishment. She was even more bewildered when she discovered the scientist nodding agreement with what Brady was saying.

"You also made the point," Brady ticked off the items one by one on his fingers, "that man's most precious commodity is time. You keep bringing that up. You insist the world needs time for the social sciences to catch up with the physical sciences."

Brady wasn't certain of his conclusion, but he took a deep breath and plunged ahead. "What it all adds up to, I *think*, is that you and your crowd *have* figured out some way to influence governments with nuclear weapons. I don't know how, but you hope to make them give up their nuclear weapons. I don't see how you could accomplish this, but for the sake of argument . . ." Brady shrugged and glanced at Ann, who sat silent through the exchange between the two men. "At the same time," Brady said, returning his attention to Mendelov, "you're restricting yourselves. Your intent is to influence or to force the action you want, but not to go any further."

"Precisely," Mendelov said quietly.

"Then are you going to enforce your demands? Because that's what it amounts to, isn't it? None of the world powers are going to listen to what you say but to what you can do."

Brady scratched his chin. "You must have a lot of muscle I haven't seen yet," he mused aloud.

Mendelov nodded. "We do."

"And you're prepared to use it even if people get hurt?"

"In view of the alternative," Mendelov confirmed, "yes."

Brady glanced at Ann. He was glad she had heard that from Mendelov directly. She seemed to have the cock-eyed idea that Mendelov could accomplish what he wanted without bruising people.

"All right," Brady said, more confident than he had been for several days. "When do you take the wraps off your little toy?"

"Very soon," Mendelov countered. "But not yet."

"That still leaves *you,*" Brady said slowly. "You are the last man in the world I would expect to get into something like this—a barefaced power play with nuclear hardware. I don't care what the stakes are; I haven't changed that opinion. So something more important than your entire lifework is involved. What is it? Why are you in the picture?"

Mendelov ignored the question and motioned for him to continue.

"So you're not trying to stop man from fighting, and you've said time is critical . . . in essence what you want to do is to keep everyone from killing themselves off." Brady was talking to himself, deep in thought. "That also means that as far as you're concerned, war is inevitable, but there's no real harm in letting

302

people hack at one another. Man's ability to reproduce far outstrips any damage he can do to himself. *Just as long as nuclear weapons are out of the picture. Is that it?*"

"It is." Mendelov said only those two words and then fell silent.

Brady ran his fingers through his hair, searching for the answer that lay at the edge of his thoughts. "There's still more to it than that," he persisted. "You're looking beyond all this, because whatever *you* do is temporary. Sooner or later things would return to where they are now, everyone getting ready for the big bang. So you're looking for a change that will be effective after you're out of the picture." Brady looked up at Mendelov. "Something that will last for a long time."

Mendelov's features were frozen.

"You're waiting for someone to take over from you."

"Yes." The word was an intense whisper from the scientist.

Mendelov's eyes seemed aflame. His huge hands gripped his chair, knuckles white from the pressure. "What we have found, Mr. Brady—I hope you can comprehend the significance of this discovery. What we have found is ... the missing link!"

"The missing link," Brady repeated softly. "Man and the apes are supposed to have descended from a common ancestor. Science has been looking for the place where they branched . . . but they've never found . . ." Again his

303

voice trailed off. He returned the unblinking gaze of Mendelov.

"They've been wrong all these years, haven't they." Brady made his words a statement.

Mendelov sat like a granite statue.

"*We* are the missing link," Brady breathed. "*The missing link is man himself.*"

Mendelov's voice came from a great distance. "And man stands in the way of the next step in evolution."

"*Homo superior?*" Brady queried.

"Some use that term," Mendelov said. "I don't. I believe that we are the predecessors of the first *humane* beings that will be seen on this planet."

". . . so you can see," Mendelov was saying, "there's a purpose that transcends all our own lives. An intellectual compassion for the first time in history spurs us on."

"That's great," Brady said dryly. "But most of the human race doesn't agree with you."

"How could they!" Ann protested. "They don't even know what Dr. Mendelov's been telling us."

"They don't know directly," Mendelov interjected. "But there is some sensing of all this. Man isn't a sane creature. Conflict is as necessary to him as eating and sleeping and reproducing. It's nature's law; man must conquer all his adversaries, take over and prepare the planet for the next phase in evolution. That's why we'll never see peace in our time. Man hasn't any choice. He's condemned by instinct

304

to fight. *Not* to fight goes against the very nature of man.

"We're certain that various members of the next race—*homo superior* was the term you used—have already made their appearance. Aristole, da Vinci, Michelangelo, Newton, Lorentz, Galileo, Plato, Kepler, Steinmetz, Einstein; many, many others of which we know. Perhaps Christ was one; I like to think so. But there must have been many denied the opportunity to flourish. From here on, it's critical they have that opportunity. It's even more critical that those of us who realize the facts take every step to assure that we'll be—"

"Replaced?" Brady offered.

"It's not a very nice word, is it?" Mendelov replied, looking from Brady to Ann.

She shook her head. "No, it's not."

"However"—Mendelov sighed—"that's the crux of it. We believe the racial sense of man is somehow aware that the next step has already begun. Man—*men*—won't consciously permit this to happen. They'll crush anyone who shows the first sign of being superior. Indeed, they'd rather drag the entire world down in nuclear flames then yield willingly to a superior animal. Have you ever considered why sane men should drive inexorably toward the ultimate holocaust? They can't help themselves. They aren't aware that racial instinct spurs them on. They'd rather die in a howling pack than to step aside gracefully. They can't help what they do.

"For more than a hundred thousand years,"

305

Mendelov said, "there hasn't been any change in the size or shape or the capacity of the human brain. Man's up against a stone wall. I believe that man, as a race, is aware of this. Because he can't get any more out of his own brain, he desperately builds artificial replicas, the advanced cybernetics systems, to compensate for his own deficiencies. The beneficial effects are unfortunately limited because man himself teaches his computers and they simply reflect man's own fear and promise of self-extinction." Mendelov spread his huge hands palms down on the desk before him and lapsed into silence.

Minutes later, Brady shifted his position impatiently. "All right," he said briskly, "there are things we've got to do."

Mendelov chuckled. "Then I take it you've joined us, after all."

Brady's words died on his lips. Damn Mendelov! Brady couldn't even recall making a conscious decision, but he knew he was in. He looked at Ann, who beamed a smile back at him. Before Brady could collect his thoughts, Mendelov thrust again.

"You didn't enjoy your dream?"

"That's one way of putting it," Brady growled. "How'd you know about it? I didn't think Taggert was reporting to you whenever I . . ." The expression on Mendelov's face ended his words. Brady took a grip on himself. "Mendelov, you've got canary feathers all over you. If I didn't know better, I'd swear you expected me to have that damned nightmare." Even as he said it, he knew he had hit dead center.

"Of course," Mendelov agreed affably. "You see, your apartment was subjected to low-frequency signals of six to twelve cycles per second. Perhaps you're aware this affects the natural frequency of the brain. It excites the alpha rhythm which, Mr. Brady, is your carrier of ideas, how you conceive mental pictures, and—"

"You mean you had me set up?" Brady was incredulous.

"No, you're wrong," the scientist corrected him. "The radiated signal assured us only that you'd dream. What's been on your mind these past days? Nuclear destruction. All we did was to prompt your subconscious fears and bring them to the surface of your dream mind. The dream, however, was yours entirely." Mendelov half smiled at the newsman. "I don't imagine it was pleasant."

"Damn you, you act awfully sure of yourself."

"I am." Mendelov admitted. "I rarely make a mistake in my choice of men."

CHAPTER XXII

Vadim Mendelov filled in the gaps in the history of the development of the discs for Ann and Brady.

"One evening in Princeton, twelve years ago now, Taggert spent several hours with me," Mendelov related. "During dinner with a group of my colleagues he'd listened to our discussions of nuclear war. We also spent some time confirming our conclusions that identified man as the missing link in the evolutionary chain. I knew," Mendelov said, nodding his great head slowly, "that something was tearing at Taggert. He was a classic example of conflicting inner emotions. Later, of course, I learned the details. If Taggert were to pursue the course that beckoned so strongly to him, he knew he'd be branded by his own country as a traitor—

there's no other word for it from the national-istic sense. We've all faced that decision. You two," he said to Ann and Brady, "have yet to realize the impact of what I'm saying. No," he said quickly, with a motion of his hand, "listen to me carefully. You haven't had time to re-flect. You must understand that making the de-cision to serve the best interests of mankind can be diametrically opposed to the best inter-ests of your country as they judge your ac-tions."

"Had Taggert developed his new drive yet?" Brady queried. He was ignoring Mendelov's warnings about his conscience. Brady figured that was up to him and no one else. As for Ann, well, Brady already knew she had decided with Mendelov.

"Yes," said Mendelov.

"I couldn't help but notice Taggert was con-taining something ready to burst free. Finally he revealed to me he'd perfected the propulsion system we now refer to as the Taggert Drive. He received my word that our conversation would remain between the two of us. It was then he described the Drive and added that he'd kept its details secret.

"Taggert kept returning to our conversation of what was needed to prevent the war we were all so convinced was inevitable. What steps would I take? How could such an organi-zation be formed and controlled? Would I prepare for him a list, known only to myself and him, of those individuals I felt were vital to such a concept? With all that Taggert told me of his Drive I was also aware he hadn't revealed anything to implicate him beyond a point where he could extricate himself from our relationship. He was testing me, of course, and I could well appreciate his caution. Taggert on his own part was already striving to bring his concept to working reality. I'm referring to the Drive. Theoretically it should work, but between the laboratory and actual flight there lies an abyss of unknown dimensions. Taggert had enlisted the aid of two men he trusted implicitly: Harry Boener, a brilliant aerodynamics engineer, and Wayne Priest, an electrical genius. Those two men applied Taggert's theory, and to the three of them we owe the discs. It was Priest who adapted the Drive as an energy beam. Not even Taggert had seen the implication of the weapon during his theoretical work.

"The next steps essentially were mechanical. I handpicked the first group the cadre, if you will. They had requested me to direct the effort. Little by little we expanded the group. Each person brought within the fold was himself convinced, beyond all doubt, that the future promised only total ruin unless the nuclear conflict was avoided. Taggert had given us the miracle we sought and the rest lay in our hands.

"Such a venture, as I'm sure you both understand, presented critical problems in organization, management, security, financing, industry, communications, and even administrative control within our expanding numbers. Drew Wilkinson has been invaluable and without his genius at organization and financing I doubt we would ever have progressed as we did. He's worth at least two or three hundred millions, and he turned over to us his entire resources. Frazer Blackburn also is a multimillionaire, but far more important than his finances was the full spectrum of Blackburn Aero which responded to all our needs.

"I'm certain you've wondered how we managed to produce the discs right under the noses of the United States Government. Actually, it was less difficult than we anticipated, thanks to Frazer Blackburn. Once the design was completed, different Blackburn plants around the country produced various components. No one element produced in Mighigan, for example, could be related to any other element without knowledge of the basic design. We used Blackburn's aircraft plants, steel mills, shipbuilding yards, forging plants, engine factories, power-generator plants—well, let's just say that Blackburn was able to bury completely within his own organization and his subcontractors the major elements of the discs. The components were delivered to the Colorado Plateau where assembly was carried out.

"Frazer Blackburn's own son was our chief test pilot," Mendelov continued. "The rest of the story is, I suppose, prosaic in its telling, but critical in its actual involvement. I understand Miss Sims has told you of the relationship with Dr. Francisco Valdivia? Good. You can imagine the roles played by Wilkinson,

Blackburn, Kroot, Valdivia, and the others. Um, you've met Professor Walton from the University of Colorado? He's been with us from the outset. Yes"—Mendelov boomed with laughter—"I can see that you have."

"You mean he's part of this, too?" Brady asked.

"Of course," Mendelov confirmed. "He's a splendid actor."

"Son of a bitch," Brady muttered.

"He's been vital to us. As the scientific head of the Air Force's UFO research effort, he's created a very effective smokescreen. Confusion is his forte, and he's been helped a great deal by the people who see all sorts of things in the sky. The discs are camouflaged neatly within the many reports. Officially the discs don't exist, which makes it difficult for the Air Force to lend credence even to those sightings when there seems absolutely no question that an artificial craft is being observed. Of course, incidents like the Cape Kennedy affair have convinced a certain element within the government that the discs—"

Brady broke in. "That film we had of the Minuteman, the one that was stolen. Did ...?"

Mendelov nodded. "Yes, we arranged the theft. We felt the dangers of the film on television would outweigh the normal confusion we could associate with the story."

Ann reached over to rest her hand on Brady's arm. So many things were falling into place now.

"Let me mention a few more of our key

people," Mendelov said. "Perhaps it will allow you better to appreciate the scope of this effort. Do you know the name Adrian Ramsey? I thought you would, since he was formerly the director of British Intelligence. Ramsey is our security chief. Thomas Carmody? Um, of course. Our inside man of policy at the United Nations. He has no confidence in the UN but his eyes and ears there are invaluable. Warren Young? A top administrator. He's one of my oldest friends and is in just the right position in the Pentagon to keep us in close touch with events there. Carl Renick. You may not know him, but he's about the best civil engineer in the business. He created this base and others like it. Well. Enough of that. Now to business.

"There's an urgency in our operations I can't exaggerate. We're about to reach the most critical juncture in our plans. . . ."

CHAPTER XXIII

Brady finished his coffee and lit a cigarette,
getting his thoughts in order. He still had
unanswered questions and the beginnings of a
plan to carry through with Mendelov, but he
didn't want to reveal his hand. Not yet.

"All right," he said to the scientist, "let's lay
it out. You've got something like thirty discs,
right? Each disc mounts an energy beam and
can operate about one month—plus a week's
emergency reserve. If you're using double
crews, you can maintain a steady operation.
That is, if you don't get knocked out of the air.
And something else. If I remember correctly,
the maximum effective range of the energy
beam is about a thousand yards?"

Mendelov nodded.

"That means you haven't got any long-range capability."

Mendelov didn't react immediately. When he did, his words were guarded. "No," he said. "Nor are we in need of any weapons of long range. Our plans—"

"What *are* you going to do with the discs?" Brady broke in. "You can tear up airplanes on the ground or even missiles in their silos and you can chew up a lot of equipment and real estate. So what? Where does it get you?"

Brady watched Mendelov carefully. For the first time since he had been face to face with the scientist, he detected less than unwavering confidence. Brady was a damned good poker player, and he knew Mendelov held something less than a sure hand.

"Our strongest weapon is psychological," the scientist replied finally. "We intend to use the discs and the energy beam with full effect in selected areas. However, that's more for demonstrative purposes than anything else."

Mendelov linked his fingers and laid them across his expansive middle. Brady recognized the gesture and felt dismay. Goddamn it, he thought angrily, don't lecture. Get your feet wet. . . .

"Over the years we've created an aura of mystery with UFO's," Mendelov went on. "Officially, as you know so well, no one sanctions the concept that any UFO is an artificial device. We have staged, deliberately, many phenomena in the air to add to the confusion surrounding UFO's. Obviously we could never operate the discs without detection, so we managed the next-best thing. Let them be seen but with the assurance that officially their existence would be denied. Again, as you know better than anyone, we accomplished our purpose.

"Everyone has an opinion about UFO's. It doesn't matter if they believe or they ridicule; they have an opinion, and they've voiced their opinions to the point where most people react to UFO stories with weariness. Our campaign has given us extraordinary freedom of movement."

Brady gestured with impatience for Mendelov to get to the issue at hand.

"So"—the scientist pursed his lips—"our weapon is of a psychological nature. The psychology of demonstrating in the most exotic and dramatic fashion that the discs—which will suddenly appear and in great number—*are* real. But no one will know where they come from. No one will know if they originate on this planet or come from somewhere in space, perhaps from another galactic system. We can see to it that the issue remains clouded in doubt. The flight performance of the discs also will generate a good psychological impact, for they will *demonstrate* a performance which on the basis of even the most advanced scientific theory cannot be of terrestrial origin. This demonstration of overwhelming performance in an astronautical science far superior to anything known on earth, coupled with the energy beam . . . well, the impact will be far-reaching

317

and attended with a real and growing doubt. A mixture of doubt and of fear."

Brady was not satisfied. "All right," he said. "Then what?"

Mendelov looked carefully at the newsman. He couldn't help but notice the furrows that reflected a conflict within Brady. Was it resentment?

Keeping a weather eye on Brady, Mendelov continued. "We plan a carefully timed sequence of appearances," he said. "Each designed for its overwhelming psychological effect. The discs will appear in different parts of the world, simultaneously. They will hover over major cities. Each disc is equipped to display flashing lights in a pattern that will indicate it is unquestionably intelligent. However, the codes will remain indecipherable. Random sequences, so to speak, but in patterns which the viewers cannot possibly *know* are random. The intent is deliberately to confuse, and to breed fear. When the authorities are unable to prove what the discs *are*, people will react in a predictable manner. They will endow the discs with an alien—extraterrestrial—origin. Some will of course reject such a belief. But most people won't. They'll believe with religious fervor that the discs come from somewhere out there"—Mendelov shook his head—"heaven-sent to warn the earth of its nuclear folly."

"Where do you go from there?" Brady's skepticism was plain.

"We have planned a method of communications with—"

"You're going to *communicate*?"

"Of course."

Brady couldn't believe it. He forced his words back and waited.

"As the discs made their second appearance around the world—everything coordinated to Greenwhich mean time—they will broadcast a message. Again, the transmissions will be carried out simultaneously. This won't be evident immediately, that everything is taking place precisely at twenty-four hundred GMT, but it will be discovered soon enough to have its effect. Each disc will broadcast its message in two languages. One will be the language of the particular area or country involved. The second will be a computer language, again intended to create serious doubts by being indecipherable. We'll broadcast on at least two frequencies. One will be a main radio or television frequency and the other will be on a major communications band, such as airport towers or air-traffic control, which are always monitored and recorded. The Taggert Drive, incidentally, provides enough power to overcome any local transmitters.

"We, um, will not broadcast with human voice." Mendelov smiled briefly. "We'll feed a message directly into a computer, where the words will be rearranged in speech electronically so that a mechanical-electronic voice will be heard. The actual broadcast won't have any tones that can be identified with a human voice. Inflection, tone, timing, well, everything will be done to create the impression that this *could* be a nonhuman voice.

"Let me go back to that artificial language I mentioned. A brilliant linguist has been running a computer program for some time to create the alien language which we believe will have a pronounced psychological impact. Hentsch has worked it out to the point where the message will be decipherable only in part. This should enhance the desired impression in the governmental and scientific community that the discs may be, ah, extraterrestrial. I'm convinced the public reactions will generate widespread fright of the power of the discs. We *want* this public consternation. We want as much controversy and tearing of hair as we can possibly generate."

"You've talked about the message," Brady interjected, "but you haven't said what it is."

"I should think that would be obvious," Mendelov chided.

"Nothing's obvious," Brady retorted.

Mendelov didn't reply for a moment. "The message will be a warning and a threat," Mendelov said. "The warning will be that the entire planet is endangered by the preparations for nuclear war. Unless the nuclear weapons are struck down, unless the missiles are removed from their silos and the submarines recalled from their positions beneath the sea, unless the planes are stripped of their nuclear bombs, unless all nuclear arms are banished—"

"You'll clobber everyone in sight. That's it, isn't it?"

"Not quite so crudely, but in essence, yes," Mendelov affirmed. "We've had under consideration some overwhelming demonstration of the power of the discs. First, no defense will be made against any attack against a disc. I'm convinced of the ability of the discs to outperform any weapon—"

"Including an antimissile missile like the Spartan? Have you ever seen that thing *move*?"

"Including the Spartan." Mendelov nodded. "Demonstrating the ability to evade any interceptor aircraft or missile without destroying the attacking weapon is more effective than direct action. The very act of disdaining to strike down the attacker has the greatest possible impact because it's our intention to demonstrate clearly that the discs are invulnerable to whatever weapons may be brought against them."

"That's a tall order," Brady said.

"The discs are quite capable of fulfilling it." Mendelov's voice was edged with arrogance. "We may use the energy beams to destroy selected military installations, again to make it absolutely clear that the discs represent a science far more advanced than anything known on earth. We would want such demonstrations before the largest possible audiences —either directly or through mass-communications media. In fact, it's in this very area that you fit in."

Brady raised his eyebrows but held back his comment.

"Immediately after the appearance simultaneously of the discs throughout the world, we intend several other demonstrations to establish beyond all question the vastly superior performance of the discs. Our pilots will seek out airliners everywhere to pace them in flight and then streak away with maximum speed. We'll do the same with the bombers of several nations. Since the discs are capable even in lower atmosphere of more than seven thousand miles per hour, their maneuvers will show just how helpless the most modern aircraft are in comparison. As a next step—"

Mendelov's voice stopped abruptly. Brady's features were contorted as he struggled to hold back his words. "Apparently there's something wrong, Mr. Brady?" Mendelov said, glancing from Brady to Ann and back to the newsman.

Brady jerked himself to his feet. "Wrong?" he shouted. "No, there's nothing *wrong*, as you put it. That'd be easy. That would even be simple. *Wrong?*" He stabbed a finger at the scientist,

"Jesus *Christ*," Brady cried. "That's the most asinine, juvenile . . ." he sputtered as he sought the words.

"Cliff!"

Brady spun around to Ann. "Shut up and stay out of this," he snapped. He turned back to Mendelov.

"Do you know what you'd be doing if you followed such a plan? You'd be playing right into their hands! You'd lose everything you've achieved so far!"

While Mendelov and Ann stared, Brady struggled to recover his composure. When he spoke again, his voice carried a reflection of his inner torment. "Do you realize what you're doing?" he cried. "You're going to *threaten* them! The men who control the most awesome power this planet has ever known! Threaten *them*? Christ, man you can't frighten those people! They've lived in the shadow of the atomic cloud for so long, they have *accepted* it's inevitability. They're the merchants of megadeath, every last damned one of them. The Russians and the Americans and the Chinese and the French and the British and whoever else is going to get the bomb. And you're going to shake them up? The hell you are!" Brady roared, shaking a fist at Mendelov. "You're going to make electronic speeches and buzz airliners and tear up a few installations and you think that's going to frighten them into standing down their weapons? Don't be childish!"

Brady's tortured breathing filled the room. He was so angry he failed to see tears running down Ann's face. Strangely, Mendelov remained silent. Brady paced furiously back and forth across the room, fists clenching and unclenching. He fought to control the rage that had erupted so unexpectedly. He spun on his heel to glare at Mendelov.

"The first goddamned moment you even *attempt* communication," Brady said, his voice cold, "you're dead. Finished. *Kaput*. The first time you try to communicate, to *deal* with these people, you and this whole damned outfit have bought the farm. You'll be playing right into their hands. I know, I know," he sneered, waving his hand to forestall an interruption from Mendelov, "you don't believe they can penetrate your disguises and your camouflage. Horse shit, they can't. They wouldn't even *care*. Don't you understand that? They wouldn't even care what or who you are or wherever the hell you're from. They're tough, determined men. They control the greatest power in history, a hell of a lot more than the fancy toys you've got here. Christ, this isn't a drop in the bucket compared to what they'll throw at you. You're offering them a *challenge*? The hell you are. You're coming down to their level, where they can get a good grip on you. Psychological impact, huh? In that kind of confrontation you'd blow it all in a few hours.

"The first time you condescend—and that's the only word for it—the first time you condescend to communicate with them, you get yourself in the position of a man trying to make a deal. You're showing them you're not nearly as strong as you look. They'll grab you and this whole outfit by the balls so fast you won't know what's hit you."

Mendelov could no longer remain silent. "Aren't you forgetting the tremendous influence of public opinion? The whole world will be aroused. There'll be great pressure brought to bear—"

"For Christ's sake, Mendelov, will you come

down from your ivory tower!" Brady shouted. *"You're turning public opinion away from you!* The only time the public becomes a force is when it becomes a mob. That's the *only* time. Public opinion, my ass!"

Brady slammed his fist on the desk. "So long as you communicate," he said, "you blow every advantage you have. You become *identified*. It doesn't matter if they *know* where you're from. If you let people have a good look at you, you're going to be identified as an enemy, a threat, a danger. You're giving the men who control power the most beautiful target they could ever want. Then you'll see public opinion, all right," Brady said bitterly. "They'll scream for your blood at any cost."

Suddenly Brady stood rock still. The change was startling as he spoke slowly and carefully. "You're dealing with a species that's psychotic. Those are your own words. A species that's compulsively bent on self-destruction, right?" He waited until Mendelov nodded confirmation.

Brady pushed the issue. "A race that's cast logic into the garbage can. Haven't you said as much?" Again Mendelov nodded.

"Then how do you expect us to behave like reasoning creatures?" Brady paused to let his words sink in. "You've told me again and again that logic and reasoning have been rejected by the human race, and then you set up your plan anticipating a reaction with the very logic and reasoning you know we don't have!"

Mendelov's voice came out flat. "You're ignoring the motivating factor. You're ignoring

325

the introduction of a wholly new source of fear. You're—"

"Is what you're offering any more fearful than Hiroshima? Is it worse than the hundred-megaton bombs we already know about? What are you threatening us with that we haven't got worse a hundred times over?"

"The discs have the element, Brady, of the unknown. They're half-seen. The instense initial reaction is what we're after. The last several years of creating an atmosphere of unknown phenomena, of distrust—"

"Initial reaction, huh? What happens *after* that initial reaction? Don't you realize you'll be considered heaven-sent by the same people you're trying to manipulate?" Brady was pleading with Mendelov to grasp what he was saying. "You yourself told me the human race would rather drag the whole civilization down in flames than allow themselves to be replaced by whatever it is in the back of their skulls that's waiting to be born. Now you're offering them an honest-to-God physical enemy, a superior being from outer space. The men who run this show would go to hell in a basket before they'd bend to any such demands, no matter how much damage you do."

Brady leaned forward, with both hands on the desk. "Mendelov, you've got to understand you're presenting them with a common enemy. You're a blessing in disguise. You're giving them every reason in the world for joining as a single force to attack . . ." Brady spread his arms and took Mendelov's huge shoulders in his grasp. He shook him for emphasis. ". . . *You*. They'll go after you, us, all this," Brady said, sweeping his arm through the air, "with everything they've got.

"They'll know the discs are real enough. You're bending over backward to make certain they understand they're real. They'll also *know* you're not extraterrestrial. Not that they care. Oh, for a while there'll be panic and a lot of running off at the mouth, but they'll know you're not from somewhere out there because the space-surveillance systems will never have given them the first suspicion that you came here to the earth. So they'll eliminate the possibilities one by one until they'll know that someone right here on earth has made the quantum jump in a new drive, and then, look out.

"*You're playing all your cards face up on the table*. You don't understand that they don't need to *know* all the answers. All they need is something on which they can act. The moment they suspect there's a major base or a couple of bases for the discs, do you know what they'll do? Think about it!"

Brady paused as he watched the changing expressions on Mendelov's face. "That's right," the newsman said, almost savagely. "They'll go after every suspected base. They'll let loose their biggest guns. What have they got to lose, Mendelov? You'll have given them every excuse there is for shooting the works. They'll use those super hydrogen bombs you've been talking about and they won't give a damn one way or the other if they wipe out half the world in the process.

"And you know something else?" Brady was shouting again. *"The whole goddamned world will agree with them!"* Brady laughed harshly. "The world will agree with them, cheer them on, because you'll have given them a danger greater than their own dictators, worse than their miseries, more frightening than all their fears. An Alien. Something *different. And* superior. That makes it the most hideous, dangerous, terrifying foe of which man can conceive. Every mother's son will be doing his best to tear the heart right out of your chest.

"You wouldn't stand a chance because they've got nothing to lose."

Silence fell heavily between them. For the first time in many minutes, Brady thought of Ann. She sat stiffly in her chair, staring at Brady as if she had never seen him before. Several times she started to speak, then shook her head and pressed her lips together. Brady agreed with her in silent sympathy. What the hell was there to say? The minutes went by and Brady poured coffee. It was barely warm, but he drained the cup without hesitation. He took his seat, trying to let the anger subside.

A sad smile appeared on Brady's face as he spoke again, this time his voice at its normal level. "You know, this sort of thing has happened before." He glanced at Ann and was pleased to see the surprise on her face. "You told me about it yourself," he said to Mendelov. "During World War Two, when our top scientists petitioned the President not to use atomic bombs against Japan. Remember? They wanted us to invite the top Japanese military leaders to a barren island in the Pacific, where we would demonstrate the power of the bomb. It looked great on paper. It was just chock-full of logic. But it wasn't realistic. The hard heads in government had a fit when the scientists made their proposal. Maybe the Japanese would have told us to shove it and refused to come. Maybe they would have shown up and the bomb might have fizzled. Or maybe they'd see it explode and be unimpressed by it because they'd be watching it explode from ten miles away. Whatever the reasons, we threw out the idea and we hit Hiroshima and Negasaki with the works, and we saved a few million lives that would have been lost in the invasion set for a few months later. It was a tough decision, and it cost the lives of thousands of Japanese civilians, but it was the inevitable decision. My point is that the best scientific minds in the United States got together, just like you're doing with your associates, and they came up with something that looked beautiful but was harebrained in reality."

Brady cracked his knuckles and looked steadily at Mendelov. "Maybe that's one of the dangers of being on top. You lose perspective. I always try to think of what happened at Singapore before the Japanese clobbered the British and took the island with hardly a struggle. The whole north shore of Singapore didn't have a single gun or bulwark or even a log for protection, although there was plenty of time and manpower and the weapons for the job. You know why that happened? Because the men commanding Singapore used logic. They said that to expend all that energy in building fortifications to resist a land invasion would be bad for the morale of their troops. They were dead right, I suppose. But it was a lot worse for their morale when the Japanese chewed them to ribbons."

Brady rubbed his eyes; he seemed to be looking for a resting place for his hands. He fidgeted for a while and then grasped the armrests of his chair. "I've spent my life studying and writing about science and scientists. You awe me . . . all of you. But who could have figured two bicycle mechanics named Orville and Wilbur Wright would prove all the experts wrong? Five years after the Wrights were flying, the best brains in the world still said an airplane couldn't fly and that the whole concept was ridiculous. Scientists in 1940 said it would take five hundred years to develop an atomic bomb and the Germans even quit at the end of 1944 because the whole thing was impossible. I remember when the biggest brains in science said it was impossible to fly faster than the speed of sound. After that was out of the way, they said man would never survive in space. Now we've been around the moon, and walking on it isn't enough. We're talking about building moon bases and going to Mars."

Brady tried, wanted to reach out to Mendelov. "I suppose," he said with a heavy voice, "I forgot that you're sometimes fallible. Maybe I shouldn't be surprised. You may know man, Mendelov, but I know *men*. What you propose to do . . . You'll be setting off a nuclear avalanche and standing right smack underneath it."

Brady stared unseeing at the floor. He was aware that Ann had come to his side, was sitting on the armrest of his chair, that she had taken his hand in hers. Brady had nothing else to say for the moment. He wasn't aware of Mendelov speaking to him until the scientist repeated his name several times.

"Cliff? You have something else in mind," Mendelov said slowly.

Mendelov had never used his first name before. Brady noticed the change and yet he felt tired. He knew Mendelov had been shaken, but he no longer felt the energy to press the other man. Finally Brady looked up, nodding.

"Yes," he admitted. "I've something in mind. You told me before, when you were talking about your meeting at Princeton, that you realized that scientists would have to shed their moral and ethical principles. I thought you meant it. Perhaps you did.

"In any case, the only way you're going to prevail is to deal with the world on its own terms. I'm afraid that means you're going to have to hurt people and kill people and possibly kill a great many of them. Unless you're prepared to go that route, I advise you to quit right now."

331

"Why do we—why is it so necessary to kill people?"

"Because if you don't, you're not going to get through." Brady wanted desperately to use the right words.

"I've listened pretty carefully to you. What you've told me has sunk in. I think it will take an insane man—insane men—to save the world from itself. The cure is drastic. It's got to be drastic or it won't work. No sane man can deliberately slaughter innocent people. But if you want a world left for that next step in evolution, you've got to do a job that's nasty, vicious, and"—Brady faltered—"insane."

He locked eyes with the scientist. "Are you prepared to do that, Mendelov? You're going to have to give orders that will result in the deaths of men, women, and children. Don't answer me yet. A few hours ago I couldn't have faced this myself. But if everything you've been telling me is true, then hundreds of millions of people, maybe even most of the earth's billions, are going to die in a nuclear war we both know is inevitable. If we *don't* do something, when we've got a chance to prevent that war, our very inaction is equivalent to permitting the holocaust to take place.

"Do you understand what I'm saying? You're going to have to sacrifice perhaps a few million people to save all the others. For once, the end is going to have to justify the means. And I don't like it any better than you do."

Mendelov's sigh was almost a soft cry of pain.

"Tell me what you propose."

The newsman shook his head. "Uh-uh. Not yet. First you've got to level with me. You haven't been doing that."

For a long moment, Mendelov paused. Then the words came. "No, I haven't."

"Unless you're prepared to be completely honest with me," Brady said, "I want out."

"What do you want to know?"

"I want to know why Stanley Hoffsommer is mixed up in all this. I think—I'm sure—I've known for a long time. But I want to hear it from you. If I'm right, then you've tried in every way possible not to use what Hoffsommer and Taggert have come up with."

Mendelov's face was contorted. The effort to answer, to unlock a doomsday's secret was a struggle.

"Yes," he said hoarsely, "you're right."

CHAPTER XXIV

It began exactly at four thirty on a Sunday morning . . .

The darkness shrouding the plains of eastern Montana vanished. Thirty feet beneath the surface of the rolling plains, beneath massive steel doors, the warhead of a Minuteman missile detonated.

The explosion was impossible. The warhead was on full safe. Acceleration triggers and other devices installed to prevent such a disaster were working perfectly. The warhead couldn't explode. It did. The warhead was designed to produce an energy yield equal to the explosion of a half million tons of TNT. Full efficiency was not achieved. Scientists later estimated the blast effect as only one tenth of design. But a blast equal to fifty thousand tons of high explosives is still an awesome event. The fireball punched up and outward in all directions. A seering gout of flame ripped nearly six hundred feet above the earth. It vaporized the missile silo as well as three other silos within reach of the fireball. The earth shock wrecked another dozen facilities for launching intercontinental ballistic missiles.

The nearest town, fifteen miles distant, suffered the blinding light, a deep rumbling thunder, and smashed windows as the shock waves tore across the ground. The earth shock collapsed more than two hundred buildings. Worst of all were the panic and the radioactive fallout. The explosion, nearly three times more powerful than the blast that destroyed Hiroshima in 1945, hurled out millions of tons of radioactive dirt and debris. Before evacuation could be started in the nearest communities downwind of the explosion, a massive fall of radioactive materials had settled onto the towns.

Outstanding emergency work by local, state, and military authorities helped evacuate communities farther downwind, and prevented heavy casualties. Considering the power of the explosion, casualties were surprisingly light. Authorities expressed gratitude that the missile silo was located in a comparatively isolated area.

Scientiests were completely at a loss to explain the terrible blast. They repeated that theoretically the warhead explosion was impossible.

The news media, quick to point out that had the bomb exploded with full power the casualties would have been substantially higher, raised the question about other nuclear weapons exploding despite their being allegedly "foolproof."

Congressman James McIntyre (D. Montana) promised a fullscale investigation by the Congress, warning that atomic bombs that had been stored for long periods of time became "unsafe" and were liable to go off without warning.

The Pentagon denied that there was any further danger.

The second bomb exploded less than forty-eight hours later, at a secret military air base in southern France. On the flight line the French Air Force kept a strike force of six Mirage III bombers armed with nuclear weapons at combat readiness. Each Mirage carried a bomb with an energy yield of one hundred thousand tons.

Shortly after three o'clock in the morning, one bomb went off. There was no way to tell which bomb was faulty. The crater was 400 feet wide and nearly 250 feet deep. As in the Montana blast, the French weapon exploded with only partial power, estimated at 15 percent of design. The force of fifteen thousand tons of high explosives in a single detonation oblitered the French air base and destroyed a nearby town. Casualties in the area immediate to the air base exceeded thirty thousand dead and nearly a hundred thousand injured or suffering from radioactive poisoning. The light of the bomb was seen for hundreds of miles.

Fortunately the prevailing winds carried most of the radioactive cloud across the Mediterranean, but it was still "hot" by the time it started drifting across North Africa. Hundreds of thousands of Arabs swarmed the streets of their cities in violent, fear-ridden demonstrations against the French, sacking embassies and other offices.

Several representatives to the United Nations rose in the General Assembly to demand the dismantling of all nuclear weapons as unsafe and of terrible danger to people everywhere. Fail-safe systems had barely prevented the triggering of an attack on equivalent bases in the Soviet Union.

The French premier assured its allies and Moscow that there could be no reoccurrence of the accident

". . . interrupt this program to bring you a special news bulletin. Britain's largest nuclear plant, producing electricity for the northwestern industrial region of England, exploded today in a mystery blast that completely wrecked the atomic installation. Witnesses said the blast was like a huge bomb going off. First reports indicate that the nuclear pile, which contains plutonium, exploded without warning. This was not an atomic explosion like that of a

338

bomb. However, the force of the blast was equal to the explosion of several hundred tons of TNT. The power plant was completely destroyed. Radioactive debris was scattered by the blast throughout nearby communities. Nearly three hundred persons are dead or missing, and a mass evacuation of the area is under way...."

".... and latest reports indicate that the explosion of an atomic bomb on the edge of Moscow has the entire Soviet nation on edge, especially after the mystery blasts in the United States, France, and England. Russian officials have clamped tight censorship on all news leaving that country, but the presence of anti-missile bases with atomic warheads in the Moscow suburbs is well known. The blast wiped out an area estimated at one square mile and caused heavy damage for another mile in all directions. Casualties are reported to be heavy, as a giant new apartment complex was caught within the blast. Foreign observers estimate anywhere from twenty to fifty thousand people killed. Soviet authorities have clamped martial law on Moscow as panic swept the Russian capital in the path of a radioactive cloud drifting across the heart of the city.

"Scientists believe the explosion to be another failure of an atomic bomb similar to the mysterious explosions in Montana and southern France. The warhead exploded with only a fraction of its full power, but due to the heavy concentration of population the casualties have been high.

"The United Nations is in an uproar with demands that . . ."

"A giant explosion seen for hundreds of miles, confirmed by Japanese scientists to be nuclear in origin, devastated a Chinese city in . . ."

". . . confirmed that the fission warhead of a hydrogen bomb in a B-52 bomber stationed on Okinawa exploded shortly after midnight, only two weeks after the first accidental blast of a missile warhead in Montana. Scientists say only a miracle kept the atomic trigger from setting off the hydrogen bomb aboard the B-52. It is well known that the hydrogen bombs carried by B-52 bombers are equal in power to thirty-two millions tons of TNT, a blast that would have destroyed part of the island of Okinawa. However, only the atomic warhead exploded, with a force estimated as equal to the old . bombs used against Hiroshima and Nagasaki in the Second World War. The military air base and an adjoining community of twelve thousand people have been completely destroyed. The radioactive cloud has been drifting to the north and it is feared it will brush the southernmost island of Japan. Hysterical demonstrations and widespread panic are sweeping the major Japanese cities. At an emergency session of the United Nations today . . ."

"Two more missile atomic warheads exploded in their silos in the western part of the United States. The radioactive fallout is headed toward ..."

"There have been at least five known nuclear explosions within the Soviet Union. Reports indicate ..."

"Wild demonstrations and panic continue to rock Spain. All American strategic bombers have left that country after threats of direct attack on bases used by the United States ..."

". . . unconfirmed reports that two nuclear-powered submarines carrying Polaris missiles with atomic warheads have been lost in mystery blasts at sea."

". . . atomic energy plant built only two years ago in the Union of South Africa exploded, killing hundreds of people. Local authorities report they are helpless to control the crowds demonstrating in the streets. All atomic energy plants are being shut down immediately. It's reported that ..."

". . . top Japanese scientist said that an unexplained increase in cosmic radiation, which is sweeping the earth with high-energy neutrons, is the cause of the mysterious explosions of atomic bombs as well as at nuclear reactors for commercial power plants. To date, nuclear reactors have exploded in the United

States, England, Russia, India, South Africa, Brazil, Sweden, and Australia. Reports indicate that all remaining nuclear plants throughout the world have been closed down. Many of these were, in fact, destroyed by wild mobs who broke into the installations with . . ."

". . . and NASA reports that none of its satellites in orbit about the earth have shown any indications of unusual activity from the sun. A new radiation-detection satellite is being rushed for immediate launching from . . ."

"Atomic bombs exploded in England and France during the last weekend. There were reports of strange glowing shapes in the sky immediately before the explosions. Authorities have identified these as plasmoids, collections of energy caused by the unusual outflow of radiation from the sun reacting in the earth's atmosphere, as was recently described by Dr. Tadashi Hashimoto of Tokyo University . . ."

"The Atomic Energy Commission denies emphatically the report from Japan that increased cosmic radiation is responsible for the nuclear explosions that have been encountered in recent weeks. There still is no valid explanation for these accidents. At the same time, as a safeguard, all research reactors in the country have been shut down. The industrial facilities producing nuclear weapons are temporarily closed and are manned only by caretaker staffs.

The AEC wishes to reassure the American public, and all the peoples of the free world, that the situations is under control, and that . . ."

"You don't trust them mothers, do you? Do you? Lissen t'me, all you people! Lissen to what I say to you! Them's white man's bombs! Them ain't been no accidental explosions! Accidental nutthin! You know what's gonna happen next? Do you know? Next time there's gonna be another accident and one of them white man's bombs is gonna land right in the middle of where we all live! You hear what I'm saying? Are we just gonna lay back and wait to be wiped out like dogs? Are we dogs or are we black people? I say we don't wait no more! I say we tear down this fence and we burn them goddamned airplanes what's carrying them bombs! I say burn them! You ready? You ready? You got your guns and dynamite and Molotov cocktails? Let's go! Go, go, go!"

". . . unconfirmed but reliable reports that two more atomic bombs have exploded somewhere within the Soviet Union."

". . . don't care *what* your goddamned scientists tell you! General, I'm telling you my men have been seeing these discs, or saucers, or whatever they are. They've been *seeing* them. There's something way out of line—"

"Colonel, shut *up*. Jesus, all we need now is a damned UFO flap on our hands! Do you realize that mobs have been storming SAC bases throughout the country? That bands of people are roaming through the hills trying to pour gasoline down missile silos and set them afire? And you come in here with harebrained stories about flying saucers... !"

". . . another nuclear explosion, this time from Alaska. Reports indicate the United States and the Soviet governments are near accord on an agreement to dismantle all nuclear weapons, and that the other atomic powers will follow suit. Following Red China's refusal to join in any international agreement, mobs sacked the government buildings in Peking and the country stands on the edge of revolt. The Russians have moved up armored divisions along the Chinese border. The United States is reported to have assured Moscow that if it becomes necessary to..."

". . . riots sweeping the major cities of almost every nation in the world. Martial law has been imposed throughout the Soviet Union, and in this country the National Guard and Army Reserves have taken up positions surrounding military airfields, missile launching sites, and nuclear submarine bases. Violent clashes are being reported as an aroused and frightened citizenry tries to remove nuclear weapons from..."

". . . so far the world has seen more than ninety atomic explosions in less than four weeks. Radioactive fallout is spreading rapidly and scientists estimate many millions are being affected. No one knows when the next bomb will explode or . . ."

"But we've got to put the blame on *somebody!* For years all our nuclear weapons have been absolutely safe. Then, suddenly, just like *that,* they start blowing up all around us. Not only us but everyone else. Maybe it *is* those damned flying saucers!"

"Are you out of your mind? You heard that scientist, that Professor Walton, from the University of Colorado. He's been studying UFO's for more than twenty years, and for all that time this country has insisted, absolutely and emphatically, that there isn't a damn thing about UFO's that's real. Now, all of a sudden, you're going to blame flying saucers for those bomb explosions! I tell you you've lost your marbles!"

"All right, all *right!* So we can't say anything to the public. But what if those discs *are real?* There's been enough of them seen the last—"

"Discs? You mean glowing shapes, don't you? *Glowing.* They're plasmas and corona discharges."

"Maybe they are and then again maybe they ain't. What do we do if they *are* real? Goddamn it, we've got to do *something.*"

"Okay. I'll buy your argument, but only behind closed doors. Not one lousy word gets out about this. I want full security right on down

345

the line. Send out these orders. All fighters with guns and missiles hot. Anytime anything shows up in the sky, no matter what, I want it identified. Immediately. If we can't identify it, shoot it down. And tell the pilots if they can't shoot it down they're to ram..."

CHAPTER XXV

The city had been thrust up from hell. All electrical power was out. Yet light heaved and tumbled everywhere, the deep orange and flickering crimson of flame diffusing the boiling clouds of dust and smoke, tossed every which way by a gusty and capricious wind. Cliff Brady and Ann Dallas pushed forward, handkerchiefs pressed against their faces, staring wide-eyed at the maelstrom about them. The bomb had exploded on the outskirts of Lincoln, Nebraska, nearly twenty hours before. It hadn't been one of the larger weapons. This time the warhead of an antimissile rocket had detonated. The fireball ripped through the earth, racked the ground with a hammering earthquake shock, and then sent the shock wave punching along one edge of the city, pulverizing buildings and other structures as it heaved through the stunned metropolis. In its wake of broken gas mains and shorted electrical systems and overturned stoves, fire crawled into being. No single huge blaze, but tens of thousands of small fires. Unchecked for lack of water, the flames fed eagerly on the twisted and tossed debris of the shock wave until fully one third of the city lay awash in a sea of growing flame.

Strangely enough, the city enjoyed a measure of fortune. The prevailing winds that night blew away from the main section of town, away from the more heavily populated areas. The winds snatched at the angry cloud mushrooming from the earth, massive and pregnant with intensively radioactive debris; snatched and pushed and bulled the cloud away from the fearful people, sending the greater part of the lethal fallout into the open countryside. Fifty thousand human beings owed their lives to that incident of wind that night.

None of them, in the hours following the ripping explosion, were aware of their "good fortune." None of them understood that a powerful warhead had exploded with only a small fraction of its power. Measurements are relative. The force of ten thousand tons of high explosives is on the low end of the nuclear-blast scale. But it is on the higher end of hell for those within the embrace of the savage shock wave.

Brady and Ann were in Omaha when the bomb explosion knifed along the edge of Lincoln. Minutes later, they knew there had been a terrible blast in the Nebraska capital. They were in the best place to receive such news— just outside Omaha, at headquarters of the Strategic Air Command. For several weeks Brady, Ann always with him, had been traveling at a nonstop pace throughout the country. Milt Parrish at World Press still didn't fathom the telephone call from Drew Wilkinson to return Brady to the WP staff. He didn't care, Parrish was still bent out of shape from his last encounter with Brady, and he took pleasure in welcoming Cliff back to the fold. When the bombs started exploding in the United States and around the world, Cliff was worth his weight in any ten men. The stories he filed during his rapid trips to the explosion sites were the best in the business. With Ann at his side, Brady covered the nation from coast to coast, seeking not only the effects of the weapons tearing up cities and countryside, but especially the reactions of people. He wanted the public pulse beat and he sought out the official reactions. Not their statements. To hell with the words. He wanted the taste and the shock and the smell of it; he wanted to be right in the middle of it. He got what he sought: the dust and the stink of fear and the aftermath.

But never this close. Brady didn't waste a moment. He and the other newsmen got the word from a tight-lipped SAC officer. His words were cryptic, as impersonal as he could make them. Brady listened to the words and concentrated on the man's eyes, on his facial expression. He found what he wanted. The unspoken questions of the man. The thought, betrayed in his eyes. Where would the next bomb go off? Who was next? What city might die tomorrow? Brady observed and made his notes and then he was asking hard questions about the latest metropolian victim. He learned that the winds were pushing the radioactive cloud to the northwest of Lincoln. They could take a helicopter to the east of the stricken city, they could approach from either the east or the southeast and they'd be upwind of the lethal, falling cloud. The closer their approach to the city—delayed nearly fourteen hours by martial law clamped on the area, until they received permission to move into a city from which thousands were fleeing in panic—the greater reality came home to them. They saw the orange glow from miles away. With each decreasing mile the flames reached higher until visual definition emerged from the glow. Finally they were so close the super-heated air smacked and chopped angrily at the helicopter and the pilot refused to go any closer. He brought the machine to ground as near as he dared. Brady and Ann continued on foot, their official passes taking them through the police barricades, the frightened and angry officials who thought they were crazy for wanting to move into hell.

They pushed their way forward no more than a mile, their path blocked by wreckage-strewn streets, abandoned automobiles, people with eyes wide and shocked. Every so often they encountered disaster forces at work, fire engines for the most part helpless, the water mains severed by the rolling earth shock of many hours before. Yet the municipal services, the police and firemen and the public-works crews, were doing their best. Which meant to save as many lives as possible, to render any vehicle as a makeshift ambulance or an evacuation vehicle. Anything to get the people away from the fires roaring out of control, spreading steadily, feeding easily on the masses of wreckage that lay everywhere.

A street sign hung awkwardly, the metal plate reading "Jackson Avenue" hanging askew. All about them smoke and dust whirled and surged like a sandstorm from a Daliesque painting of hell. Flame crackled explosively as it chewed through wreckage. Buildings collapsed in fiery cascades. Ann's ears hurt from the constant pounding of fire-noise, from sirens screaming helplessly, from shouts and cries. People emerged as ghostly wraiths from the smoke shifting before the wind. At times the clouds were so thick flame would spear a deep shaft through which blazing houses and automobiles could be seen like volcanic pits.

Ann stumbled, gasping for air, and Brady clutched her arm, kept her from falling. "Cliff . . . I—I can't take . . ." more coughing . . . "this can't . . ." Her voice trailed off in a new spasm. Brady knew they had to get out. They weren't doing anyone any good, and now their own lives were endangered. He supported Ann and they turned to retrace their steps. For a moment fear swept through him as the billowing smoke obscured the street. Then he saw the searchlights, one after the other, a serried row pointing straight up, showing the evacuees the route to safety. One street, cleared by frantic workers to provide an avenue of retreat, with every light they could commandeer from the fire engines and the police vehicles, vertically beckoning fingers. The heat-laden smoke burned Cliff's eyes and fouled his lungs and he thought they might have come too far. Sparks and firebrands whirled through the air, great glowing eyes mocking him, streaking the flame-splashed darkness.

The thought wouldn't leave him. This was their answer, their solution to the fear for tomorrow. *This?* He stared gaunt-eyed around him, helping Ann, who fought off another spasm of coughing, stumbling together, leaving the fires. *This was their solution? This was the answer? This hell they had visited on people . . . Good God!* He told himself again and again that this *had* to be the right way, that what they endured about them would be a million times worse if ever the world plunged into full-scale war. He repeated the words to himself, over and over and over. They failed to dent the rising horror, the sick helplessness that refused to leave him. For he, Cliff Brady, he and the others, Mendelov and all the rest, were responsible for this hell. Couldn't there have been another way? Wasn't there some manner to avoid suicide without *this?* They wound their way through wreckage, past bodies strewn in the streets, the broken glass crunching beneath their feet. A firebrand spun out of the air and in seconds a tiny spark of flame showed in Ann's hair. Brady cried out and thrust his hands against that tiny fire and his heart hammered within his chest.

"Come on!" he shouted. "Faster! We may be cut off!" He had to shout to be heard, and he moved more quickly now, half dragging Ann with him. Ahead of them a light jabbed through the boiling smoke, a mindless Cyclops that showed the path to safety. Then there were people all about them. They looked up and saw firemen, grimy, tired, listening to the fire-truck radio bellowing instructions.

"*Fall back . . . fall back . . . all units . . . fall back immediately to Foster Boulevard . . . regroup . . . acknowledge and . . .*"

"They're all getting out," he said to Ann, unnecessarily, wanting to hear his voice, wanting to talk with her. She nodded, swallowing the pain. Brady turned down the street, along the firelimned avenue, people moving like cloaked figures all about them in the new-flowing tide of complete evacuation. The wind had found new strength and the heat rolled over them in successive waves. Brady took off his jacket and placed it over Ann, using it as a hood to protect her against heat and swirling sparks. They had gone only two blocks when a man rushed into their midst. "The children! For God's sake, help me! Someone help me!" he cried. They stared at him until he pointed to what remained of a house, though which flames crackled like tributaries seeking a common flow. "My children!" he shouted hoarsely. "Trapped! I've got to get them . . ." Brady and several other men ran to the wreckage, coming up short as fire leaped upward. No one could be alive in there! Then two others were pulling at wooden beams, heaving wreckage, digging with cut and bleeding hands. Brady joined them, working frantically. He heard words of a collapsed floor, children in the basement. He thought he could hear a thin scream of fear, a keening sound through the fire. The flames crackled explosively, throwing them back. Brady lost sense of time. He thought he saw a dress, a print, beneath tumbled wreckage and he hurled himself at the debris, unknowingly cutting his hands. His world resolved into saving a life, into the redemption he might find here and now. Arms pulled at him, tried to drag him away. "No use!" cried a voice. "It's no use! We're too late, too late. . . ." Brady jerked himself free, shouting incoherently, wincing from the heat and the pain stabbing through his arms. He remembered only the sight of a small body, and somehow he was there, shouldering aside the wreckage, and he had the frail, unmoving form in his arms, stumbling, lurching back to the street, Ann guiding him, walking as quickly as he could, cradling the small girl, trying to protect her. He walked forever, his sense of time numbed, his awareness blunted. He knew only that he had saved the child, saved her, saved her. . . .

"Oh, my God."

She whispered the words.

Someone, a white coat, helping arms took the child from Brady. Ann watched, disbelieving, as the doctor shook his head slowly.

"Oh, my God."

The little girl was dead.

The last thin line cracked.

Brady wept.

Ann cradled his head in her arms as it spilled from Brady, racking him, deep shuddering sobs. She held him to her breast and he cried.

There was nothing else she could do.

"Physically he'll be all right," the doctor said. "But he's not trying. I mean, his body is responding and he's strong. There's no concern there." He looked up and met Ann's gaze. "But there's something else. . . ." He shrugged; they both knew the rest.

Ann nodded.

"What?"

Ann looked up with a thin, humorless smile. "Nothing, Doctor. Is there anything else I can do?"

"No, no. Just be sure he has his medicine at the times I've prescribed. Here's my number. Call me if you need me."

"You're very kind."

"I can afford to be," he said with a faint

tone of mocking himself. "His office said . . . well . . ." He shrugged again. "Anything he needs, they said."

Except, she thought, what he needs the most.

She was right. Their intimate exposure to the hell racking so many of the nation's cities had been the start of it. Repetition, horror piled upon horror, the knowledge that hundreds of thousands of human beings, helpless and innocent, had been killed, millions more injured greviously . . . all this, the inescapable, driving fact that he was one of the men responsible for the agony and the terror and the deaths, shattered the certainty of his convictions. It was not a thing of suddenness. Each successive exposure to what they had wrought chiseled deeper into the granite of his confidences, his beliefs that this was the only way. Until, finally, the granite showed the first cracks, the pieces fell willy-nilly about him, and Brady began to accept the torment of the victims as his own. As self-punishment.

The dead girl broke him. Even that, Ann knew, would have been but a passing agony. But not the hypocrisy of what happened several days later.

Another newsman had seen Brady emerge from the flame-illumined street, seen Brady stumbling, weary and cut and burned himself, carrying the little girl. It was a personal facet of a story of mass horror, and the newsman seized upon the opportunity. It made the wire services. It made Brady one of the heroes.

Cliff Brady wanted personally to kill the

man who had written the story. Ann watched him, speechless with rage, as he read of his "heroic rescue" of the child. Nothing was said in the story about the girl's being dead.

It was the last straw.

"That was the moment," she later told Vadim Mendelov, "when Cliff learned to hate himself."

For more than a month, always together, so that she knew the fiber of the emotions tormenting him, they had been witness to and part of violence, naked fear, vast suffering. And death. For weeks she and Cliff poured out to one another their feelings. They both knew they sought in and through their words the self-justification that this was the only way. Survival of the race depended upon what they might do, on the measure of success they might all achieve.

They moved through a planet different than what they had always known. A world made up of many nations, but which they now saw as a single entity, struggling through agony. The world endured the terror of bombs exploding without warning, of death always present or threatening. Only they knew why this was happening, why it was needed. But they could tell only themselves and in the logic of words between them they sought to pacify their consciences.

"It's like the pain of birth." Ann voiced her thoughts to Cliff Brady. "That's what it is to me. Pain that's necessary, that's birth, or"—she looked up, hoping he could share her thoughts more than the words for which she groped—"or rebirth. I don't know," she whispered. "I keep telling myself over and over that this is the only way." She shuddered. "But then I remember and . . ." Her words trailed away.

Yet, if not directly, then in ways similar or parallel, people everywhere, without knowing what Ann knew, shared her thoughts. They were letting it soak through their consciousness. The exploding bombs were giving the world a grim forestaste of what the threatened nuclear cataclysm would be like intensified thousands of times. Men who could think clearly, no matter where they might live on the globe, struggled to imagine the effects of thermonuclear bombs going off at full power.

Hiroshima was twenty kilotons.

Some bombs were detonating at a hundred kilotons.

The bombs waiting in the wings for World War III were set to explode with energy yields in the hundreds of millions of tons of high explosives.

It didn't take a scientist to realize that the few craters several hundred feet wide could just as easily be fifteen miles from one radioactive edge to the other. Mendelov's hopes were coming to pass. The European peoples, most of them packed even more closely together than the city populations of the United States, had rallied to the cause. Not of world peace, that nebulous goal always beyond men, but of self-preservation. There was a demand for the immediate destruction of nuclear-weapons stockpiles and emplacements that toppled governments and swept outward in the form of an irresistible tide. In the United States they were slower to react but no less severe in that reaction when finally it ripped free of its restraints.

The toll of cities grew. Lincoln, Miami, St. Louis, Pittsburgh, Los Angeles, Seattle, Oklahoma City, Dayton, Buffalo, Charlotte, Fort Worth . . . to say nothing of the bombs that went off in open countryside, in missile silos, aboard submarines, at air bases scattered throughout the nation. San Diego felt a bomb gut its innards and then, in the aftermath of a night without wind, the scattered flames fed greedily on the debris of the city and joined into a dreaded firestorm. It was the aftermath of Hamburg and Hiroshima all over again. A single fire monster nearly three miles high that howled with the throats of a million demons. The fire was visible for over a hundred miles. It burned beyond all control through the night. By ash-choked dawn more than 110,000 human beings had been consumed.

The public wanted, demanded, screamed for only one response: Dismantle every nuclear device and installation. Not next week. Not tomorrow. *Now*. Don't waste a moment, a second. Brady and Ann had seen the mobs, mixed with them, had been carried along in the smell of fear and the howls for the blood of those charged with guarding the now-dreaded nuclear machinery. The mobs stormed military installations and defending soldiers refused to fire on the throngs that often included their own families and friends. Brady and Ann watched the mobs blowing up and burning airplanes and pouring flaming oil and gasoline into and over and around anything involved with nuclear weapons.

The fear of stripping the nation of nuclear defenses had been banished. The danger of leaving the United States open to nuclear assault from her possible enemies was a tenet no longer to be endured. The bombs were exploding everywhere. No one lay in danger from anyone else. They were *all* endangered.

By the bombs right in their own backyards.

The world was stripping itself of its means to commit nuclear suicide.

But all Cliff Brady could see was a dead child in his arms.

The summons to meet with the others in Arizona came as a blessing. With Ann by his side, Brady stared through a wide picture window at the tall pines stretching across the hills and mountain slopes. His face reflected none of the serenity of the Flagstaff countryside. Brady's eyes had become sunken, his face gaunt and etched with his inner suffering. He and Ann had arrived early and waited for Vadim Mendelov and the others.

Brady knew nothing of someone else with them until he felt the hand on his shoulder. He turned to face Dr. Stanley Hoffsommer. For a long moment the two men gripped hands, stared unblinkingly at one another. Hoffsommer's face was the same, his eyes untroubled. The scientist saw within Brady what he had known himself a long time before. But he had forced from active memory the camps in Europe, and he refused now, as he had all these years, to heed the call of the suffering he had himself known behind the high barbed wire. . . .

The last time Brady and Ann had seen the weapons scientist was in Condor, deep within the caverns of the South American mountain. Brady had been told they would all be here for this meeting. No; not all. Robert Kroot was dead, victim not of a bomb explosion but of wild panic that had exploded through his neighborhood.

Sometimes you paid the price close at home.

They gathered in the conference room, uncomfortable at first with one another, troubled by what they had all seen, what they knew, what had stemmed from the power they wielded. Dr. Mendelov ill concealed his shock at Brady's appearance. The newsman, whom Mendelov had known as a volatile, energetic individual, seemed withdrawn, embittered. At the first opportunity he drew Ann aside. She told him what had happened.

The huge man nodded slowly. "I understand," he said heavily. "I wish I could say something, but . . ." She took his hand in answer. He squeezed hers in return and left to take his seat. She wondered if Cliff noticed

361

what had happened to Mendelov, if he realized how loosely the man's clothes hung on his big frame, how much weight he had lost.

Brady sat in silence. Frazer Blackburn opened the meeting with a question thrown to the group.

"It's been more than a month," he said slowly. "Has anything happened? I mean, do any fingers point to us?"

Dr. Hoffsommer shook his head slowly, a pleased smile on his face. His sigh was audible throughout the room. "No," he said at last. "We're still entirely in the clear. They're mystified, of course," he added with a chuckle, "but immediate events have trampled under the authorities. They haven't time to do anything but attend to the task at hand. Dismantle the bombs. That is the outcry everywhere. People are demanding protection from the explosions. It is like living under an overhanging rock. No one knows when the avalanche will start and everyone is afraid to move." Hoffsommer paused to light his pipe. In the midst of a world torn and frightened, he was a stark contrast of calm and assurance. No one spoke, no one wanted to interrupt. He took his time, bringing the pipe to life slowly.

"The important thing," he continued, "is that no one relates the explosions to the discs. Not directly, that is. Oh, some people are suspicious, of course," he said, gesturing with the pipe. "There's a group within the Air Force, in this country, I mean, that's convined the discs must be involved. Other people, in Europe, feel

362

the same way. But their policy isn't official. They haven't any idea of how the relationship would exist. They have even less of an idea of where the discs might come from. And since, despite their vociferous convictions, they lack proof . . ." Hoffsommer shrugged.

"Something else has happened in our favor."

Heads turned to Vadim Mendelov. The huge man was evidently pleased, but nothing could bring him to smile. His plans were successful beyond his wildest dreams. But the deaths of millions, with millions more maimed and suffering the effects of injuries and the long-term effects yet to come from radioactive exposure had suppressed within Mendelov any jubilation. He glanced at Brady, who met his gaze with almost a vacant stare. Troubled by the newsman's detachment, Vadim Mendelov forced himself to the issue at hand. "The fact that the discs were sighted by so many people," he went on, "has brought about something we apparently failed to anticipate. Brady"—he nodded to the newsman—"has seen the effects. Many people believe the sightings represent some form of divine intervention in the affairs of man. Remarkable," the scientist mused aloud. He turned his gaze to Brady. For a moment he frowned, questioning the wisdom of trying to evoke a response. "Your suggestion," he said after the pause, "certainly bore its fruit."

For a long moment Brady's eyes kept their vacancy. Finally he nodded his acknowledment. One of the ideas he had proposed was deliberately to increase the leakage of energy from the discs. It resultd in a powerful ionization effect that caused the discs to glow brightly. People no longer saw a clearly defined artificial object, a mechanical device. They saw what they had often observed when plasmoids or corona discharges were present. A glowing shape in the sky. Scientists were convinced they *were* plasma or some other electrical effect in the atmosphere.

Mendelov picked up the conversation after waiting for Brady to speak. "It's all worked out as we hoped," the scientist continued. "They know nothing of the true nature of the discs and they're completely unaware, of course, of the Taggert Drive. Neither do they know anything of the energy beam and even less—that's a paradox, isn't it? Forgive me," he said with the same humorless smile. "Well, obviously, then, they know nothing of the modification made to the energy beam."

They accepted his words without comment. The pain endured by Mendelov, one of the most gentle of men, they knew, showed clearly. He held himself more responsible than any one for the terrible casualties. Brady, wrapped in his own bitterness, had forced the issue, had demanded that Mendelov face squarely what Dr. Hoffsommer and Taggert had developed— which Mendelov had refused to countenance for use.

They made a further modification to the Taggert Drive. Instead of a destructive beam, the Drive was altered to project a loose stream of nuclear particles. Included within that invisible energy stream was a high proportion of neutrons. That would have meant little to them except for Hoffsommer's intimate knowledge of nuclear weapons.

"The nuclear devices," Hoffsommer had related to them, "operate on the implosion principle. Essentially, each bomb's energy source, its plutonium, is kept porous. The bombs contain different ingredients, such as gold cones, to soak up stray neutrons and prevent an accidental explosion. To set off the bomb you must implode, squeeze together, the plutonium, so that it forms a dense mass." Hoffsommer sketched rapidly the mechanism of the bomb as he talked. "Now, if we can generate a flood of neutrons from an outside source—the modified Taggert Drive, operating as an energy stream, so to speak—we can create what you might call an accidental explosion." Hoffsommer tapped the sketches with his pencil. "See what happens here? The plutonium remains porous, but we introduce so many neutrons that the fission process begins. We will get a partial explosion. The bomb, in other words, goes off with only a fraction of its designed power. But," he added significantly, "it goes off."

The modified beam produced a stream of nuclear particles no more visible to the eye than X rays. But they penetrated the thick bomb casings just as easily as X rays flash through the human body. Their effect on the plutonium was disastrous. Partial fission took place.

A bomb with a designed energy yield of one million tons of TNT went off with only a small fraction of its potential.

Only a small fraction.

But a blast of one hundred thousand tons of high explosives was still five times more powerful than the bomb that wiped out six square miles of Hiroshima and killed one hundred thousand human beings.

This was the weapon from which Vadim Mendelov had recoiled. Brady argued it was the only course on which they might embark with any hope for success.

They could detonate nuclear weapons anywhere they were found.

The only destruction they would cause would be from existing weapons wherever they were located and set off.

The modified energy stream was effective over a range of several miles. Only they knew that a glowing shape in the sky, regarded by scientists as a natural phenomenon, a plasmoid, could bring on the "accidental" explosion of nuclear weapons.

The pattern was clear. Atomic bombs throughout the world exploded in mysterious, "impossible" blasts at fractional power. Even nuclear reactors could be made so "hot" from the flow of neutrons that they blew themselves apart.

From one end of the world to the other the bombs exploded. Completely "safe" reactors erupted in localized but violent blasts.

No one trusted the safety of the bombs or the reactors.

Next time the bombs might go off with full power.

One hydrogen bomb could explode with a force equal to eighty or a hundred million tons of high explosives.

There were air bases and storage depots throughout the United States, where anywhere from a dozen to one hundred hydrogn bombs were kept at readiness.

It was no secret that at certain bomb-storage sites the total energy contained within a few square miles was equal to *trillions* of tons of explosive force.

The bombs could explode. At any moment. Without warning.

One such blast would wipe out virtually an entire state.

The danger of nuclear war was forgotten.

Dozens of cities throughout the world counted their dead, feared their fallout, gathered in sorrow. The specter of nuclear disaster, perhaps annihilation from existing stockpiles and weapons emplacements, was immediate.

Scientists warned that the radioactive fallout from the accidental explosions of bomb-storage centers could poison the planet.

Millions of people were already dead or living dead from the nuclear blasts and the subsequent fallout.

No one knew who would be next.

A city thirty or forty miles distant from an

air base with a hundred hydrogen bombs was as good as dead.

Cities hundreds, even a thousand miles downwind of such an explosion, and all the countryside between, and for miles to each side of the death zone, would be blanketed with radioactivity so intense it would be lethal for months afterward.

No one knew who would be next.

The specter of nuclear death crawled into every home, every office, every bedroom. It hung, invisible but terribly real, over cities and open countryside. It was there in the shadowy fear of night and in the morning light it remained.

No one knew who would be next.

Throughout the world people reacted as they could only react. Impelled by fear, compelled by survival, they rioted. They stormed through their cities, attacked military installations, searched in frenzy for bombs to destroy.

They had nothing to lose. They were right.

No one knew who would be next.

At precisely that moment, when the fear, the tension, and the violence reached its peak, Vadim Mendelov ordered the discs out of sight. They were sealed off from the world. They ceased to exist. Nothing moved into or from the secret Condor base in the South American jungle.

The UFO reports, the strange glowing plasmas, had plagued governments throughout the world. Almost always they were dismissed because of the immediacy of the exploding bombs and their effects and the horror of still more weapons going off. Yet, in the struggle for political survival, nothing could be overlooked. Every attempt was made to identify the glowing shapes that moved in such ghostly fashion through dark and stormy nights.

But there were no discs to be found. There were sun dogs and meteors, plasmoids and corona discharges, reflectional dispersion and inversion layers, balloons and planets.

But no discs.

The pressures mounted to rebellion, to open revolution. The United States and the Soviet Union assured the world they were standing down their nuclear arms. They had no choice. Even without terrified and rebellious populaces there was still the constant, impersonal, stark danger that more and more bombs would explode. Around the world the bombs were removed from planes and missile silos and submarines. The bombs were dismantled, broken down.

Few people believed the nuclear powers could be trusted.

It didn't matter.

The nuclear powers dared not trust their own weapons not to destroy them.

Delegates to the United Nations shouted for international inspection teams. The United States and the Soviet Union agreed. Why not? Neither retained their nuclear warheads. Their decisions had nothing to do with world peace. It was strictly a matter of survival, and in mutual survival they could afford to be magnanimous with one another.

Red China stated flatly it would not tolerate inspection teams. The American and Soviet governments announced immediately that unless full inspection was permitted anywhere within Red China, a massive assault would be opened at once against that country, using conventional weapons.

And biological agents.

The Chinese said they would think it over. They were given twenty-four hours.

Thus the conspirators met, finally, in the secret offices of Blackburn Aero in Flagstaff. Vadim Mendelov, Stanley Hoffsommer, Kenneth Taggert, Dianne Sims, Frazer Blackburn, Cliff Brady, Ann Dallas. Several of the others, including Drew Wilkinson, were needed elsewhere.

They left empty the chair for Robert Kroot.

They reviewed what had happened, they brought themselves to the immediate moment. They had achieved success beyond what they had dared to hope. They knew also they lacked the final success they needed. Time . . .

Finally, Vadim Mendelov spoke for them. He glanced at each face, studied the eyes of the other person. For a long moment he looked at Cliff Brady, who looked back. Uncaring. Mendelov closed his eyes, pushed aside the sorrow. "For the moment we have gone as far as we dare." His words rolled slowly, wearily, from him. "The discs must remain hidden. But it is possible, just possible, that we have succeeded. If so, then we've managed to derail the engine of nuclear destruction for this world. Those who would fight to the death of everyone else now have something to fear even more than nuclear attack from one another."

Kenneth Taggert studied his folded hands. He looked up at Mendelov. "What do we have now?"

The scientist closed his eyes. He did not open them when he answered the question.

"We wait."

But there's no waiting for him. There's no time to lose. Cliff is drowning himself in bitterness and self-hatred. He keeps seeing that little girl and he blames himself for her and all the others. If I could only reach him, if I could only let him know that all this has been worth it, the pain and the agony and the dying. They're getting rid of the bombs everywhere. There's a sense of relief sweeping the whole planet. It's as though we all stood at the edge of the cliff and were stopped only at the last moment before going over.

Ann clasped Cliff's hand with a firm, steady pressure. At times he acknowledged her presence. Most of the time he seemed not to notice. She glanced through the window at the trees, the distant hills. *There are so many ways to die*, she thought. *A child died in his arms, and Cliff died inside himself.*

She took a deep breath. Maybe she could still reach him, love him, bring him back.

Let the others save the world.

Her world was the man beside her.

THE MANITOU

"Like some mind-gripping drug, it has the uncanny ability to seize you and hold you firmly in its clutches from the moment you begin until you drop the book from your trembling fingers after you have finally finished the last page."

—Bernhardt J. Hurwood

Misquamacus—An American Indian sorcerer. In the seventeenth century he had sworn to wreak a violent vengeance upon the callous, conquering White Man. This was just before he died, over four hundred years ago. Now he has found an abominable way to return, the perfect birth for his revenge.

Karen Tandy—A slim, delicate, auburn-haired girl with an impish face. She has a troublesome tumor on the back of her neck, a tumor that no doctor in New York City can explain. It seems to be moving, growing, developing—almost as if it were alive! She is the victim

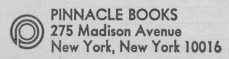

THE MANITOU
GRAHAM MASTERTON

A Pinnacle Book
P982 $1.75

If you can't find this book at your local bookstore, simply send the cover price, plus 25¢ for postage and handling to:

PINNACLE BOOKS
275 Madison Avenue
New York, New York 10016

PASSION'S DISCOVERY

"You still have not learned your lesson," Brian gritted. Before she could move to escape him, he had gripped her shoulder. "How old are you?" he demanded. With his other hand, he flipped up the hem of her scarlet smock. His fingers hooked in the edge of the breastbinder and snagged it downward. Ignoring Gillian's cry of rage, he stared at the full shapely mounds that burst free.

Twisting fearfully in his grasp, Gillian sought ineffectually to cover herself from his appraisal.

"No girl, surely," he muttered as he beheld her pale smooth skin that seemed too velvety to be real. Even as he gazed, heated blood surged through his body. As one mesmerized, he put out his hand, his fingers trembling slightly.

Her body was all too real. Beneath his fingertips the warm flesh pulsed. His eyes flew to her agonized face. Her lips parted as she gasped for air. "Oh, no," she whispered. "Oh, no."

"Beautiful," the knight sighed. The harsh man who coldly sought to inspect her body because he was accustomed to being obeyed was gone. He could not even remember why he had taken her again in his arms. He only knew the beauty of her body.

Beyond resistance, Gillian found herself responding wildly to his nearness and moaned slightly. Her pliancy acted as a command to him. His free hand smoothed the folds of the smock back over her shoulders baring her to the waist . . .

EXCITING BESTSELLERS FROM ZEBRA

HEIRLOOM (1200, $3.95)
by Eleanora Brownleigh
The surge of desire Thea felt for Charles was powerful enough to convince her that, even though they were strangers and their marriage was a fake, fate was playing a most subtle trick on them both: Were they on a mission for President Teddy Roosevelt—or on a crusade to realize their own passionate desire?

A WOMAN OF THE CENTURY (1409, $3.95)
by Eleanora Brownleigh
At a time when women were being forced into marriage, Alicia Turner had achieved a difficult and successful career as a doctor. Wealthy, sensuous, beautiful, ambitious and determined—Alicia was every man's challenge and dream. Yet, try as they might, no man was able to capture her heart—until she met Henry Thorpe, who was as unattainable as she!

PASSION'S REIGN (1177, $3.95)
by Karen Harper
Golden-haired Mary Bullen was wealthy, lovely and refined—and lusty King Henry VIII's prize gem! But her passion for the handsome Lord William Stafford put her at odds with the Royal Court. Mary and Stafford lived by a lovers' vow: one day they would be ruled by only the crown of PASSION'S REIGN.

LOVESTONE (1202, $3.50)
by Deanna James
After just one night of torrid passion and tender need, the dark-haired, rugged lord could not deny that Moira, with her precious beauty, was born to be a princess. But how could he grant her freedom when he himself was a prisoner of her love?

Available wherever paperbacks are sold, or order direct from the Publisher. Send cover price plus 50¢ per copy for mailing and handling to Zebra Books, 475 Park Avenue South, New York, N.Y. 10016. DO NOT SEND CASH.

LOVESPELL

BY
DEANA
JAMES

ZEBRA BOOKS
KENSINGTON PUBLISHING CORP.

ZEBRA BOOKS

are published by

Kensington Publishing Corp.
475 Park Avenue South
New York, N.Y. 10016

First printing: August, 1984

Printed in the United States of America

To Jim
Forever as before—
Today itself's too late!

Chapter One

Sir Brian de Trenanay lurched from the saddle of his destrier and stumbled blindly to the foot of a tree. Where his hand clutched it, the rough bark was stained red with blood. The slash below the ribs on his left side had opened despite the surgeon's stitching. Cursing flatly between clenched teeth, he lowered himself heavily to the ground. The shades of foliage in the York landscape blended into one acid green as he set his teeth and stared dizzily around him.

Damn that Saxon squire!

The coarse wool of his tunic absorbed the blood in an ever-widening circular stain. With shaking fingers Brian unbuckled the heavy leather belt around his lean hips and let it slip to the ground. Fumbling the edge of the garment upward, he exposed the jagged wound across his flank.

7

He cursed again as he pleated the material into a triple thickness and pressed it tightly against the wound. The foul words ended in an agonized groan. With leaden fingers he pulled the belt together across his lean middle and buckled it tightly.

The effort plus the pain caused by the compression of the swollen wound turned the world around him into a hazy, swirling fog. His head lolled back against the tree; his eyes closed.

The destrier continued to crop the lush grass beside the road. The grinding of its teeth and the occasional jingle of its bridle as the horse tore a particularly stubborn clump free were the only sounds in the quiet afternoon.

A bird trilled in the branches over the knight's head. A slight breeze rustled the leaves and fanned the lock of sandy blond hair plastered to the high fair forehead by the cold sweat of agony. Whether the sound or the coolness or both aroused the man from stupor, he was not to know. Hazel eyes, amber flecked with a fierce jade green, stared upward, unfocused, at the fluttering leaves. Gradually his senses returned. Weakly raising his head, he stared around him.

Grim lines of disgust and pain settled deeper into his sun-darkened skin. He was, by his own estimation, too weak to continue. He closed his eyes allowing his head to fall forward onto his chest as he exhaled the breath from his lungs in a deep sigh.

Damn! And damn again!

Damn the plague in this cursed country that had taken the life of the best squire and companion a man could ever hope to have. And damn the filthy thieving blackguard loaned him by that English knight. The swine must be laughing himself sick somewhere.

Pressing a hand tight against his side, he sought to lever himself up. The view of the landscape was suddenly obscured by dancing black spots. Sweat broke out on his forehead. At that moment he was too weak to rise. Grimly, he rested, head dropped back against the rough bark, gathering strength and will from deep reserves.

Raising his stained right hand in front of his face, he watched it tremble. His mouth curled in disgust. His temper had gotten the better of him again as it had so many times in the past. Hopefully, he looked around him, searching for some source of help.

The dastardly theft of his hauberk, plate, and weapons had so infuriated him that he had ridden at full gallop away from the rude hospital set up adjacent to the lists at Harrogate. No thieving churl in league with some English swine would make off with his armor.

He shook his head. Now miles from anywhere on a strange road, little-used by the look of it, his situation began to grow serious. Gathering his feet under him, he pushed his back against the trunk of the tree, hunching himself up until he stood panting, his legs quivering beneath his weight, his hand pressed firmly against his side, the blood seeping through his fingers.

"Ho, son." The knight's voice was a shallow tremor of its former self.

The destrier threw up its head at the unaccustomed sound from the man. Used to harsh explosive commands accompanied most frequently by the jab of a spur, it stared puzzled as if at a stranger.

Brian extended a blood-stained hand trembling with weakness. At the same time he took a lurching step away from the tree. One followed the other as he wove a twisted way toward his horse. The animal shook its bridle, snorting warily. The smell of blood did not alarm it. A battle-trained warhorse, its flanks and chest were frequently splattered with red. But the man's grab for the trailing rein was another matter. Part of its training had been to trample men on foot, especially those who came at its head to grab the bridle. Although the man on the ground was familiar, the destrier could not abandon its training, hard-learned with painful pricks from the point of a dagger on its neck. Puzzled, it shook its head up and down and backed nervously.

"Ho, son," the knight gasped again. "Damnation . . ." The destrier wheeled away and lumbered several yards down the road. Dust rose in a brown swirl drifting around the man's legs. He could taste it in his mouth as he clamped his teeth against his disappointment. The sky whirled. His knees buckled. He dropped down in the dust. A sharp stone cut his knee through his woolen chausses. The pain roused him for an instant, drawing a groaning curse from his lips before he pitched forward on his face in the road.

"Gil!" A young voice pierced the veil. "Go not near him. You cannot trust him. He may be a thief."

"What have we to steal, Kenneth?"

The older voice, preceded by an amused chuckle, carried a note of maturity and authority, yet it, too, had a high boyish quality. Strong hands touched Brian's shoulders, clutched, sought to turn him over. The twisting of his torso wrung an agonized cry from his mouth.

"Oh, poor man." The soft voice crooned in his ear. "Where are you hurt?" The youth's breath brushed his cheek.

"Side," Brian croaked. His nose was full of dust from the roadbed. His tongue felt swollen in his parched mouth. He licked his lips in an effort to produce speech. "On . . . left . . . Careful!" This last was hissed in agony.

10

"Yes. I see. Kenneth, help me turn him gently. Gently, now!" The voice reassured Brian through the haze of dust and pain.

Four hands fastened on his body along its left side carefully avoiding the area over his hipbone as they rolled him onto his back. When he opened his eyes, he stared upward into a pair of young concerned faces, obviously those of a pair of brothers.

"How did you get here?" the older youth asked. "Were you attacked and robbed?"

"If he had been robbed, his horse would be gone, Gil." The younger brother jeered importantly, visibly preening himself at having scored off the elder.

"I was robbed all right," Brian interjected hoarsely, "by my own squire."

"Poor man," the one called Gil murmured again, his fingers patting Brian's shoulder comfortingly. "And you were wounded in the encounter. Where are your friends?"

The knight's eyes closed for a minute as a sudden twinge, not altogether physical, pierced him. "No friends. Not in this cursed land," he whispered.

"Poor man." The youth's hand lifted to brush the dusty hair back from the pain-lined forehead. "Where is your home? We can take you to it."

The question elicited a weak snarl, as Brian's head rolled weakly in the dust. "Not likely you and your brother would be traveling so far as France."

"A Frenchman," the younger lad sneered, "and a knight, too, by the look of that warhorse. Best be moving on. His kind can take care of themselves, or not. He might not have any friends; but if some of his own were to ride by here, they would not take kindly to us bending over him like this."

"Nonsense. He is hurt."

"No." Kenneth rose impatiently. "Come on, Gil."

"Please . . ." With failing sense the knight fumbled for the hand that rested warm on his thigh. Closing over the slender wrist, he held on tightly, fearful that they might run away and leave him. "Please . . . will repay."

"Not necessary." The youth's dark eyes were soft with sympathy. "I will stay with you while Kenneth goes for the cart."

"Yes. All right." Brian's eyes closed in relief, but his grip on the slender wrist never relaxed.

"I hate to hear Uncle Tobin when I tell him," Kenneth objected.

"Go on. This poor man will bleed to death while you make excuses," Gil ordered. The unimprisoned hand stroked back the filthy hair again and brushed dust from around the slightly twisted mouth.

With an exclamation of disgust, Kenneth swung away, his footsteps retreating on the dusty road.

When they were alone, Brian spoke again, his eyes closed against the light and pain. "Good of you . . ."

The youth's soft voice murmured something in reply, but the knight did not catch it as he lapsed again into unconsciousness.

Drawn by a complaisant brown mare, the cart creaked down the road. Perched on its pile of fresh yew staves, Kenneth directed the driver toward the pair. "I told Gil to come away, Uncle Tobin," the boy insisted for the fifth time.

"Gil, what have you got there?" the driver growled through a grizzled curly beard.

"A wounded man, Uncle Tobin." Gil sought to pry

12

open the knight's fingers.

"Well, let him go and come away. He is naught to our business."

With a strangled moan, Brian came awake refusing to release his grasp. "No, help me. I will repay you." He coughed weakly as he raised his head from the dust. His hazel eyes swung hazily from Gil's face to the faces of the others, Kenneth and the older, bearded man called Uncle Tobin. Sweat beaded the wounded man's forehead as he sought to raise himself still further. "Sir Brian de Trenanay," he introduced himself, his lips curving in a pained travesty of an ingratiating smile.

"Tobin Walton," the older man replied coldly, his expression stony.

Brian's head slipped back into the dust. Discouraged, he closed his eyes for an instant. "If you will help me to mount my horse . . ." He sighed. "I shall be forever grateful."

"Uncle Tobin," Gil's young voice objected strongly, "he is too weak to hold up his head. How can he be put on a horse?"

At this slur on his strength, Brian grunted in protest. Hoisting himself up on his right elbow, he turned his body half over, dragging Gil's wrist with him. "Strong enough to ride . . ." he insisted, shaking his head to throw off encroaching dizziness. His lips clamped down hard as fresh blood welled from beneath the padded tunic onto Gil's hand.

Ignoring the wounded man's weak demonstration, Gil's eyes met the carter's. "We can help him onto the cart and take him back to York Minster with us. Come, Kenneth, hop down and lend a shoulder. Can you get your knees drawn up?" This was spoken to the knight who swayed dizzily.

13

"Yes," he nodded. "Jus' help me mount m' horse. . . ."

"Nonsense." A strong young shoulder wormed its way under the knight's armpit. "Put your arm around me. Kenneth!"

The smaller youth stuffed himself under the right side.

"Ready?" Gil asked. All three faces were very close together. Their eyes met.

Brian drew in a ragged breath. "Ready." He clasped each shoulder as tightly as his fading strength would allow.

"Heave!"

Accompanied by a wrenching groan, the three staggered upright and Brian's body was tipped backward onto the cart.

"Catch up his horse, Kenneth," Gil called. "Go, Uncle Tobin. The man is bleeding badly."

What Uncle Tobin's comment might have been was lost on Brian, who swooned away, even before his head rattled among the hard yew staves loaded loosely in the cart's bed. His long legs hung over the edge of the two-wheeled conveyance that swayed drunkenly from side to side as the driver turned the brown mare's head around and headed back the way he had come.

For the first time since the episode had begun, Kenneth's face broke into a grin as he approached the huge destrier. Talking soothingly, he grasped the trailing rein and patted its velvety nose.

In the cart Gil had taken the knight's head on her lap and was cushioning him against the jolts and bumps of the rough road. But Brian was insensible to everything now. His stained hands relaxed limply, palms upward; his booted feet trailed ingloriously in the dust.

Chapter Two

Gillian Fletcher tossed the long braids of wheat gold hair back over her shoulders with practiced movements of her head. Her strong fingers never faltered as she pressed firmly against the edges of the wound on the knight's side. Eyes bright with concern, she stared into the dirty sweat-streaked face of the unconscious man.

"He was poorly stitched," Tobin grunted slightly as he jabbed hard to force the point of the curved needle through the underside of the resilient flesh. It was a big needle used for sewing pieces of leather together to fashion into quivers. "Whoever did the work was careless and unskilled."

From the deep well of unconsciousness, Brian jerked upward. "'Ware my flank, you whoreson!" His hazel eyes flew open searching for the source of the pain. His arms flailed wildly, one muscular forearm narrowly

15

missing Gillian's head in its swift arc.

"Hush, Sir Knight," she whispered, her mouth close to his ear as she ducked. "Uncle Tobin, you hurt him sorely."

Grunting again, Tobin cut the knot he had tied and moved over half an inch to jab with needle again. A sardonic grin twitched the corners of his mouth upward for only an instant. "Just like most of these fellows," he averred between clenched teeth. "Brave and full of loud boasts before their senseless tournaments, but they howl loudest of all when the wounds open up." Tobin's brown eyes narrowed as he concentrated on the task at hand.

The knight stilled his thrashing, his eyes searching the face hovering over him. Brown velvet eyes in a sun-gilded face held his own. The soft mouth parted in a murmur of sympathy. "Where? . . ." His eyes flickered from her face to sweep the room. "Gil?" He sought a friendly face rather desperately.

The girl's eyes flicked to Tobin's. "He is around somewhere," the older man replied. "He has work to do . . . he and Kenneth."

Wincing as Tobin's needle dipped, Brian drew a shuddering breath. "Gil helped me," he gritted between clenched teeth. His thoughts swung dizzily as the ever-increasing pain made consistent thought almost impossible. Never in his life had anything hurt him so much. He sought to concentrate. "Repay," he gasped at last. "I will repay you all." He tried to catch Tobin's eye, but the man merely grunted. Brian's face was white to the lips. Sweat drenched his face and body. His reserves of strength were fast fading. In agony at the stitching, he forced his shoulders and head off the pallet on which he lay. To his horror the ordeal had just begun. He had

16

regained consciousness at the first jab.

Aware of the barely suppressed sounds of agony and the quivering of the flesh beneath his hands, Tobin cocked an eye toward the wounded man's face. "Mayhap if my niece would bring you a dram of ale, 'twould make the process easier to bear."

Swallowing hard, Brian nodded. "Please."

Carefully the brown-eyed girl lowered his shoulders. As she hurried away, a raw intake of breath was followed by a hoarse curse of agony.

Back at his side in a couple of minutes, Gillian found him broken, his fists clutching up handfuls of the pallet as he gnawed at his lip until the blood came.

"Here, poor man," her soft voice penetrated the terrible agony. She slipped her arm under his neck as she raised the tankard to his lips.

He drank greedily, swilling the mild alcoholic drink down his throat, willing it to numb his torn, pierced flesh. In one long gulp he consumed the bitter liquid. Then like a sick child he turned his sweating face into her breast.

Gillian wiped the wet hair from his forehead as Tobin jabbed again. An agonized shriek broke from his lips. He drove his mouth hard against the upper slope of her breast, his teeth bruising her in the violence of his pain.

His long body went limp.

Startled, fearful, she raised her eyes to Tobin, a question bright in their smoky depths.

"Passed out," the man replied phlegmatically. "Better for him. He is somewhat braver than most. I give him that."

"He is a brave man," Gillian insisted. "You hurt him sorely, Uncle Tobin. You could have used a

17

smaller needle."

"I have not a smaller needle with the proper curve."
Tobin grimaced as he jabbed again.

Even unconscious the knight's body jerked involuntarily. Gillian bit her lip as she felt the convulsive twitch along every nerve of her own body. His fevered breath burned hot against the tender skin of her breast. Peculiar sensations unique to her experience aroused a slight trembling in her hands and a singular tightening in her stomach. She slowly bent her head over his. Her lips brushed ever so slightly against his hair.

Brian regained consciousness in an unfamiliar room. His eyes focused upward on the thatch bound expertly across smoky beams. He remembered every hideous detail of the ordeal. His hand moved slowly, experimentally to touch his side, pleased that no more than a dull throbbing troubled him. He could bear that. That was child's play compared to Tobin's stitchery.

His eyes wandered across the ceiling and down the wattled whitewashed wall. A workbench occupied the entire center, an array of tools neatly arranged on hooks above it. Beneath and beside it were baskets containing staves of wood and other things beyond the line of his vision. He was obviously in a workshop of some kind. He grimaced slightly in distaste. Undoubtedly, Tobin, as well as Gil and Kenneth, were craftsmen of some kind. Grateful though he was for their care of him, he could not trust or like them.

As his body became more aware of its needs, he became aware of raging thirst. Likewise his belly felt painfully empty. He licked his cracked lips, finding them painful

18

and bruised. His mouth was so dry that he could hardly summon up enough moisture to wet them.

A sound caught his ear. He turned his head to find its source. A charcoal brazier glowed warmly beside his shoulder. Beyond that a seated figure was outlined in the light streaming through the open doorway.

Swallowing hard, Brian managed an indistinguishable croak.

The figure instantly responded. Laying down the work in hand, he came to the knight's side. "You are awake at last."

"Gil." Brian's voice was a dry whisper.

The youth sank to his knees. From a stool beside the brazier he poured ale from a pitcher into a leather tankard. A strong hand slipped beneath the man's neck lifting him and holding the drink to his lips. "Do not drink so fast. There is plenty."

Thirst satisfied, Brian sank back onto the pallet. "Thank you. I cannot remember being so dry." His voice surprised him by its weakness.

Gil's hand went immediately to his patient's forehead. "You have had a fever now for three days," he said seriously. "'Tis not surprising that you should be thirsty."

"Three days," Brian moaned. "Damn! Oh, damn!" His curse, uttered in a low whisper, was nevertheless intense and fervent. He sought to sit up, driving a wrenching pain through his side as he did so.

"You must lie still!" his nurse exclaimed, pushing his shoulders firmly back onto the pallet.

"I must get up," the knight contradicted. "The man I was using for a squire stole my armor while I was being stitched up in the surgeon's tent. He has sold it and left the country by now."

"Could he do that?" Gil asked. "Surely not. No other knight could use it. You fellows have your arms painted all over everything, do you not? No other knight could use your shield or armor." He patted the knight's shoulder soothingly. "He probably could not sell it."

A sneer curled Brian's lip. "My hauberk and plate did not have anything on them," he told the youth disgustedly.

"But are knights not the most honorable of men? What about their code of chivalry which I have heard much about?"

Brian flung an arm across his eyes. "Even if no knight would buy my armor, an English armorer would be happy to get the equipment. No questions asked." The full measure of the disaster made him weak to contemplate it. His hauberk alone had cost a small fortune, spent in palmier days. The replacement cost of it made him reel.

Beside him Gil set the tankard back on the stool. "I will fetch you some food," he suggested soothingly. "Things always look bad on an empty stomach. An honest English craftsman would not buy stolen goods, so take heart."

Brian allowed his arm to drop back limply. A rueful smile twitched across his lips. "Even if every craftsman between here and the channel were honest as your Saint George, he still would buy that armor. After all, he does not have to know that it was stolen. That damned thief would tell that I was dead and he had a right to sell the armor."

Gil's dark eyes were soft with sympathy as he regarded his patient helplessly.

With a heartfelt sigh Brian closed his eyes. "I suppose I could eat something," he agreed.

Only a very few minutes had passed before Gil was

back beside him bearing a tray. Brian's nostrils twitched as the delectable odor of meat and spices combined wafted toward him. When he opened his eyes, he beheld both boys, the older kneeling beside him as before, the younger leaning over his pallet on the other side.

Setting the tray down beside the pallet, Gil motioned to Kenneth. "We are going to raise you up and slip a bolster under your back," he told Brian. "Do not be alarmed. We will be very gentle and careful."

"Nonsense." The knight shook his head resentfully. "I can sit up by myself. I am not a babe."

His efforts to prove his statement were cut short as Gil flashed a look at Kenneth. The boy scurried away to the dimness of the shop behind Brian's head. At the same time Gil leaned forward, sliding both hands under the knight's armpits. His weight already in the youth's hands, Brian grasped the slender forearms telling himself that he was at least distributing it somewhat. Without an effort on his part, he was lifted into a half-reclining position. At the same time a bolster was shoved under his shoulders. Only a slight twinge from his left side accompanied the process.

"You can go now, Kenneth. Thank you," Gil said, reaching for a cloth on the tray. With a nod the boy left. Gil settled himself more comfortably on his knees and took one of Brian's hands in his own. The cloth was moist and warm. Deftly, Gil laved first one hand and then the other noting as he did so the strength in them as well as the crisscrossing of white scars on the back of the right hand.

"Why do you do this for me?" Brian asked suspiciously. "I vaguely remember a woman at my side the night that your uncle in his great kindness operated on

21

my side."

The youth stirred restively, his eyes downcast at his task. "Oh, you mean Gillian, my sister?"

"Yes," prompted Brian. "I suppose so."

Completing his washing, the youth folded the cloth neatly and laid it on the tray. Without answering, he picked up the bowl and spoon.

"I can feed myself," Brian objected although in truth he felt decidedly light-headed. A pallor underlay his skin and a fine film of perspiration bedewed his forehead and upper lip.

"If I feed you, you will be able to eat much more," Gil observed quietly, dipping the spoon into the steaming bowl. "Also, the soup is very hot. If you should begin to tremble and spill some, you could get a bad scald." The youth smiled sympathetically as he extended the spoon toward the man's mouth.

With a sigh and a roll of his eyes heavenward, Brian submitted. As he realized later, Gil's words had been truthful. After only a few bites, the dizzying weakness overcame him so that his head lolled back against the bolster. He was only dimly aware when Gil set down the bowl and slipped the backrest out from under his shoulders.

When he awoke, the shop was dark except for the glow from the charcoal brazier. With a weak sigh, Brian moved restively to ease a cramp in his leg.

"So you are awake," Kenneth's voice spoke from the darkness. "Wait while I fetch Gil."

The knight's voice stopped him. "Where is Gil?"

"At supper," came the curt reply. "I was set to watch

you and fetch him if you woke up."

"Wait." Brian's command brought the boy back from the shop door. "I can wait while your brother finishes his meal."

Reluctantly, Kenneth resumed his place at the side of the pallet.

"Why does your sister not care for me?" Brian asked curiously. "Surely, nursing is woman's work."

The boy's face was in shadow; his reply, hesitant. "Uncle Tobin has other work for Gillian to do."

"But surely . . ."

"Gil brought you here. He has to take care of you. Uncle Tobin said . . ." His voice trailed off in an embarrassed shrug.

"I will repay you all," Brian replied stiffly. The silence held between them for some time. "Gil seems a likely lad," he said at last.

"Gil is the best fletcher in York," Kenneth asserted proudly. "Our father taught him the craft."

Brian's forehead wrinkled into a frown. "Makes bows and arrows, does he? For hunting and the like."

"Just arrows." The boy's tone conveyed his disgust at this ignorance. "Uncle Tobin is the bowyer. Gil is the fletcher. Our family have always been fletchers. Fletcher is our name. We took it when King William wrote it down in the *Domesday Book*." Pride entered his voice. "So shall I be, too, when I grow old enough to be apprenticed."

Brian sniffed restlessly. "Gil seems a likely lad," he repeated. "He would make a good squire."

"He would not consider that," Kenneth maintained definitely. "He is the best fletcher in York."

"But I would take him and train him," Brian offered.

23

"To be a knight?" The boy sounded doubtful.

"The noblest profession in the world," the man replied. "We were with Charlemagne and your King William." When the boy opened his mouth to reply, Brian hurried on. "We make war like men with steel. Not like some peasant churls with little sticks and bits of feathers. 'Tis not honorable at all to stand afar and shoot a fellow in the eye. Good enough for rabbits and such, but not for men."

Kenneth made a disgusted sound. "Gil is . . ." he began.

"Brother," a voice interrupted from the doorway. "Why did you not call me? I told you to do so the minute he stirred."

"He would not let me." Kenneth pushed himself up from his knees.

"I bade the boy stay until you had finished your supper," Brian added. "We have been having a talk."

Gil came forward with a pan of warm water and a roll of cloth. "No doubt he has exhausted you with his chatter. You must not tire yourself. I have to change the dressing on your side. You may go to your rest, Kenneth."

Left alone he knelt beside Brian. "I shall try to be as gentle as I can. Can you turn yourself on your side?"

"I can sit up," Brian declared strongly.

"No!" Gil's exclamation was horrified.

"Yes." Brian clamped his teeth over his lower lip. "Good lord, boy, men die in bed. If I lie here much longer, I shall start growing into the pallet." So saying he spread his elbows out at his side and brought them in pushing himself upward. Although the action set the wound in his side to throbbing, the pain was not unbearable. He flashed Gil a cheeky grin. "See," he nodded. But

24

when he exerted the strain on his abdominal muscles, hot lightning streaked through him. Despite himself an agonized groan escaped him.

"Oh, please, Sir Knight," Gil reached out a hand helplessly to touch him. "Please let me help you to lie back down."

His back bowed weakly, one hand pressed hard against his left side, the other propped limply across his drawn-up knee, Brian shook his head. "Damn." His breath was almost a sob. "What did dear kind Uncle Tobin sew me up with?"

Gil's reply was low, "A quiver needle."

"Is that all?" The knight's chuckle was like a rasping cough. "I thought at least a lance point." Face white with pain, he allowed his body to slump heavily onto his right side still pressing his hand into his left.

Gil bared the wound. "Oh," he cried, "some of the stitches are bleeding. Oh, poor man." Swabbing the area with a warm wet cloth, the youth scolded his patient roundly ignoring the fact that the man had lapsed back into a feverish stupor.

A week passed. While Brian's strength was slow in returning, his temper waxed short. Lying on the pallet in the shop bored him to the point of madness. Only Gil and occasionally Kenneth came near him. Of the twin sister there was no sign.

Vaguely, the knight was aware of the long hours Gil spent in tedious labor. The three feathers had to be glued firmly to the end of each shaft and held with pins until the glue dried. Soon he began to play a game, luring the youth away from his stool in the doorway on the flimsiest of pretexts. At such times he would talk about the glories of knighthood, the honor of the position, the possibilities of a likely brave youth being knighted on the field for a gallant act.

During one such time while Gil knelt at the side of the pallet, tankard of ale in hand, a shadow filled the open doorway. Tobin Walton took in the scene before him with angry eyes.

"Gil," he growled, "leave us."

The youth sprang to his feet. His charge, sensing the battle about to be drawn between him and the other man, levered himself into a sitting position.

"Uncle Tobin, please, he is still very weak."

With a brush of his hand, the bowyer brushed him aside. "You," he commanded, "must leave."

Laboriously, Brian got his right knee under him and sought to push himself up. Though his head spun from the effort, nevertheless he attained a standing position, bracing his back against a support beam in the middle of the shop.

"Uncle Tobin, I do my work," the youth protested.

"Aye," the man agreed sardonically, "what there is of it. You know we work under commission for the Sheriff of York himself. If we do not fulfill the commission, we will lose all. The arms are being contracted through the sheriff for King Henry himself." He swung back to the knight. "You have tarried here long enough, keeping my nephew from his work, making him wait on you hand and foot. Let those of your own kind care for you."

"He is alone and wounded. He has no friends who would care for him here in England," Gil protested.

"His own kind can care for him, even as you have done," Tobin grunted. "Look, you," he swung back to face Brian. "You have done naught since you fell in our way but take our time."

"I will repay you for your care," the knight began stiffly.

Tobin snorted. "'Tis naught of pay. The food and drink are naught. We are not clutch-fisted. But time is everything. Do you not ken? You take my time, Kenneth's time, and most of all Gil's time. He cannot stay abreast of the rest of us hopping up from his stool constantly to fetch and carry for you."

"Uncle Tobin," Gil protested again, "I will work harder. Do not send him on his way unhealed. You know how deep and dangerous the wound was."

His uncle faced him, turning his back contemptuously on the knight. "You know his kind would spit on you. If you had been wounded, lying in your blood in the roadbed, he would have ridden over your prone body. His kind have naught to do with charity or kindness. You have done enough, Gil. Now is the time to think of yourself and your family obligations."

Brian straightened away from the post. Bright anger glowed in his eyes, suppressing their usually predominant hazel tone and making them blaze jade green. "Gil will meet your damned commission," he declared. "And when it is met, I will repay every groat expended on me."

Tobin snorted. "By leaving?"

"No!" Brian took a couple of slightly unsteady steps to Gil's side. He clapped his hand on Gil's shoulder. "I will work for him."

Chapter Three

The lamplight and the firelight combined to drive the shadows into strange shapes; some elongated, some compressed. It gleamed and danced in the wheat-gold hair and shimmered on the sun-gilt skin. Stripping the scarlet smock worn by the guildsmen of England from her body, Gillian unfastened the tight binder she wore across her breasts and breathed a sigh of relief. Tenderly, she rubbed her swelling mounds, each crested with a pink nipple.

Brian's presence in her workshop day after day had necessitated the tight bindings. Usually, she wore them only on the occasions when she appeared in public or took her place in the guildhall. At work she depended on her loose scarlet smock and a slightly stooped posture to insure her disguise. Her contemporaries and neighbors had accepted the fiction of a twin brother upon her father's death. He had been away working as an apprentice in London. She had summoned him to return to his rightful place in the family and take the family chair in the hall. Of course, Kenneth had been much too young. The seat would have been lost.

Hugging herself with a shiver, Gillian remembered her panic. She had cut her long hair, carefully saving it and weaving it into braids which she wore even to this day when, as Gil's sister, she appeared infrequently to do the shopping. Cold sweat dewing her palms, she had walked between the rows of chairs held by her fellow craftsmen. Trembling, her stomach a hollow pit, she had taken her place on the dais, fearful that she would lose everything she prized in the world. All would be over. The seat of the first Fletcher would be vacant for the first time since the *Domesday Book*.

But no denouncement came. They had commiserated with her at her grievous loss. William had been a fine man, a master craftsman. No one could place the vanes like William. They were delighted to welcome his son into their midst. So she had taken her place among them, her scarlet smock, her black hose, her small gold-hafted dagger in her belt. Prominent on her shoulder and on the side of her soft, crushed-velvet hat was the fletchers' badge with the scarlet dot in the center.

Of course, Uncle Tobin had vouched for her. The idea that Tobin Walton would be party to deception was beyond the ken of any who knew him in the whole of York Minster. Noted for his taciturn personality and unimpeachable honesty, as well as his bows, he would have been the last man any of his fellows would have believed capable of disguising a girl as her nonexistent twin and installing her as a master craftsman in the

30

Ancient and Honorable Company of Bowyers and Fletchers.

Standing on one foot and then the other, she stripped off the thick black hose hanging them neatly in the cabinet beside her other male garments. With a sigh she pulled out the skirt of one of the only two dresses she owned. When the deception had begun, Tobin had ordained that all her dresses be secretly donated to the abbey for distribution to the poor. Only these two had been kept to drag out at opportune moments to preserve the fiction that there were two of them, Gillian and Gil.

She had not minded. Not really. Uncle Tobin had at first decided that Gillian should die of the plague, but she had refused. When Kenneth became a craftsman, Gil would die and Kenneth would take his place as the fletcher. If she killed herself as a female, she would have nowhere to return when the time came for her to marry.

She sighed again. For a long time she had felt no desire to marry. At five and twenty, an age when most girls had been women for ten years, she was still a virgin, alone, living in an isolated world of craftsmanship away from any who might get close enough to penetrate her disguise.

Until now. Into her life had come Sir Brian de Trenanay, his long-muscled body pressed tight against hers, his hand holding onto her as if to a lover. Her peaceful, contented life was destroyed.

Closing the door of the cabinet, she walked to the commode to stare appraisingly at her body in the small mirror above the basin and pitcher. The lamplight created shadows in the hollows along her ribs. Was she too thin? She cupped her breasts in her hands, pressing them upward. Turning sideways, she regarded herself critically.

With a *moue* of disgust she smoothed her palms down over her ribs where they arched above her concave belly. Her hipbones jutted forward. Not at all like the lush bodies of some of the plump matrons whose husbands formed other members of the company with her.

No, her body was not beautiful. Perhaps she had been lucky in the role life had dealt her. Her body would not have attracted men. Although she would have been comfortably dowered had her father lived, she would not have been able to make a marriage except by contract. The thought of her body and her fortune at the service of a man who could do with it as he liked with no thought of her preferences made her shiver.

Hastily she poured water into the bowl and scrubbed herself thoroughly. The cold water made chill bumps prickle her skin and set her teeth to chattering. If her bed were not heated . . . She hurried to the bedside and thrust her hand beneath the down comforter. A smile of satisfaction lit her face. At least that had been remembered. Since her appearances as Gillian were few these days, the service was frequently lacking.

Banking the fire in the fireplace and turning down the lamp, she slipped between the warm sheets. Snuggling down in the warmth of her bed, she slid her mind back over the amazing conversation of the morning. While Tobin and Brian had faced each other growling defiance, she had stood amazed between them.

Brian's statement that he would work to repay the debt of time he had exacted from his nurse had been met with incredulity by Tobin.

"The knightly breed do not touch their hands to honest toil," Tobin jeered. "They may stain them to the shoulders in blood but not such things as paint and glue."

"I owe a debt," Brian maintained doggedly, his face flushing a dark angry red. "I am a gentleman first. A gentleman never forgoes a debt."

"I should think a few coppers thrown in the dust as you ride away would satisfy your sensitive nature," Tobin sneered. Even Gil's protesting cry could not silence his bitter tirade.

"Not even that for you," Brian observed flintily. "You would have left me lying in the dust of that road. I know well to whom I owe a debt." He turned to face Gil, purposefully blocking his hard shoulder into Tobin's chest. "For your help bestowed on a wounded traveler, young Gil, I pledge myself to your service until your commission is completed."

Despite Tobin's snort of disbelief, Gil had believed the knight implicitly. The angry scarlet color had faded as the weakness he had put aside in the heat of anger swept over him. In its place rose a pallor accompanied by a tight pinched look around the mouth as he bit his lower lip. At the same time his hand moved to his left side, covering it gently as the stitches pulled at him.

Gil's mouth quirked into a hesitant smile. "I shall be glad of your help, Sir Brian." She extended her hand.

He clasped it firmly, his callused strength engulfing hers. His hazel eyes smiled warmly as he nodded. Drawing a deep breath, he turned back to Tobin. "Is your problem solved, Master Walton? Not only will Gil be able to return to work full time, but he will have a willing helper with a strong back. I am bound to serve you." His hard hand was warm as it encompassed her own.

Lying in her bed, Gillian rubbed her fingertips gently across her palm. A faint prickling sensation skittered down the nape of her neck. She licked her lower lip tentatively. Suddenly, with a disgusted shiver, she rolled over onto her back in bed, staring into the darkness of her canopy. This man had aroused feelings in her she did not know she possessed. Too intelligent not to recognize them, she nevertheless further recognized that they must be suppressed. He was a knight. She, a fletcher. He was a member, as were all his kind, of the gentry; she, a burgesse.

Despite the romantic ballads, she knew herself to be beneath his notice. When he completed what tasks he considered to be his duty, he would ride away. Better for her if she remained a boy. Otherwise, he might desire her with no idea but his own pleasure. He would not care about her feelings. Indeed, he would be surprised to find that she had any, beyond acceptance and gratitude of the notice he bestowed upon her.

Relaxing into the warm mattress, she yawned widely. "Go to sleep," she advised herself aloud. "Tomorrow you have a busy day. And he is probably stiff as a stick anyway. Very formal and such."

Brian awaited her at the door of the shop, the next morning. Back braced against the jamb, knees drawn up, he turned his face to the rising sun. His gold-flecked eyes glittered as she approached. Bracing his feet, he pushed himself up to a stand. Only a slight tightening at the corners of his mouth revealed the pain the movement cost him. "At your service, young Gil," he smiled, drawing in a deep breath.

Standing in the door beside him, she looked doubtfully away down the street. "Are you sure, Sir Brian? You really owe me nothing. Uncle Tobin is just nervous about the size of the commission. He would have me working night and day anyway. I expect no payment. Certainly not your labor." As a boy might do, she scuffed her boot at a stain on the stoop.

"Brian," he corrected. His hand closed on her shoulder. "If you are to be my master, you should address me familiarly."

Searchingly, she stared into his eyes. Was their a hint of sarcasm? Did he regard what he was doing as a joke? Only seriousness shone in their hazel and jade depths. A head shorter than he, she felt almost ludicrous as his master, yet she could use his help. Her mouth curved in a boy's grin. "Then, Brian, we must get to work. Come inside."

He followed meekly to the workbench, where she motioned for him to pull the stool from underneath it. From a basket beside it, she selected a long slender yew rod. "Each of these"—she held it up—"must be shaped to fit into one of these." She held up in turn a broadhead. Involuntarily, Brian drew back his head. The corner of his mouth lifted at the sight of the triangular barbed shape. "This is the stole," she explained patiently, laying the steel point aside for the moment. She laid the slender rod in his hands. "If you look at the nock end, you will see the index." Taking his hand in hers, she guided the ball of his thumb over the small raised rib standing perpendicular to the nock slot itself. "Feel it," she commanded.

He nodded. "I never realized it was there," he said rubbing his thumb back and forth over it.

"An arrow is a precise thing," Gil smiled proudly. "Everything from nock to point has to be just so. The broadhead point has to be directly aligned with the nock and perpendicular to the index. Otherwise the arrow will not fly true." She watched as the man turned the length of wood over and over in his hands, his eyes intent, his brow furrowed in concentration.

"'Tis made in three pieces," he said at last.

"Oh, more than that," his master replied. "You are seeing the stole." She indicated the long yew wood shaft. "Attached to that at one end is the nock." She touched the attachment. "The bowstring fits in here, of course. And the nock index is glued to that. In the old days arrows were made all of a piece. The nock was part of the shaft and there was no index. But sometimes an arrow would be spoiled by a mistake in the nock. So now they are made separately and attached."

"What is the index for?" Brian studied the small nub of wood seeing that it indeed was glued onto the small shaft.

"A bowman can pull the arrow from the quiver and fit it into the bow without even looking at it. He can shoot faster."

Brian nodded in understanding. "I suppose that is an advantage if the game is leaping away."

Startled, Gil stared up into his face. "Uh . . . yes." Brian continued to examine the stole, running his callused fingers over the smooth joining of the nock and shaft. She cast her eyes down hurriedly to the broadhead in her hand. Its triangular steel points were designed to rip through flesh and bone, killing as much by shock as by actual destructive force. Once in, it could not be withdrawn, but had to be cut out or pushed on through. She swallowed.

"Our stoles are barreled," she hurried on, selecting one from another basket and showing him the careful taper extending slightly from the center down to both ends. "The nock must fit perfectly into the barreling, so no edges stop the flow of air past the joint. 'Tis not so important with the point end. The air will flow past anyway, so . . ."

Brian smiled sardonically, "So even a ham-fisted fellow like myself can be trusted to set the stole into the point."

"Well, perhaps not set it." Gil looked doubtful. "But perhaps you could just prepare the end to match the broadhead. I could then set them exactly."

"What about the feathers?" Brian wanted to know.

Wincing slightly at the derogatory note in his voice, Gil laid the broadhead down carefully on the workbench. "I do all the fletching," she declared, a note of pride entering her voice.

Lifting one eyebrow, he looked down at her half contemptuously, half amusedly. "Young Gil, a man can do so much more than play with glue and feathers."

A slow flush of anger rose in her cheeks. Without another word she turned away. From a third basket beside the workbench, she selected an arrow to which both nock and point had already been applied. "Do your work, Sir Brian. The tools are there. If you do not know how to use them, I will instruct you. I must be about mine, or Uncle Tobin will be seeking me out." Her back straight as one of her own shafts, she marched to the door of the shop, seated herself upon her stool, and bowed her head over her box of feathers.

Shrugging his shoulders, Brian turned to the workbench. If the boy wanted to be a knight, Brian would help him. Gil was a fine loyal lad, a squire a man could be proud of. He would be serviceable and undoubtedly was intelligent. Such boys were always welcome in the orders. A parrain could knight him on the battlefield. The opportunities were there although not so plentiful as in the old days. Still Brian determined that when he left this hovel, Gil would leave with him.

Her hands trembling with anger, Gil stared at the feathers in her box. Before her eyes they blurred. Anger turned to panic. Boys did not cry, especially ones her age with her experience. Why she should care whether this man admired her, she could not fathom. Yet his admiration and approval seemed very dear to her. The nearness and the heat emanating from his hard body, standing so close to her own, had created a flushed hot feeling coursing beneath the surface of her skin. Surreptitiously, she rubbed her hand over one cheek before turning the stroking motion into scratching and transferring it to her ear and the side of her neck.

Her vision cleared, the pheasant feathers came into sharp focus under her eyes. Carefully, she selected three, laying them out separately in the top of her box. Securing the stole in the vise, she spread the glue onto it just below the nock and in line with the nock index. Drawing a deep breath, she set the cock feather into the glue, fastening it down with a pair of steel pins. Her hands were deft and sure. All her faculties were concentrated on the delicate work. The knight-bondsman faded from her mind.

More than three hours passed before Kenneth came to call them to a meal. Sweat stood on Brian's forehead from the tediousness of the work. His days had been spent in the violent rigorous training of a fighting man. To sit still for hours on end moving only his hands in the tiniest of motions cramped his muscles.

At Kenneth's call he rose thankfully from his place barely repressing a groan as he stretched his arms wide and circled his neck on his shoulders. The heat and stuffiness of the hut made him faintly nauseous. A sharp pain racked his left side as he forgot the half-healed wound.

The young lad stared at the shafts on the workbench. "Is that all you have done?"

Nodding, Brian quirked an eyebrow. Puzzled at the question, he stared at the work. He had worked hard and steadily. He was satisfied that the amount he had done was respectable. He opened his mouth to speak.

"Kenneth! Do not disparage what Sir Brian has done." Gil's voice was stern. "He is only a helper. He has no training."

"Uncle Tobin will not like this one bit." Kenneth shook his head definitely. He studied the small collection of finished shafts with a faintly contemptuous air.

Gil tweaked her little brother by the ear. "Everyone has to learn," she insisted. "Tobin will be pleased that at least some work has been done. Something is better than nothing."

With a grunt and a shrug Kenneth turned away. "'Twill not do you much good if you have to stop fletching and do his work first."

"I would have to do the nocking anyway," Gil reminded her brother, "since you are helping Tobin with the bows."

"I like bows better. I might decide to become a bowyer," the young lad replied airily. "Come on if you want to eat."

At the door of the shop Brian caught Gil's shoulder. "I shall work faster if my work is not satisfactory."

She shook her head. "Better to work carefully and not

ruin a shaft. Kenneth is a bragging brat. He could not do much better."

"Look at me." The hard hand tightened slightly on her shoulder. "If I am too slow, perhaps I can hire someone to help me."

"Oh, no." Gil met his jade-flecked eyes. Not for the world would she let another man in her shop. The person would want to stay. She must ever work alone, so her secret would be safe. Brian was different. He would be away before long. "I will work beside you after the meal. There are some skills I can show you that should make the work go faster."

Returning together to the workbench after the cold meats and bread washed down with ale, Gil took a stool beside Brian's to assist him with the nocks. The heat of the day was upon them; the inside of the shop, stuffy. Before he resumed his seat, the knight stripped his tunic off over his head, baring himself to the waist. Unconcernedly, he tossed the garment over the edge of the basket and straddled the stool.

With a gasp Gil turned her face away. A hot blush rose from her throat into her cheeks. A frisson of something akin to fear rippled up her spine, its prickles reaching the hair on the back of her neck. At her shoulder the knight drew in a deep breath.

"That goes better," he declared. "Hot in here, is it not?"

Muttering an assent, Gil bent over the bench, trying desperately to keep her eyes trained on her work. She licked her lower lip. She must be cautious. Not by expression, not by word must she betray herself. Drawing a deep breath and straightening on her stool, she

40

forced herself to look at Brian.

His body was more magnificent than anything she could have imagined in her wildest and most romantic dreams. Revealed in profile, he sat tall on the stool. His skin glistened with sweat, highlighting the masculature of his steely right shoulder and arm. His chest, covered with curling blond hair, expanded as he drew in another deep breath of relief and bent to the work. The new position revealed the layers of muscle across his ribs, and the white bandage around his waist accentuated its taper. His chausses sagged low where they were loosely tied around his lean hips.

The magnificent body just inches away from her own, so close that she could feel the heat emanating from it, set her hands atremble. Despite her will to remain silent, a sound must have escaped her, for her benchmate turned to stare at her.

"What, young Gil? Shy like a girl? By all the saints, boy, men can look upon men." He turned to face her full front, his right hand going to rest on his right hip, with arm akimbo.

Agonized with embarrassment, bewildered and confused by the sensations that swept through her body, she squeezed her eyes shut, at the same time gripping the edge of the workbench with both hands.

The knight chuckled. "Come, boy." The strong warm hand came down on her shoulder. "'Tis hot in here. When no ladies are present, men may relax."

Opening her eyes and steeling herself, she stared straight ahead. "Of course," she nodded. "I was not concerned about your taking off . . . that is, I was only concerned that you might take a chill and sicken. You should

41

be very careful in your condition. You really are not a well man, you know."

"Nonsense." He turned her to face him. "'Tis hot as Outremer in here. You could get overheated. Come, take off your shirt. You will be better off without it." Suiting the action to the word, he reached for the hem of her smock.

Chapter Four

With a terrified gasp Gil jerked away from the knight's grasping hand, but too late. He had gripped the bottom of her smock. The heavy woolen material was strong. With a laugh Brian drew her toward him.

"Oh, no!" Both her hands flayed ineffectually at his, struggling to push the garment down. Her stool toppled over and she fell backward with it, overbalancing him. His laughter changed to a muffled oath as he fell on top of her in a welter of arms, legs, and bodies all entangled in the hard wooden legs of the stool.

The breath whooshed from her body as his forearm slammed across her middle with all his considerable weight behind it. Stunned at first, she could do little else but lie gasping, her legs spraddled. The stool lay between them and Brian's body was draped over it. Gradually, the ceiling of the shop came into focus and she became aware of his anguished moans of pain. Hastily, she pushed herself to a sitting position.

"Oh, Sir Brian, have you reinjured yourself?"

His head bowed almost against her breasts. She touched his cheek. "Damn you," he gasped, raising his head. His face, only inches from her own, was very white. Disgust and shame were written in every pain-filled line. "Damn you," he repeated. His eyes flashed angrily.

Digging her heels into the rush-strewn floor, she pushed herself out of his reach. Anger accompanied her retreat. "Why damn me?" she challenged. "You are the one who brought all this on both of us. If I had wanted my shirt off, I would have taken it off." Springing to her feet, she pulled her smock down with a violent motion, shrugging it back into a more normal position on her shoulders before smoothing it carefully. She did not look in his direction although she was fearfully aware of his harsh breathing. At last satisfied with her appearance, she looked at him.

He still remained draped over the stool. As she watched, he lifted his left hand from his side and stared at it. A disgusted growl erupted from his throat. "I am bleeding." Almost matter-of-factly he studied his stained fingers, noting without surprise that they trembled.

Instantly, she was beside him, her hands clasping his shoulders which now felt clammy to her touch. "Can you ease yourself gently over on your side?" she asked.

"Gently is the only way I dare to move," he nodded wryly. At last he lay stretched out on his back, his left hand pressed against his side, his eyes focused on the ceiling. "Damn fool thing to do," he muttered, "wrestling with a boy. Damn fool thing."

"Yes," she agreed, her face reflecting his painful disgust.

Working with methodical calmness, she peeled the bandage away from his waist to bare the wound. A sigh of relief escaped her. He looked at her quizzically. "You are very fortunate," she told him formally, rewrapping him without any further treatment. "One or two stitches were probably stretched a bit too much. There is a small bit of bleeding around them and one small corner has broken loose. But 'tis nothing serious. Everything is holding."

"How long before Uncle Tobin in his infinite mercy can take them out?" Brian's voice was a bitter rasp as she retied the knot tightly on his right side.

"I cannot say," she replied, her tone properly chiding. "If you insist on wrestling, the time may be long in coming."

He glared at her. "Look to yourself, young Gil. You may be the stronger now; but when I get my strength back, you will not crow so bravely, nor mock so loudly."

She sat back with her fists clenched on her hips. "You are the one who crows and mocks. I have done naught this entire day but my work. I did not try to force you to do something which you did not want to do." She rose to her feet, drawing herself up tall. Since he lay prone at her feet, she had the effect of towering over him while he gazed up the length of her body.

He grinned maliciously. "You are a silly boy to deny yourself comfort because of some odd shyness. Are you concerned that your body is too thin? Good lord, lad! I did not expect you would have those muscles developed." He propped himself up on one elbow to gaze contemptu-

45

ously around the shop. "Locked up in here all day bending your back over those silly sticks and bits of feathers. Why not be comfortable? Take off your shirt and let your skin breathe at least."

Gil pointed to the badge on her shoulder. A circle of white silk, it was embroidered with a black circle on the outside edge and a red dot in the center. From that dot radiated three black lines symbolic of the vanes glued to the stole. "I am the master fletcher," she reminded him coldly. "I am a professional craftsman. A certain standard of dress is expected. Would you go to a tournament improperly dressed?"

He blinked, his expression mirroring his horror at the very idea. When pageantry was everything, no knight with any pride however meager would appear garbed in anything but the best he could afford. Indeed some men accumulated enormous debts to afford the suits of chain and plate and the lavish materials for the panoply on which their heraldry was displayed. The value of such garments was staggering. Brian remembered with a sinking feeling that his had been stolen. His eyes glowed with a feral light as he stared into the middle distance remembering the agony of his ride and his anger at the thief.

With a sigh he closed his eyes for a long moment before opening them and sitting up cautiously. "I apologize sincerely, Gil Fletcher," he announced in a cool flat voice. "I was insensitive to the importance of your clothing in relationship to your office. I have not dealt often with craftsmen and then only in position of purchaser. I have had no occasion to work for them or to understand the formalities."

Warily, she studied his grave, drawn face for signs of

mockery. His gold-flecked jade eyes were deep pools. Suddenly, she realized that she could drown in those pools. A ripple of response began at the base of her spine and swept upward. Surreptitiously she swallowed in an effort to clear an unaccustomed thickness in her throat. She had lived and worked side by side with this magnificent man for a fortnight. She had bathed his body, dressed his wound, fed and comforted him. All these acts she had performed dressed as a man denying her own sexuality. His very helplessness had somehow infantilized him to her senses.

But he was helpless no longer.

Grimly, he climbed to his feet, rising well over six feet, the point of his broad shoulder even with the top of her head. The illness and fever had honed his muscles defining every curve with a fine line beneath the satiny skin of his arms and shoulders. Across his chest light brown hair curled in damp fishhooks. He exhaled painfully as he stooped to right the stools knocked over in their struggle.

"Never mind!" She leaped forward almost colliding with him, coming up short only inches from his body. Wildly, she fought the almost overwhelming urge to touch him. "You need not do any more bending and stooping for today."

Willingly, he straightened again leaving her crouched at his feet almost like a supplicant. She swallowed as she stared first at the broad columns of his legs and then at the tight-knit body that topped them. Again she swallowed convulsively. Dear God! The memory of his body bared to her touch when she had bathed him to bring down his fever rose before her.

Righting one stool clumsily, she rose. Her hands

trembled as she righted the other and pushed it under the bench. "Sit you down," she commanded, "and be on about your work. I need to check with Uncle Tobin about some of the yew rods."

Meekly, he obeyed her, straddling his place again and reaching for another stole. As one pursued, she fled out into the bright sunlight.

Alone hunched over on his stool, Brian drew a deep breath. As the pain subsided, his consternation grew. Uncertainty gripped him as he thought of Gil's panicky reaction. Surely the boy had been reared in an unnatural atmosphere. Since the time Brian had been a page, he had been used to the sight of men's nude bodies. His first duties had been to draw water for the baths of Sir Bertholdt, in whose household he had taken his training. He could understand a certain amount of shyness, particularly if a youth whose body was slim and underdeveloped were brought face to face with a man's body such as his.

He glanced down at his chest, striped in several places by dead white scars from long-healed wounds. His arms and shoulders were necessarily heavily developed; his life depended on his strength.

His mind took inventory of Gil's body. The boy's slender neck was white like a girl's; his shoulders underdeveloped in the extreme. The chest and waist concealed under the loose-fitting smock were certainly nothing out of the ordinary. Indeed Brian remembered catching a glimpse of some wrapping around the narrow chest. Possibly the lad was trying to pad himself to make his upper body seem broader.

Remembering the long straight legs, Brian smiled. The boy must have walked many miles to develop the calves and thighs. Recalling their shape as he lay staring upward as Gil rose above him, he started. His hands gripped the edge of the bench on which he worked. Carefully he went over the whole incident in his mind.

Other things began to intrude. Gil's face was beardless. Not even a thin brown down marked his upper lip. The voice was a soft clear soprano. Yet the youth was well into his late teens. Of the age, Brian was sure, for Kenneth was a teenager himself.

Frowning, Brian struggled to recall the face of the sister. What was her name? Gillian. Gillian! Gil. Briefly, a memory stirred within his mind of arms holding him, of hands brushing his fevered brow, of a faint clean smell of some lemony herb. The same smell had come to him from Gil's body as Brian had accepted the lad's help to rise and reseat himself on the stool.

The side of Brian's mouth curved sardonically. 'Twould explain much. The wary looks from Tobin and Kenneth. The extreme reserve with which Gil treated not only Brian but everyone who came into the shop. The fletcher could be merely shy. . . .

Brian chuckled suddenly. What a trick these people were playing! He shook his head. Her deception reinforced what he had always believed about bows and arrows. Real weapons could not be manufactured by a mere woman. Catch a woman making a battle-ax or a suit of chain mail. Never!

A demon entered his eyes. The chit was in a precarious position working all day alone with a man. When he left her to go on his way, she should never hire an apprentice. As easily as Brian, some other man might pierce her disguise, with most unpleasant results. Obviously, the girl was vulnerable to blackmail. Better give her a good scare,

49

then warn her.

Feeling like a tolerant uncle, Brian settled himself more comfortably on the stool. His hands performed their assigned tasks, but his mind wove fantastic plots whereby to tease and teach his youthful master.

Safe in her room, Gillian pressed herself hard against the door. Under the tight binding she could feel the nipples of her breasts prickling as their nipples hardened. She wanted him! Her arousal created such sensations in her that she sank to her knees pressing her hands tightly across her breasts in an effort to still their throbbing.

What would she do? How could she continue to work side by side with him under these circumstances? Shaking her head in despair, she bit her lip. Oh, to be a woman. To be Gillian even for a night. Did she dare? Was she the same girl who only the night before had sternly vowed to suppress her feelings and live the life of a boy?

Drawing herself up tall, she strode determinedly across her room to the table, pouring herself a drink from the carafe of water. Her mouth no longer dry, she pressed her fingertips against her temples. The situation as she had recognized it last night had not changed. Only she had changed.

Crossing to her commode, she stared at herself in the mirror. She looked the same. Her fingers trembling slightly, she opened a small door located low on one side. Carefully, she drew forth the wig she had made of her own hair. Her vision blurred. What would Brian think of her if he could see her as she really was? Would he think her attractive? Did she dare to send Gil on an errand and appear at table tonight as Gillian?

She was playing a foolish game of chance. Sighing, she let the wig rest on the commode top. Her expression mirrored her desolation.

Then a determined gleam dawned in her eyes. She would appear tonight. Be damned to her uncle and brother. Surely one time as a girl would not destroy the deception.

Her lips tight, she crossed to the wardrobe and drew forth the prettier of the two dresses she had kept for Gillian to wear. It was a gold linen *houppelande*, decorated with a pale cream-colored silk on the turned-back collar that would frame her neck and shoulders. The dress could be buttoned modestly to the neck or left open. Tonight, she told herself, as she held it against her, she would leave it open. The gold-embroidered silk belt would cinch in her slender waist.

Hanging the dress carefully out of sight in the closet, she rang for the house servant to prepare a warm bath. From the same concealing part of the commode, she drew her gold caul. Staring at it thoughtfully, she balanced her wig in the other hand.

No, she would not wear the caul and its accompanying silken veil. Sir Brian de Trenanay was accustomed to the elaborate headdresses worn by the women of the most magnificent courts of Europe. He would not be impressed with her small finery. Better leave her hair uncovered, but her plaits wrapped around her ears. Carefully adjusting the wig on her head, she coiled the braided hair into stylish swirls.

A knock at the door startled her. Frantically, she dragged the wig off and thrust it into its hiding place. At her command two servants entered, one bearing the tub; the other, two large pitchers of steaming water. Several linen towels were drapped over the side of the copper tub.

Emptying one pitcher into the tub and setting the other close at hand, the elder of the two bowed. "Will that be all, sir?"

"Er-yes," Gil's voice shook unaccountably. Were they suspicious because their master called for a bath in the middle of the afternoon? "You may leave me. I will ring if I require more. Be about your usual duties."

They had hardly closed the door behind them before Gillian began to strip the smock, hose, and breast-binder from her body.

Sprinkling the water liberally with her favorite herbs, a combination dominated by lavender and costmary, she seated herself in the comfortably warm water. Squeezing the bath sponge over her shoulder, she shivered in anticipation of the coming evening.

Despite the persistent ache in his side, Brian managed to finish setting the broadheads onto all the stoles in the basket. Just as the last rays of the sun withdrew from the shop, he stretched gingerly, rotating his neck and aching shoulders.

Damn! He would be getting a crook in his back if he did much more of this type of work. With a grudging flicker of admiration he acknowledged that at least some craftsmen had to have considerable strength and endurance to labor long hours at their crafts.

Yawning, he wondered idly how Gil, if he really were indeed a female, would have the strength. Perhaps the work he did now was always done by someone else. Perhaps Tobin ordinarily helped her. Perhaps this commission had brought an exceptional amount of business.

A cynical gleam entered his eye, turning its golden color to dark amber. Perhaps Tobin, that sly fox, had planned this from the beginning.

With a true knight's distrust for all the guildsmen whose orders and purposes he did not understand, he doubted not that the older man had conspired to exact free labor in exchange for the food and care given. Probably Gil also . . . Here he stopped himself. Gil was the only honest thing about this whole business. Even in disguise, for whatever reason, she had rescued him from the road, brought him to her home, cared for him, and fed him. He would entertain no evil thoughts about her.

Reaching for his tunic, he drew the garment over his head, noting as he did so the rank smell that enveloped him. His nose wrinkled. The odor of sweat and horses was a trademark of his profession. He even knew men who claimed to know ladies who preferred them direct from the lists. He shook his head. His tunic smelled so bad that it made his eyes water. No one could prefer this. He had worn the garment all through his illness.

Stepping out of the shop, he calculated the time. A tailor dwelt over his shop down the street. Perhaps the man might be persuaded to part with one of the rough garments he was preparing for servants' livery. Brian felt the size of his purse. Surely, he could spare a coin for the comfort of his hosts, if not for his own self-respect.

Forthwith he rousted the tailor out by the simple expediency of pounding on the shop door. "Yes," the man agreed reluctantly, "I do have several garments prepared for the duke's household. But . . ."

"When does the duke expect delivery?" Brian inquired, fingering his purse suggestively.

The little man scratched his head before cocking his

eye cannily in the knight's direction. "You be the fellow staying with Tobin down the street?"

With an engaging smile, Brian admitted that he was. "I can no longer offend my generous nurse and host," he declared in an apologetic voice. "They have cared for me, a stranger. They are most kind and gentle people." Mentally, he prayed heaven to forgive him for the lie. Tobin Walton was anything but kind, and a more ungentle man never lived.

"Aye," the tailor nodded. "That Gillian Fletcher be a sweet girl, and her twin brother so alike her. I could hardly believe my eyes when he appeared. The old man had apprenticed him to a fletcher in London. When William's untimely death brought him back, we were all amazed." Gossiping companionably, he selected a large shirt dyed in cheap woad blue, all the time eyeing the muscular body of his customer. "This be for the smithy. He has a girth that would make two of you, but your shoulders are much the same. You can belt it in to make it serve. Do you be needing hose as well?"

Brian shook his head. The feel of the rough wool under his fingers made him know he was in for an itchy time. To trust his lower parts to this man's materials was a daunting prospect. "Thank you, Master Tailor. You have given me enough to make me at least presentable tonight."

They haggled for a few minutes over the price, the tailor amused and Brian disgusted. These craftsmen's overwhelming preoccupation with money grated on his nerves. Furthermore, he felt embarrassed that he could not merely throw the man a handful of coins, more than enough to cover the cost of the wretched garment, and stalk in proud silence from the room.

His precarious position drove itself home to him as he was forced to part with two coins from his small store. Without his armor he would be long in earning more. Briefly he thought of abandoning the idea and leaving the garment. However, his stench was almost overpowering. Even the tailor stood back away from him almost half the length of the shop.

Bidding the tailor a brief good evening, he turned in the direction of the spring which bubbled up into the fountain in the center of the cul-de-sac around which the homes of Tobin and Gillian had been built. Stripping to his chausses, he splashed his neck and shoulders. The cold water set his teeth to chattering but refreshed him after the hot day in the stuffy shop. Clamping his jaws, he turned to see a servant approaching from the house.

"Is the dinner about to be served?"

"Aye, sir. Mistress Gillian sent me to remind you. She thought you might still be in the shop."

"Mistress Gillian?" Brian raised one eyebrow quizzically. "Where did she spring from?"

The servant shrugged. "She comes right frequently. She takes care of her widowed aunt over in Tolborough."

"And where is Master Gil tonight?" Brian inquired presently, drying himself with the least disreputable part of his offensive garment before slipping the fresh one over his head.

"I cannot rightly say, sir. He is away tonight. I believe he went for more yew rods."

"No doubt," Brian chuckled as he headed toward the house.

Chapter Five

Biting her lower lip in an effort to control her mounting nervousness, Gillian watched Brian saunter across the yard. The small leaden glass panes in the window distorted her face but did not, as she believed, hide her from view. His mouth twisted in a sardonic grin as he caught sight of her watching him. Genially, he raised a hand in greeting.

Hastily, she drew back. He had seen her and waved. One hand touched the wheat-gold braids wound neatly over her ears; the other adjusted the embroidered silk which belted in her full *houppelande* just below her breasts. Somewhat to her surprise, her breasts felt strange to be free of the tight binding she had worn for days. Engaged in smoothing a shadow of a wrinkle from the front of her skirt, she stood with head bowed as Brian entered.

Pausing in the doorway, he studied the gold and cream dress. For a moment he doubted his theory. Surely these softly curving lines could not be the same lines he recalled on the figure of the youth Gil.

Then she raised her eyes to his, and his doubts began to fade.

No other could have the brown velvet eyes framed by gold-tipped lashes. Privately, he had mused that the fletcher lad had eyes too beautiful for a boy. Now he recognized them. Gil Fletcher and Gillian Fletcher were one and the same. Whatever her reasons might be, she could not hide her sex from him any longer.

"My lady," he bowed low with a courtly flourish of his hand.

For an instant she stood as one turned to stone. How did one react to such gallantry? No one had ever bowed to her before. Her hands clenched in the folds of her skirt. Oh, yes . . . She extended her hand as she took a step toward him. "My lord."

He bowed low over it, his lips touching the tops of the fingers. At the same time he felt the calluses on the fingertips. Gil's hands were work-hardened. No lady of Brian's experience had such strong slender fingers. He did not consider that Gillian might have worked every bit as hard as her brother. In his own mind he was already equating her with a lady. No lady worked at anything more than her embroidery.

With a suggestion of a leer, he raised his head to stare down at her, his eyes searching her face for some nervousness, some flicker of communication of her identity. It came in the form of a blush. Fascinated, he watched as the rosy color flowed from the V of her bosom and spread upward to stain her throat and then her cheeks. He almost chuckled, but he was not satisfied to let her know he had penetrated her disguise so soon. Instead, he stepped back. "Where is your brother, my lady?"

She raised her eyebrows. "K-Kenneth? He should be around somewhere. Do you seek him, my lord, for some special reason?"

He grinned as he studied her cheeks, noting how becomingly they flushed when she became agitated. "I meant Gil," he answered softly. "He disappeared early this afternoon, mumbling something about seeing Tobin about yew-wood. He did not return."

She curtseyed, her eyelashes veiling her expressive eyes that could look as evenly as any man's when she wore her brother's clothing. Nervously, she touched her hair. "Oh, yes. I do recall that he had to go after some more shafts. I doubt that he will return before tomorrow morning. Will you have some refreshment before dinner, Sir Brian?"

"You are most gracious." Brian bowed low in his most courtly manner, his eyes on the décolletage of her dress. His appraising stare made her blush even more furiously.

Fetching a pitcher decorated with designs of roses, she poured a goblet of cool fruit juices and handed it to him. His hand touched hers in passing the drink. When she withdrew her fingers, she surreptitiously rubbed her thumb across their tips. She could not understand her own feelings. Dressed as her true self, she felt so much more uncertain of the proper responses. How did a woman react when a man stared frankly at her bosom? The hand that he had touched flew to the neckline of her gown, pressing the edges of the silk collar together where they formed a V. Suddenly she wished she had not opened her dress quite so wide. If only the shadowy valley between her breasts was not quite so apparent.

Smiling secretly behind the goblet, Brian drank. "Very refreshing," he commented. "What is it? I seem to remember it, but I cannot decide from when."

"You drank it often when you were so sick," Gillian smiled. "It is the juices of apples and pears sweetened slightly with a bit of sugar and seasoned with cinnamon. When Kenneth was little, he had a finicky stomach, but he could always drink this drink."

"Did you concoct it?" Brian asked.

"Yes," she nodded. "After our mother died, I was the woman of the household, taking care of Kenneth and Father and Uncle Tobin."

"And your brother Gil, of course," Brian reminded her with a twisted smile.

Her brown eyes swept upward to stare at him, with a slight frown. Did he suspect her secret? "To be sure," she agreed.

But his face was blank. He finished the drink and set down the goblet with a sigh of gratitude. As if with great weariness, he rubbed his side, wincing visibly as he did so. "Your brother is a rough fellow," he informed her in a conspiratorial voice. "A sick and wounded man must look to him."

Her eyebrows knitted in a frown. "What mean you, my lord? Not Gil. He would never . . ."

"Fair dragged me off my stool today." The knight transferred his hand from his side to the back of his neck. Half-closing his eyes, he watched her reaction with barely concealed amusement. "Wrestled me to the ground," he grumbled. "And me a knight. I must be weaker than I thought possible. The idea that a stripling lad, not even bearded yet, could wreak such havoc on my

60

bones is embarrassing."

The velvet brown eyes flashed in anger. "I am sure you do Gil wrong, Sir Brian. He would never drag someone from a stool. Surely you must have done something. . . ."

Brian held up his hand in mock sternness. "I merely offered to assist the lad. He took my offer in a poor spirit."

"Gil is not poor spirited!"

"I beg your pardon, Lady Gillian. You know not your brother in his dealings with men. I know you love him and must by that love defend him, but I say to you he is a very sober fellow. How a little bit of joshing sets him off!" Here Brian shook his head. "I think he needs more time spent with men. He acts more like a silly girl."

At his words Gillian started, her eyes widening, her cheeks blushing. Her mouth, opened to protest and defend, closed abruptly. She spun on her heel, her skirts swirling out. With her back straight she thought to leave the room, retreating hastily to cover her confusion. His observation, coming, she believed, as a result of her failure to preserve her disguise, terrified her. If he had seen so much, what would others who knew her better think?

Watching her hurry out, he chuckled maliciously. The evening promised to be a delightful one. He could not help but notice the delicacy of her features. How could he have been fooled even for an instant by her disguise? The deep brown eyes were Gil's, the height, the soft slightly husky voice. Yet how had she concealed the very feminine curves?

In a flash he remembered the wrapping he had glimpsed under the loose smock. His smile broadened. He had thought the youth had wrapped his chest to appear more manly. Instead, a young woman sought to conceal her curves. One eyebrow quirked. What pleasures he might find there, he could freely imagine. Perhaps after he confronted her with his discovery, they might share the joys of each other's bodies. She was only a burgesse after all. She could count herself lucky that she had attracted the attention of a knight.

A grin of anticipation spread across his face as in his mind's eye he remembered the shadowy cleft between her breasts. His body, celibate for several weeks, tightened slightly at the thought. His convalescence and self-imposed task might prove most enjoyable.

Dinner that night was a strained affair. From his place at the head of the table, Tobin Walton glowered from beneath his shaggy brows. At his right sat his nephew Kenneth, his eyes glued to the face of the man across the table. At the end in her accustomed place sat his niece dressed in her woman's garments, a flush staining her cheeks, as she, too, listened entranced to the tales Sir Brian spun of the glories of tournaments in far-off France.

"Are you saying that the knight actually had his horse led in by a girl with no clothes on?" Kenneth's voice trembled slightly over the negative.

"She appeared to have no clothes on," Brian grinned. "Of course, she was wearing a blond wig that hung almost to her knees in both front and back. She had garlands of flowers trailing around her body in the most strategic places. In truth her appearance caused quite a stir among the ladies and lords in the stands until they realized that she was wearing a closely fitted kind of flesh-colored garment."

"I should have like to have seen that," Kenneth breathed. He looked expectantly at his sister. "'Twould have been most amazing. Gil would have been shocked I bet."

"Why yes, I suppose he would," Brian agreed, pretending not to understand. "He is a foolish fellow about such things."

"Oh, well." Kenneth dipped his spoon into his soup without thinking. "What can you expect from a girl?"

At the sound of Tobin's growl of warning, Kenneth looked up guiltily, startled at what he might have revealed. His agonized expression was more confirmation for Brian.

"That is . . ." Kenneth faltered. ". . . Gillian would be really shocked. She could not even look at such a sight. *Gil* now. He would like it same as me."

Concealing a smile, Brian did not pursue the subject. Turning to Tobin, he met the man's scowl unflinchingly. "Where did you send Gil this afternoon, Master Walton?"

"To Tolborough . . ."

"To Brentharpe . . ."

"That is," Gillian explained lamely, "he went to Brentharpe to fetch some more yew and then will come back by way of Tolborough to visit . . ."

Tobin's voice rose above hers. "When and where a master craftsman chooses to go should be of no concern to a worker. Do you not have enough work to do in the shop, Sir Brian? If not, I can find more than enough to fill Gil's absent hours."

"I merely inquired, Master Walton," Brian replied coldly. "Despite my slowness, I have managed to keep working steadily. Have no fear that I shall not work on while Gil is away. I am true to my word."

"No one doubts you will work, Sir Brian," Gillian interposed hastily. "In fact if Gil does not return soon, I can always work in the shop setting the vanes. Our father taught us both the technique."

Tobin's brown eyes flashed. "You will do no such thing, lass. The guilds will not have a woman in the shops. You know the rules. Brian will work alone until Gil gets himself back." His teeth set as if he worried a tough piece of meat. "I suggested to him when he departed that he had best hurry. This trip, I dare say, will be made in record time."

What Gillian might have said was interrupted by the serving girl who carried away the soup plates. While the manservant held the roast for Tobin to carve, Brian observed that Gillian's eyes were staring downward at her lap.

"You need not fear, Lady Gillian," Brian spoke gently. "I will work as hard as I can without direction. Even if your brother is gone several days, he will find all is in order on his return."

"His errand will not take several days," Tobin declared firmly.

The rest of the meal passed in silence. Kenneth kept his lips firmly closed, considering that he had said quite enough. Feeling the full impact of Tobin's displeasure, Gillian kept her eyes on her food as the plates were set before her and removed. The evening, which she had contemplated with such anticipation, had turned into a sorry debacle. She only longed for the privacy of her room where she could discard this dress and resume her man's garb. In the morning, Gil would return and Gillian would depart for Tolborough to care eternally for an ailing aunt.

"We will now retire," Tobin announced as the savory was removed. "You, Sir Brian, must be tired from your long hours, and you so recently arisen from a sickbed. Gillian. You must depart early in the morning." The threat in his voice was undisguised. "You would never rest if your aunt were suddenly taken worse while you were away."

Drawing a deep shuddering breath, the blond girl nodded. "Yes, Uncle Tobin." Something very like a quaver made her voice wobble slightly.

Brian felt the tone rather than heard it. His eyes narrowed as he contemplated the adamant old man sitting like a stone at the head of the table. If Gil were really a boy, he would take him away from such a cruel guardian. At least he could offer Gillian, the girl, a taste of love before he left. Setting his thoughts on that goal made him feel very satisfied with himself as he rose from the table.

Tobin Walton allowed his niece no opportunity to talk to the knight, but sent her straightaway up to bed. Later beside the fire in the common room of the house, he stared at his unwelcome guest. "Sir Brian," he began abruptly, "I fear you are slow to heal. You must be on your way before long. That squire will be vanished without a trace with your armor and winnings."

Brian shrugged. "I have pledged myself to a certain labor here."

"What if you were released?" Tobin's eyes were hooded.

"None can release me but Gil," Brian replied. "I agreed to this task for his sake. I will not abandon him. He has stood against much opposition for my cause." His gold-flecked eyes glittered balefully.

Tobin drew a deep breath before nodding in agreement. "Go to your rest," he commanded gruffly. "Gil will return tomorrow. The commission should be finished in a fortnight. It *must* be finished in a fortnight. We are too far behind to complete it without your help."

With a low bow, Brian de Trenanay left his reluctant host staring at the fire.

"Your sister is a beautiful girl." Brian watched out of the corner of his eye as a pleasurable flush spread up into the cheeks of the youth sitting in his accustomed place at the door of the shop.

"Do you really think so?" For an instant the clever fingers lay idle across the stole in the boy's lap.

"Indeed." Brian smiled to himself. "You are truly identical twins. Why set side by side with her hair cut short as yours is and dressed in men's garments, she might be taken for you."

The fingers resumed their work as their guide stirred uncomfortably on the stool. "Actually, she is much different from me," the low voice insisted. "You could easily distinguish between us if you but saw us together."

"Why do you not move the aunt from Tolborough?" Brian asked with feigned unconcern. "'Twould seem an admirable solution for everyone. Gillian could live at home and take care of the household. Furthermore, Tobin could find a husband for her. She grows old."

A muffled exclamation came from the doorway. "She and I are the same age. She will marry in good time as shall I, if I am so fortunate as to live so long and keep good health."

They had been working for several hours. Brian rose from his stool, stretching himself, his hard-muscled body dwarfing the confines of the small shop. Casually, he strolled to the boy's side to regard him in the strong light. "And how old might that be?" Deliberately, he tipped the youthful face up to the full glare of the clear sunlight.

Smiling into the startled brown eyes, he studied the fair countenance as if he might draw it.

"Let me go," Gil protested, squirming.

Brian's hard hand descended on the boy's shoulder. "Not yet. I can detect no sign of a beard on that fair face." His voice assumed a serious note. "You cannot be more than sixteen, seventeen at the most, with no beard and a high girlish voice. Yet your sister seems so much older." Ignoring the squirming beneath his hands, he lowered his voice seductively. "Her breasts are so fully developed, such high firm mounds."

"You must let me go!" Gil's voice turned to a high squeal. "You . . . you should not say these things to me."

"Nonsense. This is men's talk, Master Gil." Brian's thumb dropped lower encountering the edge of the binding under the cloth of the tunic. As if to study the face more closely, he lifted Gil's body off the stool straightening it and pressing it back against the jamb of the shop door.

"Sir Brian!" Gil swallowed and lowered her voice with an effort to a deeper, gruffer tone. Her eyes slitted in the bright light of the sun. Dropping the shaft on which she had been working, she caught his wrist with both hands. Although her hands were strong, they were no match for the tough sinews of a seasoned knight. "Sir Brian! You forget yourself! Let me go! Have you gone mad?"

Her captor leered at her. "Perhaps," he suggested. "On the other hand, perhaps I suddenly see clearly."

"You know not what you do?" Gillian's voice was heavy with disgust. "Let me go!" Uncaring if she hurt him, she kicked with her left foot at the same time her right forearm slapped at his injured side.

But he was ready for her. Turning his leg, he took the blow aimed for his shin on the resilient muscle of his calf. At the same time he let go of her shoulder to block the swipe at his wounded side. "Not very effective in defense against even a wounded, weakened man," he observed archly as she drew back to pummel him again.

"Damn you!" was her only response.

"What else can you do?" he inquired politely, pressing forward with his long body and pinning hers against the doorjamb. His whole length now rested against hers.

With both hands she attacked his face, grabbing for handfuls of hair, but again he staved her off, this time by the simple expedient of letting go of her chin and catching both trim wrists in his hands. As if she were no more than a child, her arms were forced down to her sides and behind her.

The movement had the effect of arching her body into his. One sandy brow rose as he moved his body suggestively. "For a stripling boy, you feel wondrously well padded in certain places and amazingly lacking in others," he observed with a chuckle. "And your scent . . ." He dipped his face into the side of her throat, inhaling the clean lemony fragrance that he had noticed before with both Gil and Gillian. His breath tickled her skin in the hollow below her ear.

Fear shot through her. "Beast! Bully!" she cried. "You! with your knightly oath to defend the weak. How you break it to handle me so?"

Like magic he stepped back releasing her arms. Bowing low from the waist, he spread his hands. *"Mea culpa,* my lady," he said softly.

"'Tis well that you remember—" She stopped in mid-sentence, her features frozen with shock. From dark wells of despair she met his amused gaze. "What did you call me?" she whispered at last.

"My Lady Gillian, the Fletcher of York Minster, I doubt not." He bowed again in acknowledgment of her raiment and her position.

"You are mistaken," she quavered. "Now I know you are mad, fellow. I am no woman. Surely not my own sister. She has gone to Tolborough this very day to care for our sick aunt."

Brian straightened. "Shall we see?" he questioned softly. "Shall I place my hands on your body and strip off that smock you wear? Do you think that because you prevented my doing so yesterday that you would succeed in doing so today. I acted but in jest yesterday. Today I would be serious."

"You would not dare," she asserted faintly.

His voice was even, yet menacing. "If I wanted your charming body, my lady, I am as other men. I would have it. You could do naught to stop me."

"I could scream."

With a movement so swift that she could not hope to dodge him, he lunged forward, his hands grasping her shoulders. His face loomed above her. Her lips opened, but before the sound could issue, his lips closed over hers.

Chapter Six

Through long winter nights and warm summer days, lying in her solitary bed beneath the covers or dreaming while her hands lay idle over the shafts, Gillian had imagined her first kiss. Her prince, the most handsome man in the world, dressed elegantly in silks and velvets, would take her tenderly in his arms. She would close her eyes because the ladies in the romances always seemed about to swoon in ecstasy. Slowly, his lips would touch hers, warmly caressing, then withdrawing deferentially.

Brian de Trenanay, clad in a rough wool tunic, dragged her body against his hard chest. Like a falcon's swoop his lips came down on hers, covering her whole mouth, his strength pressing her head back. At the same time his tongue thrust between her lips that opened in a gasp of fear. Hotly driving into her mouth, he touched her teeth, her tongue, her velvet interior. Confused and not a little frightened, her eyes widened as she strained with puny strength against him.

The futility of her struggle became apparent to her immediately. Frustration accompanied by a feeling of claustrophobic anger swept through her. Held fast in his hard hands, her back pressed against the doorjamb, her head strained back on her shoulders, her mouth filled with the taste and scent of him, she lost her breath. Dizziness brought weakness. Her eyelids fluttered, a thin whimper escaped into his mouth.

At her pitiful sound and lack of resistance, Brian's lips softened. He had not meant to hurt her, only to frighten her a little. She must be impressed with the vulnerability of her position. Women did not masquerade as men. They did not put on men's clothing and usurp men's positions. If she were found out by someone who did not have her best interests at heart, she could be seriously hurt. Perhaps even accused of witchcraft or heresy.

Above all, he wanted to protect her from such an eventuality. She was a good friend. Whether as Gil or Gillian, she had befriended him when he was in distress. He raised his head to stare at the face turned up to his. Gently, he slipped his left arm around her shoulders, while with his right hand he brushed a lock of wavy blond hair back from her forehead.

At the feel of his hand, Gillian shivered. The brutality of the kiss had frightened her, yet her body could not help responding to his hard, warm masculinity. Her own sexuality, so long repressed, had awakened tremblingly beneath his lips. Yet how different he was from the knight errant of her dreams.

Her palms flattened against the wall of his chest. She could feel his heartbeat, strong, steady, a little rapid.

Tentatively, her tongue flicked across her bruised lips. She felt him draw a deep breath.

Suddenly, she was ashamed. Ashamed for the way she felt, ashamed for being caught out in her lie. She released her breath in a sigh of disgust. "Are you quite through?"

For answer his arms dropped from around her and he stepped back. Drawing herself erect, she leveled her fiercest gaze at him.

His eyebrow quirked in response. Placing his hands on his hips, he returned her stare. "You see," he observed at length. "If I had cared to continue, you would be here on the floor. You have done a very foolish thing to dress as a man."

Hastily, she moved away from him, sidling out of the doorway and into the interior of the shop, putting distance between them to escape his dominating maleness. "I am a master craftsman," she declared coldly, her back against the workbench.

"You are a girl."

"I am a woman. Furthermore, the two are not mutually exclusive."

"You do wrong to usurp a man's profession," his voice was primly disapproving.

She thrust out her chin stubbornly. "The tapestry weavers allow women in their guild. It is only a matter of time—"

". . . Before you are discovered," he interrupted her sternly, his hand raised to halt further arguments.

She shook her head. "'Tis little you know of what I do. I have been the fletcher for years. Kenneth was only a child when I began. No one would have known outside my family had I not made the mistake of taking you into my shop." Her voice roughened in its bitterness. "How

73

could you, who offered to help me in payment for my care of you, treat me so? Is this how you repay me? With censure and brutality?"

At the sound of the tears in her voice, he took a step toward her. Instantly, she skittered to the side. "Do not come near me, Sir Brian." From the workbench behind her, she caught up an arrow, brandishing it point first.

His eyes narrowed. For an instant he tensed, then relaxed. Cocking his head on one side, he chuckled softly. "Little girl, do you realize how ridiculous you appear? I am a seasoned knight. Weapons of all kinds are my business as is self-defense. Do you think that I could not hold my own against a little feathered stick in the hand of an untrained burgesse?" His smile was wide.

"Then leave me alone," she commanded. "Do not come closer. Let us not fight." Her voice assumed a pleading tone. "Please, Sir Brian, go away. I release you from your vow. Only do not give up my secret. To keep it will cause you no trouble. You can be on your way. With luck you may find that squire who stole your armor and be back in your beloved France in only a few weeks. What happens here in England can be of no further interest to you."

Even as she spoke, she lowered the arrow.

The gold-flecked jade of his eyes warmed as he shook his head. "What happens to you does interest me," he insisted. "You saved my life, Gil or Gillian or whatever your real name is. I fear for you. If I saw through your disguise, you are in danger."

Adamantly, she shook her head. "You are wrong. You saw through my disguise because I foolishly took you into the shop with me. I have never allowed anyone to work with me before. I have taken no apprentices, nor

74

shall I."

"How much longer," he jeered, "do you think you can go on without a beard? You are supposed to be aging. How much longer until someone looks at your smooth cheeks and realizes the truth?"

"Kenneth will become the fletcher soon," she protested.

"He speaks of becoming a bowyer."

"He will change his mind."

Brian shook his head. "You cannot know that. You will give up your chance of marriage and family." A thought struck him. "How old are you?"

She stiffened. "I do not choose to tell you that. You are too inquisitive. Remember I am still master here."

His emotions as well as his body had been aroused by their conflict. Too long without a woman, too accustomed to having his commands obeyed, her defiance angered him. His jaw hardened. "You still have not learned your lesson," he gritted. Before she could move to escape him, he had gripped her shoulder again. "How old are you?" he repeated. With his other hand, he flipped up the hem of her scarlet smock. His fingers hooked in the edge of the breastbinder and snagged it downward. Ignoring her cry of rage, he stared at the full cone-shaped mounds that burst free.

Twisting fearfully in his grasp, she sought ineffectually to cover herself from his appraisal.

"No girl, surely," he muttered as he beheld her pale smooth skin that seemed too velvety to be real. Even as he gazed, heated blood surged through his body. As one mesmerized, he put out his hand, his fingers trembling slightly.

Her body was all too real. Beneath his fingertips the

warm flesh pulsed. His eyes flew to her agonized face. Her lips parted as she gasped for air. "Oh, no," she whispered. "Oh, no."

"Beautiful," he sighed. "The gown you wore last night was charming, but it concealed much . . . as all gowns do." His breath fanned her as he bent to place a gentle kiss on her cheek beside her mouth. The harsh man who coldly sought to inspect her body because he was accustomed to having his commands obeyed was gone. He could not even remember why he had taken her again in his arms. He only knew the beauty of her body.

Beyond resistance, Gillian found herself responding wildly to his nearness. Twisting no longer, she leaned against the hand and arm that grasped her. His lips nibbled at the corner of her mouth, sending little frissons of fire and ice across her skin. She moaned slightly. Her pliancy acted as a command to him. His free hand smoothed the folds of the smock back over her shoulders baring her to the waist.

She shivered, her head sinking backward into the cradle of his shoulder and arm. The rasp of his palm on her nipple sent a jet of fire through her. Suddenly her legs would support her no longer. As she collapsed weakly, he lowered her gently to the ground, cradling her across his thighs.

The tip of his tongue traced the outline of her lips before he parted them again to caress and taste her. With fingers that trembled, Gillian touched his cheek where a heightened color began to glow. Her bare breasts brushed against the rough wool tunic as she stirred involuntarily, restlessly seeking respite from their tingling.

The knight released her mouth as he enfolded her in his arms, pressing her tightly against his chest. His lips spoke at her ear. "Do they ache, sweetheart? How cruel you are to yourself to keep them bound so tightly all day! Poor things." He whispered these last words in her ear as his tongue flicked its lobe.

His silly, soft words pleased her. No one in her memory had ever said such sweet things to her. Was this the romance she had heard of in the songs of the traveling minstrels? She smiled shyly. "I have not minded," she assured him softly, "until now."

"Shall I kiss them for you, my lady?"

She shuddered at the thought. "I . . . I . . ."

"'Tis a most pleasant thing, I do assure you," he hastened to add as he planted a row of tender nibbling kisses down her neck.

The action made her squirm and shiver. He was turning her blood to liquid fire. Already it pounded in her ears. She could feel it staining her cheeks. "I do not know if . . . if . . . Is such a thing? . . ."

He chuckled softly. "Let me show you." He bent his head.

Before he actually touched the nipple, she felt his breath. Provocatively, he blew across her fevered skin which tightened involuntarily in anticipation. "How beautifully you bloom for me," he whispered, raising his face to look into her eyes. "Like a little pink rose. I must kiss it." He hesitated, his expression questioning.

She stared at him. His face loomed above her, hard and strong, his passion leashed, but straining. Suddenly, more than she feared his kisses, she wanted his mouth on her body. The kisses she had tasted were the most pleasurable things she had ever known. Her lashes fluttered over her eyes. She shuddered slightly. "Yes," she sighed.

His tongue touched the pink tip, tracing it in warm, moist circles. First one breast received his attention and then the other. Slowly, persuasively, deliberately, he kindled the fire within her.

His teeth replaced his lips, and the tiny nibbles which had so moved her as they traced the skin along her neck seemed like tiny shocks of pleasure rather than pain. How odd that a man's teeth should feel so pleasurable! Love was certainly the strangest of . . .

A slightly harder nip wrung a moan from her lips as she clasped his face between her hands. "Oh, please," she cried, drawing her knee up and raising her lower body toward his.

"Why do you cry out?" His voice was the voice of the tempter. His eyes glittered as they searched her face so close to his own. "Why do you raise yourself to me?"

"I want. . ." She could not answer. She did not know what she wanted.

His lips, then his teeth found her other nipple, wreaking the same punishment on its swollen tip. "Tell me what you want."

She gasped for breath, her voice a sob when she answered. "I do not know. Oh, Sir Brian, believe me. I do not know."

He chuckled. "Come, my lady. You are no thirteen-year-old girl. These breasts are fully ripe. You are a woman. Do not play games with me. I want no misunderstandings later."

"Mis-misunderstandings?"

At the quiver in her voice he paused. His breathing steadied somewhat. Narrowly observing her reaction, he lowered his hand to the joining of her thighs. Her eyes flew wide with surprise as his fingers pressed firmly against her virgin mount kneading it gently.

Her fingers slid from his cheeks to clutch his shoulders as she half-closed her eyes. Like a cat she submitted to the strange pleasure his fingers brought to her body by touching that singular spot. A sigh escaped her.

Experimentally, he took his hand away, allowing it to rest gently on the top of her thigh. Her forehead creased; she opened her eyes questioningly. "You must tell me what you want," he said as if she had spoken.

She shook her head ever so slightly. Her cheek rasped against the rough wool that covered his body. His hand lay slack upon her thigh. The tension went out of her body as she became aware of the slightly precarious tilt of his thighs. She was in danger of sliding off onto the floor. To save herself, she dropped one hand off his shoulder to support herself.

Unceremoniously, he heaved her over on her side, rising and straightening his long legs. With one hand he protected his injured side while he stretched gingerly with the other. He did not look again at her breasts before he turned away to adjust his clothing over the bulge prominent in his loins.

At the sight of his broad back, she sat up. Hot blood ran into her cheeks as she dragged up the breastbinder, patting it into place, and pulled down her smock. Scrambling to her feet, she, too, turned her back on the center of the room to stare with unseeing eyes out the door at the patch of sunshine on the flagstones of the inner court.

She heard him move behind her, heard the stool creak as he sat on it.

"How many more of these damned arrows?" he croaked at last.

79

She jumped at the sound of his voice, so unlike its usual deep, pleasant tone. "We are more than half through with the commission," she replied. "Less than a week's work should finish everything. If you would like to be gone, I—"

"I shall finish what I began!" he snarled.

"There is no need," she argued. "I can finish everything. You have almost completed all the point ends. You work very fast. Your skill improves daily."

The tension of the sexual encounter began to dissipate in the fast-warming air. He drew in his breath running a hand around the back of his neck before picking up another shaft. "Think you I would make a good fletcher's apppentice, Mistress Gill . . . Master Gil?"

She grinned as she seated herself at the door. "I think you could be a master of any craft that you sought to pursue, Sir Brian. You have determination and steadiness. Your patience is not so good, but you learn quickly."

"I hate the tediousness of it," he confessed.

"It requires little in the way of exercise," she agreed.

They worked in companionable silence for a few minutes.

"I would have taken you with me," he said at last, a rueful note in his voice.

Gillian stared at his broad back. "You would?"

His back remained turned toward her. His hands kept busy as he talked. "I had never known any boy with your qualities of steadiness and trustworthiness, not to mention loyalty. I thought you were wasted here in this dismal shop working for your uncle until you got old. I would have made you my squire, trained you, taken you into battle with me. A battlefield commission is not uncommon. You could have been a knight in a few years. I would have taught you everything." His voice deepened with regret.

She bowed her head, cognizant of the compliment he was paying her. At the same time, she felt a tinge of resentment at his attitude. Had she been the boy he thought her, she would not have accompanied him, she told herself. Did he not see the deep pride she took in her work? Did he not realize the time, the years of training that she had already taken to be the master fletcher? She opened her mouth to speak, then closed it abruptly.

No. He would not understand. His attitude toward craftsmen was deeply ingrained. They were beneath him.

The day wore on. As if by common consent, when Kenneth brought some food and ale at midday, neither stopped work. Instead they ate where they were, bent steadfastly to their jobs, each taking a bite at random and washing it down without thinking.

When the interior became too dim to see, Brian moved himself to the doorway, sliding down opposite her, to take advantage of the waning light and finish the last sanding.

At length he stood. "Finished," he announced. "Every last one of them ready to set the point to."

She smiled a little wearily and straightened her back. "We have done well. I have kept up with you. Tomorrow I will show you how to set the points while I finish the fletching. We shall be ready to deliver the commission by the end of the week."

He set the arrow aside and pulled her to her feet. Seriously, he gazed into her eyes. The dying sun threw its final rays on her face. "Why did you not tell me what you wanted?" he asked seriously.

She blushed. "I do not know what I wanted," she replied simply.

"I rather thought that had been the case," he smiled ruefully. "I see I must revise my concepts of the daughters of peasants. I had heard that all farm girls lost their virtue shortly after their thirteenth birthdays. You have proved that tale false."

A wry expression twisted her mouth. "For that lesson I am sure all the farm girls thank me. But you still have to prove it with them." She shrugged away from him. "Not only was your first concept false, but your second one is likewise. I am not a peasant. Nor am I a farm girl. I am a craftsman."

He shrugged his broad shoulders. "I cannot see the difference. You work for a living. You are not a lady to the manor born. What matter if you work among feathers on or off a bird?"

Her rage boiled over. "Oo-o-ooh! You overtrained ox! You insult me without even trying. Never have I met anyone with such a lack of perception. Tell me. Is it only because you are a Frenchman? Are all Frenchmen so stupid that they cannot see anything—even the most basic concepts?"

"No," he replied haughtily. "Frenchmen see the basic concepts clearly. 'Tis only English, with their lack of appreciation for manners, for customs, for the respect that is due to rank and position, that fail to see basic concepts."

Her face was flushed with rage rather than embarrassment. "I am surprised that you could bring yourself to kiss someone so low."

He regarded her calmly. "Oh, I can bring myself to kiss almost any pretty face, mistress. I am a man as any other.

Men seek their pleasures where they find them. And I have tumbled many a peasant girl in many a hayrick along many a roadside between here and Outremer." He grinned shamelessly.

With a gasp she spun away, but he caught her, turned her back to face him, and tilted up her chin. "Furthermore, I never yet found one virginal nor unwilling." His grin changed to a gentle smile.

"Had you been unwilling, I would not have taken you," he continued softly. "My strength is not yet returned, but I am growing thirsty for a woman. Nevertheless, I would not take anyone who was unwilling. That type of lust is an acquired taste. I have seen it wreaked on the helpless after a battle by men too shocked to know what they do. It will never be my way."

His eyes held a faraway look for a second. Then he stared into her eyes again. "All my experiences have led me to recognize that you were something different. Mistress Gillian, you are a virgin rarely encountered outside a convent. You do not even know what you want. Confess. I am the first man who has ever kissed you."

She closed her eyes, somehow feeling ashamed of some inadequacy.

"No other has looked at your beautiful body, nor touched its secrets."

She nodded miserably.

He stepped back formally. "Then, my lady, I would not be the ingrate and take the babe's treasure. I am a knight. We are sworn to protect the weak and guard the pure." He bowed low. "I leave you as I found you. No man can say that Brian de Trenanay is dishonorable." So saying he left the shop to wash for supper.

Chapter Seven

When Gillian entered the common room of their living quarters, she was surprised to find Uncle Tobin there before her. The old man slumped in his chair, his arms draped limply across his knees as if he slept. To be here before her was so unlike him that she stared amazed. Tobin Walton came late to supper more often than not. When he did arrive on time, he usually rushed through the meal and returned to his beloved workshop to work far into the night by candlelight. His bows were his life as he had often said.

Thinking she would let him rest until supper, Gillian tiptoed silently away leaving him to slumber on. To her consternation the cook greeted her with an involved tale of woe about his experience at the market. In consequence he had done little to prepare the supper. Suddenly so tired she could hardly think, Gillian waved him to silence commanding him to serve broken meats from last night's roast and a lentil soup.

Her steps dragging, she mounted the stairs to her room. The heat of the upstairs room which had been closed tightly all day stifled her. Stripping away her soiled clothing, she wearily sponged her face, neck, and shoulders with tepid water before sprawling face up on the bed.

Her mind whirled as she tried unsuccessfully to sort out the happenings of the day and make some sense of the feelings that Brian had aroused in her. She was too tired to think. She would close her eyes and lie very quietly while she composed her mind. Then she would rise, dress, and go down to supper. In case the cook could prepare something edible on such short notice. In a burst of self-pity, she reflected that she had too much to do being two people. Either Gil or Gillian ended up with a neglected job. In this case Gil had no supper because Gillian had not supervised the running of the household efficiently. Disgusted with herself, she rolled over and closed her eyes. Just for a minute. Only for a minute.

At the sight of Tobin Walton's face, Brian de Trenanay sprang to his side. The older man's head lolled sideways on the back of the chair. His usual healthy flush was replaced by a grayish pallor. When Brian touched the man's forehead, he found it unnaturally cool and bedewed with sweat.

Uncle Tobin stirred feebly, fluttering his callused fingertips toward his throat. In understanding Brian loosed the man's neckcloth and tilted his head upright, gratified to hear his host's breathing ease somewhat.

"What happened? Where do you hurt?"

The breath came rasping from the slack lips. "Chest . . ." Again the fluttering hand movement.

Brian pulled aside the man's clothing but could see nothing. The deep-barreled rib cage barely moved, so labored was the breathing. Pasty white, heavily muscled, covered in the center with a mat of grayish white curly hair, the chest looked normal. Something must be amiss inside the man's chest.

Brian left the man's side for a moment to a return with a pitcher of ale from the kitchen. Pouring a draught, he held it to Tobin's colorless lips. The man could manage no more than a few sips although his eyes spoke his gratitude before they closed weakly.

Without further preamble Brian slipped his good right arm under Tobin's shoulders and heaved the man to his feet. Crouching, he guided the heavy body onto his right shoulder and lifted gingerly, using primarily the strength in his thighs. Nevertheless the weight wrenched his half-healed side, eliciting a grunt that Brian made no effort to suppress.

The knight was dripping with perspiration when he stretched Tobin's body at length on the bed. The bowyer's face looked grayer than ever; his breath came in barely perceptible movements of his chest. Ignorant of the care of such a condition, Brian covered him and went in search of Gil.

When a knock drew no response, he opened her door. In the dimness of the room her body bloomed palely opalescent. Despite the urgency of the situation, he could not suppress the instinctive tightening of his loins at the sight of her long straight limbs flung wide on the dark linen spread. He shook his head in wonder that he had ever taken her for a boy. Her femininity was so obvious.

"Gillian," he called softly, as he approached the bed. "Gillian."

She stirred groggily then buried her face in the pillow with a muffled groan.

"Gil," he called again. "Wake up."

"Uh-uh."

He touched her shoulder trying to keep his eyes from the firm clean curve of her buttocks. "Gil, you must get up. Uncle Tobin is sick."

Her eyes opened, staring uncomprehendingly at the man's thighs in her line of vision. Disoriented and unaware, she pushed herself up to a sitting position. "Uncle Tobin?"

Brian gave up all pretense of control. Staring frankly at the slender body completely nude in the fading light of day, he clenched his fists. At least he would keep his hands off her. "Uncle Tobin has had some sort of seizure. I have carried him to his room."

She ran her fingers through her hair, then childishly dug her fists into her eyes to rub the sleep from them. "I'm coming," she moaned. Not until she swung her legs over the side of the bed did she become aware of her nudity. "My God!"

Immediately, he spun around presenting her with his back. "Hurry, Gil," was all he said.

Suddenly, she giggled.

His shoulders stiffened. He glanced inquiringly over his shoulder.

She had gathered the spread around her body and stood looking around her dazedly. Was she hysterical? She giggled again.

"Gil?"

"I was just thinking . . . how you can call me Gil when you have proof incontrovertible before your very eyes. You can have no doubts about my sex." She rounded the end of the bed, trailing the spread behind her. Awkwardly she bent to retrieve her clothing from the floor.

"I never did have, my lady. Not since I have been in my right mind and caught sight of you. No two people can look so much alike as you and your twin brother pretended to do." He stirred uncomfortably as he heard the rustle of her clothing.

Then she was beside him, touching his upper arm. "I am ready." Her face was calm as she looked up into his eyes.

"Then come, Gil." He strode ahead to open the door.

Tobin Walton lay like one dead. His breath rattled faintly in his throat.

"Shall I go for a physician?" Brian offered as he stared at Gil, who bent over the bed, her face suddenly gone pale.

The girl raised anguished eyes to his. "Perhaps you had better. He is beyond my simple skills. I fear for him. Oh, Brian. I fear he has had some kind of seizure that may leave him permanently damaged. 'Twas so with my father. One day he was well. The next, stretched flat on his back. He never regained his senses." These last words were uttered in a choked voice. She put her hand over her mouth.

Brian wasted no time. "Where is the physician's office?" he asked gruffly.

"At the head of the lane where it turns into the market circle." Gil wiped perspiration from her uncle's forehead with the edge of the sheet. "Send someone to find Kenneth and bring ale, please," she begged.

Brian's fingers closed over hers in silent comfort before he hurried out. She heard him taking the stairs in great bounding strides, heard him calling for Kenneth. As in a daze she regarded her uncle, the patriarch of her family. If he died, she would be the oldest. How would she handle herself without him as a buffer?

"Uncle Tobin," she whispered. "Oh, Uncle Tobin." She pressed a kiss against his cheek. How shrunken he already appeared! Tears started in her eyes as she drew a sobbing breath.

The eyelids flickered slightly. "Lass . . ." The word slipped from between his lips on the breath he expelled.

"Oh, Uncle." She touched his cheek. "The physician will be here as soon as Brian can fetch him. You will be all right."

Beneath her fingers the head stirred slightly in negation. The eyelids flickered again. ". . . Commis . . . sion . . ."

"Oh, Uncle Tobin." She was sobbing softly now. "Please save your strength. Do not worry about the commission. 'Tis no matter. *You* matter."

The eyelids flickered again. The breath hissed faintly between the parted lips. "Bows . . ."

"Kenneth can finish them. Or he can get one of the other bowyers to help him." Frantically, she wasted a glance at the door. Where were Kenneth and Brian? A trickle of liquid slipped from the corner of her uncle's mouth. Tenderly, she blotted it with the edge of the sheet. Not even a pitcher of water was included in the Spartan appointments of her uncle's room.

Not for endless minutes did she hear the sound of hurrying footsteps on the stairs outside. Expecting Kenneth, she was surprised to see Brian bearing a tray.

Awkwardly, the knight crossed the space to the bed, his eyes fixed on the items balanced on the tray. With a sigh of relief he set them down on the floor.

Despite her concern, Gillian could not suppress a smile. The trek up the stairs probably represented the first and only time that Brian de Trenanay had ever carried anything such as a servant might do.

Wiping his hands on his chausses, he poured ale from the pitcher into the tankard and held it out to her. "I have sent Kenneth for the physician. He could run faster than I and besides . . . he knew the way." He hoisted himself gingerly favoring his side as he did so.

Gil slipped her hand under Uncle Tobin's neck. "Here is some ale for you, Uncle. Try a sip."

But the grizzled head was a dead weight in her hand while the ale trickled uselessly down the side of his mouth and into his beard. With a sob Gil gently lowered him to the pillow. Brian sought and found the weakly fluttering pulse in the flaccid wrist. "Keep up your spirits." He patted her shoulder awkwardly. "As long as he is alive, there is hope. When he regains consciousness, he will mayhap be stronger. Sleep is a great healer of wounds."

Skeptically, but gratefully, she smiled at him. A knight whose only experiences were with younger men whose bodies were in the peak of condition could not be expected to know the illnesses of older men in their declining years. Nevertheless, his words warmed her. Somehow, his presence left her feeling less alone.

Weary hours later Brian, Kenneth, and Gillian sat together in the parlor awaiting the physician's descent. The prospect was not good. Within minutes after he had made the initial examination, he had sent for the leech to bleed the patient. The family had not been allowed to stay in the room during that procedure.

Huddled against his sister's side, Kenneth shivered from time to time as nervous rigors set his body atremble. "What will become of us if Uncle Tobin dies?"

Kissing the top of his head, Gillian smiled wanly. "We will go on as before. You will be the bowyer and I, the fletcher."

"But . . ."

Brian raised a hand in warning. The bedroom door opened at the head of the stairs. The physician and his leech were descending.

Gillian sprang to her feet, her hands outstretched. Her brown eyes skipped from one to the other. The leech showed little interest. Indeed his stolid expression gave the impression that he evinced little interest in anything. His job was to gather leeches from the salt marshes. Beyond that he had no mind for anything else.

The physician's face was grave. "I have bled him, so the humors may be equalized; but I fear that some damage may have been done by the excess of blood," he intoned without preamble. "A most sanguinary man is Master Walton. I have thought several times in the past that he should have had a regular time when he should be leeched. Indeed, I spoke to him of this some while ago. But he refused." The man shook his head; his lips twitched in a slight smile.

Uttering a faint exclamation, Brian turned away and proceeded to pour himself a tankard of ale. Gillian glanced at him quickly. Beside her the man of medicine stiffened. "Evidently, you disagree with my treatment, sir," he remarked stonily.

Brian shrugged. "A man has just so much blood in

him. To let it out unnecessarily seems a waste."

"Ah, but what if he have too much?" The physician began to develop his favorite theme. "The balance of humors in the body is something that young men do not understand." This remark was directed soothingly toward Gillian, who stared doubtfully at Brian's back. "I assure you, Mistress Gillian, that my treatment will restore Master Walton to health." He paused delicately and rolled his eyes toward the ceiling. "If it be God's will that he be restored. Some things are left in the hands of the Almighty. His skill far surpasses man's."

"Far indeed," Brian snorted.

The physican drew his taffeta-lined cloak around him. "I have left a mixture to strengthen Master Walton when he revives. He should drink much water and eat nothing at all, except thin broths. Above all, give him no ale, nor strong drink, nor red beef." He looked at Brian significantly. "These things thicken and heat the blood. Master Walton's needs to be cooled."

Gillian followed him to the door where he turned back for one last word. "Tomorrow I would speak with young Master Gil. He, as head of the household now, will need to be informed of his uncle's condition."

With the door closed behind him, Gillian sank down on the bench before the fireplace. No fire had been lighted. The room was almost in darkness except for a branch of candles on the table. For several minutes no one spoke.

At last Brian broke the silence. "Has the cook prepared us some dinner?"

Both brother and sister roused at the question. Hunger asserted itself in healthy young bodies. Kenneth grinned slightly. "I had forgotten all about eating."

Gillian grinned in her turn. "'Tis the first time." Playfully, she jabbed at her little brother, cuffing him lightly on the shoulder. "Surely, Cook has prepared something although by this time it is probably cold."

The three sat silent over a meal of cold soup and hard bread. No one had the heart to do more than pick at the food. Finally, Kenneth laid down his spoon in disgust. "Enough is enough," he groaned softly. Rising he hugged his sister tightly around the shoulder. "I think things will look better in the morning," he prophesized with wisdom beyond his age.

"Good night, Kenneth." Gillian kissed him wearily on the forehead.

When the boy had left, she looked at Brian. "Will you stay in the house, Sir Brian? My bed will not be used. I shall stay in Uncle Tobin's room. I . . . I would appreciate your being near by . . . in case I need help."

"We can watch together," Brian suggested softly. His heart stirred strangely. She looked so tired. The events of the day had drawn a deep furrow between her brows. Her slender shoulders slumped beneath the fabric of her dress.

Shaking her head, she pushed back her chair. Instantly, he was beside her placing his arm around her shoulder, supporting her as he led her from the kitchen. She stiffened, remembering the near assault on her person in the shop that day. Had she been wrong to ask him to stay in the house with them? Never had she felt so alone or so vulnerable. How she longed to lay her head on his shoulder and with it her responsibilities if even for a moment.

But she dared not. The memory of what had happened in the shop, the fear of exposure of her sex to the world, the fear of what would happen if Uncle Tobin died, all seemed overwhelming. So she stiffened her spine. Brian de Trenanay might be a friend. But first, he was a man. Women were unworthy and incapable in the eyes of most men. He might decide to expose her "for her own good," considering that she was probably incompetent to assume the responsibility and therefore the destiny for her family. He might merely decide to take advantage of her unprotected state and press himself upon her physically. The debt which had bound him to her was paid. The commission was finished.

With what she hoped was a cool and assured demeanor, she stepped away from him. Instantly, he let his arm drop. "I thank you for your offer, Sir Brian, but you are tired. You have worked hard all day. I took a nap. I will sit with my uncle. If you will but be here in the house, I can summon you in case of need."

Her brown eyes seemed black in the flickering candlelight. Brian stared into their depths, reading nothing. Yet the coldness of her voice told him much. He had frightened her with his violence. He damned himself for the stupidity of his action. He had only added to her burdens. Yet his behavior might serve a useful purpose. She would be more on her guard than ever. With Tobin incapacitated, perhaps forever, she might see the futility of this disguise and abandon it.

He bowed slightly from the waist. "As you will, Mistress Fletcher. May I know whom I will address in the morning? Will it be Master Gil or Mistress Gillian?"

She flushed slightly and laid a tired hand to her forehead. "You heard the physician. He wishes to speak to Master Gil. Gillian will have to disappear for a while."

"The good people who come to visit Master Walton

will think it strange that his niece prefers to nurse some aunt in another township rather than devote herself to the care of her uncle," Brian reminded her. "'Tis time to give up this foolish masque, Gillian."

"Never!" She retreated from him, back into the shadows away from the candlelight.

"Tobin was a fool to let it begin. Now he cannot protect you."

"Leave me, Sir Brian!" she commanded angrily. "You do not have a say in this decision. What I did I would do again. If necessary, Gillian will die of the plague. What chance has she to live in this world of men unprotected? A chance to marry some lout who would use her body to get children on until she died in childbirth, a chance to be nothing in this life but a stupid and ill-used housewife." She spat the last word from her mouth.

"'Tis what you were made for," Brian argued doggedly. "There is a plan in all things. Women were made to bear children and to care for their husbands. Men were made to work and care for their families."

"Ah, but men have choices, whether to marry or not. And if they do not, they do not starve or live dependent on others. You, Sir Brian, where is your wife? You ride free from town to town, from land to land. You are respected and admired wherever you go. What if Gillian Fletcher were to try to do the same thing?"

"A woman . . ." Brian's voice was incredulous. "A woman ride about fighting in tournaments." He laughed. The idea was ridiculous.

"She might not be able to fight, but what if she were an armorer, or a surgeon, or a . . . ?" Her voice rose hysterically.

He held up his hand for silence. "You are overtired.

Mistress Fletcher. Calm yourself." The other hand came out placatingly. "Gil," he whispered. "Gil. You can trust me. I will be faithful. You have nothing to fear from Brian de Trenanay. This I swear to you."

Silence answered this pledge.

He shrugged tiredly before turning away to scatter the fire on the hearth. "I will put all to rights down here. Get yourself comfortable in Uncle Tobin's room." Behind him he heard the rustle of her clothing as she left.

When he came up the stairs, her room was empty, the spread from her bed was gone as was one of the pillows. Pulling his tunic over his head, he sat on the edge of her bed to pull off his boots. The feather mattress sank beneath his weight. Idly he realized that he looked forward to the soft sleep it would afford. Stripping off his chausses, he hung his garments over the back of the chair and yawned hugely. He was sleepy.

Clad in only his loincloth, he padded across the hall to the door of Tobin's room. "Gil," he called softly.

"What?" came the reply.

"Shall I leave the doors open? That way you can call to me if you need me."

Silence again followed his question. He was about to turn away when at last an answer came.

"Yes, thank you."

Chapter Eight

"You . . . mus . . . take . . . th' . . . th' . . . commission . . . Gil." Tobin Walton's voice was slurred, the words coming thickly from his throat with many a pause between them as he struggled to remember their sense. He smiled faintly, his mouth curving up on one side only. His right side lay almost paralyzed. Only an occasional monumental effort allowed him to twitch his thumb or stir his leg. "Pro . . . mised . . . planned . . . trip . . . .you . . . Kenneth . . ."

Tears sparkled in Gillian's eyes. Although the physician assured her that Uncle Tobin would recover some use of himself, she could not doubt but that the road to full strength was too long for a man his age. The good right hand of a craftsman was all in all. Without its capability the heart would go out of the man. "Would that you were able to make the journey?" she whispered, kissing him on the forehead.

He frowned, his left eyebrow drawing in toward the center of his forehead and giving him an unconsciously comical appearance. Clumsily, he patted her hand before his eyes closed. Finally, his breathing evened, indicating that he had drifted into a natural sleep.

With a light tap at the door Kenneth entered. He tiptoed to the bedside where he stared down at his uncle. His young face was grave. At last he motioned with his head that Gil was to accompany him out of the room.

"Did he tell you?" he asked without preamble.

"Yes," his sister replied.

"He talked to me yesternight while I sat with him. I had to leave the room afterward to weep. 'Twould worry him if he saw me weep."

"There must be someone who can take the commission to London. What about Master Jenkin?" Gil knew the answer before she asked the question.

Kenneth snorted. "That old thief. If he took his commission and ours, we would have seen the last of him. He would set up a new business somewhere else on our money."

Brother and sister were silent. The noises made by the cook preparing the evening meal sounded loudly in the quiet room. At last Gil drew a deep breath. "I must make preparations to leave without delay."

Kenneth nodded. His chin quivered. "I shall be the man while you are gone. Master Gil, the fletcher, will take the commission of bows and arrows from York Minster to London." A tear overflowed down his smooth cheek. "Perhaps you will see the king."

Gil looked inquiringly at her brother.

"The commission is for King Henry V. Uncle Tobin

100

told me yesternight. 'Twas the first time he had felt able to talk. He was afraid he might not be able to tell you. I am too young to make the journey, but not too young to stay here and take care of the shop." He snuffled slightly, wiped the back of his hand across his cheeks, and shook his head. "I can follow his direction, Gil. I know I can. As soon as he is able, Wat can carry him down to the shop. He can sit with me and direct the work. 'Twill be the chance I have waited for . . . to be a bowyer."

Frowning, Gil raised her hand in protest.

But Kenneth hurried on. "Oh, I know. You want me to be the fletcher. But, Gil, I have not the skill in my fingers that you do. My hands are strong, but not agile. I have tried and tried. The feathers drive me mad. My hands sweat and then all is ruined. You are the fletcher as our father was before you." He grinned almost happily. "When you return we will be bowyer and fletcher together. The Fletcher brothers. What a grand sight we will be in the guildhall! And Uncle Tobin will be the grand master." His eyes glowed at the thought. "I will sit with Uncle Tobin until supper," he offered. "If he wakes I can tell him all about how wonderful everything will be."

Brian found her sitting just as Kenneth had left her. Gillian's hands lay limply crossed in her lap. Her eyes stared into a frightening future. The distance to London from York appalled her. How could she hope to make the trip when she had never been more than ten leagues from her home in her life?

So lost was she in her own terrors that she did not see Brian until he dropped down beside her on one knee and took her hand. "Is . . . is Uncle Tobin worse?"

101

She shook her head. A wan smile lit her face as she stared into the knight's concerned hazel eyes. "No, he is better. He spoke to me this morning and to Kenneth yesternight."

Brian waited patiently, chafing her cold hands between his own warm ones.

She drew in a deep breath. "He gave us some instructions."

Brian chuckled wryly. "And . . ."

"Kenneth is to start work immediately as the bowyer. I am to take the commission to London." She pressed her lips tightly together to still their trembling. Her forehead creased into an anguished frown.

Brian nodded as he dropped back onto his haunches. "I had thought he would have done so."

She stared at the man aghast. "But, Brian, I do not know the way." This last piece of information came out in a wail.

He stared at her for a minute before throwing back his head and laughing. "Is that all that bothers you? 'Tis no cause to be concerned. I shall be your guide. I have paid my debt to you. The commission is completed. 'Twill be my pleasure as a knight to escort you to London." When she looked skeptically at him, he laughed. "Knights are, after all, better trained to guard and guide than to labor with their hands."

"You are so good, Brian." She bent her head over his hands that warmed her own. In a gesture as spontaneous as it was charming, she kissed the scarred fingertips.

It was the wrong thing to do. Liquid fire shot through his body. Dressed in boy's clothing, every curve of her long, shapely legs was revealed. He had seen her body and had held it. Furthermore, his celibate state had continued much longer than he had ever thought possible. His hands clenched as his breath burst from between his lips.

Startled, she flung up her head.

They stared into each other's eyes. There she read his desire, hot and passionate. He was after all a man. Although she did not understand what he was feeling, she realized that he wanted her. "Careful, Mistress Gillian," he whispered.

She pulled her hands away. Sternly, she rose to her feet, staring down into his gold-flecked eyes. "Gillian is dead," she announced. "She will never return. Only Gil will return from London to resume his rightful place as the fletcher. Kenneth will be the bowyer and I will be the fletcher."

They joined with the other craftsmen from York Minster who also carried their commissions for the king. Most had both journeymen and apprentices to add strength to the escort. Since Tobin Walton's illness was well known, all understood the odd-assorted pair of knight and youth. More than one nodded his head sagely, thinking that if Gil Fletcher had been wise, he would have taken several apprentices long ago. Had he done so, he would have had the help he now required in this emergency.

The knight rode beside the carefully packed wagon. Uncle Tobin's precious bows had been carefully shielded from the elements by oiled hides and raw wool. Gil's arrows likewise were protected in wooden barrels, covered over with the same hides and bestowed evenly along the wagon's bed. Still the weight was prodigious for the two white oxen to draw.

Though the distance was no more than two hundred miles as the crow flies, the roads zigzagged from town to town increasing the distance almost by half again. From York they would travel more west than south to Leeds where they expected to join an even larger group.

From the day he had discovered the source of the commission, Brian had grown more and more morose. The English king could not be ordering this huge supply of English weaponry unless he were planning war. And the war would most certainly be waged against France.

"You have made me a traitor," he snarled at Gil, when she inquired after his black mood. "You set me to making arrows to kill Frenchmen."

"I did not know that," she objected. "Nor do you."

"Hunting arrows indeed," he scoffed. "No wonder you looked at me so oddly when I made remarks about the game running away. An archer must shoot rapidly if he is to bring down a mounted knight before the destrier can trample him."

"I did not force you into my service," Gil reminded him. "You volunteered to pay what you considered to be a debt. I helped you freely. We all did. You know Uncle Tobin well enough now to realize his ways seem gruff, but he is a kind and generous man. He would not have turned you out."

Throwing her a hard look, Brian spurred his horse forward away from the plodding oxen. The more he thought of his labor, the angrier he became. He had been used to preparing weapons to kill his fellows. Furious at the thought, he ground his teeth to keep from roaring aloud. An old man and a girl had deceived him. He could not wreak his vengeance on the old bowyer, but the young fletcher was another matter.

Leeds lay across the Ure. They would camp on the riverbank that night. A rider on a small punch hailed him, swinging a skin of wine. His expression more a sneer than a smile, Brian accepted the offering gratefully and joined the journeyman in a drink. The wine was almost gone to vinegar, but its bite pleased Brian. Trick him, would she. She would pay.

On the wagon seat the reins slack between her hands, Gillian stared at the unlovely rumps of the slow-moving oxen. Since leaving York, she had sunk deeper and deeper into a depression. The enormity of the task before her, the responsibility facing her when she returned to York, the fear for the life as well as the health of the only member of her family older than herself, all combined to drive her spirit into the dust.

She and she alone had to take the productivity of months over hundreds of miles. Once the bows and arrows were delivered, she would have to make arrangements with the Hansa agent for a letter of credit to transfer her gold to the Hansa agent in York. The letter of credit would be issued, of course, in exchange for a small percentage of the amount, but at least the payment would not be stolen from her on the homeward trip. Indeed, if some catastrophe should befall her, Uncle Tobin could go to the agent in York and eventually, after much difficulty, receive the gold.

Her real depression came from the realization that Gillian Fletcher would have to die. She could not tell why she felt as she did. Kenneth had declared that he wanted to be a bowyer. She could give up fletching. She could marry and have a family. Perhaps her husband, if he were a good craftsman, would allow her to continue her trade. That another would *allow* her to continue her trade rankled. She had been independent too long. Angrily, she acknowledged that she would bitterly resent anyone who tried to tell her what to do.

Glumly, she recalled her haughty replies when Brian had suggested that she give up her trade and assume women's garments again. Yet her very soul cringed at the thought of abandoning her sex forever. To burn the carefully braided hair with which she preserved her disguise; to bury the last two dresses. To live alone without love.

She did not fool herself. No one could ever come near her again. Not close enough to touch her. If someone touched her as Brian had done, she would be discovered. She could have neither husband nor wife. She would never know the sweet breath of a kiss, the soft caress of a hand. A frisson terribly akin to pain slipped down her spine, coiling itself into her belly. She wanted . . .

A wicked thought tickled her mind. She was twenty-five years old. Much too old to marry anyway. No one would want such an old maid. In an age when girls married at thirteen or fourteen, were mothers at fifteen and grandmothers at thirty, she was considered ancient. What matter her precious virginity!

Brian de Trenanay desired her. She had felt his hardness against her body, had felt her own stirrings in response. He was a knight; she, a lady. Perhaps not exactly a lady, but certainly a female. She was a burgesse, not too low for him to notice her.

No, a voice whispered in her mind. No. You will pay a high price for such folly.

Her hands clenched on the reins. She sat straighter on

the wagon seat.

Yes! another voice thundered. Yes. You will never have another chance to taste the pleasure.

She looked around furtively, almost expecting to see the Devil himself as portrayed in the paintings on the front of the church altar. She shivered as with a sudden chill and clamped her teeth together to prevent their chattering. Did she dare? What if there was no pleasure, only pain?

Snatches of conversation overheard between servants, particularly maids, flitted through her mind. Tales of appalling deflorations accompanied by the most earnest entreaties and pleas for mercy. Horror stories of babes conceived without the sacred vows of wedlock.

'Twould be a horrible thing to conceive a child, but she had told so many lies that her fertile mind immediately leaped ahead to plan how such a child's birth could be explained. She smiled at the thought. Perhaps that would be the greatest pleasure of all. Brian de Trenanay was virile and strong. Surely his child would be too. She could have a son of her very own, or a daughter, although she hoped that she would not conceive such a worthless thing. The world was a hard place for daughters.

The day suddenly seemed brighter. She looked around her. The oxen crested the rise up which they had plodded. Below her lay the Ure. Lined up for some distance were the wagons of other craftsmen waiting to cross on the ferry.

Casting a knowledgeable eye at the setting sun, she reckoned that she and Brian would find a night's lodging at the huge inn built on the Leeds' side of the river. Brian, being only one person, could cross early and make arrangements for their bed and stabling. When she arrived, all would be in readiness.

He rode toward her even as she thought. How beautiful and tall he sat his destrier, the sun gilding his sandy hair, turning it to a cap of spun gold. She drew in her breath at the sight.

His anger had dissolved into a sullen black mood which sat on his frowning brow. The sight of her welcoming smile elicited only a slight sneer.

Doubtfully, she stared at him. "Is something the matter, Brian?"

He waved a gloved hand at her in the manner of a man brushing away an annoying fly. Resting the other hand on the pommel of the saddle, he hunched his shoulders and waited.

She hesitated, then shrugged. "May I suggest that you cross with one of the early loads? You could bespeak us a room at the inn as well as stable for our cattle."

One sandy eyebrow rose at the mention of a room. He swayed slightly in the saddle. Something very like a smirk flitted across his face. "Your wish is my command, my la—lad," he slurred. "Room at the inn."

As he wheeled the horse, she called after him, "Bespeak a bath as well, Brian, if such be to be had."

He waved to her to show that he had heard.

She stared reflectively after him. Evidently, he had been sharing some spirits along the way with some other men. She wrinkled her nose ruefully. He had been a sober enough man during his stay in York. Possibly he had indulged himself a bit in celebration of his being free of his labor. Settling down on the wagon seat, she prepared to wait as, one after another, the wagons crawled forward to the ferry.

Assuming a place on the next boat across, Brian dis-

mounted and held his horse's head as he stared back at
the line of wagons. He could pick her wagon easily.
'Twould be more than an hour before she could be able to
cross. He chuckled to himself. Anticipation of the
evening set his blood tingling. She would . . . she
would . . . He shook his head. Damn! He was drunk!

Drunk would never do. He should be alert and in full
possession of his faculties. He wanted to enjoy this night.
A night to remember. He had never bedded a burgesse
before. Furthermore, he had never bedded a virgin, and
she was undoubtedly a virgin. The deceitful creature! He
shook his head, staring hard at the retreating shore with
its line of wagons. Near the brow of the hill stood the
white oxen, small in the brown road and green fields. The
figure on the wagon seat was only a doll.

The Black Ox did a thriving business being the best
resting place between Leeds and York. Above the door
were carved the words, "Dame, God be here. Fellow, ye
be welcome." Brian ducked his head and entered.

"Surely an upper room may be rented for the night.
The meal will be served in the common room throughout
the evening. A bath . . ." Here the innkeeper stroked his
chin gravely and made as if to shake his head.

Meaningfully Brian jingled the purse at his belt.

"Perhaps a small hipbath . . ." the man began.

The knight withdrew a pair of silver coins.

"I can send a servant immediately."

"And when my brother arrives with the wagon, he will
require one too."

"Your brother! . . . God'amercy! With all the business
and meals to prepare . . ."

A third coin gleamed in the broad hand.

The innkeeper bowed low. "When your brother

arrives, one of the lads will bring up fresh hot water and towels."

"'Tis well," Brian nodded smoothly. "We will eat in the common room and the price of the meal will be added to the morrow's reckoning with what small gratuity as befits your service. I shall bathe now." He dropped the coins into the man's outstretched hand.

The room was so small that the hipbath could barely fit between the end of the bed and the window. Likewise, Brian's body was too broad to sit comfortably in it. He contented himself with ladling the warm water over himself and scrubbing himself with the cloth provided. A small copper coin bought him a bottle of wine and two glasses. Dressing himself again, he poured himself a sip and sat down to wait.

As the light of day faded behind the small diamond-shaped panes, the latch lifted. "Brian?"

"Here, Gil," he called from his reclining position on the bed. He could see her silhouette in the door. The long slender legs in the black hose, the scarlet smock reaching to midthigh, belted loosely around her hips and allowed to blouse over to conceal the breasts that he knew lay beneath it.

Behind her a lantern wavered. "'Tis your room, sir," came a bored voice. "Please to rest yourself. Your bath will be up directly as your older brother bespoke."

"May I have the light?" she asked.

For answer the lackey preceded her into the room, raising the hood on the lantern and lighting the candle on the small stand beside the bed. "I be right back, sir."

Standing in the tiny room, only a couple of feet from the bed, Gillian felt a tightening in the muscles of her stomach as her eyes traveled Brian's length from the foot of the bed to the head.

Hands cupped behind his head, he smiled at her warmly. "Your room, my lady, with bath."

Alarmed, she laid her finger to her lips. "Be careful, Brian. Call me Gil please. The walls of the inn might be thin. Someone might overhear who could do me harm."

Half-closing his eyes, he nodded in seeming bored agreement. "Oh, indeed, Gil. 'Twould not do for you to be harmed."

Faintly puzzled by his attitude, she gazed around her curiously. She had never been in an inn before. "This seems comfortable," she began tentatively, taking the steps necessary to bring her to the bed and pressing down on it with her fingertips. "Is the bed comfortable?"

"Very," he grinned. "Although a bit short. We shall not be too crowded."

She did not protest. They were lucky to have a room to themselves. To sleep with many men in the common upper room might reveal her identity. Nervously, she jumped back at the knock at the door.

"Your bath," Brian remarked lazily. "Enter," he called.

The servitor brought two kettles of hot water and a towel. Shaking his head at this excess of cleanliness, he departed.

Gillian stared at the hipbath at the end of the bed, then at Brian. "Will you not leave, my lord?"

"No, Gil. After all, I am your brother. My leaving might arouse suspicion."

Chapter Nine

Brian spoke in such a matter-of-fact tone that, for a full minute, Gillian gazed at him open-mouthed. Then she shook her head in disbelief. Surely, she had misunderstood. Blinking rapidly, she tried again. "I am very tired and very dirty, my lord. Please leave off your jest."

Grinning like a very devil, he propped himself up on one elbow and made a sweeping gesture with his free hand. "Your bath awaits, Brother Gil. Strip down and have at it. I have already bathed. 'Twas most pleasant, I freely admit." He rolled back against the spread with his head braced against the board. "I have never bathed so much in my life as with you Fletchers. I never thought to enjoy such a thing. But, damn, if more and more I do not feel the need. Some would say 'tis a curst habit. Today was such a time. Dusty . . ." He mused on, chuckling to himself.

113

Gillian stared at him. He was teasing. He had to be. "Please, Brian," she said evenly. "Leave off. I am so tired. My water is getting cool."

"Then use it," he urged.

Gillian moved to the end of the bed which sat on a pedestal with curtains on all four sides. If she drew the curtains over the end, she would be screened from his view, she supposed. But he *was* teasing her. No one would know or care whether her "older brother" stayed or went while she bathed.

Giving him an angry glare, she jerked the end curtains closed and emptied one pitcher into the hipbath. The water was only lukewarm when she tested it, but it would feel like heaven to her weary body. Peeking around the edge of the bed, she ascertained that he lay as she had left him. With his wine in his hand, he toasted her as he reclined smiling on the spread.

She made a face at him before ducking back behind the curtain and unbuckling her belt. In quick order she stripped off her boots, hose, and smock, laying them aside to redon when she and Brian went to dinner. Naked, she paused to listen for any sounds on the other side of the curtain.

None came.

Eagerly, she stepped into the tub and sat down. The water rose to her waist. Briskly, she splashed her chest and shoulders. Palming her breasts, she washed them and then her underarms. She was cupping water in her two hands to rinse down her back when his voice froze her.

"Care to have me wash that for you?"

He was grinning at her from the end of the bed. The curtains had been parted, and he lounged at his ease regarding her.

114

Her reaction was lightning fast. She flung the water at his mocking face. While he was cursing and mopping at his eyes, she stood up and reached for the linen towel. Unfortunately, it was not where she had left it. Looking around wildly, she spied it draped over the end of the bed under his elbow. When she dived for it, he held on tightly.

"Oh, no," he snorted, shaking the drops of water from his hair and jerking the towel out of her fingers. "Not tonight, mistress. We have a little score to settle. I paid my debt. Now you pay yours."

Splashing water over the floor, she caught up her smock and held it in front of her. "What are you talking about?"

He chuckled at her predicament, staring pointedly at her long legs and the slender curve of her hip left unconcealed by the inadequate drapery. As he stared, he observed with satisfaction the blush that rose from her throat and suffused her cheeks. This evening promised to be a night to remember. His body stirred and tightened as he contemplated it. No sense making her resentful. Women liked to believe they were loved for themselves alone. Or for their irresistible beauty and fascination. He allowed his eyes to rove over her body, so tantalizingly half revealed.

"Why the debt you have incurred with your beauty, Mistress Gillian."

She snorted, a sound perfectly in keeping with the part she had played. "I am surprised that you can tell such lies with a straight face, Sir Brian. Even more surprised that God does not send a lightning bolt to strike you dead."

Still grinning, Brian swung his legs over the end of the bed allowing them to dangle apart. His hands he spread

115

wide. "I do not lie, sweetheart. God knows the truth when He hears it."

"Stay away!" she cried, stepping out of the tub and trying to back away. The small room confined her retreat to only a couple of paces. Water dripped off her body and pooled around her feet.

He stared at it, pointedly noting as he did so that her toes curled most delightfully.

Following the line of his vision, she girlishly lifted one foot and placed it around the back of the other. "Please, Brian, stop this jesting," she begged. "'Tis not decent. 'Tis broad daylight."

He raised both eyebrows with an accompanying shrug. "So!"

"Well . . . so . . . so . . . you should not see me."

He hoisted himself over the end of the bed and stretched to his full height, flexing his shoulders and drawing a deep breath. "But it gives me pleasure to see you." His voice deepened. He moved toward her, side-stepping the tub. "Your slender white feet, your delicate ankles." Another step.

Wildly, she pressed back against the wall. He was moving too fast. Her daydream had not taken this turn. Indeed, beyond a chaste kiss after which he hugged her to him, she had only a hazy idea of what would follow. Certainly, it all would be conducted in the dark. As far as she knew, everyone made love at night, in the dark, after they went to bed. She told him so.

"Please, Sir Brian. You should wait for nightfall."

"Your softly curving hip, your smooth shoulder . . ." His hand cupped warmly over the portion of her body he described.

At his touch she gasped and closed her eyes. A shiver

116

ran through her body as his masculinity towered over and encompassed her.

". . . the velvet column of your throat . . ." His other hand slid along the skin above her collarbone until it closed around her neck, his thumb pressing into the hollow at its base. His index finger caressed the spot behind her earlobe while his other fingers slid into her close-cropped blond waves.

". . . please . . ." Her voice was a tiny whisper of sound. She caught her lip between her teeth as if to bite back the word.

". . . so made for a man's kiss . . ." His lips trailed down the other side of her neck where he felt the pulse leap wildly. The hand on her shoulder closed over the smock and drew it away. Purposefully, he moved forward, his legs almost straddling hers. The wool of his tunic pressed against her nude length. Deliberately, he moved back and forth to tantalize her nipples with its roughness.

Twisting against him, she moaned. His lips continued their soft punishment of her flesh, pulling back from his teeth, to allow them to also nip her.

"Brian . . . oh, Brian . . . please . . . I beg you . . ."

For long minutes the only sound in the room was the muffled breathing of two bodies punctuated by deep groans of pleasure and tiny gasps for mercy.

At length, it was he who broke the embrace. Stepping away from her, heady with his own success, he held her at arm's length. Surveying her blushing form, he drew a deep, if somewhat agonized, breath of satisfaction. Her nipples bloomed like painfully distended rosebuds. The pale pink aureoles also appeared swollen as if the abrasive wool had stimulated them almost beyond bearing.

117

Despite his resolve to wait, thus tormenting her further, he touched one with fingers that surprised him by their trembling.

Tantalizingly, he rolled the hardened nub between his thumb and third finger. The soft flesh of her belly jumped and quivered. She shifted from one foot to the other.

Keeping his thumb and finger at their work, he began to pat her dry with the linen towel he had draped across his shoulder. In that manner his hand covered her body, touched places never touched by a man before. In particular the tops of her thighs and the dark blond curls that covered her mount of pleasure received his loving ministrations.

When at last he was satisfied, she leaned helplessly against the wall, erotic tremors coursing through her body, her breasts hard, her lips parted by each sighing breath.

"Now," he said softly. "You will want to dress yourself so we may go down and eat."

Her eyelids flickered as if she awoke from some beautiful dream. Grinning at her, he bent for her smock. "Raise your arms," he commanded. When she did so, he could not forbear a soft kiss on each breast as her movement lifted them to him.

"B-But, Brian? . . ." Her voice was muffled within the folds as he slipped the garment over her head.

"'Tis what you wanted, Mistress Gillian," he reminded her, the corners of his mouth twitching with amusement. "Dress yourself." He had to place his hand under her elbow to guide her to the bed, so unsteady was she on her feet. While he watched her, lounging at his ease against the door, his arms crossed upon his chest, she sat down on the edge of the bed to pull on her hose and boots.

As she reached for her belt, he straightened suddenly. Pulling his purse from beneath his tunic, he poured its contents out into his hand. In a moment he came toward her, a chain with a medallion dangling from his fingers.

"Here," he said softly. "This will help you to remember where we are and what we are about." He slipped the chain over her head, and directed the medallion to slide down under her smock. At the same time, he lifted her clothing and adjusted it between her breasts.

"What is it?" she asked breathlessly.

"It is my motto," he explained. "I do not give it to you, you understand. It is mine. I wanted you to think of us while you ate. It is just a simple gold-enameled symbol, not particularly valuable." His look pierced her. Did he think she would steal it?

"What is your motto?"

"It is *Mucro Mors Cristo*. My great grandfather earned it as a Crusader. It means, 'The swordpoint is death on behalf of Christ.'" For an instant his eyes were sober.

She looked up at him solemnly. "Then I shall be extra careful."

He snorted. "You will be always at my side." His sober mood vanished. He hugged her against him. "Come."

Together they went down the rough staircase, she following behind him respectfully as a younger brother should. Across the board from each other, his knee nudged hers apart and inserted itself between.

Their food, round loaves of bread hollowed out and filled with a stew of fish and vegetables, was set before them on pewter plate. The top of the loaf was to be used as a scoop to carry bites to the mouth. No eating utensils

119

were provided, since everyone carried his own knife. Indeed some people carried their own food with them and merely paid a small charge for the innkeeper to prepare it. Pewter tankards of foaming ale were also carelessly set before them.

Gillian's hunger began to stir as she plucked the crust from the top of the loaf. Brian allowed her a few bites before nudging her with his knee. When she looked up, his eyes were smoky with desire. "Touch the medallion, Gil," he commanded.

The food stuck in her throat. Obediently, her fingers fumbled for the metal disk where it swung between her breasts beneath the cloth.

The inn was dark and smoky, crowded with noisy people. No one looked in their direction. They sat at the end of the table farthest from the kitchen and the fire.

"No," he commanded, his voice gruff. "Reach under your smock and touch it."

A blush rose in her throat. Her eyes shifted from side to side to see if they were observed.

"Do it, Gil."

Hesitantly, her hand stole under her smock sliding up between her breasts to grasp the warm gold. She swallowed.

"Are you touching it?" he asked, the gold flecks in his eyes glittering.

"Yes." Her voice was a hiss.

"Is it warm?"

"Yes."

His knee nudged hers. "Now rub it across the tip of your breast."

Her face turned crimson. She gasped as if she had been stabbed. "I cannot."

"You must. It is my command. I want to see you remember what we are going to do when we go back upstairs. I would not like for you to forget while we are eating."

As he stared at the agonized face across from him, his thoughts flashed back in time to the *comtesse* who had taught him the joy and agony of anticipation. It was almost his first bout of love. She had tortured him for hours, teasing him with her body and her voice until he thought he would burst. When at last he had been admitted to her bedchamber, she had made him wait again while she undressed, slowly and seductively baring each silken limb to his tormented eyes. The wait had been worth every anguished moment. When he had driven into her, she had screamed with pleasure, and he had exploded again and again, draining himself but almost collapsing with pleasure.

So it would be tonight. Although a virgin, Gillian was a mature woman, an unusual combination. She should be able to take everything he had to give with joy. He remembered her long strong legs. They would wrap around him tightly.

Her eyes were closed as her hand moved under the smock.

"Do you remember?" he asked softly.

"Yes. I remember."

"Take your hand away," he ordered, taking a long drink of ale.

Gillian could eat nothing else. Wordlessly, she stared at him as he finished his meal with relish and polished off the contents of the tankard. He puzzled her. How could he eat as if nothing had happened? Her body had never felt less like food. It tingled and spasmed. Blood pounded

121

through her veins; her breath hissed through her lungs. She felt a strange warmth and moisture between her legs. Surreptitiously, she shifted in her seat; but when she attempted to close her thighs, Brian's knee prevented her.

"No." He smiled silkily. "Keep yourself open for me."

Frightened at the intensity of her responses, she hung her head. Surely, everyone in the room must be watching them by now.

"Eat your dinner," was the next command.

She shook her head. "I am no longer hungry."

He nodded. "Then are you ready to go upstairs with me?"

She drew a deep shivering breath. She could not think. If he had told her to hold her hand in fire, she felt she would have done so. She tried again unsuccessfully to press her knees together.

He grinned. "How tightly you clasp me, Gil! Will you clasp me as tightly tonight?" He motioned to the servant. "Bring me the accounting and take another couple of tankards of ale to our room." He tossed a coin onto the table in payment for the service.

Chills sliding over her body, she waited until he was ready to rise. "Now, Gil," he said mockingly, releasing her knee as he did so.

She could scarcely stand.

"You foolish young one," he chided for those around him to hear. "He drinks too much, then rises dizzy. He will have a large head on him in the morning."

One man nodded in agreement, but the rest ignored the statement, intent only on filling their bellies before getting to their beds.

Brian flung an arm around her shoulder, his hand

slipping under her arm so the fingers could touch the edge of her breast. He pressed firmly against its swell. The servitor preceded them with the tankards of ale. They mounted the stairs; he, strong and ready; she, weak and breathless.

Once inside the room with the door closed behind them, he swept her up in his arms, cradling her and enclosing her in his warmth. "Oh, mistress," he crooned. "We will have a wondrous loving tonight."

Bearing her to the bed, he set her down on it and began lovingly to undress her. With each garment, he kissed her skin, commenting on its whiteness, its velvety softness. "Like damask," he vowed, running his fingers across the surface of her belly. "A pearl-like sheen to be sure. Gillian, you are as beautiful as any lady in the court of France." Stretching her out in nude splendor, he ran his hands over her body before stepping back to divest himself of his clothing.

The medallion glowed softly in the candlelight as her agitated breathing caused her chest to rise and fall. Fearful and shy, she kept her eyes closed.

"Come, Gillian," he whispered, lifting one knee to the bed beside her. "Look at me," he repeated sternly.

He was a remarkable man. Although not overly tall, his hours of training and strenuous exercise had developed his shoulders and chest to an extraordinary degree. Likewise his horseman's thighs were columns of power. The sandy hair on his chest and body had not bleached in the sun. It was therefore darker and silky fine. From out of a thatch of dark curls sprang his engorged manhood.

At the sight of its length and breadth, she gasped in fear. Horrified, she flung her hand across her eyes.

He chuckled gently. "Now, now, sweetheart. None of

123

that. 'Tis not so very big. You are made to take all of it, you know."

Trembling, she shook her head.

"Oh, yes." He sat down beside her, his fingers playing in her blond fleece, causing her to squirm slightly. "Oh, yes," he assured her. "Think for a minute. You are a tall, strong girl. God made you for the pleasure of men as He made all women. He would not make a mistake. You are just right."

So talking to her as he would a child, he found the tip of her pleasure where it hid in the joining of her thighs. Pressing it in until she gasped, then coaxing it back out again, he watched the play of sensations across her face. Dipping his fingers lower, he trailed one up and down her moist entrance before sliding it into the hot darkness.

His own need was becoming painful. He must have her very soon. He closed his eyes, struggling for control, biting his lip to maintain it.

Her breasts trembled with each agitated breath she drew.

"Sweetheart, Gillian," he whispered, stretching his body beside hers without taking his hand away. The fingers of his other hand sought the nipple of her left breast, squeezing it firmly. "Do you feel feverish and impatient?"

He could see her throat contract as she swallowed. "Yes . . ."

He moved his finger deeper into her body until he encountered her maidenhead. So that was what it felt like. Such a tiny insignificant thing. His finger stirred to find its tiny opening. "Do you ache inside?"

She drew one leg up reflexively. "Yes . . . Oh, yes . . ."

124

"Sweetheart, I feel the same. Put your hand on me."

Timidly her fingers touched his hip, his thigh, fumbled briefly, then found his hardened shaft.

"It is hot and aching for you," he explained. As he spoke, he pressed against the edges of the tiny hole in the membrane. Beneath his touch it began to open.

She gasped at the intrusion, but excitement not pain made her writhe her body. One hand closed over him while the other grasped the spread beneath her.

"Are you ready, sweetheart?"

"Yes . . . Oh! . . ."

At her word he heaved himself over her. His finger pushed aside the veil and buried in her moist depth.

Almost sobbing in his effort to control himself, he withdrew and placed himself at her entrance. With a groan, he bent to her.

Chapter Ten

Fearful of the steely strength she saw there, Gillian stared into Brian's face only short inches from her own. His square jaw clenched; his eyes slitted. She felt him at the entrance to her body, touching, probing, entering her the tiniest bit. She had heard that the first time was painful for a woman. Willing herself to endure, she closed her eyes.

"Look at me," he gritted between his clenched teeth.

Obediently, she opened her eyes.

He slipped one strong hand around her neck caressing the point of her shoulder; the other, he laid warm on her hip. "There is naught to fear," he whispered hoarsely.

She cried out more in surprise than pain as he began to slide himself into her.

"Easy," he soothed. "I will be slow. Relax. Easy. Put your arms around me." His thumb rubbed back and forth on her belly beside her hipbone.

"Brian," she gasped. "You are so big. How can I? . . ."

"Ssh. A bit at a time."

As she began to stretch, she could feel him slide deeper into her. Just when she thought she could take no more, when discomfort seemed to be about to turn to pain, he stopped. Beneath her hands that clasped his back along his ribs, she could feel his muscles bunch and tremble. He drew a deep breath.

Deep within her, nerves quivered and ached. Why did he remain still? She felt that he should move. Unconsciously, she twisted her hips. When he felt her movement, he released his breath in a sigh.

"What do you want, Sweet Gillian? Show me."

For answer she lifted her hips, thrusting them upward against him.

His smile was loving. "Do you truly, sweetheart?" He pulled himself out, then slid back in a bit farther this time.

She sighed. The sensation was not exactly pleasant, yet she wanted him to continue. Perhaps if she edged her body slightly to the left? No. Perhaps to the right?

He swore breathlessly against her neck. His hot breath burned the point between her neck and shoulder. "Sweet Jesus!" he exclaimed. "Are you sure you were a virgin?"

Affronted, she stiffened beneath him.

"Oh, no, Gillian. Ah, no, *chérie*. I did not mean to offend. I found your maidenhead with my own hand before. . . . I only meant . . . you are so . . . so . . . wonderful. Never have I . . . Never has a woman . . ." He began to move faster, pulling himself out and thrusting into her with long steady strokes.

His movements became more and more pleasant. She

quickly found that if she pressed herself up as he came down, she could drive him deeper, thus heightening the sensation. Now a wild excitement began to build within her. She felt as if something were about to happen. She clenched her teeth, determining to experience whatever . . .

Above her, Brian cried out. At the same time his hard shaft pushed deeper into her than he had ever gone.

Almost she . . . what?

Then he collapsed upon her, sweat plastering his chest to mingle with her own.

She waited. To her dismay he did nothing else. Instead, she could feel the shaft within her softening, sliding out of her. Angrily, she clenched her buttocks. She wanted him to stay in her and continue. "Brian!"

His response was a muffled groan.

She hugged him hard against her, but despite her efforts, she was empty. Had she experienced all there was to love-making? No wonder some women complained bitterly. She felt like complaining bitterly herself. She felt angry and excited and agitated and disappointed all at once. "Brian!"

As if he moved with great weariness, he eased his body to the side and rolled off onto his back. His eyes were closed; his mouth, open as he sighed gustily.

Lying beside him, her legs parted, her arms fallen back from his body, she felt foolish. Was this all there was to romantic love? It was nothing like the sweet songs of the minstrels. How could anyone get excited about it? Certainly, Brian reacted now as if he were exhausted. How could anyone find excitement in it? Of course, for a short time she had felt excited just before he had cried out and collapsed.

She shrugged her shoulders irritably. The church taught that the only function of that part of marriage was the conception of children. She supposed that Brian, being a Christian knight, had felt a duty. But how could that be when they were not married? If a child were conceived by their act, it would be a child of sin. Steps would have to be taken to conceal its true birth and legitimize it, so it could grow up in a proper family. No. He must have done that act for some other reason that she did not understand.

The candle guttered in the holder. Even though she was tired from the long drive, she felt strangely nervous. Unlike herself. Turning over on her side, she punched the bolster on the bed and pulled the cover around her shoulders. To her surprise she felt Brian cast his arm over her to draw her into the circle of his body.

Although she stiffened resentfully, he refused to let her alone. Inexorably he drew her in against him, fitted the curve of her hips into his own, drew his thighs up under hers, and cupped his hand around her breast.

"Go to sleep, sweetheart," he whispered drowsily, his lips brushing her ear with a kiss. "Tomorrow morning before we leave, you will have your pleasure too. I swear. Now sleep."

Long she lay staring into the darkness with his even breath warming her neck. Pleasure. Somehow she doubted that she would ever find much pleasure from the act they had just engaged in.

Gillian awoke before Brian. The paleness of early dawn seeped dimly in through the leaded glass. Below in the inn yard she could hear a few stirrings of ostlers and guests getting an early start. The odor of baking bread seeped through the floorboards. Suddenly, she was ravenously hungry.

Gingerly, she moved Brian's arm aside before slipping from the bed. He moaned faintly, rolled over on his back, but settled back into sleep. The medallion dangled between her breasts, striking her as she bent over to draw on her hose.

Pausing, she carried it to the window and stared at it in the strengthening light. It was a beautiful thing. Heavy warm gold, polished from constant contact with his skin, she supposed. The center was a flowering vine entwined about a sword. Around the outside of the symbol was a circlet of blue enamel with the letters of his motto raised in gold. *Mucro Mors Cristo.* She remembered well the feelings this simple object had inspired. A warm flush stained her cheeks and she stirred uneasily. In the faint dawn chill of the room she could feel her nipples harden.

Hastily, she slipped on her smock, belting it firmly around her lean waist and blousing it so that no one could even suspect that her breasts lay beneath it. She ran her fingers through her hair, fitted her cap on her head, and glanced at the sleeping man. He had not moved.

Her stomach growled noisily. Making a face in his direction, she lifted the latch and slipped out into the hallway.

Below in the dining room all was chaos. Anxious to be on their way so as to cover the most distance before nightfall, guests waited impatiently for their morning meals. Servants of both sexes and all ages dashed madly about trying unsuccessfully to provide breakfasts for the noisy throng.

Dropping down at the end of bench, Gillian reached for

the remaining small loaf of fresh-baked bread on the serving plate. The merchant whose hand had already started in that direction scowled darkly. With the cheekiness of a cocky youth, she rolled her eyes at him as she bit into the first food she had really tasted since she and Brian had pulled out of York.

While Gillian munched the roll, a heavy-breasted slattern, sweating from every pore, swept the refuse from the planking with a grimy cloth and slopped down a tureen of steaming groats with bits of pork stirred in. A lackey followed her with a fresh plate of bread. Everybody at the table fell to with alacrity.

Knives sliced the tops off the small loaves and the steaming food was then ladled into the hollow in the bread. Using the sliced off top as a scoop, the men ate until the top was consumed, then tore the bread into soaked chunks and devoured them too. Within minutes some began to leave the table, paying their scores to the innkeeper standing at the door with his lists in his fat hand.

Halfway through her breakfast, Gillian spotted Brian standing at the door, looking around the room. Waving a friendly hand, she caught his attention.

Scowling blackly, he strode in her direction. "You were supposed to remain in the room," he began without preamble.

"Oh, was I?" Gillian's pansy brown eyes widened guiltlessly.

Brian dropped down beside her, his mouth at her ear. "I promised you more," he hissed meaningfully.

"More of that." Gillian made a dismissive gesture with her hand. "I did not really want any more. I thought it too much trouble for nothing that I could see."

"Too much trouble!" Brian's roar turned heads at three tables in both directions. He glanced around him angrily as a red flush mounted into his cheeks. "Too much trouble!" he hissed, lowering his voice. "Just because *you* knew nothing at all about anything. That," he informed her loftily, "is a skill. You have to practice it. It takes many times to get it right."

"Too much trouble for what it was worth!" Gillian popped the last bite of her bread and groats into her mouth and reached for the tankard of ale.

Brian's mouth dropped open, then snapped to like a trap. His eyes narrowed. He laid a heavy hand on her forearm. "You were excited, eager," he muttered. "I have never felt . . . What do you mean . . . 'for what it was worth'?"

She glanced at the heavy hand on her, then at the face scowling incredulously down at her. "All that excitement and upset . . . and . . . work, on your part, that is, and nothing. Nothing happened." She smiled at him as if she were speaking with a somewhat spoiled child. "You strained and labored until you collapsed. Then you went to sleep."

"But . . . But . . ."

"You were tired already," she went on reasonably. "I was too. How much better we would have both felt if we could have just lain down comfortably together and gone to sleep."

So angry that he could not speak, he stared at her. A feeling of inadequacy plagued him. He had been tired. He had not taken the trouble to please her. He had settled down to sleep with merely the promise of some nebulous pleasure in the morning. But, damn her! She was a woman. Women were supposed to be reticent. Not com-

133

plaining and criticizing. How dare she?

All around them travelers were settling for food and lodgings and leaving. "We must be gone," Gillian said practically. "You break your fast and pay the reckoning. I will yoke the oxen and start out. You can easily catch up to me on your horse. That way I will not be so far back in line at the next ferry." Shaking free of his now limp hand, she took a last drink of the ale and rose. Setting her cap more firmly on her fair hair, she was gone.

Brian stared after her, the angry flush fading from his countenance. Several thoughts, none of them particularly pleasant, whirled round in his mind. Uppermost was the memory that he had settled himself for sleep almost immediately after he had rolled from her panting body. With growing shame he remembered her excitement. He could hear the agitation, the frustration in her voice. "'Brian!'"

The same slatternly woman set a tankard of ale down in front of him. "Y'r young friend be not leavin' without payin' the reck'nin'?"

"I will pay," Brian remarked absently.

"He be a fair 'un," she continued, staring across the room where Gillian walked out the door.

Brian grinned wryly. "A fair one indeed," he agreed.

"Pity ye came in so late last night," she remarked, placing her greasy hands under her sagging bosom and heaving. "Many young 'uns like a nice mature type. Gentle, y' know."

Brian stared at the huge udders thrust into his face. "I doubt that Gil would have had the stamina, mistress. He was exhausted from the long drive from York. Went right to bed."

"How about y'rself? When y' come back through, be

not forgettin' Meg." She leered at him revealing a broken tooth in her lower jaw.

"I shall remember." He took a long drink of ale before reaching for the loaf of bread.

As the creature turned away, Brian felt suddenly tired. Although his moments of ecstasy with Gillian had been sublimely satisfying, the morning after at this sordid inn seemed a repetition of too many nights and too many days. He stared disgustedly at the breakfast loaf with now-cooled and congealed groats mounded in the center. The grease from the pork had begun to harden on the rough surface.

He swallowed; his stomach threatened to turn. Looking away, his gaze encountered the broad retreating hips trembling and quaking beneath their soiled and spotted skirt. He could not eat.

Pushing back the bench, he rose, the smoky odoriferous atmosphere assaulting his nostrils. No different from other inns from the Scottish border to the plains of Provence, it sickened him as never before. Paying the reckoning including the price of his own uneaten meal to the amazed innkeeper, he thrust himself out into the foggy morning air.

Gil jumped in surprise, dropping the heavy yoke she had hoisted half off the ground. "Brian! Did you finish your meal? What? . . ."

Growling an unintelligible reply, he caught up the heavy yoke effortlessly and settled it over the necks of the placid white beasts. With efficient movements, he harnessed them to the wagon tongue, slamming the iron pin into place with unnecessary force.

Brown eyes wide, Gil stared at him. "Thank you," she murmured, climbing onto the wagon seat and lifting the reins.

"Slide over," came the curt command. Before she could protest, Brian was gone, returning moments later with his horse which he hitched to the back of the wagon. The heavy saddle and trappings, he flung into the back on top of the cargo.

Obediently, she slid over, surprised and not a little pleased by the company. Her arms felt sore and strained from hauling on the reins yesterday. If he drove even for a couple of hours today, his strength would save her much. The road to London stretched long before her.

She sighed with relief as she leaned back against the wagon seat and flexed her fingers. "I never thought to ask you to take this trouble," she began pleasantly. "But I thank you from the bottom of my heart. And my shoulders and hands thank you, too."

His eyes slid sideways as he cracked the whip above their heads and clucked his tongue loudly. "My horse needs a rest," he responded laconically as the wagon creaked forward protestingly.

The day did not clear. Instead, the skies thickened as first a light mist and then a drizzle began to fall. The ancient roadbed fast turned into a quagmire. The oxen strained mightily against the yoke to keep the heavy-laden wagon moving. Finally, the wagon ahead of them bogged down completely. If they had stopped, the oxen would have been unable to start the load again.

Cursing, Brian thrust the reins into Gil's cold, wet hands and sprang down from the seat. "Keep them moving!" he yelled dashing for their heads to turn them aside before their momentum could be slowed. Mouthing imprecations against the ancestry of the driver of the team ahead of them, Brian slid and stumbled to the beast on the left, dragging its head aside and forcing its brother to follow. The wagon heaved over the ruts and out onto the verge.

Past the bogged wagon whose driver stood on the seat cracking his whip over the backs of his bawling team, Brian guided the dirty white oxen. His fine leather boots were coated with mud; his drenched tunic, plastered to his body.

Thunder rolled as above their heads the heavens opened up. Rain poured down in torrents with such force that the knight staggered. Throwing a swift glance over his shoulder, he saw that Gil had jumped from the wagon seat.

The girl was at the other ox's off side. Plodding along together the four made their laborious way. Past wagon after wagon they continued doggedly.

"If we can find somewhere to stop, we will," Brian yelled.

She nodded drearily in reply.

Behind them he heard the pounding of hooves. Brian cast a quick glance over his shoulder. A group of horsemen were coming up fast behind them. The heavy ironshod hooves kicked clods of mud over him. Angrily, he let go of the ox and turned to face them.

As one man rode by, his contemptuous glance fell on the struggling peasants. His eyes registered shock before he pulled his hood over his face. His countenance paled at the sight of Brian de Trenanay standing arms akimbo, a fearsome scowl on his muddy face.

Too late!

Brian's hazel eyes flashed fire. The Saxon squire!

With a yell, Brian sprang at the man's thigh seeking to bring him from the saddle. But the trained horse side-stepped. Missing his hold altogether in the slippery footing, the knight fell, floundering face down in the mire.

"'Ware, robbers!" the squire cried.

Instantly, several of the men with whom he rode drew sword.

As Brian scrambled to his hands and knees, the flat of a blade across his back sent him sprawling again. Mud caked his nose and eyes. Before he could rise, a point of steel pricked the back of his neck.

"Finish him." He heard the gruff command.

"No!" That was Gil's voice shrieking. Her hands closed over his shoulders. "No! He is my brother. He is simple. He does not know what he does. Sometimes the fit seizes him. . . ."

Her words were cut off by a sharp blow. "Silence! He attacked one of my men." The sword drew blood from his skin.

"No!" Her voice was calmer now. "He is only a poor 'prentice. He cannot even do the work of a journeyman although he is so big. See him."

The sword point came away. Her hands took hold of his shoulders and turned him over face up. Her face was directly above his, her eyes sharp with meaning to warn him. "Fool," she swore. "You have disturbed the gentlemen with your play. Apologize."

Realizing that death for both of them was only a stroke away, he nodded dumbly. So muddy was he by now that he resembled nothing human. The rain spattered his mud-caked features. Pretending dizziness he sat up, holding his head between his hands and grinning foolishly at the mounted men and the two who stood on either side of him, their swords drawn.

"Apologize," came Gil's sharp command.

Instead of speaking, Brian merely moaned and swayed foolishly back and forth.

"'Tis a trick." The squire insisted. "The man attacked me."

"You probably scared him," Gil insisted. "The thunder and rain have made him nervous. He has never been away from home before. He cried like a baby all night last night. Ate no breakfast this morning." She patted the knight's broad shoulder. "Tell the nice men how sorry you are," she said gently.

As if he pouted like a scolded child, Brian sat cross-legged as the rain beat down on his bare head. "Sorry," he said gruffly.

The sword point in his line of vision relaxed visibly. "I tell you . . ."

"If you want to sit here in the rain all day arguing with a half-witted peasant," the commander growled, "so be it. Ride on." With a creak of leather and a jingle of spurs, the two who had dismounted sprang to their saddles. The horses churned mud, liberally spattering Brian and Gil where they crouched beside the oxen. The lightning crackled across the sky as the mounted troop galloped away.

Chapter Eleven

When Brian would have stared after them, Gil's hand firmly pressed against his neck. "Keep your head down or lose it," she hissed.

Brian swore graphically. "'Twas the squire who stole my armor."

"So I guessed by the way you lunged for him." She straightened cautiously, looking warily in the direction the mounted men had taken. Their forms were barely visible in the driving rain. "You can rise now. They have gone."

Soaked to the skin and plastered with mud from head to foot, Brian rolled over onto his hands and knees. Moving as if the mud weighed him down, he climbed to his feet staggering slightly. The rain beat down on his bared head. He slid his hand around the back of his neck and stared at the blood staining his fingers.

"Are you badly cut?" she asked rising on tiptoe to try to see the wound.

With lips pressed tightly together, his eyes slitted against the driving rain, he shook his head. "'Tis a nick. I have had worse being shaved."

She shuddered as she turned away to mount to the wagon seat. "I thought he would kill you."

Without comment Brian strode to the end of the wagon where he dragged his gear from beneath the tarpaulin.

Gil knelt on the wagon seat, her hands doubled into fists. "Brian! What are you? . . ."

"That bastard stole my armor," he gritted, slinging the heavy saddle over the destrier's back. "He left me split open while some damned barber quacked over me. That swine will get it back for me, or . . ."

Gil curled her fingers around the board on which she knelt. "You cannot mean to ride after him. He had friends," she pointed out, striving for reason as the rain slashed across her face.

The entire scene began to take on the quality of a particularly horrifying nightmare. Lightning slashed down the sky striking somewhere close behind them with a crackle of sound and a brilliant flash of light. Brian whirled from his task in time to see the fireball rise into the air. The thunder broke directly over their heads with a deafening explosion.

"Get off that wagon!" he yelled, leaping for the seat as he did so. Cowering beneath the noise, Gil remained frozen. Roughly, he grasped her arm and dragged her over the side and down into the mud. "Under," he growled as another flash whitened the scene and was followed almost immediately by a thunderclap of such volume that the ground seemed to tremble beneath them.

Flat in the mud beneath the wagon, they buried their faces in each other's shoulders and wrapped their arms around each other.

Again the lightning accompanied by the thunder! And again!

The destrier neighed in panic and reared. Its great weight broke the lead rope, and it whirled away into the rain.

"Damn!" Brian swore tiredly as he watched the great animal disappear within seconds. He flopped over onto his back, one arm still around the shuddering girl. Bitterly he stared at the mud-caked boards above him. This cursed country! Water poured off the sides of the wagon in sheets. Pray God the horse would not go far.

In silence they lay shivering miserably while the water pooled around and under their bodies. Gillian's throat began to ache as the cold and damp sank into her very bones. Almost weeping in her discomfort, she pressed herself harder against the knight's solid form. He seemed to her like a rock, oblivious to the elements. How grateful she was for his presence! Shuddering, she examined the propect of his riding off after his former squire and leaving her to carry the commission to London.

He *must* stay with her. He *must*. "Brian."

He did not stir except to tighten his fingers around the point of her shoulder.

"Brian." The rain began to slacken slightly. The thunder rumbled farther off. "Brian," she whispered again. "You must not go after him. You will be killed. The man who commanded him . . . he could have ordered your death with the flick of his hand."

She felt Brian's body tense beside her. "When next we

meet, I will not be on my face in the mud." He made as if to roll from under the wagon. His arm slid roughly from under her shoulder.

"No." She caught at him. "The rain—"

"I doubt that I can get much wetter," he sneered.

"Fool! You—"

"Gillian." He turned to face her; their eyes were level in the increasing brightness signaling the end of the storm. Hard as jade, his gleamed out of an unsmiling countenance from which every vestige of emotion was erased. "I go for my armor. No knight could suffer the insult I have and allow it to go unpunished if he is a true knight. The thought of that filthy knave riding so high . . ." He ground his teeth in his desire for control. His temper overcame him. Furiously, he rolled from under the wagon and sprang to his feet.

The rain had slackened to a light drizzle. Raking a muddy hand through the dripping hair plastered to his forehead, he loped away in the direction the terrified destrier had taken.

It had not gone far. In less than a hundred yards it had halted in a small grove. He found it standing dejectedly, head down, back turned to the rain, a picture of equine misery. When he approached it cautiously, it did not raise its head and made no resistance when he caught up the dragging rope and vaulted onto its back.

Meanwhile, cursing savagely, water dripping from the tip of her nose, Gillian hauled at the yoke. The oxen hunched their shoulders and strained forward, but the wagon refused to move. The soft ground held it mired fast.

As Brian rode up, she threw him a vicious look before turning away to concentrate on the team. Stepping back, she cracked the whip across their backs at the same time giving a yell that tore her already painful throat. The wagon inched forward with a sucking sound as the wheels eased upward out of the trough into which they had sunk.

Wildly elated, she cracked the whip again yelling even louder than before. The wagon lumbered forward as the oxen tossed their heads to settle the yoke more naturally on their shoulders.

Jubilant, she turned to mount to the seat only to behold Brian staggering away, his hand pressed to his side. He had thrown his shoulder against the wheel with all his strength. His herculean effort had dislodged the wagon. Instantly contrite, she dashed to his side, but he fended her off.

With a curse he flung his arm against her chest, causing her to slip to one knee on the muddy grass. "Keep them moving," he snarled as he straightened painfully. "For Sweet Jesus' sake, keep them moving, or it will all be to do over again."

Clumsily, she scrambled back yelling to the oxen as she did so. The placid beasts moved slowly, but steadily onward. Leaping onto the wagon seat, Gil gathered the reins and slapped them over the slick white backs.

Glancing behind her, she saw to her chagrin that Brian had pulled his saddle from the wagon and slung it onto the horse's back. Cinching it expertly, he mounted, favoring his left side as he did so.

"Brian!"

He held out his hand in a gesture to halt her arguments as he spurred the horse alongside. "Gillian, I *will* ride for Leeds. Do not gainsay me. Follow as you will with the wagon. I have made my pledge."

She shook her head. "Brian, you did not see the knight

with whom your squire rode. He was merciless. His face was absolutely impassive as he ordered his men to kill you."

"You need not fear for me on that score," Brian assured her. "He will regard me differently when he learns that I, too, am a knight."

"The commission," she reminded him, at the same time ashamed for her words but willing to try anything to keep him from undertaking a mission she feared would end in disaster for him.

He frowned. "You need not fear I will desert you. I will procure lodging for the night at the first available inn. If not the first on the way into town, then the second. Follow until you find the one."

She looked at him with agonized eyes. Her mouth opened to protest.

"Not a word," he commanded. "I have made you my pledge. I hold hard by my word, but I must and shall find that swine."

Shutting her mouth resignedly, she reached inside her soaked smock and withdrew the gold medallion. "Take this back then," she insisted. "It may help in some small way to convince that knight you do not lie."

Nodding in agreement, he accepted it when she drew it over her head and placed it in his hand. Dropping it around his neck, he saluted her, his smile flashing for the first time that dreary day. "Expect me when you see me, sweetheart. If I sleep not beside you tonight, then start on south tomorrow without me. I promise to catch up to you as soon as I can." Touching spurs to his horse, he galloped away.

The rain ceased altogether as Gillian's oxen pulled steadily on past the wagons mired in the road. A few feeble rays struggled through the clouds as the sun timidly sought to shine.

Restlessly, she scanned the horizon for some sight of Leeds although she knew that hours of travel drawn by the plodding beasts remained ahead of her. Her stomach tensed nervously as she remembered the glimpse of the commander's face as he dispassionately ordered a man's death. Brian had not seen him. Pray God he could not find the squire.

The Leaping Salmon boasted an arch over the entrance to its courtyard. Through it Brian rode, his hand on his sword. In the midafternoon lull only a couple of ostlers spread straw over the muck created by the morning's rains. A brindle hound slept beside the door, the weak sun warming its rough coat.

One fellow moved to take the horse's bridle as the knight dismounted to enter the inn. "Hold him," Brian commanded. "I shall be riding on."

The youth tugged his forelock obediently.

Swinging down from the saddle, Brian strode through the open door of the inn into the dimness. The interior was a trifle musty but seemed clean enough. Briefly, he hesitated. A figure rose from behind a desk across the common room.

"Have you lodgings for the night with stabling for oxen?"

A tall, thin man eyed him calculatingly. "Aye. You be here early on to get whatever you choose."

Withdrawing coin from his purse, Brian paid the fee. With a conciliatory smile, he spun an extra coin on the desk. "Mayhap a troop of men rode this way some hours earlier? Some half a score or so?"

The innkeeper stared at the coin, then shrugged contemptuously. "Many men ride this way."

Brian slipped another coin from his palm into his fingers, rubbing the two coins together. "The leader would be a lordly man, so I am told. A knight at the very least."

The innkeeper shrugged again, holding forth his palm. "Mayhap one of the hostlers did mention seeing Lord Ranulf of Briarthwaite ride by some short time ago. He usually travels in company."

"Lord Ranulf is he?"

The innkeeper sneered. "So he proclaims."

Brian glanced at the man keenly. "Where is this Briarthwaite?"

The innkeeper raised his eyebrows. Brian flipped another coin onto the desk. "Five miles out across West Riding."

Brian smiled grimly. "When my younger brother comes, tell him I have ridden in that direction. His name is Gil Fletcher from York Minster."

The innkeeper nodded curtly, slumping back onto the stool he had occupied until Brian had entered.

Briarthwaite boasted no castle. An old Norman round tower rose fifty feet above a confusion of small buildings. At the approach of Sir Brian de Trenanay a pack of hounds set up a howl.

Guiding his destrier through the welter of garbage that littered the yard that served as the bailey before the largest house in the grouping, Brian wrinkled his nose in disgust. Whatever his station, Ranulf must have fallen on hard times. The neglect and decay of the hold was everywhere.

A frisson of disquiet prickled the hairs on the back of his neck. These English were notoriously clannish. Perhaps the squire was a cousin of this Ranulf. He did not trust any of them. Would Ranulf honor his knightly vows and help him to reclaim his lost armor?

Mounting the steps of the building, he knocked heavily. The rays of the setting sun threw a bright light against Brian's back, outlining him with its beams at the same time blinding anyone who opened the door.

Silence greeted his summons. Brian glanced around inquiringly. Again he knocked, bruising his knuckles against the oaken planking. The presence of the hounds indicated that their master was at home. Perhaps this was not the main house after all. He turned away from the door to stare doubtfully in the direction of the round tower.

Behind him the door swung open. Even as he turned back, without a sound, without a warning, a heavy whip snaked round his body, pinioning his arms to his sides with a band of fire. Reacting almost without thought he spun away off the steps stumbling to his knees on the rough ground.

"'Tis him, Lord Ranulf!" It was the squire's voice shrilling excitedly. "The churl who attacked you on the road."

"Yes." A new voice hissed in agreement. "I see." The whip sang again before it landed with a harsh snap across Brian's back and shoulder. The thick wool split as if it were gauze. Brian's entire body spasmed as the white-hot jet of fire seared along his back.

Violently, he lunged to his feet. "'Fore God . . ."

The whip wrapped around his ankle tripping him into the muck. He raised himself on his forearms as the whip snapped free again.

"Hear me!"

The man with the whip circled to one side. A snarling chuckle rasped from his throat as he cracked the whip down across Brian's shoulders. The end circled his throat choking off his speech. Rolling over, Brian sought to slide his fingers under the bloody leather, so he could breathe.

Dimly Brian became aware that a line of men had formed on the steps. Their faces were clearly revealed in the last rays of the setting sun. Avidly they watched as he struggled to draw breath into his laboring lungs.

"Seize him!"

At the command two men sprang forward from the steps. Roughly, they grasped his arms, dragging his fingers away from his throat and twisting him onto his knees. Gasping for breath, his senses began to fade.

With another snap the whip tore free leaving its bloody marking behind it. "Who are you?" the man with the whip barked. "Answer truthfully and find an easy death."

Dragging in a lungful of air, Brian raised his head. "A knight of St. Denis . . ." He cleared his throat twice with the effort to speak. His larynx felt half paralyzed by the blow it had sustained. The grip on his arms tightened as he raised his head.

"A Frenchman!" The voice spat the word.

"Aye, milord." This was the squire's voice again. "A Frenchman come over to follow the tournaments. He . . ."

"I am a true and honorable knight," Brian interrupted,

struggling to get one knee under him to raise himself out of the muck. "I was wounded in the tourney outside Harrogate. That churl . . ."

"He lies," the squire yelled. "He is no knight. A thief and cony-catcher he is."

"You lie!" Brian challenged surging upward despite the two men hanging onto him. "And you shall pay for that lie."

"Milord Ranulf," the squire's voice wheedled, "he is as I have said. Beware his lying tongue. A false Frenchman to be sure."

The sun's ray had faded turning the figures to silhouettes. Brian stared futilely at the lean, rather slight figure of the man with the whip, trying to see his features.

After a moment's silence, the man turned on his heel. "Bring him inside. Fetch a light."

Figures on the steps jumped to obey as the two men who held him hustled Brian forward. The way cleared for Lord Ranulf to enter the door. After him crowded the men of his troop, muttering to themselves. Finally, the two who held Brian between them, pushed him inside.

A torch blazed from out of the darkness, then another. One was thrust into the fire pit in the center of the floor. The other was bracketed on the hall above a long trestle.

Lord Ranulf of Briarthwaite seated himself at the end of the table underneath the torch and motioned his men to bring their prisoner forward.

"Let go," Brian commanded, shrugging fiercely, but their grips held firm. One transferred his hold from arm to wrist and twisted upward. Brian cursed as the pain smote him.

Thrusting his captive down on one knee, the man

151

twisted with all his might. Only the trained sinews of a seasoned knight held together under the strain. Forced to kneel, his face turned downward toward the filthy rushes, Brian felt sweat bedew his forehead and bathe his body.

Ranulf stared at the figure for a full minute, then motioned for a stoop of ale. As he waited, the others shuffled around the tableau taking seats at the benches and stools beside the trestle.

"What seek you here?" Ranulf asked at last.

Brian shook his head. "Let me rise and speak to you face to face as men should."

A mirthless chuckle was his answer. "Your accent betrays you, Frenchman. Speak from where you are if you ever hope to raise your head again."

Gritting his teeth to control his anger, Brian complied. "I was wounded at the tournament at Harrogate," he repeated. "That lying swine left me lying under a surgeon's knife and made off with my armor."

"He lies," the squire squealed.

"You lie!" Brian threw up his head in anger twisting his shoulders in an effort to throw off his captors.

"He be a strong one, Lord Ranulf," one of the men groaned. "Mayhap if we was to put a rope on him . . ."

The man at the head of the table nodded. His eyes ran appraisingly over Brian's figure. Despite his struggles a stout stick was thrust between his elbows and his back. Thick ropes were looped over his arms binding them to the bar and then passing around to his wrists and binding them in front of him. By the time the binding was finished, Brian was wild with frustration, barely able to resist tearing futilely at the ropes.

As the two stepped back, he flung up his head. "I am a

knight of St. Denis," he repeated haughtily. "I appeal to you as a comrade by your oath . . . by your spurs. . . ."

Ranulf raised his hand. "Spare me those ravings," he snarled. "How may I know this man stole your armor?" He nodded toward the squire who lounged grinning near the other end of the table.

"Do you have my armor?" Brian countered.

"I ask the questions."

"My armor—all my trappings—are marked with my motto. The medallion hangs about my neck even yet. The swine did not have a chance to steal it."

With a lazy gesture, Ranulf motioned one of the men forward. Fumbling at the neck of Brian's shirt, the fellow finally tore the lacings aside in disgust. Pulling the warm gold out into the firelight, the man jerked it loose triumphantly.

With a curse, Brian lunged after his medallion. The other man's foot shot out tripping him neatly. Unable to stop himself or use his hands to break his fall, Brian fell heavily. Dazed by his fall, he could not forestall the cry of agony that burst from his lips as the first man's booted foot thudded against his ribs.

"*Mucro Mors Cristo*," he heard the leader's voice reading laboriously. "It appears he was telling the truth, Hob. You did indeed rob him, you fool." He dangled the medallion in the squire's face. "And from the looks of this, you made a poor job of it."

Chapter Twelve

Hob, the squire, squirmed uneasily in his seat. His eyes shifted from the glinting medallion to Brian's form twitching in the rushes before meeting Ranulf's mocking gaze. He smiled uncertainly. "Truth is . . . Truth is . . ."

Ranulf threw back his head, allowing his laugh to ring from the cobweb-festooned rafters. "I should be interested to hear your definition of truth when we have more time for you to think about it." He leaned forward, his face a mask of malicious mischief. "Tell me, Hob, would that large heavy bundle you brought with you and stowed in yon alcove contain this fellow's armor?"

The squire's eyes flickered toward the curtained area he had claimed for his own. His hand clenched nervously around the battered tankard. He shook his head. "Milord, I do just happen to have a few stray pieces of armor that my former master, the good Sir Giles of Rothingham, left me when he died. But—God spare my soul—I never saw this fellow's things."

Brian raised his head painfully. "You lie," he rasped.

Ranulf sent a contemptuous glance in his direction. "Your accusations grow tedious, Frenchman." He nodded to one of the men. "Gag him."

The fellow knelt at Brian's shoulder. In a swift motion he ripped away a piece of cloth from the torn and bloody tunic. Wadding it into a ball, he crammed it roughly between Brian's jaws.

"A couple of you fetch this churl's bundle."

Despite the squire's whining objections, the bundle was brought, its straps cut, and its contents unwrapped on the floor. A full shirt of chain mail with chausses obviously made by the same craftsman had been wrapped around a cuirass, a pair of cuisses, a pair of poleyns, and a pair of greaves. Across the chest and back of the cuirass, the replica of the medallion's motto was worked in gold and blue enamel. A fine helmet, with flowing blue scarf attached, completed the outfit.

At the sight of his precious armor, Brian twisted mightily, levering himself into a half-sitting position. His eyes blazed in the dim light as they settled on the squire.

Ranulf's man pulled the mail shirt free and held it up for inspection. A jagged gash rent the leather over the left hip and stained the whole side with the dark brown stain of blood. Ranulf laughed. "Haul the Frenchman to his feet and tear off the remains of that tunic."

When it was done as he had commanded, Brian's upper body gleamed bare in the flickering torchlight. Ranulf motioned. The man at his shoulder pushed the captive forward. Ranulf's hand slid along the white skin at Brian's waist before pushing aside the woolen chausses to reveal the fiery scar. Hard fingers touched the barely healed spot with surprising gentleness.

"Amazing coincidence, Hob," he remarked jocularly. "This fellow has a torn place here over the left hip in the same place as the mail shirt is torn. Would you like to change your story?"

An ugly flush darkened the squire's face. "Knights always getting torn up in tournaments," he argued. "That spot is a real common spot for a wound. Be the truth that Sir Giles died that way."

Ranulf clammed his tankard down on the table, spattering the ale. "Bind that lying oaf and throw him in the kennel," he commanded. Two of his men jumped to drag the whining, protesting squire away.

Slumping against his bonds in relief, Brian bowed his head before taking a deep breath. He had been believed. The gag was removed. Gratefully, he raised his eyes to the other knight.

"Now, what about your brother?" Ranulf's voice was carefully neutral.

For a moment Brian could not think whom he meant. Then knowledge dawned. "Oh, Gil." He grinned in relief. "He is not my brother. Merely a craftsman who helped me when I was wounded. He is nothing to me."

Something like a sneer curled Ranulf's thin-lipped mouth. His dark eyes glittered in the depths of the shadows cast by the torch leaping above and behind his head. "He protected you with a lie this morning," he pointed out softly.

Brian nodded uneasily. "Gil is a generous boy."

"Generous enough to follow you here to see what has happened to you?" The words were spoken lightly as Ranulf raised the tankard of ale to his lips.

Brian hesitated. He felt a prickle of apprehension. Although Gil's aid could be easily explained, he decided to absolve her altogether. "I left him when I saw that churl who stole my armor."

"You left him?"

"He was but common stock." Brian raised his head haughtily. "Release me, sir, and I will take up my armor and be on my way."

Again the dark eyes glittered from out of the shadows. "How do I know that the armor belongs to you?"

Brian drew a deep angry breath. He clenched his fists before he thought of how such defiance would look to the man seated at the long table coolly sipping ale. "You have my medallion."

Ranulf's fingers touched the gold and blue circle. "Ah, yes. I do have that." He lifted it as if to study it. "Of course, you might have stolen it. After all that wound in your side is a common enough wound for a knight on the tourney circuit."

Conscious that he was being played with, Brian raised his eyes from the table to stare straight ahead. Frustrated fury began to burn in his breast. The damnable English! Not a one of them was trustworthy. Thieving, lying blackguards all!

The man laid the medallion down on the surface of the scarred table. His hand closed around the handle of the black whip coiled on the floor beside his chair. Calmly he shook it out. "You and your brother are thieves," Ranulf asserted calmly. The whip snaked through the rushes, its forked lash gently slapping the ankle of Brian's boot.

Ranulf stood. "Take this 'thief' and chain him to the wall in my room," he commanded the men. Grinning, they grasped the wooden stake thrust between Brian's arms and spine and guided their captive away.

Knowing resistance or argument useless, Brian went with them. As they hustled him through the door, he heard Ranulf order four men to ride into Leeds and find Gil. "Bring him back here. He too will entertain us tonight."

His arms stretched wide, his wrists chained with heavy cuffs that gnawed at them, Brian clamped his jaw against his frustration. Not only had he gotten himself into a dangerous situation, but Gil as well seemed likely to share his fate. If Ranulf stripped her to the waist as he had done Brian, her identity would be discovered.

A shudder ran through him. She could expect no mercy from such as these. His tender initiation of her body had in no way prepared her for the horror these men were capable of perpetrating. She would be worse than a virgin, for her proud defiance and lack of fear would only urge them to greater atrocities.

He rattled the chains, tugging futilely at the staples that attached them to the heavy oaken walls. He must get free! With a groan he listened as the sounds of horses' hooves pounding away in the darkness outside told him that the troop had left to find her.

The door to the chamber swung open and Ranulf entered, his black whip coiled loosely over his shoulder and under his armpit. For the first time Brian could see his adversary clearly by the light of several lamps and a fire leaping on the hearth.

The man was somewhat more than medium height; his body, although tall, could not by any stretch of the imagination be called huge. His hair was dark and lank, lying in thin locks upon his shoulders, rather than cut short as Gil's was to accommodate a helmet. His thin face was clean-shaven, without even a mustache.

As Brian watched him narrowly, the man strolled to a table before the fire and poured himself a small drink from an earthenware jug. Tossing off the liquid with a gusty sigh, he turned back to Brian.

Face to face they stared at each other. The dark-haired man, the shorter of the two by several inches, smiled grimly as he read the anger and defiance in his captive's eyes.

Gently, his eyes burning with a strange light, Ranulf put up his hand to touch the red welt the whip had left around Brian's neck. In several places tiny droplets of blood had dried where the skin had broken under the impact. Curiously studying the face so close to his own, he traced the line around the strong column of the throat.

Delicately, the fingers trailed across the hard-muscled shoulder before sliding down into the curling sandy hair of the chest. Ranulf's smile never faltered as he watched the expression in the gold-flecked eyes change to one of horrified recognition.

"Come, Sir Brian," the man purred. "Surely you are not shocked. The 'celibacy' of the Templars and their kind is well known." With exquisite care his finger and thumbnail found and pinched the masculine nipple.

Flesh cringing, Brian tugged with all his might at the chains, flexing his muscles and straining.

Ranulf's smile deepened. "You cannot free yourself," he advised softly as he raised his other hand to stroke and prod Brian's lean middle, pushing the chausses down further to expose the white sheeny skin of Brian's taut belly. Where Ranulf's fingers strayed, the muscles jumped and quivered.

Furious, Brian spat a foul name into the dark smiling face.

For answer the nails sank deep into the flesh of Brian's nipple. Ranulf's smile became a sneer as the pain produced an involuntary gasp. "You should not say such things," the mocking voice advised. "I shall take offense and be forced to punish you before I can sample the delights of your powerful body."

Continuing to torture Brian's nipple, Ranulf began leisurely to untie the cord of his captive's chausses.

Brutally, intending to wound, Brian drove his knee upward aiming for the groin. His blow missed the vital spot, connecting with Ranulf's thigh and staggering the man sideways onto his knees.

The pose of cynical amusement slipped from Ranulf like a worn-out cloak. He rose spitting fury. "French pig!" he screamed. The whip rippled from his shoulder. Slinging it back to the length of his arm, he cracked it forward with all his force diagonally across Brian's chest.

The pain drove Brian's head back against the oak wall. It was as if a burning brand had been laid across his chest. And worse still was the humiliation he felt at his position. Chained to the wall in the bedroom of a catamite, his body writhing beneath the whip, he longed to scream his hatred to the very heavens. Instead he set his teeth to endure.

Opening his eyes, he glared his defiance. "English swine!"

Again Ranulf brought the whip slashing down across Brian's chest. And again! Blood began to drip from the cruel wounds. Enraged, stretched tightly between the iron staples, Brian's body twisted and spasmed as the leather tore across him and the cuffs flayed the skin on his wrists.

After a half-dozen stripes laced across his victim's chest, Ranulf drew back. "Apologize," he panted.

For answer Brian spat the foul name again.

Suddenly smiling at Brian's continued defiance, Ranulf coiled the whip and slapped Brian playfully across the cheek. "Such strength," he purred. "How I shall enjoy making you weak." He stared fascinated as a slender trickle of blood found its way down over Brian's rib cage. As if mesmerized, he touched it with his fingertips.

The hounds set up a noisy clamor in the bailey. Frowning, Ranulf paused with his arm drawn back. The thudding of a bench being overturned further disturbed him. Uncoiling his whip, he turned away from Brian. A look of annoyance stiffened his features.

At a yell of pain from the hall beyond, he glanced back at his captive. "I fear I must leave you for the moment," he growled reluctantly. "This interruption had best be important or someone will take his place beside you." So saying, he opened the door.

In the center of the hall stood Gil Fletcher, an unassuming figure in scarlet and black. Giving the lie to her slender build and size was the six-foot longbow she grasped in her left hand. She stood with legs spread apart, presenting her left side, her left arm fully extended. The thumb of her right hand was firmly hooked under her right jawbone.

At the opening of the door, she turned her body smoothly, sighting down the shaft and training the broadhead on Ranulf's chest as he came through the door. "Where is Brian de Trenanay?" Her voice was high and boyish.

Ranulf smirked. The sight of the thin boyish figure excited his already stimulated senses. The knight would be much pleasure for an evening, but his kind could never be trusted. The slim youth would be malleable. What delightful excesses could be practiced on such tender flesh. Ranulf's dark eyes sought his cowering men.

Their numbers reduced, the few who remained had sought refuge behind the table when the bravest among them had fallen writhing with an arrow in his thigh.

"Swine!" Ranulf sneered. "You let a mere boy cow you with his toys."

"Where is Brian de Trenanay?" the "mere boy" inquired again. The bow neither wavered nor trembled in his hands. Instead, deliberately, the point dipped to aim at Ranulf's thigh. "This broadhead toy can do fearful damage to a man's leg, milord," he continued conversationally.

Ranulf nodded pleasantly. "Brian de Trenanay is within," he replied. "The problem for you, my foolish young friend, is how to get to him while still keeping your shaft trained on me. If I slip behind the door as I go back into the room, how will you keep me within sight to carry out your threat?"

Gil's point never wavered. Voice coldly determined, she raised the point again to Ranulf's heart. "You, sir, will not leave the room. One of your men will go at your command and bring Sir Brian here. I do not think you would encourage your men to disobey you when your life is at stake."

The thin face darkened. From Ranulf's lips erupted a stream of curses, some directed at his men, others directed at the youth who stood so calm across the room.

163

"My arm grows weary, sir," came the boyish voice. "Likewise the fingers of my right hand might slip their grip on the string at any minute. I suggest you select a trustworthy man and send him right quickly to fetch Sir Brian."

At an angry jerk of Ranulf's head, one man crept hesitantly from behind the stool overturned at the end of the table. Nervously, he approached his master, all the time keeping a wary eye on the bow, lest it swing in his direction. At arm's length he paused and cleared his throat before muttering unintelligibly.

"What do you say, sir?" Gil inquired sharply.

The man cleared this throat before ducking his head. "The key," he grated.

The point jerked slightly. "Get it from his pocket," Gil commanded, "but be careful you do not step between me and your master. The shaft would not pass quite through you but pin you two together as neatly as chickens on a spit."

The man's frightened face became paler. Carefully, he stayed to one side as he reached one trembling hand for the keys dangling from Ranulf's belt.

"Be gone no more than a minute," Gil advised him sternly. "Otherwise your master will find himself hopping around with an arrow through his foot."

As the man hurried into the adjoining room, Ranulf stared at the youth, memorizing the delicate features. "I will remember this," he snarled. "I will likewise remember both you and that rascally thief and liar."

"Sir Brian is no thief, nor is he . . ." Gil broke off, her voice faltering, as Brian de Trenanay appeared in the doorway. Swaying he grasped the doorframe for support before he straightened himself and pushed away.

"My thanks, young Gil," he croaked. "You seem to be making a practice of saving me."

Thankful that he could walk, Gil smiled briefly. "Practice makes perfect, Sir Brian. I strive to please in all things."

Brian nodded as he spied the pieces of his beloved armor, still strewn among the filthy rushes. He motioned to the remaining men crouched behind the table. "Into that torture chamber," he commanded.

Staring nervously at Ranulf's face, now icy with the chill of suppressed fury, the men obeyed, their fear of the bow greater than their fear of their master.

Brian knelt, stacking the pieces of his armor carelessly and rolling them into his mail shirt. Hastily, he tied the straps together. Satisfied that the bundle would remain intact, he rose wearily. "Now you," he gestured toward Ranulf.

The sight of both of his intended prey escaping drove the man into a frenzy. "Neither of you will be able to run far enough to escape me," he hissed. Saliva flecked the corners of his mouth. "You," he stabbed his index finger at Brian, "will suffer the tortures of the damned. 'Twill only comfort me when I see that filthy manhood sliced off in the dirt before me."

"Into the chamber!" Brian commanded, hearing Gil's shocked gasp behind him. "You are embarrassing my young friend."

"I will do more than embarrass him," Ranulf promised, never moving from where he stood. His anger had driven all caution to the winds. "Before I am finished with him, he will beg for mercy. Let me tell you, young catamite . . ."

"You will tell him nothing," Brian interrupted the

165

enraged ravings. "Into the kennel, dog, with your pack."

"You will not escape me," Ranulf promised as he retreated. "I have friends. . . ."

"In!" Brian shouted, his control breaking. Lunging forward, he served Ranulf a terrific blow to the jaw. It staggered the man back against the door facing from which he careened into the arms of one of his men. Slamming the door, he called to Gil. "Help me drag the table in front of it," he commanded. "'Twill not hold them long, but it might give us a few more seconds."

Even as he spoke the door opened a crack. Unhesitatingly, Gil loosed the arrow. Unerringly, the feathered shaft sped through the slit. The result was a surprised cry followed by the slamming of the door. For good measure Gil plucked another shaft from the quiver swung on her hip and sent it thudding into the oak planking.

From that moment all was silent behind the door. Brian caught up his heavy bundle of armor and lumbered for the door. "How did you get here?" he asked.

"I 'borrowed' a fellow's horse," Gil replied with a shake of her head. "He will be most upset if we do not arrive back at the Leaping Salmon before morn."

Brian nodded. "We must find my destrier and ride."

"Oh, the destrier awaits outside," Gil replied sunnily.

Brian stared at her open-mouthed.

"I found a poor fellow bound hand and foot in the kennel with the hounds. They were worrying him sorely. I set him free and in gratitude he agreed to hold the horses for the three of us. He too wants to escape from this horrible place."

"The squire!" Brian spat the word like a curse. "He is the cause of all this to begin with. Gil, you fool. He has probably stolen all the horses and left with them."

Bounding through the door and out onto the steps, he was brought up short by the sight of Hob, the squire, squatting on the ground.

With a smirk the man thrust himself forward onto his knees. "Oh, praise the Lord, that the young archer was able to free you, my lord." He threw up his hands toward heaven. "I was just about to ground-stake these beasts and burst in to the rescue."

Brian stared angrily at the man. "Liar!" he snarled. "You were quietly waiting to see the outcome. If we killed each other, you would probably rob the dead."

"Brian," Gil chided. "He is here. What more proof can the man give?"

"Aye." The squire scrambled to his feet and led Brian's horse forward. "Believe me, Sir Brian, I have guarded your armor with my life these past months. I could not find you after the tournament. I thought only to protect it. I knew its great value."

"Indeed you did." Brian snarled.

"They will be out that door while you argue," Gil insisted angrily. "Mount and ride." Suiting action to words, she swung into the saddle of the 'borrowed' horse. Laying heels to its sides, she wheeled it across the bailey.

"Later," Brian promised, likewise mounting, his armor requiring the squire's help to balance it.

"I follow, my lord," the squire called.

The three galloped out of Briarthwaite together.

Chapter Thirteen

The arch over the courtyard of the Leaping Salmon
was still a dark silhouette in the lighter night sky as
Gillian with Brian and the squire Hob rode into the inn
yard. The excitement of the night had waned to be
replaced by bone-deep exhaustion for her. After driving
all day under the most adverse circumstances, she had
been greeted on arrival at the end by the news that Brian
had ridden out early in the afternoon to find Ranulf of
Briarthwaite.

The squire swung down to take the horses' heads, but
neither Gil nor Brian seemed capable of dismounting.
Balancing the unwieldy bundle of his armor, trembling
with exhaustion, Brian could only cling weakly to the
saddle. Like Gil he had done a full day's labor before bad
luck and villainy had chained him to the wall of Ranulf's
bedchamber. There he had sustained a fearful beating,

followed by a chilling ride half-naked through the wind-swept night.

"Milords?" Hob inquired curiously, staring up at their slumped figures.

"Can you move, Brian?" Gillian was the first to speak.

"In a minute," came the reply through set teeth. "Hob, take this bundle and stand where I can see you."

"Now, milord . . ." the squire whined, reaching up to take the heavy armor and staggering back under its weight.

Throwing one long leg over the saddle horn, Brian slid down from the tired destrier on the same side as the squire. Meaningfully he gestured toward the porch of the Leaping Salmon. "Set it down there and be on your way."

"Brian!" Gil's weary voice chided him as she too dismounted. "He held the horses for us. We might have been recaptured by those men if he had not been there when we needed him."

"Damn it, Gil. This fellow was in a pickle back there too. You found him in the kennels remember. How much do you think would have been left of him had you not dragged him out? He had nothing to lose by holding the horses. He was leaving anyway."

"Then why did he not leave?"

With a muttered oath Brian stomped to the porch to scoop up his precious armor. "I shall take this to our rooms, then return to help you with the horses. Do not leave him alone with them, or they, too, might disappear."

As Brian disappeared into the inn, Gil sank down on the step, too exhausted to stand. Dismally she rested her head in one hand propped on a drawn-up knee. In the other hand she clutched the bow. She was so tired she could not think.

"Milord." The squire was speaking to her. His voice seemed to come from far off. "If you will trust me, I will take the horses to the stable." His voice sounded sympathetic.

With a superhuman effort she roused from her stupor. ". . . Mus' go with you," she groaned, her voice slurred with tiredness, ". . . Return this horse to his stall."

"Yes, milord."

Staggering upright, she wove her way after Hob, who seemed to know the way unerringly. In the stable, she replaced the tired animal, ruefully hoping that the real owner would not be too disappointed with his mount's poor performance on the morrow. With a pat of gratitude and an extra scoop of oats, she turned away to find that her companion had finished attending to both the other mounts and stood waiting patiently to escort her back to the inn.

On the steps they met Brian, his spare tunic donned, his eyes searching the darkness angrily. His gruff bark of relief as they appeared was followed almost immediately by a disparaging comment. "So dishonest a man might have—"

He had said too much. Turning on him like a tiger, Gil stamped her foot. "Will you leave off?" she snarled. "We have both saved your life tonight! We have both placed ourselves in danger and made some implacable enemies for you! Do you thank us? No! Come on, Hob. There must be something in the kitchen of this inn. I am only hungrier than I am tired."

With a grin and a nod to Brian, Hob followed her through the door leaving the knight to fume and sputter in the darkness.

The kitchen of the Leaping Salmon was a dark and forbidding place until Hob, with a surprising familiarity, found the candles and flints. Lighting a couple with a flourish, he turned to Gil. "What would milord desire?" he inquired gracefully. "A little bread?" He opened a breadbox in one corner beneath the cabinets. "Some broken meats? I fear 'tis all that remains of this night's meal. Some cool ale?" His sharp eyes darted round the room to find a pantry door only waist high. Diving headfirst, or so it appeared to Gil, he drew out several jugs, placing them on a suspended table.

Giggling at his antics, Gil sat at the table and allowed the older man to spread the food before her. "A sumptuous repast," she agreed, tearing the bread in half to share with him. "But how did you know where to find everything? I would have spent an hour and probably never found the meat and drink."

The squire raised an eyebrow. "Travel, milord," he informed her. "Inns are much the same—be they Leeds or Artois."

"For that I am glad," she nodded. She took a large bite of bread and meat followed by a long drink of ale. Sighing she leaned her elbows on the table.

Behind them Brian entered scowling still.

"Sir Brian . . ." Hob rose immediately. "Seat yourself, milord, and I will serve you."

But Brian motioned the man back to the bench. Availing himself of a battered tankard, he filled it with ale before straddling the stool at the end of the scarred kitchen table. Still without speaking he helped himself to the bread and meat. The three ate in silence, ravenous after the long day and night without food.

At last Brian cleared his throat. "How did you find me?"

Gil raised her head wearily from its support on her elbow. "When I got here, I asked where you had gone. The innkeeper told me you had inquired after Sir Ranulf of Briarthwaite. A few judicious questions in the common room were all I needed to know the local tales. The man is hated and feared by everyone in the vicinity of his hold."

"I can well understand why," Brian nodded. Furtively he touched his chest hidden by the tunic he had donned before joining them. He would be bruised and scarred for many a long day. He shuddered despite his desire to remain impassive before them.

"They say he is a thief who usurped the former lord's desmesne when he and all his family died of the plague," Gil continued.

"But as a knight, he would have been awarded those lands by the king," Brian objected.

The squire snorted. "He is no knight, nor ever was one," he maintained, draining the ale from his tankard. "He knows nothing of knightly behavior except some aping of manners he has picked up here and there."

Now it was Brian's turn to snort. "And I suppose you know more?"

The squire stared at the candle flame. In its dancing light, the wrinkles on his face were deeply etched along with lines of fatigue. "Once I did." His mouth twitched. He smiled without humor. "Once I did," he repeated. "Now I know enough to pick out a *poseur* the length of a tourney list."

"You joined him," Brian reminded the squire snidely.

"Aye, milord," the man replied shortly. "I did that."

"You took my armor," Brian insisted.

Hob continued to stare into the candle flame. His curly blond hair was streaked with gray. "I saw a chance. I took it. But it did not come to pass." He shrugged. Pushing back from the table, he rose. With a short stiff bow he addressed them both. "You have recovered your armor and your chance. I shall leave you, gentles, to your better fortune."

"Oh, Hob," Gil sighed. "Sit you down. Sir Brian does not think straight at this time of night. Otherwise, he would not keep repeating the same meaningless phrases over and over." She stared wearily in Brian's direction. "Do let us go to bed . . . before I fall over on my face."

"I only took one room for the two of us," Brian reminded her coldly.

"Only one bed?" she inquired meaningfully.

"Of course."

"Perhaps we should draw lots for the spaces then," she smiled sweetly at Hob, who stood uncertainly as they argued.

"Oh, no." He shook his head. "A bed in the stable's good enough for me. After that filthy hold at Briarthwaite, 'twill seem clean and sweet."

"Brian!" Gil's voice was urgent.

Reluctantly the knight rose to his feet. "We can probably get a pallet from the common room. Wait at the foot of the stairs, Gil, while Hob and I go see what we can find."

When the two returned, carrying a pallet and a couple of blankets, they found her huddled in the corner on the first step. She had fallen asleep, her head on her outstretched arm where it rested on the third.

"A very brave lad," Hob observed, real admiration tinging his voice.

"Indeed," Brian replied softly. "Very brave. The very bravest of lads. Would that I could make him my squire?"

"Why do you not?"

Brian snorted softly as he stooped and eased her into his arms. "He has not the interest. I have asked him. He is a guildsman."

"Bowyer?"

"Fletcher." They mounted the stairs, and Brian led the way to their small room.

The squire nodded. "I guessed one or the other when I saw the way he used that bow."

Lowering his burden to the bed, Brian straightened out her limbs, before seating himself to pull off his boots. "Little bits of sticks and feathers," he groaned tiredly.

Hob spread out the pallet on the floor in front of the door. "Very powerful," he observed.

The knight pulled up his tunic and gingerly prodded the whiplashes across his chest. Deciding they were superficial and required no attention before morning, he stretched out full length. Only the moonlight and a faint glow from the hearth gave the room any light at all. As he drew the blanket over them both, he could not forbear an admiring chuckle.

"He did hold them off. They were cowering like scared sheep behind that table. Had it all planned. Ranulf never had a chance."

"Ranulf will come for revenge," the squire muttered, turning over to his side in an effort to get comfortable on the hard boards.

"We must plan how to get away as early as possible in the morning," came the sleepy reply.

A heavy weight pressed against Gil's back. Hot breath blew rhythmically in her ear. Her eyes flew open, alarmed, forgetful of where she was and with whom. The first streaks of dawn lightened the lead panes of the tiny window. The sun!

Abruptly, all the weary toil and fearsome danger of the previous day returned. She clutched Brian's wrist where it lay beneath her breasts. How serious were his hurts? Had Ranulf injured him in any way?

Turning onto her back, she stared at his face turned toward the increasing brightness. His beard was rough and stubbly. The lines around his mouth were deeply etched, as were a pair bisecting his forehead between his eyebrows. One sharp cheekbone was marred by a nasty-looking abrasion.

The overall picture was one of a face honed almost to the bone by deprivation. Even in sleep, Brian de Trenanay denied himself the luxury of total relaxation.

As her eyes moved over him, his nose twitched slightly. He mumbled something unintelligible; his hand tightened convulsively, then relaxed. She felt the strength of his fingers on her ribs. She had felt that strength before. It lay always latent yet perfectly controlled. When he had made love to her, she had been subliminally aware of its existence. When he had thrown his shoulder against the wheel of the wagon to lift them out of the muck, she had witnessed what he was capable of.

Shivering slightly, she lowered her gaze to his chest partially bared by the unlaced thong at the opening of his tunic. A cross of bruised, swollen flesh almost directly below his throat drew a faint gasp of pity from her. The ends of the cruel marks disappeared on either side beneath the tunic. How long they were or what kind of damage they had wreaked on his shoulders and rib cage, she could only guess. Involuntarily, she touched them with her fingers.

His eyes opened slowly, unfocused at first. He blinked. The lines in his face deepened in a grimace. Still half asleep he moaned, closing his eyes again as the condition of his body hit him forcibly.

He drew a deep breath, swelling his chest, and rolled gingerly over onto his back. The breath escaped him in a heartfelt groan. "God! Why did I have to wake up?"

Instantly contrite, she levered herself up on one elbow. "Forgive me," she begged. "I did not mean to touch you and waken you."

He smiled weakly. "No apology from you," he admonished her, shaking his head. "We must be gone if we are to escape that pack of dogs. I simply wanted to die rather than face warming up these muscles. I feel as though I have been beaten."

Her smile was sad. "You have," she reminded him.

He chuckled ruefully. "Oh, that. Nothing, Gil. Really nothing. Hardly scratches. That limp-wristed pig was playing with me. Probably does worse than that to his lover." But he carefully put his hand inside of his shirt to trace the lines. "Hardly broke the skin."

Abruptly, she sat up, ruffling her short hair. Despite her lack of sleep the night before, she felt reasonably able to face the day's journey. Brian's reminder of the "limp-wristed pig" had galvanized her into action. The memory of Ranulf's face as she sighted along the shaft sent a chill of apprehension over her body. The oxen were slow. To abandon the cargo and flee was unthinkable. She closed her eyes uttering a silent prayer.

"Shall I fetch a pitcher of hot water?"

Both heads turned startled toward the door. Forgetting as they threw off the numbing effects of sleep, both stared in surprise at Hob, who rose stiffly to his knees with an ingratiating grin.

"No."

"Yes, Hob!" Gil's voice rose above Brian's. "You need those 'scratches' washed," she insisted. "Look at your wrists, Brian."

He raised his arm above his face. His fist clenched at the sight of the lacerations flecked with dried blood where the cuffs had torn him as he struggled to break free. His jaw tightened as he dropped his arm across his eyes.

Dragging the pallet aside, Hob left while Gil rose and opened one of her packs. "I have a jar of salve," she murmured rummaging through her belongings. "Uncle Tobin insisted that I put it in. Ah . . ." She turned back triumphant to find Brian sitting up on the edge of the bed.

His forearms rested dejectedly on his thighs. His head hung down. His breaths were slow and shallow, as he tested his strength. "We must be away, my lady," he said softly, never bothering to raise his head. "You would not be safe from that swine."

Dropping to her knees beside him, she stared up into his face. "You would be less safe than I, milord. Those cuts and bruises need attention. Lockjaw is no pleasant

178

way to die, and many do die of it."

He sighed as he stared into her innocent face. "I did wrong," he admitted touching her cheek lightly. "I should have made thorough inquiries before I went riding out to that midden demanding my armor and depending on English honor. Anyone who would let that fellow," he jerked his head in the direction Hob had taken, "attach himself to an entourage is suspect."

Gillian rose disgusted. To talk to Brian about Hob was like talking to a brick wall. The squire had done him a bad turn. He would never have another chance. She could not argue with Brian's experience. Perhaps he was right.

Turning her back, she drew a fresh smock from her pack and slipped it over her head like a tent. Aware of Brian's stare, she fumbled under the enveloping folds, sliding her arms out of the soiled one, untying the lacings, and allowing it to drop down around her waist. She was stuffing the folds of the fresh one underneath when Brian burst out laughing.

"Sweet Jesus, Gil. What a performance to keep me from seeing your chest! Do you think that I would become so inflamed by the sight of your body that I would throw you down and ravish you before Hob comes back with the water? . . ." A knock interrupted him. "Ah, here he is now."

At Brian's chuckling call, Hob entered bearing a large steaming pitcher and several towels draped over his forearm. He glanced inquiringly at the knight whose laugh he had never heard. Setting his burdens down on the stand beside the basin, he turned to catch sight of Gil, red-faced, struggling to tuck her fresh smock through the neck opening of her soiled one.

At the expression on the squire's face, Brian burst into

another gale of laughter which collapsed him weakly onto his side on the bed.

The squire's face was a study as he sought to suppress a grin at what he believed to be painful shyness on the part of the young boy. His lips twitched and he dropped his eyes to the washstand, carefully arranging the towels and pressing imaginary creases out of them.

Scowling angrily, too embarrassed to speak, Gillian swung on Brian, having fumbled her smock over her head at last. Smoothing the fresh one into place, she flung the soiled garment at her pack and stalked to the bed. At the sight of her angry mouth creased into a tight line, Brian raised his hand and pointed weakly, going off into a fresh fit of laughter.

With a stamp of her foot, she grabbed the hem of his garment and hauled him urgently into a sitting position. As the rough wool rasped against his flesh when she pulled it over his head, his laughter ceased. His protest was muffled in the folds of his tunic.

Nevertheless, he emerged grinning, his face more relaxed than it had been in many a long day as he tried to catch her eye.

Refusing to meet his gaze, she studied the stripes, less horrified than she might have been at his condition. If he could laugh like that at her natural modesty, he must not be hurting very badly. "Hob," she called.

The squire poured water into the basin and brought it with a fresh towel to her side. At the sight of the knight's chest, his lips thinned.

Brian glanced at him a little surprised to find any emotion, much less sympathy registered there. He followed his companion's stares to his chest. The sight wiped away the smile. He swallowed, hesitated, then wiped a hand across the lower half of his face. "Looks as if I caught the wrong end this time," he remarked softly.

Gillian dipped the end of the towel into the warm water and began to wash him, beginning with the topmost weal. It lanced down halfway between his neck and the point of his shoulder. Across the collarbone, the skin had broken and lay open. Blood scabbed over the wound and trickled down into the hair on Brian's chest. Despite her gentle touch with the warm water and towel, the knight winced.

"Sorry," she muttered.

"'Tis no matter," he gritted. "Get on with it and swiftly. We must be away." He drew in a deep breath and looked at Hob. "Set that basin on the floor," he commanded, "and go make arrangements for our wagon to be hitched and the horses saddled. I assume you are planning to take the horse you stole from Ranulf."

The squire shrugged. "He never paid me."

Brian's lip curled as he nodded, his green eyes glittering meaningfully at Gil. "Begone! And bespeak a hearty breakfast while you are about it. We will follow directly."

The door closed behind him. The silence grew heavy in the air as Gillian continued to dab gently at wounds. She cleaned them as best she could, then doused his wrists in fresh water and smeared the sweet-smelling salve overall. At last she sat back with a sigh. "Shall I bandage your wrists?"

He shook his head. "They are no worse off than the rest. The air will heal them. Bandages might make them stiff."

She stared up at him. "I notice you did not bid Hob be on his way."

He shrugged as he gingerly rotated his hands, testing

181

the movability of the joints. "The man has burned his bridges with Ranulf. We probably could not depend on him for much, but little is better than nothing."

"You expect trouble."

"Oh, they might skulk on our trail for a few days before they give up and fall upon some other poor souls. 'Tis all they are capable of." He rose and stretched expansively. From his great height he smiled down at her in a manner that was meant to be reassuring. "That pack of dogs has not the courage to attack head-on. Even a boy with a bundle of sticks and feathers could hold them at bay." He drew his tunic over his head, so he did not hear her outraged gasp.

Chapter Fourteen

As if in recompense for the terrible weather of the day before, the sun shone at its very brightest. A cool breeze from the west blew away the steam as it rose from the drying earth. The landscape shimmered a vibrant green as the wagon accompanied now by two riders followed the old road southward toward London.

"We should easily make Sheffield before nightfall," Brian remarked conversationally, as he walked the destrier beside the lumbering wagon. "We are making good time."

Gil smiled wanly. Her arms ached from holding the reins and from cracking the whip across the backs of the plodding beasts. Her bottom ached from contact with the flat board of the wagon seat. Worst of all, her head was beginning to ache from exhaustion. Her all-but-sleepless night was taking its toll of her strength. Wearily, she glanced at the sun high in the sky only slightly over her left shoulder.

Misinterpreting her look, Brian looked over his shoulder toward the squire, who rode behind and to the right. "No sign of Ranulf?" he inquired.

"No, milord." Hob straightened stiffly in the saddle as though startled by the voice. He grinned sheepishly at the backs of the two ahead of him. He had in fact been dozing.

"I knew he would not have the courage to follow," Brian went on cheerfully. "He and his drunken crew are probably just now waking up. After we escaped them, they probably bandaged up that fellow's thigh and drank themselves into a stupor while they traded empty threats and promises."

"You seem to be right, milord," the squire replied dutifully.

"How far is Sheffield?" Gil asked tiredly.

"Oh, probably half a day." Brian smiled at her. "Getting tired? Shall I drive?"

"Are you sure 'tis safe?"

"As a church procession."

For answer Gil scooted over on the seat and extended the reins in his direction. The squire urged his horse around the back of the wagon and took the destrier's reins as Brian left the saddle. The exchange was made without a pause.

Within minutes, Gil found herself nodding. She did not protest when Brian guided her down onto the wagon seat and cradled her head on his thigh. "Not the most comfortable cushion, Lady Gillian," he whispered, "but certainly the best around."

Without replying she closed her eyes thankfully and

gave herself up to sleep.

And so the pattern for the next week was set. They managed to make between twenty and twenty-five miles a day by driving from sunup to sundown. Twice more it rained, but the rest of the trip was conducted in relative comfort. Of Ranulf and his men there was no sign.

After a few days Gillian forgot all about them and managed to enjoy a few of the sights of the strange towns they journeyed through. Nottingham, Leicester, Northampton, Bedford, and Luton appeared daily. She craned her neck as they drove through but dared not stop. Perhaps on her way back, she promised herself hopefully. The most important thing was the commission. It must arrive safely.

Furthermore, Brian seemed daily more and more impatient. The snail's pace maddened him. He longed to be away and into his beloved France. Neither the scenery nor the architecture pleased him. Although he had come to accept Hob and no longer sniped at him, he treated him with only grudging acceptance.

At night his temper hovered near the boiling point. Conscious of him lying stiffly in bed beside her, Gillian tried vainly to keep their bodies from touching as they slept together in the narrow beds in the inns. The pattern of the first night was repeated. Hob slept on a pallet before the door, steadfastly refusing Brian's offer to pay for an extra room.

Had not his pride prevented him from sleeping on the floor while a servant occupied the bed, Brian would gladly have changed places with Hob. In the bed, lay Gillian, her nubile body pressed innocently against his. While she lay awake, she held herself carefully away from him, properly taking up no more than her share of the bed. During this time he could manage to remain cool. Repeatedly, he told himself that he cared nothing for her scrawny body. After all she was hardly more than a boy. No shape to her at all.

But in a little while her even breathing would tell him she had fallen asleep. Her body would relax. One arm would move, seeking a more comfortable position. Her leg would be drawn up to press against the outside of his thigh. Sooner or later she would turn toward him, pressing herself against him, like a child craving warmth. Then he would set his teeth with a groan. The memory of her taut breasts, their nipples hardened by his careful touches, would rise up before him.

Why had he not wooed her with more care? Why had he stupidly lost control without bringing her to pleasure too? And why, oh why, had he turned from her to sleep, leaving her unsatisfied? He had only himself to blame. His hell was of his own making.

Roundly, he cursed the squire for joining them in the room. Yet he saw no way around the problem without revealing Gillian's secret and leaving her at the mercy of the man when they should part at the end of the trip. He could not be expected to escort her back to York. He had no intention of taking the Saxon squire to France with him when he returned. He would quickly rid himself of the fellow, even should he care to remain. He would get a French squire, one he could trust.

So he sweated, setting his teeth and clenching his fists as her sweet breath fanned his cheek and his body stiffened until he thought he would burst.

Not until they stayed for the night at St. Alban's Abbey in the magnificent gatehouse did Hob have a room to himself. Instead of large common rooms or rooms with sleeping places for two or three, the abbey provided them with small separate rooms each opening onto a narrow hall which led to the dining chamber and thence to the kitchen.

"How can an abbey have such beautiful rooms?" Gillian asked innocently as she stared around her at the small chamber with its canopied bed raised on a platform so high that three steps were required to climb into it.

His lips twisted in a cynical smile. "This abbey probably has as much or more land than the largest estate in Hertfordshire. All that money coming in plus no taxes. The money has to go somewhere. The monks get their food and lodgings. So why not live well?"

"But . . ." She hesitated. "I thought they were just poor men who begged for food."

Brian snorted. "'Tis easy to see you have never been anywhere," he observed loftily. "Monks and friars and priests—they are just men, Gil. They chose a profession that looked good to them. Some did not even get a choice. If you are dissatisfied, but you cannot quit, what do you do?"

Staring around her with eyes wide and eyebrows raised, Gillian observed the rich carpet on the floor, the dark well-polished wood of the handsome bed and chest, the leaded-glass panes through which the afternoon sun streamed. The apartment was luxurious to her unsophisticated eyes. She shook her head. "But their vows . . ."

Brian shrugged. "The English are a long way from Mother Church in Rome," he sneered. "Merely another example of their bad faith and untrustworthiness."

Gillian shot him a look of pure annoyance as he turned on his heel and strode out. He was the most irritating man she had ever known. Even among craftsmen, a breed particularly noted for its stiff-necked pride, she had not observed anything to equal Brian's support of everything French and his denigration of everything English.

Sinking down into the soft eiderdown *guedon*, Gillian stared at the folds of the tall, gracefully draped canopy above her. At times Brian was the most wonderful of men, brave, resourceful, gentle, considerate. At others he made her grit her teeth. The obstinacy, the pure blind stubbornness, of the man was hard to bear.

While he had bent every effort to repay her for her nursing, he had never really thanked Hob or her for pulling him out of Briarthwaite. To her way of thinking, such pride was ridiculous. He had been in trouble. She had saved him. He would have done the same thing for her. She would have thanked him profusely. Where was the difference? Surely he was above that silly business of women being weak and helpless. Surely he recognized that she did a man's work. She shrugged. If he did not, more fool he.

Rolling over on her stomach and drawing up one leg, she snuggled down in the soft billowing comfort. A short nap before supper. She closed her eyes with a contented sigh.

A fly tickled her nose!

Annoyed, she brushed at it.

It settled on her ear. Its tiny feet swept round the shape and down behind her lobe. Her eyes slitted open. The room in which she lay was dark. She closed her eyes. Again the tiny creature traced its way across her cheek and into the shell of her ear.

Groaning angrily, she brushed at her face. Her hand

encountered an arm.

Brian!

Rolling over on her back, she gazed up at his face, a dim white shape in the dark. "What is't o'clock?"

"You have missed your evening meal," he informed her cordially.

"Oh, no," she moaned. Her hand clapped to her stomach. "I only meant to sleep a few minutes. Why did someone not come for me?"

She felt his weight leave the bed. A scratch of flint and a candle flame flickered. "I thought you needed your sleep more."

She sat up, childishly rubbing her eyes with her fists. "And not my supper. Oh, thank you."

He turned back, a tray in his hands, his face split in a grin. "As you order, milady."

A delectable odor wafted to her from the dishes. She closed her eyes and sniffed appreciatively. "Do I smell venison?"

"Cooked in ale," was his laughing reply. "The brothers assured me it markedly improves the flavor. Although how they could tell with all the leeks they have it stuffed with is beyond me." With a flourish he set the tray down on the chest at the foot of the bed.

Eagerly, she rolled across the bed to lean over the foot and inspect the meal. Her brown eyes glowed in the candlelight. "Oh, Brian. Thank you so much for saving it for me."

He grinned as he balanced his long body on the corner of the chest. "My pleasure." He hefted the jug from the tray. "Real wine," he announced, pulling his knife from his belt and setting to work on the cork. "Not French, of course, but a reasonable vintage from Germany. Hob and

I split a bottle at supper."

She stared at it. "Am I supposed to drink it all?" she inquired incredulously.

"As much as you want," he replied, extracting the cork and pouring some of the pale golden liquid into an earthenware goblet. "What you do not drink, I will finish off." She regarded him doubtfully as he handed it to her. "Try it. See if it meets with your approval."

"I have no basis to judge." She shook her head, before touching her lips to the rim of the goblet. Tentatively, she took a sip. The liquid was cool and tart. It reminded her a little of a grape she had tasted once at a feast in the guildhall, but different. Taking a larger sip, she rolled it around on her tongue. Finally, she swallowed with a slight grimace.

Brian watched her narrowly. "What do you think?"

Privately, Gillian thought it was nothing special, but she did not like to hurt his feelings. His expression was eager. "Oh, I think it tastes fine." She smiled generously at him.

His grin broadened as if at some private joke. "Have some food," he invited her.

Instead of the usual trencher of planchet bread with a slice of meat, the venison was served on a pewter plate with turnips liberally sprinkled with pepper on the side. A small round loaf of bread and a smear of butter completed the repast.

Drawing herself up to sit cross-legged and reach over the end of the bed, she speared a piece of turnip and popped it into her mouth. The pepper made it so hot that tears sprang to her eyes and she expelled her breath in a loud huff. Fingers wiping at her cheeks, she reached for the wine goblet again.

"The cook is over generous with his spices," she remarked hoarsely, when she could speak.

"'Tis a mark of wealth," Brian shrugged. "The rich eat all their foods heavily spiced with pepper. Therefore, the cook considers it a necessity of his meal. I remember once staying at a monastery near Coventry. . . ." He was off on a story that kept her entertained throughout the whole meal.

As she drank and ate, the wine warmed her body and relaxed her tired muscles. She felt wonderful, light-headed and happy. Brian's story turned out to be uproarious. If she had tried to recall it later, she could not have done so, but midway into it, she began to giggle.

At her first mirthful response, he raised his eyebrows. Smoothly, he refilled her goblet. At the finish of his tale while she fell backward on the bed helpless with laughter, he removed her plate.

"Why not be comfortable?" he suggested blandly, producing another jug of wine as if by magic and skillfully dragging out the cork. "Take off that tight binder around your chest. You must have been miserable this past week with Hob near every moment of the time."

She eyed him suspiciously for an instant before righting herself primly. "I have not been too uncoffo—uncomfortable," she stammered, her tongue strangely thick.

Before she realized he had moved, he was sitting behind her on the other side of the bed. His arms went around her, drawing her back against him. His hands sought the buckle at her waist. "You are a brave, uncomplaining girl," he agreed as he undid her belt and let it fall away.

"Wha—what are you doing?" she gasped hazily.

"Making you more comfortable." His lips brushed her ear as his hands slid beneath the hem of her smock to enclose her waist. "We knights know how important it is to let the skin breath. I have worried about you for several days now."

"You have?" Her voice was husky as she took a deep breath.

His fingers firmly massaged the skin of her waist, slipping warmly over her ribs and even down beneath her chausses to her belly and hips. "Oh, I have," he whispered. "I have thought about you often."

Slightly dizzy, she leaned her head back against his shoulder while his hands continued to work their magic. "I thought you did not care. You never even said 'thank you' for rescuing you." This last was uttered in a childish treble.

The fingers paused, then started onward. "I did not, did I? How remiss of me, *chérie. Merci. Merci bien.*" His lips found her cheek and trailed their fire across it to her earlobe. There his lips drew back and he nipped it sharply.

"Oo-o-o-oh!"

Instantly, he kissed her cheek again and blew his hot breath into her ear until she shivered.

"You hurt me."

"Nonsense," he whispered as his palms cupped her breasts, freed as if by magic from their binding. His thumbs circled her nipples, pressing deeply into the center of each firm mound.

Involuntarily she squirmed and arched her body away from him. "What are you doing?"

"Hush. Do not speak," he commanded, pressing hard into her breasts to bring her back against him. "Drink

192

another sip of your wine."

"But . . ." She subsided against him.

Instantly, the pressure was released and the gentle circling continued. "Your breasts must be feeling much abused," he continued softly, shifting his body and beginning to kiss her other cheek. His thumbs and forefingers began to shape her nipples.

Unable to help herself, she moaned into the goblet.

"I have often thought how I would like to stop by the side of the road and lead you off into a field covered with yellow flowers. There I would stretch you out among the flowers and free your poor abused breasts to the fresh air and sunlight." Drawing back slightly, he tugged the smock over her head. With one hand he cast it aside while with the other, he took the goblet from her and set it over at the end of the bed.

Embarrassed, she covered her breasts with her hands.

"Oh, no, *chérie*." He caught her wrists and drew them away to her sides. "You must allow your skin to breathe. Allow the air to touch you. Breathe deeply yourself." Hypnotically, his voice commanded her, while his hands roamed at will over her shoulders, her back, her breasts.

Her body slumped weakly against him as he guided it back to rest on his chest. Hands lying limply where he willed them, she gave herself up completely to his ministrations. Soon her nipples stood like pale rose pearls, hard and lustrous beneath his hands.

"Do you like the way your sweet breasts feel?" he asked her, squeezing each one in turn, before rolling each firm tip and pinching it lightly.

A moan was his answer.

"Do you like for me to do this to you? Does it relax you? Make you feel good?"

A soft unintelligible murmur rasped from her throat in response to a particularly hard pinch.

"You once said that this hardly seemed worth the trouble," he reminded her smoothly. "You said it was too much trouble. Remember, *chérie*. Remember!" He punctuated his reminder with another pinch.

Dimly, she thought herself odd to respond to something ordinarily so painful with mounting excitement and pleasure. Not wanting to answer him, she turned her face into his neck, but he refused to accept her silence.

"Come, Gillian. You must answer," he whispered. One hand held her breast tormenting the nipple until she thought she must cry out, for pressure had begun to build within her belly.

As if he were a wizard or a mind reader, his other hand slid beneath the tie of her chausses and splayed across her sensitive skin, pressing downward to meet the building excitement. Two of his long fingers found their way into the soft curling hair at the top of her thighs.

A low passionate cry escaped her.

"Answer me," he commanded. "Tell me this is too much trouble."

"No!" she sobbed. "No. Oh, please, Brian."

"Please, what, *chérie*." As the heel of his hand circled gently and rhythmically beneath her garment, his fingers slid deeper into her nest to find the very core of her pleasure. Even as his index finger touched it, she cried out, pressing her teeth into his neck, unknowingly biting him in her anguish.

A fervent oath burst from his lips. *"Dieu, chérie!"*

"Oh, Brian. Please. Please. Something . . ."

"I must leave you for just a moment, Gillian," he whispered, his voice a ragged rasp.

She could not control her passionate stirrings as he stretched her body on the bed and pulled off her chausses. Her brown eyes followed him pleadingly as his hands caressed her inner thighs for an instant before he straightened up and stepped down from the platform. In a matter of moments he had divested himself and returned to her side. Naked, his body gleaming in the candlelight, his jade green eyes glittering, he straddled her, pressing her thighs together between his knees.

"Too much trouble?" he murmured in jest, his index finger sliding in to the joining of her thighs.

She cried out. Her voice a sweet sob of torment.

"I do not think you will ever say that again." His smile was the smile of a conqueror.

Chapter Fifteen

Like the breaking of a gigantic wave, intense feeling swept upward through her belly. With unbelievable gentleness, his finger insinuated itself deeper, slipped back and forth in the soft warmth. Another finger and then another joined the first, urging her to move her limbs and arch her lower body upward for his touch.

The golden flecks in his eyes gleamed in the candlelight. Gillian stared upward drinking in his masculine beauty, stirred as she had never thought possible by his love-making. Something must come of this. She could not endure such pressure as seemed to be building inside of her. She had never fainted before, had no clear idea of what a faint might be. Perhaps she would faint. She closed her eyes, her senses reeling as he continued his touches.

"Brian," she protested, arching herself against him.

He transferred some of his weight to the upper part of his body bringing down an elbow alongside her head. "Yes, *chérie*." His voice was a deep-throated purr. His knee parted her slender thighs.

Remembering the night at the Black Ox, she welcomed him as he positioned himself at her moist entrance. Catching her lip between her teeth in a gasp, she tried to push herself onto the hard muscle whose tip tantalized her so. The aching void within her craved him. Never had she felt filled with such intense longing. If she did not have him, she would die.

And if she did, she felt she would die too somehow.

A soft sob punctuated his entrance into her body. At its sound he paused. "Gillian? Did I hurt you?"

She shook her head, her eyes firmly closed, a look of intense concentration stiffening her features.

Satisfied that she was well, Brian began to move his body upon hers. His hands curved under her buttocks, lifting her so that he could drive into her more deeply.

Her lips parted; her head dropped back, arching her throat to his eager lips. He kissed it tenderly as he thrust his throbbing muscle into her to his full length. The curious mixture of tenderness and hardness wrung a whimper from her as she bit down hard on her lower lip.

He heard it dimly. His own need was burgeoning; sweat bedewed his massive shoulders and chest. Yet somehow he raised himself to search her face earnestly for signs of her distress. *"Chérie . . ."*

"Please, Brian," she whispered. "Oh, please, do not stop. I . . ." Unable to find words for the ecstasy she felt approaching, she pushed upward with her hips. At the same time her arms encircled his head drawing him down to wreak his tender havoc on her breasts. "Please," she begged through clenched teeth. "Please, kiss me . . . here again."

Smiling at the ingenuousness of her plea, he made no protest as she pulled his head down until his mouth closed over one rose-tipped point now almost thorn hard with her arousal. Gently he traced his tongue round and round before drawing the nipple up between his teeth to bite it sharply. At the same moment he stroked hard into her, grinding their loins together.

She cried out as every muscle in her body tensed in response. Then her passion burst, in an explosion of white-hot light and sensation that rushed upward from the joining at her thighs to pour into her belly, her heart, her mind.

As her muscles contracted around him, the exquisite pressure wrung from him the same climactic response. He gasped, dragging in his breath in a pained rasp before slowly releasing it. Mindful of his weight and her comfort as he had never been with any woman before, he rolled to one side, pulling her with him, keeping her locked against his chest.

She felt his hands lifting her and arranging her but could do nothing to help herself or aid him. Even as she clutched weakly at his shoulders, the waves of passion returned, less violent, but nevertheless real. The fresh agitation of their loins as he moved her had set off fresh responses. Drowning in a wash of pleasure, she shuddered helplessly Her teeth grazed his collarbone as her returning ecstasy drove her mindless.

When the sheath of muscle that encased him began to contract again, Brian groaned. Despite his not inconsiderable experience as a lover, the overwhelming response of this slender girl was new to him. He had pleasured his share of ladies some of whom had claimed to be dying for him. They had never done much more than pant and groan before collapsing limply under him. The sensations this girl had invoked were so intense as to be almost a totally new experience for him.

As he stroked her fair bobbed hair back from her hot little face, he considered the reason for such a thing. Could it be that her muscles were so much stronger because of the boyish activity she constantly demanded of them? He dropped a sleepy kiss on her forehead as he gathered her more closely against him, taking care to leave them joined together.

Gillian awoke in total darkness. The heavy breathing of her bedmate alarmed her not at all. Indeed, she had grown so used to Brian's presence in her bed that she hated to think of the time when they must part. He was so strong, so warm, so solid beside her.

Stirring slightly, she blushed as she became aware of the tangle of their limbs. Drawing a deep breath, she sought to lift her leg off Brian's hip. At her movement, he made a muffled sound. His big hand closed round her thigh just above the knee and drew it up higher almost to his waist.

The movement made her aware that their bodies were joined together in the most intimate fashion. Thank heavens the room was in darkness. Her blush must be fiery by now. How wrong she had been! What a fool he must regard her! She remembered the airiness of her dismissal when he had offered to make love to her the next morning.

His warm callused fingers rested on the outer curve of her breast where his arm encircled her body. As she became aware of their pressure, she shivered, half in ecstasy, half in embarrassment. She lay naked in his arms. The darkness made her intensely aware of his texture and shape. The curling silky hair on his chest rubbed so pleasurably against the tips of her breasts as he breathed. The smoothness of his skin over the hardness of his hipbone glided like silk against her tender inner thigh. Across the curving muscle of his bicep a raised vein throbbed gently under her fingertips.

Gently, she followed the vein with her index finger. How strong he was! How massive were his shoulders! Hours, months, years of grueling training in the arts of warfare had developed his body to its fullest extent. He could crush her almost without trying. She shuddered delicately at the thought. But he was so gentle.

A little twinge of jealousy piqued her as she realized that his skill as a lover must have been gained, as had his skill with weapons, by long practice. The unpleasant thought caused her to stir uncomfortably and try to push herself away. She pressed her palms against his chest.

His breathing altered. With a muffled groan he released her, turning over onto his back, breaking their bodies apart. She lay beside him staring upward into the darkness.

Tomorrow they would arrive in London. She would deliver the commission and then take her receipt for her gold from the Hansa merchant to carry it back to the merchant in Leeds. In this simple manner would she get her payment home. She would have little to do then but turn round and head for York with the empty wagon. The great adventure would be over.

She would bid farewell to Sir Brian de Trenanay. He would ride away out of England and out of her life. Miles and miles of land and water would separate them. To her surprise, she felt her eyes begin to fill with tears. She was weeping. A wry smile curved the corners of her mouth in the darkness.

So this was the pain of love. This was what the romances spoke and sang of. *"Alas, my love, you do me wrong to cast me off discourteously. . . ."*

She had nursed this man, worked beside him, slept beside him, joined her body to his. And he would leave her . . . probably without so much as a backward glance. And she would return to York to be a man for the rest of her life. A painful lump swelled in her throat at the thought of never experiencing this incredible ecstasy again. With one hand she brushed at the tears that trickled down her cheeks.

For shame! To lie in the darkness crying before the hurt transpires. She took a deep breath. She would try to think on the bright side. At least she had known Brian, had loved him. Clutching that thought to her, she turned on her side facing him. His arm lay between them, warm and heavy. Since they had fallen asleep on the covers, she became aware of the chill of the room. Gently she slid her hands around his upper arm and nestled close to him to wait for sleep to claim her.

As the first rays of daylight pierced the leaded panes, Brian turned to her again, wakening her with his scratchy kisses, running insistent hands over her spare white flesh. "Again," he whispered in her ear. "Please, Gillian. The feel of you, the wonder of your body. Never . . ." He punctuated his fervent speech with kisses before lapsing into breathless French, none of which she understood after the word *chérie.*

This time he did not hesitate. His love-making was swift and eager. Almost without preliminaries he pressed himself upon her, rose above her, and drove himself hard into her welcoming flesh. Again the ecstasy, the crescendo of heat and pressure. And the explosive release which left them both gasping as her body shuddered beneath the resurgent waves that went on and on until she feared she would lose consciousness. A cry of fear burst from her lips at the height of her climax as he loved her almost more than she could bear. When at last he allowed her to float trembling back to earth, she wrapped her long legs around his waist and cradled him in her body.

In her arms Brian lay with eyes closed almost senseless from the passionate explosion she had engendered. At the height of his fervor, he had been aware only of the exquisite pressure she exerted at his loins. Now as he felt his body's sweet satiety, his mind recalled with regret the cry that had burst from her lips as his pleasure had peaked.

God! He had never, never meant to hurt her. But oh, she was so sweet. He had seduced her last night to show her the joy of sex and ended with further seducing himself to the pleasures of her body.

Among men of his class the coarse tale existed that from scullery wench to chatelaine, all women were the same. Between the stalls or between the sheets they were all harlots who prattled of romance but sold their favors while they cooled their heated bodies. They each possessed a limited bag of tricks which were easily recognized after a few months on the circuit.

He opened his eyes lazily, staring across the soft mound of her breast at the dust motes floating in the sun's ray. How would he ever rise and press on to London? France seemed another world, neither real nor desirable when viewed across the delicate curve which rose and fell gently with her breathing. Beneath his ear her heart thrummed steadily and surely.

A wave of unfamiliar emotion gripped him. So intense was its grasp that he felt his muscles weaken and his head spin. The music of her heart stirred him. Her heart! He wanted to awaken with that sound in his ear for the rest of his life. His hands tightened as his thumbs pressed hard onto her narrow hipbones.

She squirmed at the pain he thoughtlessly inflicted. "Brian." Her whisper chided him gently.

Instantly, he released her. "Sorry," he murmured. He slid down her body until his mouth could touch the spots and bestow the kiss of peace upon them. "Let me kiss you, *chérie*, and make all better."

He felt her chuckle. "If you kiss me, you will only begin again."

"Would that be so bad?" His kisses trailed from one point to the other. Along the way, his tongue and lips teased and aroused her flesh.

"What will the holy brothers think?"

"That they were hasty in giving up the pleasures of the world."

She pressed her thighs against his shoulders. "We will never get to London," she mourned, then gasped as his hands gripped her buttocks and lifted her.

Odd, she thought, how she could feel no embarrassment as his mouth began to caress the point of her pleasure. At almost the first touch, her whole body responded in a manner almost painful. "Brian," she pleaded. "I beg you."

His voice was muffled. Was he chuckling? "Yes, Gillian. What do you beg? Tell me, dearest girl. What do you beg?"

She sighed as her fingers stroked through his hair cuddling him as if he were her child instead of her lover who drove her wild with his lips and tongue and teeth. As the teeth worked his sweet depredation, she moaned her answer. "I beg God to let this feeling go on forever."

Her plea went unheeded. Even as she spoke, her voice rose in ecstasy. He drove her over the peak. Swift as a swooping falcon, he pulled himself up and plunged into her again with something of wonder. He had accounted himself a lusty lover, but never had he found the inclination, much less the strength to perform again so soon. What had she done to him?

He could not get enough. Stroking slowly, he allowed the pleasure to roll over him in lazy waves. When at last he was done, he slid sideways from her body onto his stomach, breathing heavily.

Neither spoke. Gillian stared sightlessly at the folds of material that constituted the canopy overhead. Brian stared at the sun's pattern on the floor. Each was alone in thought. Weakly, he fumbled for her hand, clasped it and squeezed it.

A knock at the door disturbed them. "Gil!" Hob's voice came through the carved wooden panels. "Gil!"

"What shall I say?"

"Tell him you will be with him in a minute."

She sat up, finding the edge of the coverlet and drawing it tightly across her breasts. "What if he wants to come in?"

Galvanized into action by the thought that her disguise might be pierced, Brian leaped from the bed, staggering slightly as he hit the floor, and crossed to the door on silent feet. Gently so as not to make a sound, he slid the

205

bolt into place.

"I will be there in a minute, Hob," Gillian called from the bed. "Is Brian with you?"

"I cannot find him. His bed has not been slept in."

They stared at each other. Brian made motions of drinking from a mug.

"Perhaps he went off somewhere last night and got drunk," Gillian suggested. She reached for her hose, pulling them on as she spoke. "He will doubtless appear as we are setting out. He holds hard by his knightly word."

The squire rattled the bolt. "Doubtless," came his voice through the wood. "I say, Gil. Why not let a fellow in? I assure you, I am quite harmless."

While Brian fastened her breastbinder, Gillian brushed her hair and set her hat on her head. The smock dropped down into place. "Behind the door," she whispered.

Together they crossed the room with Brian gripping her arm just above the elbow. As her hand would have drawn the bolt, he spun her to face him and planted a quick kiss on her lips.

She grinned as she placed her hand on his naked chest and pushed him back against the wall. Her lips pursed as she shaped a kiss at him before sliding back the bolt and flinging the door back. "Here I am, Hob. This was the best bed I have slept in since I left York. . . ." She stepped hastily out into the hallway and closed the door behind her.

As the wagon rolled through the crowded thoroughfares of the outskirts of London, Gillian could not see enough. Her eyes darted everywhere trying to take in the throngs of people wearing strange clothes and driving wagons, carts, and carriages the likes of which she had never seen.

"How shall we ever find where we need to go?" she exclaimed aghast. Thank heaven she was traveling with two such seasoned veterans. A passing horseman was crowded by an oncoming carriage into the side of one of the oxen. The normally placid beast lowed nervously.

"What is your guess?" Brian asked Hob's advice. He had been in London several times, but his stay had been limited to inns near the lists and temporarily erected pavilions. Not possessing goods to deliver, he had no idea where such a business might be transacted.

"Likely Cheapside," Hob replied after a brief pause. "The middles and commons deal over there. The lords and clergy, this side."

Gil listened to this pronouncement with growing trepidation. "'Tis so strange. We have come this far without knowing where we are going. I am sure Uncle Tobin knows. He has taken many a commission to London. I suppose he did not think to tell me."

Brian shifted in the saddle. "He was ill," he reminded her.

She laughed dryly. "The exact destination should have been the first thing I thought to learn. What did I expect? Someone standing eagerly at the roadside to reach out and take the oxen's bridle."

Hob listened with interest to this conversation. "I have wondered how you two came to be riding together."

"A long story." Brian straightened angrily in the saddle, the abrupt motion causing his wound to catch slightly. His sandy eyebrows drew together in a frown which he directed at the squire. "You figure prominently in it, and not to your credit."

Hastily, Gillian interrupted this train of thought. "Night will be here soon. We need to find lodgings. Nothing can be done now. Where is this Cheapside?"

Brian's frown did not relent. "I like not the idea of staying on the south bank of the Thames. 'Tis a place of cutthroats and vagabonds. We would do better to stay in one of the inns on the northbank."

Then it was Hob's turn to protest. "I disagree. Gil, this side of the river is strewn with inns charging exhorbitant prices for the same services that we can get for much less on the other side. Since the commission in all likelihood will be delivered to the other side, let us save money."

"But . . ."

Hob cut across the protest. "I know a place on the other side. In Southwark. A clean tavern . . . reasonable. Some of these places . . ." He snorted in disgust. "Just waiting to rob the unwary." He looked meaningfully at Brian.

The knight shrugged his shoulders, his lips compressing into a thin line as a sign that he would say no more.

Gil looked from one man to the other, then resolutely slapped the reins on the oxen's broad white backs. "Lead on, Hob," she called as the beasts threw their shoulders into the yokes and the wagon's pace increased slightly.

Through the noisy, filthy streets of London he led them. For Gillian, town bred though she was, the press of humanity going about its final chores before nightfall was unsettling. Everyone seemed to be rushing, with slightly furtive looks about them. Their cloaks seemed drawn more tightly than absolutely necessary. Their hats and hoods, pulled down a bit farther than ordinarily to conceal their eyes.

Few women were about. Only at the head of one lane that led off the broad street into the heart of the city did Gillian see a couple of females. At first glance they looked little different from the wenches in the taverns she had stayed in all along the way. Why did they lounge against the corners of dirty hovels at the entrance to a cul-de-sac? Why not be about their business? Her face flushed beet red when she realized that they were about their business.

By the time Gillian was almost exhausted from the crowds and the stench, the trio finally crossed London Bridge and turned east.

"Into the slums," Brian muttered loudly enough to be heard. "I might have known."

Hob shot him a quick glance. "You ride high now, my fine French lord. But wait until you get a bit older. You will pray that places like this exist where your weary old bones will be welcome for a few pence."

"Where do we go, Hob?" Gillian glanced furtively around her as the shadows lengthened.

"To a place that I hope is still there," the man admitted. "'Tis quite a time since I stayed there. Not since my father died. But at that time it was good and clean. Good people stayed at it. People from everywhere. Nuns and priests, merchants and landowners. Knights too." He threw a glance in Brian's direction. "My father and I."

"Who owns this eminent hostelry?" Brian sneered.

"Old Harry Bailey," the squire replied. "The name of the place is the Tabard Inn."

Chapter Sixteen

A bar dexter, the upper bend painted in garish red with a crude lion rampant, the lower bend divided into a field of black and white cheque, constituted the sign of the Tabard Inn.

"Amazing arms for an innkeeper," Brian sneered. "If I am not mistaken the gold lion is the royal animal."

"Old Harry never misses a trick," Hob grinned without embarrassment. "He probably took the lion because somebody who stayed here one time had a relative who knew the king's groom."

Sitting on the wagon seat between the two, Gillian giggled. More and more often, Hob seemed to be playing with Brian, teasing the seriousness and bitterness out of him, refusing to rise to the bait the Frenchman cast. Hob was a jolly fellow, Gillian decided.

The squire threw one leg over the saddle bow and slid

gracefully down to the flagstones laid in a semicircle in front of the porch. With grand insouciance he threw his reins to the glum-faced boy who received them with some reluctance. Mounting to the porch, Hob turned and spread his arms wide. "I speak for Harry when I say, 'Welcome to the Tabard Inn. The beds be cleanly, the food be hot, the wine be mellow.'"

"He probably gets a commission from the tavern keeper for everyone he brings here," Brian muttered as he dismounted on the other side of the wagon.

Shaking her head, Gillian jumped down onto the flagstones and followed Hob into the tavern. Brian trailed along behind the two of them, muttering faintly. He did not trust Englishmen in general and Hob particularly had given him no reason to change his opinion.

"Harry Bailey!" Hob bawled.

A heavy-chested man with shirt sleeves rolled back to expose forearms like small hams raised himself from a seat behind the desk in the lobby. Watery blue eyes stared expectantly at the squire. "Tell me not," he commanded. "I never forget a guest. No matter how long ago." He studied the face. His brow wrinkled as he mentally erased the lines and plucked out the gray hairs.

Behind the squire, Gillian and Brian entered, moving to the side to witness the reunion.

Suddenly, the broad rubicund face smoothed into a grin. "'Tis long years indeed since you came this way, Howard of Rothingham, but you are welcome."

For an instant Hob's grin faded. His face looked gray beneath the weathered skin. Then he recovered himself. His lips forced themselves into a rearrangement that passed for pleasant. "A very long time, Harry," he grimaced. "I have not heard that name in more than a

212

dozen years. Not since my father died."

Harry Bailey in turn lost his grin. "Ah, lording, how sad to hear you say such! We do pass. We all do. But one so worthy . . ." He shook his head.

The squire was silent. A glint suspiciously like tears appeared in his eyes. Almost imperceptibly he shook himself. "Not lording, Harry. No longer. I am plain Hob."

The innkeeper made a face. "Oh, no, lor—Hob. You might be Hob, but never plain Hob."

"Ah, Harry, the bloom has faded from the rose."

At this point Harry Bailey grinned, including the two who had obviously come with his old friend. "Be that like unto the romances of old, lordings? Ah, could he not spin the words right out of his mouth, and the ladies right out of the bowers? Why some nights around here he slept no more than did the nightingale."

Obviously somewhat discomfited, Hob reached out and drew Gil forward. "Enough about old times, Harry. My friends and I are weary and hungry. We travel on a king's commission and have a king's thirst. Here be my young friend, Gil Fletcher from York Minster. And this fine gentleman is Sir Brian de Trenanay of France."

Gillian made a respectful bow to the host who smiled his approval of such manners. Brian raised his eyebrows and smiled frostily.

"*Ne parlez pas anglais, monsieur?*" Harry inquired politely. "*C'est bon. Je parle français aussi.*"

Irritated at Brian's rudeness, Gil frowned. "Brian . . ."

"I speak English," Brian replied stiffly, "when there is something to speak about."

Catching Hob's expression, Gillian hastened into the breach. "We are very tired, Master Host. We came all the way from St. Albans today. Have you rooms for us for the night?"

Beaming a broad smile at the thought of renting his rooms, the innkeeper turned back to his desk. "To be sure. You will want a private parlor and beds for the three of you. You shall have the best in my house, and at only the price you would pay if you took the poorest." He slid a glance at the knight to gauge his reaction to this generous offer. When none was forthcoming, he shrugged and turned his attention to his old friend.

"Will you take supper in my own private rooms tonight, Howard of Rothingham?"

The squire drew himself up. His eye glittered in the lantern light. "I should be honored, mine host."

"Then I shall send a boy to conduct you to your rooms. There you may wash, after which he will conduct you to my private apartments."

"Will your good wife be present?" Hob inquired as the other two followed a youth who had entered from the hall at a motion of Harry's hand.

"My wife is dead," Harry said softly.

The squire sighed. "I grieve for your loss, good friend."

"She was a good wife, all in all," Harry nodded, his face grave. "I miss her even now. Had a deal of trouble living with her. Now I find 'tis a deal more trouble living without her." He shook his head over the book on the desk as Hob turned sadly away up the stairs.

The boy opened the door to a private parlor with two connecting chambers. "This be King Henry's Chambers," he announced proudly, scratching a bright red bump on the side of his jaw. "The master always keeps them nice and fresh. Fresh straw in the mattresses, fresh linen on

214

the beds. Coals ready to light in the fireplace should you be needing such a thing." He stumped to the small bricked opening in the wall and peered in anxiously. Pulling his head back out, he straightened formally and recited, "Everything here for your comforts, milords."

His face lightening somewhat before the boy's earnestness, Brian slipped a farthing from his purse and pressed it into the boy's hand. "I am sure we will be very comfortable," he agreed.

When they were alone, Gillian turned to Brian. "You were rude, milord, to the host," she chided gently.

He stiffened angrily. "No more, Gillian. I warn you."

"You do not deny that these rooms are comfortable," she insisted. "Hob has gotten us here with no difficulties. 'Twas just as he said it would be. The man is obviously an old friend who is willing to give us a very reasonable rate on these rooms." She entered the bedroom to the right. "Clean sheets," she observed. "Scented with lavender and costmary. My favorite scents."

He ground his teeth. "Gillian," he protested. "I do not mean to distress you, but we will probably be murdered in our beds. If not then at the very least robbed blind. This treacherous Saxon . . ."

She sighed gustily, her expression one of tolerant boredom. "I am a Saxon of sorts, Brian. Although allow me to remind you that there really are no such things as Saxons anymore. We are English. All of us. Whether Angles, Saxons, or Jutes. We are *English*." She emphasized the word as if speaking to a deaf person.

Behind his back the door opened. Hob stepped inside, a hesitant smile on his face. "Is all to your liking, milord?"

Brian swung round. "Gil is pleased," he replied grudgingly. He allowed the remark to hang on the air, his meaning clear without a word being spoken. He felt Gil's fingers in the middle of his back at his waist. Suddenly, she pinched him. Surprised, he started slightly.

Another boy appeared behind Hob, bearing a tray with pitcher and goblets. "Master sends some fine light ale to refresh yourselves before supper," he announced in a singsong voice.

"How very thoughtful." Gil brushed by Brian and indicated the small table before the fireplace. "Shall I pour some for all of us?" Without waiting for an answer, she splashed some clear pale liquid into the goblets and handed one in turn to each of her companions. Lifting a third for herself, she toasted them. "To friendship."

Brian scowled, but lifted his also and drank. Over the top he stared at Hob, his eyes studying the older man as if taking a new measurement. He lowered the empty cup. "Howard of Rothingham?" He raised one eyebrow.

The other flushed and turned away. "'Twas a long time ago. I had not thought Harry would have such a long memory."

"I seem to recall your mentioning someone named Giles of Rothingham," Brian continued.

"My father," the squire admitted. "He was a knight."

"Was?"

"He died. An old man rich in years and memories." As if the memory pained him even yet, Hob set down his goblet. With a short bow he excused himself, entering the other bedroom and closing the door behind him.

Angrily, Gillian whirled on Brian, who threw up his hands in mock fear. "*Mea culpa*," he begged. "I just asked him a question. How was I to know he would be so easily piqued?"

"You never think that anyone but you has feelings,"

she snapped. "You have the sensitivity of a charging boar." Pouring herself another goblet of ale, she strode into the other bedroom leaving him alone and feeling very put upon.

The dinner that night in Harry Bailey's apartments was one of the most delicious that Gillian had ever tasted. Even Brian allowed himself to unbend sufficiently to admit the wine to be of excellent French vintage. The meal consisted of roasted capons, one for each, stuffed with chestnuts, leeks, and sausage. A fine salad of spinach leaves seasoned with oil, vinegar, and garlic accompanied the meat. Hot round rolls of white bread were offered to each in turn by the serving boys.

"Good bread, good meat, good companionship," Hob commented, over his third glass of strong wine. "Ah, Harry, you do the innkeeping business proud." His tongue was slightly thick. He waved the goblet at Brian. "Saw this man set down thirty people at a time to tables just like this." He waved his hand expansively. "Still taking people to Canterbury, Harry?"

"Oh, now and again," the host beamed. "Now and again. But the groups are smaller now. The old days are going fast. Not so many people visit the holy places anymore. Thinking too much. Not keeping the faith."

"I should love to go to Canterbury someday." Gillian smiled. "I have heard all my life of blessed Saint Thomas, whose blood heals the sick."

"That it does," the host agreed quickly. "That it does. Cures the most fearsome diseases. I have seen it. I can tell you."

Brian looked skeptical. "Who is this Saint Thomas?"

"England's holy martyr Saint Thomas à Becket."
Harry crossed himself piously.

"I have heard of him, now you remind me." Brian
nodded. "He was a Norman Frenchman." His grin was
broad and satisfied.

"His parents were Norman," Harry corrected him.
"He was born right here in Cheapside."

"Even the king of England in those days was French."
Brian snorted.

Rolling her eyes heavenward, Gillian poured the
knight another goblet of wine. "Drink up, Sir Brian.
There is still plenty here." The look she threw the other
two at the table indicated that she would like to see her
arrogant French escort unconscious. "Perhaps you can
help us, Master Bailey?"

"For you, young gentleman and friend of my friend, I
am at your disposal."

"I am a fletcher from York, come all this distance with
Brian and Hob as escorts to deliver a commission of
arrows to the king's quartermaster. I was not supposed to
make the delivery at all, but my uncle grew desperately ill
and so it fell to my lot." She smiled ruefully. "The only
thing is . . . I do not know where to make the delivery. I
am utterly stupid. Were it not for my good fortune in
meeting these two, I might be wandering the streets of
London tonight searching vainly for I know not what."

Harry Bailey nodded sagely. "Many a one comes to
town and does not know where to go," he comforted her.
"Hob steered you right though in bringing you to me.
Little happens on either side of the Thames that I do not
hear about."

"Then you know where I may take my load."

"Go east to Greenwich," Harry advised. "King Henry

218

marshals his forces there while he readies them."

"Readies them for what?" Brian roused to ask suspiciously.

Harry Bailey turned a bland face in his direction. "I really cannot say, lording. The king has not deigned to stay at the Tabard this month."

Brian subsided and buried his face behind his wine goblet.

"The commission was a large one," Gillian offered after a slight silence. "Quite the largest we were ever given. If bowyers and fletchers all over England were given orders of the same size, something important must be going to happen."

The three men nodded in agreement, while each considered his own private reasons. Harry Bailey contemplated with pleasure the extra customers a general marshaling of men and supplies would mean for his business. A broad smile spread across his face as he signaled one of the boys to refill each drink in turn.

Hob considered the possibility that he might find a position in the retinue of some lord close to the king. A high placement in some noble household might offer him a chance at easier living. He calculated that he was getting too old for the tourney circuit with its chancy fortunes to be made, but more importantly lost, in the lists.

Brian de Trenanay welcomed the trip to Greenwich to take note of the preparations. Should the English king be arming for a major campaign, he could listen to the talk and discover what were the army's strengths and weaknesses. Although he despised himself for any violation of his knightly oaths, he could satisfy his conscience by reminding himself that he had sworn fealty to the Dauphin.

"Did you go to Canterbury with Harry Bailey?" Gillian interrupted their thoughts.

The squire smiled. "Aye, that I did. My father and I. I had just turned twenty. I was hoping to get a battlefield commission the next place we went. My father was bound for Canterbury. He had an old wound that was bothering him and a pain from time to time in his shoulder and arm. Near to forty-five was my father," he explained.

"But a strong man." Harry interceded. "And wonderfully polite. A gentle, perfect knight."

Brian sat up a bit straighter at this compliment to one of his own kind. "All knights should be," he agreed.

"All men should be." Harry nodded sagely. "But many are not."

Brian threw the host a suspicious glance, but the man's rubicund face remained bland as white pudding.

Across the table Gillian coughed slightly as she stared into the bowl of her wine goblet.

"I am concerned with knights," Brian insisted. "We all take oaths by which we swear fealty to God and to our sovereign lords. No man should become a knight if he cannot hold fast to his word."

"But some do," Harry argued quietly. "However, Sir Giles of Rothingham was not such a one. He was true."

"He was a man," the squire interposed softly. "All in all, with a man's strengths and a man's weaknesses." He closed his eyes as his mouth thinned into a hard line as if to shut out the memories.

"But why did you not become a knight?" Harry questioned gently. "I know such a position for you must have been your father's dearest wish."

Howard of Rothingham shrugged his shoulders. In the

flickering light he looked older than his forty-two years . . . and very tired. "He died before we ever fought again," he sighed. "He should have quit long before he did, but he wanted to go on. He had fought on the circuit for years, until he got too old. Too many young ones knocking him off his horse. He began to lose too often. Someone was bound to keep his armor. So he went to work as a mercenary as long as he was able."

"Hired his sword?" Brian's voice was grim.

Hob's blue eyes flashed in defiance. "So long as he was able," he repeated. "To last until he could get me a chance at a battlefield commission. We fought for Christian and for Moslem. From Spain to Russia. But we always fought fair."

"Mercenaries!" Brian spat the word.

"Is not the tourney circuit a fight for pay proposition?" The squire faced his adversary squarely.

"Prizes," Brian flung back at him.

The squire made a rude noise. "Pay!" he insisted.

"The tourneys keep a knight's skills sharp and give him a chance to work out against the best of his kind. The prizes are just extra. No one really cares about their monetary value, just the honor of the thing."

"Tourneys *were* a way to keep knights busy and out of trouble between wars," Hob argued. "Then they got too big and dangerous, so the church outlawed them. Now all they really are is tilting in the lists, but still the men get hurt and killed. You, for example. You almost died. I thought you were dead. When they carried you off that field with your side split open, I had never seen a man survive a wound like that. If you had not bled to death, the lockjaw would have killed you within a few days."

221

"You can always find ways to excuse your dishonorable behavior," Brian snarled angrily. "Fight for pay, steal from a 'dying' man, ride with rogues."

"Be quiet!" Gillian interrupted, her voice cutting across the argument. "This argument will not be resolved. Brian. Hob. Both of you are not to discuss this again. When two men think each is right and the other is wrong, then they cannot see each other's side at all. You both have much to thank each other for. Forget the past and let these things be bygone."

"Well spoken, young Gil," Harry Bailey applauded. "You are both right and both wrong, lordings. I bid you make peace between yourselves and stand together. All need friends in this world, not enemies."

"This Frenchman"—Hob emphasized the word in a way calculated to raise Brian's ire—"this Frenchman will never be satisfied until he has laid me under the sod."

"You left me to die," Brian snarled.

"I left you for dead. There is a difference."

Both men rose from their chairs. Brian was half a head taller than the squire and close to ten years younger. His hard hands flexed as they itched to bring the matter to a head. The Englishman, as Gillian insisted on calling him, would finally get his reward for his treachery.

Hob squared his shoulders. His jaw firmed. No coward he. The Frenchman would not emerge from this fight unscathed. The sight of the massive shoulders and heavily muscled chest revealed to him that he had no chance of winning, but he knew a trick or two. This knight who prated so about honor and prizes might not stand well against one who had actually fought for his life. The rules did not apply on the battlefield. He stepped around from behind the table.

"No!" The host and the fletcher exclaimed in the same instant.

"Have you lost your minds, both of you?" Gil continued, her voice shrill with fear. These two had changed before her eyes. The killing look was upon them.

"Keep out of this, Gil." Brian moved her aside as easily as if she had been a child.

Chapter Seventeen

With a mocking bow Howard of Rothingham stepped aside to allow Brian to precede him from the private apartments. Brian glowered fiercely, his brows drawn together as he regarded the man whom he could not forgive.

"Brian." Gil caught at his arm again. "Please stop this nonsense. You are being foolish."

"Foolish!" he snarled. His voice was slightly slurred from the effect of the drink.

"Listen to yourself! You are reeling drunk." Like a small fury she placed herself in front of him, pushing hard against his chest. Proving the truth of her words, he staggered back. His hip banged against the side of the table, and he careened off it, grabbing for Hob's shoulder to steady himself.

The shorter man caught at Brian's elbow and steadied

him upright. Realizing his would-be opponent's condition, the squire cast Gillian a tolerant glance over the massive shoulder.

She smiled apologetically. Her long association with Brian had created a sense of responsibility. He was her knight. She acknowledged her affection that could very easily strengthen into something more, if she would allow herself to care, or if she were unable to control the mounting passion and affection she felt. Gently, her hand slipped around Brian's waist.

Haughtily albeit unsteadily, the knight straightened himself and brushed his enemy aside. "Tripped," he muttered, staring down at the floor to find the object that had thrown him so foully.

"Brian." Gil ducked under his arm and came up with it over her shoulder. "Let me help you to the chamber that Harry has kindly provided. You must be exhausted from the travel today."

"No!" he muttered. "Not too tired to take the skin off this varlet." He glared at Hob, who stepped back behind the table, his thumbs hooked nonchalantly in his belt.

"Any time," the squire smiled pleasantly. "I will be here in the morning, Sir Brian. Perhaps a good night's sleep may serve to give you a new outlook on life."

"No!"

But Gillian was already drawing him toward the door.

"Well, perhaps. Sleep tonight," Brian flung over his shoulder. "Challenge at dawn."

One hand on the latch, Gillian looked up at him. "We have to leave early in the morning, Brian, to take the commission to Greenwich. Maybe you and Hob should plan it for a later date." Her brown eyes were soft and glowing as she raised them to him.

Forgetting that she was in disguise, he smiled down at her. "Anything you say, my pretty Gil."

Before she could prevent him, his mouth swooped down to plant a kiss somewhere in the vicinity of her mouth. Frantically, she pushed his face away staggering back as his tottering weight was thrown off balance. Another minute and her identity would be pierced. She made a grab for the latch.

"Need any help?" Hob's voice sounded concerned.

Perhaps the kiss had gone unnoticed. Brian's shoulders should have shielded her from view. Perhaps the words 'my pretty Gil' might be taken innocently. She lowered her voice as much as she could. "No. I can manage him. He really got too drunk tonight. I should have suggested that we not drink that last round."

Harry Bailey came around on her side and opened the door. "You are not his keeper, young lording," he reminded her kindly.

"He helped me," she argued. "I could not have made the trip alone."

"A fine and loyal lad." Harry tipped an imaginary hat to her. "A good sleep to you tonight. To you both." He patted the knight's shoulder as the two swayed and staggered through the door and out into the hallway.

As the door closed behind Harry, Brian's mouth caressed her ear. "Make love to you now. Kill him later," he slurred.

"You are impossible," she hissed, glancing furtively over her shoulder to assure herself that they were not being observed.

"Know what I like," he insisted. "Like you. Nobody else like you. Be my squire, Gillian. Take care of you always."

They arrived at the door of their apartment. Ignoring his questing mouth and roaming hands, she let them inside and closed the door thankfully behind her.

Immediately, his hands closed round her body. So slender was she that his arms completely encircled her rib cage allowing the strong callused fingers to press seductively against the sides of her breasts. His warm mouth, tasting headily of wine, closed over her own. The kiss was deep and seemed to go on a long time.

Then he chuckled deep in his throat and pulled his mouth away with a loud smack. "There," he said. "See how well I make love to you." His smile was fatuous as he swayed slightly almost succeeding in tugging her off balance with him.

Taking advantage of his tipsy state, she guided him across the private parlor to the room where they were to sleep that night. Lowering his weight onto the bed, she bent to pull off his boots. As soon as his head touched the pillow, he was asleep. As the last boot came off, a muffled grunt followed by a snore announced to her that he was out for the night.

With a grin, she rolled him over on his side and covered him lightly. "Sleep well, Brian," she whispered. His face was youthful and flushed in the candlelight. An impulse overcame her. Gracefully, she stooped to plant a kiss on his forehead. When he stirred slightly, brushing at her as if the touch of her lips tickled him, she drew back in embarrassment. But no one had seen her and he did not wake.

How she hated to leave him! How she wished he could somehow return with her to York. *If wishes were horses* . . . His world lay across the channel with the pomp and panoply of knighthood. Hers lay in the dim recesses of her shop. Closing her eyes against the pain the thought of parting gave her, she touched her lips where they had brushed his forehead. He would never know, she promised herself. She would ride away in the morning before he awakened. When he awoke she would be long gone on her way to Greenwich. Without reason to follow her, his promise accomplished, he would ride away toward France and think of her after a while, if he remembered her at all, as a pleasant bedfellow.

The road to the borough of Greenwich took her away from the city of London and the Thames. Away from the Tabard Inn she guided the sleepy oxen, past the Bell. So early in the morning did the wagon creak over the bumpy cobblestones, that not a man was to be seen starting home from his night of pleasure.

Half asleep, the end of the long trip in sight, Gillian dozed on the wagon seat. Neither of her companions had been in any condition to rise when she had deemed the time was right for her to leave. Overcome with melancholy after the events of last night, she felt she could not face them when she departed lest she embarrass herself by bursting into unmanly tears and exposing her sex to Hob.

A very sleepy innkeeper had given her somewhat confusing directions into Greenwich, assuring her that the way was clearly marked. If she became lost, anyone could direct her, he promised. So she drove alone, feeling exceedingly tired and experiencing an encroaching weariness, resulting she was sure from the abnormal demands she had made on her body, along with a general depression now that her quest was almost ended. Stifling a yawn, she slapped the reins across the rumps of the team.

Never varying their pace, nor flicking a placid ear, they moved along steadily through the silent lanes. As they neared the Thames, banks of silvery mist stirred around their knees, hiding the roadbed from her eyes. A strange feeling of loneliness sent cold prickles along her spine. She was the only person in this silent floating world. Kenneth and Uncle Tobin—York itself, the shop—seemed more like a dream than ever. What was she doing here so far from home, so solitary in this strange muffled atmosphere?

A grim gray building rose out of the mist beyond several rows of thatched-roof neighborhoods. Within the neighborhoods people began to go about their daily business of cleaning, cooking, caring for livestock, opening the doors of their shops. As the brightening sun burned away the mist, the lane began to fill with vehicles and pedestrians.

Gillian welcomed the change. Concentrating on weaving the oxen in and out of the traffic took all her attention, keeping her mind off the companions she was leaving behind.

Grunting placidly, a drove of swine meandered across the road. As the oxen moved on unperturbed through their numbers, the smaller animals scattered. The swineherd shook his fist at Gillian, cursing her in a patois unfamiliar to her north of England ears.

Probably just as well, she thought as she ignored his imprecations. A couple of horsemen approaching from the other direction received his ire as their horses drove the now frightened pigs back across the way, scattering them hopelessly. Their grunts turned to squeals.

One horsemen pulled his mount as the animal reared in alarm when one small piglet, its tiny tail upraised ran noisily between its legs. When the rider brought his mount down, his thin face was even with Gillian's.

Ranulf of Briarthwaite!

Hastily she pulled her cap down over her eyes and snapped her whip over the oxen's backs. As familiar to her as the face of the devil in the Christmas morality plays was the face of the man who jerked his horse's head aside and guided it onward through the swirling traffic. His thin dark face unbearded, its dark eyes slitted against the rising sun, he surely had not recognized her in that brief minute. When last they had met, he had only seen her face for a few minutes.

Nevertheless, a chill of foreboding hunched her shoulders. She ducked her head, refusing to look behind her until the thud of hooves faded. Best get the business behind her and head back for York. She would have to make the journey quite alone. At least, she knew the places to stay and could make good time with the empty wagon.

The sight of yeomen archers in motley, but with the badge of Lancaster sewn on their caps, encouraged Gillian. She was nearing her destination. The great gray building!

Ahead of her in the lane were several wagons such as hers. A line began to form. The king must be preparing for a great expedition indeed. Gillian's blue eyes gazed in wonder at the enormous wagonloads of supplies which preceded her and began to close in behind her.

Never in her experience had she seen so many men and animals. Certainly, never in York, on its most crowded fair day, had so many people assembled in one place. The noise made by cursing men and bawling grunting animals intimidated her. The stench of sweating bodies and piles of manure made her feel faint. She hesitated to open her mouth or try to draw a deep breath. Close to the river, the steamy heat of the day added to the discomfort and tempers.

An hour crept by, then two. She slumped listlessly, half sick on the wagon seat. Without food or water she realized she had planned very poorly. Ruefully, she grinned at herself. How stupid to start off in such a fhurry to be away from the Tabard Inn that she neglected to eat or provide for herself.

Finally, her stomach growling, her mouth as dry as dust, she drove the oxen through the palisade into the inner court. From that moment men accustomed to the business of receiving goods took over. With bored efficiency they consulted their lists, inventoried the goods, consulted again, signed and countersigned, delegated others to unload the wagon, and directed her to a stone depot erected in the center of the bailey.

There like a king on his throne sat Johannes Gisze, the Hansa banker. An appreciative smile turned up the corners of Gillian's mouth for the first time that wretched day. The problem of handling payment in gold for the commission was eliminated by the League which had companies in London and outlying large cities in England including Leeds. Apart from a small percentage paid into her hand for the journey home, the gold for her goods delivered would never be her responsibility.

Without preliminary greetings, the German held out his square hand with its stubby fingers. Into it she placed the written receipt for the bows and arrows she had cared for and carried for so long. Without comment he recorded figures and names in various places on hand-copied documents.

Efficiently, he pushed the documents toward her and extended the quill. Gillian signed where he indicated by stabbing at the bottom of the pages with his blunt index finger. *"Ist gut."* He folded one over and over until no edges were left exposed. With hot wax he sealed the flap he had created by the intricate process. Finally, he buried a heavy seal in the soft glob and pushed the packet across the desk.

"I want ten pounds in small coins for the return trip," Gillian insisted when he would have closed his book and begun to motion her away.

The banker frowned in a disapproving way before drawing a metal box from beneath his desk. "I must make changes in the letters," he growled in heavily accented English. "Why did you not ask for this before?"

Shaking her head apologetically, Gillian shrugged. "I did not know . . . I . . . 'Tis my first time to deliver the commission and deal with the Hansa." She smiled slightly. "Everyone says that you are completely fair and honest."

Gisze looked at her suspiciously from beneath heavy-lidded eyes. "We are honest," he nodded. "We are more honest than the Church. Like priests we live. The English King Henry does well to build us this fine depot here. We assure fair profit for everyone."

While Gillian smiled her most angelic smile, the banker counted out her money and slipped it into the leather purse she drew from beneath her loose smock. "Thank you."

"Bitte," came the gruff reply. Not a suggestion of smile flickered across the square face. Already the heavy-

lidded eyes were studying the face of the man who had come up behind her.

With a great weight lifted from her slender shoulders, Gillian suddenly longed for the opportunity to shout for joy. She had done it. She, a girl, had done what many men had not.

How she longed to share her feeling of accomplishment with someone! Her thoughts turned wistfully to her brother Kenneth and Uncle Tobin at home in York. Was her uncle recovering? Was Kenneth managing to keep everything in order and operating smoothly?

As the oxen ambled slowly out of the palisade, she regarded their white rumps disgustedly. Why could the beasts not hurry? Surely the now empty wagon should move more quickly. She cracked the long whip above their backs to be rewarded only with the slightest increase in speed.

The trip home would indeed be a long one, she realized.

Where was Brian? Was he thinking of her? Had he dismissed her from his mind and ridden away in the direction of France after his head had stopped aching this morning? She smiled to herself remembering the nights when he had drunk too much.

A shiver of regret coursed down her spine. She would never forget him. Before she realized what she was about, a tear trickled down her cheek. How would she sleep without Brian beside her tonight? She had become so used to his warmth; she dreaded the chill and the loneliness. As Gil Fletcher she would never know another man.

But she knew she would never want another. Despite his stubbornness, despite his narrow-mindedness, despite his prejudice against the people he called "Saxons," the integrity and generosity of Brian de Trenanay had won her heart. A man of unstained honor, he manifested everything that her youthful dreams had ever created.

Mucro Mors Cristo.

Another shudder as she felt her nipples harden remembering the first night he had loved her, when he had commanded her to rub the warm gold over her breasts. Another tear slipped down her cheek as she paid little attention to where the oxen meandered.

If only he had cared to pursue the craft, he could have been a fine fletcher. Although his hands were heavily callused, they possessed great dexterity. His whole superbly trained body obeyed his every command perfectly. She sighed, remembering the rippling muscles of the massive back and shoulders. How she had caressed them while he had moaned with pleasure!

She would almost be willing to be his squire. The outrageous idea whispered through her mind like the hiss of the tempter serpent. With genuine regret she shook her head. The problems of posing as a man were enormous in the controlled environment of her own home in York with Uncle Tobin and Kenneth to intercede between her and accidental company. The problems would only be compounded by accompanying a man in close proximity to other men where bathing, dressing, sleeping, all the most intimate of body functions were carried on without thought of privacy. Her disguise would be penetrated in no time at all. Thereafter she would become the prey of lustful men whenever Brian's back was turned. And if he should be killed or seriously wounded . . .

She was approaching the turn into the lane leading back to the Tabard Inn. Should she take the turn or go farther? The shadows were lengthening. Whether Brian still lodged there or not, she needed a place to stay the night. Tugging at the reins she swung the oxen's heads.

As she did so, a horseman urged his mount into the road. Startled, Gillian stared hard at the figure. "What? . . ."

On both sides of the wagon, she heard the scuffle of rushing footsteps. As she half-rose from the seat, they were upon her. Rough hands grasped her arms and tugged her upright.

"Get away!" she gasped. "Let me go! You have no right!" Realizing that her words were availing her nothing, she raised her voice. "Help!"

Only one cry could she utter before a man threw his arm around her neck and pressed his forearm into her throat, effectively and painfully silencing her.

Weak with fear, she ceased her struggles. Her eyes focused on the mounted figure in the road ahead. "I have no gold," she managed to rasp as the man guided his mount past the oxen and came even with the wagon seat. "Only a few pounds and the team. Take them if you will, but let me go."

A soft chuckle answered her. "Oh, I was sure you did not have money," the dark figure replied.

Ranulf of Briarthwaite had recognized her. For added surety he must have known about the Tabard Inn from Hob's conversation while in Ranulf's company. Too weak or cowardly to try to attack them together, he had watched and waited until they separated. She found cold comfort in the fact that she could not have known of his intentions. As frightened as she had ever been in her life and utterly helpless, she waited.

The wait was incredibly short. "Tie his hands," came the barked command.

Immediately, a rough rope was wrapped around her

wrists and knotted so tightly it wrung a pained protest from her.

"Careful," Ranulf cautioned, his voice silky. "Do not bruise the tender flesh. So young and fair a lad would bruise most easily."

"I have nothing," Gil repeated, her voice thin and high with fear.

For answer Ranulf made another gesture with his arm. Another pair of men rode out of the dark. One led a mount. "Take him in front of you," he ordered the slighter of the two riders.

"No," Gil protested. "No, please. I really have nothing but this old wagon. I am worth nothing. Please."

Unceremoniously, ignoring her protests, the one whose arm encircled her neck urged her to the side of the wagon. One of the riders guided his mount alongside. A rough hand slipped under her thigh and tossed her astraddle. The rider's arms went round her.

"Make a sound," Ranulf warned her, "and Wat will throttle you. A most unpleasant experience, believe me."

The horses cantered forward into the pitch blackness away from the direction in which she was traveling, away from the Tabard Inn, away from Brian and Hob and Harry Bailey. A sob escaped her. Terrified, she bowed her head as the man who held her spurred his horse into a gallop to keep abreast of Ranulf.

Chapter Eighteen

The man called Wat thrust out his foot and sent Gillian sprawling headfirst into the dark room. With her hands bound behind her, she could not break her fall. The wind whooshed from her lungs as she fell flat, her shoulder slamming into the leg of a heavy piece of furniture. Above and behind her she heard his harsh laugh.

"Gently, Wat." A flint struck fire and a lantern's light illuminated what she feared would be her torture chamber. Remembering the whip marks on Brian's chest, she lay too terrified to whimper. If she pretended to be unconscious, she might postpone . . .

Ranulf grasped her shoulder and rolled her over into the light. Her cap fell off disclosing the pale yellow hair cut in the boyish bob to curl like soft feathers around her face. He knelt beside her running his hand down her upper arm before resting it on her hipbone. Since her hands were bound beneath her body, her entire pelvis thrust upward prominently.

"You may leave us, Wat," Ranulf purred, running his thumb gently over the bone. "I expect most of the fight has been knocked out of this fine archer."

With a dry chuckle of agreement, the henchman sauntered out, closing the door behind him. Brown eyes wide and pleading, Gillian watched him leave. Almost paralyzed she turned her gaze on Ranulf, who grinned pleasantly, his teeth flashing whitely in his face.

"Such big brown eyes," he remarked, gently touching her cheek. "Such big, terrified, brown eyes. Like a fawn. You need not be afraid of me, little wild thing. I only seek to tame you to my hand." His voice was soft and crooning, like a woman's. He slid his arm under her shoulder and helped her to a sitting position.

"Wat was a brute to you," he continued, massaging the shoulder that had slammed against the table leg. "Of course, you were quite rough with his cousin, you know."

Gillian swallowed. "I? . . ." she croaked.

"Oh, yes, you." Ranulf's grip tightened painfully on the bruised flesh causing her to wince away from him. "He was the man you shot in the leg when you gallantly rescued your huge friend. Had an awful time, did Wat's cousin. Almost died. Wat was up day and night nursing him and cursing you."

"I . . . I am truly sorry. . . ." she hesitated.

Ranulf's fingers encircled her throat, drawing her toward him again. "Of course, you are. Never believed for an instant that you were not. Still you might remember that Wat would love to get his hands on you. I really had quite a time keeping him from abusing you

240

more than he did." His beardless chin nuzzled her cheek.

A shudder ran through her. Her flesh crawled at the touch of this man. The horror was compounded by the knowledge that he believed she was a boy. Her vision blurred. In another instant she would faint if he continued to touch her in this dreadful familiar manner.

"Please, sir," she whimpered twisting away from his lips. "Please, sir, I have not drunk nor eaten since last night. I am weak from hunger." If he left the room, she might have a chance of wriggling free and escaping.

"Poor dear boy," Ranulf murmured, lifting her to her feet. He placed a hand familiarly around her hip and patted her buttock. Hastily, she stumbled away. He grinned unpleasantly. In his experience, young boys such as this one frequently hated his touch at first, but they soon came round.

Taking a coil of rope from the bench drawn up to the table, he looped it through the bonds around her wrists. Her spirits sinking, Gillian turned to face him, her head thrown back in an outwardly defiant stance which she was far from adopting inwardly. Their pupils dilated so her brown eyes appeared almost black with tiny pinpoints of light reflected from the lantern. Unblinking she surveyed her captor.

Ranulf's grin deepened as he wrapped the coil of rope round and round his hand shortening her leash. "Ah, at last the true colors begin to show. You thought to fool me into leaving the room so you might escape. You pretended to be weak and terrified. But I remembered you standing with your bow drawn, the arrow aimed at my heart. I shall certainly have to punish you for that."

He led her to the fourposter bed in a dark alcove of the room. When her steps faltered and she sought to resist, he merely exerted his superior strength and spun her around. At last standing her up against one of the bedposts, he tied her to it, looping the rope tightly through her bonds and knotting it at her back.

"Now, wait here for me, sweet." He stood in front of her, hands on his hips surveying her with pleasure. "I will return with food and wine to break your fast. You must have all your strength. Furthermore, it is my duty to see to your comfort. You are my guest." With a mocking bow, he left her.

Even as the door closed, Gillian began to twist futilely at her bonds. The left wrist felt a little looser than the right. She pulled and tugged, desperately trying to press the heel of her hand and her thumb into her palm so the rope would slip off.

It was coming. Only a fraction of an inch more would slip the knot over the big knuckle at the base of her thumb. She could feel hot moisture flowing over her hand. She was bleeding. Only a fraction of an inch . . . Setting her teeth against the pain, she pulled with all her strength. Suddenly, the hand came free, tearing the skin off her knuckle.

Instead of crying out as she would have done a few weeks ago, she let fly with one of Brian's particularly vivid curses. It seemed to help. Spinning around, she set her fingers to the task of freeing her other hand. The knots were now tightened, so she could not budge them. Blood trickled off her thumb, making her grip slippery. Sobbing in frustration, she bent and tackled the tangle with her teeth.

Dear God! Please . . . It was so tight. She could taste her own blood and sweat on the rope. Please . . .

The door opened behind her. Instantly, she swung

around, her heart pounding. Tears sparkled in her eyes at the sight of her captor leering at her from the doorway.

Face alight with malicious pleasure, Ranulf motioned Wat to set a tray down on the table. With a malevolent glance at Gillian now braced upright against the bedpost, the henchman departed again.

Alone the two stared at each other. With subtle menace Ranulf uncoiled the whip he wore slung over his shoulder and under his armpit. Raising his arm in her direction, he snapped the leather violently.

Terrified, Gillian spun around, straining frantically at the remaining bond. The man was crazy! And here she stood tied like an animal at the slaughter block.

Behind her the leather cracked again, the tip slashing so close to her ear that she could feel the rush of air. Involuntarily, she winced away, then scrambled onto her knees on the bed to put the post between her and Ranulf.

"How appropriate!" He chuckled delightedly. "On your knees in bed." He moved inexorably toward her. The whip lashed across the end of the bed when she would have thrust her legs over the footboard. In terror, she drew her legs under her.

Frantically, she ducked her head behind the protection of the post and tried again with her teeth to tear loose the knots. Tears of fear and pain streamed from her eyes as the futility of her struggles sank home to her.

Then Ranulf's hand clutched a handful of her fair hair jerking her backward. The fragile face, deathly pale, glistening with sweat and tears and contorted with terror excited him almost beyond control. He burned and throbbed to penetrate that virginal flesh, to impose his will, to conquer this fresh innocence.

Determined to go down fighting, Gillian twisted her

head to sink her teeth into his wrist. Like a bulldog she bit, grinding her teeth to reach the tendons. The hot salt blood welled into her mouth.

Screaming like a woman, Ranulf chopped his fist at her temple, stunning her temporarily. With her jaws relaxed he was able to pull his wrist from between her teeth. Instead of deterring him from his purpose, the pain acted as a spur for his already overexcited sexuality. Her body, struggling feebly between his legs, rubbed against the insides of his thighs. Her hip twisted sideways thrusting against his protuberant manhood. He could no longer control himself. With a shuddering cry he exploded, falling forward upon her, both of them fully clothed.

Only the heavy breathing of the two broke the silence for several minutes. As her senses returned, Gillian began to struggle again, pushing at Ranulf's heavy body, ignorant that the danger was over for a few minutes at least.

His passion spent, Ranulf allowed himself to be rolled away onto the bed where he lay staring up at the ceiling. In a few moments rage and disgust would assert themselves, but for now he rested. His body felt drained, yet not satisfied. Cynically amused, he wondered at himself and the attraction this youth had for him.

Panting, her head reeling with pain, Gillian slid her legs over the foot of the bed. With the bedpost between her and Ranulf, she bent again to free her wrist. But the sight drove her back, trembling in despair. Her right hand was a purplish blue to the fingertips. A roll of puffy flesh smeared with blood stood out around the cutting rope. The knot was almost buried beneath it. Only a knife wielded with great care could free her.

Drawing a deep breath, she looked at the man sprawled

on the bed. The expression on his face made her shudder. Through slitted lids the opaque eyes studied her, while the thin lips curled back in a vulpine grin. Ranulf propped himself lazily on one elbow.

"Given up, my pretty sweetbrier?" he asked silkily, his voice soft and husky. "Your poor little hand must be hurting dreadfully. But it will hurt much more when I finally release you. So I think that for now you must stay as you are." He spoke as if explaining something to a child.

Thoroughly enjoying himself, he punched the bolster up under his head and straightened his body on the bed. Between his booted feet, he stared at the pale slight figure. "What is your name?"

Instead of answering, Gil tried to slip her index fingernail under the rope to relieve some of the tingling pain which tormented her whole arm.

Lazily, Ranulf reached for the whip where it snaked about on the bed. "Answer me!" he barked.

"Gil Fletcher," came the hoarse reply. Gillian's throat was so dry, she could barely form the words.

"Ah, yes. The little archer. Are you also the arrow-maker?"

"Yes."

"How interesting! 'Tis obvious you have mastered the craft as well as the use of the product. Wat's cousin can testify to that."

Gillian opened her mouth to protest, then closed it without speaking. She had no answer. Brian had been in danger. The man had tried to attack her. She had shot him. She would do so again if she were confronted with a similar situation. Furthermore, she knew if the situation had been reversed, Ranulf or any of his men would not have been content with merely wounding her but would have killed her without compunction.

Ranulf waited a few moments eying the upright figure, the thrust of the defiant chin. Already he could feel himself hardening slightly. How exciting the youth was! How defiant! What hours and hours of pleasure awaited him! He licked his lips in anticipation.

"Take off those garments," he commanded.

"Go to hell!"

"Do not be foolish, my young sweetbrier. I intend to have you naked in my bed for days to come. The sooner you strip for me, the sooner you will have that painful rope removed from your wrist. I can even have a pan of cold water brought for you to plunge your hand in when it is released. The pain will be so intense that you will need some little help to stand it."

She swayed on her feet, reaching out blindly for the bedpost to steady herself. She must not faint, but the pain and her own hunger and thirst were fast overwhelming her.

Ranulf swung his legs leisurely over the side of the bed and came around to put his arm familiarly across her shoulders. Beneath his hand, he felt her shudder with revulsion. He almost smelled her fear along with the cleanly odor of her hair. Tenderly, he gathered her back against his chest, guiding the fainting head beneath his chin. With arms encircling her he began to undo the leather belt at her waist.

"No. Oh, no," she whispered faintly.

For answer she felt Ranulf's lips brush her temple where only moments before he had struck her. "Such a defiant little fighter," he murmured.

The belt dropped to the floor under their feet.

His long fingernails delicately scored the skin around her navel and up under her ribcage. Again she shuddered, as this new misery added to the pain that already wracked her. "Please, sir . . ."

Pressing his palms against her ribs, he rubbed them upward expecting to find the flat casement of a male. Instead, he encountered the swathe of linen about her breasts. Puzzled he ran his fingers along its lower edge. "Have you been wounded, sweetbrier?" he asked, surprising concern in his voice.

She rolled her head helplessly on his chest. "No. Oh, no. Please, please let me go."

Finding the ties at the back, he unfastened them, unwrapping her and letting the cloth fall to the floor. At last his hands closed over the swollen mounds. He stiffened, unable to believe what he had found.

Devoid of sensuality as if he had been doused with cold water, he squeezed them painfully. To his horror he embraced a female!

Ranulf spat an oath so foul that she could only guess at its meaning. Furiously, he pushed her away to sprawl half on the bed. "A woman! A female!" His voice rose shrilly. "Why did you not disclose yourself?"

As she lay there almost in a stupor, Gillian herself was hard put to think why she had not immediately told him. Only long habit, the rigorous conditions she had set for herself to maintain her identity at all costs, had prevented her. Why had she not? Oh, why had she not stood on the wagon and declared herself? *Unhand me, sirs, I am a woman.*

Fear was her answer. The men's garments were a shield in ordinary instances against that most horrible of all atrocities—rape. A woman whose body had been well loved loathed the thought of rape as much or more than the ignorant virgin. Of what Ranulf of Briarthwaite had planned for her had she been the lad he thought her, she had no conception. Not the slightest hint had ever been dropped before her of what men did to other men. Caught between the prospect of two evils, she had chosen to avoid the devil she knew rather than the one she could only guess at.

Behind her, she dimly heard the growling, cursing voice continuing. A stunning blow caught her left buttock, booting her higher onto the bed as it sent pain rocketing up her spine. She grunted hoarsely, unable to make more response from her parched throat. He had kicked her.

Possessed of rage so great he could not contain it, her captor grabbed her shoulders, dragging her from his bed and off onto the floor where she hung upright by her abused wrist. A slash of the rope that bound her to the bedpost left her sprawling limply at his feet. Again the boot rolled her over on her stomach. A quick twist of the rope and her left wrist was again bound to the right one.

He grasped her hair and jerked her head up again. "You!" he spat into her face. "You dare to trick me. You do not deceive me and escape."

As he let go her hair, he pushed downward to fling her from him. The point of her chin struck the floor. Blessedly, she lost consciousness.

Unfortunately, her oblivion was short-lived. When the man called Wat caught her by her bound wrists to drag her to her feet, the searing pain made her cry out.

"Conscious, is she?" Ranulf's voice had resumed its icy silkiness.

"She whimpers like she is," Wat's reply was deep with satisfaction.

"Good. Good. Push the little slut down into that chair and let her hear exactly what I have planned for her and for that monstrous brute she was whoring for."

Barely conscious, her stomach roiling, Gillian was pushed down into the chair. When she would have fallen sideways, Wat's hard hand held her upright.

"Give her a drink of ale," Ranulf commanded. "Not that I want to relieve your suffering," he hastened to inform her. "I merely want you revived enough to know what is happening."

His blurred face finally came into focus over the top of the mug as Gillian swallowed the bitter ale. "You, my girl, will disappear tonight. I would offer you to my men." Here he glanced at Wat significantly. "But they are all too discriminating to sully themselves with a whore, no doubt from the army's tail if you were following a knight."

Wat lowered the mug grinning as he waited for her to beg for mercy. Too exhausted to realize what was happening, Gillian disappointed them both by merely listening dazedly.

"The ship of a very good friend of mine is outward bound across the channel this very night for France," Ranulf continued, his eyes studying her avidly for signs of terror and pleas for reprieve. "He owes me several favors and will be glad to repay by giving passage to an extra cabin boy." The word *boy* spat from between his tight lips.

"Then Wat will drive your oxen close to the Tabard Inn where your knight and his squire are still staying.

They will come looking for you, suspecting rightly that you have met with foul play. I will arrange to leave clues that will lead them here, but not too quickly nor too obviously. They will work for more than forty-eight frantic hours trying to find you. They will be exhausted and upset—careless—when they arrive. We will be waiting for them." He laughed nastily as he helped himself to the ale.

Wat chuckled also, his hand tightening on her upper arm.

"What say you to that?" Ranulf prodded.

Gillian cleared her throat. The ale had dampened it, so painful husky speech was possible. "You waste your life in revenge," she whispered.

Her answer did not please Ranulf. He took another long drink. "The ship is bound for France," he repeated unnecessarily. "Do you speak French, whore?"

When Gillian shook her head, he smiled again. "Of course, the destination should be of no concern to you. You will never reach the port. I shall simply pay my friend to drop you over the side in midchannel. Actually, that way is cheaper. He has not the problem of disposal once you arrive. You will disappear from the face of the earth. Good riddance to all of your sex I say."

"Here, now!" Wat's voice sounded dimly in her ear. "She's sliding off again."

"Revive her," Ranulf commanded. "I want to watch her terror."

But she could not feel the blows. Her hands were numb. Only the sound of roaring filled her ears. Was she already at sea? She was slipping, floating down, down, down into blackness so deep that she could never climb back out. Briefly she thought of Kenneth, of Tobin, of

Brian, but only in flashes like pictures. They did not speak, nor move. Like lights they blinked on, then off in her brain before she knew no more.

"Shall I take her now, milord?" Wat asked. "Likely, she'll not regain her senses for hours." He tilted the face upward by placing his hand under the chin. "She looks half dead already."

Ranulf shuddered at the fair youthful face, now bruised and beginning to swell. Disappointed and enraged, he felt the deep dissatisfaction that his own ungratified lust had created. "Leave her be," he commanded, moving to pour a mug of ale for himself and another for Wat. "She will keep for the minute." His hand closed over the shoulder of his henchman. "Come," he smiled invitingly, rubbing his fingers into the lean muscles. "We have many hours before the ship sails."

Chapter Nineteen

The wind snapped the sails viciously under the gray glowering sky as the small heavily loaded merchant vessel wallowed her way creakily from the mouth of the Thames toward the open sea. Low in the water from the weight of her cargo, she constantly blew her horn at approaching small craft that scudded back and forth across her path.

Truth to tell, her bottom was befouled. Old, long overdue for a drydocking, she was nevertheless called upon to make the voyage in and out of small bays and inlets between the mouth of the Thames and the Isle of Thanet, south to Dover and across the straits to Calais. She was an English vessel, *The Maudelayne*, sailing only to English ports but carrying whatever trade goods she was paid to, with no questions asked.

Consequently, the hold into which Wat's burden had

been unceremoniously dropped was redolent of many past voyages, some bearing cargo in deplorable condition. The smells of vinegary wine and rancid fat, of dead rats and bilge, assaulted Gillian's nostrils, forcing her at last into a state of semiconsciousness.

Immediately, her stomach heaved violently, but she had nothing to expel. Finally, the spasms abated, and she rolled over onto her back staring wretchedly upward. Through the grating over the hold, she could see only dull gray sky. Around her was utter darkness alive with creaking, groaning sounds and disgusting odors.

Gradually, the sounds began to separate themselves. The primary sound all around her was the slap of water. She was on a ship! They had done it. She was on her way out into the ocean. She would be dropped overboard, drowned like an unwanted kitten. A tear slid down from the corner of her eye.

In abject misery she lay in the foul damp hold, staring through the grating far above her head. A gull flapped across the tiny patches of sky. Free! It was free. She closed her eyes, giving herself up to self-pity and weakness. Her whole body, especially her arms and hands, hurt in varying degrees. Her parched, bruised lips moved experimentally. A low whimpering sound escaped her as her dry swollen tongue rasped across her lips. She hurt so badly she wanted to die.

In the darkness beyond her head she heard a loud squeaking and scuffling. A rat! Oh! A rat! She hated rats. Galvanized into action by thoughts of the furry, slick-tailed creatures with sharp teeth and nasty claws, she lunged upright. Dizzily she reeled from side to side in the hold, rebounding off crates and bales. The motion of the ship set her staggering drunkenly, but by some miracle she managed to keep her legs under her.

When her body finally came to rest, wedged in a corner formed by two crates, the skylight seemed much nearer than it had before. After all, she thought hopefully, she might see a way out of here. If she could just manage to get her hands free . . . Experimentally, she moved her fingers. To her surprise she found that she could still do so, although they felt like sticks of wood, without tips.

A sharp metal edge on one of these crates might serve as a knife, if she could only find such a thing. Sometimes the metal hoops of barrels had upper edges sticking out. Carefully feeling with her palms, she brushed her way around the surfaces against which she leaned.

No luck there. All were wooden and bound with ropes. The sharp point of a nail scratched her, but on investigation it proved to be only a bare quarter of an inch long, unsuitable for her purpose.

Ah, barrels. Bracing herself, she lunged in their direction as the ship rocked and pitched under her. Twice she measured her steps backward as the deck beneath her feet rose. The sky through the grating was fast turning from gray to purplish black. Thunder rumbled far off.

Despite her feverish desire to find a means to free herself, Gillian could not forbear glancing at the sky. If the storm broke before she could get her hands free, she might be tossed about so badly that she would be unable to stand. Her present condition, already considerably weakened by hunger, might become so much worse that a long storm would render her helpless.

Frantically, her palms slid over the barrels. At last, she found what she sought—a sharp edge bent outward and split from rough handling. The jagged edge of the split was perfect for her purpose.

Fumbling and cursing inwardly, she finally maneuvered her hands into the proper position. Body bent at an odd angle, her feet braced against the pitching deck, she doubted her strength within less than a minute. She could not. . . . But what had she to lose. If she succeeded, she might get free and hide herself until the ship reached France. If she did not succeed, she would be here when they came for her. Might as well expend her energy in the struggle for freedom as lie like a helpless rat in a trap.

A rat! The thought gave her precious seconds of vitality. When she finally had to pause, she was shaking with weakness. The ropes felt infinitely tighter from the strain she was putting on them.

Above her the thunder rolled. A voice bawled orders. She could hear the sound of running feet overhead. Rain began to fall, spattering through the grating and beginning to flood the hold. As the ship pitched, the water began to slosh backward and forward. Already her boots were wet. Thank heaven, she was not still lying where she had been thrown under the grate. She would be wet and cold already. Here only a fine spray touched her.

Revived by the thought that she had something to be grateful for, she continued her efforts. She was beginning to get a rhythm going. The ship swayed beneath her; thunder crashed. Lightning flashes illuminated the hold time and again. Violent bouts of seasickness swept over her causing her stomach to heave, but she could bring nothing up. Cold, salt spray constantly spattering her face kept her conscious.

The ropes were parting. She could feel the frayed ends snapping back against her wrists. With all the strength of her shoulders and arms, she tugged at the ends. Still not enough. Sobbing with frustration, she continued rubbing, rubbing, rubbing. Her arms threatened to drop from their sockets. Her wrists and hands felt as if she had thrust them into fire.

At last, the rope split. Only a few stretched strands held it. With a weak pull, she managed to part it completely.

Her arms felt wrenched as she gingerly brought them in front of her and held her hands in front of her. In the grayness, she could not see clearly. Perhaps it was better not to see them; the sight would likely depress her. Closing her eyes, she slid down the barrel onto the damp floor. Better sit than fall, she thought. Drawing a deep breath, she lifted her right hand to her mouth and began to gnaw at the knot with her teeth.

When at last the rope came free of her right hand, she could not control the sobs of pain. The blood flowing back into that abused extremity burned like acid and oozed from the wounds in her wrist. Thousands of tiny pinpricks of returning life tormented her so that she beat her hand against her thigh in a futile effort to gain some slight relief.

She cast her eyes upward toward the squares of grayish purple sky. Teeth clenched against the pain, she realized that she could not bear to free her left wrist. So intense was her present agony that more would make her faint. Shutting the pain into one area of her mind, she stared round her, studying her surroundings with desperate intensity.

A short wooden ladder led upward to one side of the hatch opening. Although the grate appeared to fit tightly, she might be able to slide it aside and sneak out. Watching overhead for some sign that she was observed, she cautiously mounted the ladder.

A bolt of lightning bright enough to illuminate the entire hold blinded Gillian's upturned eyes. Thunder exploded in a deafening clap directly overhead. As if from a gigantic bucket, water poured down through the squares in the grate. She was drenched to the skin with icy water, but she welcomed its cleansing touch. She was sure her wounded wrists would never heal without scars, but at least they would stand a better chance of not becoming infected.

Her head butted against the grate. Dare she raise it? From somewhere in back of her, she could hear commands bawled in a hoarse voice.

She had no idea how long she had lain unconscious. Was it most of the day? When had she been dumped into the hold? Certainly, the cover of the storm with its darkness and alarm seemed a heaven-sent opportunity to escape. Water poured in through the openings. Cautiously, she pushed upward.

At first the grate did not budge. Gritting her teeth, she pushed again, this time hunching her shoulder against it. It rose a few inches. Grimly, she waited, her thighs trembling under the weight. If someone noticed . . . No cry of alarm reached her above the howling wind and roaring water.

Gathering her strength, she stepped up on the next rung of the ladder. Bowing her back, she pressed upward using the strength of her legs. A crack appeared between the heavy grate and the edge of the hold.

Salty spray stung her eyes. Before her was little more than open sea. Only a few feet of deck and a wooden railing separated her from rolling, churning water. Even as she stared, aghast, a great wave crashed over the side, driving the water through the opening and into her mouth and eyes. Coughing, sputtering, half-blinded, she nevertheless held her position and even managed to raise the cover another few inches.

The sky was dark purple, illuminated occasionally by brilliant flashes of forked lightning. The ocean was an ugly gray, almost black, with white foam on the crest of each gigantic wave.

Only her desire to escape the hold, fortified by the knowledge that she would be drowned at the first opportunity, gave her the strength to conquer her terror. How she longed to pull back into the hold and cower down! She had never even been out in a boat before. She could not swim. Her feet had always been planted firmly on dry land.

She raised the cover another few inches. With surprising ease she had created enough space to crawl out of the hold. Like an eel she slipped her leg over the edge and felt for the deck with her toe. In one quick motion, she pulled herself through the opening and slid prone onto the heaving boards. The hatch cover thudded down behind her.

For a moment, she could only lie flat with her face pressed into her hands to shield herself from the storm's fury. The wind slammed against her with such force that she doubted her ability to stand upright. How did anyone manage such a feat on a heaving slippery deck? Salt water stung her eyes. Soaked to the skin and shivering uncontrollably, Gillian realized she must move.

Pressing her hands flat, she took a deep breath. At that moment a hand dropped onto her shoulder.

"Up wi' ye, lad. Hang onto the rail like I told ye. Never

come away from it. 'Tis safest closest to the sea." The strong hard hand hauled her up and dragged her to the railing. The hoarse voice continued instructing her to hang on and move hand over hand.

Midst the darkness and the slashing rain, he must be mistaking her for one of the crew. Gratefully, she obeyed his instructions and followed where he led. She would watch carefully for an opportunity to duck away and hide when they got in out of the driving rain.

Gillian did not dare to raise her face to stare around her at the vessel on which she rode. Keeping her head well down and her eyes glued to the legs of the man she followed, she did not see the chaos around her. The *Maudelayne* wallowed from side to side almost as much as she heaved up and down. Like a fat old crone, she waddled through the waves that rose in peaks above her bow and washed over her decks.

The door to a companionway opened and steps led down toward a dim light. Fearfully she paused. If she followed her guide into the light, he would recognize her or, as the case was, not recognize her. Frozen on the top step, she tried to survey her surroundings in the darkness, searching vainly for a hole to hide in, a door to slip through, an escape of any kind.

But even as the man ducked into the light at the bottom of the steps, she was knocked forward and down by the sudden opening of the door behind her. Another man had burst in through it.

"Sorry," came the gruff voice behind her as she staggered down the steps and into the light. "Did not mean to give you such a swat, but 'tis wretched cold and wet out there, as you might have seen." The sailor came down the steps two at a time. "Give us a warm drink, Cookie," he called.

The instant Gillian had staggered into the lighted room, she had thrown herself to one side. Pressing herself against the wall like a cornered animal, she stared fearfully around her waiting for the outcry that she knew must come. Her hands clenched into fists. She was not very good as a fighter, but she silently vowed she would not allow them to throw her overboard like a sack of meal. She would resist.

Gradually, she realized that the five or six other occupants of the cabin were not paying the slightest bit of attention to her. Two sat slumped over a heavy oaken table, their hands laced around thick mugs of steaming drink. The one who had guided her into this cabin did not glance in her direction before he, too, slumped down tiredly at the head of the table, at right angles to the others.

The one who had catapulted her into the room followed him, threw his leg over the bench, and called again for the cook who ambled forward with two more mugs of the steaming brew.

"Your watch," her guide informed the two who had been in the room when he entered.

"Aye, Skipper." The two rose almost simultaneously. Regretfully, one drained the contents of the mug while the other fastened his clothing more securely around him.

"Any signs that we might run out of it?"

The man addressed as Skipper shook his head, burying his face in the mug, before answering. After a long swallow he wiped his heavy gray beard with the back of a gnarled hand. "Not likely. We will be on the French coast before we know it."

"Oh, aye," came the snorted reply. "Or the Danish."

The skipper did not comment further, but signaled to the cook for more steaming brew. The two lumbered up the steps and out into the howling night, a blast of noise through the open door signaling their exit.

When the cook brought the skipper's drink, he also brought another mug which he thrust into Gillian's frozen hand as he passed her. With a silent nod, he indicated a place at the table.

Suddenly, her physical condition reasserted itself. She had been distracted by the sea and the storm. The elements combined with the imminence of discovery had forced her multiple pains from her mind.

Now she clutched the steaming mug as if it contained the elixir of life. Lifting it to her lips with shaking hands, she almost choked on the hot wine. The liquid burned her tongue and her throat as it warmed her all the way to her stomach. Like lava the warming brew sped along her veins to every part of her numbed abused body.

She shuddered at the taste, but immediately drank again, gratefully gulping it down. At any minute her identity would be discovered. This might be her last drink on earth. At least it was a warming one.

"Sit ye down, lad."

Senses instantly alert, she stared over the rim of the mug at the skipper, who sat unconcernedly at the head of the table. Could he be talking to her, ordering her to sit at the table with him? The minute she stepped into the light spilled from the swaying lantern hung above the center of the table, he would know she was not the person he thought her to be.

Trying to think what to do, she hesitated, the now empty mug held before her face like a mask.

"I thought you were a goner for sure," the other man joined in the conversation. "Thought you went over the side when that big wave hit us. I looked one minute and you were there by the rail and then the wave hit."

Cautiously, not daring to hope, Gillian lowered the mug. Neither man appeared in any way suspicious. Wondering if she were in a nightmare, she raised one trembling hand to her face. The bruises on it felt puffy.

"Uh ..." she began, then paused and cleared her throat gruffly. "Uh . . . I fell down. Banged my face up pretty bad on the deck."

"Too bad," the skipper sympathized mildly. "'Twill take ye a day or two to get your sealegs, lubber that ye are."

A tingle of hope danced along Gillian's nerves. "Yes . . . uh . . . aye, sir. I guess so."

"Come on and sit down. Serve us some of that stew, Cookie."

"Aye, Skipper." Heavy plates, a matched set with the mugs, were placed in front of the two men. "Come on, lad, sit you down." The cook set a plate down in the spot vacated by one of the two who had gone above.

Maybe if she kept her head bowed . . . Gillian thought. She could not just stand here forever. The ship heaved as thunder rolled above decks. The motion added impetus to her cautious step, staggering her into the table which she caught with both hands. The same movement set the lantern swinging wildly. More to keep herself from falling than anything else, she sank onto the bench where the plate had been set for her.

The cook went around filling plates with a white stew made of fish, barley, and onions. Its savory smell rose around her, making her nostrils twitch and her stomach growl. The skipper and the crewmen paid no attention to her. They had accepted her presence as a member of the crew. Perhaps in broad daylight, they might recognize her, but tonight in the semidarkness with the lantern swinging wildly, she was not scrutinized.

Besides who else could she be? Not some vagabond off the streets.

Drawing a shivery breath, she set to work on the stew, swiping the liquid up with a crust of bread and spearing the pieces of fish with a knife. Her chill body began to warm. The cook poured her more hot wine. Despite the danger, she began to relax. Her head began to nod.

"Turn in, lad," the skipper ordered. "'Tis been a rough beginning for a life at sea."

Helplessly, she stared at her clean plate. Now would come the discovery.

"Come." The other man rose from the table and motioned. "This way. You can use this hammock." He led her through a door behind the galley to a larger room strung with hammocks and warmed by a potbellied stove with coals of fire glowing warmly through its grate.

Shivering in her soaked clothing, she held her hands toward its warmth.

"Get out of those wet things," the other man advised, as he shed his boots and oilskin coat.

Again Gillian tensed. She had nothing to put on. If she should be so stupid as to undress in front of these men, such a move would mean instant recognition, probably accompanied by her shameful rape, before they threw her body overboard. She shook her head dizzily, almost overwhelmed by her exhaustion and the drink. She could not think. She must make some excuse.

"There be your gear," the man pointed to a bundle on

the floor under the hammock. "Change into your dry things, before the bloody cold gets into your lungs."

So saying, he swung himself into his own hammock, wrapped the bedding around him and fell almost instantly to sleep, even as Gillian stared at him.

With a now-or-never feeling, she slipped to her knees on the floor beside the gray bundle. Untying it, she found rough but heavy and serviceable shirts and trousers that would buckle below her knees with hose to cover her feet and legs.

Almost before one might blink an eye, she had stripped off her sodden shirt and replaced it with the rough full one. It fitted her well enough, being sufficiently long in the arms and body to more than adequately conceal her femininity. Stripping off her chausses, she donned the rest of the clothing thankfully. At last she was dry.

Kneeling in a welter of wet garments, she looked around her. There was no escape from the room except through the galley. And then where would she go? Great weakness and dizziness overcame her. She had to rest.

Clumsily she climbed into the hammock and pulled the damp musty covers around her. Wrapped in the smelly cocoon, she swung back and forth as the ship rode the waves. Terror and pain faded away. Like a dead man, she slept.

Chapter Twenty

"Your watch, laddie!" The hoarse voice growling so close to her ear barely stirred Gillian, so deep in exhausted slumber did she lie.

With a faint groan she sought to move her arms, to stretch them above her head. The cocoon of bedding in the hammock bound her so tightly that she could free only her fingertips, wriggling them out of the mass experimentally.

The hammock swayed as violently as ever, testimony to the storm's continuing fury if the thunder's sullen rumble were not enough.

"Come on, laddie," the weary voice commanded irritably. "Your turn. I be dead on m' feet."

"Yes, sir." Gillian worked her whole hand free and began to pull the musty woolen blankets down from around her ears. Without another comment the man

turned away, shedding his wet outer garments in a
sodden pile before climbing into his hammock. Actually
fighting the bedroll then, as if it were about to strangle
her, the girl at last got a foot free and swept her arms and
legs outward. The hammock promptly pitched violently,
then flipped over dropping her onto the cold wet floor
with a painful thump.

On hands and knees, she looked around her quickly,
embarrassed by her clumsiness and afraid of discovery.
The figure in the hammock was already asleep. As the
ship rolled, the sounds of the roaring, foaming sea filled
her ears until she thought the whole world must be dis-
solving in chaos.

"Watch," he had said. She must find her shoes
somewhere on the wet floor in the near darkness. Cautiously, she began to feel around, her fingers trailing
through tiny salty slips of water on the uneven floor. At
last, she located one, then the other, and dragged them
over her feet. It was like putting on sodden leather rags.
She began to shiver immediately.

The door from the galley opened, framing the cook's
rotund body and the skinny legs hanging out from
beneath his apron. "The skipper bade us let you sleep,"
he informed her in a friendly manner, "but he needs you
topside now. Come eat a bite and drink another mug of
wine to warm your innards."

At the mention of more food and drink, Gillian
scrambled to her feet, catching at the hammock rope as
the deck lurched crazily beneath her feet.

"Aye," the cook advised her. "Hold on tight. We be
running before the storm. But the old *Maudelayne*'s a
good stout lady. She may be a bit creaky here and there,
but she can weather with the best."

Privately, now that she had begun to recover her interest in staying alive, Gillian doubted that any man-made object could weather such chaotic elements as the North Sea storms. Even as she reached the table, the ship seemed to stand on the crest of a tall wave, teeter backward and forward for heartstopping seconds, then plunge downward almost perpendicularly. Its action flung her into the side of the table, bruising her hip. Hanging onto the massive oak with one hand, she rubbed her injury with the other and stared in amazement at the cook, who seemed to be anchored by lead soles on his shoes. With each motion of the ship, he swayed with practiced rhythm in the opposite direction.

"How can you stay upright?" she gawked.

He shrugged, moving with a weaving gait around the end of the table to fetch her a piece of bread and more of the hot wine from last night. "Not too much to drink now," he cautioned. "Just a bit to warm ye. Then down the bread and off ye go. Ye don't want to be drunk. To be drunk in this sea is dangerous. Just warmth for a few minutes until yer body gets used to the bite of the air."

"What do I do?"

"Report to the skipper. He be the one to assign ye to the watch."

Still keeping her head down, her face concealed by the shadows or the cup from which she drank, Gillian hesitated. "Where are we?"

The cook shrugged. "Hard to say at this point. Somewhere in the middle of the sea near the coast of France." His lack of interest amazed Gillian at the same time that it reassured her. This man had no fear of the elements. Or perhaps he simply had no special interest in them.

The roar of the storm now intruded on her consciousness, which had been selecting his voice and obscuring all else. A cowardly shivering began at her spine and transmitted itself to her feet, her hands, her stomach. Her teeth began to chatter violently, clacking against the rim of the mug. Wrapping both hands around it, she lowered it to the table.

The cook shot her a tolerant glance. "Best be going," he advised. "We be in the heart of the storm. Not much chance of a letup."

Her hands released the cup, shifted to the edge of the table, and pushed her upright. Her only chance was to do the job they thought her hired for.

"Take one of those oilskin capes." The cook pointed to a heavy gray garment hanging on a peg by the outer door.

With only a moment's struggle, she donned it, tying the ends of an oiled hood around her head and low on her forehead. She was ready.

The wind struck her like a gigantic hand almost throwing her back down the companionway. How could anyone even stand in this, much less make a way through it . . . or stand watch in it? She stared around her through slitted eyes trying to locate the skipper. Seeing nothing before her but rolling sea, she staggered along the wall of the cabin to a small ladder that led to the upper deck. Cautiously, she mounted it.

The full fury of the storm struck her in the face as her head came over the top of the deck. Heavy salt spray filled her eyes with tears. When she gasped, the air was so water laden that she wondered if it would drown her.

A sort of low canvas tent had been erected on the deck. To this she made her way and stumbled in. Two men crouched inside, their faces drawn. One did not even glance in her direction. The other, the one she recognized as the skipper, nodded grimly. "Took ye long enough, lad."

"Sorry, sir."

"Ye need to do better. Other men have stood their watches and are depending on ye to relieve them so they can go below."

Nervously, Gillian glanced in the direction of the other man who nodded to the skipper before he crawled out of the small tent. The wind filled its canvas sides whooshing them out, threatening to carry the frail structure away into the darkness and the storm.

The skipper handed her a spyglass, drawing it out to its length and closing it back again. "Now, lad, keep watch. Time and again ye keep this trained outside through the holes toward the horizon. If ye spot anything, anything at all, ye pull this cord. Pull it hard, lad, and keep pulling it until I get up here. Do ye understand?"

Gillian nodded, keeping her head down and her shoulders hunched.

The skipper stared at her closely. His eyes narrowed suspiciously. "Ye gave your face a bad bashing," he remarked at last. His gnarled hand reached out to take her chin between thumb and index finger and turn it up to face him in the semidarkness.

She stiffened, ready to fight for her life. With a full belly and a night's sleep, her spirit had rejuvenated. But he merely turned her head from side to side as he studied her bruises.

At last he let go of her chin. "Ye look somewhat younger than I thought at first. Hardly a sign of a beard."

"'Twill make no difference," she assured him huskily. "I can do my work."

"Oh, I doubt not, lad." His chuckle was the only dry thing about the wretched day. As he pulled himself through the opening in the tent, a blast of storm-breath threatened to take the canvas again.

Bravely, she turned the spyglass to the hole just in front of her. This was a real exercise in futility she thought. She could see nothing. Not even the horizon. The deep purplish gray of the stormy sky was reflected in the water. The waves rose higher than the ship in all directions. Thunder rumbled periodically.

Miserably cold and wet, Gillian stood her watch. The hot wine she had drunk was only a sweet memory. Her teeth chattered, and her chilled fingers ached from gripping the spyglass and holding it horizontally from her eye.

After an hour she cradled the instrument across her lap and bared her left wrist. The rope with which she had been bound was still knotted tightly around it. The ends dangled free when she pushed back her sleeve. With shivering fingers she plucked at the knot. Her hand was too weak. Raising her wrist to her mouth, she gnawed at the offensive thing. It was hard and cold and very salty. Furthermore, the soaked knot was rocklike. At first she could make no progress.

Resting, she pulled the spyglass up to her eye and made a circuit of the horizon. The sky seemed to be lightening slightly behind them. Perhaps the storm was passing them.

Cradling the glass again, she continued gnawing at the rope. As she sat, she tried not to think of her predicament. Suppose the skipper had figured out who she was. Would he merely wait until the storm abated to drop her over the side? Her stomach lurched as a tremor of fear ran through her. She had not thought about being seasick in a long time. Perhaps she was not going to be seasick any longer. Thank God for small favors. At least she could die on a quiet stomach.

Suddenly, the knot began to pull apart. She could scarcely believe she was actually succeeding in freeing herself. When she could have grasped the rope with her fingers, she bit down on it and tugged backward like a hound. Ruefully, she chuckled to herself. "Good dog," she whispered as she lowered her wrist and pulled the knot apart with ease.

As the rope fell away, a peculiar sensation gripped her. As if it were a symbol of bondage, it had weighted her with more than intrinsic weight. Her left hand tingled to its fingertips, torturing her with the sweetness of the pain. Gasping, she allowed her head to roll back as with eyes closed she accepted the agony of returning life. Before she was aware, soft tears squeezed from the corners of her lids and trickled down her cheeks.

For a full minute she massaged her wrist. At last she straightened her body to look at her hand. The rope lay in her lap, like a dark serpent coiled obscenely across her calf. In a wash of anger, she caught it up. Despite the howling storm, she crawled from beneath the tent. Standing erect in the whipping rain, she hurled the rope into the wind. With a shudder of satisfaction, she watched as the gale carried it, writhing away, into the darkness.

Taking advantage of her freedom despite the chill, she scanned the horizon in every direction. Still nothing. The *Maudelayne* creaked and groaned like a soul in torment but seemed to be weathering the storm well.

Breathing easier than she had since Ranulf had

captured her, Gillian slipped back inside the tent and resumed her watch. Perhaps by the time the storm was over, the skipper and the rest of the crew would have accepted her so they would not even question her identity. At the first port she would slip away and find passage back to England. The business of hiding her sex from the crew did not daunt her. She was familiar with all the tricks of concealment.

Gradually, she began to relax. Her only problem became staying awake. Because of the sameness of the weather, she had no clear impression of day or night. Likewise, she had no idea how many hours had passed since she had been captured by Ranulf.

He had taken her prisoner just at dusk. The hour had been late when he had discovered her identity and knocked her unconscious. The time that had elapsed until she regained consciousness in the hold of the *Maudelayne*, and the hours she had slept before being awakened for her watch were the unknown factors.

In the middle of the ocean, she had no idea in which direction the ship was being borne. As these thoughts flitted through her mind, she became further aware of her isolation. She was alone in the middle of a stormy sea with not one friend around her. If not surrounded by enemies, she was amidst men who would probably kill her without compunction.

The sky behind them became lighter and lighter. Either the storm was blowing itself out or was outdistancing them. The rain began to slacken its fierce pelting. Yawning widely, Gillian opened the tent flap and peered out. The motion of the ship settled to a more gentle rocking. Although the waves were still high, they seemed farther apart.

As she stared out, the rain stopped entirely. The sky overhead lightened to a pale gray with a tinge of blue. Tentatively, she sniffed the air finding it clean and fresh with only a hint of saltiness.

Behind her in the direction the ship had sailed, she could hear the roaring still. The storm was definitely passing on. She wondered idly when she would be relieved of her watch. She was sleepy and hungry too. A hot plate of fish stew with a crust of hard bread to scoop it up with would go well right now. She was hungry enough to eat anything.

A door opened on the deck beneath her. The skipper stepped out and strolled toward the bow of the ship. His distinctive rolling gait identified him, as did the fierce grizzled whiskers that tangled around the sides of his cheeks and stuck out in gray tufts on either side of his head.

Immediately, Gillian ducked back inside her tent, closing the flap except for a slit through which she could peek. As she watched, the old man knelt on the grate over the hold in which she had been imprisoned. Cupping his hands around his face to accustom his eyes to the dark interior, he peered down intently. He was looking for her, Gillian realized instantly. A cold chill spread from her belly to her heart, stopping her breath in her throat.

The skipper glanced keenly in her direction, seemed satisfied, then stepped down off the hatch and slid the cover aside. As Gillian watched with clenched fists held against her mouth, he disappeared into the hold.

Frantically, Gillian waited. When he discovered his victim was missing, what would be his reaction? Would he immediately connect the unfamiliar face of the new deckhand with her, or would he not make the connection at all? Trembling, she waited for what seemed hours.

In her mind she could see him searching in the dimness, confidently at first, then with progressive irritation as his prey seemed to have hidden herself well. Finally, he would become angry, tossing barrels aside with his rough gnarled hands as he cursed under his breath.

How long would he continue the futile search? The answer was not long in coming. His head appeared above the hold. On deck again, he scratched his beard in a puzzled fashion. Hands on hips he stared around him at the expanse of calming sea in the wake of the *Maudelayne*. The man's entire aspect bespoke perplexity. Where was she?

His thick grizzled brows beetled together as he frowned at the tossing waves. Suddenly he stiffened. Watching from the slit in the tent flap, Gillian recognized the change in his aspect.

His shoulders hunched as if anticipating a knifethrust. Slowly he turned. His hands dropped to his sides where they clenched into tight fists. His eyes narrowed against the lightening day. As if the canvas were not around her, he stared at her. In the minute of recognition the two regarded each other as if each was stripped bare.

She saw his lips move in the tangle of his beard. Then he started forward, his rolling gait carrying him across the deck and up the ladder with frightening swiftness. Shoulders hunched and teeth clenched, she waited for his hand to grasp the tent flap. But he never swept it aside.

Instead, the alarm bell began a fearful clamor. The line with its wooden peg attached to the end jumped and twisted within the confines of the tent. Dazedly, she stared at it, its meaning eluding her. Was he calling the others to help him drag one lone girl from beneath a frail piece of canvas? Would he require the help of the entire crew to consign her to the depths?

Suddenly, jarringly, the *Maudelayne* jolted against something in her downward pitch. Through the canvas she heard the skipper curse loudly and fervently. The cries of the crew were added to his noise. The vessel slewed violently sideways.

Gillian was slung against the side of the tent with such force that the canvas ripped loose from its moorings. At the same time the skipper crashed through the top, his body tangling in the welter of canvas and lines. Scrambling to her hands and knees, Gillian shook her head in disbelief.

A sandy expanse of beach stretched before her almost under the bow of the ship. They had run aground. Watching the skipper, she had neglected her duty. The wind-driven vessel had rammed head-on into the sand bar that guarded the beach.

Gillian glanced over her shoulder at the struggling skipper, who continued to spit forth a string of oaths, the meaning of which she could only guess at. He had managed to flop his body over on his belly, at the same time tangling himself more hopelessly in the whipping lines and ripped swathes of wet canvas. The face he turned toward his sometime deckhand glowed bright red. His mouth contorted into a mask of hatred while his eyes promised murder. The tangled grizzled beard shook wildly as he screamed imprecations at her.

Her decision was made. Springing to her feet, she avoided the gnarled hands clutching at her and dashed to the bow of the vessel. Only a moment she stared down into the churning, boiling surf. How deep it was, she had no idea. It was her only hope. The skipper would do worse than drown her if he caught her.

"*Stop him!* Blast your eyes. A gold piece to the man who catches that . . ."

She never heard what he called her. Taking a deep breath, her eyes concentrating hopefully on the sandy beach that glimmered like silver in the strengthening light, she leaped out as far as she could beyond the grinding bow. Icy water closed over her head, causing her to gasp for breath and at the same time swallow some of the unfamiliar salty liquid.

Down she slid into the churning water. Her eyes stung like fire, but she refused to shut them. She could bear the pain. She must see where she was going. Desperately she kicked with her legs and flailed with her arms.

She was sinking. She could not keep afloat. Through blurred eyes she glimpsed the shoreline. So close. She took a deep breath as the waves closed over her again.

Miraculously, her feet touched the sandy bottom. The distance from the top of her head to the surface could be no more than a couple of feet. Pushing downward with her hands and jumping, she drove herself forward and upward. Her progress was agonizingly slow, but each time she could take a breath before she sank again. Her terror subsided slightly.

Fortunately, the waves slapped at her back as she came to the surface. Their power carried her forward. Now she could touch bottom with her toes while her head was out of the water. Then her shoulders.

In her ears she could hear more and more faintly the shouts of the crew, but she dared not look around. The pounding surf, the whirling white water around her waist now, seemed almost warm as she exerted herself to the utmost. Her clothing dragged her down. She was getting winded, but the beach was ahead of her. She was almost to dry land.

Risking a glance over her shoulder, she saw that the attention of the men of the *Maudelayne* had turned from her. The skipper had turned his back to the beach and stood gesticulating wildly. His crew scurried to and fro, their full attention centered on obeying his commands and getting the vessel afloat again.

Her spirits rose at the same time her breath rasped in her throat in great agonizing gasps. The salty water that she had swallowed burned like fire. But she was moving. The water was swirling around her thighs. Then her knees. Throwing herself forward, she began to run, splashing the white water in all directions.

In water only an inch deep, she fell, gasping, panting, her eyes and throat burning. The last few feet she accomplished on hands and knees. The tears began to come then. Great gulping sobs of thanksgiving tore from her. She would not drown. She was free from the old barge with its menacing piratical skipper. She had escaped the horrible death Ranulf had planned for her.

Only a moment did she allow herself to lie on the cold damp sand. Rolling over on her back, she hoisted herself on her elbows to watch the efforts of the crew to get the ship afloat. Not a jot of remorse stirred within her. They had callously taken the job of murdering her. She hoped their rotten old ship stayed on the sand forever.

The sea wind plastered her wet clothing against her body. Her teeth started to chatter. Hurriedly, she pulled herself to her feet and surveyed the shoreline. A discernible path wound away into the dunes. At the end of the path hopefully were people with whom she could shelter until she could arrange for passage back to England. Clenching her teeth to still their chattering, she loped away from the rolling sea.

At the crest of the dune, she turned and looked back. They were still working futilely. A brief smile curved her face as she raised her hand to thumb her nose in their direction.

Chapter Twenty-One

Still yoked to the empty wagon, the white oxen stood disconsolately in the courtyard of the Tabard Inn. Rain pelted their soaked hides and formed muddy pools around their hocks. Finally, one drew in a deep breath and gave forth with a mournful bawl.

A sleepy ostler peered out, gesturing obscenely from the window. A flash of lightning, followed immediately by a deafening clap of thunder, set the second ox to bawling. Within the inn itself Harry Bailey rose sighing. The quality of help he was able to hire these days left much to be desired. Perhaps he was really getting too old for innkeeping.

Yawning and shaking his head at the thunder, he began to dress. Again a loud bawl drew him to his dormer window overlooking the courtyard and the brilliantly painted sign. The oxen looked familiar somehow. Suddenly, the identity of their owner dawned upon him.

Hastening from his room, he knocked on the door of the suite where his friends had spent the night. "Howard! Hob! Awake! Brian de Trenanay! Sirs! Awake!"

His pounding brought the squire almost immediately. Dressed only in his hose and shoes, and rubbing the sleep from his eyes, Hob regarded Harry sourly. "By God, Harry, it cannot be time to pay the reckoning this early. You used to allow the guests at least time for breakfast before rousting them out."

Harry looked hurt. "Your friend Gil Fletcher's oxen and wagon have returned without him," he announced.

Hob's forehead wrinkled. Shaking his head worriedly, he drew a deep breath. "Best wake up Sir Brian. He paced the floor until the wee hours worrying about the boy. Seems he was right to fear."

Harry nodded glumly. "The young one must have met with foul play."

Entering the bedchamber, Hob roused Brian with only a touch.

"Gil . . ." The knight's eyes flew open. At the sight of the squire bending over him, he tightened his jaw. Wide-awake, he sat straight up searching the room beyond where he caught sight of Harry standing stolidly in the doorway, his hands clasped over his apron. "Has Gil returned—"

The older man shook his head. "The team is standing in the courtyard bawling, but of the boy there is no sign."

Icy fear gripped Brian in the pit of his stomach. Cursing vividly, he flung back the covers and swung his muscular legs over the side of the bed. "No sign of him, you say?"

The squire shook his head stepping back as Brian

began to draw on his clothing with frantic haste.

"That fool boy."

Hob nodded sadly. "He had his commission to deliver. We were drunken. But he should not have left without an escort."

Brian drew on his boots. "What does the wagon look like?"

"I have not looked at it. I thought to rouse you immediately."

Brian nodded. "Right. Put on your tunic and follow me down straightway." He regarded the shoulders and chest of the man he had challenged to fight to the death. Although of slighter build than Brian's, Hob's shoulders were strongly muscled. His chest likewise was well developed for his size. A sprinkling of gray hairs among the blond ones did not deceive Brian into believing that the contest would have been an easy victory for himself.

As Hob hurried into his own room, Brian confronted Harry Bailey. "Has anyone investigated the wagon?"

Harry turned to lead the way. "Come, my lord, we will go down together now that you have covered yourself."

Brian mounted to the wagon seat, the rain slashing at his face, plastering his fair hair to his forehead. The wagon was empty. To assure himself, he climbed into the bed and knelt behind the seat. Only the neatly folded canvas that had been used to cover the load lay carefully tucked underneath. A black tip of cloth peeped from behind it. Pouncing on it, he drew it forth.

Emotional pain pierced him so that, desperate, he clutched at his wound in sympathy. The crumpled cloth was her hat. Her black hat with its red and gold insignia. He crushed it in his hand as he rested his forehead against the rough boards before him. She must have been snatched from this very seat.

Sitting back on his heels, he started to examine his find when Harry Bailey called to him. "Come in out of the driving rain, Sir Brian. You will catch the lung fever and be to bury. 'Twill do Master Gil no good at all."

Recognizing the truth of the innkeeper's admonition, Brian vaulted over the side of the wagon. Harry signaled to the ostler to lead the cattle into the stable and care for them. In the taproom, Hob thrust a tankard of ale into Brian's hand. "What did you find?"

"Her hat . . ." Brian held it out.

"*Her!*" Both men stared aghast at Brian's words.

Brian shook his head, turning the piece of velvet cloth over and over in his hands. "I did not mean to tell. Forgive me, Gillian," he muttered.

"You mean Gil Fletcher . . . *Master Gil Fletcher . . .* is a girl!" Hob's voice stammered in surprise.

"She poses as her own twin brother to retain the family seat in the guildhall," Brian explained, his fingers moving ceaselessly over the soft velvet. "My God!" he gasped, his voice trembling.

"What have you found, my lord?"

"A crusted stain, Hob. Unless I am wrong . . . and I have seen too many on velvets . . . this hat has a bloodstain in the band." The eyes that the knight raised to his sometime squire were dark with pain.

Hob reached out for the hat, bending Brian's icy fingers away from the crushed velvet. "It could be anything." His own voice was hoarse. He had liked and admired the young man Gil Fletcher. Now his tender heart, trained in the ideals of courtly love, went out to the imagined suffering of a gentle damsel.

Harry Bailey cleared his throat. "Sit you down, gentlemen," he ordered, taking Brian's arm and guiding him to one of the tables. "We must think clearly about this. First. Whence came the team?"

"The team? . . ." Brian's forearms rested on the edge of the board, his hands curved limply, palm upward. "Why I suppose they returned here after she was taken."

"Why here?"

Hob slapped his palm on the table. "Why indeed?"

Brian straightened, staring at one man and then the other. "Of course. They would have no association with here. They could have wandered anywhere. Someone brought them here."

Hob nodded excitedly. "Someone who wants you to come after him . . ." His lip curled upward sardonically. "Someone who cares not for young damsels, but who lusts for massive men."

"Ranulf," Brian growled.

"Aye, Ranulf of Briarthwaite."

Brian shook his head wiping his hand across the lower part of his mouth. The hideous picture of the slender, gentle girl in the hands of that perverted fiend rose in his mind. His hand sought the medallion beneath his shirt. His green eyes glittered with the intensity of his feeling. *Mucro Mors Cristo.* Never had the motto meant more than it did at that moment. The ungodly Ranulf would die on his sword point. He swore it.

"We must be off on the trail." Brian pushed back the bench with a violent shove of his legs.

Hob grabbed his wrist. "But carefully," he advised, looking up into the man's set face. "Carefully. Cautiously. Sit back down and let us plan." When Brian would have jerked away, the smaller man's grasp tightened. "Please. You can do nothing to save her from what

285

they have done to her at first. I dare say she was taken yesterday sometime in the afternoon as she left the depot."

At the suggestion that she had been maltreated, Brian swore graphically.

Beside him, Harry Bailey nudged his elbow. "You have to keep a cool head, my lord," he admonished.

"They wanted me!" Brian rounded on Harry, his voice rising to a roar. "She has suffered this . . . this atrocity for my sake. *I* got her into this. *I* was so sure that because that swine claimed to be a knight, I could just walk in and remind him of his vows and all would be well. Damn! Damn his soul to everlasting hell."

The other two sat silent unable to gainsay him.

"I must go to her," Brian rose from the table and headed for the stairs. "I shall follow the route to the quartermaster depot. Undoubtedly, they waylaid her somewhere between here and there and carried her away. They want me to find them. I shall do so. They will leave clues. The rats want the cat to chase them until they can surround him and drag him down."

"I will be your shield at your back, Sir Brian," Hob volunteered, springing after him.

"You—"

"The lady was always kind to me," the squire reminded Brian. "She is a brave and true lady."

"She is a little fool, with more pride than sense," Brian fussed as he reached the room.

"She did not seem so foolish the night she rescued you," Hob reminded him.

"They will be after her blood for that," Brian sighed as he buckled on the heavy fustian tunic that went under his armor.

"Will you dress in full armor?" Hob could not suppress the disbelief in his voice.

"No," Brian replied. "But this will give me a modicum of protection. "I will wear my mail shirt. That will turn a few points."

Within minutes Brian was dressed. At the door of the inn they found Harry had ordered their horses saddled. "Go with God." The innkeeper embraced Hob, patting him long on the back and hugging the younger man to his heart. "Return here when you have rescued her," he called, raising his hand in farewell. "You can all stay free." His lips twitched into a semblance of a smile.

"God and Saint George," Hob swore. "Harry must have taken a real liking to young Gil. He never promised anyone a free night before."

As the pair galloped out of the inn on the road toward Greenwich, Ranulf, at his post among the dripping trees, chuckled. He congratulated himself that he had not waited long. Brian de Trenanay was so predictable. All honor and no brains. He would be a most amusing man to play with for a time.

The squire was another matter entirely. Turncoat scum! Ranulf closed his fist tightly over the handle of his whip. Too bad he had not had Hob in his hands last night. The skipper of the *Maudelayne* could have disposed of two as easily as one. The price might have been a little higher, but the results would have been worth it.

Ranulf frowned. The presence of the squire complicated things slightly. He presented the distinct possibility that the man loitering near the depot to supply Brian with false information might be recognized. Ranulf shook his head. What difference! If the fellow's story were convincing enough, the two would follow his false clue even better because they believed him to be one of Ranulf's men.

With a smile that did not reach his eyes, Ranulf turned his horse and rode down the other side of the hill to the small inn he had made his headquarters.

Throughout the miserable ride to Greenwich, Brian managed to sustain himself on his anger. Amidst rumbling thunder and torrential rain, he pushed the destrier to the limit. His own skin was burning hot; his face, flushed. The blood of battle drummed in his ears. Desperately, he pushed the images of Ranulf's cruelties to the back of his mind.

The guards at the palisade passed them through without comment. Yes, according to their records a commission from York Minster had been delivered the day before. The signatures were in order. Would Brian care to see them?

Brian shook his head. No one but Gillian would have delivered the commission. She had guarded it with her life. She would not have trusted it to anyone else. What had she done with the payment?

The quartermaster waved his quill pen. "The gold was paid directly to the man who made the delivery. If he carried it away with him, there is the end so far as we are concerned. If he chose to risk robbery and probable murder on his way home, those things are his business. If he chose the easy sensible way, Gisze will have a record." He indicted the stone depot.

Without inquiring, Brian knew Gillian would have made a Hansa deposit. His own strength and pride in his independence, combined with the fact that he had never had much gold in his possession, had precluded his dealings with the merchant bankers, but he knew their reputed honesty. Craftsmen and tradesmen who dealt with money had developed the League to protect themselves when they transported goods to be sold at distant spots. His little fletcher would not have taken a chance on carrying gold in her wagon across the length of England.

Brian turned bleakly to Hob. "She was here," he confirmed unnecessarily. "But where she went after she left here, or how long since she left is a mystery."

The squire nodded staring round the almost deserted bailey. In contrast to the usual bustle, the violence of the storm had kept activity to a minimum. "Will you step into the mess with me, my lord?" he asked at last. "We could make inquiries there or perhaps pick up a word of gossip."

Brian pushed the cowl of his tunic back and ran a hand through his soaked hair. "A good idea." He nodded without much conviction. As Hob turned to lead the way, Brian caught the other's arm. "Forget about calling me my lord. We are not part of a pageant or a joust. Just two men trying to find a friend who is lost and in deep trouble."

Hob's mouth quirked up at the corner in a suggestion of a smile. "We are that," he nodded. Other comments leaped to mind, but he firmly shut his mouth. He could not tell how long the truce with the Frenchman would last. The man was insufferably arrogant at the same time he was incredibly naïve. The combination made for an uncomfortable association. With just the hint of a shrug, the man who had been Howard of Rothingham led his companion out of the rain.

Brian's accent immediately set him apart from the men he sought to question. A couple of them stared at him blankly. Then one burly yeoman marked him for the others by spitting contemptuously into the rushes at Brian's feet. With an effort the knight controlled himself. Such effrontery before one's betters would have been handled summarily in France. But this was not France. He realized his own life might very well be in danger in this room which fairly bristled with hostility.

Again he controlled himself, backing away from the hard eyes that regarded him from all sides. For Gillian's sake he would put aside his pride. The thought gave him satisfaction. When he got Gillian back, he would tell her . . . what? He eased himself back into an unobtrusive position near the door. There he folded his arms and waited, trying not to appear anxious as his eyes followed Hob around the room.

At last the squire returned, shaking his head. "No one knows anything," he reported in a low voice. "Or if they do, they will not speak. Damn! I should have remembered your French accent. You can easily pass for an Englishman with your fair hair and pale complexion. We think of Frenchman as small and dark. But that damned accent gave you away. Next time keep your mouth shut."

Huffily, Brian stiffened. "If there is a next time."

"You want to find her, do you not?"

A man somewhat younger than the others approached Brian. "Did the lad you are seeking get into trouble?"

"Can you tell us anything?" the knight asked eagerly. His eyes scanned the face of the one who spoke. Such a young lad might have had conversation with Gillian. She might have given some hint. "Did he speak of going directly home?"

The youth looked slyly around him. "I might have heard him say something. And I might be mistaken."

"Anything you can tell us," Brian urged, his fists clenched in frustration. "We have nowhere to go from here."

The youth looked at the squire who stood at the knight's left shoulder. Hastily, his eyes slid away. He raised a hand and wiped the lower part of his face. "He said he was on his way back to York." The youth swallowed hard and licked his lips as if his throat were dry. "Has he gotten into trouble?"

"We fear so," Hob replied, his face revealing nothing.

"Too bad. Lots of sad things happen to young men these days."

Hob's bright blue eyes narrowed slightly. "Indeed," he agreed.

"Can you give us some direction? Did you see him when he left?" Brian asked impatiently.

"No." The youth shook his head emphatically. "We just talked a bit. He said he was going home directly. Said he missed his home. Been away a long time, he had."

"'Tis true," Brian agreed.

The youth peered from beneath his lashes. "He asked me the quickest way across the river."

"And you told him," Hob supplied quietly. The squire had been staring at a spot on the wall seeming to be paying no attention.

The youth flashed him a swift glance before looking directly at Brian. "I told him about the ferry over to the east about half a mile."

Brian hit one fist into the palm of the other. "A ferry a mile to the east." He turned to Hob eagerly. "Shall we try for it?"

Hob appeared to be chewing on something. "Oh, by all means," he smiled pleasantly into the face of their informant. "I have a feeling that we may have struck the trail, thanks to you. How may we repay you for this valuable information?"

The young man held up his hands in protest. "Oh, I want no pay. Just hope you find your friend all right. He was a real kind person. Real friendly. I liked him when I met him."

Hob nodded cynically, but Brian withdrew some coins from his purse and pressed them into the youth's hand as he shook it. "Use these to buy something for another friend, if you do not want them yourself. *Merci. Merci beaucoup.*"

Outside, Hob trailed behind when Brian hurried toward the horses. As the Frenchman swung up and would have galloped off, Hob caught the bridle. "You are the most credulous man I have ever met," he sighed.

"What mean you? Leave off. Mount and ride. Every minute the trail grows colder." Brian tugged on the reins impatiently.

"Ride without the palisade," Hob commanded, "but do not be so hasty as to take the lane to the ferry." His English blue eyes were cold and steady brooking no further argument.

Sullenly, Brian did as the squire commanded.

"Did you never think that man might have been looking for us to give us information?"

Brian scratched his chin. "He must have overheard us making inquiries."

"He might, except that he was lounging near the door all the time we were talking. I doubt that he could have heard anything."

"Perhaps someone else told him that we were asking about Gil."

Raindrops spattered the squire's face as he faced Brian. The corner of his mouth lifted in a cynical smirk. "Perhaps he is one of Ranulf's men, if man he may be called. I have seen him only once or twice. He is one of the *gentlemen of the chamber*."

Brian swore, reining his horse around as if to head back to the depot.

"Wait, Brian." Hob's voice betrayed his irritation. "For God's sake, think. You cannot ride back into the English garrison and take one of the men. They would be on you in an instant. You would do Gil no good."

Brian pulled the destrier back. "You are right." His urgency subsided. "What shall we do? Wait until he leaves and then follow him."

"For a time." The squire smiled at the idea that Brian would allow any man who was not a knight to give commands. "Then we will take a hostage of our own. Ranulf will not want his lover harmed."

Chapter Twenty-Two

"Ah, Hereward." Ranulf greeted the young man with open arms, dragging him against his chest and planting a kiss on the youth's rain-dampened cheek. "You did your work well. They did not suspect."

Hereward stood stiffly in the arms of his lover, his eyes sliding uncomfortably over Wat, who raised an eyebrow and nodded in mock salute. Wat lounged insolently, one long leg thrown over the arm of the carved wooden chair at the head of the table. His flat gray eyes never blinked.

"I took care, my lord Ranulf."

"I knew you could. To be sure. You are a clever boy. Did I not say he was a clever boy, Wat?" Ranulf patted Hereward on the back with uncommon affection.

"You did, my lord."

Ranulf laughed gustily as he strode to the table and poured ale for the three of them. "So they are on their way to the ferry below Greenwich."

"Yes, my lord."

Ranulf cupped both of Hereward's hands around the flagon and lifted the drink to his petulant lips. "Drink deep. You deserve a reward for performing this task so well." He chuckled excitedly as the youth drank. "Let them ride all day in the rain. Let them exhaust themselves and their horses. Let them catch the lung fever if God so wills." He transferred one hand to the youthful shoulder, rubbing seductively with his thumb.

"I hope they have sense enough to let Guy find them," Wat snorted contemptuously.

"They will be searching and asking everywhere." Hereward's expression was blank as he lowered the cup. Sensing Wat's antipathy, he could appreciate the threat the man brought to his own position as lover to Ranulf. A man of small stature and smaller expectations, he had submitted to the lord of Briarthwaite without demur. The relationship had brought a measure of comfort and security . . . until now. He stared at Wat from beneath lowered lids.

Ranulf stared from man to man, another wave of excitement shivering through him. He bared his teeth between his thin lips. Their obvious rivalry for his favor promised delicious nights ahead. His eyes slitted as he breathed deeply to calm himself.

A peremptory knock broke the tense silence. Ranulf glanced at Wat inquiringly, receiving a shrug in reply. "Answer it, sweetbrier," he bade the youth. Sullenly, Hereward flung the door wide without actually looking to see who stood on the threshold.

Brian de Trenanay rested his hand on the hilt of his sword. Eyes like dark jade, he strode into the room. So tall, so menacing, so deadly, the embodiment of his own motto, he moved amongst them and they fell back before him. Behind him Hob closed the door decisively and leaned back against it with arms folded. The light glinted off the uplifted point of a dagger in front of his left shoulder.

Ranulf paled, his colorless eyes shifting from his adversaries to his two allies. The boy Hereward fell back almost paralyzed by shock, but Wat was another matter. Galvanized into action, he sprang up, drawing the dagger he carried ever at his belt. Placing the heavy walnut chair between himself and Brian, he waited for the command.

Knowing the odds better than even, Ranulf recovered himself. "Ah, Sir Brian, so good of you to drop by to renew our acquaintance. May I offer you some ale? Hereward can just step downstairs for another flagon."

"I did not come for social amenities." Brian extended his arm to detain the youth. "I remember too well your treatment of visitors."

Ranulf smiled unpleasantly. "Well, perhaps I was a trifle rough, but big fellows like you sometimes turn so savage. I promise you, you would have ended enjoying yourself."

Brian's face turned a dull red, but he controlled his rage. "Where is Gil?" he asked through set teeth.

"Your disgusting little friend?" Ranulf waved his hand dismissively. "Oh, he, or more correctly she, is where she can be reached if you intend to become unpleasant."

Ranulf's words reassured Brian, but Hob noticed a stiffening in Wat's figure along with a flicker of surprise in the henchman's face. Gillian was not all right, if Wat's demeanor were any indication.

"Let her go," Brian demanded. "Send this catamite with Hob to take her away and I will submit to whatever you want. I swear."

Ranulf ran his tongue across his lower lip. The thought of the big savage knight bowing to him stirred him mightily. The man's muscles were like steel bands; his legs, like tree trunks. And best of all, the man would be compelled by his own knightly oath and his fear for the girl. "Ah, but for how long? You would ride away when you saw your transvestite friend safe," he turned his back as if the conversation bored him.

In a movement swifter than the henchman could forestall, Brian caught the man's shoulder. "You would discover my methods of persuasion, Ranulf?" he questioned angrily. "I bear you no love. You deserve a taste of your own medicine."

Ranulf looked contemptuously at the callused hand despite the agonizing force of the grip. "You will never discover her that way," he sneered. "Come, Sir Brian, is a term in my . . . employment so loathesome? Certainly it would be preferable to a term spent laying a seige or fighting a series of skirmishes. Much less dangerous too."

"How long a term?"

Ranulf smiled. His eyebrow lifted languidly. "I would hope we might become friends. You might find you would desire to stay longer."

"How long?" Brian felt his skin prickling.

"How long do you usually take to become friends with someone?"

Brian swallowed. "A week."

"Why one hardly gets to know a person in a week."

"A fortnight," Brian bargained. An angry flush

stained his cheeks.

"Do you swear?"

"When Gil is released into Hob's care, when I see them ride away safe together then I swear to be your"—he swallowed convulsively—". . . your man or whatever you want . . . for a fortnight."

Ranulf's mind was working rapidly. The girl was already dead. Her fate had been sealed the moment she had been dumped into the hold of the *Maudelayne*. But Wat could lead Hob away and dispose of him. In the meantime a drug in Brian's ale would render him unconscious until he could be chained up. "Hereward does not know where she is kept," Ranulf explained. "He shall remain here to wait upon us while Wat takes your squire to fetch the little slut." His tone eloquently portrayed his disgust with both of Brian's companions.

"I think not . . ." Brian began.

"A reasonable arrangement, my lord." Hob spoke from behind him for the first time. "Everyone should be satisfied by that arrangement."

Brian turned to peer intently at his squire, trying to read the message in that stony face. At length he shrugged. Hob was no novice. He would not allow the henchman to get behind him.

When Brian turned back, the tableau had broken. Wat moved from behind the chair, skirting the center of the room. Hereward melted back into the shadows of the corner. After refilling his flagon of ale, Ranulf took the chair that Wat had vacated. Unconsciously he adopted almost the same posture as the younger man had held. The difference lay in the fact that his position really was a pose. Through slitted eyes he watched the two leave before returning his attention to Brian.

"Sit," he gestured jovially. "Bring ale, Hereward. Fresh ale. You know Hereward is really the most charming young man," he declared expansively. "So inventive and receptive to all my suggestions for gratifying my needs."

Brian sat stiffly at the bench. His stomach jumped and quivered. Gillian had been held captive by this swine for over twenty-four hours. The thought of her pure innocence at Ranulf's mercy drove him frantic.

When he got her back, he vowed he would lavish on her long hours of tender care to restore her spirit as well as her body. She had suffered because of him and his stupidity. He would not trust this creature out of his sight. Yet he kept his face impassive effectively concealing his thoughts.

The boy entered, bearing the laden tray which he presented to Ranulf, who inspected it nonchalantly. With a wave he sent it to Brian. "This is poor stuff," he apologized softly, watching to see that the knight took the flagon meant for him. "The ale of Briarthwaite is justly famous all around Leeds."

Brian said nothing but regarded his would-be tormentor steadily.

"Come. Drink up." Ranulf suited his words with the action. "The day is stormy, but we are warm and dry here. A bit of liquid refreshment will help to while away the hours. Wat has quite a long way to take the squire. And once there they will have to return."

Brian lifted the flagon to his mouth, moistening his lips, taking only a tiny sip. It was bitter as Ranulf had said. Yet he was thirsty. He took a mouthful.

Ranulf smiled, brushing a lock of his lank hair back from his temple and trailing his hand down his neck. "I would never have seriously hurt you, you know." His voice was soft and gentle, like a woman's. "You angered me."

Brian's hand tightened around the stem of the flagon. He took a swallow in an effort to clear the evil taste from his mouth. "You are a knight!" he blurted at last.

Ranulf shrugged; his shoulder rose in a contemptuous shrug. "And what is a knight? A hired killer. A thief with a nobleman's permission to loot and rape."

"No." Brian denied. "We are the first to live by our word. We pay homage to the lord and defend his honor with our own."

Ranulf chuckled softly. "How many lords do you swear allegiance to, Sir Brian?"

Brian looked surprised. "My homage to my liege is paramount," he replied stiffly.

"And who is your liege," Ranulf inquired suavely, "when you are not in France, that is?"

"I owe no Englishman my allegiance," Brian insisted.

"Oh, of course not." Ranulf made a stiff face in mockery of Brian's icy expression. "How did you happen to be bringing our little arrowmaker to London?"

"I owed her a debt."

"And to discharge your debt you guarded her journey to deliver her arrows to the arms depot of Henry V. . . ."

Brian took another drink from the flagon. Despite his discomfiture as he realized the direction the conversation was taking, he did not feel his muscles tensing as they might have done. He shook his head to clear a faint buzzing from his ears. "I owed her . . ." he insisted. His tongue felt slightly thick. He looked suspiciously at the flagon. "Besides arrows cannot damage castle walls or go through a well-made piece of armor plate."

"Castle walls . . ." Ranulf sneered. "Cannon, my dear fellow. Cannon *can* and do knock down castle walls. Time was when a lord could hide behind his walls and send his knights out to attack whatever threatened him while he stayed safe and sound. Those days are gone forever." He made a sweeping gesture with the hand that held the flagon, ending up with it tipped to his mouth.

"Cannon are almost as dangerous to the one who fires them as to the one they are fired against," Brian observed.

"But they will improve," his adversary replied smoothly. "They will improve. Mark my words. I have not bothered to rebuild the fortifications that were around Briarthwaite. A waste of money, not to mention, time."

Brian shook his head again focusing his eyes carefully on Ranulf's face which through a trick of light seemed to blur slightly. "A knight should not be concerned with money."

Chuckling cynically, Ranulf rose from the chair to help himself to another flagon of ale. "Why do you insist upon those outmoded ideals?" He strolled over to Brian studying him interestedly.

"They are not outmoded. They are . . . They are . . . God given."

His lips curling into a smile, Ranulf brought his slender fingers to rest on Brian's shoulder. The knight shrugged irritably seeking to throw off his adversary, but Ranulf merely moved his hand inward toward the side of Brian's neck. "God given . . ." Ranulf shook his head, his eyes reflecting his amazement. "God given." He pushed Brian gently back against the edge of the table.

Brian's head tilted back on his shoulders as he stared

defiantly up into Ranulf's dark eyes. "I made my vows to God," he insisted. "My motto is my bond. *Mucro Mors Cristo.*"

Ranulf tapped him on the cheek. "How fierce," he murmured gazing down into the gold-flecked green eyes. "And how naïve."

Brian carefully set the flagon down and took a grip on the edge of the table. Using his hand as a prop, he levered himself up until he forced the slighter man to step backward. "I have fought in tournaments in England and France for years," he declared coldly. "Sometimes I have been bested, but most of the time I have won handily. But each time I have fought fairly giving God the victory. When I have fought in battles, I have fought always for France."

He had pulled himself erect and stood steadily. Now the effort seemed too much. He subsided onto the bench. He felt a taste of brass in his mouth. Licking his lower lip, he reached for the flagon. Over its rim he stared at Ranulf's back.

"The king or Burgundy?" Ranulf threw over his shoulder contemptuously.

Brian paused nonplused.

Ranulf swung round, one eyebrow lifted quizzically. "The old mad king or the Duke of Burgundy—or, for that matter, the party of Orléans." He watched Brian draw in a deep breath. "Come, come! You must have some concept of the politics of your native country. To which of those estimable gentlemen do you owe allegiance. Or do you owe allegiance to them all."

"The king," Brian choked.

"Ah, the king." Ranulf nodded sarcastically. "But the king is mad."

"He is still my king."

"As Harry of Monmouth is mine. But these are troubled times. When I was a boy, the king was Richard of Bordeaux, but Harry's father killed him. How can you decide which one deserves your allegiance? Defend the murdered and end up murdered yourself. Swear allegiance to the man who pays you. That is my motto."

"I will fight for lilies of France."

"But who will wear them? The king, the new Duke of Orleans, or Burgundy? Oh, we hear across the channel," Ranulf smiled his sardonic smile. "'Tis for the reason of this rivalry that we prepare for war. If the lion of England were to wear the lilies of France, would you fight for him?"

Angrily, Brian rose again. "That will never be," he prophesied. "France will never have an English king."

"England had a French king a few hundred years ago," Ranulf reminded him smoothly as he slipped his hand under Brian's arm. "But I have upset you. Here, let me pour you another drink. Hereward can fix a pallet on the floor for you, or you can lie down on my own bed. Are you ill?"

"Hot," Brian whispered. His eyes glazed. Feverishly he licked his lips. "The drink, the drink."

Ranulf sighed as Brian staggered crazily away, falling to one knee. "Yes, the drink. You really should learn to get over this naïve trust, Sir Brian." Setting his flagon down on the table, he followed his quarry across the room.

Brian fumbled at his belt for his sword.

"Oh, no!" Ranulf wrested the weapon from his trembling hand. "None of that. After all, you promised to submit yourself. Here you are resisting and trying to draw your sword." The Lord of Briarthwaite made a clucking sound with his tongue as he disarmed Brian completely.

"P-Promised to submit when . . . Gillian . . . freed."

"True. But there is no reason to wait around," Ranulf sneered. "She may be a long time coming. We are here together through the long evening."

Clumsily Brian struck out, his long arm cuffing Ranulf across the ear. Even drugged as he was, his strength against the slighter man was prodigious. Ranulf staggered sideways, the smile slipping from his face to be replaced by a grimace of pain and anger. "Keepsh m' vow when I shee Gil . . . an' Hob," Brian insisted. "'Til then . . . keeps y'r dishtance."

"I could send for my men to tie you," Ranulf reminded him. His slender hands were doubled into fists. "I could chain you so tightly you could not move a finger."

"But thash not wha' y' want." Brian shook his head like a beleagered bull. "Y' want me willin'." He grinned a travesty of a grin. His lips felt stiff as uncured leather. He could not make them move as he willed.

Suddenly, Ranulf relaxed. "You are right." He nodded, his face assuming its pleasant lines. "Of course. Please be seated, Sir Brian. The strain of keeping yourself upright must be terrible."

"I c'n handle m'self," Brian insisted, reeling on his feet. Sweat drenched him. His blond hair was plastered to his forehead in damp dark fishhooks. A growing nausea seemed to swell in his belly. Swallowing with difficulty, he welcomed it. When the time came, he could void his stomach of the disgusting brew and be little the worse for wear. Now he concentrated on remaining moderately alert. Let Ranulf think he was helpless or virtually so.

The man would grow overconfident.

Ranulf, for his part, regarded the reeling man with satisfaction. No stranger to the effects of the drug he had employed, he recognized the first signs of paralysis. As the mighty muscles relaxed, the man would grow more and more helpless. He would be able to feel everything but would be unable to move a hand. His body would lie open to Ranulf's caresses and punishments, too. Able to feel everything, but unable to resist. The thought made Ranulf shiver with anticipation.

"Where's Hob?" Brian peered round him. The room seemed murky.

"Why we sent him with Wat to fetch the little arrow-maker," Ranulf replied silkly. "Surely you remember?"

"Hard t' see," Brian rasped. "Need t' stay 'lert."

But Ranulf was beside him. The gentle fingers trailed down Brian's cheek. "Of course, you need to stay alert." He snickered. "But 'tis a difficult act with so much ale. You should have been more cautious, my dear fellow."

The door creaked behind them. Ranulf threw a glance over his shoulder, then froze. His fist clutched the material of Brian's tunic. With a squeal of alarm he swung Brian around so that the knight's wide body formed a shield between him and the door.

Wat's bleeding figure stumbled into the room. The henchman dropped to his knees before falling face down, groaning, one leg kicking feebly. Hob stood in the doorway, his dagger drawn. "Let him go, Ranulf," he commanded. "Your man has admitted that 'twould be hard to bring the lady to our side short of the French coast."

The words "French coast" alerted Ranulf. He glanced at Wat, who lay face down, his hands bound behind him.

"What did he do to the girl?" Ranulf stepped from behind Brian, feigning surprise. "I ordered him to keep her safe," he shrilled.

"Oh? . . ." Hob's face was steely. Disbelief rang in the single syllable.

"What did you do, you savage?" Ranulf snarled at Wat's prone figure.

With a groan the man stirred, rolled over on his side, and lifted his head. "I dropped her in the hold of a barge bound for France," he whispered. "Safe enough. She might get a little hungry if they fail to discover her before they unload the cargo."

Brian pulled himself away from Ranulf and staggered past him to Hob's side. He did not turn back to face the room. "Ge' me out o' here," he whispered.

The squire put a sympathetic hand on the knight's upper arm. "Can you make the horses? They are just below."

At Brian's nod Hob patted his shoulder. "Go on. I will finish here."

Brian paused. "Didsh y' fin' out th' name of ship and ish port?"

Hob shook his head. "He said he just picked one with the cargo hatch open."

"He lies. 'Twas planned. Run a blade under 'is ribs if he doesn't speak."

Hob knelt beside Wat.

"The *Maudelayne* for Calais!" the man screamed before the dagger could touch his garments.

Hob smiled thinly. "I bid you good night, gentlemen." He backed for the door through which Brian had left. Slamming it behind him, he heard Ranulf's raging curse.

Chapter Twenty=Three

Hob raced down the stairs to catch Brian's stumbling figure halfway across the inn yard. Throwing an arm around the massive shoulders, he guided the knight toward their waiting mounts. Oblivious to the squire's assistance, Brian concentrated on lifting his foot the almost impossible distance to the stirrup. Even with his toe finally in place, he would have measured his length back into the yard had not Hob boosted him.

"What happened?" the squire gasped, heaving with all his might to lift the larger man into the saddle.

"Drugged me." Brian's stomach roiled alarmingly. His legs felt leaden; he could not feel his feet at all. Perspiration drenched his clothing and dripped into his eyes stinging and blinding them.

"Fool!" Hob snarled. "Why did you drink with Ranulf?"

Laboriously, Brian swung his leg over his horse's withers. Only instinct enabled him to sit a saddle. He could not find the stirrup on the right side and allowed his leg to dangle uselessly. "Play 'long," he mumbled. "Learn 'bout G-Gil. . . ."

Hob shook his head disgustedly. Catching up the trailing reins, he tried to thrust them into Brian's hand but found the fingers too numb to hold them. The heavy body sank forward in semiconsciousness, his cheek pressed against the horse's neck. "Hang on!" Hob shouted in Brian's ear. His fingers tangled in the long mane.

Not a moment too soon, Hob sprang to his saddle. The occupants of the inn would be roused by Ranulf soon. Hob dug spurs to his mount and galloped from the inn yard, dragging Brian's mount behind him.

The motion of the horse further stirred Brian's nausea. Grimly, he set his teeth to endure, clenching his hands into weak fists in his effort to hang on and not to hinder their escape. Suddenly, Hob swerved the horses aside into the inky darkness of a grove of trees.

The twist of his mount's body slung Brian from the saddle. He landed with a bone-shattering thud in the middle of the road. The fall left him completely paralyzed for a moment, limp as a sack of meal, too weak even to curse.

Fortunately for the downed man, Hob halted the horses in the depth of the copse. With an exclamation of alarm, the squire sprang down and dashed on foot back to the road. The sound of retching guided him. "Brian," he called softly. Wide sweeps of his hands soon located the huddled figure in the roadbed. Encountering the hip first, the squire ran his hand up the shuddering frame to the shoulder and finally to the forehead.

Brian gratefully accepted the strong hand that brushed his soaked hair back as it supported him in his weakness. "Sorry," he muttered.

"We must get into the trees," Hob insisted. Even as he spoke, the vibrations of approaching hooves shook the road. Dragging himself up to his hands and knees, Brian made his way, with Hob's help, to the side and into a ditch. The violent effort brought on a recurrence of the heaving that had rendered him helpless on the road.

Hob patted the Frenchman's shoulder sympathetically. "I am going back to the horses. If their pursuit stops along here, I will make a noise to try to lead them away." With that he was gone.

"Good man," Brian murmured between clenched teeth. Too weak even to express his thanks, he concentrated on getting his body under control. His terrible sweats had suddenly given place to chills. The night air had changed from ministering spirit to tormentor as it blew against the knight's soaked head and plastered his clothing to his shivering body. Dear God! What had he drunk? Dizzily, he shook his head, then moaned as that motion only increased its swimming sensation and brought on another bout of vomiting.

Like all strong men Brian had been secure in his strength. The idea of a few sips of liquid rendering him helpless had been absurd. Now the treachery of his own body, his inability to control its most basic functions, tormented his spirit. When Gillian needed him, when Hob had to take the responsibility for them both, when Ranulf threatened them all, he could only lie in a muddy ditch and shiver.

Distant thunder rumbled. The horses slowed to a brisk

311

trot but continued on without pause past the place where he lay. Drops of rain splattered his bowed neck with painful icy force.

Hob called softly from the darkness, "Sir Brian?"

"Here."

"Can you stand? We must be away."

"I can try." Brian braced himself upward on arms that trembled alarmingly. "Damn! Weak as a baby."

"Hurry."

Laboriously, Brian straightened to his knees. The squire led the horse forward until Brian could grasp the stirrup and pull himself up hand over hand.

The rain was coming down in earnest now. Great pelting sheets of it washed the sweat away. As he pulled himself erect, Brian tilted his head back, welcoming the coolness into his mouth.

"For God's sake," the squire whispered trying to steady the swaying man.

"Mouth tastes like a mucky stable." Brian shook the rain from his eyes and climbed into the saddle.

"Let us away," Hob urged.

"For the harbor," Brian insisted.

"No!" Hob shook his head disgustedly. "Think, man. Back to Harry's. We need dry clothes, as well as our other garments and belongings. The voyage to Calais is not a short one."

"Er . . . right," Brian muttered in a chastened voice. "I just . . ." He paused, swallowing hard. "I just . . ."

"I know. Your lady may be in desperate peril, but we cannot help her this night." Hob thrust the reins into the larger man's hands and led the way back through the building storm.

Brian for his own part hunched miserably in his

312

saddle. As feeling gradually returned to his extremities and his stomach settled into a more normal mode, he faced the more painful thorns of a guilty conscience. He had caused all of this turmoil by his own actions. If he had not been so sure that Ranulf was a gentleman by virtue of knighthood, the three of them would not have been pursued. If he had not been so determined to continue his senseless quarrel with Hob and if he had not gotten stupidly drunk, Gillian would never have set out alone and unprotected to Greenwich.

Gillian! Hob had called her his lady. Brian could not gainsay him. Yet how different she was from the ladies of the romances. His mind wandered over her slender body, her straightforward gaze, her strong hands that caressed him to such delirious heights of passion. She was no shy and modest maid, nor one to weep and pray for him when he was in danger. Not she! She had caught up her bow and arrows and come to his rescue. He could still see her standing straight and tall, her eye trained down the shaft of the arrow.

The thought of her peril wrung his heart. Almost he moaned aloud at the thought of her in Ranulf's cruel hands. What had that perverse beast done to her? Especially when he'd discovered her true sex. Creatures of that kind had no use for females. Yet this one might appeal to him. Her slender form dressed in boy's garments might have excited him to . . . Brian cursed softly. He could not think of such depredations. They would drive him mad.

A streak of lightning lanced the sky, grounding somewhere close by, and was accompanied in the next instant by an ear-splitting clap of thunder. What if she were dead? Brian writhed in the saddle. He could not imagine a future world if he had to live knowing that Gillian were not inhabiting it somewhere.

Limned in the flames of whatever the lightning had struck, Hob jumped from the saddle. "We must lead the horses," he shouted. "Keep their heads down as much as possible. Thank God, you are not wearing your armor."

Brian nodded wearily as he swung down. That armor was becoming more trouble than it was worth, he decided as he plodded head down behind the dripping rump of Hob's horse.

"You have no obligation to follow me to France." Brian tied the last of his armor to the back of the destrier before turning to say farewell to his host.

Hob ignored the comment as he, too, fastened the belongings he'd rolled inside his kit. "'Tis long since I have been in France," he announced as if they discussed travel arrangements of no importance. "No problem with the language. France is nice this time of year."

"You owe me no obligation," Brian insisted.

"I understand that . . . but you need a squire, and I need a knight. I may not be your first choice, but at least I know the lady we are seeking. Two may look in twice as many places."

A warm feeling spread about Brian's heart. He turned to offer his hand, a smile on his face. "So long as you understand that I still have little use for Englishmen. Although you are the exception. Are you sure you are not French?"

"With a name like Rothingham . . ."

Brian chuckled. "Mount up, Howard of Rothingham." With a wave to Harry Bailey, the two galloped out of the Tabard.

Muddy and bedraggled, Gillian Fletcher nevertheless grinned in satisfaction as she strode along on dry land. The feel of firm rocky ground under her feet restored her drooping spirits. She had escaped death twice now. When the icy waters of the North Sea had closed over her head, she had been almost paralyzed with terror. But when her feet had touched the sandy bottom, she knew she was going to live. Clearly, she was not born to be drowned. Where she was bound, she did not know, but so long as she moved inland away from the sea, she felt she was moving in the right direction.

At the top of a rise, several hills' distance from the sea, she paused to study her surroundings. Only the gray line of water now appeared in the west. Even the *Maudelayne* and its bloody crew had disappeared. To the north and east lay forested acres, their trees concealing any signs of habitation. Away to the south, the path she had followed became a road. Go where the people are, she advised herself. Find some good merchants and earn your passage home.

Her stomach rumbled softly. She was hungry, but her hunger was not an emergency. She could go for the rest of the day without food. The welcome sun began to burn away the clouds, drying out her clothing, leaving it stained and stiff with salt but otherwise comfortable.

Grimacing, she raised both hands and ran her fingers through her tangled hair. She could just imagine what she looked like. Before her eyes she saw her damaged wrists. Best keep her sleeves pulled down. Catching sight of those bruised and scored members, someone might

315

think her an escaped felon. She had been lucky beyond belief to cheat the fate Ranulf had ordained for her.

The thought of her deliverance thrilled her. Luck had been with her. She spared a minute of sympathy for the youth lost overboard in the storm. His death, whoever he might have been, had saved her life. She must remember to light a candle for him and pay for a mass for his soul. As for Ranulf, she condemned him to everlasting fire with her next thought. At the memory of his anger when he'd discovered her sex, she shook her head in wonderment. The world was certainly full of strange people outside the walls of York Minster.

Pulling her shirt sleeves down over the backs of her hands, she started down the road. Before long her natural buoyant spirit brought forth a tuneless whistle. Instinctively she felt she was heading for home.

She walked and rested alternately for the greater part of the day. The sun was well down in the sky before she beheld the tip of a church spire over the distant hill. The sight quickened her step.

On the outskirts of the town, she came to a large, well-appointed manor house. Did she dare try to find shelter and work there? What language these people spoke, she could not guess. French was a good possibility, although it could be Dutch or Danish for all she knew. She shrugged philosophically. She had a working knowledge of only one language, her own native English. All others including church Latin were incomprehensible to her.

Running her fingers through her hair again and straightening her sea-stained smock, she passed through the gate into a small inner courtyard. A large brindle hound sprang silently, teeth bared, from the shadows beside the door.

The speed and unexpectedness of the attack tore a shriek from Gillian. Terrified she flung herself at the low branch of a tree that overshadowed the flagstones of the court. Swinging herself up, barely ahead of its snapping jaws, she clung in panic.

"Ee-ee-easy." She hoisted herself farther above its slavering fangs. The silent attack had given way now to hoarse staccato howls, loud enough, Gillian was sure, to waken the dead in the small private burial ground she had observed outside the gate on the other side of the road. Probably some of those in their graves were this monster's personal victims.

The shaggy creature growled fiercely and stretched his length into the air, forepaws on the rough bark, jaws agape to tear and rend should his treed victim seek to come down.

The door to the manor opened. A servant, identifiable by his livery, stood regarding the situation with quiet disinterest. At last he snapped a command to the dog. Instantly, the animal turned without a backward glance and trotted to the man's side. There it crouched, shaggy tail twitching slightly, regarding her balefully.

"Please, sir," she cried, holding out one hand in supplication. "Please, I beg you. I meant no harm. Please call off your hound."

The servant, a man of indeterminate age, thin as a rake, his eyes dark and unreadable in his sallow face, shook his head. His voice low and rasping, he spoke to her in a language she could not understand.

Her spirits sank.

Another voice, softer, more melodious, came from the interior of the house. Hopefully, Gillian looked beyond the servant who turned back obsequiously. The

317

hound rose to his feet, its hackles settling, its tail wagging eagerly.

An elegant lady stood framed in the door, the point of her metal caul extended upward almost touching the top of the entrance. A drapery of purest sendal wrapped her chin and wove its way through gold mesh until it burst from the top of the headdress and flowed down her back like water. Her gown was blue velvet with a sideless surcoat of brocaded silk accenting her splendid figure.

One tiny black wing of an eyebrow rose quizzically as she stared at the scene before her. *"Jehan, qu'aves-vous ici?"*

Shrugging, the servant replied in the same language. "Please," Gillian called. "Please, milady. I swear I mean no harm. I am a stranger."

Her face paling slightly, the lady glanced at the servant. *"C'est bien, Jehan. Descendez, mon fils."* Jehan's mouth opened as if he wished to protest before it closed with a snap. He bent and grasped the heavy studded collar of the hound. The lady motioned hospitably, a timid smile playing about her mouth.

Trembling from reaction and strain, Gillian dropped weakly to the ground. "Oh, thank you, madame." Struggling to rearrange her clothes, she bowed from the waist.

Acknowledging the bow with an imperious nod, the lady gave what could only be orders to the servant. The man raised his hands in protest, releasing the hound as he did so. The animal growled softly at Gillian, who retreated a couple of steps.

Throwing Gillian an apologetic glance, the woman snapped her fingers sending the beast back to the shadows from whence he had risen. Again she spoke to the servant, who withdrew obsequiously. With another gesture, she instructed Gillian to follow where she led. Then she turned and entered the house, her long drapery of sendal trailing behind her like a soft breath of mist.

Seated at a scarred table in a kitchen at the back of the house, Gillian could scarcely believe her good fortune. With a pleasant smile an old man, his white beard hanging down almost to his ample girth, set a loaf of hard brown bread in front of her. While she watched, he expertly cut off the top and scooped out the center to make a generous trencher. From a pot at the back of the fire, he ladled a delicious smelling *pot-au-feu* into the cavity. Smiling her thanks as well as voicing them in English, she dipped her crust.

At the first bite, she closed her eyes in pleasure, chewing slowly to savor the rich flavors. When she opened them, the cook uncorked a bottle of dark red wine and set it on the table in front of her. Her eyes widened. What generosity! What a wonderful country!

She could appreciate Brian's boasts about his homeland. Her brown eyes glinted with tears. So long as she was in peril among strangers, she could be strong. However, kindness broke through her reserve. Another minute and she would be bawling. To break down would surely reveal her sex. She did not need that problem added to the rest. Clenching her fist in her lap, she smiled a bright smile and murmured her thanks.

The strong wine made her cough at the first draught, but after a few more bites of food the next swallow seemed not so unpalatable. When she had finished, a maid servant, her slumberous eyes appraising the strange male, came to lead Gillian to a tiny room off the stable.

Scarcely had she slumped down on the cot beneath the tiny window than she fell into a deep sleep.

The room was full dark. Only the sounds of the night creatures disturbed the silence. The door opened; its leather hinges made no sound other than the faintest creaking. A crouching figure was outlined briefly against the paler gray of the night sky before it slipped into the room, shutting the door as silently as might be.

Senses long overwrought warned Gillian that someone was in the room with her. The complacent girl of a few weeks ago was gone forever. Danger, as well as the strain of the journey, had honed her nerves to a fine edge. Although the interloper made almost no sound, Gillian's eyes swept open, staring into the darkness, icy shudders of terror trailing along her spine.

Flee! her senses commanded her. Coiling her legs under her, she crouched waiting for the next sound, so that she could move away from it.

"Boy!"

The word was but an explosion of breath. For an instant, Gillian could not believe her ears. Someone was calling to her in English.

"Boy, where are you? I cannot find you in the dark. Oh, please, wake." The voice dissolved into a whimper. The rustle of heavy silk material marked the prowler's movements across the room.

Gillian relaxed slightly. No one would enter to do her harm and then announce his presence. She opened her mouth to speak.

Again the soft whisper. "Boy! Oh, please answer. Oh, please do not be gone." The voice was closer still. Against her face Gillian could feel the movement of air as if someone had swept a hand in an arc trying to find the cot. "Oh! . . ."

The last syllable became a terrified squeak as Gillian

320

made a grab in the dark and her hand closed over a velvet-clad arm. "Who are you? What do you want? If you seek to rob me, I have nothing except the clothes on my back."

A purely feminine sob burst from the captive who twisted ineffectually in Gillian's strong grip. "Oh, please. I do not seek to rob. I will not harm you. Please . . ."

"What do you want then?" Conscious of her man's role, Gillian dropped her voice to a low growl. "Speak, wench!"

"Oh, please . . . you are hurting me."

Smiling to herself in the darkness, Gillian loosened her grip. She doubted seriously that the lady was in much pain. Probably fear had played its part on her over-burdened senses. "Speak! Why are you sneaking around in the dark disturbing a man's sleep?"

With a soft thump the form sank to its knees beside the cot. The hand already in Gillian's grasp was joined by another. Together the two were clasped as if in prayer. "Please . . ." The voice was under control now, low and melodious. "Please, kind sir. Please help a fellow countryman."

"How can I aid you?" Gillian started in surprise, her hand falling away from the fragile wrist.

"Take me back to England with you."

Chapter Twenty=Four

Certainly if Gillian had been asked to guess the purpose of her nocturnal visitor, she could never have provided the right answer. For a full minute the two sat frozen in time: one, shocked and amazed by the total improbability of the request; the other, trembling slightly, hardly daring to breathe as her whole future hung on the answer she would receive.

At last Gillian cleared her throat noisily. "Who are you—"

The hands groped in the dark to close over Gillian's knee. "Oh, please, my name is Alys. I must return to England. When I recognized the language, I thought that my prayers had been answered. Oh, please, take me back with you."

Gillian's head whirled. How could she answer this fervent plea? The soft hands clasping her knee trembled; the fingers twisted nervously.

"Oh, please," Alys whispered again. "You are my only hope. If you do not help me, I have no hope left. I had given up. Then you appeared out of nowhere, speaking English. I had almost forgotten the sound of the tongue."

Sensing the desperation in this soft voice, Gillian patted the clutching fingers. "Why do you need a stranger to take you to England, lady?"

The question brought silence although the soft fingers closed round the hand that patted them.

Gillian made her voice stern. "What crime have you committed that you seek to escape?"

The hand withdrew. "I can help you," the lady promised anxiously. "You do not speak the language. I could do all the talking for us. I could dress as an old man and be your father. I could make arrangements for our passages, even pay for them. I have some jewels that truly belong to me." Her dress rustled softly as if she stirred restlessly. "I would go alone except that I . . . I am afraid. I know nothing of inns or ships . . . or—"

"You have no idea what you are undertaking," Gillian interrupted. "You are a lady, to the manor born. The way is hard. I am bound for Calais—"

Alys interrupted in her turn. "Calais! But that is perfect. The *ville* beyond the manor is Montchambeau. It lies less than twenty leagues from Calais, or so I have heard. The journey takes only a matter of a couple or three days."

Gillian snorted. "Not walking." Her voice betrayed her disgust. "Or do you have some horses 'that truly belong to you'?"

"Well, no . . . But I am strong. Truly I am. I was not gentle born. That is why I must escape." Her voice trembled again. "I must escape," she repeated.

Gillian hesitated. Her better judgment admonished her to wait until the bright light of day to look at this problem. They should talk in the light when she could see the face of this person and judge the truth of her words by her expression.

Furthermore, she herself needed time to think, to weigh both sides of this singular request. In the morning the offer of a translator and gold to finance her speedy return to England might not appear so fair.

"I must think on this, Lady Alys."

Her words drew a soft cry of protest from the kneeling figure. "Oh, please, do not refuse me. I will do anything . . . anything that you ask of me. I can bear anything but the fate my stepson has set for me."

The faintest of gray was stealing into the room through the tiny window. The lady's face was a white shape in the gloom. Gillian covered the quivering lips with her fingers. "Say no more, Lady Alys." She spoke sternly to forestall more tears. I have not said I will *not* accept your good offer. You are right in thinking that I do not speak French. Your aid would be invaluable. I am shipwrecked from an English vessel and need to return to my native land as swiftly as I—"

"Oh, then . . ."

Gillian pressed her fingers firmly against the soft lips. "I want to return in good health, milady. Your . . . er . . . stepson may have good reason for what he does. Remember a woman must obey her liege lord. If your stepson is your liege, then I could be killed for helping you."

Alys subsided. Placing her hands on the edge of the cot, she climbed to her feet. Visibly she straightened as if reclaiming the reserve she had abandoned in her impas-

325

sioned plea. "May then I summon you to a discussion in the arbor after breakfast?" she inquired distantly, her voice calm as a saint's.

"At that time we can talk more practically," Gillian agreed.

"I bid you *bonne nuit*." Alys walked to the door.

"Lady Alys," Gillian called softly. The woman paused but did not turn back. "Are you English?"

"Indeed," came the low response. "Born at Southhampton." And so saying, she passed out through the door and closed it quietly behind her.

In the arbor, the big brindle hound at her knee, Lady Alys of Bellepaix stared with frightened intensity around her. "We must be quick. They watch me closely now. What do you want to know about me? I will tell all that you wish to know. Anything to convince you of my dire need. If Jules finds out, he can do no more than beat me to death." The flatness of her voice robbed the words of their melodrama. Lady Alys obviously had herself well in hand.

Gillian regarded her narrowly. "What does your stepson plan for you that you find flight with a perfect stranger preferable? Surely, there are servants here who are your friends. Would you not be safer traveling with one of them to Calais?"

The lady smoothed an imaginary crease in the lustrous material of her skirt. "I am, as I have said, an Englishwoman. My father was a merchant whose wealth rescued my husband's manor. 'Tis an old story. The very oldest where women are concerned, I suppose. My place in this house was always as an inferior. Never were my husband's servants my friends. Now they are my guards. My stepson will do as he wills. He is their lord now. They would obey him even if they sympathized with me. Which they do not," she added unhappily.

Gillian was silent. Lady Alys was pale as death. Her eyes, a soft sky blue, were the only color in her face. Still she had not told this terrible fate that she feared so.

Swallowing, the lady raised her eyes heavenward. Her hands twisted the scrap of linen in her lap. "Jules will send me to the Poor Clare nunnery near Amiens. I cannot join the sisterhood. Indeed, I would not want to. But he will not pay for me to enter except as an indentured servant. I cannot leave. The sisters are under a vow of silence. Some choose death in life. To be buried alive in sight of the altar. I cannot . . . I cannot . . ." Her breath came short in her throat. Her heart beat against the confines of her dress so that Gillian actually saw it beating.

Alys's words spoken in such quiet desperation created a cold feeling in the pit of Gillian's stomach. Reared in a world of middle-class men, she knew little of nunneries and monasteries. The control of the Roman Catholic Church in York Minster was strong; all paid their tithe unquestioningly. Yet no one in Gillian's acquaintance had actually chosen the church as a vocation. A few older women sometimes retired behind its walls voluntarily when their husbands died. Gillian's own free life; with choices open to her as if she were a man, made her shudder at the thought of Alys's virtual imprisonment. Nevertheless, she tried to voice an objection. "I suppose you have told your stepson you do not wish to go."

"Of course," Alys sighed hopelessly. "I even volunteered to give up all my dowry if he would only let me return to England. He refused. He hates me. He feels I influenced his father against him."

"Did you?" Gillian's eyes locked with the older woman's. The crucial question had to be asked and answered truthfully.

Without blinking Alys answered. "Yes. I was young and foolish. I hoped to have sons of my own. I did not know . . . could not have known . . . that Floris was barely able to perform as a husband more than half a dozen times. In the end Jules remained his only heir. He is right to hate me; but, oh, I cannot bear the thoughts of what he plans."

Her confession complete, Alys bowed her head. Gillian drew in a deep breath. What had she stumbled into? She found Alys's story impossible not to believe, especially in the light of the confession of her wrongdoing. For what acts the unfortunate Jules now sought revenge, Gillian could not guess. The rest of the sordid story was unimportant. Could she leave a fellow countrywoman to virtual slavery? Her own life as an independent freeworker had taught her to love freedom.

Still she tried once more. "How can you be sure that your nephew will accept you in England? Perhaps you go from a life of quiet toil in a nunnery to something much worse."

Alys raised her head. "Rather the devil I know than the devil unknown?" She shook her head. "I do not dread the unknown, *mon fils*. I came to France as a young girl. I lived for many years with an old cruel man. He was not hard to influence. He hated his son. If Jules would only admit it, he was better served to live apart from his father. But the Bellepaix men were ever crazed. Once an idea gets into their heads, it remains."

When Gillian still hesitated, Alys struggled to her feet, her voice breaking at last. "I will show you!" she exclaimed, her blue eyes flashing hysterically. Stooping, she pulled up the full skirt of her velvet gown. Above the silk stockings and prettily tied garters encasing her lower limbs, her thighs gleamed white. "See," she whispered. "See what Floris did to me one night shortly after we were married."

Marring the smooth skin was a puckered scar. Faded with the years, it nevertheless was the result of a deep burn. Holding the skirt with one hand, Alys caught up Gillian's wrist. "Feel." She guided the reluctant fingers over the spot. "He branded me with the brand he used for his serfs."

Sick with horror, Gillian had little strength to resist. Alys's hand steadily dragged the stronger girl's fingers over the white indentation almost two inches in diameter. "'Tis very deep," Alys continued. "He held the iron against me a long time while I screamed and twisted. No one can tell what the mark was meant to be."

With an indistinct exclamation of horror, Gillian wrenched her hand away. "Good Lord, milady! How could you endure such as that?"

"A woman endures what she must." Alys dropped her skirt philosophically. "I was younger then. But now I will not suffer at the hands of the son of that sadist. I long so desperately to be free of this house. Oh, please . . ." She clasped her hands. "Please, take me with you."

Gillian closed hers over them. "The way will be hazardous . . . but I will take you."

They were an odd pair, Gillian thought. A tiny lady

dressed in the purloined garments of an elderly man-servant, her fair golden hair docked short and whitened with flour and face powder, and herself, a woman dressed in the salt-stained garments of an unknown sailor. Heavy rucksacks on their backs, they nevertheless strode out briskly along the coast road toward Dunkerque.

How long Lady Alys could continue at the pace was questionable, but Gillian intended to push both herself and her charge as fast as possible. Alys had been unsure as to the time Jules would arrive. Anxiously, she had pressed for a departure as swift as possible. The genuine fear in her convinced Gillian as nothing else could have done of the necessity for haste.

Alys did not know that she traveled in the company of another female. The habits of concealment born of so many years made Gillian wary. To her knowledge, no one outside her immediate family except Brian de Trenanay and his nemesis Ranulf knew what she was. The fewer people who knew, the better. Alys would doubtless have more faith in her if she believed her escort to be a youth.

The road was crowded with all sorts of vehicles, mostly heavily laden. At last Gillian spotted an empty one. Grabbing Alys's arm, she pointed. "Ask him politely if he minds us riding with him as far as he is going."

Alys stared at the burly man nodding over the reins. "But . . ."—she sniffed expressively—". . . he is a fish-monger from somewhere along the coast. He has used his cart to carry fish to market."

"Right. He should be going in the same direction we want to go for a time."

"Why not ask someone else?" Alys looked around hopefully.

"Because no one else has an empty cart." Gillian gave

her a slight shove. "Go on."

While Alys hesitantly approached and bowed low at the cartwheel, Gillian struck a pose at the side of the road. The fishmonger answered readily enough, pointed to the road ahead, then slapped the reins on the horse's back and drove on.

Alys turned back, shrugging her shoulders expressively but not quite meeting Gillian's eyes.

"What did he say?"

"He said we are about fifteen leagues from Calais." Alys picked up her bundle. "We had best walk steadily if we want to get over halfway tonight."

Gillian caught her arm as she bent over. "Why did he not offer us a ride?"

Alys drew a deep breath. "Because I did not ask him for one." At her admission, she flinched away fully expecting a blow. When none was forthcoming, she stared at Gillian. "Why do you not beat me?"

"I am waiting for your reason. Then if it is not a good one, I will beat you."

Alys sighed. "It is not a good one. I hate the smell and sight and taste of fish." She stood with head bowed waiting for Gillian's blow to descend.

Gillian shrugged angrily. "Fifteen leagues is a long walk because you happen to dislike something."

"It makes me violently ill if I have to eat it."

"You are a spoiled fool."

Alys murmured something too low to catch in reply. "I shall walk faster," she promised.

"And carry me on your back," Gillian grumbled.

But Alys was already heading down the road, almost at a trot.

They settled down for the night in a haystack. The surf

sang somewhere to the northwest. The prevailing wind was cool and smelled of salt. Alys happily spread a blanket down for them, then held out her arms.

Gillian stared at her in astonishment. "What? . . ."

Alys smiled shyly. "I fully mean to pay my way," she said softly. "I am old enough to be your mother, 'tis true, but I am experienced in many ways to please men."

Gillian stepped back a couple of paces, shaking her head. "'Tis not necessary," she protested. "Believe me, I will never ask such a sacrifice of any woman." A secret smile played around her lips.

Alys's arms dropped; her mouth quivered. "Is it that I am so much older than you? I know I am past my youth, but I will do anything you ask of me. Floris needed much 'coaxing.' Sometimes he would punish me because he could not." She swallowed hard, her blue eyes luminous with tears of remembered pain. "At length he found that only by causing me pain could he become excited enough to perform the man's part."

Gillian sat down across from her on the blanket. "Believe me, Lady Alys, what you offer is generous, but unnecessary. I will take you to Calais and get you on a boat and thence to England, if luck holds. I will not desert you. You may believe me. I will do all that I say without a reward."

Alys regarded the fletcher steadily. With the tip of her tongue, she moistened her lips. Her hands twisted in her lap. At last she spoke. "I believe you. You are a brave and honest youth. Would you like to make love to me because I can give you pleasure then? Not as payment, but as if I were your lover?" She blushed painfully. "I would like that very much. I have never been loved by anyone but Floris," she admitted.

In that moment Gillian pitied her. Her own experience with Brian had taught her the joy of physical pleasure. The idea of the act of love with anyone but her knight was distasteful in the extreme. Especially distasteful was the picture Alys created of her husband beating and burning her in order to arouse himself. What a horrible experience Alys must have endured!

Should she tell this woman her secret? Her mouth opened to reveal herself, then closed abruptly. She did not entirely trust Alys to do what she was ordered to do. She might betray Gillian if a better opportunity came along.

But how to refuse without betraying herself? Unbidden came the memory of Ranulf and his strange love for men. Carefully Gillian raised her hand to her temple and smoothed her hair back as she had seen him do. "I really cannot help you more, milady." She made her voice light and bored in imitation of Ranulf.

Instantly, Alys's face changed. Her lip curled slightly. "I see," she said. "Forgive me. I did not realize your feelings. You seemed so . . . Forgive me. I am grateful for your escort. I shall not embarrass you with unwanted offers again."

Briskly, she pulled a blanket from Gillian's rucksack and wrapped it around herself. "I must get some sleep," she said huskily as she stretched out with her back to Gillian. "I shall need all my strength to walk to Calais in the morning."

Sadly, Gillian regarded her stiff form. Had she destroyed the camaraderie of the day with her pretense? But how much more would Alys's confidence have been destroyed had she learned she was traveling with another woman!

Gillian, too, rolled herself into her blanket and stretched out in the sweet-scented hay. By the end of the day tomorrow, should all go well, they would arrive in Calais. There her work would begin. She would be responsible for finding them a ship sailing for home. If none were in port, she would have to find rooms at an inn. They had no money, only a few jewels which someone might think they had stolen. Pray God there was a ship leaving immediately.

At the same time she longed to be away, Gillian shuddered at the thought of having to set forth again in a rolling, pitching boat. Once back home in England, she would think twice before taking a ferry across a river.

A farmer with a load of turnips gave them a ride a league from Calais. "You are not sickened by the sight of turnips, are you?" Gillian asked with mock politeness, when Alys started to climb onto the cart's tail.

But Alys groaned with the effort of dragging her weary body up. "I would ride down the road now even if I were heaving over the side of the wagon," she vowed, slumping back against the load. "I swear the soles of my feet are one solid blister."

"Very likely," Gillian agreed. "Mine are no better. I never walked so far in all my life."

Alys lay silent for several minutes as the cart creaked along behind the plodding draft horse. "As a sailor I suppose you have never had to," she said at last. "Is your profession, away from land and women, why you do not care for us?"

"I am not a sailor," Gillian said before she thought.

"No?"

"I was shipwrecked, true enough. But I am a fletcher by trade."

Alys digested this bit of information. "My father was a merchant. 'Tis terrible to be neither wellborn nor lowborn. You are neither up nor down, neither high nor low."

Gillian shook her head. "I did not find it so. I am a member of the Guild of Fletchers and Bowyers. Only the finest craftsmen are allowed in this guild. We are very proud of our profession."

Alys shook her head doubtfully. "Perhaps it is different for a man," she sighed. "For a woman . . . Perhaps if I had been able to do as you have done, I would feel differently about myself. Perhaps the problem is with being born female."

"Perhaps so." Gillian was forced to agree.

Alys yawned widely in the warm sunshine. Her eyelids drooped, then closed. "No wonder you prefer men," she whispered. "Who in his right mind would prefer a woman?"

Chapter Twenty-Five

The Calais docks were a confusion of cacophonous sounds, exotic smells, and bizarre sights—not all of them pleasant. Small and large ships from all over the world docked at this English port on the seacoast of France. All the languages of every seafaring country in the world flowed around their heads, but the common language was French. Alys hung on Gillian's sleeve as much as she dared, cowering back because the many exchanges in guttural peculiar accents frightened her.

"Whatever shall we do?" she whispered. "I have never seen so many people." She staggered backward as a duffel bag, swung from the shoulder of a passing sailor, brushed against her.

"Ask about a ship bound for England."

"Ask who?" Alys was close to tears. Blotches reddened on her cheeks due to her effort to restrain herself.

Gillian pulled her into a niche created by barrels and bales piled in front of a warehouse. "Brace up!" she commanded gripping Alys's shoulders and glaring hard into her pale blue eyes. "You must do the talking, unless we find an English ship. Then I will do it."

Alys shook her head despairingly. "I—"

"Think of Jules. Think of the nunnery."

"Perhaps I was wrong. . . ."

Gillian snorted her disgust. "A fine time to think that. Listen, Alys, if you burst into tears like a woman, I will slap you. You are dressed like a man. Act like one."

Alys sniffed, shaking her head slightly.

"You can do it. Remember to keep your voice trembly like your old husband's." She caught Alys's chin and lifted it. "Of course . . . Be your old husband. How would Floris behave? Think of yourself as Floris."

Alys stared into the intense face stooping to her level. "Like Floris?" she whispered. "Like Floris." She blinked, then drew a deep breath. She looked past Gillian's shoulder. "Shall we try that ship first?" Her voice had dropped at least four notes. With a peculiar limping gait she swaggered across the dock to the gangplank of a small barge.

With a smile of relief Gillian followed her. The persistence that Alys had displayed in getting Gillian to take her this far would go a long way. Once Alys set her mind, she was as determined as the Bellepaix men who would not change.

Some vessels had just docked; others loaded cargo preparing for departure. "Ask at those first," Gillian advised as Alys came down the third gangplank shaking her head.

They walked along noting ships taking on cargo, and inquiring at those first. The morning passed swiftly.

Those vessels bound for England seemed, one and all, to have full crews. One mate offered to take Gillian, but refused to take Alys, who, to Gillian's disgust, had overplayed her part as an old man.

Tired and hungry, they sat on a couple of barrels staring at the gray water and the ships floating at anchor in the harbor. "Somewhere out there is the ship for us," Gillian insisted.

Alys's stomach rumbled. "If we find it before we starve to death."

"We will. We have not really tried very long. You are doing so well," she added truthfully to the older woman.

The compliment braced Alys. "Forward," she murmured with a dry smile.

At the end of a long dock a short man directed the unloading of a pair of horses. Gillian stared at his back. Somehow he looked vaguely familiar. As the sling lowered the big destrier to the boards, the animal lost its footing and went down on its knees.

A string of oaths leaped from the man's mouth as he sprang to the horse's head. Although the language was French, the voice, too, seemed familiar.

"Try here," Gillian suggested.

"But they are unloading," Alys protested.

"Yes, I know. . . ." Gillian stopped in mid sentence.

A tall man with massive shoulders strode down the gangplank. His cloak blew around him; his sandy hair tossed in the wind. Even at a distance his features were marked by deep grooves around the mouth and between the eyebrows.

"Brian," she whispered. "Brian. I am dreaming." Stumbling slightly, she started forward. The dock seemed endless. Expecting him to disappear at any moment or to become someone else as she came closer, she walked slowly at first almost hesitating. It could not be he. Not here in France. Not arriving on this dock on the day she needed him most. His presence was the stuff of magic and of wishes.

Flinging his cloak back, he strode toward the destrier adding his voice to the smaller man's. Together they hauled the horse to its feet.

She was halfway, her steps hurrying. She could vaguely hear Alys behind her calling her name inquiringly. At the sound of her name, the big man turned.

A look of incredulous gladness lighted his stern features. He dropped the horse's bridle and bolted toward her. "Gillian!"

She flung herself against him throwing her arms around his body, crying and laughing at the same time. "Brian! Brian! Oh, dear God, Brian. I have been so afraid. . . ."

"When I found Ranulf had taken you captive . . ." Leaving his sentence unfinished, he bent his head and kissed her full on the mouth, his tongue burrowing into her as if to assure himself of her reality. His arms clasped her so hard against him that she could not breathe. His prodigious strength was cracking her ribs, yet she did not care. His big palms roved up and down her slender body pressing her tightly against him as he reassured himself.

"Gillian." He gasped her name against her mouth. "Gillian! Oh, I feared . . . Oh . . ." He flung his head back, his eyes heavenward in an attitude of silent thanksgiving. His right hand cupped the back of her head pressing her face against his chest. She could feel his heart pounding beneath her cheek.

"Ah, Brian . . ." Her eyes brimmed with tears of joy. He was holding her; she was safe in his arms. He felt so good. Smiling she tilted her head back to be greeted by another impassioned kiss delivered accompanied by a joyous laugh.

This time the kiss lasted longer. His lips turned tender; his tongue, caressing. She could feel a new hardness to his body as her own began to tingle. A languor began to invade her, a melting softening that caused her to lean impossibly closer to him.

All around them the workers on the dock stared, their faces registering every emotion from utter shock to frank outrage.

At last the two pulled apart, breathless, their eyes smoldering with desire. From far off Hob spoke. "Thank God you are safe, *Gil*." He emphasized her name drawing them partially back to reality.

Brian stepped back grinning. "Are you really all right?" He surveyed her critically, taking in the strange clothing, salt-stained and much the worse for constant wear. "You are thinner." Unable to keep his hands off her, he ran them over her ribs, pressing meaningfully. A dockhand dropped the end of the bale he was carrying to stare in open-mouthed astonishment.

"You too," she acknowledged, taking in the harsh lines around his mouth and the sunken hollows of his cheeks.

"I was frantic, *chérie*," he admitted softly.

"Who is your companion?" Hob asked, breaking in again and drawing Brian's attention.

Suddenly conscious of the cold, speculative looks of men on the dock, Brian set her gently from him. Over her shoulder he saw a little old man dressed in the livery of a servant, a hat shading his face against the glare.

At the same time, Gillian swung away from Brian's embrace and motioned to Hob to come forward. Affectionately, she shook his hand and patted him on the shoulder. His blue eyes gleaming, he drew her in against him. "'Tis good to see you safe, mistress," he rasped in her ear.

Startled, she pulled back.

"Brian told me," he grinned. "When we found the oxen tied outside Harry Bailey's, he went mad. In his ravings he revealed all about you."

She shrugged. "Ah, well, since Ranulf knows, you might as well too." Gillian felt Brian's arm around her waist. Looking up at him, her joy in her eyes, she slid her hand into his and leaned her head against his shoulder. "I have missed you both." She drew a deep breath.

"'Tis obvious you missed Sir Brian more than I," Hob teased.

"Certainly," Brian grinned. His fingers squeezed her waist.

"M-Master Gil," Alys stammered shyly.

The three broke apart self-consciously, like children whose secret club must be protected against intruders at all costs.

Brian eyed the little old man suspiciously; but almost at first glance, Hob's face broke into a grin. "Who might this be?" His voice was light and warm.

Gillian smiled gently at Alys. "Brian. Hob." She motioned to her traveling companion to come forward. "This is Alys."

Hob's grin broadened. He thrust forth his hand in manly style. "My pleasure, *m'sieur*."

Alys smiled warily as she placed her small hand in his.

"These are friends of yours, Gil?" she questioned anxiously.

"Oh, yes," Gillian replied, looking fondly from knight to squire. "The best of friends."

An awkward silence followed as Alys stared aghast at the person she believed to be a slender youth locked in the embrace of one tall man while she held the arm of another. At last she swallowed gamely. "Well, I think that is lovely. To meet one's friends so surprisingly. How well . . . met. . . ." She trailed away. "I—"

"What has happened to you?" Brian asked.

"The story is too long to tell standing on the dockside." Gillian smiled. "Neither Alys nor I have any money. Nor have we eaten all day. I know my lady is faint from weakness."

Hob sprang forward gallantly to offer his arm to Alys. One old sailor on the dock spat disgustedly as he loosened the sling from around the destrier's belly. Hob looked uneasily around him and dropped his arm embarrassed.

Brian chuckled. "Join the group, Hob."

Alys's face turned beet red. "I am a woman," she hissed at Brian.

"But they do not know you are." He raised one cynical eyebrow. "What does that make all of us?"

"We had best find an inn some distance from here." Hob glanced around him hurriedly. Most men were stolidly ignoring the scene, but a few muttered and growled among themselves, pointing and sneering.

"I will take Gil and his companion to *La Reine d'Or*," Brian said decisively. "Follow with the horses and gear as soon as you can. I shall secure rooms for all of us."

The squire touched his hat. "I shall hurry," he smiled, his eyes on Alys, who returned his smile hesitantly.

343

"Best order a full meal to be served immediately. They both look nigh done."

Gillian smiled thankfully at Hob, while Brian growled, "I can take care of them without any advice from you. Give me credit for knowledge of the courtesies due a lady."

Motioning them both to accompany him, he led the way muttering as he went.

"Still at odds with Hob," Gil observed sadly as she strode along beside him and Alys trotted along bringing up the rear.

Brian slowed his pace. "Not at all," he denied. "He practically saved my life. Only Hob thinks I have no common sense."

Gil shot him a teasing glance from under raised eyebrows.

Brian squared his jaw stubbornly. *"La Reine d'Or* is just ahead. We can continue this conversation over supper."

Ordering with a lavish hand, Brian bade Hob open a bottle of wine. "Ah, *chérie"*—he smiled at Gillian—"at last I can treat you to some of the delicate wines of my country. The stuff that the English import is poor stuff by comparison."

He had seated her within reach of his right hand, his knee pressing against her thigh under the table. If he thought about how they must appear to Alys, he chose to disregard appearances.

The nearness of him stirred Gillian's senses almost unbearably. The sight of his dear face, his green-flecked gold eyes, his strong jaw filled her vision. The intimate warmth of his knee sent tremors of weakness into the center of her body. When he offered her the goblet of wine, she deliberately caressed his fingers where they grasped the bowl.

Hob seated himself across from Brian with Alys on his right. He grinned at the sight of the knight, once so imbued with the inherent snobbishness of the knightly kind toward the middle-class craftsmen. The man could not take his eyes off his little fletcher, while she gazed at him with her heart in her luminous eyes, her lips trembling as he spoke to her.

With a twinge of loneliness the squire turned to the lady on his right. Late thirties, he judged her to be by the tiny wrinkles around her eyes. Her hands were soft and white as befitted a lady, her figure in the men's garments shapely. He doubted very much if she had borne children, since the results were usually readily evident in sagging breasts and bulging belly.

Flushing under his scrutiny, she concentrated on her meal. "Oh, I do appreciate this," she remarked to the table in general as she reached for the wine. "I was desperately hungry. Several times when I went on board a vessel to inquire about passage, I would smell food cooking in the galley. Even fish was beginning to smell good." She smiled apologetically at Gil.

"Fish makes Alys ill," Gillian explained. "She refused to ask a carter for a ride yesterday because he had been hauling fish in his cart."

Brian's face grew grave. "How far did you have to come?"

"From Montchambeau," Alys supplied. "A distance of some twenty leagues."

"No wonder you are both tired," Hob observed sympathetically. "How long did the journey take?"

"Two and a half days," Gillian said. "We ran out of food yesterday."

"I have some jewelry, but Gil would not let me try to sell it." Alys turned to Hob. "Perhaps you would sell it for me?" she asked. "Then I could pay for my passage back to England."

"I was afraid that someone might think we had stolen it and ask too many questions. I would have risked it today, if we had not found you." Gillian shivered slightly at the comforting pressure of Brian's knee under the table.

"You must not wander away on your own again," he said sternly.

Gil turned on him indignantly. "I did not wander away. I rose early and delivered the commission to the depot. On the way back I was waylaid by Ranulf and made a prisoner. I was returning to the Tabard."

"You should not have gone without escort," Brian argued. "Both Hob and I would have risen shortly and accompanied you."

"The last words between the two of you the night before bespoke a more serious business the morning after." Gillian reminded him of his drunken challenge.

Swallowing his wine hastily, Hob leaped into the conversation. "What happened to you after Wat threw you into the hold of the boat?"

Gillian smiled grimly. "Ranulf told me that the captain of the vessel was to throw me overboard when she was in the middle of the channel." Brian cursed angrily. "So I worked myself free, determined to hide somewhere on board. A great storm blew up and drove us before it to the French coast. Evidently some poor sailor new to the ship

346

was washed overboard in it. In all the confusion and fear, I was mistaken for him. They fed me and gave me his hammock and clothes." She plucked at the filthy garments.

"They set me to watch for the coastline, but I was distracted and they ran aground. I jumped overboard and made the shore. When last I saw them, they were trying to get free from the sand bar."

Hob looked amazed. "Wat said he threw you in the hold of the *Maudelayne*. Did he really do so, or did he lie?"

Gillian shook her head. "I really do not know the name of the ship. I suppose . . . oh, yes, I remember. The cook told me her name. It was the *Maudelayne*."

Hob sat back regarding her with awe. "You escaped one of the terrors of the channel," he declared. "A tall man with a grizzled beard that bristled in every direction on his face."

"Yes."

"He is a pirate and a thief. Dangerous. Whenever he takes a ship, he throws his captives overboard. He would have done just as Ranulf commanded him."

Gillian shuddered.

Brian shook his head, his hand closed over her own. "Think no more about it," he advised. "You are safe. But do not leave my side again."

"No," she whispered.

"How long was it before you appeared in my apple tree?" Alys asked to break the awkward silence.

"Oh, about a day. I was very hungry. Your hound attacked me without warning. I barely made the lower limb with my life." Gillian grinned in mock terror.

"You were like an angel to me." Alys smiled warmly.

347

"So young and golden and speaking the first English I had heard in many a long year. I could scarcely believe my ears."

"Nor I," Gillian agreed. "I must learn some French." She turned to Brian.

"I mean that you should." His eyes regarded her warmly, stripping the coarse garments and imagining her naked while he taught her the parts of her body.

"We came to find you," Hob told her. "Ranulf had left clues to lead us on a chase all over the south side of the Thames, but we found him sooner than he expected."

"Obviously, you were successful," Gillian complimented them. "You arrived in Calais very quickly."

"He tried some nasty tricks, drugging Brian and sending me to be killed by Wat, but we were able to get out of his trap and come after you. Although," the squire added quietly, "I frankly never expected to see you again. Ranulf would never have allowed you to live."

Gillian stared into the wine in her goblet. "I cannot think why the man bears me such enmity. I did not harm him. I did not even do permanent harm to Wat's cousin when I shot him."

Brian drew a deep breath. "Ah, but you did best him," he reminded her. "Alone, you with your little feathered sticks held him and his retinue captive. You freed me and robbed him of his pleasure. Most important you embarrassed him, made him lose face with his men. And the reason he will not tolerate that is well known to you if you will only think on it a minute."

Soberly she nodded. "I only sought to rescue you."

Brian drained the last of the wine. The meal had been a long one, for the candles were nigh to guttering in the candelabra. Alys was drooping, her elbow on the table,

348

her palm supporting her cheek. "'Tis time to retire. We have two rooms at our disposal. Gil and I will take the inner room. Hob, summon the manservant to make up beds in here for you two."

"Lady Alys may not care to sleep in the same room with me," Hob reminded the knight who even now was guiding an exhausted Gillian to her feet.

"Oh, no," Alys sat up startled and straight. "Oh, I will be fine anywhere. I do not want to be a burden. Just a pallet on the floor. I have spent the night with Gil these past two days. I trust his friends equally." She looked from one to the other, her blue eyes resigned.

Hob hid a smile behind his hand. Alys obviously believed them all to prefer men to women. For himself he would enjoy disproving that belief. However, tonight when she was so exhausted was not the time. "We shall do very well in separate beds in the same room," he declared.

"Good night," Gil mumbled as Brian led her into the bedchamber. His hands were already caressing her as the door closed behind them.

Chapter Twenty-Six

As if mighty forces had thrown them together, Gillian and Brian clasped each other's bodies. His mouth came down on hers, sealing them in all ways but one as their hands clutched and their arms strained. The only sound in the still room was their labored breathing followed by the faint whimper of protest Gillian made when his strength became too much for her slender body to bear.

At the sound Brian reluctantly raised his head and loosened his grip, allowing her to draw in a shuddering breath. "Forgive me, *chérie*," he murmured. "I could not get enough of you."

"'Tis the same with me," she whispered. "I ached to hold you. I could not get you close enough."

He kissed her again, less violently, but not less emotionally. "First to get you out of these rags," he told her, lifting the bottom of the sailor's smock and tugging it off over her head. Her comments were muffled in the enveloping material. "Ah, beautiful," he grinned as he tossed the smock over his shoulder and cupped her breasts. His thumbs circled her nipples as she moaned with pleasure.

"You . . . you . . ." she protested softly.

"Yes, sweetheart," he agreed, kissing each in turn. "Me . . . me . . ."

The drawstring holding up the coarse, gathered pantaloons yielded to his questing fingers. Efficiently, he peeled the rough, salt-stiffened garments, along with the hose under them, down around her knees. There he knelt to pull her boots off.

On his knees before her, his eyes swept up her naked body, swaying slightly in the firestorm of her passion. With a fierce exclamation, he clasped his hands over her buttocks and drew her body toward his mouth.

Embarrassed, she pushed against his shoulders, but he would not be denied. Exultantly, he pressed a kiss against the nest of pale curls at the jointure of her thighs. She moaned as the intimacy of his act shook her uncontrollably. Then with her body shuddering beneath his mouth, he brushed his beard back and forth across her lower belly.

"Oh, God, Brian . . . Oh, no . . . please . . . pl-please . . ." she babbled hysterically. Tiny giggles of laughter burst from her throat as she gripped his hair and pulled back. But when he complied, allowing his head to drop away, she drew him toward her.

"A woman can never make up her mind." He chuckled. His tongue traced fantastic patterns from her navel to her groin. Weakly she collapsed, able only to fall back limply as his hands on her buttocks supported her gently to the floor.

In mock irritation he rose straddling her. "What am I going to do with you?" he growled. "No stamina. No strength. A man loves you and you just pass out on him— on the floor."

"Yes, Brian," she whispered, her eyes half closed as she took sweet revenge for his criticism. Watchful of his reaction, she allowed one hand to stray to her breast where her thumb and forefinger gently pinched her nipple.

The movement drew a sharp intake of breath from him. Swiftly, he tore off his clothing, careless of any damage he might do. As he stood aside to strip off his hose, her other hand strayed down over her belly to twine her fingers in the tangled curls.

"Witch!" he gasped feverishly as his naked manhood hardened even more at the sight of her deliberate abandon.

She laughed. A shivery throaty laugh. All woman, all temptress, she arched upward, lifting her swollen breasts to him.

With an unintelligible cry he dropped down, parting her thighs roughly. Iron-hard, he positioned himself against her glistening opening. "I cannot . . ." He drove into her without finishing his sentence.

She cried out, a high shriek of pained pleasure, and clasped him to her, with the hot velvet walls of her sheath as well as her arms and thighs and mouth. They were as one, sealed to each other.

A trembling began within her as she felt his throbbing hardness against the mouth of her womb. The vibration caressed his shaft, stimulating it. Sweat beaded his body as he groaned in virtual agony at the sweet torment.

Every atom of his manhood screamed at him to move, to thrust, to relieve himself of this awful building pressure. Yet the experience was too sweet to forsake. Grimly, he hung on, his hands flexing, his fingers bruising her spine and digging into her buttocks.

The sounds of his breathing hummed in her ears as did the drumming of her own blood. Every tremor that began in the pit of her stomach drove lightning along her nerves to every part of her body. Her tongue explored the interior of his groaning mouth, tasting him and lapping up the sweet nectar of him. Her turgid nipples aching unbearably, she sought relief instinctively by rubbing them against the blond mat on his chest.

"Gillian! Oh, God!"

He must come closer, he must come . . . Responding to desires she did not know she possessed, she drove her fingernails into the heavy muscles across his shoulder blades. The pain drove him harder into her. In his ecstasy he ground against the throbbing core of her womanhood between her thighs.

His was the final movement. An explosion of feeling burst from that point to roll in powerful waves throughout her body. So intense was its lightning that she seemed to leave the floor, clasping herself to him impossibly tighter.

"Gillian! Oh, love!"

His throbbing sword was helpless in her grip. Wave after wave of sweet motions rippled around him, gripping and releasing so powerfully that he could contain himself no longer. He, too, exploded; his body splintering into a thousand tiny shards, each one a separate atom of pleasure. In his ecstasy, he shouted his love into her gasping mouth.

For an interminable time neither of them moved. Finally, feeling a need for air in her lungs which labored under Brian's considerable weight, Gillian stirred weakly.

"Am I too heavy?" he moaned softly.

"Of course," she whispered. "How can you doubt it?"

"But you are so soft and comfortable," he protested, lifting himself on hands and knees and sliding limply aside to sprawl on the floor.

A disgusted mutter was her only reply.

Both lay side by side with hands limply clasped, staring at the brown vacancy of the ceiling. At last she stirred. "Is there a bed?" she whispered.

"Somewhere over there," he murmured.

"A long way away?"

"Um-hum. A *very* long way away."

She lay silent for a few moments. "You are the knight," she said at last. "Are you not supposed to bear me away somewhere, say to a bower, or at least a bed?"

"Only before I ravish you," he sighed. "Not after."

She sat up dizzily, pressing her face into her hands. "Missed my chance again."

"We have the whole night before us. I promise to do better next time."

She rubbed her elbow, then shifted slightly onto one hip. "I think I have a splinter."

"Probably several." He rolled over on his side, pillowing his cheek on his bent arm. Appreciatively, he studied her naked form. "Hopefully in some very interesting places. It will be my duty as a knight to render aid to you, my lady, and help to alleviate your suffering." He leered suggestively at the white curve of the buttock she displayed.

She raised her eyebrows haughtily. "I can find my own splinters."

"'Twill be more fun if you let me help you." He smiled.

She raised a hand to her forehead as if shading her eyes to look into the far distance. "I think I see the bed over there in the shadows."

He reared up on one elbow. "By God, you are right. It is a bed," he agreed.

She looked at him expectantly. "I can make it if you can."

"Done!" Lazily, he climbed to his feet, stretching unashamedly in front of her. The sight of his nude body viewed at her leisure excited her again. He was so beautiful. Like a sculptor's rendering of a perfect male body except for the pale scars that here and there laced his skin.

Lithe as a cat, she sprang; her hands clutched his thighs. As he gasped in surprise, she fastened her mouth on the tender flesh of the inside of his thigh. Her tongue licked him, tasting the salt on his skin. Inhaling deeply, she smelled the stirring masculinity of him.

"Oh, God, Gillian . . . Please . . . not . . . Aahh!"

Obeying desires older than mankind, she touched her lips to the tip of his manhood. Instantly, the muscle stiffened jumping against her mouth as a tormented groan burst from him. Her fingernails dug into his suddenly taut buttocks as she held him firmly and closed her mouth around him.

"Woman!" he cried, bowing his head as shudder after shudder of delight poured over him.

She pulled back her head. "Yes?" She smiled seductively.

With a fervent oath he clutched her shoulders and hauled her to her feet. Accustomed ever, by virtue of his size and strength, to take the lead in lovemaking, the intensity of emotion aroused by this small girl, combined with the force of his own arousal angered him. "You go too far!" he grated.

Dragged against him so her body touched his from loins to breasts, she allowed her head to loll back on her shoulders. Perhaps she should have been afraid. She had shocked him with her ardor, yet she could not fear him. Smiling lazily into the face of his irritation, she dared to tease him. "*Now* will you bear me away to the bed and ravish me?"

"Damn!"

He swept her high on his chest and bore her where she asked with swift steps. Almost flinging her onto the coverlet, he followed her down and buried his face between her breasts.

They lay for a long time. His hands clasped her waist tightly while her fingers trailed ever and ever through his hair.

At last he sighed. "I want you again," he whispered. "My body is beginning to ache as if I never had you."

She shifted slightly, arching her back and digging her heels into the soft mattress. "Do you?"

"Yes." He kissed her breast closing his lips over her nipple and tonguing it gently.

She moaned softly. Her stroking never ceased, but her fingers trembled.

"May I have you?"

"Why not let me make love to you?"

When he did not reply, she lay in breathless silence, fearful that she might have angered him again. At last he sighed deeply. "Whatever would please you." He rolled away from her onto his back.

Galvanized with excitement, she sat up. Her eyes moved down the length of his body. He lay quiescent, his arms at his sides, hands lying limply with palms turned upward. Only a tightness about his mouth betrayed the restraint he had placed on himself. That and the fact that his eyes glowed like green flames in his suddenly pale face.

Hesitantly, trembling, she slid her hands up along the flat plains of his chest. The soft blond hairs curled around her fingers. Beneath her palms his tiny male nipples hardened and rasped against her skin. Sensing she had found a sensitive spot, she swept her hands in small tight circles, finally, ending with her thumbs caressing him. When a tiny moan escaped him, her eyes flew to his face studying it as he half-closed his eyes and caught his lower lip between his teeth.

A quivering began in her belly as she recognized the same signs in him that she had felt in herself. Feeling strangely powerful, she bent to catch one of the tiny nubs of taut flesh between her teeth. Nipping lightly at first, she immediately kissed him with the next breath. Her lips and tongue laved the flesh she had punished the instant before.

Beneath her mouth Brian moaned again, this time accompanying the sound by a convulsive closing of his hands into tight fists.

Smiling, she repeated her attention to his other nipple. This time his chest arched slightly before she had finished.

Dimly surprised at her own inventiveness and daring, she rose above him and straddled him. His eyes flew open

358

as she settled herself so her soft moist nest brushed the hard bulging maleness at the joining of his thighs.

Leaning forward, her belly and breasts resting against his counterparts, she began to kiss him, running her tongue into the sensitive satin interior of his mouth, touching his teeth and tongue. At the same time her hands fondled his nipples, pinching and caressing them, treating him to tiny stabs of pain followed by infinite gentleness.

His fist clenched in the coverlet, pulling it as he sought to restrain his desire. His breath was a series of raw gasps as he bucked his hips upward to meet her. As she rode him, she twisted her body from side to side and up and down adding immeasurably to his pleasure as her own body began to glow with moisture from the heat of her exertions.

He spoke into her mouth. "Ah . . . please . . . I cannot . . ."

Sitting up straight, she raised herself and guided his throbbing stiffness into her sheath. As she slid down upon him, twisting her hips as she did so, he was unable to completely choke back a cry of unalloyed pleasure. Now her hands slid forward across his flat belly upward across his ribs to cover his chest. Her fingers found his nipples tormenting them while her palms gave her leverage to move up and down on his staff. With each stroke she grew more confident and less afraid. What she did felt so right.

For Brian, her love-making carried him into a sphere of pleasure he had never conceived. He had had his share of ladies of the court, but none had ever even . . . Beyond the earth-shattering pleasure was the helpless feeling of bewilderment. A woman should not . . . Of course, she had spent a great deal of her life as a man. . . . A knight should . . . A lady should . . . But . . . "Aaaaahhh!"

A primeval scream burst from his lips. His heels dug deeply into the mattress lifting them both off the bed, thrusting his exploding manhood higher into her than she had ever imagined possible.

Her own cry of painful ecstasy exploded as she was tossed wildly to her own climax.

Almost weightless, their bodies floated back to earth, perspiring limbs entwined. Breast to breast, they lay, her face pressed into the column of his neck. When he softened and slipped from her, she sighed in the drowsy half-world of pleasurable exhaustion.

For a time they slept thus. First one and then the other would wake to be assured of the beloved's presence. A few moist kisses delivered to the portion of skin closest to the lips, a tightening of the arms, and then sleep would close over them again.

As the first rays of dawn slid through the lead panes, Brian opened his eyes. His lips touched Gillian's forehead and she stirred slightly.

"Love?" she whispered.

"Yes." He kissed her again. His hand stroked her tangled ringlets. "We must never be separated again," he said at last.

"No," she agreed dreamily.

"Do you know why?" he continued.

"Because you love me too much?"

"That too." She felt him nod against her hair. "But mainly because we would kill each other the next time we came together after a long parting. I, for one, would not survive the encounter."

She chuckled throatily. "I thought you enjoyed it."

She laughed. "You seemed to be enjoying it at the time."

He slapped her buttocks affectionately. "Wrong," he whispered. "I almost died. The agony was unbearable. Only a knight could have endured the pain. Did you not hear my moans?"

"I did indeed," she agreed. "I shall never, never treat you so cruelly again. And this I swear." She sat upright, placing her hand ceremoniously across her naked breast and bowing her head.

"Perhaps I spoke hastily." He smiled, drinking his fill of the sight of her silken skin in the pearly light. "Actually, I would like you to do that often. The experience gives me a chance to toughen myself."

"I will toughen you," she vowed, punching him gently in the stomach. "Tell the truth, Brian de Trenanay. You loved every minute."

"I loved every minute." He chuckled, dragging her down and kissing her soundly.

They lay together silent for several minutes.

"Brian?"

"Umm?"

"Would you tell me something if I asked you?"

"If I know the answer, I will tell you."

She swallowed hard in embarrassment. "How could Ranulf . . . how could he . . . you know? . . ."

He drew a deep breath. "You mean how could he make love to another man as I have made love to you?"

"Yes . . . and why would he want to?"

"Many men have needs which they feel they must satisfy even when they are in company for long periods of time with other men. Some men do so, but they never have the taste for it. Others find they prefer other men to women."

"I can understand that."

"Furthermore, some men are so brutal or so ugly that women find them repulsive. They, too, turn to other men, who may be stronger and more able to bear their brutality."

"Alys told me her husband beat her so that he might become excited enough to use her. He branded her too." Gillian hid her face against Brian's neck. "Can you imagine anything so hideous?"

Brian's arms tightened around her. "Poor gentle lady," he agreed. "I have heard of such and more."

She pressed a kiss against the pulse beat at the base of his throat. "I could not believe, would not believe until she showed me."

"You are a gently reared girl. Innocent as a baby. 'Twas a bad day for you when Tobin became ill." He stroked her shoulder reassuringly.

She shuddered. Still the question plagued her. "But how could a man make love to another man?"

"When you took me into your mouth," Brian reminded her, "'twas more than pleasant."

"Oh . . ."

"Yes, oh."

Still hideous thoughts would not disappear. "When Ranulf held me captive," she whispered, "he threw me down on the bed on my stomach. And then he straddled me." Her voice quavered at the memory that had haunted her midnight hours.

Brian kissed her forehead. "Tell me, sweet. Did he hurt you badly?"

She shook her head bitterly. "Only the terrible pain in my wrists where he bound me, but something else happened. He cried out while he was on top of me. I am sure he . . ." She could not go on. Her embarrassment was too great.

"Were you naked?"

"No . . ." Gillian's voice was outraged. "I would have died. No one has ever seen me naked except you."

Brian took a deep breath. She wanted to know. The knowledge might help her guard herself sometime. His voice deepened. "If you had been naked, he would have hurt you badly." Her hands clutched him. "He would have used an opening other than the natural one created for our pleasure."

She was silent, the brutal physical aspects gradually dawning in her innocent mind. Suddenly, she began to shudder. "Oh, God. How hideous! How revolting!" She clutched him tightly.

"Put it from your mind," he commanded her. "You wanted to know. Now you know. But you should not dwell on it. It can have no meaning to you." He put his hands on either side of her head and raised her face from his chest. "Kiss me," he ordered. "I will make the horror go away."

Chapter Twenty=Seven

"I must be away as soon as possible," Lady Alys announced at breakfast. "I am nervous every moment I remain on French soil. Even now Jules will have set servants to find me."

"You need have no fear, milady." Brian tried to reassure her. "You are under my care. Besides, surely your stepson can have little idea where to find you."

"He knew of my deep desire to return to England." Alys's voice trembled with fear. "The servants will tell of the youth who spoke the language only I could understand. They will tell that the livery is missing. He will be on his way." She clasped her hands tightly in her lap. Her face was very pale.

"Surely you are overfearful?" Hob's voice was gentle with concern.

"I have many reasons to fear for myself," Alys

insisted, "and almost as many to fear for you. He is implacable in his hatreds. He hates me. I know he plans to drag me off to the living death of the nunnery. What is more, if he finds me with you and knows you aided me, he might kill you and say you were abducting me."

The two men looked at each other skeptically. A woman frequently exaggerated things for effect. In all likelihood her stepson would be delighted to return home and find her gone. His attitude would be good riddance since her disappearance saved him the trouble of disposing of her properly. To their way of thinking the nunnery was the only place for her.

"We shall see to the booking of your passage immediately." Brian nodded to Hob, who shrugged agreement.

The four sat at table in the outer room where Brian had bespoken their breakfast. Gillian stared at Alys in concern. In her own mind she had begun to doubt the strength of Alys's will. Perhaps a life of quiet contemplation might not be so bad. "Are you really, really sure that England is where you want to go, Alys? After all, you have not been there in many years."

"Not since I was a girl," Alys admitted, her eyes downcast.

"Are you sure there will be something to go home to?"

"I have a nephew who is a merchant as his father and my father were before him. He is the male relation closest to me in blood." She sighed pathetically. "I am his duty."

Tears of pity misted Gillian's eyes. The injustice of Alys's situation, coupled with the precariousness of it, disturbed her deeply. Being reared to be a cosseted and cared-for possession of men seemed fine until the possession was no longer desired. What of the possession when it was cast aside? A garment, a weapon, a tool had no feelings, but a woman was capable of great depths of emotion. The inherent cruelty of every man who had ever known Alys was obvious.

Hob cleared his throat. "Can he reclaim some of your dowry, milady?"

Alys stirred uncertainly. "I doubt it. Bellepaix was in a precarious position, else Floris would never have married me. I am sure the bulk went into rebuilding and refurbishing within a few months of our marriage."

Again there was silence at the table.

At last Alys drew her slender purse from inside the servant's shirt. Gravely, she handed it to Sir Brian. "Will you see to the sale of these items, milord? You may be sure the jewelry is mine to sell. I beg you to get the very best price you can. It must pay my passage to Southhampton and provide some means of transport to my nephew's house."

Brian weighed the pittance in his hand. Even if the items enclosed were solid gold, their value would be nominal. He doubted very seriously if Alys had enough there to pay for passage to Dover. He tossed the purse to Hob, who weighed it similarly. The two exchanged meaningful glances.

During this exchange Gillian gathered her courage. Although the thought of leaving him tore her heart, she must return. "We were both seeking passage," she reminded them timidly.

Brian frowned at her. "You need not be concerned about your own passage. After all, in a way 'twas my fault you are here to begin with. When the time comes for you to return, I will arrange everything. But surely you do not mean to leave France before you have seen some of its beauty?"

Her eyes misted with tears, Gillian nodded solemnly. "I must. I have been away for so long. My business will not take care of itself. I do not know whether Uncle Tobin is alive or dead. Kenneth might be all alone in York trying to maintain the family trade by himself."

At the mention of her business, Brian's face darkened. Gilliam remembered that he did not care for Tobin Walton. "The money for the commission should have reached them by now," he pointed out coldly. "No. I wish to talk to you very seriously before you make any decision about returning to York."

"Perhaps Alys and I should take the purse and see about her passage?" Hob suggested hastily, sensing the tension in the air. He knew well Brian's stubborn unbending nature, but Gillian had proved herself a very independent lady. The vicinity of these two for the next few minutes would not be pleasant.

"Oh, yes," Alys agreed eagerly, sliding out of her chair and adjusting her smock. "I shall feel every confidence if you make all the arrangements, milord."

Hob held the door for her. "I am not a lord, milady. I am just an humble squire."

She smiled at him, her eyes meeting his as she passed through. "And I was only milady by marriage. Since the marriage is over, I am just a humble widow."

As the door closed behind them, Gillian raised her mouth to receive Brian's kiss. When it came, warm and tender, her heart beat faster with love.

When it was over, his hands caressed her shoulders as he drew her to her feet. "You must remain with me."

She took a deep breath. "Surely you must see that I cannot." Her voice was low, almost a whisper as she hid her face against his throat.

For a long moment, he did not answer. His body was stiff against hers. At last he spoke in a voice harsher than usual. "I see nothing of the kind. You are the woman I love. I will dress you in women's clothing and take you to my home outside Amiens. My mother will meet you and welcome you."

"To what?"

"Why to our family."

Leaning back in his arms, she stared up at him. "I do not even speak your language. What would I do in a French family?"

He gave a sigh of impatience. "She would instruct you in the household arts. You could learn the language quickly. I have some money and a small portion of land."

"What about *my* arts?"

He laughed softly as he smoothed her hair. "You can put aside the sticks and feathers forever, love. You can let your beautiful hair grow long so that I may wind it round your white throat."

His laugh was like a knife driven into the pit of her stomach. "Then I am to become your possession?"

"My wife," he corrected her. "You will be my wife and the mother of my children." His voice was so tender. His green-flecked eyes caressed her everywhere as he bent to kiss her again.

She swallowed hard. Only one chance remained in this tangle. Gently, she extricated herself from his arms and stepped back. When he would have followed her, she held up her hands. "Wait," she commanded him. "Wait right there. I cannot think clearly when you are kissing me."

His eyes were soft with love. "That is as it should be."

"Wait," she begged him again. "Listen. Can I not

be both?"

"Wife and mother, assuredly."

"No. Wife and fletcher?"

He stared at her, his face mirroring changes of emotion. Incredulity. Amusement. Recognition. Disbelief. "N-no . . ." he stammered. At last he smiled uncertainly. "But why should you want to? I will take care of you from now on. You need never work again."

Gillian pulled him down on the bench where Hob had slept. "Does your mother work?" she asked.

Brian thought a minute. "Of course. She works all day long, sewing, embroidering, seeing to the household, managing the servants."

"So you would expect me to work at those tasks?"

He nodded, pleased that she grasped the situation so quickly. "Those tasks are woman's work."

"But I do not wish to do those tasks. A good woman could be hired to do those. Alys, for example. We could let her come to us. She could take care of the house, and I . . ."—she paused to draw a deep breath—". . . I could continue fletching."

Had she suddenly grown two heads, he could not have stared at her harder. At last he shook his head. "This cannot be."

"Why not? Why can I not choose the work I prefer to do rather than the work that would be boring and onerous to me? Some provision could be made for me to sell my work through Tobin. I could not take the fletcher's chair in the hall, but I would not mind so badly giving it up to be your wife." Her jaw tightened as those words were uttered. She knew she would mind terribly, but she would do it. She must be willing to compromise.

"What of the children?"

"They would be taken care of by nurses as all good children are. I would spend just as much time with them as I would if I were doing all sorts of household tasks. Your mother does not take care of children while she is embroidering or trading with merchants. She has nurses to do that."

Brian shook his head. Gradually, the humor drained from his face as he saw that she was serious. Incredulously, he stared around him as if trying to find the strength to control his mounting irritation and anger. "You will be my wife!" he burst out at last, springing to his feet and beginning to stomp back and forth across the small room. "You will be my wife! You do not need to work." He turned suddenly as an argument occurred to him. He crossed his arms across his chest, his disapproving frown etching his forehead deeply. "You would not expect to sell these things."

She looked at him amazed. "But of course. I would not work for nothing."

His control broke completely, exploding in the form of a fervent curse. Wincing, Gillian congratulated herself on her ignorance of the French language. "For money," he repeated. "You would *sell* those silly things."

"Well, what is the harm in that?" Gillian countered irritably. "You were fighting on the tourney circuit. Hob told me so. You fought for pay."

"The pay was incidental," he replied with injured hauteur. "I fought to sharpen my skills."

"Well then"—she mocked his tone—"we shall say that my pay is incidental. I merely make arrows to while away the time."

The scowl grew so deep on Brian's flushed face that Gillian feared he would be scarred. "I am a knight. You will be my lady," he groaned at last. His teeth were set, his jaw clamped tight. "You will obey me. 'Tis God's law."

Tears filled her eyes. The argument was over. He had invoked God's law. To make contradiction was heresy. "Then we shall not marry," she sighed.

He raged. He stamped. He clenched his fists and cursed in French.

She remained adamant.

"Why?" he begged. "Can you think of one reason why you will not let me take care of you?"

She looked at him, a strange expression in her eyes. "You have only to look at Alys to see one reason made flesh."

Her answer rocked him back on his heels. For a moment he gaped, nonplused. At last he found his answer. "Ah . . . but she married an old husband. I am young and strong. You would have many sons by me. Sons who would take care of their mother."

"Suppose I did not. Suppose I were barren. I have not conceived as yet. Perhaps I may not be able to. What if you were killed in a tournament? What if your estate fell to the nearest male heir?" She looked at him squarely. "What would be my lot but to sell my few trinkets in a desperate effort to get home to Kenneth, who would by that time have forgotten my existence?" She rose, her face calm now. The anguish of the past few minutes seemed wiped clean by a new resolve.

"Gillian . . ." he put out his hand.

The conversation was interrupted by Hob's bursting into the room. "Brian! Gillian! Come quickly. . . ." The squire's face was bloody about the mouth. An eye was closing above a bright red bruise on his cheekbone. Once in the room he slipped to one knee.

Brian caught him with a growl, lifting him into a chair. Gillian poured some wine from the pitcher on the table and held it to his lips.

"What has happened?" Brian asked when Hob had swallowed a little of the restorative. "Who dares? . . ."

"Alys and I were beset as we walked down the dock together," he groaned. "Her stepson Jules ordered his lackeys to beat me and throw me to the fishes." He grinned crookedly and rubbed his knuckles. "Evidently they thought I was you, Lady Gillian. They were quite surprised when I fought back."

"We must get her back." Gillian sprang to her feet. "She truly fears what Jules may do to her. She says he is as crazy as her husband, his father."

"What direction would they take her?" Brian asked.

Hob drained the wine and flexed his hand again, wincing in pain. "I heard him boast to her about taking her immediately to the convent. He promised her that he would request that she be made to begin a period of rigorous fasting and self-denial to cleanse her soul of her unholy thoughts."

"Oh, poor Alys." Gillian turned to grasp Brian's arm. "She is to be sent to the convent of the Poor Clare's near Amiens. It is a very strict sisterhood. They take a vow of silence."

Brian looked doubtful. "Perhaps that is the best thing for her. . . . Women without men . . ." He bit his lip. Alys's problems faded for a moment as the truth of what Gillian had said dawned on him.

"Brian?" Hob asked doubtfully as he staggered to his feet.

Gillian, too, stared at the knight as emotions played

across his handsome face. Bitterly, she realized that at least he recognized her problems even if he could not sympathize with them. "Sir Brian," she prodded him gently. "You know the countryside. Which route would they take to Amiens?"

Blinking, he came back to the room. Gillian and Hob were waiting for him deferentially as the natural leader to direct them. He smiled at the feelings their confident expressions engendered. "Which way to Amiens? Did they ride away?"

"I believe so. A man nearby was holding some horses." Hob shrugged. "I cannot say for certain. Is there another way?"

"Assuredly. They could take ship here at Calais and sail around the coast to the mouth of the Somme. A small boat could take then thence from Abbeville to Amiens." He thought a moment. "That might be the logical way to carry her. A person is easily held captive on a boat. The boat itself is a prison. No embarrassing questions need be answered if the prisoner gets noisy, so long as the captain and the crew are well paid."

Remembering her own experience with the captain of the *Maudelayne*, Gillian shuddered. "There are probably plenty of captains who would make money any way they could."

Both men nodded.

"Should we try to hire a boat and follow them then?" Hob asked.

Gillian stiffened. She had vowed to herself that only the return trip to England would get her on a boat again and that the voyage would be made on the calmest day of the year. Nervously, she glanced through the window at the bright blue sky.

"I think not," Brian was saying. "'Tis no more than thirty leagues to Amiens by horse. The roads are good. We can be there before them. They will not be expecting us. With a bit of luck on our side, we can greet them as they disembark."

"What about guards?" Gillian looked meaningfully at Hob's bruised, cut face.

"They are not professional," Hob laughed. "Just a few burly servants. Clods all, they could barely swing their fists. I threw all three of them into the channel."

"We must select a suitable mount for Gil." Brian began to gird himself for riding.

"I shall take care of that," Hob offered.

"No." Brian stopped him eying the injured face also. "I suggest you lie down for a space and rest. "Gil and I will see to the preparations. When all is ready, we will come for you." When Hob would have protested, the knight raised his hand imperiously. "The extra rest will help to restore you. We will ride fast. Although you are strong, you have had a shock."

Hob grinned gratefully. "As you command, my lord." He bowed formally before sinking down on the cot. "But knight's are not supposed to cater to their squires. Quite the contrary, you know."

On the street Brian led the way, with Gil flanking him on the left shoulder. "You really are a kind, considerate man," she told him at last.

He did not stop. If anything, his strides lengthened as though he did not want to hear what she was saying.

Still she felt compelled to say more. "You look after Hob as if he were your own, yet you claim he left you to die. You love me and care for me, even though I am not of your class and your debt is long paid. Now you hie off across France after a woman whom you do not know, whose cause you do not heartily espouse."

"She is a lady in distress," Brian reminded her stiffly, still staring straight ahead of him. "A knight is supposed to rescue such a one."

"Ah, yes," Gillian smiled. "The code of chivalry. I quite forgot about that."

"I never do," Brian remarked forbiddingly as he strode into the dimness of the stable.

The horse for Gillian constituted more of a problem than Brian had at first supposed. She could not ride. At least not well enough to ride the two iron-mouthed mounts the stable owner would rent. Wicked-looking, ill-trained animals both, they intimidated her even standing in their stalls.

Seeing the size of the youth and noting the growing disgust of the knight, the owner cleared his throat hesitantly. "I have a palfrey," he suggested. "A rather nice little thing, she be. A lady's mount to be sure; but since the lad be not a rider, perhaps she would be just the thing."

With a fierce scowl, Brian nodded. The man hurried off to another aisle of stalls. "Just the thing for you," Brian told her aside. "I would have asked for it first, but I feared he might become suspicious. We have enough trouble without someone discovering your sex."

The stable man trotted out the small gray animal leading her around and patting her nose with something like affection. "Nice mount," he explained. "Just small. The lady to whom she belonged died. The widower was selling off all her things. Quite heartbroken, he was."

"Do you have trappings to go with her then?" Brian inquired.

"Full gear."

"How much?"

While the two chaffered, Gillian patted the velvety nose. "You are a dear thing," she whispered in the black ear that flicked back to hear the compliment. "You will not be so ill mannered as to throw me will you?" The small mare snuffled into her hand.

"Saddle the three then," Brian ordered. "Bring them round to the front of *La Reine d'Or* in half an hour."

"Milord." The man pulled his forelock as he pocketed a sizable profit.

Pulling Gillian away from the mare, Brian led her out of the stable. "You had better change your mind about marrying me," he said severely. "You are costing me a fortune. I should hate to spend all this money for nothing."

"I will pay you back," she replied haughtily. "Remember I make my own money."

Angry at her answer, he hastened off down the street.

Chapter Twenty-Eight

Jules de Chambeaux preened against the rail of the Somme River barge that drew him nearer and nearer to his goal. His black eyes glowed with a savage light as they scanned the tiny deckhouse in the stern. Alys would not enjoy her last moments of freedom, he vowed.

He had taken great pleasure in locking her inside, refusing her all food, and keeping her dressed in the same worn soiled clothing. The sight of her would add to the severity of the welcome the abbess would bestow on her. He chuckled grimly, relishing the thought of his stepmother's embarrassment.

Turning back to the rail he stared hard. The twin spires of Amiens cathedral, built almost two hundred years earlier, rose dimly in the distance. Soon. Soon his revenge would be complete.

Leisurely, he extracted the key from his pocket. By evening this last pitiful symbol of parental authority would be safely locked away, imprisoned in what he hoped would be a living hell for the rest of her natural life. An unpleasant smile played about his thick lips as he strolled to the door and unlocked it.

"Ah, *ma mère*." He bowed mockingly as he paused in the door of the dim cabin, his eyes taking in the drooping figure sitting in the center of the room in the only chair.

The despairing woman hardly stirred. Exhausted and terrified, Alys had ceased to hope. When escape seemed within her grasp, Jules had appeared out of nowhere, seizing and beating Hob despite Alys's tearful pleas that Hob was not the man with whom she had escaped, that he was innocent. Had her cries not threatened to draw a crowd on the dock, she had no doubt that Jules would have stayed to see him killed instead of dragging her away.

Now she did not move as Jules strolled across the cabin. Shivering at his touch, she endured his hand on her shoulder.

"Look at me," he demanded exerting such pressure that her slight bones ground together.

Like a trapped and dying animal, she raised her tear-drenched eyes to his face. The signs of his debauchery and self-indulgence were evident in his corpulent form, in the double chin that hung over the filthy collar of his undertunic. Staring at his greasy pock-marked skin, she shuddered.

With a snarl he spat in her upturned face.

Flinching, she turned her head away and wiped her cheek, but his persistent and painful grip on her shoulder brought her back.

"Your disposal will complete my revenge, madame," he chortled. "When you are safely locked away at Amiens, I shall have finished with all who abused me in my lifetime." He waited, hoping she would beg, but he was doomed to disappointment. Angrily, he pushed her aside. The force of his thrust upset the chair, toppling it over backward with Alys in it.

He laughed as she wallowed helplessly in a tangle of legs and arms. Strolling around in a circle, regarding her prone form from all angles, he threw back his head and laughed. "I shall have a new motto for Bellepaix," he bragged. "'Vengeance is mine.' Sounds good. Sounds strong."

He nudged her weakly struggling form with his boot. "What do you say?"

"Why?" she whimpered. "Why do you feel the need for such awful vengeance? I was willing, eager to return to England. I would never have bothered you more."

He dropped down on one knee beside her, his face only inches from hers. "Ah, but you might have been happy," he snarled. "And I could not risk that. No." He resumed his pacing, enjoying the sight of her huddled on the floor. "No, I could not bear the thought that somewhere in the world, one who had done me a wrong might be prospering."

Alys buried her face in her hands.

"Do not hide your face from me, dear Alys," he warned. "I want to see those lovely tear-drenched eyes of English blue. I want to dream about them at night. They will comfort me."

Wearily, she raised her head, her eyes staring steadily at a small spot on the wall above his shoulder. "The convent will be peaceful after this," she observed with only a hint of spirit.

"Think you so?" He laughed. "You cannot imagine the things I have planned for you. The things I will whisper in the ear of the Mother Abbess. I have told them you are an English whore who was given to my father in marriage. He was deceived, I have said, and bitterly regretted his wife. You will enter the convent without dowry to work for your keep."

"I was no whore," Alys averred softly.

Ignoring her comment, Jules went down on one knee. Gripping her slender wrists, he pulled her hands toward him. "Such white soft hands," he purred. "Oh, how it pleasures me to think of them gnarled and rough, with blisters and chilblains throbbing as you try to sleep on a rough board with only a thin blanket for covering."

Her eyes widened in horror as they stared at each other, face to face. "Monster!" she hissed at last.

"You are the monster," he insisted. "You had me removed as a youth from my home, sent away to that wretched school. I never saw my father alone again. Never! You wrecked my life. Furthermore, you sought to supplant me in my father's favor. If you could have conceived a child for him, you would have had me disinherited. It would have been so easy." He laughed. "Except that the old fool was quite exhausted by the time he married you." He sprang up and strode around the room, laughing wildly. "Exhausted. Oh, the richness of it. Just like the manor of Bellepaix. Exhausted until your tainted riches rebuilt it."

"I think you might at least thank me for that," Alys begged. "Without my fortune you would have nothing to inherit."

Again he ignored her. "I shall suggest to the abbess that you be forced to wear a hairshirt," he crowed. "And you shall be fed only the scraps from the table. And you shall be required to scrub all the floors on your knees."

In terror Alys cowered. Flecks of spittle whitened his lips. Suddenly, he lunged at her. "But first you shall serve me."

The thing she had dreaded most was upon her. A swift blow to the side of her face cut short her scream of horror. Releasing the violence he had worked himself up to, he ripped and tore her clothing aside giving his hands access to her breasts.

Again she screamed in agony as his hands squeezed her and his fingernails tore at her white flesh. "Mercy! Oh, please, Jules. No . . . oh, God . . ."

"I wanted you!" he snarled ravening at her mouth like a dog. "I wanted you. Father should have married you to me instead of taking you for himself. If you had been nice to me, we could both have had what we wanted. But you spurned me. I was a stripling youth beneath your notice. I watched how you bared your white breasts around Father. I watched him fondle you when you first came to the house. You never noticed me. But now you will. Now you will!"

Even as he shouted at her, he tore her hose away, ripping them down over her legs, exposing her most private parts to his frenzied lust. Pulling aside his codpiece, he lunged forward into her body.

Alys thought she would be torn in two. Like a file he rasped the unprepared chamber of her body. Celibate for several years even before her husband's death, she was tight as a virgin. Her screams as he pulled back and lunged again turned to agonized sobs. Sweat dripped from him, splashing in her eyes and on her bosom. Blinded as well as crushed, she slumped lifelessly under him.

With a curse he thrust again and again, the sense of victory lessened only minimally by his victim's insensibility to the ultimate triumph. Grunting and panting, he pumped his seed into her body and collapsed.

When he could move at last, he rolled over and sat up. The stuffy deckhouse was now unpleasantly hot. His clothing stuck to his gross body as he grimly fastened himself up and rose laboriously to his feet.

Without a backward glance he staggered toward the

door. As he opened it, he heard a faint moan behind him. "Get your clothing in some kind of order," he commanded her over his shoulder, "else I lead you through the streets of Amiens as you are—half naked."

When the door slammed behind him, Alys rolled over sobbing. The heat and the sickening odors of the cabin assailed her senses. Her abused body ached fearfully. But worse was the knowledge that her own stepson had raped her. Would even God forgive her for the hideous sin to which she had been a party? In her mind she had been a party to incest, an abomination of the most damnable sort. And so she wept, great gulping sobs that finally trailed away into a sort of comatose sleep.

She was unconscious for only a few minutes, though for all she knew, the time might have been longer. Sounds—shouting, thudding of bodies, the clashing of steel on steel—aroused her. She struggled to sit up, then slumped back in a despairing heap. What matter what went on outside? She closed her eyes.

"Lady Alys!"

Someone was shaking her shoulder.

"Good God! What has he done to her?"

That sounded strangely like Gil's light voice.

"The swine has undoubtedly raped her."

"Y-yes," Alys whispered. "Please . . . help me. . . ."

"We will, my lady." Hob slipped his arm around her shoulders and lifted her upright.

"Get something to put around her," Gil pleaded. "We cannot carry her away in that condition. But we must get her from this awful place."

Embarrassed despite her terrible shock, Alys plucked ineffectually at the ragged edges of her garments. "My clothing . . . Yes . . . He tore . . . my . . ." She broke off with a sob. A great swirling blackness swept in from the corners of her mind as Hob lifted her to her feet.

Gillian's body shuddered with nausea as she staggered to the door of the small deckhouse. With difficulty she made the railing before giving up all she had.

Brian glanced over his shoulder, then swung round alarmed at the sight of her. Drained of all color except for a greenish tinge around the mouth, her face shocked him. A couple of swift strides took him across the deck to support her with an arm around her shoulders.

Taking advantage of the distraction, Jules de Chambeaux attempted to rally his men who had been cowering back against the rail, held on their knees by Brian's deadly blade.

"Seize him!" he hissed, dragging one burly brute to his feet.

Shaking his head in fear, the man hung back. "He has a sword, milord."

"I know that, fool. Seize him while his back is turned. Up, you mongrels! Up! Earn your keep." Jules's wrath exploded over his servants' heads as he kicked and pummeled them uselessly.

Brian turned from his attention to Gillian. "What have you done, bastard? What did she see?"

Before Jules could reply, Hob bore the unconscious Alys through the door. Her fair face lolling sideways over the squire's arm looked like a dead woman's. Paths made by tears and sweat furrowed her dusty cheeks.

Brian's face contorted in pity. "Is she dead?"

"No, alive, but barely," came Hob's terse answer as he made for the gangplank.

Furious at their interference, Jules sprang to bar the way. "You are kidnapping my kinswoman!" he screamed.

Hob's reply was sharp as a blade. "If she is your kinswoman, why have you treated her in this manner? You owe her your protection not abuse.''

Jules clenched his fists; his black eyes glowed redly in his anger. ''She is mine to do with as I see fit. I have made arrangement for her housing in the Convent of the Poor Clares. She is to spend the rest of her life in penance for her sins.''

Brian had moved to stand at Hob's back, his arm supporting a barely recovered Gillian. ''Is she willing to embrace this life?''

''I have convinced her that she should.'' Jules planted himself in front of the gangplank to bar their progress.

''How?'' In her anger and disgust, Gillian's voice cracked and trembled. ''By rape?''

''Is that what the whore told you?'' Jules sneered. ''How like her to lie to appear innocent. She tried to seduce me. Tore off her clothing and offered me her filthy body. I resisted, of course. But afterward, righteous rage overcame me. I punished her perhaps a bit severely for her evil acts.''

''Liar!'' Gillian accused.

Jules glared at her. ''Are you the youth whom she persuaded to take her away? I suspect you were easily deceived because of your young years. She is dipped in sin, make no mistake.''

''In that case,'' said Hob smoothly, ''you should be glad to get her off your hands. We will take her with us and be gone. Step aside.'' He moved to shoulder past the fat man.

''No!'' Jules cried. ''She is my duty and my chattel. I demand that you give her up to me.''

''So that you may beat her and rape her again,'' Gillian snarled.

''So that I may take her to the care of the abbess at the convent,'' Jules argued. ''Perhaps there she will find salvation for her soul. Otherwise she is surely damned."

"We are wasting time." Brian laid a hand on Hob's shoulder. "Let me show him the edge of my steel."

Hob stepped aside, and Brian raised the heavy broadsword, pointing it at Jules's ponderous belly. "I promise you, sir, on my honor as a knight that if this lady truly wishes to enter the convent, we will bear her there and save you the expense and trouble. You need concern yourself no more with her."

Jules stepped back down the gangplank. "You will regret this," he whined. "She is a whore and will seduce you all. You will be damned as will she. I only seek the salvation of her soul. Punish the body to cleanse the soul," he recited piously.

Steadily, Brian advanced, the gleaming blade flashing fire in the last slanting rays of the dying sun. Menacingly, he moved the sword in a small circle as if sighting the best target for his attack.

Jules held up his hands. "Have a care, sir knight. This gangplank may be slippery. Have a . . ." His heel came down in thin air. Precariously he teetered for a moment; his arms windmilled furiously. His own bulk made him unwieldly. Like a great stone he dropped over the edge of the plank and into the slow-moving waters of the Somme with a tremendous splash.

Grinning like a very devil, Brian sprang to the dock and bowed low, pointing the way with his swordpoint. "Come, Hob. Come, Gil. Clear the gangplank. I am sure M'sieur Chambeaux's servants need the space to fish their master out of the river."

Alys did not stir as Hob bore her through the street away from the quay and into the interior of the town. "Where shall we take her?" he asked anxiously.

Brian shook his head. "Her condition undoubtedly complicates things. She cannot ride the mount I hired for her."

"I would feel safer were we away from here," Gillian cast a nervous glance over her shoulder. "I know Jules has not given up. He sent a man to follow us."

Looking over his shoulder, Brian cursed fervently in French. "I shall put a stop to that," he said as the fellow in Jules's livery ducked in at the door of a small shop.

"No." Gillian put a hand on his arm. "We are already attracting too much attention. In truth, we are kidnapping her from her lawful guardian bearing her to a nunnery. Our actions are indefensible to any sheriff or bailiff that Jules might care to call in."

"Gil is right," Hob agreed. "Let us get the horses and ride. I can carry the lady for a while. If we hurry, we can perhaps make some inn in the countryside before the darkness gets too deep. If not, we can sleep in the open, but let us quit this town."

"Oh, yes," Gillian urged. "Let us do as Hob says. Jules is utterly mad. You did not see the condition of Alys's body as I did. And the room where she was imprisoned was unbelievable."

Surrendering to her impassioned plea, Brian held out his arms to take Alys from Hob. "Go before us," he commanded. "Saddle the horses and purchase what supplies you can. We shall wait for you outside the city at the fountain by the Abbeville gate."

As Alys's unconscious body was passed between them, Hob's cloak fell away from her side exposing her bare breast. Brian drew in his breath at the sight. Jules's nails had left hideous scratches radiating inward toward the aureole. A trickle of blood stemming from the nipple had dried on the underside of the swollen bruised mound.

Accustomed to sights of carnage on the battlefield, the knight nevertheless could not remain unmoved by this evidence of deliberate torture. "Poor lady," he murmured.

Hob nodded, the lines of his face more deeply etched than ever. Gently as if bestowing a benediction, he covered the tormented form. Then he turned and dashed off down the street.

Dusk was falling. Fog rising from the river began to filter in through the streets and alleyways. The pleasant cathedral town began to take on a sinister appearance as merchants closed their shops and locked their doors. Shutters were firmly fastened from the inside on all windows. The night watch had not yet made his rounds to light the lamps so the entire town seemed to be deserted.

"Follow close to me," Brian commanded Gillian. "In fact, hang on to my cloak. That way if you should stumble you can catch yourself."

Gillian shivered uncontrollably. Not only the chill fog from the river but also her terror of Jules preyed on her mind. A pure innocent only a short time out of York Minster, her experiences with Ranulf, the captain of the *Maudelayne*, and now Jules combined to drive her to the brink of hysteria. Like a child in a nightmare she followed Brian through the streets, clutching at his cloak with hands that were cold as ice.

All around her was ghostly silence, broken only occasionally by a strange sound. The fog that muffled their footsteps also muffled the footsteps of their pursuers, she reasoned fearfully. As they passed the door of a house, a hound bayed thunderously. Gillian gave a terrified scream as she threw herself against Brian's back. Simultaneously, the creature could be heard flinging itself against the closed door with a muffled thud followed by a confusion of scufflings and scratchings as it sought to get out to attack.

"Easy," Brian's voice came, strong and comforting in the darkness. "Easy, my love. We will win through safely. It cannot get to us."

But the hound's growls which followed them down the street were a light in the darkness, Gillian thought, to lead the pursuers after them. As its voice finally ceased, she listened feverishly, trying to pick up the sounds of footsteps in the fog.

"How much farther?"

Brian stumbled as his foot turned on the uneven cobblestones. With a curse he righted himself. "I cannot tell. This damned fog."

"How can we find the fountain?" Gillian whispered. "For that matter, how can we find the gate? Are you sure you know the way?"

Indeed, Brian himself was beginning to doubt his direction. Amiens was no different from all medieval towns in that the maze of streets turned and twisted like rabbit warrens. Built purposefully in that manner to break the force of the wind and conserve heat in the dwellings, the seemingly insane configuration also allowed several dwellings to utilize the same walls. Furthermore, the presence of neighbors within calling distance made for security.

Suddenly, out of the darkness torches flickered faintly. "The gate!" Brian exclaimed. Sure enough, the Abbeville gate to the town loomed before them, its huge wooden doors closed and barred for the night, its torches smoking fitfully in the damp air.

"How can we get out?" Gillian stared aghast.

"Through the sally port," Brian whispered. "We may have to grease the porter's palm to get it opened, but I think he will oblige us."

"If Jules has not gotten to him first," Gillian breathed.

Chapter Twenty-Nine

That thought had also occurred to Brian. While one part of his mind was intent on finding their way through the winding streets, the other mulled over the distinct possibility that Jules had set men to guard the only two exits from the walled town.

Inwardly, he cursed himself for sending Hob away from him. Though valuable time would have been lost, the absence of the squire, a seasoned fighter, left him with sole responsibility for two women. As he came to a halt, Gillian grasped his shoulders and pressed herself against his back. He could feel her shivering through the double thickness of their clothing.

"What shall we do?" Her voice was barely a thread of sound in the darkness. Her breath brushed his ear, so close did she press against him.

He shook his head. "'Tis a problem. Of course, the

gate may be unguarded. We may be able to walk up, pay the guard, and pass through without a murmur."

"Otherwise?"

"At the very least, a man may run to tell Jules that we left the city by the Abbeville road." She felt his great shoulders shrug. "At the very worst, we may be walking into a trap."

He felt her shudder. Her voice was high and weak yet steady. "Shall I go ahead and investigate?"

"Gillian!" he chided aghast. "I am the knight. I am supposed to defend you."

She squeezed his arm at the same time she nuzzled her cheek against his shoulder. "I know. You do it so well. But if they are there, they are expecting you. All of Jules's men saw you and will remember you forever. I could muffle my cloak about my face and attract no attention."

"You were in Jules's house for twenty-four hours," he reminded her sternly. "They would remember you."

Gillian straightened herself away from him. Pulling her hat down low over her forehead, she tossed the cloak around her shoulders. "They would not be expecting you to send me," she declared reasonably. "No fighting man in his right mind would send a boy."

"No!" Before he could say more, she strode away from him toward the flickering torches. The fog swirled and billowed around her legs before it swallowed her figure entirely. "Gillian!"

More terrified than she would let him know, Gillian hesitated before the door of the porter's box. Actually it was a small hut built in the side of the wall in front of the sally port. The port therefore could only be reached by rousing the porter and getting him to open first his door and then the chained and barred inner door in the thick stone wall.

Strange thudding sounds reached her ears muffled by the dense fog. Her heart. She pressed her hand against her bosom. The sounds were inside her, not out. Dear God! But she was cold and scared. Above the gate, the flambeau smoked and wavered fitfully.

She closed one hand around the other, forcing her chilled fingers to make a fist. Then tucking her chin and mouth more securely within the folds of her cloak, she rapped strongly. At first no one answered. As she listened nervously, again the only sound she heard was the pounding of her heart.

Time stretched agonizingly along her already frayed nerves. She rapped again more loudly and pressed her ear against the door. Did she hear a sound? No. Drawing away in disgust, she looked to right and left in the cold muffling darkness.

"Gillian . . ." Brian strode toward her out the dense fog, bearing Alys, who at last stirred feebly in his arms.

"S-s-ssh! No one seems to be about, unless someone is hidden inside."

Behind her she heard a dry rasping sound as if someone were dragging a heavy bundle across an uneven floor. A tiny peephole in the door swung open. Only the faintest of lights shone through.

"Who goes?"

Brian spoke behind her. "Travelers for Hangest, monsieur." Drawing close to him, Gillian cleared her throat. "We are friends. Ah . . . that is . . . my family and I must leave the city tonight."

"Gate's closed." The peephole started to close.

"Oh, but one of us is sick," Brian hastily interposed.

393

Alys moaned pitifully, and Gillian gave a hacking cough for effect. "And I am feeling so bad. We all want to get home . . . tonight."

She thought the porter spoke to someone; then his face reappeared at the peephole. "Stand in the light of the torch."

At Brian's nod, Gillian moved nearer to the wall, pulling the cloak around her more tightly and shrinking inside it as if she were shivering uncontrollably.

Brian staggered slightly as he spoke. "Please, sir, for God's sake. Let me go through with my old father and my wife's little brother. Father is bad sick. All feverish and swollen."

"Swollen!" The porter's voice sounded instantly alert. "Swollen where?"

"Oh, up around the throat and down around the privates."

Following this information an excited conversation could now be heard. The gatekeeper was clearly arguing loudly. The words *plague* and *buboes* rose above all the rest.

Gillian judged the time was right to throw in a fervent plea. She thrust her face up close to the peephole, coughing painfully. *"S'il vous plaît, m'sieur, mon père est . . ."* Since she had exhausted her vocabulary, she fell away from the door coughing so deeply that she thought she would tear her throat.

Evidently, the porter did too, for he slammed the peephole to and unbarred the heavy door. Sagging on its hinges, it swung back, leaving a quarter-circle groove in the hard-packed earth and making a fearful grating sound.

"Wait!" he snarled. "Do not enter until I tell you,

then go straight through touching nothing. Do you understand?"

"*Oui, monsieur.*" Gillian tried again. Brian gathered the cloak more tightly around Alys, who, too, began to cough.

They heard the chains rattle, the bolt grate. "Go!" The porter drew back against the wall. "Touch nothing."

Another man also pressed back against the wall of the hut, but he did not cower. Instead he stood upright, taking in Brian's tall broad-shouldered form and that of the cloaked figure he bore. Midway across the room, he stepped forward. "Stop!"

Gillian froze in her tracks. If only she had her bow . . . Prepared to fling herself upon the villain, she tensed. But help came from out of nowhere. "Are you mad?" Seizing the other man by the collar, the porter spun him around and shoved his body into the corner. "They have the plague. The old man is dying of it. They must get out of the city." He spun back. "Go. . . ."

But they were already gone. With a growl of satisfaction he slammed the port and shot the bolt.

"I can walk," Alys whispered when the door closed behind them.

"Rest easy, dear lady," Brian replied. "The distance we go is but a few steps. Then we will all rest and wait for Hob to join us."

The sound of trickling water drew them through the fog. "How will Hob get here?" Gillian asked nervously. "We would never have gotten out at all had you not thought of the plague."

Brian set his burden down on a stone bench beside the fountain and rotated his shoulders to ease the strain. "Hob should have no trouble at all. Jules's spy will have gone to report to his master. When Hob comes, the only problem he will have is getting the horses and supplies through the port. The porter might not be willing to open again."

"I have caused you no end of trouble," Alys mourned softly. "I should have submitted gracefully and gone into the convent. It might not have been so bad," she faltered.

"If you did not want to go, dear lady," Brian observed, "it would have been very bad indeed. The cloistered life is not for everyone."

"I can think of nothing worse," Gillian agreed.

Brian chuckled suddenly. "Certainly, I can think of no one less inclined for the monastic life than you, Gil. Also your French was very good. You sounded almost like a Frenchman."

She blushed in the dark. "I had a good teacher. When I ran out of words, I just coughed. Did I really do well?" Both Brian and Alys assured her that her accent was superb. "You must teach me many more words."

They sat, huddled companionably in their cloaks, Lady Alys on the stone bench, Brian on the ground beside her with his arm around Gillian, holding her back against his chest. Together they taught her all the words they could think of as well as how to string them together in sentences.

Despite the chilly dampness of the night, the time was a time of peace. Alys said nothing about the two she believed to be men sitting in a close embrace at her feet. In her gratitude for her saviors, she had cast aside all her past attitudes. They loved. She was pleased for them. Indeed a twinge of envy touched her at the warmth they shared while she sat alone.

Long past midnight Gillian had fallen asleep on Brian's

shoulder and Alys, too, had wrapped herself in her cloak and lain down on the hard stone bench. Brian roused himself when he felt rather than heard the vibration of approaching hoofbeats. Several horses moved slowly through the fog.

Easing Gillian gently to the ground and covering her closely with both their cloaks, he started in their direction. He would encounter whoever was approaching away from the girls. He loosened his sword in its scabbard.

Dark silhouettes appeared out of the fog. "Hob!"

"Brian. Thank God!"

"What are you doing so far off the road?"

"I left by the Peronne gate," the squire chuckled. "Encountered a fellow that I knew must have been Jules's man. Knocked him down. The porter was not pleased but declined to argue with a sword at his throat."

Brian chuckled in his turn. "We encountered one at the Abbeville gate. The porter knocked him down for us."

"No! How did you manage that?"

"Another story for another time. Gillian and Alys are alone asleep at the fountain. We must rouse them and put distance between Amiens and Jules before dawn. This fountain is practically under the wall. Let us go quickly."

And quickly they did depart. Steadily, Brian led his group through the night. Alys and Gillian both insisted they were well rested and strong enough to ride. So four horsemen clattered across the Somme River bridge at Hangest.

"Where are we bound?" Hob asked while they rested

the horses on the east bank.

"We make for Beauvais," Brian told him. "My home. Jules will not look for us in this direction. The ride is not so long."

"But . . ." Hob began.

"It is best," Brian declared repressively.

Hob shrugged. He was a squire. Where the knight led, the squire followed. But he hated to think of Lady Gillian's wrath when she discovered that Brian had led them deeper into France.

By late evening the next day, the weary party reached Château de la Forêt. Alys had been riding pillion since the last rest stop when her courage had failed her. She could no longer bear the pain in her abused thighs. Hob had taken her up behind him.

In the twilight the château looked shaggy somehow. Great swaths of ivy trailed across its windows and quite covered most of the chimneys of the house. One of the chestnuts in the lane running beside the low wall was dead, its skeletal limbs lifted like a pleading hand to the indigo heavens.

Dismayed and a little concerned at the appearance of the château, Brian nevertheless led his exhausted troop onward. A stodgy peasant youth in smock and drooping hose challenged them at the gate. In a slightly startled tone, Brian identified their party.

"The Sire de Trenanay does not expect you. He would have told me. He gave strict orders—"

"Damn!" Brian spurred his tired horse past the dull youth. "Follow me!" he called as he led the way past the wall and up toward the château.

Even in the twilight the once-elegant formal gardens looked decidedly seedy and overgrown. The hedges, formerly cut in fantastic shapes, had lost their identities and run wild.

"The *forêt* certainly seems intent on reclaiming its own," Hob whispered dryly over his shoulder to Alys who slumped against him.

The lady raised her drooping head, but all around her was little to be seen. "Are we still in France?" she whispered.

"I fear so."

"God protect me."

Hob squeezed her hands where they clasped him at his waist. "I feel we have seen the last of your stepson, lady. He could not know which direction we traveled. We left by different gates and were observed. *Voilà!* Conflicting reports! He will expect us to head for the coast . . . either west or north. We ride south."

She shuddered. "I pray God you are right, but I long for England. Sometimes I do not think I shall ever see it again."

Ahead of them Brian's destrier clanged and clattered under the carriage arch.

"How can you see where you ride?" Gillian asked, disgust evident in her voice.

"We were not expected," Brian mumbled apologetically. "Father and Mother would have sent escorts to greet us had I been able to send Hob ahead with news of our arrival."

"Are you sure they still live here? This place looks deserted." Gillian did not move from the saddle. Despite being almost weary unto death, she could barely control her blazing anger at what she considered to be Brian's trickery. When he came to her side and held up his arms, only with great reluctance did she allow him to help her down.

Leaving her leaning against the balustrade, he climbed the staircase and banged the lion's-head knocker authoritatively. The hollow sound echoed and reechoed in the rooms beyond.

Complete darkness filled the inside of the carriage arch. Behind him Brian could hear Hob stumble and curse as he helped Alys down. Worriedly, he lifted the knocker again.

His father must be alive. The gatekeeper had mentioned him. In the old days the lamps on either side of the carriage arch as well as on either side of the door were always kept lighted.

Still no answer. "Wrap your cloak around you and sit down, Alys. Looks like we sleep out tonight again." Gillian's voice dripped sarcasm. "Ah . . . *la belle France.* The stories I shall tell when I reach home . . . if I ever reach home."

Angry and exhausted, Brian raised his voice in a bellow. "Father! Mother! Stephen!"

Alys jumped and whimpered faintly as the stentorian challenge bounced off the walls of the carriage arch. "Maybe they have moved away. How long have you been gone?" Gillian called bitingly as she put her arm around the smaller woman to comfort her.

"Four years," replied Brian, his voice gruff with worry.

From behind the door came a faint shuffling sound; a bolt was drawn. The heavy oak door slid open a few inches. A man's outraged face appeared at the aperture. "Be gone! Have you no respect? The Sire de Trenanay is near to death." He started to slam the heavy door.

With a vicious oath Brian smashed his strong shoulder against the paneling. The door exploded inward catapulting the servant across the entry. "Enter and welcome!" the knight called to his companions.

Like tired children they filed in after him and huddled together in an entryway lighted by a huge iron lantern suspended on a great chain from the second story. A stone staircase, the extension of the one they had mounted from the carriage entrance, curved upward.

A woman stood midway up, her withered face stiff with outrage. As Brian's foot touched the first step, he saw her. "Mother!"

"Brian." The voice was cold and cracked, the voice of an old woman, although her black-clothed body was firmly erect. Not a twinge of emotion other than faint annoyance appeared in her face. He might have been arriving late for supper, rather than returning home after a long absence.

"Mother, the servant said that Father is near to death." Brian advanced several steps upward to meet his mother.

With measured stately tread she came slowly down the steps. Repressively, she extended her hand, allowing him to drop to his knee and kiss it. Then she withdrew it from his grasp and continued her descent. She did not exactly brush him aside, Gillian decided, but she certainly did not gather him into a welcoming embrace. "He is instructed to do so. The lie is convenient to keep away unwanted visitors."

The woman who was Brian's mother crossed the floor of the entry, pausing momentarily before the huddled group. Dark eyes regarded them from out of her pale face as she might have regarded some particularly loathesome creatures that Brian might have brought home with him.

"Where is Stephen?" Brian trailed her across the floor. She pushed back the heavy oak door that opened into an ancient baronial hall.

"Stephen is dead," the woman said coldly as her son came abreast of her.

"Stephen? Dead?" The words were a cry torn from Brian's throat. As if he had been struck, he fell to his knees. Gillian sprang forward, clutching his arm, supporting him as he moaned in anguish, pressing the heels of his hands into his eyes. The terrible strain of the past few days when he had been the sole protector and leader of the group, the sleepless nights, the forced marches, all combined to break him, coupled as they were with the terrible news.

Hob, who had been assisting Alys, released her and stepped forward to put his hand on Brian's shoulder.

Gillian flashed an enraged glance at the woman who stood aside holding the door open and surveying the scene with a smirk of satisfaction about her mouth. "Brian," she murmured. "Brian, take heart!"

"Stephen," he moaned.

Alys hurried across the flagstones to pull a dusty chair from the end of a banquet table. A startled exclamation escaped her at the sight of the festoons of filthy cobwebs spun across the armrests. Steeling herself not to think about the spiders who had spun them, she wiped them away with her hand. Hastily, she swiveled the chair around to accept Brian's staggering form as the other two helped him to it.

With something suspiciously like a sob, Brian slumped down in the chair, bowing his head and shading his eyes with his hand. Gillian knelt in front of him to place a comforting palm against his cold cheek.

"Brandy?" Hob snapped.

With a desultory wave of her hand the woman indicated the sideboard. Perhaps two inches of murky brown liquid remained in a dusty carafe. Wiping a glass on the inside lining of his cloak, Hob poured a generous amount. Cautiously, he smelled it, then sipped it, before carrying it to Brian's lips.

The knight downed it on one swallow. Gillian lovingly brushed back his sandy hair from his ashen face. "Who is Stephen?" she asked softly.

"My brother . . ."

The woman laughed nastily from the doorway. The four stared at her as she advanced menacingly. The light of malevolence shone so strongly from her eyes that Alys crossed herself involuntarily. Trailing her black garments across the stones, she stopped within a yard of Brian.

"Your half brother," the woman sneered. "Stephen was never your full brother. When he died, how I enjoyed telling Trenanay the truth. You are my son, but not his."

Chapter Thirty

At the instructions of the chatelaine of La Forêt, the servant had shown the four of them to separate chambers in a distant wing of the château. Gillian had waited until he had gone before slipping noiselessly into Brian's chamber.

He did not stir from where he sat slumped in a chair before a cold fireplace, a single candle burning beside him. His eyes were closed; his hands, clenched around the chair arms. As she studied his still face, a muscle jumped in his jaw testifying to the iron control he was exercising over his body.

The bed had not been made, Gillian saw to her disgust. Apparently, no amenities were to be offered to the bastard son. Her whole body began to tremble in sympathy for the spiritual and mental agony he was enduring. She had seen him weak with pain, torn by wounds, his flesh pierced over and over by Tobin's needle. He had endured all, yet instinctively, she realized that never had he seemed so brave as now when his mind and spirit were pierced over and over by the sharp words of his own mother.

She came close to him and rested a hand on top of one of his. "Brian," she breathed softly.

He flinched, jerking his hand out from under hers as if she had touched him with fire. "Leave me," he snarled, his voice unrecognizable.

"No, Brian, I will not leave you. I came to help you. Let me get you undressed and into bed before the candle burns out. Everything will look better in the morning."

"Not here," he whispered. "Never here. I want to wait until the candle burns out."

"But why, Brian?" Gently she knelt to pull off his boots. His hat she laid aside on the table. Then she reached for the buckle of his belt.

"This is Stephen's room. She put me in Stephen's room."

Gillian's hands froze. "Oh, no."

"Do you understand why I cannot bear to look—why I must wait until the candle burns out?" His voice was a singsong.

Gillian realized that he was not really thinking rationally. The multiple shocks had numbed him. "Stand up," she urged him firmly, grasping his hands and tugging on them.

"No . . ." But he had no will to resist. Like a recalcitrant child he allowed himself to be hauled to his feet and undressed. Leading him across the room, she pulled back the musty coverlet. Thank heaven the bed had sheets.

She would not have been surprised to find those missing in this neglected household.

Pushing him down on the edge, she stroked his pale cheek. "Climb in."

Closing his eyes to hide the tears, he turned his head to kiss her palm.

Stripping off her garments, she climbed in beside him and gathered him into her arms.

"This is Stephen's bed," he grated through clenched teeth.

"Good." She stroked his sweaty hair back from his forehead. "He would be glad you could use it."

"I am not so sure about that anymore."

They did not speak after that. She pulled his tired head into the circle of her arm, his face pressing against the side of her breast. He adjusted himself carefully so she would not take the weight of his head, but he could rest his lips against her smooth warm skin. His arms enclosed her waist and fitted her against him as if he sought to draw her into his body and somehow make her a part of him.

For her part she stroked her fingers rhythmically over his hair and cheek, his neck and shoulders, and across his chest. Wherever she could reach, she touched him, bestowing on him the gifts of warmth and reassurance. Despite her best intentions to remain awake until he was asleep, she drifted off within minutes, her exhausted body bent on restoring itself.

For him there was no such peace. His nerves jumped and quivered. Periodically, rigors would shake his body as if he had a fever. When these occurred, he would tighten his arms around her and clench his hands at her waist. Over and over again, the horrifying questions tortured him. Why? How? Who?

The next day the two people who could give him the answers sat in high-backed chairs at opposite ends of the solar. Flanked by a reluctant Gillian, Brian confronted them both at noon.

Even a cursory glance revealed that the Sire de Trenanay had not long to live. The man's naturally short, thin body appeared shrunken. The once black hair was thin and gray; the sallow skin was deeply tinged with yellow. From beneath scabby eyebrows, black eyes stared at Brian. Recognition flamed, as if for only an instant the man longed to reach out to embrace the boy he had once believed to be his son. Just as quickly it died, to be replaced by a look of loathing.

Brian raised his hands toward his father before he, too, remembered and let them fall. Awkwardly, he shuffled his feet in the rushes. Embarrassed, he glanced at Gillian. What could he say?

From her chair, the chatelaine of La Forêt viewed the exchange with a cackle of satisfaction. Her fingers curved into talons as she raised them, rolling her eyes upward as if thanking God for the day. Her withered face radiated an unholy joy.

Then she clasped her hands together before her and turned her gaze on her husband. From where she stood, Gillian could see her green eyes, gold-flecked as Brian's own, blazing triumphantly. "He is not yours!" She exclaimed, spacing each word with torturous emphasis. She pushed herself out of her chair, her black garments swaying. "I warned you. You would not listen. You doubted me and my intent. I waited long. Now feel my sword."

Brian turned toward his mother. "Who was my father, if not Trenanay?"

She shrugged. "A passing knight. An Englishman, if I remember correctly." She chuckled. "The enemy then— the enemy now."

Her husband writhed in his chair. Her words kindled the flames of hell behind his dark eyes.

"You lie," Brian denied flatly. "I am a son of this house. You have run mad."

She snarled like a panther. "Mad am I not. Had you not wondered where your coloring and size came from? Not from Trenanay, that miserable stripling."

"From you and from your father."

She laughed. "I told you that. You believed it. So did he. 'Tis true enough our eyes are of a color, but nothing else. Your father had the same sun-streaked blond hair which even now glistens in the sun on your head. If he stood here before you today, you could look him in the eye. His very body, broad shoulders and chest, tall, powerful. Just like you. Poor Stephen! Even with my blood, he never grew but an inch above me."

"But why did you wait 'til now to reveal this secret?" Brian's voice shook with pain as he accepted the truth of what she said.

His mother laughed. "Because Stephen was the heir," she explained patiently, as though he were not particularly bright. "So long as Stephen lived, I could only rejoice in secret. I had put horns on Trenanay, but I would profit nothing by telling him so. He would simply disinherit you and perhaps kill me. He might even get another wife."

Fiercely, she lunged at Trenanay, where he huddled in his chair. "You would have done that," she accused.

"With pleasure," he snarled.

She turned back to her son. "You see. I could not have him set me aside. He has not come to my bed in years. Soon after Stephen was born, he took a serving wench into his bed. Then another. Then another. His bastards populate the countryside." Suddenly, her voice quavered as remembered shame and grief overcame her. "I was his wife. I was young and not uncomely. He preferred the sluts. Said they gave him a better time in bed. I was too cold, too . . ." Her voice fell away in a cry of mingled rage and disgust.

Brian heard his mother with nausea clawing at him, a clammy film of perspiration coating his skin. How had she concealed all this hatred all these years? If her husband had not come to her bed, how had she managed to fool him when Brian was born?

Breathing heavily, her chest heaving beneath the rusty black weeds, she pointed her finger at Trenanay. "Then he informed me that he intended to visit my bed again. For insurance for the succession, he called it. Not for pleasure, not for affection, not even for desire. I could have born all those reasons. But for insurance. 'Twas then I looked afield. I planned carefully. No mistakes. I had to be sure. He lay almost every night for a fortnight, and each time before he came I blocked his passage."

"Abomination," the Sire de Trenanay cried. Frantically, he made the sign of the cross in the air before his chair. He was wild with rage. Gillian realized that he could not walk. His skeletal legs in their drooping wrinkled hose, hung down from the chair like dead things. Only the upper half of his body contorted in

410

agony. The man was quite literally in a living hell of mind and body.

His wife flew across the room, crouching before him, just out of reach. "Shall I tell you again what I did, old man? I pushed a vinegar soaked sponge up inside me. You were too insensitive to care that I seemed tight and that your hammering away on me did not go in deep. I pretended to moan and beg for mercy, and you laughed. 'Tight as a virgin,' you said. Called me a stick whom no man would want and laughed at me."

"Abomination! Witch!" her husband screamed. "You are damned to prevent the conception of a Christian soul."

"Would not your sluts and serving girls have given much to know my trick?" she laughed. "They conceived your Christian bastards and you cast them out. I learned the trick from one of your whores, by the way."

She whirled away from him, her motion bringing her face to face with Brian. "And then he came . . ." she jeered. "He came riding through the forest with a small troup of mounted archers. He begged to stay the night at the château. Trenanay had left for a long stay at his hunting lodge doubtless with another of his mistresses. I offered them lodging. I offered him my bed. He was surprised. He was pleased. He called me beautiful. He kissed me as he moved above me. For the next fortnight I was well and truly loved. And then he rode away."

Brian gasped at the pain. "Who was my father?"

She hesitated. Then shook her head. "I cannot remember his name."

Brian screamed. His hands closed round her throat before Gillian could make a move to stop him. "Witch!" he screamed, throttling her. "Monster!"

411

"Brian!" Gillian yelled, leaping to drag her weight down on his arm.

"Kill her!" the Sire de Trenanay urged fiercely.

"Brian! For God's sake. For the sake of your own soul." Gillian forced her slim body between Brian's arms so that her face came between his and his mother's. "Brian," she pleaded. "She is your mother. Do not damn your soul."

Slowly his hands relaxed. His victim fell to the rushes of the solar in a dusty black heap and lay still. "Gillian," he muttered softly. She put her arms around his waist and hugged him hard.

Behind them they heard the old man's fierce hiss of anger and disgust. "Whoreson! Catamite!"

Brian set Gillian carefully aside. "Why? Does my lover offend you, Trenanay? At least no poor tortured girl sobs out her anguish because I have given her a bastard. At least no shamed wife plots revenge against me." He pointed at the feebly stirring figure. "She has destroyed your house. Her knife cuts deepest of all. Your line is destroyed along with my name. We were both better off dead."

The black eyes glittered; the death's head grinned slyly, speculatively. "You can do the house of Trenanay one last favor. One last act of expiation. Expiation for the sins of all." The voice sank to a whine. It cajoled. It fawned. "You with your mighty body and your precious golden principles. Ah! You thought I had forgotten them. How holy you felt when you won your spurs! I was a little bit ashamed of myself considering what I was."

Gillian caught at Brian's arm. "Do not listen to him, Brian. Come away. We will go to England. France has nothing for you anymore. Your father is English. Come."

Brian shrugged her off. "Expiation," he whispered. "Expiation."

"The sins of the fathers. The Scriptures speak of them."

"Brian! How can you listen? You have no sins. He is not your father."

"Pay my debt and your mother's," the voice begged. "Marshal Boucicaut has called for six knights and twenty men-at-arms from La Forêt to join with him to drive the English king from our shores. I cannot go. Nor have I any men to lead. But you could go. You could fight for France. You could die for the honor of Trenanay. The last of the line. I am dying even as I speak. I would acknowledge you as my son in this."

"Brian! For God's sake!"

He looked at her as if he had never seen her before. "He offers me the only course. To die with honor. I cannot live a bastard, a landless, nameless bastard."

She shook him. "Brian. You are talking to Gil. You are you. No one cares about these insane people anymore. Let us leave here now."

He nodded. "Yes. We will leave here now. I will go to my destiny. Hob will see you home." He touched her shoulder. "Let us leave here now," he repeated. As one in a trance, he led the way from the room.

Shivering in the grip of pure hatred such as she had never thought herself capable of, she glared at the two who remained. "Monsters!" she spat. "Monsters!" Whirling, she ran after him.

"No, Hob. I thank you, but I ride alone. You are an Englishman. I go to fight for France."

Hob shook his head. "You are an Englishman too, from what Lady Gillian tells me. You should join with Harry. Not Charles."

"My mother was French. A Frenchman reared me." Brian swallowed hard as he remembered the pain of Trenanay's rejection. "I could not . . ."

"Then I will accompany you," Hob promised simply. "A squire should go with his knight. I followed my father from Russia to Algeciras. We fought for whoever would pay for our sword . . . Christian or pagan. The squire obeys the knight."

Brian felt a lump rise in his throat. How could he ever have doubted this man? He shook his head. "If you will obey me, then you must see the ladies back safe to England." He pulled a heavy purse from beneath his fustian tunic. "Here is everything. I will leave all I own here at La Forêt. My fa— The Sire de Trenanay reluctantly agreed to buy it from me for gold. Likewise, the amount he would have given me for personal expenses has been included. Take it. It is a fair sum. Whatever is left after you and Alys are safely fixed should go to Gillian."

Hob took the purse, a velvet and doeskin pouch. Worked in dark gold was the motto, *Mucro Mors Cristo*.

"I should like Gillian to have the purse also. She does not understand, but someday she may. Perhaps the motto will help her to come to that understanding and to forgive me."

Hob drew a deep shuddering breath. His blue eyes searched Brian's face. "To tell the truth, I do not understand either," he admitted. "But I will not argue. You are the knight."

414

"Yes, I am." Brian turned away.

Brian ordered a supper served to him and Gillian in Stephen's room that evening. Before the food was brought, he arranged for hot baths before the fire. When Gillian came, he was waiting for her, garbed only in a robe of forest green wool.

"My lady." He knelt to her. "Tomorrow I go to fight for king and country."

She smiled uncertainly. Clearly he wanted her to play a part. Although she hated the thought of his going, she could not change his intent. If he wanted this scene, she would do her best for him. "My lord."

Rising, he drew her into his arms to kiss her. He kissed her hair, her eyes, her cheeks, her lips. His tongue caressed the interior of her mouth arousing her while his hands moved over her body. When she was shivering with need, he stood her away from him. "Now I shall undress you."

With tormenting slowness, he drew each garment from her body. As he cast each aside, he kissed the soft skin he revealed, teasing her unmercifully with teeth and lips and tongue.

"Brian," she sobbed, "oh, Brian."

"I love you. Gillian. I love you so."

Her naked body melted in his arms, her legs so weak they would not bear her weight. With a sad smile he lifted her. "Time for your bath."

Standing her in the small tub, he dipped the sponge in the warm water and laved her gently with its silken caress. The flickering firelight threw its colors over her pale skin and made it glow through the clear water. Like a man worshiping a goddess, he touched her satin smoothness, the swelling of her breasts, the trimness of her waist and hips, the golden curl of hair at the jointure of her thighs. On each of these he pressed his lips, his own body swelling with love.

At last he dried her body with a clean linen towel and surveyed her as a sculptor might survey his greatest handiwork. "Now to bed." He lifted her again holding her tightly against his chest. He slipped her in between clean white sheets and pulled the covers only to her waist. "To await me," he whispered.

Swiftly, he pulled off his robe and stepped into the tub. Catching up a rougher sponge than the one he had used for her, he scoured his body, repeatedly rinsing it until finally he was satisfied with the cleansing.

As she watched him, Gillian realized he was performing a ritual, the ancient purification ceremony preceding the battle. When his skin was glowing, he lifted a bucket of warm water and poured it over himself, letting it sluice down over his face and body. Stepping out, he dried carefully.

At last when she was trembling uncontrollably with desire at the sight of his magnificently muscled nude body, he was satisfied. His face, which had been serious throughout the bathing, now smiled. Purposefully, he strode toward her, his expression relaxed yet eager, his manhood hard.

Beside the bed he paused, one hand on the post, gazing down at her, looking his fill at her white skin, her wavy mass of honey-gold hair, her pale pink nipples stiffened with desire and crowning her swelling breasts. "You are so beautiful," he breathed. With the other hand he uncovered her lower body, allowing the sight of its perfection to rouse him to even greater heights of desire until he was hard as metal.

"My lord"—she faltered—"will you come into me?" As though she pleaded for his love, she raised her arms and spread her thighs, arching her bosom upward.

"Gillian!" With a cry of delight he positioned himself and slid into her welcoming body. Thereafter, he rode her silently. As each lunge was fiercely delivered, each withdrawal was punctuated with kisses assuring her of his eternal love.

At last when they could no longer bear the bliss, they came together in a shuddering climax. Brian cried her name aloud, his body stiffening in that ecstasy which was like the end of everything and yet the beginning. Gillian clasped him to her with legs and arms. Her open mouth she pressed against his shoulder hiding her face against his neck, so he would not see her tears.

They arose together at dawn. She dressed in her men's clothes and then assisted him to garb himself for war. Only the plate armor would be carried on the back of his saddle.

Silently, she buckled on his sword, her eyes glistening with tears. 'Twas the last step in the ritual. He was ready. Face to face they stared into each other's eyes. From around his neck he lifted the golden medallion she knew so well. It was a part of him. Whenever they made love it struck her breasts; she had kissed it often in her passion. Now he placed it around her neck. "I give you my life, my love, and my honor. With this token I wed you in the sight of God."

With a cry of pain she broke. "You fool! You magnificent, honorable fool! How can you throw away what we have? What are those two miserable people up there in that solar that you should expiate their sins? Suppose your mother lied. She lied to your father all these years. I doubt if she knows the truth herself. They are both deranged with grief and hatred. Brian . . ." She fell to her knees. "Do not go! Come with me to England. You can be whatever you want to be."

His eyes longed for her, his mouth softened. For a moment he wavered. Then the expression was gone. "Farewell, my lady. I go to fight for the king." He turned on his heel and left her sobbing brokenly.

Chapter Thirty-One

"And you could not dissuade him?" Alys stared at the purse Hob weighed in his hand.

"He goes to die. For him honor is everything. Both Gil and I knew the destruction his mother wrought when she told him he was a bastard. His unsullied name has meant everything. He is like a Galahad, an Arthur, a Roland. Despite all the troubles he has gotten himself into, he still believes that people are essentially honorable and good."

Alys smiled up at the squire. "His true friends have done nothing to disavow him of that notion."

He quirked an eyebrow at her. "I am not good, Lady Alys."

"Nor I, but I am not so deep-dyed in evil that I cannot admire it and recognize it when I see it."

Hob stared at the pouch, then thrust it back under his tunic. "I must go," he muttered. "Gil is with Brian now.

He will be well cared for. Get a good night's sleep. We must rise in the morning early. I want to be away from this ruin as soon as possible. No good can come of remaining here."

"The chatelaine is obviously deranged. Her husband is a cripple according to Gil. He is near to death. She controls everything." He shrugged his shoulders. "Who can say? Best be on our way to England as quickly as may be."

"I thank you for coming to me with this news." Alys walked with him to the door of her room. There she leaned against the facing as he swung it open. Smiling sweetly, she crossed her arms across her chest. "Get a good rest."

Hob paused in the doorway regarding her fair form speculatively. Faint dark smudges still remained under her eyes, and her skin had a fragile translucent quality. Not only her courage but her physical strength had been sorely tried since she had thrown herself on the mercy of strangers. He was a man, with a man's desires; but as his fortunes had fallen, a natural fastidiousness as well as a certain snobbishness had forbade him to seek release with wenches from the taverns and whores from the army's tail.

Tentatively, fearful of frightening her, he raised his hand to touch her cheek. The rough tan fingers looked strange against the pearly skin. Her gaze remained steady at his touch. Encouraged, he allowed his thumb to trace the corner of her mouth and the indentation of a dimple next to it.

Her breathing altered slightly and her arms dropped away to her sides. Mesmerized by his touch, she allowed her eyelids to veil the ardent response.

Emboldened by the reactions he knew so well, he

trailed his fingers down the side of her cheek until the side of his hand rested under her chin. Pressing his thumb gently to her lower lip, he tilted up her face. Carefully he searched for some sign of revulsion or fear.

None was forthcoming. Instead she seemed to be waiting for him. Gently he touched her lips with his own. They were sweet as he had imagined they would be. He felt a powerful surge of desire. His other arm went round her waist drawing her to him. He felt her arms encircle his neck.

As he lifted her against him, he stepped backward pushing the door closed with a nudge of his shoulder. Her soft breasts pressed against him through the material of her garments. He could feel her nipples hardening. Suddenly, he wanted to see them. He wanted this woman badly.

To take her against her will would destroy the camaraderie of the journey. With just the three of them, he did not dare to create hostility. Dizzily, he held her at arms length. "Alys," he began huskily, "I am a man, my lady, with a man's desires. I must . . ."

She smiled winningly, her hands caressing the back of his neck. "Of course, you are. I know you must. And I am a woman. And I have been without a man for longer than I care to remember. I am not even sure I remember how this is done."

He grinned at her. "Allow me to be your teacher, lady."

As he informed her later, she needed very little instruction. Alys had spent her younger days arousing an old man. If she failed to arouse him, she would be beaten. Her skills brought Hob quickly to a heartstopping climax. Because he had been used to taking the lead in love-

421

making, he was unprepared for the pleasure she brought him to. Wildly, he writhed beneath her eager lips and knowing hands until he lost control and exploded helplessly like an untried youth.

Later, when he had recovered himself, he repaid her with a long slow titillation of her senses until she was moaning and panting for release. When he sheathed himself within her, her cries of pleasure and gratitude rang out in the still room.

"I have never known such pleasure," Alys admitted later as they lay together in her bed. Naked beside him, her hands woven behind her head, she allowed him free access to her body, reveling in his gentle caresses. No one had ever touched her in such a manner. Her breasts had only been mauled and bruised by her husband. Never had someone kissed and admired them. Tears trickled from the corners of her eyes at the thought of so many wasted years of pain and degradation.

Hob lay with his cheek against her belly, his hands clasping her rounded hips. "You were made for pleasure," he whispered, his breath tickling her so that she stirred and arched slightly. "What a terrible life you must have led. Yet how lucky I am."

"What do you mean?" she asked amazed.

"I have never been made love to like that before. Never has a woman set about so purposefully and skillfully to bring me to pleasure. I could not control myself. You were the mistress in all things."

She blushed. "I am glad you were pleased."

"Pleased." He raised himself on his elbows to stare into her eyes. "I am in heaven. I am in ecstasy." Complimenting her extravagantly, he began to rain kisses over her bare flesh while she giggled and twisted with pleasure at the tickling of his lips and breath.

So they passed the night, alternately sleeping and waking to make love joyously.

When Hob finally woke to daylight streaming in the window, he found Alys sitting up in bed, staring at nothing. "What are you thinking?"

She smiled. "I am thinking how wonderful it will be to look back on this as well as any other times we may steal. These lovely memories will sustain me for the rest of my life in my nephew's house, or wherever I go."

Rolling over on his side, he propped himself up on his elbow. His chunky frame, laced with scars and covered with a thick mat of coarse blond hair, could by no means be called handsome. While he was slipping gracefully into middle age, he was not the fair-skinned youth he had once been. He sighed. "I regret that such as I would be the stuff of your memories, Alys."

She looked at him frankly, then she smiled again. "You are much more than I ever dreamed, Hob. Believe me. I am so happy." Gently, she bent to kiss him on the mouth. Then drew hastily away. "We must go. Gil will be searching for us. No doubt he has garbed Sir Brian for his war. We must go and bid him farewell and good luck."

Brian had already departed when they descended. Instead the chatelaine of La Forêt confronted them. Her face reminded Alys of an ancient apple that had somehow escaped being eaten during the long winter. Lipless, her eyes reduced to glittering slits, she concealed the rest of her body completely, even wearing a black wimple that covered her hair and forehead to the eyebrows.

Whereas the night they had first seen her she had been

cold and still, now her eyes darted everywhere and her taloned hands plucked nervously at the air. "He has gone like a fool!"

Hob choked with anger at her first words. "Are you sure, madam, that you are the mother of that man? Better would I believe him to be a bastard sired by your husband and foisted on you. None of your blood could ever be anything but evil."

A slight smile flashed across the mummy face and as quickly disappeared. "Think you not, impudent wretch?"

"I *know* not, madam." He bowed slightly. "I come to tell you that the three of us will depart as soon as may be."

"By your leave, madam," Alys interposed. "I thank you for your hospitality. I will leave you now to prepare our packs." Without waiting to be dismissed, Alys hurried back up the stairs.

The woman in black sighed. "You do well to leave immediately. Trenanay is furiously angry. The sight of Brian coupled with the knowledge that he did not sire him has made him mad. He talks incessantly of hellfire and damnation." Her eyes took on a beseeching look.

Without a trace of pity Hob returned her look. "Then if I were you, madam, I would look to my soul. Call a confessor and obtain unction."

She looked away. "I cannot expect unction," she quavered. "I am not sorry for my sins."

"Then God pity you, madam," Hob said as he, too, turned to go.

"Sir!"

He stopped, his hand on the door.

"Send the young man who accompanied my son yesterday. I would have words with him."

"Gil Fletcher. I do not know whether he will come. But I will deliver your message."

"What can that witch want with me?"

"Do not go," Alys advised. "She only wants to wound and insult. She has no pity for either father or son. What a monster!" She shook her head as if she had difficulty in believing what she had witnessed.

Gil looked to Hob for guidance. The squire shrugged. "If you wish, Gil, then go. Otherwise, we will leave immediately." The three started down the stairs together. Halfway down, a servant met them.

He bowed courteously to Gil and addressed her in labored English. "My lady bids you wait upon her, if you please. She bade me tell you she will require only a few minutes of your time so as not to delay your departure."

Gil glanced questioningly at Hob, who shrugged his shoulders. "We will wait for you," was all he said.

"Please, sir."

"Oh, very well." Although she dreaded the encounter, her curiosity was aroused. She followed the servant back up the staircase and into another wing of the château.

At last the man knocked on a door at the end of a long hall. After a brief moment, he opened it and stepped back obsequiously. The familiar cracked voice invited her into the room. "Wait without, Cavilon," she instructed the servant.

Gil stepped into a room remarkable in the Château de la Forêt for its color and light. On three sides were windows that looked out over the forest, while the heavy old furnishings were draped and cushioned with bright blues and greens. Seated in a heavy curule chair before

425

an embroidery frame was Brian's mother. Like raven's wings, her black garments fluttered around her as she gestured to Gil to come closer.

"My son appears to have more than a passing affection for you," she sneered.

Concealing her surprise that the woman knew English, Gil clamped her jaws tightly. One part of her longed to set the record straight about the relationship between Brian and her. On the other hand, she could not be sure that the fact she was a woman, traveling in men's clothes, posing as a boy, would really improve this woman's opinion. Furthermore, she did not really care what they thought, she decided. Silently, she waited.

The woman gestured impatiently. "Come closer."

Gil crossed to the windows.

"In the light you are not ill favored." The gold-flecked eyes glittered. "So much for my son's chances of fathering. 'Tis probably as well." She stared out across the forest.

Gil cleared her throat. "I assume you did have some purpose in bringing me here," she remarked with exaggerated politeness.

The chatelaine shrugged. "Yes, I suppose so. Yes." After a moment's hesitation, she pointed with an index finger, frightfully crippled with arthritis. "Open yonder chest and bring the small casket you find hidden in it under the blankets."

Puzzled, Gil did as she was bidden. The blankets were old and musty-smelling with signs of powdery mildew in their creases. Brushing them aside with a wary hand, she uncovered a small ornately carved casket, studded with small blue stones and inlaid with gold.

"Bring it here," the chatelaine grumbled impatiently.

Gil set it on the small table at her right hand and stepped back.

With hands that fumbled and shook slightly, the woman opened the lock and lifted the lid. The interior, lined with green velvet, contained several pouches made of the same material. Gently, the taloned fingers brushed the soft stuff. The wrinkled face flushed slightly as if precious memories flooded into her mind which had been kept locked as tightly as the chest had been.

"Sit down," she rasped, indicating a chair beneath a window. "Pull that thing over here, so I can show you."

When Gil had obeyed, the lady of La Forêt lifted the first pouch and pulled it open. "Hold out your hand." Twenty gold pieces slid warmly onto her palm. At Gil's astonished expression, the lady cackled. "Part of my marriage dot. I kept a portion of it back, in hope that some day I might be able to leave here. But I never did." She tossed the empty pouch onto Gil's lap. "Now put them back in."

Puzzled, Gil slipped the heavy gold coins back inside the velvet and drew the string.

"Now, these"—the lady opened another pouch— "were given me by my mother. She loved pretty things and my father was very extravagant. He loved to dress her in elegant clothing and jewels and parade her around for all the nobles in Normandy to see. She was a beauty and he was rich. They had a fair exchange." She held up a necklace, two matching bracelets, and a ring of gold all set with magnificent baroque pearls. "I never really cared for these," she sniffed, handing them in turn to Gil to put back in their pouch. "Pearls make me think of fish. But my mother was stunningly beautiful in them."

Brian's mother opened two more pouches containing

sets of jewels, one of rubies and one of dark green jade, which she declared to be the most valuable of all. "Do you know where jade comes from, foolish boy?" she snapped. Before Gil could shake her head, she began to explain. "From Cathay. All the way from Cathay. And the darker green, the more expensive and rare it is. These gems are very, very rare. Worth a king's ransom as the romances say."

She handed away each in turn, then came to the last pouch. "These are my jewels," she said bitterly. Ripping open the last green pouch she emptied the contents onto the table. A simple betrothal ring, a marriage ring, and a small gold medallion clattered onto its hard surface. She laughed softly. Scooping up the rings onto the ends of her fingers, she waved them at Gil. "These Trenanay gave me." Contemptuously, she allowed them to drop into Gil's hand from off her fingers. "And this," she held up the medallion, "was given me by the man who was Brian's father. There is a name on it. But that name remains with me only. Brian has no need of either of these two men. Neither was particularly good. But at least one was preferable to the other."

Still clutching the medallion to her breast, she handed the casket to Gillian. "Put all the pouches back in and take the casket."

"Yes, lady. Where shall I take it?"

The woman looked disgusted. "With you, you fool."

Gillian almost dropped the box. Her mouth gaped open. "Why?"

"Good God! Do you want me to say it? Or are you really that stupid? Because you are my son's love. Because I have hurt him irreparably. Because I wish to make amends in some small way. I would give these things to his wife, but he will probably not live to have one. So I give them to you." Her voice was a rasping quaver.

"B-But you think . . . that is . . . you know I am a . . . boy."

"And I am an adulteress. What stones have I to throw at you? Perversion is no new thing in this old, corrupt world."

Gillian stared aghast.

The chatelaine coughed deeply, her fist containing the gold medallion pressed tightly against her chest. "Get out. . . . Take your hoard and go!"

Faintly nauseous, Gillian headed for the door.

"Wait!" The old voice was only a breath of sound. Gillian froze, her scalp prickling. "If Brian should by some miracle survive, he will come to you. I know it. Tell him . . ." The silence was pregnant.

"What shall I tell him?"

Then a sigh. "Tell him what you will. . . ."

Gillian closed the door quietly behind her.

"You must go quickly, sir." The servant Cavilon touched Gillian's arm. "No. Not that way. The Sire de Trenanay has already placed guards at the main doors."

"But my friends . . ."

"They have been escorted ahead of you."

Suspicious, yet having no choice, Gillian clutched the casket tightly under her arm. "Where are you taking me?"

"If *m'sieur* will please follow closely. The way is somewhat tedious here. We must go carefully, yet swiftly."

Fearfully, Gil stared around her at the cobwebs festooning the dark low passage. Only the servant's candle lighted the way. "Where are you taking me?" she demanded. "I . . ."

"*S'il vous plaît, m'sieur,* bend very low."

Scuttling along in a crouch, following the servant's lead, the walls closing in around her, she could do little but obey his instructions. Suppose the sire had planned this. Would she be knocked in the head and buried down here? With her free hand, she felt for Brian's medallion dangling between her breasts inside her smock.

Poor Brian! What a terrible experience! Poor Gil! And Hob and Alys perhaps lying dead somewhere ahead. She shuddered.

The servant came to a small door.

She heard the clinking of a chain, the rattle of a bolt. A small door only about three feet high was dragged inward.

"Go, *m'sieur.*" She squeezed past him and out into the dim light of a grove of trees.

"Hob! Alys!"

Hob swung her horse around for her. "Mount up, Gil. We must ride fast. The Sire de Trenanay wants to kill us."

Gillian caught hold of the reins. "But why? We have done nothing."

"The sire is shamed," Alys explained. "He wants no one to spread the word that Brian is not his son. Cavilon told me that only he among the household staff knows the real truth. He fears for his own life but will not leave his mistress." She regarded Gil curiously. "What have you there?"

Gil unfastened her pack from the back of the saddle and unrolled it. Carefully she placed the jewel casket within it and retied the straps. "The most amazing thing has happened. . . ."

"Save it," Hob advised. "We must escape."

Springing into the saddle, Gillian wheeled her mount to follow the other two. Silently, they walked their horses among the dark trees. A heavy stand of evergreens with long needles had dropped a thick mat over the forest floor, effectively muffling the sounds of passage. No birds called from the branches. Once they heard the stirring of some small creature. Once a group of mounted men rode by some distance away, but they were screened from view.

They rode for more than two hours before Hob called a halt to rest the horses. "What did the old witch want to see you about?" he asked.

Gil shook her head. "She feared for her soul, I suppose. She gave me some of Brian's heritage."

"Poor Brian," Hob said softly.

"What a terrible family!" Alys agreed.

Her comment ended the conversation. They sat silent until at last Hob signaled them to move on.

Bringing up the rear as they rode onward, Gillian imagined once or twice that she could smell smoke.

Chapter Thirty-Two

"Do you know where we are?"

Hob smiled wearily. "Our exact location, no. These forests are thick and stretch for miles. As you may have observed, one tree looks much the same as the next."

Gil perked an eyebrow in Alys's direction. "At least we shall be jolly though lost."

"However," the squire interrupted her sarcasm, "I do know the direction we should be traveling in. *Et voilà!* We are traveling north and west."

"Toward?"

"The channel, what else?"

"Of course, the channel. And when we arrive we will easily ride our horses in and let them swim across."

Hob grinned. "If you prefer to swim your horse across, Gil, you may do so. Knowing your aversion to sea travel, I can imagine that you would. However, Lady Alys and I, less adventurous creatures, will take ship at Dieppe for England."

Gillian laughed. "I have a much greater aversion to drowning, sir. I shall take ship with you although 'twill be a frightful experience. I swear that once home in England, I shall think carefully before bathing."

Alys swayed in her saddle. They had been riding with only short stops for rest since leaving the château. Hob guided his horse back to her. "About ready to rest for the evening?" He patted her hands where they crossed on the horse's withers.

"Oh, I can continue." Alys sat up straight and smiled at him alertly. "I am fine. The good night's rest at the château gave me much strength. Truly."

Gil, too, guided her horse to ride beside Alys. "Well, I am wretchedly weary and sore. Horses are another thing I shall regard doubtfully once I get home to York."

"I was hoping we would come out of the woods and find somewhere to spend the night," Hob told them. "But I fear we will have to sleep on the ground. Without fresh water."

"We can ride on," Alys protested. "I can . . ."

Hob flung up his hand for silence as a distant drumming of hoofbeats interrupted the conversation. Gillian and Alys both looked at him in alarm. Motioning them to follow him, he reined his horse round and led off in the direction of the sound.

The forest began to thin. The trees were farther apart; the underbrush was thicker. Although it presented no problem for the horses, the soft muffling qualities of the pine needles were replaced by rustling and crackling as the mounts breasted the scrub. Through the trees wound a gray road and beyond it a dark river.

Hob raised his arm and pointed. "Unless I miss my guess, 'tis the Bethune."

Gillian came up beside him. "You really do know the country," she commented admiringly.

He eased himself in the saddle, his tiredness showing in the deep lines on his face and the droop of his shoulders. "I rode all over Flanders, Artois, and Picardy with the cavalry some twenty years ago," he acknowledged. "I will admit 'twas easier then. I was younger. 'Twas then I learned to speak the language."

The sounds of horsemen approaching roused him to alertness. "Back into the trees," he commanded.

Immediately, Alys turned her horse and cantered away.

Gil hesitated. Hob was not moving. "Hob?"

"Go on, my lady," he urged. "I shall parley with these people. If they be good honest men, mayhap they will allow us to journey with them. My guess is that they are, since they ride openly taking no care to go quietly."

"And if they should not be?"

"Then you and Alys are safe."

"I will stand my ground with you."

He had not time to argue. Four horsemen appeared in the deepening twilight. At the sight of the two ahead of them, they slowed their mounts to a walk. A look of incredulity spread over Hob's face as they approached.

Their garments were ordinary enough, being merely black cloth jackets which came down over their black hose. Although each wore a badge, the day was already too far done to discern its inscription. But strung over the shoulder and across the chest of each one was a fine yew bow. One's head was bare, but the other three wore conical hats familiar to every Englishman.

"By God!" Hob exclaimed. "Mounted archers. What cheer, lads?" He raised his voice at the same time he urged his horse toward them.

"English?" came the incredulous exclamation.

"Right. Howard of Rothingham." Hob clasped arms with the first archer who grinned through a grizzled beard.

"Nicholas Warrenby from Winchelsea. What do ye here so far from home?"

"Esquire to Sir Brian de Trenanay until he released me from his service. I will not fight against good English lads." Hob shook hands round with the other three before motioning for Gil to come forward.

"Here is Master Gil Fletcher from York Minster, one of the finest fletchers in the north parts as well as bowman master."

Nicholas Warrenby cast a calculating eye at Gil's slender form. "Mayhap you'd be willin' to replace one of the good lads that died in this wretched land," he suggested.

Hob held up his hand before Gillian could speak. "Gil is just a boy, Master Warrenby. He is a good archer, true, but you and I both know too many good archers who have not the stomach for fighting."

Nicholas made no reply to Hob's observation, but changed the subject. "Where be ye bound?"

"For the port at Dieppe there to take ship back to England. Gil and I are accompanied by Gil's old father who even now waits in the woods. Fetch him, Gil."

The mounted archer grinned. "The English army crossed the bridge at Arques this very day. The Castellan was so terrified of Young Harry that he provided us with bread and wine. Tonight we enjoy the feast, and

436

tomorrow we march on for Calais. At least join us for the meal."

Hob looked doubtful until Gil rode up with Alys drooping miserably in the saddle. Her posture, her matted whitened hair, her general air of despair and exhaustion changed his mind. "With pleasure, Master Warrenby."

The camp of Henry V on the north side of the Bethune was a scene of confusion. Four days march from Harfleur had brought them almost a third of the distance to Calais. Resistance had been encountered at three towns and summarily disposed of with almost no losses. Though the weather was unseasonably hot and muggy, the French wine made all things bearable.

Nicholas himself showed them a place to unroll their gear and bed down for the night before inviting them to sup with men in his own troop of mounted archers. The black-garbed men dispensed with their weapons and leather caps and lounged at ease round the watch fire.

"Was Harfleur a long seige?" Hob wanted to know.

"Just over three weeks," Nicholas growled. "Long enough to get everybody sick with the damned trots. We've lost more to dysentery than to the French. The Earl of Suffolk, himself that was so strong, turned up his toes. Duke Clarence, the king's own brother, is terrible weakened."

"Aye," one of Nicholas's troop observed. "Likely to die in the winter, he is. That kind of thing really runs a man down."

"We'd still be lying there up to our ankles in our own filth were it not for us miners," a man squatting on the outside of the circle avowed.

Nicholas rolled his eyes to the heavens. "You miners,"

he sneered. "Dig a trench, and the French dug another one right opposite and blocked yours up. We'd have been there 'til doomsday if we'd waited for you."

The miner looked hurt. He rose to his feet with injured dignity. "The king could never have got his guns in place without us."

Nicholas relented. "Why right you are on that score!" He grinned at Gillian. "I warrant you'd like to have been there, lad, to hear 'The King's Daughter' open up. Knocked the walls right down she did. She and 'The Messenger.'"

Gillian nodded uncertainly. "But what about the people inside the town . . . and the soldiers. Were many of them killed?"

Nicholas shook his head. "Only if they was dumb enough to stick their heads over the walls and out from behind the screens. Cannons like those big gunnys are for knocking stones out of walls."

"And was the king ordering the cannons?"

"Why, bless him, he was! Hardly slept did Young Harry. I recollect one night when I was standing guard, he come by me. Right handsome man he is, hair shaved up the back of his neck just like his men. He asks me my name, and I tells him right out, 'Nicholas Warrenby, Your Majesty.'"

"'What do you call me when I am not standing before you, Nicholas,' he says."

"Well, before I thought, I blurted right out, 'Young Harry, Your Majesty.'"

"'To make a difference between me and my father, Old Harry,' he says."

"I was that upset. I didn't know what he might do to me, but he just laughs sort of quiet like and pats me on the shoulder. I nodded my head. 'I was with your father at Shrewsbury,' I says, 'when I was a young man.'"

"'Then we are brothers,' he says. 'I wonder how many more are here today that were at Shrewsbury.' He tucks his head and walks on with his hands behind him, like he's thinkin' about it and rememberin'."

The miner snorted. "Every time Nicholas tells that tale it gets longer. Before long King Henry will have invited him to sup."

"How did you finally get in?" Hob pressed. Battlewise himself, he knew enough to discount many soldiers' tall tales. The truth was under all the embellishment. But one had to keep searching for it.

"The gunners kept poundin' away at the barbican," Nicholas explained.

"Nearly every gun," another man added excitedly. "Whoo-ee! The noise was something fierce. We all had padding from our jackets stuffed in our ears."

"Well, the French saw we were about to knock it down, so they came charging out, riding right for the gun emplacements. And it was cut and hack. I don't mind tellin' you it was pretty bloody there for a few minutes."

Gillian turned pale. "I should not like to see men killed, or to be forced to kill one myself."

"But they're French, lad," Nicholas insisted. "French."

"I know," Gillian tucked her head, thinking of Brian. Sharp pain lanced through her at the memory of their love. Where was he tonight? Was he thinking of her, regretting the loss of her as bitterly as she regretted the forces that pulled them apart? Or . . . she closed her eyes as the pain stabbed deeper . . . was he lying wounded or dead in some lonely field? And why? The innocent recipient of his parents' vengeance.

Nicholas continued the story. "When they came chargin' out, 'course that's when we came in. Right, lads?" He looked round him at his grinning troop. They had all heard the story many times before, but like children, they loved to hear it again.

"We came galloping up on our horses and let fly with a steady stream of arrows. They hardly touched those gunners. We was too strong for them. The French can't stomach English broadheads. And that's a fact."

Hob saluted them all with the jug of wine that they had passed him. "Right!" he exclaimed. "I remember a yeoman archer who used to ride with my father. Tough man. Could let loose a half a dozen arrows while you blinked, and hit a man's thumb at three hundred yards. He liked peacock feathers for fletching," Hob remarked aside to Gil.

"Peacock's good," Nicholas nodded, "but duck's the best."

"Get on with the story, Nick," someone urged.

"That I will, lads. Just let me wet my throat." Nicholas accepted the jug hastily offered by Hob and turned it up, drinking noisily. "As I was saying . . . The French comes chargin' out and we rides to meet them. There was several groups of us, but the main one was led by young Johnny Holland. He yells 'Huntingdon! A Huntingdon!' for that was his father, you know. We all knows he's our leader and follows him. Right over the barbican . . ."

At this juncture one of the troop extended his feet toward Gil to show how his boots were charred. "Like runnin' through hell," he nodded seriously.

". . . across the barbican and it blazin' away, through the rubble in the moat, and over the palisade . . ." Nicholas's hands made wild gestures to mime slipping

440

and sliding and climbing.

"They knew we was in," said the man with burned boots. "They started hollerin' for peace."

"That they did," Nicholas declared. "That they did. And we won through." He looked around with a satisfied grin and took another long drink of wine.

The little group around the watch fire had grown as more and more came to hear Nicholas's story. The wine was passed around again and again.

Gillian began to feel dizzy. Her nose felt numb at the very tip as did her lips. "Wha's wrong wi' me?" she whispered to Hob.

He grinned at her. "You are drunk, Gil. Mayhap you had better find your way to our place and roll up beside Alys."

She shook her head. "I'll jus' not drink anymore. But, oh, Hob, 'tis exciting. I jus' can't go bed."

Someone broke into a ribald song about an archer and a lass who liked him to draw his bow and shoot straight. Gillian turned bright red but held her ground.

Again Hob questioned Nicholas. "Why are you heading for Calais?" He looked around him. "You *are* heading for Calais I assume."

A silky voice broke in between the squire and Gillian. "*Chevauchée*, my dear Hob, and dear Gil too. How amusing and amazing!"

"Ranulf!" Gil leaped to her feet in terror. The alcohol fumes vanished from her brain as if they had never been. The mellow evening had become suddenly dark with menace.

Ranulf caught her arm and steadied her. "Ah, my little fletcher." He laughed. Before Hob's tired, slightly drunken brain could function, Ranulf had dragged her

441

away from the fire.

Despite her desperate struggles in the darkness, Ranulf's hands were like manacles of steel around her wrists. "Be still!" he snarled, his breath hot in her ear. "Otherwise I tear that smock off you and expose you as the whore you are. These men are drunk. What do you think will become of you if they discover you are female?"

The threat, coupled with the pain in her wrists where Ranulf squeezed them, subdued her. Ranulf herded her farther away into the darkness. Behind them he heard Hob's alarmed voice. "This way, Hob," he called.

As the squire thudded up to them, Ranulf held Gillian tightly against his chest. "That is quite far enough," he warned. "Her bones are so fragile. Just a small amount of pressure could crack one or maybe both of them in each wrist. So painful."

Hob flexed his muscles, groaning at his own failure to look out for her.

Ranulf grinned. "Why not just wander back over to where Master Warrenby is embroidering his tales?" he invited. "He is quite entertaining. I have heard his stories. In fact this little march has been quite boring except for old Nick. That is, until tonight," he finished silkily.

"Let her go!" Hob grated.

"Moan for him, dear girl," Ranulf whispered, giving her wrists a vicious twist. Agonizing pain shot through her as she bent double under his hands. A small cry sprang from her mouth as sweat popped out on her forehead.

"Not quite a moan," Ranulf mocked her. "We might

442

have to practice on that. Be off with you, Hob. I promise not to hurt her more than she can bear. She will be quite all right on the morrow. I just want to spend a part of my evening with her, renewing old acquaintances."

Hob dropped his hands. "I will go back to the fire on one condition."

Ranulf waited, never relaxing his grip on Gillian's wrists.

"You must stay here, where I can see the two of you talking."

Ranulf drew a deep mocking sigh. "Oh, very well. But I swear I was not going to savage her. Not here. Not a valuable bowman like her. But you must leave us alone, Hob. Otherwise, I shall be forced to reveal her identity to the men of this camp. Most of them like a wench from the army's tail . . . not being so fastidious as I."

Slowly Hob withdrew, leaving Gillian alone in the dark with the man who had paid good money to have her dropped into the channel. As the squire went back toward the fire, Ranulf eased his hold on her wrists. "Straighten up, my dear. If you give me your promise you will do nothing stupid, I will even release your wrists."

In a voice tight with pain Gillian promised.

Instantly, his hands fell away. Quickly she turned to face him, backing a step away from him. He raised his hands with palms up. "Peace, I swear."

"You do not know the meaning of the word."

"Peace?"

"No. Swear."

He chuckled. His eyes glittered in the dark as he assessed her figure up and down. "You look much the worse for wear," he said at last. "And skinnier too. I felt you. All knobs and bones."

Gillian said nothing. Nervous rigors racked her body. Only the fear of what he could do to her by exposing her sex made her able to stand and face him.

"I must admit that I was amazed to see you. At first I did not recognize you. I could not believe my eyes."

"I am not surprised. You must have thought the dead w-were walking." Gil's teeth chattered so that she could hardly speak.

"Cold?" Ranulf questioned softly. "But 'tis a warm night."

Something very like a sob escaped her. "I have done you no harm. Not ever," she quavered.

Ranulf appeared to be considering. He placed one hand on his hip while the other he lifted to lay alongside his cheek. "Well, in one sense, I suppose you have not. But in another. Oh, Gil—by the way, what is your real name?"

"Gillian Fletcher?"

"Gillian. Pretty. As I was saying, in one sense you have not, but in other ways, you have done me many disservices. For example, Wat has left me."

Gillian did not know what to say. The tone of Ranulf's last sentence was different from the mocking silky sound that he usually adopted. There was a touch of sincere sadness.

Ranulf drew a deep breath. "Yes, Wat left me. And took Hereward with him."

Following a moment of awkward silence, during which the sounds of the camp seemed to move farther and farther away, Gillian cleared her throat. "I am very sorry," she said huskily. "Friends are rare."

"Ah, yes." Ranulf's voice was angry. "Friends are rare

and hard to come by. So are lovers," he added significantly.

"But surely you cannot blame me for their leaving." Gillian raised her hand in a gesture of appeal. "I had nothing to do with Wat, and I did not even know the other man."

"If you had not interrupted my pleasure with Brian, I would have quickly dispensed with him and gone on to pay proper attention to Wat and Hereward. As it was, they became jealous of my interest in him and sought solace in each other."

Gillian gasped, too amazed at his statement to be afraid. "That is the most twisted piece of reasoning I have ever heard."

Ranulf laughed. "Yes, it is. I rather pride myself on thinking of things like that. But people like you will have to have explanations for my behavior. I simply think up outrageous ones. The real reason is that I do things because I want to. The idea occurs to me. It tickles my fancy, and I do it."

"But . . . but . . ."

"Gillian, the truth is that I am without a single person whom I feel real affection for. In fact, I hardly know anyone. The young man I was . . . er . . . traveling with on the *Catherine* caught this terrible dysentery and died in agony. I was prepared to be bored for a long time. These soldiers are such louts, no delicacy, no sensitivity. And then I saw you."

"But I am a female."

"I know, dear. But you are so easy to tease and torment. It will quite take my mind off the boredom of the trip. So I want you to bid good-bye to that lout, Hob. Send him on his way to join the king's troops. They all need squires over there. So many poor lads dead, you know."

Gillian felt a sick helplessness. "And come with you?" she gasped.

"Exactly." Ranulf smiled delightedly. "See how quick and intelligent you are. You will provide me no end of pleasure."

Chapter Thirty-Three

"Ah, the *chevauchée*," Ranulf declaimed over his shoulder to Gillian. At his instructions she now rode as a good servant should, slightly behind him on his left.

"What, Ranulf?" Her eyes restlessly searched the horizon. Since he talked almost constantly for the sheer joy of listening to his own ravings, she had decided to pay as little attention to him as possible.

He pulled his horse, waited for her to come abreast, and then rapped her smartly with his leather thong. The lash slapped her thigh and forearm both thickly covered in the archer's black padded jacket. "Pay attention to me, Gillian," he commanded angrily. "I was extolling the virtues of the *chevauchee*, both as a tool of war in the hands of our good King Henry, and as an opportunity for clever men to turn a profit."

While the lash had not even stung through her thick

clothing, the humiliation of being struck without being able to retaliate infuriated Gillian. She bent on him a look of utmost loathing. "You mean as an opportunity for looting, do you not?"

"Nonsense. The French are our enemies." He smiled blandly as he patted a heavy purse which he had taken great pleasure in showing her the first night of their enforced companionship.

"The king considers that these are his subjects," she reminded him stiffly. "He has issued stiff rules for their protection. 'No man shall rob either merchant, vitaler, surgeon, nor barber.'"

"Very well recited," he sneered scathingly. "But keep your mouth shut around the marshal, or your little secret will be out also. Remember."

"I will," she nodded angrily. Defiance stiffened her spine. "But you put away that lash, or I will tell. If you try to hurt me too much, I might decide that others would be kinder to me than you."

Suddenly, he threw back his head and laughed. His teeth were very white, and the eyeteeth, very sharp. He reminded her of a fox. His dark eyes flashed as he smiled. "Threats. Ah, Gillian. What a pleasure it is to match wits with you. Your tongue is most acerbic, my little fletcher. Are you sure you are not really a boy disguised as a girl disguised as a boy?"

She shot him a fulminating look.

"Perhaps I should have those clothes off you tonight to check for sure. I might have been mistaken. Perhaps those protuberances are merely pasted on." He made curving motions with his hands to illustrate the protuberances to which he alluded, then laughed uproariously when she blushed and touched spurs to her horse's flanks.

She had endured this kind of talk for twenty miles the day the army had left Arques. While waiting their turn to cross at Bresle, he had insisted that they sit together on a grassy bank. There he had regaled her with an explicit description of one of the techniques by which he made love to the men he called his lovers. When she had tried to break away, he had caught hold of her ankle and gripped it tightly while he pinched and stroked her calf.

Remembering her rage and humiliation of yesterday, she seethed with suppressed anger. She had had no opportunity to speak to Hob or Alys after Ranulf had dragged her away. A worried look on her face, Alys had waved at her when she rode across the bridge with the rest of the retainers in the baggage train. Gillian had pasted a big false smile on her face and waved back gaily. No sense in worrying Alys.

Now the sun's heat combined with a pervading stillness to create a sultry, unpleasant day. The archer's heavy black clothing absorbed the sun's rays. Gillian could feel perspiration trickling down her face and steaming out of every pore of her skin. Her whole body was bathed in it, and the rough English wool itched abominably.

Ranulf caught up with her. "The *chevauchée*, as I was saying," he continued as if no interruption had occurred, "is a time-honored military practice. In this case, however, many of the nobles did not want to make it. The king himself knew if practiced as it should be, it was impossible. So we are compromising." He looked at her narrowly to be sure that she was listening.

She sighed. "How are we compromising, Ranulf?"

"Call me 'milord.' We are compromising because we

should be moving from Harfleur to Rouen to Paris thereby conquering France. Instead we are actually moving north toward Calais. The nobles know the king cannot take Paris with only six thousand men. The king knows it too."

As she digested this information, Gillian found herself paying attention to his lecture. "Then why this?" she asked. "Why march through the country following the seacoast? If we are going to take ship at Calais, why not take ship at Harfleur and go home?"

Ranulf rolled his eyes. "Because, you stupid creature, the king cannot just turn around and run home with his tail between his legs like some whipped cur. He must at least *claim* all this land, even if it is the seacoast. He would look like a fool, if he did not."

Gillian grimaced both at the appellation and the explanation. "But we are just riding through it. We cannot change the people. They feel no loyalty to the king just because he rode through their land."

"Right. That is what several of the king's advisors probably told him. But he must make the grand gesture." Ranulf waved his hand emulating the king's grand gesture and then doubled it into a fist. "For the stupidly honest, this march is an exercise in futility. But for the soldier who has any sense it is an opportunity to make himself a tidy profit at the expense, of course, of the nation's enemies."

Gillian looked at him disgustedly. "You are nothing but a thief," she accused.

"Nonsense. I am much more than a thief. I am a lecher, as well, but only for members of my own sex. I do not lust after women, nor do I impregnate them and leave little bastards running around the countryside." He glanced significantly at Gil's stomach.

"A paragon of virtue . . ."

"*Au contraire.* Have you noticed how much my French is improving? I am a paragon of vices. Shall I continue to enumerate them for you?"

"Why not just ride along silently?" she suggested hopefully. "The day is really too hot for debate."

"You do look rather red in the face, my dear. Are you sure you feel all right?"

She shrugged. In point of fact she felt ill. Vague nausea weakened her insides. The sun beat down on the black leather helmet Ranulf had insisted that she wear until she was sure her brains were frying. She licked her lips, tasting the salt on them.

Suddenly, a cry went up in the line ahead. A small troop of French knights swept out of the trees. Less than a dozen in all, they thundered straight at the line of marching men.

Horrified, Gillian stared open-mouthed. The mighty destriers, their foreheads and breasts covered with armor plate, galloped full tilt into the English at the point where the king's standard was displayed.

Ranulf was shouting something in her ear, but she could not understand him, so stunned was she by their frightful killing power. In horror she watched the men break and scatter, fleeing for their very lives. The screams of the wounded beneath the iron lances and swinging maces drove her mad. Shutting her eyes tightly, she covered her ears with her hands.

"Damn it!" Ranulf shouted, grabbing one of her wrists and pulling her hand down. "Use that bow!"

She blinked at him. The screams were awful. The entire line was thrown into confusion. Men and horses shoved and toppled each other like dominos as the point of the line meant to receive the charge collapsed and fled.

"Damn it!" Ranulf grabbed for the bow. "This! Use this!"

Her mind was a blank, but when her hands closed over the bow, she began to act on instinct. One hand found the arrows at her belt, drawing one. Turning in the saddle to drop the bow alongside her leg, she nocked an arrow into the string.

The French knights had done their worst, charging through the line, killing men not only with weapons, but also in the panicky crush their charge created. Now one of them charged up the center of the road, his great broadsword swinging. The English dived to either side, dodging behind trees and flinging themselves into the underbrush.

Mesmerized, Gillian could not move. Ranulf was screaming in her ear, but her horse's reins were on its neck as she stood upright in the saddle, her bow drawn, the arrow aimed.

Broadsword arcing round his head, the basinet with visor down covering him completely, the knight charged toward her. The men between them dived aside. She could hear Ranulf. She could hear the screaming. Then she could hear nothing. Her thumb was at her ear. Between his breastplate and his gorget was a gap. He had lost the protective seam plate on the right side.

The broadsword whistled in the air. A scarlet mantle fluttered from the basinet. Sighting along the arrow she placed the tip an inch above the gap. She held her breath. Her fingers released. The bowstring twanged.

She heard the fleshy thunk as the shaft buried itself in his body just below the shoulder. The steel broadhead tore into his chest. He had been leaning forward, but the force drove him backward in the saddle. Only the high cantle saved him from being overset. The broadsword went flying and the convulsive tug of the reins to the right pulled the destrier aside.

Upright on her horse, her fingers automatically reaching for the next arrow, Gillian surveyed the melee on the road. The wounded and dead lay in their blood. The living had scrambled to comparative safety. Some two hundred yards ahead of her the remaining Frenchmen were wheeling their horses to ride back the way they had come.

One separated himself from the group and galloped toward her, lance couched. A blue and gold scarf fluttered from his helmet. A blue and gold enamel medallion shone on his armor. Her arrow was in the string. Even with visor down she knew him. His size, the way he rode the horse were unmistakable. Across the quickly diminishing space behind lance and broadhead, they stared at each other. Suddenly, he raised his lance and swung his mount off to the side.

Following him with her eyes, Gillian saw him intercept the knight she had shot. The knight of the blue and gold scarf retrieved the rein from the neck of the other's horse and led him away.

Other bowmen, recovering from their shock, were following Gillian's example. A hail of arrows bouncing harmlessly off the powerful armor plate on the Frenchmen's backs followed their retreat. The skirmish had lasted less than ten minutes.

All around her, men were climbing back onto the road. Several gathered about her horse, their faces turned up to her. They were speaking. She could see their mouths moving. Gradually the sense of their words entered her brain.

"Great shooting!"

"That's keeping a cool head, lad."

"Did you see that? Never gave an inch."

"What a shot!"

Ranulf rode up beside her. Silent, his face blank, he relieved her first of the arrow. When his hand touched her fingers curled round the bow, he found them icy cold. Where her face had been flushed from the heat of the day, he found it greenish white, the pupils of her eyes dilated with shock until they almost filled the irises. Ordering the others away, he caught up her reins and led her off the road.

Beneath a tall chestnut whose wide trunk to some degree hid the carnage on the road, he dismounted and held up his arms. "Gillian." His voice was low and surprisingly devoid of mockery. "Gillian."

She blinked again. Remembrance flooded into her eyes. Her body jerked; her hands clenched. She opened her mouth.

"Gillian!" Ranulf placed his hand on her thigh.

"Where is he?" The tears formed in her eyes. "Where?" She looked wildly around her.

Ranulf snapped his fingers to attract her attention, then held up his hands to her. Gratefully, she went into them, throwing her leg over the pommel and allowing him to lift her to ground. But when he tried to stand her on her feet, she collapsed. Her face was hidden in his padded tunic. Her hands clutched at his arms.

His expression embarrassed, he put his arms around her. Uneasily he looked around, but no one was paying any attention to them. "Gillian," he muttered. "Gillian.

Get hold of yourself." He patted her awkwardly.

"Oh, Ranulf. Did you see him?"

"Who? The man you killed? I should say I did. Great shot, Gillian."

"The man I killed!" She drew back in horror; her face, if anything, went whiter. "Did I kill a man?"

He nodded grinning. "Most likely, my dear. Shot him right through the body. Found the hole in the armor plate and went for it. So far as I know . . ."

With a low moan she fainted. Had his arms not been around her, she would have fallen.

Consternation on his face, he lowered her to the ground. Kneeling beside her, he patted her hand awkwardly before unfastening the tight leather cap and pulling it from her head.

Her fair hair was plastered in darkly gold fishhooks about her head. Tossing the damp leather aside he pushed the hair back from her forehead and waved his hand back and forth in front of her face to stir up a breeze. "Fool girl," he muttered. "Have no idea what to do with you. A girl. If you were a boy, I know what I would do." He grinned slightly. "Actually, I cannot imagine what I would do if you were a boy. No boy I ever knew fainted on me."

Untying the strings on her padded woolen jacket, he pulled it aside. It, too, was wet as was her clothing under it. The small mounds of her breasts were clearly outlined beneath his gaze. No question about her sex, he thought wryly.

At the rush of comparatively cool air to her head and body, she stirred weakly and moaned.

"Time for a drink," he said heartily, lifting her head and shoulders onto his knees and uncorking the leather bottle of wine he had carefully stowed after the crossing at Bresle. He held it to her lips, his other hand supporting the back of her head as she drank.

After a weak swallow, she coughed and opened her eyes. "Did I really kill someone?"

Ranulf raised an eyebrow. "You held your ground against a knight charging full tilt and swinging a broadsword."

She moaned and closed her eyes. Her hand reached for the wine, closed over his fingers and guided the bottle to her mouth. "Oh, dear God!"

"Everyone was most impressed," Ranulf chuckled. "You sighted along your arrow, found the chink in the armor, and let fly. At twenty yards the shock knocked him backward. His sword went flying, the horse veered off to the right and you were left the field. Most impressive. I take my hat off to you." He grinned down at her.

She shuddered. More tears trickled down her cheeks from under her closed eyelids. "I never meant to kill anyone."

He stared at her. He had forgotten the pain and nausea he had felt when he had killed his first man. A youth at the time, not much older than this girl, he had been violently ill while tears spouted from his eyes. The old soldier with him at the time had laughed and scoffed. Later the man had said that he had done so to make Ranulf behave like a man. But the laughter and scorn had made Ranulf resentful. His own very genuine suffering had been treated as somehow shameful and of no consequence.

"It was him or you," Ranulf said soberly at last.

"Perhaps I did not kill him," Gillian glanced at him hopefully.

Ranulf shook his head. "Not much chance of that. If he is not already dead from loss of blood and shock, the surgeon will probably kill him getting it out."

"Oh, no . . ." Gillian rolled off Ranulf's lap and crawled on hands and knees away from him. Her body convulsed and trembled as she retched.

He sprang after her and supported her head, drawing a scarf from beneath his tunic to wipe her face. At last when she had given up all she had, he pulled her up and half carried, half dragged her over to the tree. Setting her down with her back to its trunk, he positioned himself on his knees in front of her.

Taking both her hands in one of his, he mopped her colorless perspiring face. "Now listen to me," he said sternly. "When you dress like a soldier, you do a soldier's job. Except you do it better than most. That Frenchman was out to kill English soldiers. He thought you were a soldier. If you had not found the hole in his armor, he would have sliced you in two."

She gave a moan of anguish and pressed her hand against her mouth.

"Stop that," Ranulf frowned disgustedly. "I do not like the odor." When she had managed to get control of herself, he continued, "That knight should have been jerked out of the saddle and put an end to before he ever started that sweep down the line. But none of those 'brave lads' had the presence of mind to do what they were trained for. And as a result they died."

Her eyes started to fill with tears again.

"And stop that too!" He held up his hand, his dark eyes

hard as obsidian.

She gulped and swallowed.

"I yelled at you to use that damned bow . . . and you did." At her negative shake, he nodded. "Oh, yes, I did. And you heard me and did exactly what you had practiced hundreds of times. The way he went backward, the chances are he never knew what hit him."

"Oh, no!"

"Stop it! No more of that!" He handed her the wine jug and watched her while she drank. The color began to return slightly to her cheeks. Suddenly, he grinned wickedly. "By the way, Gillian, my dear, while you were unconscious, I checked to see if those protuberances really were pasted on."

She choked. Her cheeks flamed. "Damn you, Ranulf! Oh, damn you. How dare you? You . . ."

He sat back on his heels laughing like a very devil. "I just had to find out, my dear. After that performance with the bow in the face of such terrible danger, I just could not believe that you were not really a boy. I mean women. Bah! Screaming, crying, shrinking creatures. I would not believe that one was capable of even drawing a bow, much less using it effectively. So I checked."

Her hands flew to her breasts now concealed by the tunic which had flapped down across her when she stood. Her eyes flashed fire. Bright color stained her cheeks. Her mouth opened, then closed as she could think of no words strong enough to convey her disgust and hatred of him.

Laughing, he rose and struck a pose. "Your color is good now, my dear. I really suggest you pull your . . . er . . . self together. We have many miles to ride before nightfall. I believe the carnage has been cleared away."

Suddenly, she turned pale again. "I did not hurt anyone else, did I?"

"No, my dear."

"The knight who charged toward me with his lance. I did not shoot him, did I?"

Ranulf shook his head. "No. Evidently, that fellow thought better of charging into your arrows, my dear. He reined his horse off to the right and rode to aid his comrade whom you dispatched so efficiently. Good thinking on his part, say I."

Gillian pushed herself to her feet. "He was Brian," she hid her face in her hands. The emotion coursing through her was too intense. She would show it in her face, and Ranulf would mock her for it.

"Who was?"

"The knight who turned away. I recognized him. The blue and gold scarf. The medallion on the breastplate." Drawing a deep breath, she dropped her hands.

"You cannot be sure," Ranulf told her, his face no longer mocking.

"I am sure."

He whistled softly. "I would laugh about this. I really would, but somehow I think you would kill me if I did."

Without speaking she began to lace the strings of her tunic. The full horror of what she had almost done made her weak in the knees again. "Is there any more of that wine left?" she asked when she was decently covered again.

Ranulf had been watching her closely. Helping himself to a hearty mouthful first, he passed it to her. "Finish it."

She threw back her head and poured the raw red liquid down her throat without flinching. With scarcely a shudder, she swallowed.

"'Tis not easy," Ranulf mused as if he were speaking to himself, "to have someone you love on the other side in a battle."

She nodded. "I might have killed him today."

Ranulf patted her shoulder awkwardly. "Come," he said. "They are reforming the lines."

Chapter Thirty-Four

Brian swung wearily from the saddle. Stripping the leather cord that held the tippet to the basinet, he shoved the face covering aside and pulled the basinet from his head. With the heavy metal pieces dangling from one hand, he pushed the mail hauberk back around his neck. Enjoying the rush of blessed coolness, he drew in a deep breath.

With a touch of uncustomary mockery, he lifted the basinet and stared at it. Had he really worked and trained all his young life for the privilege of boiling alive inside that?

The pointed tippet with its down-slanted eye slits and regular lines of perforations over the cheeks and mouth faintly resembled some predatory bird. It regarded him silently. He shook his head. He really was deranged.

He had delivered the knight of the scarlet mantle to the

surgeons. No words had been exchanged between them, but the raspy shallow breathing inside the visor along with the sluice of blood that dyed the knight's mail skirt, the saddle, and the horsecloth had told their own story.

Brian accepted a cup of cool wine from a man appointed to esquire him. Docilely, he stood while the fellow unbuckled the various straps and undid the leather lacings. Like a cicada shedding its shell, his body emerged from the heavy metal. Then the chain-mail hauberk was slipped off his arms. At last the body servant slipped off the fustian shirt that protected his body from the sores caused as a natural consequence of metal rubbing against skin.

Shivering slightly as the breeze cooled his skin, he stood in his breechclout to have his body rubbed dry with a linen towel.

"That was a bad wound," the man remarked conversationally as he patted gently at the skin over the reddish-pink gash at Brian's waist.

"Yes," Brian agreed draining the wine and holding out the cup to be refilled.

The servant obliged, then held a soft robe for Brian to slip over his head. "Looked well treated though. The stitching held fine."

"Hurt like sin," Brian remarked drily. "It should have held fine." To close the conversation, Brian turned away, staring across the grassy areas toward Marshal Boucicault's pavilion. The old wound in his side ached with a dull throbbing pain. It weakened his concentration allowing his thoughts to turn ever and again to the home that was no more and the love that he had renounced.

Gillian! The body servant glanced at him questioningly. Flushing, Brian coughed as if he had caught something in his throat. He must have muttered her name. The pain increased. He feared it would be with him always, and he had little defense against it.

Even the English archer today. Fierce fellow that one. Standing in his stirrups, bow drawn back, arrow nocked, waiting for him. Waiting until Brian came so close that the arrow would pierce the armor plate. Cool, deadly, the eyes dark wells, the face expressionless . . . The face . . . Gillian's face . . .

Suddenly, he knew. Somehow Hob and Gillian had joined up with the English army. Of course, they would take an archer of her caliber. He remembered the night she had saved him from Ranulf by loosing an arrow through the slit in the door. Like lightning she was with a bow and more than accurate.

The thought made him momentarily weak. Only his own concern for his wounded fellow had made him swerve his horse away to intercept instead of riding the archer down and skewering him on the tip of the lance. He smiled ruefully. Or being shot himself. The chances were good that she could have spotted a chink somewhere in his own armor. Then he would be the one whose life drained away while the surgeons worked vainly to remove the steel broadhead buried somewhere within his body.

Had she known him? He doubted it. His own armor concealed him completely. Many knights wore blue and gold scarves. He had not come close enough for her to recognize the medallion on his breastplate.

Wearily, he passed a hand across his eyes. Fate had played with him most cruelly in the last few months. His comfortable world of honor and chivalry, firmly anchored to the security of family ties, had been crushed beneath a series of gigantic blows. Likewise the type of woman he had always expected to love and cherish as the idealized wife of his dreams and mother of his children had metamorphosed into the slender waiflike figure whom he loved without restraint even while she drove him wild with her shocking ideas.

And now fate had played its cruelest trick. The woman whose life should have been joined to his stood on the opposite side of the world facing him over the very arrows he had helped her to make. Exhausted and despairing, he squeezed the bridge of his nose tightly between his thumb and third finger. He could not face the Marshal of France with tears on his cheeks.

The skirmish which Brian had volunteered to lead against the English had confirmed their diminished numbers. They had crossed the Bresle and were now making for the Blanche-Taque ford on the Somme. In his own mind, Brian was sure the marshal intended to prevent the Somme crossing, drive the English back into France, and hold them trapped until reinforcements could arrive to crush them and their upstart king once and for all.

The guard before the marshal's tent stood aside for Brian to enter.

"De Trenanay." Jean Boucicault's shrewd dark eyes took in the deep lines grooved in the hollowed cheeks and the pinched look about the mouth. "Sit down, man." He indicated a camp chair beside a field table overlaid with maps. "More wine." He pointed to Brian's half-empty flagon, and it was instantly refilled. "Drink up. Drink up."

Brian shook his head, preferring to make his report first. "The English are as we suspected, sir. About five to

464

six thousand men-at-arms, mounted archers, and archers on foot. We tested them a few miles south of Bailleul. The line broke but rallied quickly. De Montville was injured."

Boucicault sighed. "Good man. I shall send word that he is to have special attention."

"Thank you, sir."

"Undoubtedly, they will try to cross at Blanche-Taque, but they must be prevented from doing this. If we can hold them at the Somme until Alençon and D'Albret arrive, we can drive them back and forth across Picardy until they are exhausted and surrender." The marshal bent over his maps staring closely at them with his brilliant black eyes.

"Without ever having to engage them in a serious battle," Brian added hopefully. His concern for Gillian had changed his outlook on the war.

The marshal raised his head in surprise. Never in his experience had he heard a knight approve of a tactic that did not lead to instant battle. Trenanay must be more exhausted than he looked. Perhaps he was not well. When he had joined the force, he had looked impassive although a bit strained. But a careful study of the younger man's face revealed nothing.

Shrugging, Boucicault returned to his maps. "Exactly. Fabian tactics. Run from the enemy. Make him chase you. Then when he catches you, make him run. Never engage anyone. Particularly when their force is as strong as yours or stronger." As he spoke, he continued to pore over the maps.

Brian sipped his wine. The marshal's stock was much better than the *vin ordinaire* supplied for the common soldiers. Since he had joined the army without retinue, he had eaten the rations supplied to the lowliest soldiers and servants.

Boucicault ordered a squadron sent out to drive strong, sharp stakes in the slow-moving swampy passage. "For the ford is wide. It is a bad place to fight, but not impossible as the rest of the river is. We do not want them to come at it in a rush and push us back. A strong, determined detachment of mounted archers could make the difference. They must not get across."

His face concealed in his cup, Brian nodded. Surely, fate had tormented him long enough. If Boucicault had only known, he would have been surprised to find himself cast in the role of good angel.

Ranulf swore crudely and viciously. One side of his jaw was swollen and his personal supply of stolen wine had run out. "Gil!"

The girl came to kneel at his side, a cup of steaming liquid in her hands. "Drink this, Ranulf. Hold it in your mouth a bit before each swallow. The heat will ease the pain."

"What is it?" he asked suspiciously.

"Beef broth."

Again the man cursed. "Beef broth. Cursed beef. All we've had to eat for three days is dried beef and walnuts. Walnuts! No wonder I broke a tooth."

She nodded soothingly. "Both are hard to stomach as a steady diet. Drink up. I had Alys make it for you. She is good at cooking. Practically the only one in the train who is."

"All the cooks who did not die of dysentery stayed in Harfleur. No fools they." Ranulf leaned sulkily back against his saddle. Tentatively he sipped at the cup, then made a face. "Bah! Tastes like she boiled shoe leather."

Gil returned to her seat across the fire from him. She agreed with him wholeheartedly about the taste, but it made a change from the constant gnawing required to turn a strip of dried beef into something edible. Besides Ranulf loved to complain.

"Not a damn thing in this wretched countryside. The moors are scenes of mass confusion by comparison."

"Also the last man who was caught stealing something from the countryside got hanged," Gil reminded him.

"He stole from a church. A pyx. *Jesu Maria.*" He crossed himself piously. "I would never . . ." He was off again. Gillian closed her eyes and allowed her mind to drift.

For five days the English had marched down the Somme ever deeper into France, ever farther from Calais. Their food was almost exhausted. Ever on the far bank were the French.

Gillian thought of Brian. Did he think of her? Had he recognized her? Was that the reason he had swerved aside? The memory of the day had dimmed somewhat. Her own perceptions had changed. Perhaps the charging knight had not been Brian after all. As Ranulf kept insisting, blue and gold were very common colors for a knight.

She hugged her arms about her body and rolled tightly into her blankets. The nights were getting colder. October was finally turning autumnal.

Ranulf was shaking her shoulder. The night was pitch-dark, but all around her could be heard the stirrings of the camp. "We march tonight," he informed her without preface. "Roll out and roll up. Mount your horse and stick close to me."

Teeth chattering, she followed him. The line was eerily silent as the semiexhausted, dispirited men stumbled along. Within a mile Gil heard the change in the hoofbeats. Hollowly, they echoed as the animals and men moved out onto what seemed to be a bridge or causeway.

"The Somme," Ranulf growled excitedly. "We must be moving over it. Thank God! We might see England again after all."

Gillian caught his excitement and for a few minutes her blood stirred at the thought of home. Almost a lifetime had passed since she had sat in her shop in York. She had left a green girl; she would return a mature woman with a woman's problems to be faced in the future.

"The bridge is knocked out."

The word went up and down the line. Anguished whispers conveyed the message. "Damn!" Ranulf snarled. All around them were their own muffled sounds rising above the faint soughing of the wind over the water of the Ingon marsh.

Then in a clatter of shod hooves, Nicholas Warrenby rode out of the graying dawn. "I need two hundred archers to wade across on foot," he informed Ranulf. "I thought immediately of you and yon Gil Fletcher. I heard what you did, lad, knocking out that knight. We need cool heads like yours."

"We are mounted archers," Ranulf tried to protest. "We . . ."

"Follow me." Warrenby reined his horse around on the narrow causeway and trotted away toward the east where the pale pink streaks of dawn began to creep up the sky.

"I am deathly afraid of water and I cannot swim," Gillian protested to Ranulf.

"With you that makes two of us," he swore fervently. "Damn! Why did you stand up to that knight? You could have panicked and dived for cover like everyone else. I did."

"You told me to shoot him," she reminded him. "The fault is with you, 'milord.'"

His dark gaze was vitriolic. "Now you call me 'milord.' You never do anything that I tell you at the right time. I know for certain that you are a woman."

They dismounted and joined Warrenby's detachment. In the pearly light of morning, they hopped and scrambled from rock to rock of the broken causeway. They had shed their heavy jackets and leather and wicker caps. Some men had shed their shirts as well.

"Stay in front of me," Gillian hissed spitefully in Ranulf's ear. "If I get this old smock too wet, you lose your hold over me."

"If I could be sure you would drown, I would push you into the water," he snarled.

At last they reached the Somme itself. "It looks cold," he complained.

"Bows and arrows overhead," came back the command.

"Oh, Lord," Gillian breathed, her teeth chattering as much from fear as from cold. The water rose above her knees. At any minute she expected to step in a hole and go under, but the water rose no farther than her waist in midstream.

At last on relatively dry ground, Warrenby sent them into the woods in all directions to attack and hold off any French.

"What do we do now?" Gillian asked from her position of concealment by a broken stone wall that overlooked the Athies road.

Ranulf lounged with eyes closed, his face and sparse brown beard turned upward to the afternoon sun. "We rest tonight." He wriggled his body into a more comfortable position.

"And then what?"

"Tomorrow? I expect tomorrow we run like hell for Calais."

"They have crossed, sire."

"Damn!" Boucicault's face registered his extreme disappointment. "Where?"

"At Voyennes."

The marshal's expression became murderous. "I gave orders that the causeway across the Ingon be destroyed."

"The fools only broke up about half a mile of it and left the debris in the marsh. A detachment of archers got across and held the bridgehead while the engineers repaired it."

Boucicault struck his fist into the palm of his hand. His oath was so foul that the messenger blanched. "Assemble my council. We must plan new strategies."

That evening in Peronne only six miles from Athies, the marshal called his council. Although the flower of France sat at his table, he knew the real battle would be fought around it. Beside him sat Constable D'Albret, an experienced soldier. He could be counted on to realize the importance of strategy. The others . . . Boucicault braced himself.

Besides the duke of Alençon, the marshal faced the

dukes of Bourbon and Orléans, who had already issued a challenge to Henry V to name the place to do battle.

"We expect him to reply forthwith," the duke of Orléans was saying *sotto voce* to the counts of Eu and Richemont.

"He could do no less," Richemont agreed. "But do you trust him to choose a battlefield where fair opportunities may be seized on all sides to achieve honors?"

"Gentlemen." Boucicault interrupted them. His face remained impassive as he stared at Orléans's fair young face. Before the strained eagerness to do battle, the marshal felt infinitely old. "I gather from your conversation that you too have heard the tragic news. The English king has managed to get his army across the ford at Voyennes."

"Bravo!" the count of Eu declared. "He is now in a more sporting position to fight. I mislike having to attack a man as he is coming out of the water. He is under a terrific disadvantage."

"Of course, best is not having to attack him at all," D'Albret inserted softly. At his comment the nobles turned as one to stare at him as if he were some strange creature.

Bourbon broke the silence. "The duke of Berry will have disgraced himself forever in the sight of the king. When we win this great victory here, he will fly into such a rage at being foolishly persuaded to stay away."

"We will take pains to capture the English king and bring him with a halter around his neck to Charles," Orléans promised with a chuckle. "I should first like to lead him back through all the towns he has threatened, so that all the cowardly officials who presented themselves to him may spit upon him."

Above the general laughter Boucicault called for order. "Milords, I propose that we delay our attack and allow our enemy to further exhaust himself."

"Not to attack immediately?"

"What is this? Not attack?"

"Never. We have issued the challenge."

"The honor of France demands—"

"We are not fighting a duel, gentlemen. Nor yet a tournament. We are fighting . . ." The marshal's voice thundered above them, but he was shouted down in his turn.

"He is a knight first and a king second. He will adhere to the principles of chivalry." This from Orléans, who had half-risen from his seat and leaned across the table with clenched fist.

"How can you be sure of that?" The marshal's cold voice and dark eyes drove the young man back to his seat.

"He has behaved in honorable fashion all across the north of France," Bourbon replied haughtily. "We have had no reports of looting, burning of crops, nor killing of the people."

"He would be a fool to do such as that," Constable D'Albret argued. "The people in the first town he approached surrendered, and he treated them well. Thereafter everyone surrendered. He has not left a trail of enemies behind his back."

"They have even given him gifts of bread and wine," Boucicault pointed out. "No, Henry Lancaster is not a foolish man. But acts of good sense do not prove he will adhere to the rules of chivalry. In fact . . . quite the opposite."

His final remark brought a fierce growl from those around him. Alençon pushed his chair back and stood. "I think you forget yourself, Jean Boucicault," he threatened. "You are here at our request to handle the details of outfitting and training the commons. Because each of us is leader of his own army, we allow you to act as a sort of mediator among us. Remember your place."

The marshal drew a deep angry breath. "You do not understand your adversary. Have you forgotten what happened to your great-grandfathers at Crécy? The duke of Berry remembers Poitiers. His own brother was captured there. The English have a habit of winning. This Henry will not want to break that habit. The great-grandson of Edward III will win at all costs, or die trying."

"Then he will die!" Alençon thundered.

"We have issued the challenge," Orléans repeated. His mouth twitched; he could not control his delight. He broke into a high hysterical laugh. "Honor will be satisfied."

Bourbon rose, signaling the end of the council. "Then it is decided. We shall wait until he sets the time and place, then crush him with one blow. No Englishman shall ever forget the lesson we will teach."

Chapter Thirty-Five

Howard of Rothingham stared up into the darkness of the tent. He should have been asleep. His most basic needs had been more than satisfied by the loving ministrations of Alys. As if by magic, she had produced a light stew made from the dried beef they ate habitually but artfully flavored with wild onions and wine. He suspected that she had saved some of her ration of bread to thicken it. But however she had done it, he had dined better than the king that night.

Afterward, she had caressed him untl he was wild with desire, holding him off, increasing his pleasure until he writhed and groaned. Finally, she had opened her sweet thighs to him and guided him into her. Despite his firm resolves he had lost all control, shuddering and plunging deep into her until he had exploded in a burst of fiery delight. His ecstatic cry he had muffled against her shoulder. He knew his teeth had bruised her, for he had felt her wince under him.

Now pressed against his side, her regular breathing warmed his neck while the motion of her firm breasts caressed his chest. He tightened his arms around her, rubbing his fingertips gently across the satiny skin of the inside of her arm.

All his life he had chased the dream of romantic love. His exploits with the cavalry in this very country twenty years ago had been chiefly so he might have such deeds to boast of when courting a lady. His education, his arts had all been achieved so that a lady would be pleased and impressed when he wrote poetry to her and then sang his love songs.

Love as the jongleurs and bards had sung of it was a bubble rather like the bubble of chivalry. It had never really been there and yet it always had. He had longed to be a knight, sacrificed for it, suffered for it. When it escaped him, he had even been tempted to steal for it, thereby ironically destroying the honor he must leave unstained to achieve the chivalric ideal.

Yet all around him lesser men achieved and then were forsworn a dozen times. Most of the men in whose midst he had been, including the king, played the game of chivalry, but in the serious business of fighting a war, they recognized that games must be left behind.

Romantic love was a game also. He hugged Alys closer until she moaned faintly in protest. But when the real business of love came into one's life, romance and all its posturings fled out the window.

"Alys," he whispered. "Alys."

She stirred, grasped convulsively at his neck. Her fingers slid down and twined around the thick mat of hair on his chest. He felt her lips move against his skin.

"Alys."

"Hob?" Her voice was just a whisper in the darkness.

"Alys, I love you."

She did not answer. He might have thought she had fallen asleep without understanding his words except that she was very still. He waited patiently until she exhaled with almost painful slowness.

"Will you marry me? I want you badly for my wife," he hurried on. "When we return to England, instead of going to your nephew you could go with me. Brian gave me some money to take care of you and to see me on my way. I could give up the tourney circuit. I know all about armor. How to make it, how to mend it. I could set up a shop. I know dozens of knights on the circuit who would come to me for repairs and replacements. People who know armor best are the ones who have actually worked in it."

Moved by the excitement in his voice, she sat up. "You are serious."

"I have been thinking about it all night."

"But you love chivalry. Your dream—"

"—is a dream." He took her hands which she had pressed against his chest. Lifting them he kissed each palm in turn. "Alys, I am forty-two years old. Chivalry will die right here in France if King Henry has to fight. He will win hands down. Gillian proved that."

"Gillian?"

"She stopped a knight's charge and killed him. A girl. He never came close to her."

"But surely? . . ."

"The king took Harfleur. You did not hear what Nicholas Warrenby said. The engineers blasted away with the big cannons and knocked the wall down. The day of the walled city is over. An ordinary man can just pull up a cannon and blow the wall down. And the knight's armor is just like the wall of the city. Listen, I saw a handgun once. Someone will get round to perfecting those things so each man may carry his own cannon. Then the knight's armor is gone."

"Are you saying that you do not want to be a knight?"

"No, I suppose I shall always wish to be a knight. Dreams die hard and with their deaths comes a sense of failure. But I can survive. I can become something else. For years people will continue to want armor for all sorts of things. The tourney circuit will last so long as men are willing to get their bodies smashed and people are willing to give prizes to see them do it."

Alys smiled in the dark. "I suppose there will always be ladies so long as men are willing to pay to have them grace their houses."

He laughed softly, pulling her down onto his chest. "You will not be a lady, Alys," he promised her. "You will be a woman and my wife."

She began again to caress him, but he rolled her over onto her back. "No!" he growled fiercely. "No more of that tonight. You are the one who should be pleased and caressed. By God, Alys, you are like a drug. I could lie on my back like a Muslim and have you, the pearl of my harem, do all the work for the rest of my life."

He gathered her wrists together in one hand and pushed them above her head. "Now leave them there," he told her fiercely. "Pretend you are chained and I am your master."

She shivered deliciously at the thought. And then she could think no more as with hands and mouth he began a

478

slow assault on her senses. His lips covered every inch of her skin, kissing, nibbling, delivering little nipping bites, and then apologizing with wildly extravagant phrases. Her beauty had driven him mad. She was so delicious that he could not forbear to taste her delicate flavor.

When she forgot herself and pressed his head against her belly, he chastened her sternly, reminding her where her hands belonged. Hastily she replaced them above her head, panting with delight as he gripped her buttocks and lifted her to meet his questing mouth.

Finally, when she could not suppress her cries of pleasure, he pulled himself up and entered her, covering her mouth with his own. Thus impaling her with his tongue as well as his manhood, he held her strongly while she writhed and twisted in her ecstasy.

As she achieved her peak of pleasure, he lunged hard, driving himself over the edge, so they fell spiraling down together.

"I love you," she admitted. "I never thought I would love anyone. Not after . . . But you have taught me gentleness and kindness. I do not care to be a lady if I can be a woman for you."

He lay beside her then, his hand clasping hers. "And I do not care to be a knight, if I can be a man for you."

She too stared at the roof of the tent, now grayed by the first streaks of dawn. "I pray there will be no battle," she said wearily, thinking as she did that they had loved the night away and would have to suffer through tomorrow without sleep. "Yet I feel it in my bones. The very air is charged with anger. Perhaps this time you will win your golden spurs."

He laughed as he sat up. He should be waking up the knights to whom he had been assigned. "How strange to win the spurs when I no longer care!"

Word of the ducal challenge spread through the ranks like wildfire. The three heralds rode through the lines of soldiers resting from their exhausting crossing of the Somme. Their flamboyant costumes drew loud catcalls from the muddy, ragged men dressed mostly in black except for the red crosses of St. George many wore on their tunics. They came bearing the lilies of France on their standards as well as the banners of Orléans and Bourbon.

"Lovely, lads," Ranulf remarked mockingly to Gillian. "That slight blond fellow in the middle. So sweet, so virginal."

She pretended to study the herald closely. "I agree about the slight. But he has little pig eyes and a smallish mouth. My guess is that he pouts when he cannot get his own way."

He raised his eyebrows. "You are not nearly so much fun to tease as you once were. I have been looking around in the ranks for a suitable replacement, but everyone looks too big and savage."

"Poor Ranulf! You may have to join the rest of the world in its sexual preferences."

He looked at her slender figure speculatively. "Are you perhaps volunteering your services to make a good Christian man out of me, Gillian?"

"Of course not." Horrified, she jumped away tugging her jacket tightly across her chest.

He laughed loudly at her, making a sideswipe which she ducked and then cheering when she darted away among the other archers. He had found a new aspect to tease. His eyes returned to the heralds being led by the duke of York to the king's pavilion. His face grew hard at the thought that he might not have much longer to tease anybody; or, alternatively, no one to tease.

No one remained at ease. The heralds were dismissed after only a brief time. Heads up and standards waving, they rode out of the camp each a hundred gold crowns richer for his bravery.

Gillian joined Hob, whose position as esquire put him closer to the king. "What did the Frenchmen want?" she asked excitedly.

"To know when the king will fight."

"Did he tell them? That seems stupid. If you are going to kill someone, you ought to go do it, not let him get prepared." Gil looked disgustedly at the royal pavilion with its standard-bearer standing stiffly in front.

"We shall soon know," Hob pushed her slightly in front of him so she might get a better look. "Here he comes."

Henry of Monmouth was a handsome man, Gillian thought as she stared in awe. Although not above medium height, he carried himself like a god. His brown hair cut short in soldier's fashion was like a cap on his well-shaped head. Wearing the coat of arms of England, he mounted his small gray horse.

"He always rides that horse when he has something important to do," Hob whispered.

With a pat to the animal's neck, the king of England touched spurs to his mount's dappled flanks and rode into the midst of his men. Behind him his uncles York and Camoys mounted their horses also to fall in behind.

As the knots of men began to straighten out into lines, he stopped ever and again to speak to them. The men's faces as they listened were grave. Many glanced over their shoulders in the direction the heralds had taken toward the walled city of Peronne.

As he came abreast of Gillian with Hob standing behind her, his hand on her shoulder, he reined the gray horse around to face them.

"Who is the archer among the squires?"

Gillian gulped, looking from side to side for a means to melt back into the crowd. Hob patted her shoulder. "This is Gil Fletcher of York, Your Majesty. He is a fletcher and bowman master."

The king stared hard at her slight figure. His clear hazel eyes reminded her of Brian's. Timidly, she smiled. Her hand found the sheaf of arrows hung from her shoulder and she ran her fingers across the feathers nervously.

Henry smiled back, his lips parting to expose very even white teeth. "I seem to know the name."

York leaned forward. "That is the archer who wounded the French knight before the ford at Blanche-Taque."

Henry raised his eyebrows, then looked her up and down again. Suddenly, he laughed. A rather sober laugh to be sure, but a laugh. "Brave work, lad," he congratulated her.

"Thank you, sir."

"And excellent shooting, so I was told." He glanced at Hob. "You spoke truth when you called this one 'bowman master.'" He raised his voice to include the rest of the men standing close at hand. "They tell me to name the time and place, lads. They say they will never let us reach Calais but will take revenge."

He paused for effect, his eyes seeking out the faces of

all within his hearing. "We told them, 'Straight we march for Calais, and if our enemies try to disturb us in our journey, it will not be without the utmost peril. We do not intend to seek them out, but neither shall we in fear of them move either more slowly or more quickly than we wish to do. We advised them again not to interrupt our journey, nor to seek what would be its consequence: a great shedding of Christian blood.' What say you to this, lads?"

"More of theirs than ours," one man shouted.

"Why you say right," the king replied, smiling his sober smile. "And what says Gil Fletcher?"

Gillian paled. The king of England wanted her to say something. Instinctively, she knew he wanted her to say something he could use. "God brought you this far, Your Majesty. He must love you very much."

Around her she could hear the men muttering agreement. The duke of York smiled a winsome smile. Henry Lancaster smiled too. "And you, too, Gil Fletcher. He will bring us all safety through." Clicking his tongue and slapping the reins against the gray neck, he urged the little horse down the lines of waiting men.

For three days in the cold driving rain of October they marched, with the signs of French soldiers ever about them. On the next day after the heralds had delivered the challenge, the Bapaume-Peronne road was a sea of mud. As her horse bogged down, even beneath her slight weight, Gillian stared at the mess bewildered. "I do not understand," she complained to Ranulf who had dismounted minutes before her and was leading his mount beside hers. "Why is this part of the road so muddy? The rest has not been so bad."

He did not answer immediately. At that precise
moment, only his hold on the reins prevented him from
sprawling full length in the muck. When he was able with
much cursing and panting to regain his footing, he began
to curse her too. "Stupid, stupid," he snarled. "Too
stupid to be believed. The whole of the damned French
army passed across this road sometime today, and you
cannot even figure out what made it this swamp. Have
you not eyes?"

Shivering and exhausted, she regarded him through
the driving rain. To answer him would be useless. She
had nothing to apologize for. Indeed she was too weary to
take offense. She slid off her mount and sloshed to its
head. The clinging mud clogged her boots to her knees.
Seizing the bridle, she pulled manfully to get the horse
started. He must not sink to his knees now. If she had to
leave him behind, she had just as well stop herself.

Ranulf caught her mount's bridle from the other side.
"Up, you—" The name he called the animal made Gillian
blush. It was bad even for Ranulf. As if offended, the
horse gave a snort, bowed its neck, and struggled forward
heaving its hindquarters out of the mud.

"Thanks," Gillian muttered.

"My pleasure," he sneered. "Cursing stupid animals is
my pleasure." He slogged back to his horse and led it
forward again.

"Then this must be your lucky day, 'milord,'" she
murmured.

"Why do they not attack?" Alys asked Hob for the

fifteenth time. "They are all around us. From what you say there are thousands . . . tens of thousands. We are so badly outnumbered that they could almost ride us down without swinging a sword."

Hob coughed deeply. The torrential rain and chill had settled a cold in his chest. "Knights hate to fight in the rain," he explained when he could catch his breath. "Their horses are too heavy to move swiftly under the best of circumstances. The weight of mud on their hooves and trappings exhausts them. Worse, if a knight falls off his horse in the mud, he is like to drown before anyone can get to him. Especially if he falls face down."

Alys shivered as she handed him a cup of hot broth. "I cannot imagine why anyone in his right mind would want to be a knight."

"When I start enumerating all the difficulties to you"—Hob grinned—"I cannot either."

"Do you think," Alys asked hopefully, "that if the rain continues for the next several days, we might reach Calais without them attacking us?"

Hob patted her hand. Smiling slightly, he shook his head. "The grand dukes of France are out there in the darkness. They are very close to us. Probably no more than a couple of miles away. They have issued challenges. They outnumber us at least five to one . . . maybe more. They will attack before too much longer. If we escape, their honor would be stained."

She hugged him hard against her, weeping tears into his tunic.

"Stop that," he chided her. "'Tis already wet enough without your adding to it. I hate a crying woman anyway." With those words he kissed her soundly on the mouth. And she pushed him down on his back to work her special magic with him.

On the eve of St. Crispin's Day, the word flew round the ranks. The French army blocked the way they must march tomorrow. Nicholas Warrenby brought the word to Ranulf and Gillian as they sat huddled side by side for warmth beneath a small tree. The *ville* of Maisoncelles had not had nearly enough huts to accommodate the army. His grizzled beard dripped with water as the rain spattered into his face. His eyes glowed hotly. "Well, we almost made it, lads," were his first words as he surveyed the miserable pair.

"Made what?" Ranulf sneered.

"The port of Calais."

Ranulf raised his head sharply. His jaw tightened. "Is it to be tomorrow then?"

Warrenby nodded. The wind whistled harshly through the tree above them, and the water brushed off the leaves joined the downpour in pelting them even harder. "Your tree leaks," he observed.

"Stay and eat," Ranulf snarled sarcastically, flinging a walnut at the bowman master.

Warrenby chuckled. "Save that fight for the French," he advised. "And you, Gil?" He crouched down by her side. "How be ye?"

"I feel all right," she whispered doubtfully.

"Good lad!" He patted her shoulder. "Put him at your side tomorrow, and watch out for him," he commanded Ranulf.

"Aye. But he can watch out for himself. I put him by my side so he can watch out for me." Ranulf chuckled edging himself closer to Gil. "He is by far the better shot."

Warrenby stood up. "The king has given the order. The camp is under a rule of silence. Everyone is to rest peacefully tonight. If someone breaks the rule, he will lose his right ear. See ye obey." With a terse good-night, he strode away to the rest of his rounds.

The water dripped from the tree. Gil shivered, her teeth chattering and clacking. I may not have to worry about tomorrow morning, she thought. I shall freeze to death tonight. At that moment a stronger gust of wind dropped a great shower of drops onto her head. Or drown, she added wearily.

"Gil," Ranulf's voice was so hoarse, it had lost all of its resonance.

"Yes."

"I am f-freezing."

"Me too."

He was silent for a moment. "Come over here with me," he said at last. "I promise not to do anything."

She hesitated. She had lived side by side with him for almost two weeks. She could hardly remember why she hated and feared him.

"Please."

The word was whispered so low, she could not be sure she had heard aright. "What did you say?"

The rain pelted on in the silence. At last, he spoke a bit louder. "Please, damn it."

Smiling, she rolled toward him, tugging her roll with her. He opened his arms to drag her in against him and combine the warmth of their bodies.

Chapter Thirty-Six

Wide-eyed, white to the lips, Gillian stared at the might of the French forces. "What are they waiting for? Why are they just staring at us?" she muttered for the fourth time.

"They want us to get so scared we piss in our pants," Ranulf replied coarsely. His voice was only a shadow of its former self. When he cleared his throat, he grimaced as if his throat were sore. "Just as you are about to do. For God's sake, Gil. Get hold of yourself. You are going to make me so nervous that I shall lose faith in you."

As it had before, his coarse language had the effect of angering and steadying her. The French enemy was forgotten in her disgust and anger at the Englishman beside her. "God! Ranulf, but I despise you."

"I am delighted to hear you say that," he jeered. "After we slept together last night, I was afraid you might

489

develop tender feelings for me. After all, I am a handsome fellow as men count handsome features. I did not want you to suffer from disappointed love."

She laughed mirthlessly, "I am trying desperately to conceal my growing affection. I think you will agree that I am succeeding."

"You would do well to." He nodded. "For myself I appreciated the warmth, but the . . . ah . . . protuberances got in the way."

"Ranulf! . . ." What she might have told him was interrupted by the command to move.

"Advance banner! Advance banner!"

Her eyes locked with Ranulf's. The time had come. She tightened her lips to still their trembling. Ranulf, too, was white. He closed his eyes for a minute, then blinked and stared about him. On the right the woods of Trame-court and on the left those of Agincourt were green walls closing around them.

"Advance banner!" From the center of the line of men-at-arms Henry rode forth. Out onto the pale green field of newly sewn autumn wheat galloped the king of England, wearing both the lions of England and the lilies of France. His golden crown decorated with fleurons encircled his helmet. He had not yet donned the visor but wheeled his horse to face his men.

All along the line some five hundred yards wide, they watched him as his little gray palfrey pawed the earth. As one, five thousand men held their breath, their eyes trained steadfastly on the man they followed as they loved God. "Advance banner!" he called again. "In the name of Jesus, Mary, and Saint George!"

Like the wind, like the rumble of thunder, like the rattle of rain, their voices took up the call. Camoys and

York moved on the left and right each at the head of his group of men-at-arms. And between and on the outside, in four divisions, each formed in a wedge, each wedge shaped like the broadhead of an arrow, came the archers, their longbows strung, their double-pointed stakes hoisted over their shoulders. "Advance banner! Advance banner!"

Each man went down on his knees, making the sign of the cross in the earth with his hand and then placing his lips to the center of the cross.

"Jesus, Mary, and Saint George! Saint George!"

Gillian struggled with her stake as Nicholas Warrenby's troop stepped forward. The brief business of balancing all the pieces of wood gave her something to concentrate on. Suddenly, she was not afraid. Hefting the load awkwardly, she grinned a faint apology at Ranulf, who had hoisted his easily and was waiting, his lip curled faintly in impatience.

Surprisingly, he grinned back, a sardonic grin to be sure, but a grin nevertheless. Beneath their feet the new wheat was crushed into the muddy earth.

Two hundred yards, then four, then six. The outermost wedges of archers stood with their flanks in the trees on either side of the field.

The French lines were barely three hundred yards away. "Do we have to get so close?" Ranulf muttered.

Gillian's eye measured the distance. She was sweating profusely both from excitement and from the labor of carrying her load so far. "We are just about close enough. A good bow range."

He wiped his forearm across his mouth. "Any closer and we could stab them with the arrows."

The command came to implant the stakes. With ease

Ranulf drove his into the soft earth. "Glad to see the end of that damned thing," he commented dusting his hands. "Here, let me." He took Gillian's from her and drove it into the ground with a mighty overhead swing.

Together they arranged themselves shoulder to shoulder with the rest of Warrenby's troops to stare over their frail palisade at the massed lines.

"Better armed, better dressed, and many, many more of them," was Warrenby's succinct evaluation. "Now, lads. Make every arrow a good one."

Gillian pulled a dozen arrows from her quiver at her belt. Not broadheads these, but slender barrels with steel tips no wider than the shaft itself. If there was a chink to be found in the armor, these would find it. Dropping all but one on the ground beside her foot, she nocked it into position on the string. Smoothly her arms flexed, the left pushing outward at the same time the right pulled back. The gray cock feather brushed her cheek. Simultaneously, she took aim. Her eyes picked out a tall fellow fiddling with his windlass. Dumb crossbowman was her thought as she leaned back slightly to allow for arc and released.

A sound like the rushing of water over a weir vibrated in her ears. The air was dark with whirring, whishing death.

She did not wait to see whether her arrow had found the mark or missed. To do so would be to arouse herself to pity. These are targets, she said. Targets only. They are like painted circles far down the green on Sunday in York. York. Her mind went carefully blank. Like an automaton she bent, caught up another arrow, nocked it, drew back, and let fly.

All around her, people were doing the same. And from

492

three hundred yards away came the screams.

"Here they come!" Ranulf tugged at her sleeve, pointing wildly to right and left as from each flank of the French position charged some six hundred knights, in full panoply. Armored from helm to heel they lumbered forward. Their horses likewise armored wore full horse cloths over the heavy saddles.

Galloping, galloping through the cloggy mud, they swept out from the flanks and crowded each other as they sought to form a line in front of the panicky crossbow-men. Twelve hundred men could not ride abreast in the narrow space between the woods. Already some were pulling their horses. Those that led the charge began immediately to channelize themselves, aiming their lances for the English knights, instinctively avoiding the death hail of the archers.

Nearer they came, their heads bowed, charging sight-less like bulls. No one wanted an arrow through the eye slit. Or and argent, gules and azure, sable and vert and purpure. A mass of moving color thundered toward the stakes, divided in every conceivable fashion: cross and saltire, fess and bar, pale and chevron, pile and bend. A menagerie of animals threatened them: lions and leopards, wolves and boars, dolphins and harts, eagles and martlets, as well as mythological griffins and dragons.

The ragged, muddy black-garbed archers took no notice. With rhythmical precision, they sent their arrows into the charging mass, bouncing them off helms and cuirasses, shoulder plates and breastplates, and occasionally finding chinks. Sometimes a muffled cry would follow the arrow as a knight would break ranks either falling to the ground or pulling his destrier in an effort to get himself out of the charging line.

"Aim for the horses!" Ranulf screamed in her ear.

Without questioning him, Gillian lowered her aim to the shoulder of a green and black horse cloth. Less than fifty yards away now, the horse screamed in agony as the arrow tore into its shoulder. Rearing and caracoling, it unseated its rider, who was flung headlong into the path of the mount on the right. Both mount and rider stumbled and crashed over the steel obstruction thrown so suddenly in the way. The wounded horse galloped in panic back through the knights who had restrained their mounts and into the lines of crossbowmen.

All along the front the wounded fell in the paths of the ones charging behind them and were buried under the stumbling bodies of their comrades. The few mounts that reached the stakes were impaled, unseating their riders in their death throes.

As a knight struggled to climb to his feet in front of them, Ranulf dropped his bow. "Cover me," he yelled and leaped between the stakes, drawing his dagger. The Frenchman managed to get one knee under him. He had broken the lance intended to be used at close quarters in the charge. With the point he stabbed awkwardly at Ranulf, who laughed nastily; then side-stepped as easily as a dancer and slapped an arm around the mailed shoulders. The point of the dagger slid between the gorget and breastplates and into the jugular. The mailed figure gurgled horribly before toppling slowly backward into the mud.

A terrified horse galloped down the lines headed straight for Ranulf. Gillian sent an arrow into its side through the horsecloth. It neighed shrilly before plunging back the way it had come adding to the havoc.

"That knight is mine," Ranulf declared to the archers around him as he darted back between the stakes and picked up his bow.

No one bothered to reply, for the number of dead and wounded was piling up high in front of them. They would all have rich pickings from the gold and jewels to be found under the armor.

"Nice to remind us," one man called. "I almost forgot what we were really fighting for."

"I claim the big black fellow yonder," yelled another. "Got to be rich. Look at the brass fittings on the armor."

"You want to fight me for him," came an answering growl. "My arrow took out his horse. He was trampled before you ever shot him."

Strangely the horror of the exchanges did not affect Gillian. The melee of writhing groaning bodies on the field had no human factors. The screams and pleas for mercy echoed hollowly from inside the helmets. No flesh showed anywhere. The scarlet tides sluicing out from between plates or through slits might have been red paint, spilled from buckets. Even the horses were covered from poll to hooves with armor and trappings.

Three hundred yards back up the field, the French archers and dismounted men-at-arms tried manfully to move forward at the commands of Marshal Boucicault and Constable D'Albret.

"Montjoie! Saint-Denis!" came a few hoarse cries. But more often could be heard screams as the hail of arrows resumed its flight over the writhing mass of agony a couple of hundred yards before them. In order to see, the men were forced to raise their heads to avoid the panicky dashes of the riderless horses as well as the retreat of the rear echelon who had lost their leaders and were galloping back straight through the lines of archers instead of returning to the flanks.

"Here they come again!" The English braced for the renewed attack. Seasoned veterans knew the first line had been a mere probe, a test of strength. But Gillian turned to Ranulf, "Surely they will not charge again? They could not make any headway." She looked around her hastily. "Everyone is standing. I cannot see a single man wounded."

His lips curled slightly in a pitying smile. "Oh, they will charge again. Use your eyes. We might have killed a couple of hundred. They have thousands over there. Keep shooting and pray!"

"But they have to come at us over their own dead and wounded!" Gillian's eyes widened with horror as she beheld the knights forming again despite the bodies lying still or feebly struggling in the mud between.

"They have no choice. They cannot charge through the woods. Low hanging limbs are hell on horsemen." Ranulf nocked another arrow and let fly, striking a crossbowman as he frantically cranked his winder. The man went over sideways, clutching at his shoulder. "Got him."

Again the charge. Shouting fiercely, the French slogged through the churned-up morass toward the lines. As they neared, they tried to increase speed to produce the greatest shock of impact. In the lead Boucicault with D'Albret on his left and Alençon on his right bloodied his spurs in the destrier's flanks with little success. The mighty animal could not manage to gallop through a field of liquid mud almost knee-deep.

Alençon pulled his horse to the left closing in tight beside the marshal. "The king!" he yelled to the men following his lead, crowding the middle of the line. "Capture the king!"

Boucicault mentally reeled at the words. The fool was pressing in too close. They would have no room to fight. He himself could not move to the left because of crowding D'Albret. And ever the arrows spattered and twanged.

The duke and the marshal struck the center of the line almost at the same time, their doubled contact sending the mounted English men-at-arms reeling backward. We are lost, Boucicault thought when he realized that he could not raise his arms to strike the enemy.

As Alençon's force surged forward, the mount directly behind the leader slipped sideways and went down. Immediately the charge turned to chaos as knights and animals fell. Helpless to rise in the clinging mud, overrun by their own men coming on behind, they lay in their monstrous cocoons of steel and waited for death.

"Stay close, little girl!" Ranulf shouted in her ear. "Leave the bow and follow me." A merciless killer, he was in his element. His eyes flashed black fire as he drew the short sword and plunged from behind the walls of stakes.

"I cannot!" she cried. And yet she did. They were not like men. Again she closed her mind to the screams and pleas. She did not hear them. Anything that stirred, she stabbed. Steel rang against steel. Her arm vibrated, and pain shot from palm to shoulder.

"I cannot," she whispered, as her blade slid in under the armpit of a knight struggling to rise. A scarlet stream poured out as she twisted the blade to withdraw it. Its hilt slipped out of her sweaty palm.

"Gillian! Behind you!"

She whirled to see a steel monster looming over her. But luck had claimed her for its own. An unhorsed knight who had managed to clamber to his feet slashed downward with his great sword. Had she not turned, the blade would have cut her in two. She screamed shrilly as she tried to leap away. A terrible blow struck the side of her thigh.

Her mind whirled. One thought remained uppermost as she saw the blood on his blade, saw it drawn back to slash across her body. If I fall, I will drown in the mud. As if she had not been injured, she leaped back.

The leg was numb; she dragged it after her. He was pursuing her, slashing at the air again. He too must be wounded, she thought vaguely. He may be bleeding too. Still she stayed ahead of him hopping frantically.

Ranulf flung himself at the back of the knight. The fellow was taller than he. Damn his lack of height! His hands closed over the eye slits in the visor. "Gillian! Kill him!"

The sword slashed crazily in the air. Ducking under it, she flung her weight hard against the knight's chest. Her teeth clicked together with shock as she rammed her shoulder against the steel plate. With Ranulf clinging to his back, it was enough to overbalance him. He fell backward like a tree, his arms flailing the air.

Ranulf's breath whooshed out of his lungs as the steel-clad body came down on top of him. For a moment he could only lie face up in the mud, his body half buried.

Weak and nerveless, her muscles turning to jelly with shock, Gillian could not find her weapons. Terrified that the knight would push her aside, rise up and kill her and Ranulf, she screamed for help. Please God! Tears spouted from her eyes. Lancing pains shot through her shoulder and into her chest. Her leg burned like fire. "Help! Help! Oh, please! . . ."

Ranulf was stirring feebly, but the weight of the downed knight with Gillian perched on his chest was too much for him. He struggled to draw air into his crushed lungs. Then from out of his field of vision another archer with a dagger dispatched the fallen knight.

"Oh, thank you. Thank you!" Gillian cried grasping the hand of Nicholas Warrenby and pressing it to her cheek.

"Steady now, lad. Don't take on so." He pulled his hand away embarrassed. "Just straighten yourself up and step off that Frenchman. He be dead, but your friend be about crushed from the weight of both of you."

With a groan of dismay, Gillian hoisted herself off the breastplate. "Ranulf." She hopped on one foot, afraid to lean her weight on the other. "Ranulf?" She called uncertainly. Desperately, she pulled at the mailed arm at last succeeding in raising the body slightly. "Ranulf, can you slide out from under?"

"Damn you!" He began to curse. Mud was in his mouth and in his eyes. "I must be bruised from head to toe."

Heartened by his complaining and cursing, she pulled doggedly. At last she got the body rolled half over where it stayed balancing precariously. Ranulf braced himself up on his elbows, got a foot free and drove it into the back of the body. At last it rolled all the way over, leaving him free.

Most of his face was black with mud. The part that was still clean was dark with anger. "Damn you! I told you to kill him, not push him over on me. I cannot believe you. Sitting on his chest and crying for help." He grabbed her arm and shook it.

Suddenly, she began to tremble. "Ranulf, I did the best I could. I lost my sword." She hung her head in shame. She had behaved badly. Ranulf was right. "Please forgive me."

Amazingly, he chuckled. "Where did you lose your sword?"

"Right over there." She pointed.

"Are you badly hurt?"

She thought about that, trying to take a mental inventory of her abused parts. Aside from a burning in her leg and an ache in her shoulder, she seemed to be fine. At last she shook her head. He knelt swiftly before her, ripping the mantle from the helm of the dead knight they had killed together. "Hold still while I tie this tight," he ordered. "'Twill keep the worst of the muck away from it until we can look at it."

"Saint Denis! Saint Denis! To me!" The duke of Alençon had found another horse. Mounting it, he ripped off the visor of his helm and called to the knights of the rear guard who had held back out of the melee. His strong voice carried well above the noise, and the English knights made a concerted effort to reach him. Swinging his sword above his head, he fended them off, then guided his horse between the knots of bodies back toward the second line.

"Saint Denis! To me, you cowards!" But the rear guard, fearing to suffer the fate of the advance, retreated. Tears of fury and frustration streamed from his eyes. The damned English should not have this day. His words the night of the council returned as a vow. The English king must die.

Swinging the sword above his head, Alençon spurred

the destrier for the center of the English line which had already begun to reform. Shouting his challenge, his mouth open, his body leaning far forward in the stirrups, he forced the pain-wracked animal to leap over a grisly clot and made for the unmistakable figure of the king.

The duke of Gloucester, Henry's younger brother was down. Henry straddled him, fighting on foot to protect him until the duke's own retinue could rally to his side.

Alençon flung himself from his horse. A few Frenchmen still on their feet closed in behind him and together they made for the pair. "The king is mine!"

His loud voice carried to the king, who whirled to meet the attack. Parrying the first swing, Henry Lancaster riposted, slipping under the duke's guard, his sword clanging off the armor and staggering the surprised nobleman.

Beneath the Frenchman's feet, blood and muddy water collected in pools. His steel boots slipped from under him and he fell ignominiously onto his back. The king's swordpoint halted an inch from his mouth. The death he had arrogantly planned for Henry terrified him.

Honor forgotten, he raised his hand. "I am the duke of Alençon," he called, "and I yield myself to you."

The king lowered his sword and extended his hand. Like a striking snake the duke's dagger flashed for the throat.

"'Ware, Hal!" Humphrey of Gloucester's sword stabbed upward burying itself in the duke's body.

Chapter Thirty-Seven

The French knights lunged forward as Alençon's body fell backward, impelled by Gloucester's stroke. The king's guard closed with them. For the first time that terrible day, the battle was cut and hack in the ancient manner of a hundred years ago.

Although lightly armored with bits and pieces he had managed to acquire from the armorers in the camp, Howard of Rothingham gloried in the challenge. For years he had trained, for years he had yearned. Now the opportunity was here. He fought to defend the king of England. Instinctively, he knew that should they win the day, he would win all. The years rolled back and he was a young squire on his first *chevauchée* in this same country.

With a mighty swing, he dented the shield of a knight in a purple and white surcoat. Staggering back, the man swung wide with his sword striking Hob's shield and denting it in turn. Evenly matched in skill, neither would give ground. Joyously, Hob absorbed and delivered blows, banging away with fierce enthusiasm. He almost hated to end it, but the Frenchman was lowering his guard. His shield must be tiring his arm.

With a breathless laugh, Hob redoubled his strokes, driving this opponent to his knees with both hands raised to support the shield above his head. With a final mighty blow, Hob drove in underneath. His sword point found the seam between breastplate and skirt. The knight toppled backward, pulling himself free of the sword, and Hob with a last glance of satisfaction turned to find another.

The fighting had begun to thin somewhat, but Hob's experienced eye caught the concerted movement of some eighteen or twenty knights toward the king.

Swinging his sword round his head, he sprang forward with a yell. "Defend the king! To Henry! Saint George! Saint George!"

The king's guards closed ranks with Hob in their center presenting a wall of bodies between the king, who waited until his brother was helped away before dashing up behind them, and the French knights.

"Your Majesty! Stay back!"

The Lion of England pushed his way through to stand shoulder to shoulder with his guard. "I let no man do my fighting. We fight together."

The French knights charged with swords upraised. Their cries of "Saint Denis" mingled with answering challenges of "Saint George." Their youthful voices, muffled behind their visors, sounded like children's.

Gradually, the seasoned men of the king's guard recognized the age and experience of their opponents.

"What?" called one. "Do the French now send boys against us?"

"Boy!" the youthful voice cried. "I will show you—" Ganiot de Bournonville swung wildly, allowing his shield to drop. The guardsman struck him a fearful blow on the side of the neck, caving in the gorget and breaking the young man's shoulder.

"Yield!"

"Never!" Bournonville's voice came in a desperate sob of pain. The weight of the shield buckled around his left arm pulled it down straight. He could no longer defend himself.

Pitying his youth, the Englishmen stepped back.

With a maniacal scream Bournonville flung himself at the king. The wildly swinging sword bounced off the king's helm striking a fleuron from the golden circlet and sending it cartwheeling into the mud. As the king staggered, the guardsman, with a roar of rage, brought down his blade with all the force of both arms. The steel cut through the metal plate and split the body beneath from shoulder to waist.

As it toppled spouting blood, the other guardsmen redoubled their blows, sending some members of the cortege fleeing while others sustained wounds that felled them on the spot.

"Who called the warning?" The king rested panting on his sword. His head rang from the blow he had taken, but otherwise he knew himself to be whole.

"I, milord." Hob limped forward. His light armor had not sustained a blow to his body. The mail hauberk was ripped open above his left thigh. Blood streaked the dangling leather flap.

"You are wounded," Henry observed.

"Not badly, Your Majesty."

The steady hazel eyes inspected the thigh as well as the face of the man. "Our own physician shall attend you. Report to him when you will. What is your name?"

"Ho-Howard of Rothingham," he stammered, tugging the basinet off his head and running a trembling hand through his sweaty locks.

"We do not know the name, but it has a noble sound."

"It is my own, so please you."

"We cannot doubt it." The king straightened wearily. His head was beginning to ache. "Kneel."

His hands cold and his throat dry, Hob dropped down in the mud, his hands clasped over the hilt of his sword.

The king touched the flat of the blade to the shoulder in the time-honored ritual of chivalry. "We dub you Knight. Rise, Sir Howard."

His blood staining the mud under his left knee, Howard staggered to his feet. He could find no words. The dreams of a lifetime achieved in the mud of France. Stunned, his only thought was that he could hardly wait to tell Alys.

"Time to move," Ranulf drawled in Gillian's ear.

A bleak sun had finally broken through for a few minutes at midday, but it had been quickly covered with dark gray clouds. A chilly wind began to blow out of the northwest. The French had deserted the field. Only the great mounds of dead and dying remained. Their moans of pain and cries for help had replaced the fierce shouts of "Mountjoie" and "Saint Denis."

All around Gil the archers were moving out from behind the stakes that had protected them so efficiently from the knights' charge. In only a few places had the defenses been breached. In most of those places the opening had been closed immediately by the body of the horse that had been ridden onto it.

Ranulf sliced through the leather straps that held the armor on the man he had killed earlier that day. Excitedly, he held aloft a heavy gold chain with a medallion swinging from it. The trophy gleamed dully in the gray afternoon. "What did I tell you? Pull off those gauntlets, Gil, and see what rings he wears."

Curling her lip in distaste, she shook her head. "I think I would rather leave the robbing of the dead to you."

Disgusted, he crossed over and jerked the gauntlets off the stiff fingers. A brilliant gold signet ring intricately molded and set with precious stones caught the light. "No share for you then, milady." He sneered. "Just follow along with me and carry the stuff. Surely you have the stomach for that."

Handing her the ring and the medallion, he squelched through the grayish-pink muck to the nearest mound of fallen. The pile reached higher than their heads and would have measured more than ten feet long. Those who had fallen first had blocked the passage of those that came behind, who in turn had tried to clamber over their bodies. Loving the targets outlined plainly against the sky, the archers had dropped them with deadly accuracy on the hill they sought to climb.

Pulling a gauntlet off an outstretched hand about waist high in the pile, Ranulf began to work the ring off the finger. The hand flexed.

"Ranulf! That man is still alive." Gillian tried to find a place to push at the mound without putting her palms in blood.

"Why so he is," Ranulf agreed unconcernedly, tugging the ring free and handing it to her.

"Help me get him free," she cried. "He may be badly wounded."

"If he is, then he is better off dead. If he is in good condition, he can wait until we get down to him. If he can be held for ransom, some rich knight will get richer. If he can be exchanged, he might live." Ranulf looked around him speculatively as he began to pull at a steel boot hanging over the top of the pile. "I doubt that many will be exchanged though. None of us were captured." He chuckled as the body came sliding down.

Gillian wandered away after a few minutes. The stench of blood, mixed with other things too foul to think about was making her sick. Carefully, she skirted the mounds of dead, trying not to step in the puddles that were too brightly stained.

All the brave young men. Their lives cut short for such a stupid reason. Their bodies lying in mud.

Brian! Her eyes filled with tears. Since the battle began, she had not thought of him. In order to do the job she had been commanded to do, she had closed the personal side of her nature. It had been locked away safe in her brain where it would not be too scarred by what she had been forced to do. Her hands sought the medallion hanging between her breasts where Brian had placed it. How long had they been apart? Forever.

Her eyes swept over the terrible battlefield toward the French lines. No one blocked the Calais road now. Soon. Very soon, she suspected the English army would move on, taking what spoils men like Ranulf could carry. Fervently she hoped that somewhere out there . . .

But suppose he were here, somewhere around her, lying dead or dying. She had not watched for a knight caparisoned in blue and gold. She turned and ran back to Ranulf, who had made his way almost to the bottom of the pile. A French knight lay on his side, moaning slightly, his hand pressed beneath his mail skirt in an effort to stop the red flow that puddled sluggishly beneath him. She dropped down beside him. *"Monsieur,"* she began haltingly, *"connaissez-vous le Sire Brian de Trenanay?"*

The wounded man groaned and raised his head, staring at her through the eye slits. Again she had the impression that there was nothing human inside the steel cocoon.

"Le Sire de Trenanay? De la Forêt?"

The helmed head swung slowly back and forth.

"What are you asking?" Ranulf asked.

"I was asking about Brian, but he does not know him."

Ranulf paused in his pillage. "I had completely forgotten about him. I wonder if he could be around here under some of these." He looked around him.

The field was now busy with the English archers and men-at-arms as they systematically worked over the bodies. Once in a while she would hear a cry as someone slit the throat of a man deemed too badly wounded to survive.

She caught Ranulf's hand. "Please help me look for him," she begged. "If two of us look, we stand a better chance of finding him than one."

He shook his head. "If I come to him, I will promise to save him for you. But this is business. He caused me almost as much trouble as you did, and now you refuse to help me again."

Throwing down his hand, she stormed away. "Ranulf! Rot in hell!" she screamed. Hopelessly, she stared round her. She would do her best, she promised herself. And all the time she would reassure herself that she was wasting her time, that Brian was not really there but had been held back in reserve and had not fought at all.

As she moved along, she suddenly realized that Ranulf was doing the same thing covering a portion of the field she was not. She straightened and stared at him.

He stared back defiantly. "I was about to get more than I could carry," he snarled. "What was he wearing when you say you saw him the other day?"

"A blue and gold scarf. And he had a blue and gold medallion decorating the breastplate."

Ranulf nodded as he bent over a body half buried in the mud. "I remember." He chuckled. "Something *Mors Cristo!*"

"Yes," she said. "*Mucro Mors Cristo.* Thank you, Ranulf."

"Will you retract your curse now?" he sneered.

"I retract it. May you live long and go straight to heaven."

"I doubt I can handle that." He laughed.

As they bandied words, they moved across the field. Simultaneously, they spied a trail of blue and gold scarf streaming from under a pile of bodies.

Gillian ran toward it, her heart pounding in her throat. The knight whose ring Ranulf had stolen had been alive under the pile, she told herself. But he had been lucky. Many had been crushed by the weight of the bodies on top of them so they could not breathe. "Brian," she gasped. "Brian."

Together she and Ranulf pushed at the mass. It did not move.

"Have to pull them down one at a time," Ranulf

panted as he grabbed for a mail shoulder and sent a corpse sliding off. "Control that heaving stomach and get to it, Gil."

"I will," she sobbed. "Oh! . . ." She jumped back to avoid a falling corpse with an arrow through one of the breathing holes in the faceplate.

At last the upper body of the knight with the blue and gold scarf was exposed. No identifying medallion gleamed from the breastplate. Ranulf turned to go.

"No wait," Gillian begged. "At least help me open the visor."

"But . . ." Ranulf protested.

"Help me." Her fingers trembled as she unbuckled the leather straps. Lifting aside the visor, she sighed, "'Tis he."

"Damn! I cannot believe it." Ranulf helped her push aside the rest of the bodies lying across Brian's arms and legs. "Is he still alive?"

"His lips are blue." She felt the still face. It seemed warm. Holding her fingertips beneath the nostrils, she thought she could feel the slight stirring of breath.

Ranulf knelt beside her, his knowledgeable hands cutting the leather straps that held the breastplate across his chest. "This thing is badly caved in," he muttered almost to himself. "Probably crushed by the pressure from above. I doubt if the Frenchman is alive, Gil."

"I can feel his breath. I know I can," she argued, unable to control her sobs of despair.

Tossing aside the breastplate, Ranulf shook his head as he cut into the mail hauberk. "Unbuckle the gorget from about his throat," he ordered. "Let him breathe."

Tears flowing down her cheeks, she twisted around to find the buckles.

A faint moan and a gasp for breath brought her upright. "Did you hear that? Ranulf, he breathed!"

"He did indeed, little girl. He did indeed." Ranulf smiled at her joy. "I suppose I can go through the rest of the bodies on this pile while you finish reviving him. I might find that gold medallion of his. I would guess it has slipped off somewhere. As I recall it was solid gold. Valuable thing." He continued muttering as he stood up and began to pull aside pieces of armor on corpses.

"Ranulf," she called.

He raised his head, one eyebrow raised in inquiry.

"I love you."

"My God! How dare you?" He turned away and bent hurriedly back to his task.

Tearing the silken scarf that trailed from the top of Brian's helm, she sprang down from the pile and dipped it into a pool of water, less gray than most. Although the water was dirty, at least its coolness might revive him. Gently, she bathed his cheeks.

He groaned again. One gloved hand lifted feebly to knead against his chest as if to tear the pain away. Gently, she laved his cheeks again and touched the moisture to his lips.

He opened his eyes to stare blankly upward at the lowering sky. His mouth opened, gasping like a fish as he sought to draw air into his lungs that had been compressed by more weight than his ribs could bear. He closed his eyes against the pain. Someone was speaking to him. He could feel the stroking of a moist cloth on his face. The pain in his chest and limbs racked him. He wanted to scream, but he could not draw in enough breath to scream. Someone was speaking. It sounded like . . . "Gillian."

"Brian." She was crying. "Brian. Oh, Brian. We found you alive."

"Hurt . . ." He kneaded his chest again. Suddenly, he choked, then coughed. The pain in his bruised ribs made him try to roll over, but he could not move. Gradually he became aware that he lay sprawled on a most uncomfortable mound.

"Can you move your limbs, Brian? Ranulf's here and we can get you up, but we are afraid to move you just yet."

"Ranulf?"

"Here, dear man."

Brian turned his head slightly. His neck was almost too stiff to move. He wondered if his spine were broken. Wondered if he were crushed. He remembered the destrier stumbling over a mailed body impossible to avoid. Then he had been thrown. Something had slammed into his back as he had tried to rise. He had struggled up again, only to be kicked in the chest by a terror-stricken horse. The force of the blow had slammed him down onto a mass of rocks. Then he had lost consciousness.

"Can you move your legs?" Ranulf asked gently, taking one of Brian's steel-capped boots in his hand.

"I—I can barely feel them."

"Can you feel that?" He gave the boot a harsh jerk.

Brian nodded. He got his elbow under him and raised himself slightly. "What am I lying on? My God!" The sight of the bodies beneath him shocked him. His gorge rose, and he flung himself sideways retching painfully. The searing pain of his bruised ribs made him sicker and he could not control himself.

Gillian steadied his shoulders as best she could while

Ranulf unbuckled more of the crushing armor.

At last, when he could relieve his stomach no more, Brian collapsed back against her. "Get me off here," he begged. "Please, Gillian, get me off here."

"Just a minute," Ranulf grunted. "He is too heavy to lift with all this iron on him. I remember what a big fellow he is. So muscular and tall."

"Ranulf," Gillian chided. "He is in pain. I doubt he appreciates your humor."

Ranulf flashed her a quelling look. "It always worked with you," he reminded her. The greaves fell free. "Ready."

Gillian put her arms under Brian's shoulders. The chain mail cut into her wrists. Biting her lip, she lifted with all her might. Brian managed to get his knees doubled and tottered to his feet. With Ranulf on one side and Gil on the other, they brought him down.

Standing swaying, he looked around him. His face, already unnaturally pale, turned gray at the sight.

"Come," Gillian urged. "We must get you back to safety. The French may attack again."

The two pulled his arms over their shoulders and turned him back toward the English lines. Their banners still bravely flew above the field. The rows of stakes still standing in their wedge shapes still marked the archers' lines no one had breached. And between was the carnage.

Sick unto death, Brian lowered his eyes to the ground. Even there the horror of the loss tortured him. His steel boots sank into the mud and sloshed through pools of pinkish-gray water. The blood of France. He said it aloud. "The blood of France."

Gillian was panting beside him as with every step his

weight sagged heavier and heavier on her slender shoulders.

"Why did I live?" he sighed.

Ranulf snorted disgustedly. "I ask myself that when you make stupid dramatic statements like those. You live because of her. Because she dragged me away from my profit-making to search through the bodies for you."

When Brian said nothing, Ranulf cursed mildly. "Can you manage him the rest of the way, Gil?"

She gasped something in reply.

"I take that for yes. *Adieu* until later." He slogged back onto the field.

Behind the stakes, Gillian helped Brian to sit down, then knelt before him to strip off the helmet and push back the chain mail. He raised his head as the chilly wind cooled his overheated scalp. "Feels good," he said at last.

"I love you," she smiled. "You are going to be all right."

Bleakly, he nodded as he stared between the stakes at the French lines now deserted.

Chapter Thirty-Eight

His exhausted face nevertheless radiant, Sir Howard of Rothingham made his way across the field. Despite various nicks and scratches, despite a multitude of bruises, some so deep they would take weeks to fade, his body felt wonderful. Exhilaration pelted through his veins.

He had not thought to fear for Gillian during the course of the afternoon. His conscience smote him as he remembered his neglect. Yet he could have done no differently. She had acquitted herself so nobly in the earlier skirmish that he had firmly believed she would do as well in battle.

As he neared the spot where Nicholas Warrenby's troop had set their stakes, he saw her. Ragged and dirty, her fair hair matted and tangled, she kneeled awkwardly as she cared for someone. Perhaps Ranulf. The swine deserved killing instead of being carefully tended and waited on hand and foot by a gentle, merciful lady.

"Hob!" Her glad exclamation was punctuated by a wave of her hand.

The man to whom she ministered lay as one dead.

"Gil! Are you all right?"

"Good. A scratch here and there and scared out of the next year of my life."

Hob dropped down beside them. "Sir Brian! . . . Milord? . . ."

Brian did not stir. His long body was still clad in armor from the waist down. Flat on his back he lay, his chest bared as Gillian bathed the myriad cuts from the metal links of his mail. His hazel eyes flickered open, and he smiled slightly in recognition.

"How goes it, milord?"

Brian rallied his strength. "Like my horse had fallen on me. Which he did."

"We found him under a pile of dead," Gillian explained. Her face was grave as she flung away the sodden, soiled scrap of material and pulled the fustian tunic across Brian's chest. "You must not get a chill," she told him.

"Good as new in a few minutes," he murmured. "My ribs feel like they might be bent somewhat but not broken."

"His armor was all caved in," she told Hob worriedly.

"It probably saved his life."

"Yes," Brian agreed.

"We all fared well today," Gillian said thankfully. "You are not wounded, Hob?"

His face crinkled into a smile. Deliberately, he rose to his full height. "Sir Howard of Rothingham, Lady Gillian," he corrected her, bowing slightly.

Her eyes sparkled with tears of joy. Climbing to her feet, she limped to him to throw her arms around his neck. "Oh, Hob, I mean, Howard . . . I am so happy for you." She planted a delighted kiss on his muddy, unshaven cheek. "Congratulations, Sir Howard."

Brian smiled wanly. "To the victors belong the honors. The day has been a great one for you. Congratulations."

"The French fought gallantly, milord."

"But stupidly, I fear." He shifted, grimacing as if a shaft of pain had racked him.

Gillian dropped down beside him. "Is it bad?" She caught his hand in both of hers.

"No." Their fingers entwined. "No, my love. I winced remembering how I made fun of your little bits of sticks and feathers."

She bowed her head and kissed his hand. His eyes misted with love for her as he brushed her hair with his other hand.

Hob left them without disturbing them further. His obligations to Gillian and to Brian were dissolved. He was his own man with his own lady to see to. Eagerly, he hurried back toward the town of Maisoncelles.

The king had ordered the baggage called from the town and drawn up to the left of the original line. There the sick, the pages, and the sumpters had been sheltered and partially hidden by the trees and underbrush.

A hundred yards from the woods, he heard the noise. A rabble of shouting, cursing peasants were dragging the baggage from the carts. The pages, merely lads, were being knocked aside as they tried futilely to defend the food and supplies. A few sick men had been dragged from the wagons. As he charged forward, Hob saw a knight, obviously a leader of the rabble drive his sword into the body of one who sought to resist.

"Saint George!" Hob whirled. Cupping his hands around his mouth, he shouted at the top of his lungs. "'Ware robbers! To me! Saint George!" But the lines seven hundred yards away were abandoned. The archers and men-at-arms were occupied with the business of sorting through the battle dead and tending their own wounded. No one paid any attention to him. "Saint George!" he cried again, his throat torn by the effort.

Drawing his sword, Hob broke into a run. The peasants at the very edge of the woods saw him coming. Lightly armored, he moved faster than they expected. With a fierce swing, he chopped one down. The others scattered. Their sticks were no match for the steel of his thrusting sword.

Still shouting for help, he burst into the scene of carnage. The baggage was strewn from the wagons. On the ground as well, lay the bodies of several young pages, their innocent blood staining the grass.

"Alys!" Hob's heart froze. He heard her scream. She ran toward him from behind an overturned wagon. Her arms outstretched, she took two steps into the open.

"Saint Denis!" A mounted knight in full armor galloped between the carts. His sword swinging in a wide whistling arc, he made for the Englishman.

"Hob!" Alys threw herself at him. Her hands almost touched him before the metal chest plate of the destrier struck her. Like a doll flung away by an angry child, her slight body catapulted helplessly through the air to fall crumpled amid the broken chests of a nearby wagon.

"*Alys!*"

Automatically, he caught the knight's broadsword on

his own. The downward arc had been deflected when the destrier had broken stride. As the man reined the champing warhorse in a circle, Hob stepped back and straightened. His chances on the ground with only a sword were slim. The knight's armor was virtually impenetrable coupled with the fact that no mortal wound could be delivered below the waist.

Hob drew his dagger with his left hand. Crouching slightly, eyes blazing, he waited as the knight spurred his mount forward again. The tired horse lumbered forward.

Leaping nimbly aside, Hob dodged the deadly broadsword and stabbed his dagger into the horse's flank as the animal plunged by. With a shrill neigh it reared and bucked, unseating the rider who tumbled sideways from the saddle. Weapons ready, Hob walked cautiously toward the downed knight who lay stunned.

From behind him came a shout. Another knight charged, his lance couchant. Hob barely had time to turn. His sword only partially deflected the tip before it ripped into his body. The shock plummeted him backward throwing him to the ground. Curiously, he felt nothing at all. He stared upward, puzzled, at the colorless sky before his vision faded completely.

The pain was so great that he could not bear to open his eyes. He could not, dared not move. One side of his chest throbbed with each uneven beat of his heart. Alys . . . Hob opened his eyes.

With a great effort of will he rolled his head to one side. She lay as the knight's destrier had thrown her. One arm flung over her head. Her face was turned away from him. Even from where he lay, he could see her body was twisted unnaturally.

Alys. Tears rolled down his cheeks. With a superhuman effort he rolled over on his side. The pain blinded him for a moment before it subsided. His left side was paralyzed, yet not numb. Every severed nerve sent its excruciating message to his brain.

His good right arm levered him up and hitched him along. His right leg, too, pushed weakly, but its connections were feeble. My lower body is growing numb, he thought. I must be bleeding to death.

He did not look at his body. Instinctively, he knew he could do nothing more for it ever. Instead he glued his eyes on Alys's crumpled body. Tears made it blur as if he looked through a clear pool that rippled only faintly. Someone was moaning. Terrible moans of agony roared in his ears. Someone must be badly hurt, he thought idly.

Alys had not moved. He licked his lips, surprised to find salt on them. "Alys," he whispered. He could not hear his own voice. He licked his lips and tried again. Now there was more salt on them. It must be blood. Not much of a romantic lover with a bloody lip.

He was almost to her. His good right hand touched the fabric of the old gray smock. Gently, he tugged at it. Her body rolled over on its back across his arm.

"Alys?" he begged her softly. "Alys, open your eyes."

Arched over his arm, her chest did not move. He lowered his weary head to her breast listening, hoping despite what he knew to be true.

"Alys . . . love . . ." He hunched himself forward until he could rest his tired body against her own. "Alys . . . came to tell you . . . no longer just plain Hob. Sir H-Howard of Rothingham."

A pressure began to build in his chest. He rested his cheek against her hair. "You will be my lady, Alys . . . my lady. I . . . your knight. Just like in the ballads." His bloody hand touched her cheek. "Love . . ."

From somewhere he heard the sound of heralding trumpets. "The king . . . gathers his forces. Battle over." He closed his eyes. "Knighted by the king . . ."

News of the attack on the baggage spread through the English lines. Some French knights had led a thieving, murderous sortie of vengeance. At this time when in battle men fought only men, the deliberate slaughter of these innocents was greeted with fierce retaliation. Many of the prisoners were killed on the spot, their heads bashed in by furious Englishmen.

Gillian started up. "Hob must have gone to the baggage to tell Alys," she gasped.

"Help me up," Brian commanded.

"No. You are too weak."

"He was my squire," he reminded her. He laboriously pulled himself to his knees. Grimacing at the pain of expanding his lungs fully, he drew a deep breath and climbed to his feet. He tottered a few steps. "Where is the baggage?"

"In the trees to the left, behind where we were this morning."

"Lead the way."

In the end Gillian found she could move no faster than Brian. Her thigh had stiffened badly. The weight of her wet, muddy clothing exhausted her as did trying to slog through the soft, churned-up field. Each breath Brian drew was a moan, and he walked bent over holding his side like an old man, but he still managed to move.

By the time they arrived, priests and some squires had already begun to move the dead and put the baggage to rights.

Gillian ran first to the bodies that were laid out side by side. "Not here. Oh, Brian, neither of them is here. Perhaps . . ." Her hand flew to her mouth as she looked where he pointed. "Hob! Alys!"

They lay together as if they were asleep. Except that his whole side from armpit to knee was dyed in shining red.

Gillian ran to them, sinking to her knees at his side. Brian followed and knelt beside Alys. When he lifted her hand, it was already stiff and cold, but he felt for the pulse anyway. Wordlessly he shook his head. Gillian sobbed aloud burying her face in her hands.

At the sound, Hob's eyelids flickered. "M' lady . . ."

Unashamed of her tears, she caught his bloody hand. "Oh, Hob . . ."

His eyes were glazed. "Can't see you. . . ."

"We are here, Hob. We are both here. Brian and me."

"Alys? . . ."

Gillian looked at Brian, who shook his head.

"She is right beside you."

"Ah . . ." His right hand moved feebly patting Alys's shoulder. "Die for my lady . . ."

The tears streamed Gillian's cheeks almost drowning her in her effort to keep from sobbing aloud.

". . . golden spurs . . ." he muttered.

Brian detached a spur from the heel of his boot. "Here, Sir Howard."

Two fingers caressed the chased metal before the hand slipped back limply to lie against Alys's breast.

Side by side they waited as each breath seemed his last. At length he drew a deeper breath. His eyes opened, searching for Gillian. "Tell Harry Bailey . . ." His life went out as that breath escaped from his body.

Gillian cried out. Brian waited a minute before reaching across to close his eyes.

A squire stood over them, his young face grave. "Is that Hob?" he asked.

"Yes." Gillian whispered softly.

"He was a good man. I thought he was a knight at first."

"He was a knight," Brian informed him, climbing heavily to his feet. "Sir Howard of Rothingham."

The squire nodded. "Thought he might be. He always acted like one. He knew everything about chivalry."

"Can we bury him with his . . . father?" Gillian gasped, trying to suppress the worst of her sobs.

The squire smiled sadly. "You mean Lady Alys?"

Her head shot up. She stared at him intently. "Yes, with Lady Alys." Numbly, she felt Brian take her arm to lead her away.

"Better hide, Frenchman," Ranulf warned Brian. "The English have blood in their eyes. They are killing all the wounded and most of the prisoners."

"He is my prisoner," Gillian said quietly. "No one shall kill him."

Ranulf raised his eyebrow. "Better say he is an Englishman. Someone could run right over you, little fletcher, and bash his brains out while he stood."

"I am a Frenchman—" Brian began stiffly.

"Ranulf may be right," Gillian interrupted. What she had witnessed on the battlefield before they had found Brian had sickened her. The dispatching of badly wounded men had been done with a sort of cold-blooded mercy. Hot with anger over the deaths of the pages and wounded, what would they do to Brian?

"Believe me, Sir Brian," Ranulf snapped, "I care nothing about you personally. Nor her either for that matter. I just hate to see the time that I spent looking for you go to waste. If you consider how much profit I let slip through my fingers while I was looking for you, you understand my meaning." He hoisted a heavy leathern bag significantly. "Still I managed to collect quite a fortune."

"Robbing the dead," Brian swore fiercely. "What depths will you not sink to?"

Ranulf smiled sweetly. "Never try to tell me or yourself that your French countrymen would not be out there doing the same thing to us if they had won and we had lost. Why do you think the baggage was attacked in the first place? A knight killed your friend Howard. He was a good fighter. Too good for a rabble of peasant scum. A knight killed him. Am I right?"

Brian cursed again. His fists clenched in frustration. "Yes," he ground out.

"I rest my case." Ranulf made a motion as if he dusted his hands. Grinning his devil's grin, he turned to Gillian. "I like the idea of you and him working for me until we get back to England," he gloated, handing her the bag to carry back to their packs.

Brian growled and would have flung himself upon Ranulf to throttle him, had not Gillian stepped between them and soothed him with soft words. "I will see you in hell before I work for you!"

"How interesting! I am sure Warrenby would love to know that one of his best archers is a girl. Likewise I am sure the rest of the men in camp would like a little private time with her." He smiled at Brian. "You might be able to fight one, but if they also happened to find out that you were a French knight . . ." He shrugged eloquently.

"Brian!" Gillian begged. "We have come so far. Let us do as Ranulf says and get out of this awful place."

"Damned catamite!"

"Sticks and stones!"

Gillian stepped from between them. They were both spoiling for a fight. She was exhausted and thoroughly disgusted with them both. Her leg ached with a fierce throbbing pain. Whenever she thought of Howard of Rothingham and Lady Alys, her throat ached from trying to stifle the tears. Without a backward glance she limped away to find the packs she and Ranulf had carefully stowed before the battle.

Before Ranulf turned away to follow Gillian, he tossed a black jacket to Brian. "Put this on," he commanded. "And take off that metal and throw it away."

"This is an archer's uniform," Brian objected.

"Very clever of you to recognize it," Ranulf sneered. "You hardly got close enough to see them today."

"But I . . ." He swallowed. His hands crushed the cloth, then relaxed.

"Keep the hauberk over your head. Otherwise your haircut might make someone suspicious. Get rid of all the armor. Just toss it out onto the field. Nobody will even notice."

"Why did you do this for me?" Brian wanted to know.

But Ranulf turned away without an answer and hastened after Gillian. Catching up with her as she knelt by the packs, he squatted down beside her to open his and stow the heavy bag of gold ornaments inside. "Stretch out beneath the tree," he commanded, not looking at her.

527

"What?"

"Lie down. I thought your hearing was good."

Protesting softly, she slid over on her side, staring at him suspiciously.

With practiced hands he caught hold of her leg and began to untie the bandage he had wrapped around it hours before. She lay quiet, too tired to argue as he examined the wound with a touch gentle as a woman's.

From under his jacket he drew a flask. "Good French brandy," he informed her, uncorking it. Ripping the muddy hose away from the wound, he grinned again. "Grit your teeth and keep your mouth shut. My nerves will not stand a howling woman."

With these instructions as preamble, he poured the brandy over the wound. Like liquid fire it burned the raw flesh, cleansing as it did. "Two things good for a wound," he told her. "This is one. Two is let it alone." He took a clean cloth from his pack and wrapped it around her thigh, tying it firmly but not too tightly.

She lay on her side, her head on her crooked arm, staring at him. Her brown eyes were fathomless depths. "Thank you," she said at last.

He grinned. His hand began to stroke the inside of her thigh.

"What are you doing?"

He laughed. "I was touching you as a man should touch a woman. Frankly, I do not see what there is in it."

"Then leave me alone."

He bowed mockingly. "Rest well. You have had a terrible day. She is all yours." He rose as Brian dropped down beside her, a scowl of warning on his face.

The *Non nobis* and *Te Deum* droned from the woods and across the field. King Henry V, mounted on his little gray

528

horse and followed by a squire leading a magnificent destrier white as the snow, passed along the line of troops. Each man among the English knew the gray palfrey was being honored above all other animals as even the warhorses paid homage to it.

Above the woods on the northwest loomed the round towers of a gray castle. Pausing beside a small knot of prisoners who had been spared because of their exalted rank, he pointed with his steel-gauntleted hand. "What castle is that?"

For a moment no one answered. Then Montjoie, the Principal Herald of France, stepped forward. "The castle of Agincourt, so please Your Majesty."

The king nodded. His voice rose loud enough for the Englishmen in his close proximity to hear and tell the rest. "Then as all battles should bear the name of the fortress nearest to the field on which they are fought, this shall forever be called the Battle of Agincourt."

Bowing obsequiously, the herald stepped back.

Chapter Thirty-Nine

Twenty-three English dead were honored at dusk at the head of the battlefield. Their bodies were placed in a barn located not far behind the original line from which the cry "Advance banners!" had been given. There with a great pile of supplies and armaments taken from the bodies of their French victims they were burned while prayers and hymns followed the smoke and flames into the sky all through the night.

The bodies of the duke of York, King Henry's uncle, who had commanded the line on the right, and of the youthful earl of Suffolk, whose father had died at Harfleur, were preserved to be carried home for burial in England.

The king caused three grave pits to be dug in the field beside the Calais road, each twelve feet wide and twenty-five yards long. Into these pits nearly six thousand bodies were tipped. A large wooden cross was placed at the head of each. Three days later the army marched into Calais.

"Now is the time to really use that French," Ranulf urged out of the side of his mouth to Brian. "We need a room to stay in. For myself I have been sleeping out in the open so long, I think I am an animal."

Brian looked at Gillian. How long had she been without a bed and a bath? Since she left La Forêt he guessed. Likewise how long since she had eaten a full meal? She was thin to the point of emaciation and caked with mud to her eyes. Poor girl. How he loved her! He made an obscene gesture toward Ranulf. "For you," he sneered, "anything."

The price of a room had tripled at the rat-infested inn on the waterfront. Ranulf cursed stringently when Brian calmly relieved him of a fine gold necklace from the leathern bag. "You could have done better. You were probably too honorable to chaffer for a fair price."

"A room with some hot water for a bath." Brian untied the packs from Gillian's saddle and from his own. "If you think you can do better, please do so. We will stay here tonight and move into your cheaper, more luxurious rooms tomorrow."

The room was poor indeed. The beds were only frames with ropes laced across them and mattresses stuffed with grass. One scuttle of coal was provided to take off the damp chill.

"At least we will not be rained on tonight," Gillian smiled thankfully.

"Even that statement is open to conjecture," Ranulf snarled, glaring at the ceiling.

532

"Ranulf, if you would like to desert from the army, we will not try to stop you," Brian suggested hopefully. A remarkable change had occurred in him since the day of the battle.

He no longer carried himself so stiffly. No longer did he struggle to maintain a dignified façade. References to chivalry and honor were notably absent from his conversation. Once or twice he had even gone so far as to respond in kind to Ranulf's incessant teasing and tormenting.

"When does the bath arrive?" Gillian wanted to know. She had dropped her pack beside the middle bed and was now stretched out on it. "Oh, lord, this feels good. I have forgotten how to sleep without twisting my body around rocks."

Brian smiled at her. "It even has a sheet and blanket."

"In that case I may try to peel off these clothes. In the places they are not rotted through from the mud they are stuck to my skin."

At a knock, Brian opened the door to admit a servitor bearing a tray with a vessel of wine and three flagons on it. "We will desire the bath as soon as possible." Speaking in his educated French, he slipped a coin into the waiting hand. The man gave a surly nod before withdrawing. "This may be an English port, but the sympathies of many are French," he informed them as he poured three liberal drinks.

He passed each of his companions a flagon and toasted them silently. Together they drank, letting the sharp red liquid run down their throats and spread its balm through their tired bodies.

For a long time no one spoke. Gillian remained on the bed, her flagon perched on her stomach, her feet crossed at the ankles. Ranulf sprawled across two chairs on one side of the small table. He too held the wine on his stomach staring dolefully into its dark red pool. Brian sat slumped over the other side of the table. His shoulders hunched, his elbows braced. From time to time one or the other would take a sip.

The sounds of roistering soldiers floated up from the streets. Darkness fell and the sounds increased.

When all the wine had been drunk, Ranulf rose and stretched widely, his hands fell to his ribs and he scratched himself. "All this warmth," he complained, "makes a man soft. Those fellows in the street seem to be having a wonderful time. A celebration is what a man needs to drive the ghosts away."

Neither of his companions moved.

He shrugged. "Ah well. I perhaps wasted my breath. One of you has nothing to celebrate and the other is not a man." He strolled to the door. "Never mind the bath. You may take two, young fletcher, one for you and one for me."

Hand on the latch, he paused. "Good night," he smiled sardonically. "Enjoy whatever it is you two do together." With those parting words, he was gone.

Brian raised his eyebrows. "I would not have credited him with so much sensitivity."

Gillian smiled faintly. The wine, the warm room, the bed had all combined to make her more than a bit drunk. "He is a very sensitive person in some ways. He just cannot show it. He knows he is already hated and despised before people get to know him. Therefore, he builds walls around himself and keeps people out by firing volleys of insults at them."

Before Brian could respond, another knock at the door

signaled the arrival of their bath, a small tub with two buckets of water, both barely lukewarm, and a couple of threadbare squares of linen.

"When I get back to York, I shall fix me a bath with water so hot I will scald myself," Gillian promised herself outloud. "I shall hire someone to pour water over and over me until I am clean. And than I shall sit in the hot tub until I am wrinkled like a prune."

Brian grinned at the thought. "Come." He came to the end of the bed and began to unlace her boots. "I may not be able to do much for that dream, but at least you can have one bucket of water poured over you."

She smiled lovingly as he undressed her. Beneath her black jacket, she still wore the stained and faded smock of the lost sailor. She wondered what her own scarlet smock with its fletcher's badge would look like. She had almost forgotten. How long ago had she worn it?

"You will be going home very soon," he reassured her as he lifted her clothing over her head. Then he choked, his control almost broken. Between her breasts hung his gold and blue enamel medallion. His motto, the code by which he had planned to live his life, tore at him unbearably. Agincourt had changed all that. No longer would a man's sword point be death on behalf of Christ. *"Mucro Mors Cristo"* belonged in the grave pits beside the Calais road.

Gillian immediately pressed her cheek to his. "You are still the same man," she whispered, taking his face between her palms and looking into his eyes. "The man who gave me this medallion was alive in the chivalric code. So long as that code lives in you, you may wear this with pride."

Accepting her kiss humbly, he shook his head. "I shall

never wear it again. Truly I am not sure I want to. The sword and the armor were getting very heavy. I was almost glad to put them down."

"Truly?"

"Truly." He kissed her long, letting his love pour into her.

Glorying in it, luxuriating in his care of her, she allowed him to stand her in the small tub and pour in the first bucket of tepid water. "Can you sit?" he chuckled.

"I . . ." She had barely room for her feet, much less her buttocks as well.

"Then we will wash your body first," he laughed, swinging her up and setting her down.

Her feet and legs hung over the rim. She whooped with laughter when he tickled her arch. "I love a ticklish woman." He grinned as he picked up one of the squares of linen, wrung it out, and began to lave her belly and thighs.

"I wish we had a piece of soap," she complained. "I could wash my hair. I can imagine what it looks like by what yours looks like."

Washing her breasts with loving attention that made her squirm, he pinched her nipple. "Mine looks wonderful in comparison to yours," he teased her. "After all, I only slept on the ground three nights. You have slept on it for two weeks."

"My God! I am surprised that you can bear to look at me. I must be hideous beyond belief."

"You are." He dipped the washcloth and began to scrub her face with unnecessary vigor while she struggled and sputtered.

After he had washed her thoroughly, he stood her on her feet and attended to her legs and feet, taking special care to wash the wound on her thigh. To his relief it seemed to be healing cleanly. Finished, he helped her out and began to dry her too-slender body. She had lost so much weight during the ordeal, that she in truth resembled a gangling youth.

Wherever the towel went, his lips followed, until she was blushing furiously. Tormented by his tongue, she backed away until her buttocks came against the table. "Brian . . ." she whispered.

"What?" His lips were nibbling at her navel before trailing down the center of her flat belly to blow his breath into the downy triangle at its base. Aroused by his ministrations, her body was already beginning to heat.

"Brian . . ."

"Yes?" Swiftly he lifted her onto the edge, before kneeling before her and sliding in between her thighs. He lifted each one so that they rested on his shoulders. With gentle fingers he found the central core of her being and parted the soft blond curls that concealed it.

She moaned ecstatically, calling his name over and over. Her senses were overcharged, tingling, aching for the fulfillment he offered. She had been so long afraid, so long in pain, so long miserable and uncomfortable. His mouth offered her release from all that. She knew it and she wanted it. Never had she thought such craving possible.

Wild with desire, she locked her ankles together and pressed her heels into him to bring him against her. Her fingers sank into his hair and held him while the heat and moisture of his tongue carried her higher and higher.

When her peak came, she began to sob. Great gusty sobs of pleasure followed the release his love had brought her. She had needed him so much. When he had begun,

537

she had welcomed the physical arousal and fulfillment. Now she experienced the emotional catharsis she had sought instinctively. She was no longer a girl, but a woman who had dealt with life and death.

He left her sobbing on the table, sprawled limply, one hand drooping over the edge. Her legs, too, he left apart, one knee drawn up, the other outstretched, her lower leg and foot swinging limply.

Quickly, he bathed his own body, scrubbing himself thoroughly before using the other bucket of water to rinse. Wet as he was, his skin gleaming, the curling hairs plastered to his body, he came to her.

His hands grasped the underside of her thighs and pulled her toward him again so that her hips rested on the edge of the table. This time he placed her legs around his waist.

Gillian's eyes were still closed; her sobs had subsided to choking gasps.

Brian slapped her lightly on the cheek. "Enough," he commanded, his face serious. "I want you now. Give me everything. Hold back nothing."

She shuddered. "Yes," she whispered, tightening her legs.

He drove hard, burying himself in the warm darkness of her body. As her eager flesh closed around him, he cried out in pleasure. A compulsion arose to drive deeper and deeper, to hide himself in her until somehow he could be reborn, a different person.

In a very real sense he was a different man. The younger son of the Sire de Trenanay had never really lived. The knight of the gold medallion was dead, buried under the weight of the arrow-riddled bodies of his brothers on the field of Agincourt. From the body of this

538

Englishwoman he would take his new identity. His mother had told him his father was English. Although he would never know him, he would take that knowledge as his talisman and put away the old life forever.

With a cry of dedication, he spilled his seed into her body.

Accepting him with her whole being, aflame with love, Gillian encompassed him with arms and legs. Her mouth pressed against his throat, kissing the strong column where the blood pounded ecstatically. When his hard weight collapsed on her, she felt no pain, only the delicious sense of completeness. They were one flesh, one heart, one mind.

At last Brian stirred. Rotating first one wrist and then the other to ease the strain, he braced himself on his elbows to stare down into Gillian's face. "Did you die?" he asked at last, planting a kiss on the tip of her nose.

She opened her eyes, staring dreamily past his head. Her face was soft with love; her eyes, velvet pools; her slightly parted mouth bore the imprint of his impassioned kisses.

"You look well loved," he observed with satisfaction. He touched one finger to her lower lip. "Is this sore?"

"No . . ." Her answer was a whisper.

He bent and kissed it, taking it between his two lips to caress it lovingly. "It is so red," he told her. "I feared I might have hurt you."

"Oh, no . . ." Again the mesmerized whisper.

He shifted slightly, rubbing their lower bellies together. "Am I too heavy for you?"

This time she merely shook her head and tightened her arms slightly.

He snorted in disbelief. By his own best estimate, he

539

weighed over fifteen stone. His hand caressed the fragile shoulders, tracing the collarbones where they pushed upward through the nearly translucent skin. As thin as she was she would be lucky to weigh seven. Reluctantly he disengaged her arms from around his neck and pushed himself up.

Protesting wordlessly, she tightened her legs, but he forestalled her by slipping his hands under her buttocks and carrying her to the bed locked to his body. She rested her head on his shoulder.

"This is nice. Can you carry me back to England like this?"

He paused as if considering. "We would get awfully cold."

"Nonsense. I never felt warmer." She twitched her hips suggestively. At the movement, he felt himself tighten within her.

His sharply indrawn breath was music to her ears. Her fingers splayed across his shoulder blades. Their bodies were still locked together as he lowered himself to the bed. "At least, let me hold you for a while." He chuckled as his manhood burgeoned within her.

Stretching out full length on the bed, he let her move at her own pace, blissfully teasing and caressing him until they climaxed together again. His last conscious act was to pull the blanket over their bodies to protect them from the chill of the room.

"I have something to show you," Gillian knelt on the bed beside him, her breasts only a few inches from his eyes as she reached across his body for her pack.

"I am delighted," he observed, raising his head to brush one pendant nipple with his mouth. "Although I have seen it before, it is a sight one does not grow tired of."

Closing her eyes against the sexual thrill, she struggled for control. "I did not mean that."

"Oh?" He transferred his mouth to the other breast, while one hand stole up her thigh to cup her bare buttock. "Then why did you offer them to me so seductively. I can think on nothing else I would rather be shown." His lips drew strongly on the nipple.

"Please stop," she whimpered, writhing above him. "I really need to show you this. I cannot think when you do . . . that?"

He bit the small scrap of impudent flesh, taking pleasure in her tiny cry. "What a prospect!" he laughed. "I shall keep you naked and mindless, a perfect mistress."

"Stop!" she commanded pushing his hands away and jerking herself upright. "Stop that this instant. I have something important to show you."

Grinning a huge mocking grin, he made an elaborate show of lacing his fingers together and putting them behind his head. "Show away!"

Carefully avoiding the trap she had fallen into before, she pulled the blanket tightly around her before getting out of the bed to reach her pack. Bringing it back to the bed, she sat down cross-legged, her body decently covered. Untying the strings, she pulled out the ornately carved casket. Without preamble, she set it on Brian's chest.

"This is for you," she said.

He stared at it puzzled. "A woman's jewel box?"

"Your mother's."

His mouth hardened. One hand flashed down to sweep it away.

Gillian caught it. "No! She gave it to me to give to you."

He turned his head away staring in mutinous anger at the wall.

Gillian placed her hand beneath his chin and brought him back to face her. "Listen! She loved you. These are proof incontrovertible that she loved you more than anything in the world."

"She destroyed my life."

"Perhaps." Gillian shook her head. "Perhaps not. Would you ever have been happy in that decaying rubble?"

"It was Stephen's."

"But he was dead. The responsibility for it was to fall to you. She hated your father. What passed between them is for them alone to know. But she loved you. She arranged for us to get out of that house when the Sire de Trenanay would have killed us."

Brian opened his mouth in horrified protest. "He would not! Why kill you, my innocent friends?"

"To hide his shame. He was mad."

Gillian looked pityingly at him. "You know he was. She did too. She gave me these because she recognized me as your love."

Brian shrugged. "That was nothing. I made no secret of my feelings for you."

"She believed I was a boy," Gillian reminded him gently. "What does that make of you? Of me? Of our obvious love for each other? Ask Ranulf how people feel

542

about people like him."

Brian shot up. "I have never—"

"But she did not know that you 'never,'" Gillian insisted. "She accepted what she believed to be your sin and loved you anyway. Can you not accept her sin and love her a little bit?"

Brian dropped back, throwing one arm across his face, his fist clenched tightly. His mouth was set in a thin-lipped line of pain.

"Look." Opening the casket Gillian began to draw forth the velvet pouches. "Look, Brian," she insisted. "First is the twenty gold pieces from her dowry."

Slowly, he lowered his hand from his eyes. His face was white and grave.

"Here are the sets of jewels that her father gave her mother. Look. These are what your grandfather gave your grandmother in love and pride. Pearls. Rubies. Jade. Your mother told me that the jade is the rarest of all because it is dark green." She pressed the necklace into Brian's fingers.

He turned it over and over, studying its rich color, its intricate design. "What is in the last pouch?"

Gillian drew her breath. "Her marriage and betrothal rings from Trenanay. She gave it all to me, to give to you if you lived. If you died, then they were for me, because I was your love."

Brian shook his head. "Such things cannot pay for what she took from me."

"She did not expect them to. But they were all she had to give." Gillian's eyes filled with tears. "At least accept them as a gesture. Think of what we know happened to Alys. Think of what her life must have been

543

like with Trenanay."

"She was his wife."

"She had no choice. Words and gestures are the only weapons that a woman has to fight with. Try to think of her as a brave fighter."

He sighed. "Close the casket and put it back in your pack. Perhaps later I can accept it."

Chapter Forty

The triumphal army knelt on the beach at Dover while the king prayed. To Gillian the sight of the magnificent white cliffs, the feel of the sand beneath her feet, the white clouds scudding across the gray-blue English sky were too much to bear unmoved. Tears flooding down her cheeks, she sank down to gather handfuls of the cold white sand in her fists. To her the feel of England was as precious as gold and rubies. Her prayer was one of deliverance and thanksgiving.

Brian knelt at her side, his white face impassive. He would never see France again. He faced an unknown future among people who were strangers. When he tried to recall the faces of Tobin and Kenneth, they floated in and out of shadows. These were the men he would have to work among. The job he would have to learn was one he had regarded with contempt. But the product he would be expected to make, he could only treat with respect. He squared his shoulders and prayed for strength.

At Canterbury Cathedral the procession stopped again.

"Blast!" Ranulf complained. "We are never going to get home at this rate. My knees are getting knobby."

Gillian prodded him in the ribs. "Hush!"

"You fought hard," he reminded her, catching her hand. "Why should you and all the rest of us not have the glory? I swear I did not notice God drawing a bow or swinging a sword."

"He sent the rain."

"And almost drowned us in the process. It did not rain only on the French side of the field."

As their horses clattered into the inn yard of the Tabard, Gillian could not help smiling. Harry Bailey had outdone himself. A painting on cloth hung over the sign. Its subject was clearly King Henry V riding, triumphant, through a field of prone Frenchmen. Around the edge of the picture were painted the words to the newly composed tune of the day:

> Then went oure Kynge, with alle his oste,
> Thorowe Fraunce for all the French boste;
> In Agincourt felde he faught manly;
> He had both the felde, and the victory.

"I wonder if he has King Henry's Chambers ready?" Gillian laughed.

Brian grinned. "Undoubtedly. And the king shall stay the night whether he knows it or not."

Ranulf hesitated as they dismounted. "Perhaps 'tis time for me to move on. I have been long from Briarthwaite. Those scurvy villeins that I left in charge have probably robbed me blind."

Brian made no comment but stood with arms folded regarding him coldly. He neither liked nor trusted Ranulf.

But Gillian extended her hand. "Nonsense. 'Tis drawing on toward evening. Stay the night and continue in the morning."

Ranulf took her hand hesitantly. "I think I would cast a shadow on the festivities."

Gillian shook her head. "You are a returning hero." She grinned. "Besides Harry Bailey would never forgive us if you did not part with some of your gold at his establishment."

His mouth curved in a sardonic smile, Ranulf swung down. "I almost forgot." He cast a significant glance at Brian. "A man's worth and desirability are always judged by the weight of his purse."

Harry sat behind the desk, as was his wont. At the sight of them he threw up his hands in thanksgiving. "Sir Brian. Praise God you found the lady safe. Welcome, gentles all." Swiftly, he rose and came round the desk to greet them, shaking the hand of each in turn. "I do not know you, sir."

"I am Ranulf of Briarthwaite," was the stiff reply.

"Welcome! Welcome to the Tabard Inn. We have beds and food for all." He looked expectantly toward the open door through which they had come.

Gillian laid her hand on his arm. "Sir Howard of Rothingham is dead, Harry."

His watery blue eyes suddenly filled. Compressing his lips between his teeth, he turned away. In the silence of the lobby his sharply indrawn breath betrayed his grief. After a moment he turned back. His face was calm, but very red. "Sir Howard, you said?"

"Knighted by the king's own hand at Agincourt," Brian supplied heartily.

Harry swallowed hard, wiping his hand hastily across his eyes. "Why then he died happy as a man could," he said at last.

"He spoke of you at the end," Gillian said. "He wanted you to know."

"Always a good lad," the host agreed. "We shall speak later of this, my lady Gillian. For now the best beds and the best wine for my friends."

That night over a sumptuous table the story of Agincourt was told and retold. Gillian thought she had never tasted such delicious food, even given the circumstance that she was half starved and had been eating little fit for human consumption in almost a month. Harry kept the wine flowing freely, until all three of his guests slumped happily in their chairs.

Gillian yawned widely, her eyelids drooping. "My compliments to the host." She smiled. "I believe I will retire. The thought of your excellent bed in . . . er . . . The King's Chambers tempts me more than the excellent wine."

Brian rose only a trifle unsteadily. "I shall escort my lady to her chamber," he declared. He presented his arm with a courtly bow.

"'Tis unnecessary, Brian," Gillian replied cheerfully. "I think I would really like to go alone tonight. You have good wine and good friends. Please stay and enjoy yourself."

Brian hung his head in sorrow. "She loves me not," he

confided half-seriously to Ranulf.

The master of Briarthwaite smiled. "Oh, I think she loves you very well. She is tired." He rose also, bowing slightly. "I give you good night, Gil."

Her brilliant smile encompassed the room. Brian blinked. In clean garments, her hair a soft cloud around her face, her cheeks flushed from the wine, Gillian was very close to beautiful. "Good night, Ranulf. Harry. Brian."

"She left us," Brian noted, his voice faintly surprised.

Ranulf dropped back into his chair, reaching as he did for the wine. "You take her too much for granted. Because she has played a man's part for so long, you forget that she has less strength than you."

Brian scowled at the smaller man. "Are you taking it upon yourself to instruct me in how I should treat a woman?" he asked in amazement.

Ranulf grinned a self-mocking grin. "Seems incredible, I grant you. I of all people."

"She is a very special lady," Harry Bailey noted. "I have been an innkeeper for over twenty years. To my knowledge I never met another one like her."

Brian listened to them resentfully. "She does very well," he said at last.

Ranulf's dark eyes hardened. His mouth curled in a sneer. "She saved your skin at least twice that I know of. Did you ever so much as thank her?"

Brian opened his mouth.

Ranulf held up his hand. "No, hear me. To my eternal shame she suffered agonies because of me. She stared death in the face on that battlefield and never flinched. She starved, froze, and almost drowned, but she never complained. She behaved like a soldier when men in

549

front of her were diving for cover. If you mistreat her and take advantage of her love . . ."

Brian interrupted. "I have no intention of mistreating her. I love her. I simply feel that she may be wrong to be living such an unnatural life."

Ranulf spat a rude name.

"Gentlemen . . ." Harry interceded softly.

"You know nothing about unnatural. Perhaps she is living the most natural life of all. Do you really want to know why I cannot get interested in women? Because they are so damn stupid. How many of them do you know who have anything at all to offer a man except the bed-chamber? They are reared to be so ignorant that most can barely converse, so weak that many do not survive the first year of marriage. Whether you acknowledge it or not, Sir Brian, the things you love in Gillian are the things you want her to give up."

"She will not give them up," Brian gritted out. "I asked her to when I asked her to marry me the first time. She refused. I wanted to leave her then, but I could not."

"Then you must take her and love her for the rare jewel that she is." Ranulf spread his hands. "I think that if you do not, you will be a most unhappy man, not to say stupid."

Brian regarded the two somberly. Ranulf's dark eyes and Harry's light blue ones were calculating his worth. He felt extremely uncomfortable as he hid his face in his wine cup.

The master of Briarthwaite rose before the sun the next morning. Calling for his horse, he thought to settle the account with the host and ride away before the others

550

were stirring.

"Ranulf."

He winced at the sound of her voice. He had especially hoped to ride away without sentimental good-byes. Assuming a faintly bored expression, he turned to see her coming down the stairs.

"Will you join me for breakfast?" she invited him.

He hesitated. "I must be away," he muttered.

"Just some fresh hot bread and ale." She held out her hand. "Please."

Heaving a sigh of resignation, he capitulated. "Lead the way."

They sat facing each other while a boy brought the bread with fresh churned butter and some dried fruit drenched in honey.

"I must away as soon as can be." He took a bite, concentrating on his food and not looking at her.

"I know."

His dark eyes flicked upward then dropped. "I have been a long time away from my lands. I shall probably have to fight my reeve for my rents."

She took a sip of ale. "I doubt not you will win handily."

He nodded. "I had not planned to get so much experience in fighting when I left Briarthwaite. The whole thing rather got out of hand."

She grinned. "Certainly for me. I was just delivering the king's commission."

Suddenly, his face twisted. He drew in a shuddering breath. "Gil Fletcher. Damn you!" His voice was a snarl. "How does one apologize for all the wrongs I have done you? What do I say?" He clenched his fists in agonized frustration.

551

She smiled. "Let us begin here. I am Gil Fletcher from York. So pleased to meet you Ranulf of Briarthwaite." She extended her hand across the table. "Now there is nothing to apologize for. We just met today."

He took the hand she offered but shook his head. "Too easy. When you do that, you wipe away all the good things too. No. I have to live with my sins, black and damnable as they are."

She changed the subject. "I suppose that Brian and I will leave today too. We will journey much more slowly than you would wish to travel. The oxen, you know. Still we must make all haste. I do not know what I shall find when I return to my shop."

He drained his ale and rose, tossing several coins on the table to pay for both their breakfasts. "Then fare you well."

She rose also, her face sad and still. "Fare you well, Ranulf."

He extended his hand, not to shake in parting, but to lead her out of the common room and into the hall. The entryway was still dark.

"I have a mind to try a short experiment," he said softly.

She threw him a quick look. Was he teasing again?

He pulled her up against him with a twist of his arm. The other arm he closed round her waist. His dark eyes searched her face carefully for some sign of revulsion. Finding only acceptance, he touched his lips to hers.

It was a brother's kiss, Gillian remembered later. When it might have become something more, he shivered slightly and stepped back, his face unreadable. "Fare you well," he repeated.

She smiled. "If you are ever in York, you have a

friend. Remember friends are rare and hard to find."

He set his cap on his head. "I will remember." He walked toward the door. His slight spare figure paused silhouetted in the light. "Gillian, are you sure you are not a boy disguised as a girl disguised as a boy?" He did not wait for her answering chuckle.

"I think I may take a pilgrimage to Canterbury for the soul of my good friend," Harry told them as they bid him good-bye. "I met him on a pilgrimage to Canterbury, you know. Him and his good father over twenty years ago."

Brian nodded soberly. "I believe that in his ending, he redeemed all. Yet no man can have too many friends to pray his soul from Purgatory."

Gillian smiled painfully. "We will light candles in the great cathedral in York. Certainly so many will speed his journey."

As the oxen pulled out of the inn yard, she looked back over her shoulder. Her last glimpse of Harry was as he raised the corner of his apron to his face.

The inner court of her home had never looked so dear. Springing down from the wagon seat, Gillian flung open the door. Everything was just as she remembered. "Kenneth! Uncle Tobin!" she shouted.

From the back of the house, the cook answered. "Master Gil! Praise be to God. Master Kenneth be in the shop. Master Walton he be with him. How be ye, Master Gil. We feared for ye being gone so long."

"Fine. I am fine." Gillian dashed from the house and across the court to the shops. "Kenneth."

"Gil." Kenneth's voice was shrill with delight. "Oh, Gil." Her younger brother flung himself into her arms. "What happened to you?"

"So many things that you would not believe. I have been to France."

"No! Uncle Tobin. Did you hear that? Gil has been to France."

Keeping her arm tightly around her brother, she made her way into the bowyer's shop. Tobin Walton seemed shriveled. The arm and leg on his left side maintained a horrible stillness, while the rest of his body strained forward to see her.

"Gil." His eyes filled with tears. His dear familiar voice was hoarse with emotion. "I feared you dead or worse."

"Uncle Tobin . . ." She knelt beside him, throwing her arms around him while he held her close. "Oh, Uncle Tobin. How are you?"

"Good. Excellent. Now that you are returned, I am wonderful. You will be fletcher and Kenneth will be bowyer." The old man's face, sadly drawn down on the left, glowed with excitement.

"Yes," Gillian agreed, hugging them both. "We shall be as we were before, except more."

"More?"

She kissed Uncle Tobin on both cheeks. When she would have done the same to Kenneth, he drew back. "Stop kissing me. I knew you would come home safely. I told everybody. Did you bring me a present?"

She thought about his request. "Well, I brought you an archer's jacket and cap."

He looked at her suspiciously. "Where did you get them?"

"They were mine, but I give them to you." With

pleasure, she thought. "They are the real thing worn by King Henry's archers."

Kenneth still looked skeptical.

"Ask Brian." Eagerly, she drew him into the room from where he had waited, his large frame filling the doorway.

"Gil fought with the king's army at Agincourt," Brian told him in answer to his doubting look.

Tobin Walton bent a hostile eye on the knight. "I thought we had seen the last of you," he growled.

Brian shook his head. "Never, sir. Gil has accepted my proposal of marriage."

Tobin's face turned dark red in anger. He turned to Gil. "Will you give up everything?" he snarled.

Gil started to protest, but Brian raised his hand. "Believe me, Master Walton, she will give up nothing. We will be married in secret. I will apprentice myself to Gil Fletcher and learn the trade."

"Sir Brian de Trenanay, Fletcher?" Tobin snorted. "Not likely."

"No. Master Brian Forest, Fletcher."

Tobin stared from man to woman. Her face was serenely happy; his, serious but resolved. "Why?" he said at last.

Brian laughed dryly. "Oh, many reasons." He took her hand. "Not the least of which is that she took me prisoner. I have to work to pay my ransom."

"In bondage for the rest of your life," Gillian agreed happily.

After supper that night, they retired to her room. On her own bed, spread with sheets scented with lavender and costmary, he made long and leisurely love to her. Then when she had cried a little for pure happiness, they both lay breathless, their bodies warm and satisfied.

Gillian spoke dreamily. "What a wonderful prospect"—she sighed—"you beside me in this bed every night for the rest of our lives."

Beside her, Brian brushed a wisp of hair back from her temple and blew in her ear. "Yes, and in the mornings too."

"Oh, yes. I had forgotten the mornings."

"We could take long naps in the afternoons."

She giggled. "Uncle Tobin will be furious. We will never get the commissions done on time."

Brian rose on one elbow. "I will work hard, Gillian. This I swear to you. You gave me my life twice over. I can never repay you."

She frowned. "Do you talk of payment?"

"No." His voice was low and serious. "Never. I said I could never repay you. It is hard for me to explain."

She waited in the darkness. Brian had talked little on the return journey. Except for the most commonplace observations about the scenery and the weather, he had remained silent, only reassuring her of his feeling with his affection and passion. Each night he had made love to her with studied care, bringing her to pleasure again and again before holding her secure in his arms until she fell asleep. He almost seemed to be demonstrating how he would behave toward her.

"You owe me no explanation," she said as the silence lengthened.

"I think I do," he replied. "You need to know what to expect." He pulled away and sat up in the bed. The moon cast its brightness through the panes, making pale patterns of light on the floor.

556

"When I threw away the last of my armor, I felt relieved," he whispered. "I had wanted to die. In a sense I think I did die. I was unconscious a long time. And when I awoke, all around me were dead knights. We had all died." He shuddered at the memory.

She sat up and put her arms about him, leaning her head on his shoulder. "Think not on it."

"I must say it. Then I will be free. You and Ranulf woke me. Do you see?"

She waited, puzzled.

"You and Ranulf. You represent the new world. He was a knight who had sense enough to see knighthood for what it was. You were an archer whose weapons spelled the end of knighthood for all time. You had both taken the trouble to come and seek me out. To dig me up, if you will."

"Brian, I love you. I came to seek you out for that reason only."

He turned and took her into his arms, caressing her cheek and kissing her forehead. "I know. But I belong to you now. I belong to your world. And I shall hold hard by the life you gave me."

"What if you find you dislike fletching?" she asked seriously. "Kenneth cannot manage it. He says his fingers fumble over the feathers."

"Then I shall be a bowyer, or an armorer, or a carter, or who knows what. But I shall earn money as you do and love you and honor you every day." He kissed her tenderly.

She thought her heart would burst from loving him so much. Lifting her hands to his hair, she held him to her in a long, long kiss.

"We can have a wonderful life," she assured him.

"I know. I have only one request." He squeezed her suggestively.

"Name it."

"Be a woman for me occasionally."

With a small feminine sigh she lifted her breasts to his kiss. "I shall be a woman for you every night. . . ."